PHOTO FINISH
and two other
GREAT MYSTERIES

PHOTO FINISH
and two other
GREAT MYSTERIES

Ngaio Marsh

NELSON DOUBLEDAY, INC.
Garden City, New York

This edition by arrangement with Little, Brown and Company

Printed in the United States of America

Contents

Cast of Characters

(in order of appearance)

Isabella Sommita (née Pepitone)
Ben Ruby, her manager
Montague V. Reece, her friend
Rupert Bartholomew, her protégé
Maria, her maid

Chief Superintendent, Roderick Alleyn, C.I.D.
Troy Alleyn, R.A., his wife
His Assistant Commissioner, Scotland Yard

Bert, a chauffeur
Les, a launch man
Marco, a manservant
Ned Hanley, Mr. Reece's secretary

Signor Beppo Lattienzo, the Sommita's Master of Singing
Roberto Rodolfo, a tenor
Sylvia Parry, a mezzo-soprano
Hilda Dancy, a contralto
Eru Johnstone, a bass
Sir David Baumgartner, a critic
Mrs. Bacon, housekeeper
Dr. John Carmichael, M.D., a guest

Inspector Hazelmere, Rivermouth Constabulary
Detective Sergeant Franks, Rivermouth Constabulary
Detective Sergeant Barker, Rivermouth Constabulary
Dr. Winslow, medical examiner

CHAPTER I

The Sommita

I

ONE OF THE MANY MARVELS of Isabella Sommita's techniques was her breathing: it was totally unobservable. Even in the most exacting passages, even in the most staggering flights of coloratura, there was never the slightest disturbance of the corsage.

"You could drop an ice cube down her cleavage," boasted her manager, Ben Ruby, "and not a heave would you get for your trouble."

He had made this observation when sitting in a box immediately above the diva at the Royal Festival Hall and had spoken no more than the truth. Offstage when moved by one of her not infrequent rages, La Sommita's bosom would heave with the best of them.

It did so now, in her private suite at the Chateau Australasia in Sydney. She was *en négligé* and it was sumptuously evident that she was displeased and that the cause of her displeasure lay on the table at her elbow: a newspaper folded to expose a half-page photograph with a banner headline, "Cross-Patch?" and underneath, "La Sommita is not amused!"

It had been taken yesterday in Double Bay, Sydney. The photographer, wearing a floppy white hat, a white scarf over his mouth, and dark spectacles, had stepped out from an alleyway and gone snap. She had not been quick enough to turn her back, but her jaw had dropped and her left eye had slewed, its habit when rage overtook her. The general effect was that of a gargoyle at the dentist's: an infuriated gargoyle. The photograph was signed "Strix."

She beat on the paper with her largish white fist and her rings cut into it. She panted lavishly.

"Wants horsewhipping," Montague Reece mumbled. He was generally accepted as the Sommita's established lover, and he filled this role in the manner commonly held to be appropriate, being large, rich, muted, pale, dyspeptic, and negative. He was said to wield a great deal of power in his own world.

"Of course he needs horsewhipping," shouted his dear one. "But where's the friend who will go out and do it?" She laughed and executed a wide contemptuous gesture that included all present. The newspaper fluttered to the carpet.

"Personally," Ben Ruby offered, "I wouldn't know one end of a horsewhip from the other." She dealt him a glacial stare. "I didn't mean to be funny," he said.

"Nor were you."

"No."

A young man of romantic appearance, in a distant chair behind the diva, clasped a portfolio of music to his midriff and said in a slightly Australian voice: "Can't something be done? Can't they be sued?"

"What for?" asked Mr. Ruby.

"Well—libel. Look at it, for God's sake!" the young man brought out. "Well, I mean to say, *look!*"

The other two men glanced at him, but the Sommita, without turning her head, said, "Thank you, darling," and extended her arm. The intention was unmistakable: an invitation, nay, a command. The young man's beautiful face crimsoned, he rose, and, maintaining a precarious hold on his portfolio, advanced crouchingly to imprint a kiss upon the fingers. He lost control of his portfolio. Its contents shot out of their confine and littered the carpet: sheet upon sheet of music in manuscript.

He fell on his knees and scrabbled about the floor. "I'm so sorry," he gabbled. "Oh hell, I'm so bloody sorry."

The Sommita had launched a full-scale attack upon the Australian press. Rupert, she said, indicating the young man, was absolutely right. The press should be sued. The police should be called in. The photographer should be kicked out of the country. Was he to be suffered to wreck her life, her career, her sanity, to make her the laughingstock of both hemispheres? (She was in the habit of instancing geographical data.) Had she not, she demanded, consented to the Australian appearances solely as a means of escape from his infamy?

"You are sure, I suppose," said Mr. Reece in his pallid manner, "that it's the same man? Strix?"

This produced a tirade. "Sure! Sure!" Had not the detested Strix bounced out of cover in all the capitals of Europe as well as in New York and San Francisco? Had he not shot her at close quarters and in atrocious disarray? *Sure!* She drew a tempestuous breath. Well, she shouted, what were they going to do about it? Was she to be protected or was she to have a breakdown, lose her voice, and spend the rest of her days in a strait-jacket? She only asked to be informed.

The two men exchanged deadpan glances.

"We can arrange for another bodyguard," Montague Reece offered without enthusiasm.

"She didn't much fancy the one in New York," Mr. Ruby pointed out.

"Assuredly I did not," she agreed, noisily distending her nostrils. "It is not amusing to be closely followed by an imbecile in unspeakable attire who did nothing, but nothing, to prevent the outrage on Fifth Avenue. He merely goggled. As, by the way, did you all."

"Sweetheart, what else could we do? The fellow was a passenger in an open car. It was off like a bullet as soon as he'd taken his picture."

"Thank you, Benny. I remember the circumstances."

"But *why?*" asked the young man called Rupert, still on his knees assembling his music. "What's got into him? I mean to say, it doesn't make sense and it must cost a lot of money to follow you all over the globe. He must be bonkers."

He recognized his mistake as soon as it escaped his lips and began to gabble. Perhaps because he was on his knees and literally at her feet the Sommita, who had looked explosive, leaned forward and tousled his blond hair. "My poorest!" she said. "You are quite, *quite* ridiculous and I adore you. I haven't introduced you," she added as an afterthought. "I've forgotten your surname."

"Bartholomew."

"Really? Very well. Rupert Bartholomew," she proclaimed, with an introductory wave of her hand.

". . . d'you do," he muttered. The others nodded.

"Why does he do it? He does it," Montague Reece said impatiently, reverting to the photographer, "for money. No doubt the idea arose from the Jacqueline Kennedy affair. He's carried it much further and he's been successful. Enormously so."

"That's right," Ruby agreed. "And the more he does it the more"—he hesitated—"outrageous the results become."

"He retouches," the Sommita intervened. "He distorts. I know it."

They all hurriedly agreed with her.

"I'm going," she said unexpectedly, "to dress. Now. And when I return I wish to be given an intelligent solution. I throw out, for what they are worth, my suggestions. The police. Prosecution. The Press. Who owns this"—she kicked the offending newspaper and had some difficulty in disengaging her foot—"this garbage? Who is the proprietor? Attack him." She strode to the bedroom door. "And I warn you, Monty. I warn you,

Benny. This is my final word. Unless I am satisfied that there is an end to my persecution, I shall not sing in Sydney. They can," said the Sommita, reverting to her supposed origins, "stuff their Sydney Opera House."

She made her exit and did not neglect to slam the door.

"Oh dear," said Benjamin Ruby quietly.

"Quite," said Montague Reece.

The young man called Rupert Bartholomew, having reinstated his portfolio, got to his feet.

"I reckon I'd better—?"

"Yes?" said Mr. Reece.

"Take myself off. I mean to say, it's a bit awkward."

"What's awkward?"

"Well, you see, Madame—Madame Sommita asked me—I mean to say she said I was to bring this"—he indicated, precariously, his portfolio.

"Look out," said Ben Ruby. "You'll scatter it again." He did not try to suppress a note of resignation. "Is it something you've written?" he said. It was more a statement than an inquiry.

"This is right. She said I could bring it."

"When," Reece asked, "did she say it?"

"Last night. Well—this morning. About one o'clock. You were leaving that party at the Italian Embassy. You had gone back to fetch something—her gloves I think—and she was in the car. She saw me."

"It was raining."

"Heavily," said the young man proudly. "I was the only one."

"You spoke to her?"

"She beckoned me. She put the window down. She asked me how long I'd been there. I said three hours. She asked my name and what I did. I told her. I play the piano in a small orchestra and give lessons. And I type. And then I told her I had all her recordings and—well, she was so wonderful. I mean to me, there in the rain. I just found myself telling her I've written an opera—short, a one-acter—sort of dedicated to her, *for* her. Not, you know, not because I dreamt she would ever hear of it. Good God, no!"

"And so," Benjamin Ruby suggested, "she said you could show it to her."

"This is right. This morning. I think she was sorry I was so wet."

"And have you shown it to her?" asked Mr. Reece. "Apart from throwing it all over the carpet?"

"No. I was just going to when the waiter came up with this morning's papers and—she saw that thing. And then you came. I suppose I'd better go."

"It's hardly the moment perhaps—" Mr. Reece began when the bedroom door opened and an elderly woman with ferociously black hair came into the room. She held up a finger at Rupert, rather in the manner of summoning a waiter.

"She wanta you," said the woman. "Also the music."

"All right, Maria," said Mr. Ruby, and to the young man, "Maria is Madame's dresser. You'd better go."

So Rupert, whose surname was Bartholomew, clutching his opera, walked into La Sommita's bedroom like a fly, if he'd only known it, into a one-way web.

"She'll eat that kid," Mr. Ruby said dispassionately, "in one meal."

"Halfway down her throat already," her protector agreed.

II

"I've wanted to paint that woman," said Troy Alleyn, "for five years. And now look!"

She pushed the letter across the breakfast table. Her husband read it and raised an eyebrow. "Remarkable," he said.

"I know. Especially the bit about you. What does it say, exactly? I was too excited to take it all in. Who's the letter *from,* actually? Not from *her,* you'll notice."

"It's from Montague Reece, no less."

"Why 'no less'? Who's Montague Reece?"

"I wish," said Alleyn, "he could hear you ask."

"Why?" Troy repeated. "Oh, I know! Isn't he very well off?"

"You may say so. In the stinking-of-it department. Mr. Onassis Colossus, in fact."

"I remember now. Isn't he her lover?"

"That's it."

"All is made clear to me. I think. Do read it, darling. Aloud."

"All of it?"

"Please."

"Here goes," said Alleyn and read:

Dear Mrs. Alleyn,

I hope that is the correct way to address you. Should I perhaps have used your most celebrated soubriquet?

I write to ask if from November 1st you and your husband will be my guests at Waihoe Lodge, an island retreat I have built on a lake in New Zealand. It is recently completed and I dare to hope it will appeal to you. The situation is striking and I think I may say that my guests will be comfortable. You would have, as your studio, a commodious room, well lit, overlooking the lake, with a view of distant mountains and, of course, complete freedom as to time and privacy.

"He sounds like a land-and-estate agent—all mod. cons. and the usual offices. Pray continue," said Troy.

I must confess that this invitation is the prelude to another and that is for you to paint a portrait of Madame Isabella Sommita, who will be staying with us at the time proposed. I have long hoped for this. In my opinion, and I am permitted to say in hers also, none of her portraits hitherto has given us the true "Sommita."

We are sure that a "Troy" would do so quite marvelously!

Please say you approve the proposal. We will arrange transport, as my guest, of course, by air, and will settle details as soon as we hear, as I so greatly hope, that you will come. I shall be glad if you will be kind enough to inform me of your terms.

I shall write, under separate cover, to your husband, whom we shall be delighted to welcome with you to the Lodge.

I am, believe me, dear Mrs. Alleyn,
Yours most sincerely,

[in spiky writing] *Montague Reece.*

After a longish pause Troy said: "Would it be going too far to paint her singing? You know, mouth wide open for a top note."

"Mightn't she look as if she were yawning?"

"I don't *think* so," Troy brooded and then with a sidelong grin at her husband, "I could always put a balloon coming out of her mouth with 'A in alt' written in it."

"That would settle any doubts, of course. Except that I fancy it refers to male singers."

"You haven't looked at your letter. Do look."

Alleyn looked. "Here it is," he said. "Overposh and posted in Sydney." He opened it.

"What's he say?"

"The preamble's much the same as yours and so's the follow-up: the bit about him having to confess to an ulterior motive."

"Does he want *you* to paint *his* portrait, my poor Rory?"

"He wants me to give them 'my valued opinion as to the possibility of obtaining police protection in the matter of the persecution of Madame Sommita by a photographer, of which I am no doubt aware.' Well, of all the damn cheek!" said Alleyn. "Travel thirteen thousand miles to sit on an island in the middle of a lake and tell him whether or not to include a copper in his house party."

"Oh! Yes. The penny's dropped. All that stuff in the papers. I didn't really read it."

"You must be the only English-speaking human being who didn't."

"Well, I did, really. Sort of. But the photographs were so hideous they put me off. Fill me, as I expect they say in Mr. Reece's circles, in."

"You remember how Mrs. Jacqueline Kennedy, as she was then, was pestered by a photographer?"

"Yes."

"It's the same situation but much exaggerated. The Kennedy rumpus may have put the idea into this chap's head. He signs himself 'Strix.' He's actually followed the Sommita all over the world. Wherever she has appeared in opera or on the concert stage: Milan, Paris, Covent Garden, New York, Sydney. At first the photographs were the usual kind of thing with the diva flashing gracious smiles at the camera, but gradually differences crept in. They became more and more unflattering and he became more and more intrusive. He hid behind bushes. He trespassed on private ground and cropped up when and where he was least expected. On one occasion he joined the crowd round the stage door with the rest of the press, and contrived to get right up to the front.

"As she came into the doorway and did her usual thing of being delighted and astonished at the size of the crowd, he aimed his camera and at the same time blew a piercingly loud whistle. Her jaw dropped and her eyes popped and in the resulting photograph she looked as if someone had thumped her between the shoulder blades.

"From then on the thing ripened into a sort of war of attrition. It caught the fancy of her enormous public, the photos became syndicated, and the man is said to be making enormous sums of money. Floods of angry letters from her fans to the papers concerned. Threats. Unkind jokes in the worst possible taste. Bets laid. Preposterous stories suggesting he's a cast-off lover taking his revenge or a tenor who fell out with her. Rumors of a nervous breakdown. Bodyguards. The lot."

"Isn't it rather feeble of them not to spot him and manhandle him off?"

"You'd have thought so, but he's too smart for them. He disguises himself—sometimes bearded and sometimes not. Sometimes in the nylon stocking mask. At one time turned out like a city agent, at another like a Skid Row dropout. He's said to have a very, *very* sophisticated camera."

"Yes, but when he's done it, why hasn't somebody grabbed him and jumped on the camera? And what about her celebrated temperament? You'd think she'd set about him herself."

"You would, but so far she hasn't done any better than yelling pen-and-ink."

"Well," Troy said, "I don't see what you could be expected to do about it."

"Accept with pleasure and tell my A.C. that I'm off to the antipodes with my witch-wife? Because," Alleyn said, putting his hand on her head, "you are going, aren't you?"

"I do madly want to have a go at her: a great, big flamboyant rather vulgar splotch of a thing. Her arms," Troy said reminiscently, "are indecent. White and flowing. You can see the brush strokes. She's so shockingly sumptuous. Oh, yes, Rory love, I'm afraid I must go."

"We could try suggesting that she waits till she's having a bash at Covent Garden. No," said Alleyn, watching her, "I can see that's no go, you don't want to wait. You must fly to your commodious studio and in between sittings you must paint pretty peeps of snowy mountains reflected in the lucid waters of the lake. You might knock up a one-man show while you're about it."

"You shut up," said Troy, taking his arm.

"I think you'd better write a rather formal answer giving your terms, as he so delicately suggests. I suppose I decline under separate cover."

"It might have been fun if we'd dived together into the fleshpots."

"The occasions when your art and my job have coincided haven't been all that plain sailing, have they, my love?"

"Not," she agreed, "so's you'd notice. Rory, do you mind? My going?"

"I always mind but I try not to let on. I must say I don't go much for the company you'll be keeping."

"Don't you? High operatic with tantrums between sittings? Will that be the form, do you suppose?"

"Something like that, I daresay."

"I shan't let her look at the thing until it's finished and if she cuts up rough, her dear one needn't buy it. One thing I will *not* do," said Troy calmly. "I will not oblige with asinine alterations. If she's that sort."

"I should think she well might be. So might he."

"Taking the view that if he's paying he's entitled to a return for his cash? What is he? English? New Zealand? American? Australian?"

"I've no idea. But I don't much fancy you being his guest, darling, and that's a fact."

"I can hardly offer to pay my own way. Perhaps," Troy suggested, "I should lower my price in consideration of board-and-lodging."

"All right, smarty-pants."

"If it turns out to be a pot-smoking party or worse, I can always beat a retreat to my pretty peepery and lock the door on all comers."

"What put pot into your fairly pretty little head?"

"I don't know. Here!" said Troy. "You're not by any chance suggesting the diva is into the drug scene?"

"There have been vague rumors. Probably false."

"He'd hardly invite *you* to stay if she was."

"Oh," Alleyn said lightly, "their effrontery knows no bounds. I'll write my polite regrets before I go down to the Factory."

The telephone rang and he answered it with the noncommittal voice Troy knew meant the Yard.

"I'll be down in a quarter of an hour, sir," he said and hung up. "The A.C.," he said. "Up to something. I always know when he goes all casual on me."

"Up to what, do you suppose?"

"Lord knows. Undelicious by the sound of it. He said it was of no particular moment but would I drop in: an ominous opening. I'd better be off." He made for the door, looked at her, returned, and rounded her face between his hands. "Fairly pretty little head," he repeated and kissed it.

Fifteen minutes later his Assistant Commissioner received him in the manner to which he had become accustomed: rather as if he was some sort of specimen produced in a bad light to be peered at, doubtfully. The A.C. was as well furnished with mannerisms as he was with brains, and that would be underestimating them.

"Hullo, Rory," he said. "Morning to you. Morning. Troy well? Good." (Alleyn had not had time to answer.) "Sit down. Sit down. Yes."

Alleyn sat down. "You wanted to see me, sir?" he suggested.

"It's nothing much, really. Read the morning papers?"

"The *Post.*"

"Seen last Friday's *Mercury?*"

"No."

"I just wondered. That silly stuff with the press photographer and the Italian singing woman. What's-her-name?"

After a moment's pause Alleyn said woodenly: "Isabella Sommita."

"That's the one," agreed the A.C., one of whose foibles it was to pretend not to remember names. "Silly of me. Chap's been at it again."

"Very persistent."

"Australia. Sydney or somewhere. Opera House, isn't it?"

"There is one: yes."

"On the steps at some sort of function. Here you are."

He pushed over the newspaper, folded to expose the photograph. It had indeed been taken a week ago on the steps of the magnificent Sydney Opera House on a summer's evening. La Sommita, gloved in what seemed to be cloth of gold topped by a tiara, stood among V.I.P.s of the highest caliber. Clearly she was not yet poised for the shot. The cameraman had jumped the gun. Again, her mouth was wide open, but on this occasion she appeared to be screaming at the Governor-General of Australia. Or perhaps shrieking with derisive laughter. There is a belief held by people of the theatre that nobody over the age of twenty-five should allow themselves to be photographed from below. Here, the camera had evidently been half-a-flight beneath the diva, who therefore appeared to be richly endowed with chins and more than slightly *en bon point*. The Governor-General, by some momentary accident, seemed to regard her with incredulity and loathing.

A banner headline read: "Who Do You Think You Are!"

The photograph, as usual, was signed "Strix" and was reproduced, by arrangement, from a Sydney newspaper.

"That, I imagine," said Alleyn, "will have torn it!"

"So it seems. Look at this."

It was a letter addressed to "The Head of Scotland Yard, London" and written a week before the invitations to the Alleyns on heavy paper endorsed with an elaborate monogram: "I.S." lavishly entwined with herbage. The envelope was bigger than the ones received by the Alleyns but of the same make and paper. The letter itself occupied two and a half pages, with a gigantic signature. It had been typed, Alleyn noticed, on a different machine. The address was "Chateau Australasia, Sydney."

"The Commissioner sent it down," said the A.C. "You'd better read it."

Alleyn did so. The typed section merely informed the recipient that the writer hoped to meet one of his staff, Mr. Alleyn, at Waihoe Lodge, New Zealand, where Mr. Alleyn's wife was commissioned to paint the writer's portrait. The writer gave the dates proposed. The recipient was of course aware of the outrageous persecution—and so on along the already familiar lines. Her object in writing to him, she concluded, was that she hoped

Mr. Alleyn would be accorded full authority by the Yard to investigate this outrageous affair and she remained—.

"Good God," said Alleyn quietly.

"You've still got a postscript," the A.C. observed.

It was handwritten and all that might be expected. Points of exclamation proliferated. Underscorings doubled and trebled to an extent that would have made Queen Victoria's correspondence appear by contrast a model of stony reticence. The subject matter lurched into incoherence, but the general idea was to the effect that if the "Head of Scotland Yard" didn't do something pretty smartly he would have only himself to blame when the writer's career came to a catastrophic halt. On her knees she remained distractedly and again in enormous calligraphy, sincerely, Isabella Sommita.

"Expound," the A.C. invited with his head on one side. He was being whimsical. "Comment. Explain in your own words."

"I can only guess that the letter was typed by a secretary who advised moderation. The postscript seems to be all her own and written in a frenzy."

"*Is* Troy going to paint the lady? And do you propose to be absent without leave in the antipodes?"

Alleyn said: "We got our invitations this morning. I was about to decline, sir, when you rang up. Troy's accepting."

"*Is* she?" said the A.C. thoughtfully. "*Is* she, now? A good subject, um? To paint? What?"

"Very," Alleyn said warily. What *is* he on about? he wondered.

"Yes. Ah well," said the A.C., freshening his voice with a suggestion of dismissal. Alleyn started to get up. "Hold on," said the A.C. "Know anything about this man she lives with? Reece, isn't it?"

"No more than everyone knows."

"Strange coincidence, really," mused the A.C.

"Coincidence?"

"Yes. The invitations. Troy going out there and all this"—he flipped his finger at the papers on his desk. "All coming together, as it were."

"Hardly a coincidence, sir, would you say? I mean these dotty letters were all written with the same motive."

"Oh, I don't mean *them*," said the A.C. contemptuously. "Or only insofar as they turn up at the same time as the other business."

"What other business?" said Alleyn and managed to keep the weary note out of his voice.

"Didn't I tell you? Stupid of me. Yes. There's a bit of a flap going on in the international drug scene: the U.S.A. in particular. Interpol picked up a lead somewhere and passed it on to the French, who talked to the F.B.I., who've been talking to our lot. It seems there's been some suggestion that the diva might be a big, big girl in the remotest background. Very nebulous it sounded to me, but our Great White Chief is slightly excited." This was the A.C.'s habitual manner of alluding to the Commissioner of the C.I.D. "He's been talking to the Special Squad. And, by the way, to M.I. 6."

"How do they come into it?"

"Somewhere along the line. Cagy, as usual, I gather," said the A.C. "But they did divulge that there was a leak from an anonymous source to the effect that the Sommita is thought to have operated in the past."

"What about Reece?"

"Clean as a whistle as far as is known."

" 'Montague Reece,' " Alleyn mused. "Almost too good to be true. Like something out of *Trilby*. Astrakhan coat collar and glistening beard. Anything about his origin, sir?"

"Thought to be American-Sicilian."

During the pause that followed the A.C. hummed, uncertainly, the "Habañera" from *Carmen*. "Ever heard her in that?" he said. "Startling. Got the range—soprano, mezzo, you name it, got the looks, got the sex. Stick you like a pig for tuppence and make you like it." He shot one of his disconcerting glances at Alleyn. "Troy'll have her hands full," he said. "What?"

"Yes," Alleyn agreed, and with a strong foreboding of what was in store, added: "I don't much fancy her going."

"Quite. Going to put your foot down, are you, Rory?"

Alleyn said: "As far as Troy's concerned I haven't got feet."

"Tell that to the Fraud Squad," said the A.C. and gave a slight whinny.

"Not where her work's concerned. It's a must. For both of us."

"Ah," said the A.C. "Mustn't keep you," he said and shifted without further notice into the tone that meant business. "It just occurs to me that in the circumstances you might, after all, take this trip. And by the way, you know New Zealand, don't you? Yes?" And when Alleyn didn't answer: "What I meant when I said 'coincidence.' The invitation and all that. Drops like a plum into our lap. We're asked to keep a spot of very inconspicuous observation on this article and here's the article's boyfriend asking you to be his guest and Bob, so to speak, is your uncle. Incidentally, you'll be keeping an eye on Troy and her termagant subject, won't you? Well?"

Alleyn said: "Am I to take it, sir, that this is an order?"

"I must say," dodged the A.C., "I thought you would be delighted."

"I expect I ought to be."

"Very well, then," said the A.C. testily, "why the hell aren't you?"

"Well, sir, you talked about coincidences. It so happens that by a preposterous series of them Troy has been mixed up to a greater and lesser degree in four of my cases. And—"

"And by all accounts behaved quite splendidly. Hul-*lo!*" said the A.C. "That's it, is it? You don't like her getting involved?"

"On general principles, no, I don't."

"But my dear man, you're not going out to the antipodes to involve *yourself* in an investigation. You're on observation. There won't," said the A.C., "as likely as not, be anything to observe. Except, of course, your most attractive wife. You're not going to catch a murderer. You're not going to catch anyone. What?"

"I didn't say anything."

"All right. It's an order. You'd better ring your wife and tell her. Morning to you."

III

In Melbourne all was well. The Sydney season had been a fantastic success artistically, financially, and, as far as Isabella Sommita was concerned, personally. "Nothing to equal it had been experienced," as the press raved, "within living memory." One reporter laboriously joked that if cars were motivated by real instead of statistical horsepower the quadrupeds would undoubtedly have been unhitched and the diva drawn in triumph and by human propulsion through the seething multitudes.

There had been no further offensive photography.

Young Rupert Bartholomew had found himself pitchforked into a milieu that he neither understood nor criticized but in which he floundered in a state of complicated bliss and bewilderment. Isabella Sommita had caused him to play his one-act opera. She had listened with an approval that ripened quickly with the realization that the soprano role was, to put it coarsely, so large that the rest of the cast existed only as trimmings. The opera was about Ruth, and the title was *The Alien Corn.* ("Corn," muttered Ben Ruby to Monty Reece, but not in the Sommita's hearing, "is dead right.") There were moments when the pink clouds amid which Rupert floated thinned and a small, ice-cold pellet ran down his spine and he wondered if his opera was any good. He told himself that to doubt it was to doubt the greatest soprano of the age, and the pink clouds quickly re-formed. But the shadow of unease did not absolutely leave him.

Mr. Reece was not musical. Mr. Ruby, in his own untutored way, was. Both accepted the advisability of consulting an expert, and such was the pitch of the Sommita's mounting determination to stage this piece that they treated the matter as one of top urgency. Mr. Ruby, under pretense of wanting to study the work, borrowed it from the Sommita. He approached the doyen of Australian music critics, and begged him, for old times' sake, to give his strictly private opinion on the opera. He did so and said that it stank.

"Menotti-and-water," he said. "Don't let her touch it."

"Will you tell her so?" Mr. Ruby pleaded.

"Not on your Nelly," said the great man and as an afterthought, "What's the matter with her? Has she fallen in love with the composer?"

"Boy," said Mr. Ruby deeply. "You said it."

It was true. After her somewhat tigerish fashion the Sommita was in love. Rupert's Byronic appearance, his melting glance, and his undiluted adoration had combined to do the trick. At this point she had a flaring row with her Australian secretary, who stood up to her and when she sacked him said she had taken the words out of his mouth. She then asked Rupert if he could type and when he said yes promptly offered him the job. He accepted, canceled all pending appointments, and found himself booked in at the same astronomically expensive hotel as his employer. He not only dealt with her correspondence. He was one of her escorts to the theatre and was permitted to accompany her at her practices. He supped with her after the show and stayed longer than any of the other guests. He was in heaven.

On a night when this routine had been observed and Mr. Reece had retired early, in digestive discomfort, the Sommita asked Rupert to stay while she changed into something comfortable. This turned out to be a ruby silken negligé, which may indeed have been comfortable for the wearer but which caused the beholder to shudder in an agony of excitement.

He hadn't a hope. She had scarcely embarked upon the preliminary phases of her formidable techniques when she was in his arms or, more strictly, he in hers.

An hour later he floated down the long passage to his room, insanely inclined to sing at the top of his voice.

"My first!" he exulted. "My very first. And, incredibly—Isabella Sommita."

He was, poor boy, as pleased as Punch with himself.

IV

As far as his nearest associates could discover, Mr. Reece was not profoundly disturbed by his mistress's goings-on. Indeed he appeared to ignore them but, really, it was impossible to tell, he was so remarkably uncommunicative. Much of his time, most of it, in fact, was spent with a secretary, manipulating, it was widely conjectured, the stock markets and receiving long-distance telephone calls. His manner toward Rupert Bartholomew was precisely the same as his manner toward the rest of the Sommita's following: so neutral that it could scarcely be called a manner at all. Occasionally when Rupert thought of Mr. Reece he was troubled by stabs of uncomfortable speculation, but he was too far gone in incredulous rapture to be greatly concerned.

It was at this juncture that Mr. Reece flew to New Zealand to inspect his island lodge, now completed.

On his return, three days later, to Melbourne, he found the Alleyns' letters of acceptance and the Sommita in a high state of excitement.

"Dar-leeng," she said, "you will show me everything. You have photographs, of course? Am I going to be pleased? Because I must tell you I have great plans. But such plans!" cried the Sommita and made mysterious gestures. "You will never guess."

"What are they?" he asked in his flat-voiced way.

"Ah-ah!" she teased. "You must be patient. First the pictures, which Rupert, too, must see. Quick, quick, the pictures."

She opened the bedroom door into the sitting room and in two glorious notes sang, "Rupert!"

Rupert had been coping with her fan mail. When he came in he found that Mr. Reece had laid out a number of glossy, colored photographs on the bed. They were all of the island lodge.

The Sommita was enchanted. She exclaimed, purred, exalted. Several times she burst into laughter. Ben Ruby arrived and the photographs were reexhibited. She embraced all three men severally and more or less together.

And then with a sudden drop into the practical, she said, "The music room. Let me see it again. Yes. How big is it?"

"From memory," said Mr. Reece, "sixty feet long and forty wide." Mr. Ruby whistled. "That's quite a size," he remarked. "That's more like a bijou theatre than a room. You settling to give concerts, honey?"

"Better than that!" she cried. "Didn't I tell you, Monty, my dar-leeng, that we have made plans? Ah, we have cooked up *such* plans, Rupert and I. Haven't we, *caro*? Yes?"

"Yes," Rupert said with an uncertain glance at Mr. Reece. "I mean—. Marvelous."

Mr. Reece had an extremely passive face, but Rupert thought he detected a shade of resignation pass over it. Mr. Ruby, however, wore an expression of the deepest apprehension.

The Sommita flung her right arm magnificently across Rupert's shoulders. "This dear child," she said, and if she had made it "this adorable lover" she could have scarcely been more explicit, "has genius. I tell you—I who know. *Genius.*" They said nothing and she continued. "I have lived with his opera. I have studied his opera. I have studied the leading role. The 'Ruth.' The arias, the solos, the duets—there are two—and the ensembles. All, but all, have the unmistakable stigmata of genius. I do not," she amended, "use the word *stigmata* in the sense of martyrdom. Better, perhaps, to say 'they bear the banner of genius.' *Genius,*" she shouted.

To look at Rupert at this moment one might have thought that *martyrdom* was, after all, the more appropriate word. His face was dark red and he shifted in her embrace. She shook him, none too gently. "Clever, *clever* one," she said and kissed him noisily.

"Are we to hear your plan?" Mr. Reece asked.

The hour being seven o'clock, she hustled them into the sitting room and told Rupert to produce cocktails. He was glad to secrete himself in the chilly pantry provided for drinks, ice, and glasses. A few desultory and inaudible remarks came from the other three. Mr. Ruby cleared his throat once or twice. Then, so unexpectedly that Rupert spilled Mr. Reece's whiskey and soda over his hands, the piano in the sitting room sketched the opening statement of what he had hoped would be the big aria from his opera, and the superb voice, in heartrending pianissimo, sang: "Alone, alone amidst the alien corn."

It was at that moment with no warning at all that Rupert was visited by a catastrophic certainty. He had been mistaken in his opera. Not even the

the fancy to take a picture up at the head of the Pass. Where we have lunch."

"I don't think that's likely," Troy said.

"You're going to paint the famous lady: is that right?"

His manner was sardonic. Troy said yes, she was.

"Rather you than me," said the driver.

"Do you paint, then?"

"Me? Not likely. I wouldn't have the patience."

"It takes a bit more than patience," Alleyn said mildly.

"Yeah? That might be right, too," the driver conceded. There was a longish pause. "Would she have to keep still, then?" he asked.

"More or less."

"I reckon it'll be more 'less' than 'more,'" said the driver. "They tell me she's quite a celebrity," he added.

"Worldwide," said Alleyn.

"What they reckon. Yeah," said the driver with a reflective chuckle, "they can keep it for mine. Temperamental! You can call it that if you like." He whistled. "If it's not one thing it's another. Take the dog. She had one of these fancy hound things, white with droopy hair. The boss give it to her. Well, it goes crook and they get a vet and he reckons it's hopeless and it ought to be put out of its misery. So *she* goes crook. Screechin' and moanin', something remarkable. In the finish the boss says get it over with, so me and the vet take it into the hangar and he chloroforms it and then gives it an injection and we bury it out of sight. Cripes!" said the driver. "When they told her, you'd of thought they'd committed a murder." He sucked his teeth reminiscently.

"Maria," he said presently, "that's her personal help or maid or whatever it's called—she was saying there's been some sort of a schemozzle over in Aussie with the papers. But you'll know about that, Mr. Alleyn. Maria reckons you've taken on this situation. Is that right?"

"I'm afraid not," said Alleyn. Troy gave him a good nudge.

"What she reckons. You being a detective. 'Course Maria's a foreigner. Italian," said the driver. "You can't depend on it with that mob. They get excited."

"You're quartered there, are you? At the Lodge?"

"This is right. For the duration. When they pack it in there'll only be a caretaker and his family on the Island. Monty Reece has built a garage and boathouse on the lakeshore and his launch takes you over to the Lodge. He's got his own chopper, mind. No trouble. Ring through when required."

The conversation died. Troy wondered if the driver called his employer "Monty Reece" to his face and decided that quite possibly he did.

The road across the plains mounted imperceptibly for forty miles, and a look backward established their height. Presently they stared down into a wide riverbed laced with milky turquoise streaks.

At noon they reached the top, where they lunched from a hamper with wine in a chiller kit. Their escort had strong tea from a thermos flask. "Seeing I'm the driver," he said, "and seeing there's the Zig-Zag yet to come." He was moved to entertain them with stories about fatal accidents in the Gorge.

The air up there was wonderfully fresh and smelled aromatically of manuka scrub patching warm, tussocky earth. They were closer now to perpetual snow.

"We better be moving," said the driver. "You'll notice a big difference when we go over the head of the Pass. Kind of sudden."

There was a weathered notice at the top. "Cornishman's Pass. 1000 metres."

The road ran flat for a short distance and then dived into a new world. As the driver had said, it was sudden. So sudden, so new, and so dramatic that for long afterward Troy would feel there had been a consonance between this moment and the events that were to follow, as if, on crossing over the Pass, they entered a region that was prepared and waiting.

It was a world of very dark rain forest that followed, like velvet, the convolutions of the body it enfolded. Here and there waterfalls glinted. Presiding over the forests, snow-tops caught the sun but down below the sun never reached and there, threadlike in its gorge, a river thundered. "You can just hear 'er," said the driver, who had stopped the car.

But all they heard at first was bird song—cool statements, incomparably wild. After a moment Troy said she thought she could hear the river. The driver suggested they go to the edge and look down. Troy suffered horridly from height vertigo but went, clinging to Alleyn's arm. She looked down once as if from a gallery in a theatre on an audience of treetops, and saw the river.

The driver, ever informative, said that you could make out the roof of a car that six years ago went over from where they stood. Alleyn said, "So you can," put his arm round his wife, and returned her to the car.

They embarked upon the Zig-Zag.

The turns in this monstrous descent were so acute that vehicles traveling in the same direction would seem to approach each other and indeed did pass on different levels. They had caught up with such a one and crawled behind it. They met a car coming up from the Gorge. Their own driver pulled up on the lip of the road and the other sidled past on the inner running with half an inch to spare. The drivers wagged their heads at each other.

Alleyn's arm was across Troy's shoulders. He pulled her ear. "First prize for intrepidity, Mrs. A.," he said. "You're being splendid."

"What did you expect me to do? Howl like a banshee?"

Presently the route flattened out and the driver changed into top gear. They reached the floor of the Gorge and drove beside the river, roaring in its courses, so that they could scarcely hear each other speak. It was cold down there.

"Now you're in Westland," shouted the driver.

Evening was well advanced when, after a two hours' passage through the wet loam-scented forest that New Zealanders call bush, they came out into more open country and stopped at a tiny railway station called Kai-kai. Here they collected the private mailbag for the Lodge and then drove parallel with the railway for twenty miles, rounded the nose of a hill, and there lay a great floor of water: Lake Waihoe.

"There you are," said the driver; "that's the Lake for you. *And* the Island."

"Stay me with flagons!" said Alleyn and rubbed his head.

The prospect was astonishing. At this hour the Lake was perfectly unruffled and held the blazing image of an outrageous sunset. Fingers of land reached out bearing elegant trees that reversed themselves in the water. Framed by these and far beyond them was the Island and on the Island Mr. Reece's Lodge.

It was a house designed by a celebrated architect in the modern idiom but so ordered that one might have said it grew organically out of its primordial setting. Giants that carried their swathy foliage in clusters stood magnificently about a grassy frontage. There was a jetty in the foreground with a launch alongside. Grossly incongruous against the uproarious sunset, like some intrusive bug, a helicopter hovered. As they looked, it disappeared behind the house.

"I don't believe in all this," said Troy. "It's out of somebody's dream. It can't be true."

"You reckon?" asked the driver.

"I reckon," said Troy.

They turned into a lane that ran between tree ferns and underbrush down to the lake edge, where there was a garage, a landing stage, a boathouse, and a bell in a miniature belfry. They left the car and walked out into evening smells of wet earth, fern, and moss and the cold waters of the Lake.

The driver rang the bell, sending a single echoing note across the Lake. He then remarked that they'd been seen from the Island. Sure enough, the launch put out. So still was the evening they could hear the putt-putt of the engine. "Sound travels a long way over the water," said the driver.

The sunset came to its preposterous climax. Everything that could be seen, near and far, was sharpened and gilded. Their faces reddened. The far-off windows of the Lodge turned to fire. In ten minutes it had all faded and the landscape was cold. Troy and Alleyn walked a little way along the water's edge, and Troy looked at the house and wondered about the people inside it. Would Isabella Sommita feel that it was a proper showplace for her brilliance and what would she look like posing in the "commodious studio" against those high windows, herself flamboyant against another such sunset as the one that had gone by?

Troy said, "This really *is* an adventure."

Alleyn said, "Do you know, in a cockeyed sort of way it reminds me of one of those Victorian romances by George Macdonald where the characters find a looking glass and walk out of this world into another one inhabited by strange beings and unaccountable ongoings."

"Perhaps," said Troy, "the entrance to that great house will turn out to be our own front door and we'll be back in London."

They talked about the house and the way in which it rose out of its setting in balanced towers. Presently the launch, leaving an arrowhead of rippled silk in its wake, drew in to the landing stage. It was a large, opulent craft. The helmsman came out of his wheelhouse and threw a mooring rope to the car driver.

"Meet Les Smith," said the driver.

"Gidday," said Les Smith. "How's tricks, then, Bert? Good trip?"

"No trouble, Les."

"Good as gold," said the helmsman.

Alleyn helped them stow the luggage. Troy was handed on board and they puttered out on the Lake.

The driver went into the wheelhouse with Les Smith. Troy and Alleyn sat in the stern.

"Here we go," he said. "Liking it?"

"It's a lovely beginning," said Troy. "It's so lovely it hurts."

"Keep your fingers crossed," he said lightly.

II

Perhaps because their day had been so long and had followed so hard on their flight from England, the first night at the Lodge went by rather like a dream for Troy.

They had been met by Mr. Reece's secretary and a dark man dressed like a tarted-up ship's steward, who carried their baggage. They were taken to their room to "freshen up." The secretary, a straw-colored youngish man with a gushing manner, explained that Mr. Reece was on the telephone but would be there to meet them when they came down and that everyone was "changing" but they were not to bother as everybody would "quite understand." Dinner was in a quarter of an hour. There was a drinks tray in the room, and he suggested that they should make use of it and said he knew they would be angelic and excuse him as Mr. Reece had need of his services. He then, as an apparent afterthought, was lavish in welcome, flashed smiles, and withdrew. Troy thought vaguely that he was insufferable.

"I don't know about you," she said, "but I refuse to be 'quite understood' and I'm going to shift my clothes. I require a nice wash and a change. And a drink, by the way."

She opened her suitcase, scuffled in it, and lugged out a jumpsuit, which was luckily made of uncrushable material. She then went into the bathroom, which was equipped like a plumber king's palace. Alleyn effected a lightning change, at which exercise he was a past master, and mixed two drinks. They sat side-by-side on an enormous bed and contemplated their room.

"It's all been done by some super American interior decorator, wouldn't you say?" said Troy, gulping down her brandy-and-dry.

"You reckon?" said Alleyn, imitating the driver.

"I reckon," said Troy. "You have to wade through the carpet, don't you? Not walk on it."

"It's not a carpet; it's about two hundred sheepskins sewn together. The local touch."

"All jolly fine for us to snigger. It's pretty smashing, really, let's face it. Not human, though. If only there was something shabby and out of character somewhere."

"Us," Alleyn said. "We're all of that. Drink up. We'd better not be late."

On their way downstairs they took in the full effect of the hall with its colossal blazing fireplace, display on the walls of various lethal weapons and hangings woven in the Maori fashion, and a large semiabstract wood sculpture of a pregnant nude with a complacent smirk. From behind one of the doors there came sounds of conversation. An insistent male voice rose above the rest. There followed a burst of multiple laughter.

"Good lord," said Alleyn, "it's a house party."

The dark man who had taken their baggage up was in the hall.

"In the drawing room, sir," he said unnecessarily and opened the door.

About a dozen or so people, predominantly male, were grouped at the far end of a long room. The focal point seemed to be a personage with a gray imperial beard and hair *en brosse,* wearing a velvet jacket and flowing tie, an eyeglass, and a flower in his lapel. His manner was that of a practiced raconteur who, after delivering a *mot* is careful to preserve an expressionless face. His audience was barely recovered from its fits of merriment. The straw-colored secretary, indeed, with glass in hand, gently tapped his fingers against his left wrist by way of applause. In doing this he turned, saw the Alleyns, and bent over someone in a sofa with its back to the door.

A voice said, "Ah, yes," and Mr. Reece rose and came to greet them.

He was shortish and dark and had run a little to what is sometimes called expense-account fat. His eyes were large, and his face closed: a face that it would be easy to forget since it seemed to say nothing.

He shook hands and said how glad he was to receive them; to Troy he added that it was an honor and a privilege to welcome her. There were, perhaps, American overtones in his speech, but on the whole his voice, like the rest of him, seemed neutral. He introduced the Alleyns formally to everybody. To the raconteur, who was Signor Beppo Lattienzo and who kissed Troy's hand. To a rotund gentleman who looked like an operatic tenor and turned out to be one: the celebrated Roberto Rodolfo. To Mr. Ben Ruby, who was jocular and said they all knew Troy would do better than *that:* indicating a vast academic portrait of La Sommita's gown topped up by her mask. Then came a young man of startling physical beauty who looked apprehensive—Rupert Bartholomew—a pretty girl whose name Troy, easily baffled by mass introductions, didn't catch, and a largish lady on a sofa, who was called Miss Hilda Dancy and had a deep voice. Finally there loomed up a gentleman with an even deeper voice and a jolly brown face, who proclaimed himself a New Zealander and was called Mr. Eru Johnstone.

Having discharged his introductory duties, Mr. Reece retained his hold on Alleyn, supervised his drink, led him a little apart, and, as Troy could see by the sort of attentive shutter that came over her husband's face, engaged him in serious conversation.

"You have had a very long day, Mrs. Alleyn," said Signor Lattienzo, who spoke with a marked Italian accent. "Do you feel as if all your time signals had become"—he rotated plump hands rapidly round each other—"jumbled together?"

"Exactly like that," said Troy. "Jet hangover, I think."

"It will be nice to retire?"

"Gosh, yes!" she breathed, surprised into ardent agreement.

"Come and sit down," he said and led her to a sofa removed from that occupied by Miss Dancy.

"You must not begin to paint before you are ready," he said. "Do not permit them to bully you."

"Oh, I'll be ready, I hope, tomorrow."

"I doubt it and I doubt even more if your subject will be available."

"Why?" asked Troy quickly. "Is anything the matter? I mean—"

"The *matter*? That depends on one's attitude." He looked fixedly at her. He had very bright eyes. "You have not heard evidently of the great event," he said. "No? Ah. Then I must tell you that the night after next we are to be audience at the first performance on any stage of a brand-new one-act opera. A world premiere, in fact," said Signor Lattienzo, and his tone was exceedingly dry. "What do you think about that?"

"I'm flabbergasted," said Troy.

"You will be even more so when you have heard it. You do not know who I am, of course."

"I'm afraid I only know that your name is Lattienzo."

"Ah-ha."

"I expect I ought to have exclaimed, 'No! Not *the* Lattienzo?' "

"Not at all. I am that obscure creature, a vocal pedagogue. I take the voice and teach it to know itself."

"And—did you—?"

"Yes. I took to pieces the most remarkable vocal instrument of these times and put it together again and gave it back to its owner. I worked her like a horse for three years and I am probably the only living person to whom she pays the slightest professional attention. I am commanded here because she wishes me to fall into a rapture over this opera."

"Have you seen it? Or should one say 'read it'?"

He cast up his eyes and made a gesture of despair.

"Oh dear," said Troy.

"Alas, alas," agreed Signor Lattienzo. Troy wondered if he was habitually so unguarded with complete strangers.

"You have, of course," he said, "noticed the fair young man with the appearance of a quattrocento angel and the expression of a soul in torment?"

"I have indeed. It's a remarkable head."

"What devil, one asks oneself, inserted into it the notion that it could concoct an opera. And yet," said Signor Lattienzo, looking thoughtfully at Rupert Bartholomew, "I fancy the first-night horrors the poor child undoubtedly suffers are not of the usual kind."

"No?"

"No. I fancy he has discovered his mistake and feels deadly sick."

"But this is dreadful," Troy said. "It's the worst that can happen."

"Can it happen to painters, then?"

"I think painters know while they are still at it, if the thing they are doing is no good. I know I do," said Troy. "There isn't perhaps the time lag that authors and, from what you tell me, musicians can go through before they come to the awful moment of truth. Is the opera really so bad?"

"Yes. It is bad. Nevertheless, here and there, perhaps three times, one hears little signs that make one regret he is being spoilt. Nothing is to be spared him. He is to conduct."

"Have you spoken to him? About it being wrong?"

"Not yet. First I shall let him hear it."

"Oh," Troy protested, "but why! Why let him go through with it? Why not tell him and advise him to cancel the performance?"

"First of all, because she would pay no attention."

"But if he refused?"

"She has devoured him, poor dear. He would not refuse. She has made him her secretary-accompanist-composer, but beyond all that and most destructively, she has taken him for her lover and gobbled him up. It is very sad," said Signor Lattienzo, and his eyes were bright as coal nuggets. "But you see," he added, "what I mean when I say that La Sommita will be too much engagée to pose for you until all is over. And then she may be too furious to sit still for thirty seconds. The first dress rehearsal was yesterday. Tomorrow will be occupied in alternately resting and making scenes and attending a second dress rehearsal. And the next night—the performance! Shall I tell you of their first meeting and how it has all come about?"

"Please."

"But first I must fortify you with a drink."

He did tell her, making a good story of it. "Imagine! Their first encounter. All the ingredients of the soap opera. A strange young man, pale as death, beautiful as Adonis, with burning eyes and water pouring off the end of his nose, gazes hungrily at his goddess at one A.M. during a deluge. She summons him to the window of her car. She is kind and before long she is even kinder. And again, kinder. He shows her his opera—it is called *The Alien Corn,* it is dedicated to her, and since the role of Ruth is virtually the entire score and has scarcely finished ravishing the audience with one coloratura embellishment before another sets in, she is favorably impressed. You know, of course, of her celebrated A above high C."

"I'm afraid not!"

"No? It's second only to the achievement recorded in the *Guiness Book of Records.* This besotted young man has been careful to provide for it in her aria. I must tell you by the way that while she sings like the Queen of Heaven, musically speaking this splendid creature is as stupid as an owl."

"Oh, come!"

"Believe me. It is the truth. You see before you the assembled company engaged at vast cost for this charade. The basso: a New Zealander and a worthy successor to Inia te Wiata. He is the Boaz and, believe me, finds himself knee-deep in corn for which 'alien' is all too inadequate a description. The dear Hilda Dancy on the sofa is the Naomi, who escapes with a duet, a handful of recitatives, and the contralto part in an enfeebled pastiche of 'Bella figlia dell' amore.' There she is joined by a mezzo-soprano (the little Sylvia Parry, now talking to the composer). She is, so to speak, Signora Boaz. Next comes the romantic element, in the person of Roberto Rodolfo, who is the head gleaner and adores the Ruth at first sight. She, I need not tell you, dominates the quartet. You find me unsympathetic, perhaps?" said Signor Lattienzo.

"I find you very funny," said Troy.

"But spiteful? Yes?"

"Well—ruthless, perhaps."

"Would we were all."

"What?"

" 'Ruth'-less, my dear."

"Oh, *really!*" said Troy and burst out laughing.

"I am very hungry. She is twenty minutes late as usual and our good Monty consults his watch. Ah! We are to be given the full performance—the Delayed Entrance. Listen."

A musical whooping could at that moment be heard rapidly increasing in volume.

"The celestial fire engine," said Signor Lattienzo, "approaches." He said this loudly to Alleyn, who had joined them.

The door into the hall was flung wide, Isabella Sommita stood on the threshold, and Troy thought: "This is it. O, praise the Lord all ye Lands, this is it."

The first thing to be noticed about the Sommita was her eyes. They were enormous, black, and baleful and set slantwise in her magnolia face. They were topped by two jetty arcs, thin as a camel-hair brush, but one knew that if left to themselves they would bristle and meet angrily above her nose. Her underlip was full, her teeth slightly protuberant with the little gap at the front which is said to denote an amorous disposition.

She wore green velvet and diamonds, and her celebrated bosom, sumptuously displayed, shone like marble.

Everyone who had been sitting rose. Alleyn thought: A bit more of this and the ladies would fall to the ground in curtseys. He looked at Troy and recognized the quickened attention, the impersonal scrutiny that meant his wife was hooked.

"Dar-leengs!" sang La Sommita. "So late! Forgive, forgive." She directed her remarkably searching gaze upon them all, and let it travel slowly, rather, Alleyn thought, in the manner of a lighthouse, until it rested upon him, and then upon Troy. An expression of astonishment and rapture dawned. She advanced upon them both with outstretched arms and cries of excitement, seized their hands, giving them firm little shakes as if she was congratulating them on their union and found her joy in doing so too great for words.

"But you have COME!" she cried at last and appealed to everyone else. "Isn't it wonderful!" she demanded. "They have COME!" She displayed them, like trophies, to her politely responsive audience.

Alleyn said "Hell" inaudibly and as a way of releasing himself kissed the receptive hand.

There followed cascades of welcome. Troy was gripped by the shoulders and gazed at searchingly and asked if she (the Sommita) would "do" and told that already she knew they were *en rapport* and that she (the Sommita) always *"knew."* Didn't Troy always *know?* Alleyn was appealed to: "Didn't she?"

"Oh," Alleyn said, "she's as cunning as a bagload of monkeys, Madame. You've no idea."

Further melodious hoots, this time of laughter, greeted the far from brilliant sally. Alleyn was playfully chided.

They were checked by the entry at the far end of the room of another steward-like personage, who announced dinner. He carried a salver with what was no doubt the mail that had come with the Alleyns and took it to the straw-colored secretary, who said: "On my desk." The man made some inaudible reply and seemed to indicate a newspaper on his salver. The secretary looked extremely perturbed and repeated, loudly enough for Alleyn to hear, "No, no. I'll attend to it. In the drawer of my desk. Take it away."

The man bowed slightly and returned to the doors.

The guests were already in motion and the scene now resembled the close of the first act of an Edwardian comedy, voices pitched rather high, movements studied, the sense, even, of some approach to a climax which would develop in the next act.

It developed, however, there and then. The bass, Mr. Eru Johnstone, said in his enormous voice: "Do I see the evening paper? It will have the results of the Spring Cup, won't it?"

"I should imagine so," said Mr. Reece. "Why?"

"We had a sweep on Top Note. It seemed a clear indication," and he boomed up the room. "Everybody! The Cup!"

The procession halted. They all chattered in great excitement but were, as actors say, "topped" by the Sommita, demanding to see the paper there and then. Alleyn saw the secretary, who looked agitated, trying to reach the servant, but the Sommita had already seized the newspaper and flapped it open.

The scene that followed bore for three or four seconds a farfetched resemblance to an abortive ruck in Rugby football. The guests, still talking eagerly, surged round the prima donna. And then, suddenly, fell silent, backed away, and left her isolated, speechless and crosseyed, holding out the open newspaper as if she intended to drop-kick it to eternity. Alleyn said afterward that he could have sworn she foamed at the mouth.

Across the front page of the paper a banner headline was splashed:

"Sommita says NO FALSIES."

And underneath:

"Signed statement: by famous prima donna. Her curves are all her own. But are they????"

Boxed in a heavy outline, at the center of the page, were about nine lines of typescript and beneath them the enormous signature,

"Isabella Sommita."

III

Dinner had been catastrophic, a one-man show by the Sommita. To say she had run through the gamut of the passions would be a rank understatement: she began where the gamut left off and bursts of hysteria were as passages of rest in the performance. Occasionally she would come to an abrupt halt and wolf up great mouthfuls of the food that had been set before her, for she was a greedy lady. Her discomforted guests would seize the opportunity to join her, in a more conservative manner, in taking refreshment. The dinner was superb.

Her professional associates were less discomforted, the Alleyns afterward agreed, than a lay audience would have been and indeed seemed more or less to take her passion in their stride, occasionally contributing inflammatory remarks while Signor Rodolfo, who was on her left, made wide ineffable gestures and, when he managed to get hold of it, kissed her hand. Alleyn was on her right. He was frequently appealed to and came in for one or two excruciating prods in the ribs as she drove home her points. He was conscious that Troy had her eyes on him and, when he got the chance, made a lightning grimace of terror at her. He saw she was on the threshold of giggles.

Troy was on Mr. Reece's right. He seemed to think that in the midst of this din he was under an obligation to make conversation and remarked upon the lack of journalistic probity in Australia. The offending newspaper, it seemed, was an Australian weekly with a wide circulation in New Zealand.

When the port had been put before him and his dear one had passed for the time being into a baleful silence, he suggested tonelessly that the ladies perhaps wished to withdraw.

The Sommita made no immediate response, and a tricky hiatus occurred during which she glowered at the table. Troy thought, Oh, to hell with all this, and stood up. Hilda Dancy followed with alacrity and so after a moment's hesitation did wide-eyed Sylvia Parry. The men got to their feet.

The Sommita rose, assumed the posture of a Cassandra about to give tongue, appeared to change her mind, and said she was going to bed.

About twenty minutes later Alleyn found himself closeted in a room that looked like the setting for a science-fiction film but was Mr. Reece's study. With him were Mr. Reece himself, Mr. Ben Ruby, Rupert Bartholomew, and the straw-colored secretary, whose name turned out to be Hanley.

The infamous sheet of newsprint was laid out on a table around which the men had gathered. They read the typewritten letter reproduced in the central box.

To The Editor
The Watchman
Sir: I wish, through your column, to repudiate utterly an outrageous calumny which is circulating in this country. I wish to state, categorically, that I have no need of, and therefore have never resorted to, cosmetic surgery or to artificial embellishment of any kind whatsoever. I am, and I present myself to my public, as God made me. Thank you.

Isabella Sommita.
(Picture on page 30)

"And you tell me," Alleyn said, "that the whole thing is a forgery?"

"You bet it's a forgery," said Ben Ruby. "Would she ever help herself to a plateful of poisonous publicity! My God, this is going to make her the big laugh of a lifetime over in Aussie. *And* it'll spread overseas, you better believe it."

"*Have* there in fact been any rumors, any gossip of this sort?"

"Not that we have knowledge of," said Mr. Reece. "And if it had been at all widespread, we certainly would have heard. Wouldn't we, Ben?"

"Well, face it, old boy, anyone that's seen her would know it was silly. I meantersay, look at her cleavage! Speaks for itself." Mr. Ruby turned to Alleyn. "You've seen. You couldn't miss it. She's got the best twin set you're likely to meet in a lifetime. Beautiful! Here! Take a look at this picture."

He turned to page 30 and flattened it out. The "picture" was a photograph of the Sommita in profile with her head thrown back, her hands behind her resting on a table and taking the weight. She was in character as Carmen, and an artificial rose was clenched between her teeth. She was powerfully décolletée and although at first glance there seemed to be no doubt of the authenticity of the poitrine, on closer examination there were certain curious little marks in that region suggestive of surgical scars. The legend beneath read, "Seeing's believing!"

"She never liked that picture," Mr. Ruby said moodily. "Never. But the press did, so we kept it in the handouts. Here!" he exclaimed, jamming a forefinger at it. "Here take a look at this, will you? This has been interfered with. This has been touched up. This has been tinkered with. Those scars are phony."

Alleyn examined it. "I think you're right," he said and turned back to the front page.

"Mr. Hanley," he said, "do you think that typewriter could have been one belonging to anybody in Madame Sommita's immediate circle? Can you tell that?"

"Oh? Oh!" said the secretary and stooped over the paper. "Well," he said after a moment, "it wasn't typed on my machine." He laughed uncomfortably. "I can promise you that much," he said. "I wouldn't know about hers. How about it, Rupert?"

"Bartholomew," explained Mr. Reece in his flattened way, "is Madame's secretary." He stood back and motioned Rupert to examine the page.

Rupert, who had a tendency to change color whenever Mr. Reece paid him any attention, did so now. He stooped over the paper.

"No," he said, "it's not our—I mean my—machine. The letter *p* is out of alignment in ours. And anyway it's not the same type."

"And the signature? That looks convincing enough, doesn't it?" Alleyn asked his host.

"Oh, yes," he said. "It's Bella's signature."

"Can any of you think of any cause Madame Sommita may have had to put her signature at the foot of a blank sheet of letter paper?"

Nobody spoke.

"Can she type?"

"No," they all said, and Ben Ruby added irritably, "Ah, for Chrissake, what's the point of laboring at it? There've been no rumors about her bosom, pardon my candor, and, hell, she never wrote that bloody letter. It's got to be a forgery and, by God, in my book it's got to be that sodding photographer at the bottom of it."

The two young men made sounds of profound agreement.

Mr. Reece raised his hand and they were silenced. "We are fortunate enough," he announced, "to have Mr. Alleyn, or rather Chief Superintendent Alleyn, with us. I suggest that we accord him our full attention, gentlemen."

He might have been addressing a board meeting. He turned to Alleyn and made a slight inclination. "Will you—?" he invited.

Alleyn said: "Of course, if you think I can be of use. But I expect I ought just to mention that if there's any idea of calling in the police, it will have to be the New Zealand police. I'm sure you will understand that."

"Oh, quite so, quite so," said Mr. Reece. "Let us say we will value, immensely, your unofficial expertise."

"Very well. But it won't be at all startling."

The men took chairs round the table, as if, Alleyn thought, they were resigning themselves to some damned lecture. The whole scene, he thought, was out of joint. They might have arranged between themselves how it should be played but were not quite sure of their lines.

He remembered his instructions from the A.C. He was to observe, act with extreme discretion, fall in with the terms of his invitation, and treat the riddle of the naughty photographer as he would any case to which he had been consigned in the ordinary course of his duties.

He said: "Here goes, then. First of all: if this was a police job, one of the first things to be done would be to make an exhaustive examination of the letter, which seems to be a reproduction in print of an original document. We would get it blown up on a screen, search the result for any signs of fingerprints or indications of what sort of paper the original might be. Same treatment for the photograph, with particular attention to the rather clumsy faking of surgical scars.

"At the same time, someone would be sent to the offices of the *Watchman* to find out everything available about when the original letter was received and whether by post or pushed into the correspondence box at the entrance or wherever of the *Watchman*'s office. And also who dealt with it. The *Watchman*, almost certainly, would be extremely cagey about this and would, when asked to produce the original, say it had not been kept, which might or might not be true. Obviously," Alleyn said, "they didn't ask for any authorization of the letter or take any steps to assure themselves that it was genuine."

"It's not that sort of paper," said Ben Ruby. "Well, look at it. If we sued for libel it'd be nothing new to the *Watchman*. The scoop would be worth it."

"Didn't I hear," Alleyn asked, "that on one occasion the photographer—'Strix' isn't it?—dressed as a woman, asked for her autograph, and then fired his camera at point-blank range and ducked out?"

Mr. Ruby slammed the table. "By God, you're right," he shouted, "and he got it. She signed. He got her signature."

"It's too much, I suppose, to ask if she remembers any particular book or whether she ever signed at the bottom of a blank page or how big the page was."

"She remembers! Too right she remembers!" Mr. Ruby shouted. "That one *was* an outsize book. Looked like something special for famous names. She remembers it on account it was not the usual job. As for the signature she's most likely to have made it extra big to fill out the whole space. She does that."

"Were any of you with her? She was leaving the theatre, wasn't she? At the time?"

"I was with her," Mr. Reece offered. "So were you, Ben. We always escort her from the stage door to her car. I didn't actually see the book. I was looking to make sure the car was in the usual place. There was a big crowd."

"I was behind her," said Mr. Ruby. "*I* couldn't see anything. The first thing *I* knew was the flash and the rumpus. She was yelling out for somebody to stop the photographer. Somebody else was screaming, 'Stop that woman' and fighting to get through. And it turned out afterwards, the screamer was the woman herself, who was the photographer Strix, if you can follow me."

"Just," said Alleyn.

"He's made monkeys out of the lot of us; all along the line he's made us look like monkeys," Mr. Ruby complained.

"What does *he* look like? Surely someone must have noticed something about him?"

But, no, it appeared. Nobody had come forward with a reliable description. He operated always in a crowd where everyone's attention was focused on his victim and cameramen abounded. Or unexpectedly he would pop round a corner with his camera held in both hands before his face, or from a car that shot off before any action could be taken. There had been one or two uncertain impressions—he was bearded, he had a scarf pulled over his mouth, he was dark. Mr. Ruby had a theory that he never wore the same clothes twice and always went in for elaborate makeups, but there was nothing to support this idea.

"What action," Mr. Reece asked Alleyn, "would you advise?"

"To begin with: *not* an action for libel. Can she be persuaded against it, do you think?"

"She may be all against it in the morning. You never know," said Hanley, and then with an uneasy appeal to his employer: "I *beg* your pardon, sir, but I mean to say you *don't*, do you? Actually?"

Mr. Reece, with no change of expression in his face, merely looked at his secretary, who subsided nervously.

Alleyn had returned to the *Watchman*. He tilted the paper this way and that under the table lamp. "I think," he said, "I'm not *sure,* but I *think* the original paper was probably glossy."

"I'll arrange for someone to deal with the *Watchman* end," said Mr. Reece, and to Hanley: "Get through to Sir Simon Marks in Sydney," he ordered. "Or wherever he is. Get him."

Hanley retreated to a distant telephone and huddled over it in soundless communication.

Alleyn said: "If I were doing this as a conscientious copper, I would now ask you all if you have any further ideas about the perpetrator of these ugly tricks—assuming for the moment that the photographer and the concocter of the letter are one and the same person. Is there anybody you can think of who bears a grudge deep enough to inspire such persistent and malicious attacks? Has she an enemy, in fact?"

"Has she a hundred bloody enemies?" Mr. Ruby heatedly returned. "Of course she has. Like the home-grown baritone she insulted in Perth or the top hostess in Los Angeles who threw a high-quality party for her and asked visiting royalty to meet her."

"What went wrong?"

"She didn't go."

"Oh dear!"

"Took against it at the last moment because she'd heard the host's money came from South Africa. We talked about a sudden attack of migraine, which might have answered if she hadn't gone to supper at Angelo's and the press hadn't reported it with pictures the next morning."

"Wasn't 'Strix' already in action by then, though?"

"That's true," agreed Mr. Ruby gloomily. "You've got something there. But enemies! My oath!"

"In my view," said Mr. Reece, "the matter of enmity doesn't arise. This has been from first to last a profitable enterprise. I've ascertained that 'Strix' can ask what he likes for his photographs. It's only a matter of time, one imagines, before they reappear in book form. He's hit on a money-spinner and unless we can catch him in the act he'll go on spinning as long as the public interest lasts. Simple as that."

"If he concocted the letter," Alleyn said, "it's hard to see how he'd make money out of that. He could hardly admit to forgery."

Rupert Bartholomew said: "I think the letter was written out of pure spite. She thinks so, too; you heard her. A sort of black practical joke."

He made this announcement with an air of defiance, almost of proprietorship. Alleyn saw Mr. Reece look at him for several seconds with concentration as if his attention had been unexpectedly aroused. He thought: "That boy's getting himself into deep water."

Hanley had been speaking into the telephone. He stood up and said, "Sir Simon Marks, sir."

Mr. Reece took the call inaudibly. The others fell into an unrestful silence, not wishing to seem as if they listened but unable to find anything to say to each other. Alleyn was conscious of Rupert Bartholomew's regard, which as often as he caught it was hurriedly turned away. "He's making some sort of appeal," Alleyn thought and went over to him. They were not removed from the others.

"Do tell me about your opera," he said. "I've only gathered the scantiest picture from our host of what is going to happen, but it all sounds most exciting."

Rupert muttered something about not being too sure of that.

"But," said Alleyn, "it must be an enormous thing for you, isn't it? For the greatest soprano of our time to bring it all about? A wonderful piece of good fortune, I'd have thought."

"Don't," Rupert muttered. "Don't say that."

"Hullo! What's all this? First-night nerves?"

Rupert shook his head. Good Lord, Alleyn thought, a bit more of this and he'll be in tears. Rupert stared at him and seemed to be on the edge of speech when Mr. Reece put back the receiver and rejoined the others. "Marks will attend to the *Watchman*," he said. "If the original is there he'll see that we get it."

"Can you be sure of that?" Ruby asked.

"Certainly. He owns the group and controls the policy."

They began to talk in a desultory way, and for Alleyn their voices sounded a long way off and disembodied. The spectacular room became unsteady and its contents swelled, diminished, and faded. I'm going to sleep on my feet, he thought and pulled himself together.

He said to his host, "As I can't be of use, I wonder if I may be excused? It's been a long day and one didn't get much sleep on the plane."

Mr. Reece was all consideration. "How very thoughtless of us," he said. "Of course. Of course." He made appropriate hospitable remarks about hoping the Alleyns had everything they required, suggested that they breakfast late in their room and ring when they were ready for it. He sounded as if he were playing some sort of internal cassette of his own recording. He glanced at Hanley, who advanced, all eager to please.

"We're in unbelievable bliss," Alleyn assured them, scarcely knowing what he said. And to Hanley: "No, please don't bother. I promise not to doze off on my way up. Goodnight, everyone."

He crossed the hall, which was now dimly lit. The pregnant woman loomed up and stared at him through slitted eyes. Behind her the fire, dwindled to a glow, pulsated quietly.

As he passed the drawing room door he heard a scatter of desultory conversation: three voices at the most, he thought, and none of them belonged to Troy.

And, sure enough, when he reached their room he found her in bed and fast asleep. Before joining her he went to the heavy window curtains, parted them, and saw the Lake in moonlight close beneath him, stretching away like a silver plain into the mountains. Incongruous, he thought, and impertinent, for this little knot of noisy, self-important people with their self-imposed luxury and seriocomic concerns to be set down at the heart of such an immense serenity.

He let the curtain fall and went to bed.

He and Troy were coming back to earth in Mr. Reece's airplane. An endless road rushed toward them. Appallingly far below, the river thundered and water lapped at the side of their boat. He fell quietly into it and was immediately fathoms deep.

CHAPTER III

Rehearsal

I

TROY SLEPT HEAVILY and woke at nine o'clock to find Alleyn up and dressed and the room full of sunshine.

"I've never known you so unwakable," he said. "Deep as the Lake itself. I've asked for our breakfast."

"Have you been up long?"

"About two hours. The bathroom's tarted up to its eyebrows. Jets of water smack you up where you least expect it. I went downstairs. Not a soul about apart from the odd slave who looked at me as if I was dotty. So I went outside and had a bit of an explore. Troy, it really is quite extraordinarily beautiful, this place; so still; the Lake clear, the trees motionless, everything new and fresh and yet, or so one feels, empty and belonging to primordial time. Dear me," said Alleyn, rubbing his nose, "I'd better not try. Let's tell each other about what went on after that atrocious dinner party."

"I've nothing to tell. When we left you the diva merely said in a volcanic voice, 'Excuse me, ladies,' and swept upstairs. I gave her time to disappear and then followed suit. I can scarcely remember getting myself to bed. What about you?"

Alleyn told her.

"If you ask me," Troy said, "it needs only another outrage like this and she'll break down completely. She was literally shaking all over as if she had a rigor. She can't go on like that. Don't you agree?"

"Not really. Not necessarily. Have you ever watched two Italians having a discussion in the street? Furious gestures, shrieks, glaring eyes, faces close together. Any moment, you think, it'll be a free-for-all, and then without warning they burst out laughing and hit each other's shoulders in comradely accord. I'd say she was of the purest Italian—perhaps Sicilian—peasant stock and utterly uninhibited. Add to that the propensity of all public performers to cut up rough and throw temperaments right and left when they think they've been slighted, and you've got La Sommita. You'll see."

But beyond staring bemusedly out of the windows, Troy was not given much chance of seeing for herself. Instead, she and Alleyn were to be taken on a tour of the house by Mr. Reece, beginning with the "studio," which turned out to be on the same level as their bedroom. Grand pianos being as chickenfeed to Mr. Reece, there was one in here, and Troy was given to understand that the Sommita practiced at it and that the multiple-gifted Rupert Bartholomew acted as her accompanist, having replaced an Australian lady in that capacity. She found, with astonishment, that an enormous easel of sophisticated design and a painter's table and stool had been introduced into the room for her use. Mr. Reece was anxious, he said, to know if they suited. Troy, tempted to ask if they were on sale or return, said they did and was daunted by their newness. There was also a studio throne with a fine lacquer screen on it. Mr. Reece expressed a kind of drab displeasure that it was not large enough to accommodate the grand piano as well. Troy, who had already made up her mind what she wanted to do with her subject, said it was of no consequence. When, she asked, would she be able to start? Mr. Reece, she thought, was slightly evasive. He had not spoken this morning to Madame, he said, but he understood there would be rehearsals for the greater part of the day. The orchestra was to arrive. They had been rehearsing, with frequent visits from Bartholomew, and would arrive by bus. The remaining guests were expected tomorrow.

The studio window was of the enormous plate-glass kind. Through it they had a new view of Lake and mountains. Immediately beneath them, adjoining the house, was a patio and close by an artificially enclosed swimming pool, around which and in which members of the house party were displayed. On the extreme right, separated from the pool and surrounded by native bush, was an open space and a hangar which, Mr. Reece said, accommodated the helicopter.

Mr. Reece was moved to talk about the view, which he did in a gray, factual manner, stating that the Lake was so deep in many parts that it had never been sounded and that the region was famous for a storm, known locally as the Rosser, which rose unheralded in the mountains and whipped the Lake into fury and had been responsible for many fatal accidents.

He also made one or two remarks on the potential for "development," and Alleyn saw the look of horrified incredulity on his wife's face. Fortunately, it appeared, pettifogging legislation about land tenure and restrictions on imported labor would prohibit what Mr. Reece called "worthwhile touristic planning" so that the prospect of marinas, high-rise hotels, speedboats, loud music, and floodlit bathing pools did not threaten those primordial shores. Sandflies by day and mosquitoes by night, Mr. Reece thought, could be dealt with, and Troy envisaged low-flying aircraft delivering millions of gallons of kerosene upon the immaculate face of the Lake.

Without warning she was overcome by a return of fatigue and felt quite unable to face an extended pilgrimage of this unending mansion. Seeing her dilemma, Alleyn asked Mr. Reece if he might fetch her gear and unpack it. There was immediate talk of summoning a "man," but they managed to avoid this. And then a "man" in fact did appear, the dark, Italianate-looking person who had brought their breakfast. He had a message for Mr. Reece. Madame Sommita wished to see him urgently.

"I think I had better attend to this," he said. "We all meet on the patio at eleven for drinks. I hope you will both join us there."

So they were left in peace. Alleyn fetched Troy's painting gear and unpacked it. He opened up her old warrior of a paintbox, unstrapped her canvases and set out her sketchbook, and the collection of materials that were like signatures written across any place where Troy worked. She sat in a chair by the window and watched him and felt better.

Alleyn said: "This room will be desterilized when it smells of turpentine and there are splotches of flake white on the ledge of that easel and paint rags on the table."

"At the moment it can*not* be said to beckon one to work. They might as well have hung 'Please Don't Touch' notices on everything."

"You won't mind once you get going."

"You think? P'raps you're right," she said, cheering up. She looked down at the house party around the pool. "That's quite something," she said. "Very frisky color and do notice Signor Lattienzo's stomach. Isn't it superb!"

Signor Lattienzo was extended on an orange-colored chaise longue. He wore a green bathrobe, which had slid away from his generous torso, upon which a book with a scarlet cover was perched. He glistened.

Prompted, perhaps by that curious telepathy which informs people that they are being stared at, he threw back his head, saw Troy and Alleyn, and waved energetically. They responded. He made eloquent Italianate gestures, which he wound up by kissing both his hands at once to Troy.

"You've got off, darling," said Alleyn.

"I like him, I think. But I'm afraid he's rather malicious. I didn't tell you. He thinks that poor beautiful young man's opera is awful. Isn't that sad?"

"Is *that* what's the matter with the boy!" Alleyn exclaimed. "Does *he* know it's no good?"

"Signor Lattienzo thinks he might."

"And yet they're going on with all this wildly extravagant business."

"She insists, I imagine."

"Ah."

"Signor Lattienzo says she's as stupid as an owl."

"Musically?"

"Yes. But, I rather gathered, generally, as well."

"The finer points of attitudes towards a hostess don't seem to worry Signor Lattienzo."

"Well, if we're going to be accurate, I suppose she's not his hostess. She's his ex-pupil."

"True."

Troy said: "That boy's out of his depth, altogether. She's made a nonsense of him. She's a monster and I can't wait to get it on canvas. A monster," Troy repeated with relish.

"He's not down there with the rest of them," Alleyn pointed out. "I suppose he's concerned with the arrival of his orchestra."

"I can't bear to think of it. Imagine! All these musical V.I.P.s converging on him and he knowing, if he *does* know, that it's going to be a fiasco. He's going to conduct. Imagine!"

"Awful. Rubbing his nose in it."

"We'll have to be there."

"I'm afraid so, darling."

Troy had turned away from the window and now faced the door of the room. She was just in time to see it gently closing.

"What's wrong?" Alleyn asked quickly.

Troy whispered: "The door. Someone's just shut it."

"Really?"

"Yes. Truly."

He went to the door and opened it. Troy saw him look to his right.

"Hullo, Bartholomew," he said. "Good morning to you. Looking for Troy, by any chance?"

There was a pause and then Rupert's Australian voice, unevenly pitched, not fully audible: "Oh, good morning. I—yes—matter of fact—message—."

"She's here. Come in."

He came in, white-faced and hesitant. Troy welcomed him with what she felt might be overdone cordiality and asked if his message was for her.

"Yes," he said, "yes, it is. She—I mean Madame Sommita—asked me to say she's very sorry but in case you might be expecting her she can't—she's afraid she won't be able—to sit for you today because—because—."

"Because of rehearsals and everything? Of course. I wasn't expecting it and in fact I'd rather *not* start today."

"Oh," he said, "yes. I see. Good-oh, then. I'll tell her."

He made as if to go but seemed inclined to stay.

"Do sit down," said Alleyn, "unless you're in a hurry, of course. We're hoping someone—you, if you've time—will tell us a little more about tomorrow night."

He made a movement with both hands almost as if he wanted to cover his ears but checked it and asked if they minded if he smoked. He produced a cigarette case; gold with a jeweled motif.

"Will you?" he said to Troy and when she declined, turned to Alleyn. The open case slipped out of his uncertain grasp. He said: "Oh. Sorry," and looked as if he'd been caught shoplifting. Alleyn picked it up. The inside of the lid was inscribed. There in all its flamboyance was the now familiar signature: "Isabella Sommita."

Rupert was making a dreadfully clumsy business of shutting the case and lighting his cigarette. Alleyn, as if continuing a conversation, asked Troy where she would like him to put the easel. They improvised an argument about light and the possibility of the bathing pool as a subject. This enabled them both to look out of the window.

"Very tricky subject," Troy muttered. "I don't think I'm up to it."

"Better maintain a masterly inactivity, you think?" Alleyn cheerfully rejoined. "You may be right."

They turned back into the room and there was Rupert Bartholomew, sitting on the edge of the model's throne and crying.

He possessed male physical beauty to such a remarkable degree that there was something unreal about his tears. They trickled over the perfect contours of his face and might have been drops of water on a Greek mask. They were distressing but they were also incongruous.

Alleyn said: "My dear chap, what's the matter?" and Troy: "Would you like to talk about it? We're very discreet."

He talked. Disjointedly at first and with deprecating interruptions—they didn't want to hear all this—he didn't want them to think he was imposing

—it could be of no interest to them. He wiped his eyes, blew his nose, drew hard on his cigarette, and became articulate.

At first it was simply a statement that *The Alien Corn* was no good, that the realization had come upon him out of the blue and with absolute conviction. "It was ghastly," he said. "I was pouring out drinks and suddenly without warning, I knew. Nothing could alter it: the thing's punk."

"Was this performance already under consideration?" Alleyn asked him.

"She had it all planned. It was meant to be a—well—a huge surprise. And the ghastly thing is," said Rupert, his startlingly blue eyes opened in horror, "I'd thought it all fantastic. Like one of those schmaltzy young-genius-makes-it films. I'd been in—well—in ecstasy."

"Did you tell her, there and then?" asked Troy.

"Not then. Mr. Reece and Ben Ruby were there. I—well I was so—you know—shattered. Sort of. I waited," said Rupert and blushed, "until that evening."

"How did she take it?"

"She didn't take it. I mean she simply wouldn't listen. I mean she simply swept it aside. She said—my God, she said genius always had moments like these, moments of what she called divine despair. She said *she* did. Over her singing. And then, when I sort of tried to stick it out she—was—well, very angry. And you see—I mean she had cause. All her plans and arrangements. She'd written to Beppo Lattienzo and Sir David Baumgartner and she'd fixed up with Roberto and Hilda and Sylvia and the others. And the press. The big names. All that. I did hang out for a bit but—"

He broke off, looked quickly at Alleyn and then at the floor. "There were other things. It's more complicated than I've made it sound," he muttered.

"Human relationships can be hellishly awkward, can't they?" Alleyn said.

"You're telling me," Rupert fervently agreed. Then he burst out: "I think I must have been mad! Or ill, even. Like running a temperature and now it's gone and—and—I'm cleaned out and left with tomorrow."

"And you *are* sure?" Troy asked. "What about the company and the orchestra? Do you know what they think? And Signor Lattienzo?"

"She made me promise not to show it to him. I don't know if *she's* shown it. I think she has. He'll have seen at once that it's awful, of course. And the company: they know all right. Roberto Rodolfo very tactfully suggests alterations. I've seen them looking at each other. They stop talking when I turn up. Do you know what they call it? They think I haven't heard but I've heard all right. They call it *Corn*. Very funny. Oh," Rupert cried out, "she shouldn't have done it! It hasn't been a fair go: I hadn't got a hope. Not a hope in hell. My God, she's making me *conduct*. There I'll stand, before those V.I.P.s waving my arms like a bloody puppet and they won't know which way to look for embarrassment."

There was a long silence, broken at last by Troy.

"Well," she said vigorously, "refuse. Never mind about the celebrities and the fuss and the phony publicity. It'll be very unpleasant and it'll take a lot of guts, but at least it'll be honest. To the devil with the lot of them. Refuse."

He got to his feet. He had been bathing, and his short yellow robe had fallen open. He's apricot-colored, Troy noted, not blackish tan and coarsened by exposure like most sun addicts. He's really too much of a treat. No wonder she grabbed him. He's a collector's piece, poor chap.

"I don't think," Rupert said, "I'm any more chicken than the next guy. It's not that. It's her—Isabella. You saw last night what she can be like. And coming on top of this letter business—look, she'd either break down and make herself ill or—or go berserk and murder somebody. Me, for preference."

"Oh, come *on!*" said Troy.

"No," he said, "it's not nonsense. Really. She's a Sicilian."

"Not *all* Sicilians are tigers," Alleyn remarked.

"Her kind are."

Troy said, "I'm going to leave you to Rory. I think this calls for male-chauvinist gossip."

When she had gone, Rupert began apologizing again. What, he asked, would Mrs. Alleyn think of him?

"Don't start worrying about that," Alleyn said. "She's sorry, she's not shocked and she's certainly not bored. And I think she may be right. However unpleasant it may be, I think perhaps you should refuse. But I'm afraid it's got to be your decision and nobody else's."

"Yes, but you see you don't know the worst of it. I couldn't bring it out with Mrs. Alleyn here. I—Isabella—we—"

"Good Lord, my dear chap—" Alleyn began and then pulled himself up. "You're lovers, aren't you?" he said.

"If you can call it that," he muttered.

"And you think if you take this stand against her you'll lose her? That it?"

"Not exactly—I mean, yes, of course, I suppose she'd kick me out."

"Would that be such a very bad thing?"

"It'd be a bloody good thing," he burst out.

"Well then—?"

"I can't expect you to understand. I don't understand myself. At first it was marvelous: magical. I felt equal to anything. Way up. Out of this world. To hear her sing, to stand at the back of the theatre and see two thousand people go mad about her and to know that for *me* it didn't end with the curtain calls and flowers and ovations, but that for *me* the best was still to come. Talk about the crest of the wave—gosh, it was super."

"I can imagine."

"And then, after that—you know—that moment of truth about the opera, the whole picture changed. You could say that the same thing happened about her. I saw all at once, what she really is like and that she only approved of that bloody fiasco because she saw herself making a success in it and that she ought never, *never* to have given me the encouragement she did. And I knew she had no real musical judgment and that I was lost."

"All the more reason," Alleyn began and was shouted down.

"You can't tell me anything I don't know. But I was *in* it. Up to my eyes. Presents—like this thing, this cigarette case. Clothes, even. A fantastic salary. At first I was so far gone in, I suppose you could call it, rapture, that it didn't seem degrading. And now, in spite of seeing it all as it really is, I can't get out. I can't."

Alleyn waited. Rupert got to his feet. He squared his shoulders, pocketed his awful cigarette case, and actually produced a laugh of sorts.

"Silly, isn't it?" he said, with an unhappy attempt at lightness. "Sorry to have bored you."

Alleyn said: "Are you familiar with Shakespeare's sonnets?"

"No. Why?"

"There's a celebrated one that starts off by saying the expense of spirit in a waste of shame is lust in action. I suppose it's the most devastating statement you can find of the sense of degradation that accompanies passion without love. 'La Belle Dame Sans Merci' is schmaltz alongside it. That's your trouble, isn't it? The gilt's gone off the gingerbread, but the gingerbread is still compulsive eating. And that's why you can't make the break."

Rupert twisted his hands together and bit his knuckles.

"You could put it like that," he said.

The silence that followed was interrupted by an outbreak of voices on the patio down below: exclamations, sounds of arrival, and unmistakably the musical hoots that were the Sommita's form of greeting.

"Those are the players," said Rupert. "I must go down. We have to rehearse."

II

By midday Troy's jet lag had begun to fade and with it the feeling of unreality in her surroundings. A familiar restlessness replaced it and this, as always, condensed into an itch to work. She and Alleyn walked round the Island and found that, apart from the landing ground for the helicopter and the lawnlike frontage with its sentinal trees, it was practically covered by house. The clever architect had allowed small areas of original bush to occur where they most could please. On the frontal approach from the Lake to the Lodge, this as well as the house itself served to conceal a pole from which power lines ran across the Lake to a spit of land with a dado of trees that reached out from the far side of the Island.

"For the moment," said Troy, "don't let's think about what it all cost."

They arrived at the bathing pool as eleven o'clock drinks were being served. Two or three guests had arrived at the same time as the quartet of players, who turned out to be members of a South Island regional orchestra. The musicians, three men and a lady, sticking tightly to each other and clearly overawed, were painstakingly introduced by Rupert. The Sommita, in white sharkskin with a tactful tunic, conversed with them very much *de haut en bas* and then engulfed the Alleyns, particularly Troy, whose arm and hand she secured, propelling her to a canopied double seat and retaining her hold after they had occupied it. Troy found all this intensely embarrassing but at least it gave her a good opportunity to notice the markedly asymmetric structure of the face, the distance between the corner of the heavy mouth and that of the burning eye being greater on the left side. And there was a faint darkness, the slightest change of color, on the upper lip. You couldn't have a better face for Carmen, Troy thought.

The Sommita talked of the horrible letter and the touched-up photograph and what they had done to her and how shattering it was that the activities of the infamous photographer—for of course he was at the bottom of it—should have extended to New Zealand and even to the Island, when she had felt safe at last from persecution.

"It *is* only the paper, though," Troy pointed out. "It's not as though the man himself was here. Don't you think it's quite likely that now the tour of Australia is over he may very well have gone back to his country of origin, wherever that may be? Mightn't the letter have just been his final effort? You had gone and he couldn't take any more photographs, so he cooked up the letter?"

The Sommita stared at her for a long time and in a most uncomfortable manner, gave her hand a meaningful squeeze, and released it. Troy did not know what to make of this.

"But," the Sommita was saying, "we must speak of your art, must we not? And of the portrait. We begin the day after tomorrow, yes? And I wear my crimson décolleté which you have not yet seen. It is by Saint Laurent and is dramatic. And for the pose—this."

She sprang to her feet, curved her sumptuous right arm above her head, rested her left palm upon her thigh, threw back her head, and ogled Troy frowningly in the baleful, sexy manner of Spanish dancers. The posture provided generous exposure to her frontage and gave the lie to any suggestions of plastic surgery.

"I think," Troy said, "the pose might be a bit exacting to maintain. And if it's possible I'd like to make some drawings as a sort of limbering up. Not posed drawings. Only slight notes. If I could just be inconspicuously on the premises and make scribbles with a stick of charcoal."

"Yes? Ah! Good. This afternoon there will be rehearsal. It will be only a preparation for the dress rehearsal tonight. You may attend it. You must be very inconspicuous, you understand."

"That will be ideal," said Troy. "Nothing could suit me better."

"My poor Rupert," the Sommita suddenly proclaimed, again fixing Troy in that disquieting regard, "is nervous. He has the sensitivity of the true artist, the creative temperament. He is strung like a violin."

She suspects something, Troy thought. She's pumping. Damn.

She said: "I can well imagine."

"I'm sure you can," said the Sommita with what seemed to be all too meaningful an emphasis.

"Darling Rupert," she called to him, "if your friends are ready, perhaps you should show them—?"

The players gulped down the rest of their drinks and professed themselves ready.

"Come!" invited the Sommita, suddenly all sparkle and gaiety. "I show you now our music room. Who knows? There may be inspiration for you, as for us. We bring also our great diviner, who is going to rescue me from my persecutors."

She towed Troy up to Alleyn and unfolded this proposition. Her manner suggested the pleasurable likelihood of his offering to seduce her at the first opportunity. "So you come to the salon too," she said, "to hear music?" And in her velvet tones the word *music* was fraught with much the same meaning as *china* in *The Country Wife.*

Troy hurried away to get her sketching block, charcoal, and conté crayon. Alleyn waited for her and together they went to the "music room."

It was entered by double doors from the rear of the main hall. It was, as Mr. Ruby had once indicated, more like a concert chamber than a room. It was tedious to insist upon the grandiloquences of Waihoe Lodge: enough to say that the stage occupied one end of this enormous room, was approached from the auditorium by three wide steps up to a projecting apron and thence to the main acting area. Beautifully proportioned pillars were ranged across the back, flanking curtained doorways. The musicians were in a little huddle by a grand piano on the floor of the auditorium and in the angle of the apron. They were tuning their instruments, and Rupert, looking ill, was with them. The singers came in and sat together in the auditorium.

There was a change, now, in the Sommita: an air of being in her own professional climate and with no nonsense about it. She was deep in conversation with Rodolfo when the Alleyns came in. She saw them and pointed to chairs halfway down the auditorium. Then she folded her arms and stood facing the stage. Every now and then she shouted angry instructions. As if on some stage director's orders, a shaft of sunlight from an open window found her. The effect was startling. Troy settled herself to make a drawing.

Now the little orchestra began to play: tentatively at first with stoppages when they consulted with Rupert. Then with one and another of the soloists, repeating passages, making adjustments. Finally the Sommita said, "We take the aria, darling," and swept up to stage center.

Rupert's back was turned to the audience and facing the musicians. He gave them the beat conservatively. They played and were stopped by the Sommita. "More authority," she said. "We should come in like a lion. Again."

Rupert waited for a moment. Troy saw that his left hand was clenched so hard that the knuckles shone white. He flung back his head, raised his right hand, and gave a strong beat. The short introduction was repeated with much more conviction, it reached a climax of sorts, and then the whole world was filled with one long sound: *"Ah!"* sang the Sommita. *"A-a-a-h!"* and then, *"What joy is here, what peace, what plentitude!"*

At first it was impossible to question the glory, so astonishing was the sound, so absolute the command. Alleyn thought: Perhaps it hardly matters what she sings. Perhaps she could sing "A bee-eye-ee-eye-ee sat on a wall-eye-all-eye-all" and distill magic from it. But before the aria had come to its end he thought that even if he hadn't been warned he would have known that musically it was no great shakes. He thought he could detect clichés and banalities. And the words! He supposed in opera they didn't matter all that much, but the thought occurred that she might more appropriately have sung: "What joy is here, what peace, what platitude."

Troy was sitting two seats in front of Alleyn, holding her breath and drawing in charcoal. He could see the lines that ran out like whiplashes under her hand, the thrown-back head, and the wide mouth. Not a bit, he thought remembering their joke, as if the Sommita were yawning: the drawing itself sang. Troy ripped the sketch off her pad and began again. Now her subject talked to the orchestra, who listened with a kind of avid respect, and Troy drew them in the graphic shorthand that was all her own.

Alleyn thought that if Rupert was correct in believing the players had rumbled the inadequacies of the music, the Sommita had ravished them into acceptance, and he wondered if, after all, she could work this magic throughout the performance and save poor Rupert's face for him.

A hand was laid on Alleyn's shoulder. He turned his head and found Mr. Reece's impassive countenance close to his own. "Can you come out?" he said very quietly. "Something has happened."

As they went out the Sommita and Roberto Rodolfo had begun to sing their duet.

The servant who had brought the Alleyns their breakfast was in the study looking uneasy and deprecating.

"This is Marco," said Mr. Reece. "He has reported an incident that I think you should know about. Tell Chief Superintendent Alleyn exactly what you told me."

Marco shied a little on hearing Alleyn's rank, but he told his story quite coherently and seemed to gather assurance as he did so. He had the Italian habit of gesture but only a slight accent.

He said that he had been sent out to the helicopter hangar to fetch a case of wine that had been brought in the previous day. He went in by a side door and as he opened it heard a scuffle inside the hangar. The door dragged a little on the floor. There was, unmistakably, the sound of someone running. "I think I said something, sir, 'Hullo' or something, as I pushed the door open. I was just in time to catch sight of a man in bathing costume, running out at the open end of the hangar. There's not much room when the chopper's there. I had to run back and round the tail, and by the time I got out he was gone."

Alleyn said: "The hangar, of course, opens on to the cleared space for takeoff."

"Yes, sir. And it's surrounded by a kind of shrubbery. The proper approach follows round the house to the front. I ran along it about sixty feet but there wasn't a sign of him, so I returned and had a look at the bush, as they call it. It was very overgrown, and I saw at once he couldn't have got through it without making a noise. But there wasn't a sound. I peered about in case he was lying low, and then I remembered that on the far side of the clearing there's another path through the bush going down to the lakeside. So I took this path. With the same result: nothing: Well, sir," Marco amended and an air of complacency, if not of smugness, crept over his face, "I say 'nothing.' But that's not quite right. There was something. Lying by the path. There was this."

With an admirable sense of timing he thrust forward his open palm. On it lay a small round metal or plastic cap.

"It's what they use to protect the lens, sir. It's off a camera."

III

"I don't think," Alleyn said, "we should jump to alarming conclusions about this but certainly it should be followed up. I imagine," he said dryly, "that anything to do with photography is a tricky subject at the Lodge."

"With some cause," said Mr. Reece.

"Indeed. Now then, Marco. You've given us a very clear account of what happened, and you'll think I'm being unduly fussy if we go over it all again."

Marco spread his hands as if offering him the earth.

"First of all, then: this man. Are you sure it wasn't one of the guests or one of the staff?"

"No, no, no, no, no," said Marco rapidly, shaking his finger sideways as if a wasp had stung it. "Not possible. No!"

"Not, for instance, the launch man?"

"No, sir. No! Not anyone of the household. I am certain. I would swear it."

"Dark or fair?"

"Fair. Bareheaded. Fair. Certainly a blond."

"And bare to the waist?"

"Of course. Certainly."

"Not even a camera slung over his shoulder?"

Marco closed his eyes, bunched his fingers and laid the tips to his forehead. He remained like that for some seconds.

"Well? What about it?" Mr. Reece asked a trifle impatiently.

Marco opened his eyes and unbunched his fingers. "It could have been in his hands," he said.

"This path," Alleyn said. "The regular approach from the front of the house round to the hangar. As I recollect, it passes by the windows of the concert chamber?"

"Certainly," Mr. Reece said and nodded very slightly at Alleyn. "And this afternoon, they were not curtained."

"And open?"

"And open."

"Marco," Alleyn said, "did you at any point hear anything going on in the concert chamber?"

"But yes!" Marco cried, staring at him. "Madame, sir. It was Madame. She sang. With the voice of an angel."

"Ah."

"She was singing still, sir, when I returned to the clearing."

"After you found this cap, did you go on to the lakeside?"

"Not quite to the lakeside, sir, but far enough out of the bush to see that he was not there. And then I thought I should not continue, but that I should report at once to Signor Reece. And that is what I did."

"Very properly."

"Thank you, sir."

"And I," said Mr. Reece, "have sent the house staff and guests to search the grounds."

"If I remember correctly," Alleyn said, "at the point where Marco emerged from the bush, it is only a comparatively short distance across from the Island to that narrow tree-clad spit that reaches out from the mainland towards the Island and is linked to it by your power lines?"

"You suggest he might have swum it?" Mr. Reece asked.

"No, sir," Marco intervened. "Not possible. I would have seen him." He stopped and then asked with a change of voice, "Or would I?"

"If he's on the Island he will be found," said Mr. Reece, coldly. And then to Alleyn: "You were right to say we should not make too much of this incident. It will probably turn out to be some young hoodlum or another with a camera. But it is a nuisance. Bella has been very much upset by this Strix and his activities. If she hears of it she might well begin to imagine all sorts of things. I suggest we say nothing of it to tonight's guests and performers. You hear that, Marco?"

Marco was all acquiescence.

Alleyn thought that if what was no doubt a completely uncoordinated search was thundering about the premises, the chances of keeping the affair secret were extremely slender. But, he reminded himself, for the present the rehearsal should be engaging everybody's attention.

Marco was dismissed with a less than gushing word of approval from his employer.

When he had gone, Mr. Reece, with a nearer approach to cosiness than Alleyn would have thought within his command, said: "What do you make of all that? Simply a loutish trespasser or—something else?"

"Impossible to say. Is it pretty widely known in New Zealand that Madame Sommita is your guest?"

"Oh yes. One tries to circumvent the press, but one never totally succeeds. It has come out. There have been articles about the Lodge itself and there are pressmen who try to bribe the launch man to bring them over. He is paid a grotesquely high wage and has the sense to refuse. I must say," Mr. Reece confided, "it would be very much in character for one of these persons to skulk about the place, having, by whatever means, swimming perhaps, got himself on the Island. The hangar would be a likely spot, one might think, for him to hide."

"He would hear the rehearsal from there."

"Precisely. And await his chance to come out and take a photograph through an open window? It's possible. As long," Mr. Reece said and actually struck his right fist into his left palm, "as long as it isn't that filthy Strix at it again. Anything rather than that."

"Will you tell me something about your staff? You've asked me to do my constabulary stuff and this would be a routine question."

"Ned Hanley is better qualified than I to answer it. He came over here from Australia and saw to it. An overambitious hotel had gone into liquidation. He engaged eight of the staff and a housekeeper for the time we shall be using the Lodge. Marco was not one of these, but we had excellent references, I understand. Ned would tell you."

"An Italian, of course?"

"Oh, yes. But a naturalized Australian. He made a great thing, just now, of his story, but I would think it was substantially correct. I'm hoping the guests and performers will not, if they do get hold of the story, start jumping to hysterical conclusions. Perhaps we should let it be known quite casually that a boy had swum across and has been sent packing. What do you think?"

Before Alleyn could answer, the door opened and Signor Beppo Lattienzo entered. His immaculate white shorts and silken "matelot" were in disarray and he sweated copiously.

"My dears!" he said. "Drama! The hunt is up. The Hound of Heaven itself—or should I say Himself?—could not be more diligent."

He dropped into a chair and fanned himself with an open palm. " 'Over hill, over dale, through bush, through briar,' as the industrious fairy remarks and so do I. What fun to be known as 'The Industrious Fairy,' " panted Signor Lattienzo, coyly.

"Any luck?" Alleyn asked.

"Not a morsel. The faithful Maria, my dear Monty, is indomitable. Into the underbrush with the best of us. She has left her hairnet as a votary offering on a thorny entanglement known, I am informed, as a Bush Lawyer."

Signor Lattienzo smiled blandly at Mr. Reece and tipped Alleyn a lewdish wink. "This," he remarked, "will not please our diva, no? And if we are to speak of hounds and of persistence, how about the intrepid Strix? What zeal! What devotion! Though she flee to the remotest antipodes, though she, as it were, go to earth (in, one must add, the greatest possible comfort) upon an enchanted island, there shall he nose her out. One can only applaud. Admit it, my dear Monty."

Mr. Reece said: "Beppo, there is no reason to suppose that the man Strix has had any part in this incident. The idea is ridiculous and I am most anxious that Bella should not entertain it. It is a trivial matter involving some local lout and must not be blown up into a ridiculous drama. You know very well, none better, how she can overreact and after last night's shock—I really must ask you to use the greatest discretion."

Signor Lattienzo wiped the sweat away from the area round his left eye. He breathed upon his eyeglass, polished it, and with its aid contemplated his host. "But, of course, my dear Monty," he said quietly, "I understand. Perfectly. I dismiss the photographer. Poof! He is gone. And now—"

The door burst open and Ben Ruby strode in. He also showed signs of wear and tear.

"Here! Monty!" he shouted. "What the hell's the idea? These servants of yours are all saying bloody Strix is back and you ought to call in the police. What about it?"

IV

Mr. Reece, white with annoyance, summoned his entire staff, including the driver and the launch man, into the study. Alleyn, who was asked to remain, admired the manner in which the scene was handled and the absolute authority which Mr. Reece seemed to command. He repeated the explanation that had been agreed upon. The theory of the intrusive lout was laid before them and the idea of Strix's recrudescence soundly rubbished. "You will forget this idiotic notion, if you please," said Mr. Reece, and his voice was frigid. He looked pointedly at Maria. "You understand," he said, "you are not to speak of it to Madame." He added something in Italian—not one of Alleyn's strongest languages, but he thought it was a threat of the instant sack if Maria disobeyed orders.

Maria, who had shut her mouth like a trap, glared back at Mr. Reece and muttered incomprehensibly. The household was then dismissed.

"I don't like your chances," said Ben Ruby. "They'll talk."

"They will behave themselves. With the possible exception of the woman."

"She certainly didn't sound cooperative."

"Jealous."

"Ah!" said Signor Lattienzo. "The classic situation: mistress and abigail. No doubt Bella confides extensively."

"No doubt."

"Well, she can't do so for the moment. The *recitazione* is still in full swing."

Ben Ruby opened the door. From beyond the back of the hall and the wall of the concert chamber but seeming to come from nowhere in particular, there was singing: disembodied as if heard through the wrong end of some auditory telescope. Above three unremarkable voices there soared an incomparable fourth.

"Yes," said Signor Lattienzo. "It is the *recitazione* and they are only at the quartet: a third of the way through. They will break for luncheon at one-thirty and it is now twenty minutes past noon. For the time being we are safe."

"I wouldn't bet on that one, either," said Ben Ruby. "She likes to have Maria on tap at rehearsals."

"If you don't mind," Alleyn said, "I think I'll just take a look at the terrain."

The three men stared at him and for a moment said nothing. And then Mr. Reece stood up. "You surely cannot for a moment believe—" he said.

"Oh, no, no. But it strikes me that one might find something that would confirm the theory of the naughty boy."

"Ah."

"What, for instance?" asked Ben Ruby.

"This or that," Alleyn said airily. "You never know. The unexpected has a way of turning up. Sometimes. Like you, I wouldn't bet on it."

And before any of them had thought of anything else to say, he let himself out and gently closed the door.

He went out of the house by the main entrance, turned left and walked along the graveled front until he came to a path that skirted the western facade. He followed it and as he did so the sound of music and of singing, broken by discussion and the repetition of short passages, grew louder. Presently he came to the windows of the concert chamber and saw that one of them, the first, was still open. It was at the end farthest removed from the stage, which was screened from it by a curtain that operated on a hinged bracket.

He drew nearer. There, quite close, was the spot in the auditorium where the Sommita had stood with her arms folded, directing the singers.

And there, still in her same chair, still crouched over her sketching block, with her short hair tousled and her shoulders hunched, was his wife. She was still hard at work. Her subject was out of sight haranguing the orchestra, but her image leaped up under Troy's grubby hand. She was using a conté crayon, and the lines she made, sometimes broadly emphatic, sometimes floating into extreme delicacy, made one think of the bowing of an accomplished fiddler.

She put the drawing on the floor, pushed it away with her foot, and stared at it, sucking her knuckles and scowling. Then she looked up and saw her husband. He pulled a face at her, laid a finger across his lips, and ducked out of sight.

He had been careful not to tread on the narrow strip of earth that separated the path from the wall and now, squatting, was able to examine it. It had been recently trampled by a number of persons. To hell with the search party, thought Alleyn.

He moved farther along the path, passing a garden seat and keeping as far away as was possible from the windows. The thicket of fern and underbrush on his right was broken here and there by forays, he supposed, of the hunt, successfully ruining any signs there might have been of an intruder taking cover. Presently the path branched away from the house into the bush to emerge, finally, at the hangar.

Inside the hangar there was ample evidence of Marco's proceedings. The earthy shortcut he had taken had evidently been damp, and Alleyn could trace his progress on the asphalt floor exactly as he had described it.

Alleyn crossed the landing ground, scorching under the noonday sun. Sounds from the concert chamber had faded. There was no bird song. He found the path through the bush to the lakeside and followed it: dark green closed about him and the now familiar conservatory smell of wet earth and moss.

It was only a short distance to the Lake, and soon the bush began to thin out, admitting shafts of sunlight. It must have been about here that Marco said he had spotted the protective cap from the camera. Alleyn came out into the open and there, as he remembered them from his morning walk, were the Lake and overhead power lines reaching away to the far shore.

Alleyn stood for a time out there by the lakeside. The sun that beat down on his head spread a kind of blankness over the landscape, draining it of color. He absentmindedly reached into his pocket for his pipe and touched a small hard object. It was the lens cap, wrapped in his handkerchief. He took it out and uncovered it, being careful not to touch the surface: a futile precaution, he thought, after Marco's handling of the thing.

It was from a well-known make of camera, which produced self-developing instant results. The trade name was stamped on the top.

He folded it up and returned it to his pocket. In a general way he did not go much for "inspiration" in detective work, but if ever he had been visited by such a bonus, it was at that moment down by the Lake.

CHAPTER IV

Performance

I

EARLY IN THE MORNING of the following day there came a change in the weather. A wind came up from the northwest, not a strong wind and not steady, but rather it was a matter of occasional brushes of cooler air on the face and a vague stirring among the trees around the house. The sky was invaded by oncoming masses of clouds, turrets and castles that mounted and changed and multiplied. The Lake was no longer glassy but wrinkled. Tiny wavelets slapped gently at the shore.

At intervals throughout the morning new guests would arrive: some by chartered plane to the nearest airport and thence by helicopter to the Island, others by train and car and a contingent of indigenous musical intelligentsia by bus. The launch would be very active.

A piano tuner arrived and could be heard dabbing away at single notes and, to the unmusical ear, effecting no change in their pitch.

Sir David Baumgartner, the distinguished musicologist and critic, was to stay overnight at the Lodge, together with a Dr. Carmichael, a celebrated consultant who was also president of the New Zealand Philharmonic Society. The remainder faced many dark hours in launch, bus and cars and in midmorning would be returned wan and bemused to their homes in Canterbury.

The general idea, as far as the Sommita had concerned herself with their reaction to these formidable exertions, was that the guests would be so enraptured by their entertainment as to be perfectly oblivious of all physical discomfort. In the meantime she issued a command that the entire house party was to assemble outside the house for Mr. Ben Ruby to take a mass photograph. They did so in chilly discomfort under a lowering sky.

"Eyes and teeth to the camera, everybody," begged Mr. Ruby.

The Sommita did not reappear at luncheon and was said to be resting. It was, on the whole, a quiet meal. Even Signor Lattienzo did little to enliven it. Rupert Bartholomew, looking anguished, ate nothing, muttered something to the effect that he was needed in the concert chamber, and excused himself. Mr. Reece made ponderous small talk with Troy while Alleyn, finding himself next to Miss Hilda Dancy, did his best. He asked her if she found opening nights trying and she replied in vibrant contralto, "When they are important," clearly indicating that this one was not. After Rupert had left them she said, "It's a crying shame."

"A crying shame?" he ventured. "How?"

"You'll see," she prophesied. "Cannibal!" she added and, apart from giving him a dark look which he was unable to interpret, though he thought he could make a fairly good guess, she was disinclined for any further conversation.

After luncheon the Alleyns went up to the studio, where he related the story of the interloper and the camera cap. When he had finished and Troy had taken time to think it over, she said: "Rory, do you think he's still on the Island? The photographer?"

"The photographer? Yes," he said, and something in his voice made her stare at him. "I think the photographer's here. I'll tell you why." And he did.

For the rest of the afternoon Troy brooded over her drawings and made some more. Sounds of arrival were heard from time to time. Beyond the great window the prospect steadily darkened and the forest on the far shore moved as if brushed by an invisible hand. "The arrivals by launch will have a rough trip," said Alleyn. The helicopter flapped down to its landing place and discharged an imposing personage in a black overcoat and hat. "Sir David Baumgartner, no less," said Alleyn and then, "Troy, you saw me outside that window, didn't you? Do you think you would have been bound to notice a photographer if one had operated through that same window?"

"Oh, no," she said, "not bound to at all. I was working."

"So you were," he agreed. "I think I'll take a look."

And he went downstairs to the concert chamber. When he arrived, there was no one to be seen but Hanley, who was evidently stage manager for the production, superintending three imported electricians in the management of the lights and seeming to be in a state of controlled dementia. Whatever the climate outside might be, inside it was electric.

Alleyn heard Hanley demand at large: "Well, where the hell is he? He ought to be *here*. I've never seen anything like it."

The curtain that separated the apron from the stage proper was open and the acting areas were prepared for the performance. A realistic set had not been attempted. A blue cloth had been hung behind the pillars and the central entrance was flanked by two stylized sheafs of corn. Three sumptuously draped seats completed the decor.

Alleyn sat where Troy had sat to make her drawings. The window in question was still uncurtained and open. Such had been her concentration that he thought she would not have noticed him if he had not leaned over the sill.

Hanley said to the electricians, "It's easy, really. You've marked the areas where Madame Sommita stands, and you've got them covered. Fade up when she's there and fade down when she moves away. Otherwise there are no lights cues: they stay as set throughout. Cover the windows and we'll run it through once more."

He turned to Alleyn. "Have *you* seen Rupert?" he asked. "He was to be here half an hour ago to give the music cues. They went all to blazes at the dress rehearsal. Honestly, it's too much."

"I'll see if I can find him," he volunteered.

"Super of you," gushed Hanley with a desperate return to his secretarial manner. "Thank you *so* much."

Alleyn thought that a hunt for the unhappy Rupert might well turn out to be as fruitless as the one for a problematical photographer, but he struck it lucky, if that was the appropriate word, at the first cast, which was Mr. Reece's spectacular study.

He wondered if a visitor was expected to knock or even to make an appointment before venturing upon this sanctum, but decided to effect an entrance in the normal manner. He opened the door and walked in.

The actual entrance was shut off from the room by a large leather screen, the work of a decorator much in vogue. Alleyn came in to the sound of Mr. Reece's voice.

"—remind you of the favors you have taken at her hands. And this is how you would choose to repay them. By making her a laughingstock. You allow us to engage celebrated artists, to issue invitations, to bring people of the utmost distinction halfway across the world to hear this thing, and now propose to tell them that after all there will be no performance and they can turn round and go back again."

"I know. Do you think I haven't thought of all this! Do you think—please, *please* believe me—Bella, I beg you—"

"Stop!"

Alleyn, behind the screen and about to beat a retreat, fetched up short as if the command had been directed at him. It was the Sommita.

"The performance," she announced, "will take place. The violin is competent. He will lead. And you, you who have determined to break my heart, will sulk in your room. And when it is over you will come to me and weep your repentance. And it will be too late. Too late. You will have murdered my love for you. Ingrate!" shouted the Sommita. "Poltroon! So!"

Alleyn heard her masterful tread. As he had no time to get away, he stepped boldly out of cover and encountered her face-to-face.

Her own face might have been a mask for one of the Furies. She made a complicated gesture, and for a moment he thought that actually she might haul off and hit him, blameless as he was, but she ended up by grasping him by his coat collar, giving him a ferocious précis of their predicament, and ordering him to bring Rupert to his senses. When he hesitated, she shook him like a cocktail, burst into tears, and departed.

Mr. Reece, standing with authority on his own hearthrug, had not attempted to stem the tide of his dear one's wrath nor was it possible to guess at his reaction to it. Rupert sat with his head in his hands, raising it momentarily to present a stricken face.

"I'm so sorry," Alleyn said; "I've blundered in with what is clearly an inappropriate message."

"Don't go," said Mr. Reece. "A message? For me?"

"For Bartholomew. From your secretary."

"Yes? He had better hear it."

Alleyn delivered it. Rupert was wanted to set the lights.

Mr. Reece asked coldly, "Will you do this? Or is it going too far to expect it?"

Rupert got to his feet. "Well," he asked Alleyn, "what do you think, now? Do you say I should refuse?"

Alleyn said: "I'm not sure. It's a case of divided loyalties, isn't it?"

"I would have thought," said Mr. Reece, "that any question of loyalty was entirely on one side. To whom is he loyal if he betrays his patrons?"

"Oh," Alleyn said, "to his art."

"According to him, he has no 'art.'"

"I'm not sure," Alleyn said slowly, "whether, in making his decision, it really matters. It's a question of aesthetic integrity."

Rupert was on his feet and walking toward the door.

"Where are you going?" Mr. Reece said sharply.

"To set the lights. I've decided," said Rupert loudly. "I can't stick this out any longer. I'm sorry I've given so much trouble. I'll see it through."

II

When Alleyn went up to their room in search of Troy, he found her still suffering from jet lag, fast asleep on their enormous bed. At a loose end, and worried about Rupert Bartholomew's sudden capitulation, Alleyn returned downstairs. He could hear voices in the drawing room and concert chamber. Outside the house, a stronger wind had got up.

Midway down the hall, opposite the dining room, there was a door which Mr. Reece had indicated as opening into the library. Alleyn thought he would find himself something to read and went in.

It might have been created by a meticulous scene painter for an Edwardian drama. Uniform editions rose in irremovable tiers from floor to ceiling, the result, Alleyn supposed, of some mass-ordering process: classics, biographies, and travel. There was a section devoted to contemporary novels, each a virgin in its unmolested jacket. There was an assembly of "quality" productions that would have broken the backs of elephantine coffee tables, and there were orderly stacks of the most popular weeklies.

He wandered along the ranks at a loss for a good read and high up in an ill-lit corner came upon a book that actually bore signs of usage. It was unjacketed and the spine was rubbed. He drew it out and opened it at the title page.

Il Mistero da Bianca Rossi, by Pietro Lamparelli. Alleyn didn't read Italian with the complete fluency that alone gives easy pleasure but the title was an intriguing surprise. He allowed the half-title page to flip over and there on the flyleaf in sharp irregular characters was the owner's name, M. V. Rossi.

He settled down to read it.

An hour later he went upstairs and found Troy awake and refreshed.

The opera, a one-acter which lasted only an hour, was to begin at eight o'clock. It would be prefaced by light snacks with drinks and followed by a grand dinner party.

"Do you suppose," Troy wondered, as they dressed, "that a reconciliation has taken place?"

"I've no idea. She may go for a magnificent acceptance of his surrender or she may not be able to do herself out of the passionate rapture bit. My bet would be that she's too professional to allow herself to be upset before a performance."

"I wish he hadn't given in."

"He's made the harder choice, darling."

"I suppose so. But if she does take him back—it's not a pretty thought."

"I don't think he'll go. I think he'll pack his bags and go back to teaching the piano and playing with his small Sydney group and doing a little typing on the side."

"Signor Lattienzo did say there were two or three signs of promise in the opera."

"Did he? If he's right, the more shame on that termagant for what she's done to the boy."

They were silent for a little while after this and then Troy said: "Is there a window open? It's turned chilly, hasn't it?"

"I'll look."

The curtains had been closed for the night. Alleyn parted them, and discovered an open window. It was still light outside. The wind had got up strongly now; there was a great pother of hurrying clouds in the sky and a wide vague sound abroad in the evening.

"It's brewing up out there," Alleyn said. "The Lake's quite rough." He shut the window.

"Not much fun for the guests going home," said Troy and then: "I'll be glad, won't you, when this party's over?"

"Devoutly glad."

"Watching that wretched boy's ordeal, it'll be like sitting out an auto-da-fé," she said.

"Would you like to have a migraine? I'd make it sound convincing."

"No. He'd guess. So, oh Lord, would she."

"I'm afraid you're right. Should we go down, now, darling, to our champagne and snacks?"

"I expect so. Rory, your peculiar mission seems to have got mislaid, doesn't it? I'd almost forgotten about it. Do you, by any chance, suppose Mr. Reece to be a 'Godfather' with an infamous Sicilian 'Family' background?"

"He's a cold enough fish to be anything but—" Alleyn hesitated for a moment. "No," he said. "So far, there's been nothing to report. I shall continue to accept his hospitality and will no doubt return empty-handed to my blasted boss. I've little stomach for the job, and that's a fact. If it wasn't for you, my particular dish, and your work in hand, I'd have even less. Come on."

Notwithstanding the absence of Rupert and all the performers, the drawing room was crowded. About thirty guests had arrived by devious means and were being introduced to each other by Mr. Reece and his secretary. There were top people from the Arts Council, various conductors and a selection of indigenous critics, notably a prestigious authority from the *New Zealand Listener*. Conspicuous among the distinguished guests from abroad was a large rubicund man with drooping eyelids and a dictatorial nose: Sir David Baumgartner, the celebrated critic and musicologist. He was in close conversation with Signor Lattienzo, who, seeing the Alleyns, gave them one of his exuberant bows, obviously told Sir David who they were, and propelled him toward them.

Sir David told Troy that it really was a great honor and a delightful surprise to meet her and asked if it could be true that she was going to paint the Great Lady. He chaffed Alleyn along predictable lines, saying that they would all have to keep their noses clean, wouldn't they? He spoke gravely of the discomforts of his journey. It had come upon him, to put it bluntly, at a most inconvenient time and if it had been anybody else —here he gave them a roguish glance—he wouldn't have dreamed of—he need say no more. The implication clearly was that *The Alien Corn* had better be good.

Lobster sandwiches, pâté, and miniature concoctions of the kind known to Mr. Justice Shallow as "pretty little tiny kickshaws" were handed round and champagne galore. Sir David sipped, raised his eyebrows and was quickly ready for a refill. So were all the new arrivals. Conversation grew noisy.

"Softening-up process," Alleyn muttered.

And indeed by ten minutes to eight all signs of travel fatigue had evaporated and when Marco, who had been much in evidence, tinkled up and down on a little xylophone, he was obliged to do so for some time like a ship's steward walking down corridors with a summons to dinner.

Ben Ruby and Mr. Reece began a tactful herding toward the concert chamber.

The doors were open. The audience assembled itself.

The chairs in the front rows were ticketed with the names of the houseguests and some of the new arrivals who evidently qualified as V.I.P.s. Troy and Alleyn were placed on the left of Mr. Reece's empty chair, Sir David and Signor Lattienzo on its right, with Ben Ruby beyond them. The rest of the élite comprised the conductor of the New Zealand Philharmonic Orchestra and his wife, three professors of music from as many universities, an Australian newspaper magnate, and four representatives of the press—which press exactly had not been defined. The remainder of an audience of about fifty chose their own seats, while at the back the household staff was feudally accommodated.

The collective voice was loud and animated and the atmosphere of expectancy fully established. "If only they keep it up," Troy whispered to Alleyn. She glanced along the row to Signor Lattienzo. His arms were folded and his head inclined toward Sir David, who was full of animation and bonhomie. Lattienzo looked up from under his brows, saw Troy, and crossed the fingers of his right hand.

The players came in and tuned their instruments, a sound that always caught Troy under the diaphragm. The lights in the auditorium went out. The stage curtain glowed. Mr. Reece slipped into his seat beside Troy. Rupert Bartholomew came in from behind the stage so inconspicuously that he had raised his baton before he had been noticed. The overture began.

Troy always wished she knew more about music and could understand why one sound moved her and another left her disengaged. Tonight she was too apprehensive to listen properly. She tried to catch the response of the audience, watched Rupert's back and wondered if he was able to distill any magic from his players, wondered, even, how long the ephemeral good nature induced by champagne could be expected to last with listeners who knew what music was about. She was so distracted by these speculations that the opening of the curtain caught her by surprise.

She had dreamed up all sorts of awful possibilities: Rupert breaking down and walking out, leaving the show to crawl to disaster; Rupert stopping the proceedings and addressing the audience; or the audience itself growing more and more restless or apathetic and the performance ending on the scantiest show of applause, and the audience being harangued by an infuriated Sommita.

None of these things took place. True, as the opera developed, the boisterous good humor of the audience seemed to grow tepid, but the shock of that Golden Voice, the astonishment it engendered note by note, was so extraordinary that no room was left for criticism. And there was, or so it seemed to Troy, a passage in the duet with Hilda Dancy—"Whither thou goest"—when suddenly the music came true. She thought: That's one of the bits Signor Lattienzo meant. She looked along the row and he caught her glance and nodded.

Sir David Baumgartner, whose chin was sunk in his shirt frill in what passed for profound absorption, raised his head. Mr. Reece, sitting bolt upright in his chair, inconspicuously consulted his watch.

The duet came to its end and Troy's attention wandered. The show was well dressed, the supporting artists being clad in low-profile biblical gear hired from a New Zealand company who had recently revived the York

Cycle. The Sommita's costume, created for the occasion, was white and virginal and, if it was designed to make Ruth look like a startling social misfit amidst the alien corn, succeeded wonderfully in achieving this end.

The quartet came and went and left no mark. Sir David looked irritated. The Sommita, alone on stage, sailed into a recitative and thence to her big aria. Troy now saw her purely in terms of paint, fixing her in the memory, translating her into a new idiom. The diva had arrived at the concluding *fioritura,* she moved toward her audience, she lifted her head, she spread her arms and rewarded them with her trump card—A above high C.

No doubt she would have been very cross if they had observed the rule about not applauding until the final curtain. They did not observe it. They broke into a little storm of clapping. She raised a monitory hand. The performance entered into its penultimate phase: a lachrymose parting between Ruth and Signor Rodolfo, plump in kilted smock and leg strappings and looking like a late photograph of Caruso. Enter Boaz, discovering them and ordering the gleaner to be beaten. Ruth and Naomi pleading with Boaz to relent, which he did, and the opera ended with a rather cursory reconciliation of all hands in chorus.

The sense of relief when the curtains closed was so overwhelming that Troy found herself clapping wildly. After all, it had not been so bad. None of the horrors she had imagined had come to pass, it was over, and they were in the clear.

Afterward, she wondered if the obligatory response from the audience could have been evoked by the same emotion.

Three rapid curtain calls were taken, the first by the company, the second by the Sommita, who was thinly cheered by back-benchers, and the third again by the Sommita, who went through her customary routine of extended arms, kissed hands, and deep curtseys.

And then she turned to the orchestra, advanced upon it with outstretched hand and beckoning smile, only to find that her quarry had vanished. Rupert Bartholomew was gone. The violinist stood up and said something inaudible but seemed to suggest that Rupert was backstage. The Sommita's smile had become fixed. She swept to an upstage entrance and vanished through it. The audience, nonplussed, kept up a desultory clapping which had all but died out when she reentered, bringing, almost dragging, Rupert after her.

He was sheet-white and disheveled. When she exhibited him, retaining her grasp of his hand, he made no acknowledgment of the applause she exacted. It petered out into a dead silence. She whispered something and the sound was caught up in a giant enlargement: the northwest wind sighing round the Island.

The discomfiture of the audience was extreme. Someone, a woman, behind Troy said: "He's not well; he's going to faint," and there was a murmur of agreement. But Rupert did not faint. He stood bolt upright, looked at nothing, and suddenly freed his hand.

"Ladies and gentlemen," he said loudly.

Mr. Reece began to clap and was followed by the audience. Rupert shouted, "Don't do that," and they stopped. He then made his curtain speech.

"I expect I ought to thank you. Your applause is for a Voice. It's a wonderful Voice, insulted by the stuff it has been given to sing tonight. For that I am responsible. I should have withdrawn it at the beginning when I realized—when I first realized—when I knew—"

He swayed a little and raised his hand to his forehead.

"When I knew," he said. And then he did faint. The curtains closed.

III

Mr. Reece handled the catastrophe with expertise. He stood up, faced his guests, and said that Rupert Bartholomew had been unwell for some days and no doubt the strain of the production had been a little too much for him. He (Mr. Reece) knew that they would all appreciate this and he asked them to reassemble in the drawing room. Dinner would be served as soon as the performers were ready to join them.

So out they all trooped and Mr. Reece, followed by Signor Lattienzo, went backstage.

As they passed through the hall the guests became more aware of what was going on outside: irregular onslaughts of wind, rain, and, behind these immediate sounds, a vague ground swell of turbulence. Those guests who were to travel through the night by way of launch, bus, and car began to exchange glances. One of them, a woman, who was near the windows, parted the heavy curtains and looked out, releasing the drumming sound of rain against glass and a momentary glimpse of the blinded pane. She let the curtain fall and pulled an anxious grimace. A hearty male voice said loudly: "Not to worry. She'll be right."

More champagne in the drawing room and harder drinks for the asking. The performers began to come in and Hanley with them. He circulated busily. "Doing his stuff," said Alleyn.

"Not an easy assignment," said Troy and then: "I'd like to know how that boy is."

"So would I."

"Might we be able to do anything, do you suppose?"

"Shall we ask?"

Hanley saw them, flashed his winsome smile, and joined them. "We're going in now," he said. "The Lady asks us not to wait."

"How's Rupert?"

"Poor dear! *Wasn't* it a pity? Everything had gone *so* well. He's in his room. Lying down, you know, but quite all right. Not to be disturbed. He'll be *quite* all right," Hanley repeated brightly. "Straight-out case of nervous fatigue. Ah, there's the gong. Will you give a lead? Thank you *so* much."

On this return passage through the hall, standing inconspicuously just inside the entrance and partly screened by the vast pregnant woman whose elfin leer suggested a clandestine rendezvous, was a figure in dripping oilskins: Les, the launch man. Hanley went over to speak to him.

The dining room had been transformed, two subsidiary tables being introduced to form an E with the middle stroke missing. The three central places at the "top" table were destined for the Sommita, her host, and Rupert Bartholomew, none of whom appeared to occupy them. All the places were named and the Alleyns were again among the V.I.P.s. This time Troy found herself with Mr. Reece's chair on her left and Signor Lattienzo on her right. Alleyn was next to the Sommita's empty chair, with the wife of the New Zealand conductor on his left.

"This is delightful," said Signor Lattienzo.

"Yes, indeed," said Troy who was not in the mood for badinage.

"I arranged it."

"You what?" she exclaimed.

"I transposed the cards. You had been given the New Zealand maestro and I his wife. She will be enraptured with your husband's company and will pay no attention to her own husband. He will be less enraptured, but that cannot be helped."

"Well," said Troy, "for sheer effrontery, I must say!"

"I take, as you say, the buttery bun? Apropos, I am much in need of refreshment. That was a most painful debacle, was it not?"

"Is he all right? Is someone doing something? I'm sure I don't know what anybody *can* do," Troy said, "but is there someone?"

"I have seen him."

"You have?"

"I have told him that he took a courageous and honest course. I was also able to say that there was a shining moment—the duet when you and I exchanged signals. He has rewritten it since I saw the score. It is delightful."

"That will have helped."

"A little, I think."

"Yesterday he confided rather alarmingly in us, particularly in Rory. Do you think he might like to see Rory?"

"At the moment I hope he is asleep. A Dr. Carmichael has seen him and I have administered a pill. I suffer," said Signor Lattienzo, "from insomnia."

"Is she coming down, do you know?"

"I understand from our good Monty—yes. After the debacle she appeared to have been in two minds about what sort of temperament it would be appropriate to throw. Obviously an attack upon the still-unconscious Rupert was out of the question. There remained the flood of remorse, which I fancy she would not care to entertain since it would indicate a flaw in her own behavior. Finally there could be a demonstration as from a distracted lover. Puzzled by this choice, she burst into a storm of ambiguous tears and Retired, as they say in your Shakespeare, Above. Escorted by Monty. To the ministrations of the baleful Maria and with the intention of making another delayed entrance. We may expect her at any moment, no doubt. In the meantime the grilled trout was delicious and here comes the coq au vin."

But the Sommita did not appear. Instead, Mr. Reece arrived to say that she had been greatly upset by poor Rupert Bartholomew's collapse, which had no doubt been due to nervous exhaustion, but would rejoin them a little later. He then said that he was sorry indeed to have to tell them that he had been advised by the launch man that the local storm, known as the Rosser, had blown up and would increase in force, probably reaching its peak in about an hour, when it would then become inadvisable to make the crossing to the mainland. Loath as he was to break up the party, he felt perhaps . . . He spread his hands.

The response was immediate. The guests, having finished their marrons glacés, professed themselves, with many regrets, ready to leave. There was a general exodus for them to prepare themselves for the journey, Sir David Baumgartner, who had been expected to stay, among them. He had an important appointment looming up, he explained, and dared not risk missing it.

There would be room enough for all the guests and the performers in the bus and cars that waited across the Lake. Anyone so inclined could spend the tag end of the night at the Cornishman's Pass pub on the east side of the Pass and journey down-country by train the next day. The rest would continue through the night, descending to the plains and across them to their ultimate destinations.

The Alleyns agreed that the scene in the hall bore a resemblance to rush hour on the Underground. There was a sense of urgency and scarcely concealed impatience. The travelers were to leave in two batches of twenty, which was the maximum accommodation in the launch. The house staff fussed about with raincoats and umbrellas. Mr. Reece stood near the door, repeating valedictory remarks of scant originality and shaking hands. Some of the guests, as their anxiety mounted, became perfunctory in their acknowledgments; a few actually neglected him altogether, being intent upon maneuvering themselves into the top twenty. Sir David Baumgartner, in awful isolation and a caped mackintosh, sat in a porter's chair looking very cross indeed.

The entrance doors opened, admitting wind, rain, and cold all together. The first twenty guests were gone: swallowed up and shut out as if, Troy thought—and disliked herself for so thinking—they were condemned.

Mr. Reece explained to the remainder that it would be at least half an hour before the launch returned and advised them to wait in the drawing room. The servants would keep watch and would report as soon as they sighted the lights of the returning launch.

A few followed this suggestion, but most remained in the hall, sitting round the enormous fireplace or in scattered chairs, wandering about, getting themselves behind the window curtains and coming out, scared by their inability to see anything beyond streaming panes.

Eru Johnstone was speaking to the tenor, Roberto Rodolfo, and the little band of musicians, who listened to him in a huddle of apprehension. Alleyn and Troy joined them. Eru Johnstone was saying: "It's something one doesn't try to explain. I come from the far north of the North Island and have only heard about the Island indirectly from some of our people down here on the Coast. I had forgotten. When we were engaged for this performance, I didn't connect the two things."

"But it's *tapu**?" asked the pianist. "Is that it?"

"In very early times an important person was buried here," he said, as it seemed unwillingly. "Ages afterwards, when the *pakehas* came, a man named Ross, a prospector, rowed out to the Island. The story is that the

* *Tapu*—Maori word signifying sacred and forbidden.

local storm blew up and he was drowned. I had forgotten," Eru Johnstone repeated in his deep voice. "I suggest you do, too. There have been many visitors since those times and many storms—"

"Hence 'Rosser'?" Alleyn asked.

"So it seems."

"How long does it usually last?"

"About twenty-four hours, I'm told. No doubt it varies."

Alleyn said: "On my first visit to New Zealand I met one of your people, who told me about Maoritanga. We became friends and I learnt a lot from him—Dr. Te Pokiha."

"Rangi Te Pokiha?" Johnstone exclaimed. "You know him? He is one of our most prominent elders."

And he settled down to talk at great length of his people. Alleyn led the conversation back to the Island. "After what you have told me," he said, "do you mind my asking if you believe it to be *tapu*?"

After a long pause Eru Johnstone said: "Yes."

"Would you have come," Troy asked, "if you had known?"

"No," said Eru Johnstone.

"Are you staying here?" asked Signor Lattienzo, appearing at Troy's elbow, "or shall we fall back upon our creature comforts in the drawing room? One can't go on saying goodbye to people who scarcely listen."

"I've got a letter I want to get off," said Alleyn. "I think I'll just scribble it and ask one of these people if they'd mind putting it in the post. What about you, Troy?"

"I rather thought—the studio. I ought to 'fix' those drawings."

"I'll join you there," he said.

"Yes, darling, do."

Troy watched him run upstairs.

"Surely you are not going to start painting after all this!" Signor Lattienzo exclaimed.

"Not I!" Troy said. "It's just that I'm restless and can't settle. It's been a bit of a day, hasn't it? Who's in the drawing room?"

"Hilda Dancy and the little Parry, who are staying on. Also the Dr. Carmichael, who suffers excruciatingly from seasickness. It is not very gay in the drawing room, although the lissom Hanley weaves in and out. Is it true that you have made drawings this afternoon?"

"One or two preliminary canters."

"Of Bella?"

"Mostly of her, yes."

Signor Lattienzo put his head on one side and contrived to look wistful.

In spite of herself Troy laughed. "Would you like to see them?" she said.

"Naturally I would like to see them. *May* I see them?"

"Come on, then," said Troy.

They went upstairs to the studio. Troy propped her drawings, one by one, on the easel, blew fixative through a diffuser over each, and laid them side by side on the throne to dry: Signor Lattienzo screwed in his eyeglass, folded his plump hands over his ample stomach, and contemplated them.

After a long pause during which vague sounds of activity down in the hall drifted up and somewhere a door slammed, Signor Lattienzo said: "If you had not made that last one, the one on the right, I would have said you were a merciless lady, Madame Troy."

It was the slightest of the drawings. The orchestra was merely indicated playing like mad in the background. In the foreground La Sommita, having turned away from them, stared at vacancy, and in everything that Troy had set down with such economy there was desolation.

"Look what you've done with her," Signor Lattienzo said. "Did she remain for long like that? Did she, for once, face reality? I have never seen her look so, and now I feel I have never seen her at all."

"It only lasted for seconds."

"Yes? Shall you paint her like that?"

Troy said slowly: "No, I don't think so." She pointed to the drawing of La Sommita in full cry, mouth wide open, triumphant. "I rather thought this—"

"This is the portrait of a Voice."

"I would have liked to call it 'A in Alt' because that sounds so nice. I don't know what it means but I understand it would be unsuitable."

"Highly so. *Mot juste,* by the way."

" 'A in Sop' wouldn't have the same charm."

"No."

"Perhaps, simply 'Top Note.' Though why I should fuss about a title when I haven't as yet clapped paint to canvas, I can't imagine."

"Has she seen the drawings?"

"No."

"And won't if you can help it?"

"That's right," said Troy.

They settled down. Signor Lattienzo discoursed cosily, telling Troy of droll occurrences in the world of opera and of a celebrated company, half-Italian and half-French, of which the Sommita had been the star and in which internal feuding ran so high that when people asked at the box-office what opera was on tonight the manager would intervene and say,

"Wait till the curtain goes up, madame!" (or "dear boy!") "Just wait till the curtain goes up." With this and further discourse he entertained Troy exceedingly. After some time Alleyn came in and said the launch had been sighted on its return trip and the last batch of travelers were getting ready to leave.

"The wind is almost gale force," he said. "The telephone's out of order —probably a branch across the line—radio and television are cut off."

"Will they be all right?" Troy asked. "The passengers?"

"Reece says that Les knows his job and that he wouldn't undertake the passage if he thought there was any risk. Hanley's swanning about telling everyone that the launch is seaworthy, cost the earth, and crossed the English Channel in a blizzard."

"*How* glad I am," Signor Lattienzo remarked, "that I am not on board her."

Alleyn opened the window curtains. "She could be just visible from here," he said, and after a pause, "Yes, there she is. Down at the jetty."

Troy joined him. Beyond the half-blinded window, lights, having no background, moved across the void, distorted by the runnels of water streaming down the pane. They rose, tilted, sank, rose again, vanished, reappeared, and were gone.

"They are going aboard," said Alleyn. "I wonder if Eru Johnstone is glad to have left the Island."

"One would have thought—" Signor Lattienzo began and was cut short by a scream.

It came from within the house and mounted like a siren. It broke into a gabble, resumed, and increased in volume.

"Oh *no!*" said Signor Lattienzo irritably. "What now, for pity's sake!" A piercing scream answered him.

And then he was on his feet. "That is not Bella's voice," he said loudly.

It was close. On their landing. Outside their door. Alleyn made for the door, but before he could reach it, it opened and there was Maria, her mouth wide open, yelling at the top of her voice.

"Soccorso! Soccorso!"

Alleyn took her by the upper arms. *"Che succede?"* he demanded. "Control yourself, Maria. What are you saying?"

She stared at him, broke free, ran to Signor Lattienzo, beat him with her clenched fists, and poured out a stream of Italian.

He held her by the wrists and shook her. *"Taci!"* he shouted and to Alleyn: "She is saying that Bella has been murdered."

IV

The Sommita lay spread-eagled on her back across a red counterpane. The bosom of her biblical dress had been torn down to the waist and under her left breast, irrelevantly, unbelievably, the haft of a knife stuck out. The wound was not visible, being masked by a piece of glossy colored paper or card that had been pierced by the knife and transfixed to the body. From beneath this a thin trace of blood had slid down toward naked ribs like a thread of red cotton. The Sommita's face, as seen from the room, was upside-down. Its eyes bulged and its mouth was wide open. The tongue protruded as if at the moment of death she had pulled a gargoyle's grimace at her killer. The right arm, rigid as a branch, was raised in the fascist salute. She might have been posed for the jacket on an all-too-predictable shocker.

Alleyn turned to Montague Reece, who stood halfway between the door and the bed with Beppo Lattienzo holding his arm. The secretary, Hanley, had stopped short just inside the room, his hand over his mouth and looking as if he was going to be sick. Beyond the door Maria could be heard to break out afresh in bursts of hysteria. Alleyn said: "That doctor—Carmichael, isn't it?—he stayed behind, didn't he?"

"Yes," said Mr. Reece. "Of course," and to Hanley: "Get him."

"And shut the door after you," said Alleyn. "Whoever's out there on the landing, tell them to go downstairs and wait in the drawing room."

"And get rid of that cursed woman," Mr. Reece ordered savagely. "No! Stop! Tell the housekeeper to take charge of her. I—" he appealed to Alleyn. "What should we do? You know about these things. I—need a few moments."

"Monty, my dear! Monty," Lattienzo begged him, "don't look. Come away. Leave it to other people. To Alleyn. Come with me." He turned on Hanley. "Well. Why do you wait? Do as you're told, imbecile. The doctor!"

"There's no call to be insulting," Hanley quavered. He looked distractedly about him and his gaze fell upon the Sommita's face. "God almighty!" he said and bolted.

When he had gone, Alleyn said to Mr. Reece, "Is your room on this floor? Why not let Signor Lattienzo take you there. Dr. Carmichael will come and see you."

"I would like to see Ben Ruby. I do not require a doctor."

"We'll find Ben for you," soothed Lattienzo. "Come along."

"I am perfectly all right, Beppo," Mr. Reece stated. He freed himself and actually regained a sort of imitation of his customary manner. He said to Alleyn: "I will be glad to leave this to you. You will take charge, if you please. I will be available and wish to be kept informed." And then: "The police. The police must be notified."

Alleyn said: "Of course they must. When it's possible. At the moment it's not. We are shut off."

Mr. Reece stared at him dully. "I had forgotten," he conceded. And then astonishingly—"That is extremely awkward," he said, and walked out of the room.

"He is in trauma," said Lattienzo uncertainly. "He is in shock. Shall I stay with him?"

"If you would. Perhaps when Mr. Ruby arrives—?"

"*Sì, sì, sicuro,*" said Signor Lattienzo. "Then I make myself scarce."

"Only if so desired," Alleyn rejoined in his respectable Italian.

When he was alone he returned to the bed. Back on the job, he thought, and with no authority.

He thought of Troy—of six scintillating drawings, of a great empty canvas waiting on the brand-new easel—and he wished to God he could put them all thirteen thousand miles away in a London studio.

There was a tap on the door. He heard Lattienzo say: "Yes. In there," and Dr. Carmichael came in.

He was a middle-aged to elderly man with an air of authority. He looked sharply at Alleyn and went straight to the bed. Alleyn watched him make the expected examination and then straighten up.

"I don't need to tell you that nothing can be done," he said. "This is a most shocking thing. Who found her?"

"It seems, her maid. Maria. She raised the alarm and was largely incoherent. No doubt you all heard her."

"Yes."

"She spoke Italian," Alleyn explained. "I understood a certain amount and Lattienzo, of course, much more. But even to him she was sometimes incomprehensible. Apparently after the performance Madame Sommita was escorted to her room by Mr. Reece."

"That's right," said the doctor. "I was there. They'd asked me to have a look at the boy. When I arrived they were persuading her to go."

"Ah yes. Well. Maria was here, expecting she would be needed. Her mistress, still upset by young Bartholomew's collapse, ordered them to leave her alone. Maria put out one of her tablets, whatever they are. She also put out her dressing gown—there it is, that fluffy object still neatly folded over the chair—and she and Reece did leave. As far as I could make out, she was anxious about Madame Sommita and after a time returned to the room with a hot drink—there it is, untouched—and found her as you see her now. Can you put a time to the death?"

"Not precisely, of course, but I would think not more than an hour ago. Perhaps much less. The body is still warm."

"What about the raised arm? Rigor mortis? Or cadaveric spasm?"

"The latter, I should think. There doesn't appear to have been a struggle. And that card or paper or whatever it is?" said Dr. Carmichael.

"I'll tell you what that is," said Alleyn. "It's a photograph."

V

Dr. Carmichael, after an incredulous stare at Alleyn, stooped over the body.

"It'd be as well not to touch the paper," said Alleyn, "but look at it."

He took a ball-point pen from his pocket and used it to open out the creases. "You can see for yourself," he said.

Dr. Carmichael looked. "Good God!" he exclaimed. "You're right. It's a photograph of her. With her mouth open. Singing."

"And the knife has been pushed through the photograph at the appropriate place—the heart."

"It's—grotesque. When—where could it have been taken?"

"This afternoon, in the concert chamber," said Alleyn. "Those are the clothes she wore. She stood in a shaft of sunlight. My wife made a drawing of her standing as she is here. The photograph must have been taken from outside a window. One of those instant self-developing jobs."

Dr. Carmichael said: "What should we do? I feel helpless."

"So, believe me, do I! Reece tells me I am to 'take charge,' which is all very well, but I have no real authority."

"Oh—surely!"

"I can only assume it until the local police take over. And when that will be depends on this blasted 'Rosser' and the telephone breakdown."

"I heard the young man who seems to be more or less in charge—I don't know his name—"

"Hanley."

"—say that if the Lake got rougher the launch man would stay on the mainland and sleep on board or in the boatshed. He was going to flash a lamp when they got there from the second trip to show they were all right. I think Hanley said something about him ringing a bell, though how they could expect anyone to hear it through the storm, I can't imagine."

"Eru Johnstone said the 'Rosser' usually lasts about twenty-four hours."

"In the meantime—?" Dr. Carmichael motioned with his head, indicating the bed and its occupant. "What should be the drill? Usually?"

"An exhaustive examination of the scene. Nothing moved until the crime squad have gone over the ground: photographer, dabs—fingerprints—pathologist's first report. See any self-respecting whodunit," said Alleyn.

"So we cover her up and maintain a masterly inactivity?"

Alleyn waited for a moment or two. "As it happens," he said, "I have got my own working camera with me. My wife has a wide camel's-hair watercolor brush. Talc powder would work all right. It's a hell of a time since I did this sort of fieldwork, but I think I can manage. When it's done the body can be covered."

"Can I be of help?"

Alleyn hesitated for a very brief moment and then said, "I'd be very glad of your company and of your help. You will of course be asked to give evidence at the inquest, and I'd like to have a witness to my possibly irregular activities."

"Right."

"So if you don't mind, I'll leave you here while I collect what I need and see my wife. And I suppose I'd better have a word with Hanley and the hangovers in the drawing room. I won't be long."

"Good."

An onslaught of wind shook the window frames.

"Not much letting up out there," Alleyn said. He parted the heavy curtains. "By George!" he exclaimed. "He's signaling! Have a look."

Dr. Carmichael joined him. Out in the blackness a pinpoint of light appeared, held for a good second, and went out. It did this three times. A pause followed. The light reappeared for a full second, was followed by a momentary flash and then a long one. A pause and the performance was repeated.

"Is that Morse?" asked the doctor.

"Yes, it reads '*O.K.*,'" said Alleyn. "Somewhat ironically, under the circumstances. It was to let us know they'd made it in the launch."

The signals were repeated.

"Here!" Alleyn said. "Before he goes. Quick. Open up."

They opened the curtain wide. Alleyn ran to the group of light switches on the wall and threw them all on.

The Sommita, gaping on her bed, was, as she had always demanded she should be, fully lit.

Alleyn blacked out. "Don't say anything," he begged the doctor, "or I'll muck it up. Do you know Morse?"

"No."

"Oh, for a tiny Boy Scout. Here goes, then."

Using both hands on the switches, he began to signal. The Sommita flashed up and out, up and out. The storm lashed the windows, the switches clicked: *Dot, dot, dot. Dash dash dash* and *Dot, dot, dot.*

He waited. "If he's still watching," he said, "he'll reply."

And after a daunting interval, he did. The point of light reappeared and vanished.

Alleyn began again, slowly, laboriously: "*S.O.S. Urgent. Contact. Police. Murder.*" And again: "*S.O.S. Urgent. Contact. Police. Murder.*"

He did it three times and waited an eternity.

And at last the acknowledgment.

"*Roger.*"

Alleyn said: "Let's hope it works. I'll be off. If you'd rather leave the room, get a key from the housekeeper. Lock it from the outside and wait for me on the landing. There's a chair behind a screen. Half a minute; I'd better just look round here before I go."

There was another door in the Sommita's enormous bedroom: it opened into her bathroom, an extraordinarily exotic apartment carpeted in crimson with a built-in dressing table and a glass surrounded by lights and flanked by shelves thronged with flasks, atomizers, jars, boxes, and an arrangement of crystal flowers in a Venetian vase.

Alleyn looked at the hand basin. It was spotless but damp and the soap, wet. Of the array of scarlet towels on heated rails, one was wet, but unstained.

He returned to the bedroom and had a quick look around. On the bedside table was a full cup of some milky concoction. It was still faintly warm and a skin had formed on top. Beside this was a glass of water and a bottle of tablets of a well-known proprietary brand. One had been laid out beside the water.

Dr. Carmichael met Alleyn at the door. They left the room together. Alleyn took charge of the key, and locked the door.

"If it's all right," said the doctor, "I thought I'd have a look at the young chap. He was rather under the weather after that faint."

"Yes," said Alleyn. "So I gathered. Did you look after him?"

"Reece asked me to. The secretary came round to the front in a great taking-on. I went backstage with him."

"Good. What did you find?"

"I found Bartholomew coming to, Madame Sommita shaking him like a rabbit, and that Italian singing master of hers—Lattienzo—ordering her to stop. She burst out crying and left. Reece followed her. I suppose it was then that she came upstairs. The ingenue—little Miss Parry—had the good sense to bring a glass of water for the boy. We got him to a seat and from there, when he was ready for it, to his room. Lattienzo offered to give him one of his own sleeping pills and put him to bed, but he wanted to be left to himself. I returned to the drawing room. If it's O.K. by you, I think I'll take a look-see at him."

"Certainly. I'd like to come with you."

"Would you?" said Dr. Carmichael, surprised. And then: "I see. Or do I? You're checking up. Right?"

"Well—sort of. Hold on a jiffy, will you?"

Below in the hall a door had shut and he caught the sound of a bolt being pushed home. He went to the head of the stairs and looked down. There was the unmistakable, greatly foreshortened figure of their driver: short ginger hair and heavy shoulders. He was coming away from the front door and had evidently been locking up. What was his name? Ah, yes. Bert.

Alleyn gave a not too loud whistle between his teeth. "Hi! Bert!" he said. The head tilted back and the dependable face was presented. Alleyn beckoned and Bert came upstairs.

"G'day," he said. "This is no good. Murder, eh?"

Alleyn said: "Look, do you feel like lending a hand? Dr. Carmichael and I have got a call to make, but I don't want to leave this landing unguarded. Would you be a good chap and stay here? We won't be too long. I hope."

"She'll be right," said Bert. And then, with a motion of his head toward the bedroom door: "Would that be where it is?"

"Yes. The door's locked."

"But you reckon somebody might get nosy?"

"Something like that. How about it?"

"I don't mind," said Bert. "Got it all on your own, eh?"

"With Dr. Carmichael. I *would* be grateful. Nobody, no matter who, is to go in."

"Good as gold," said Bert.

So they left him there, lounging in the chair behind the screen.

"Come on," Alleyn said to Dr. Carmichael. "Where's his room?"

"This way."

They were passing the studio door. Alleyn said, "Half a second, will you?" and went in. Troy was sitting on the edge of the throne looking desolate. She jumped to her feet.

He said, "You know about it?"

"Signor Lattienzo came and told me. Rory, how terrible!"

"I know. Wait here. All right? Or would you rather go to bed?"

"I'm all right. I don't think I really believe it has happened."

"I won't be long, I promise."

"Don't give it another thought. I'm O.K., Rory. Signor Lattienzo seems to think it was Strix—the photographer. Is that possible?"

"Remotely, I suppose."

"I don't quite believe in the photographer."

"If you want to talk about it, we will. In the meantime could you look me out my camera, a big sable brush and a squirt-thing of talc powder?"

"Certainly. There are at least three of the latter in our bathroom. Why," asked Troy, rallying, "do people perpetually give each other talc powder and never use it themselves?"

"We must work it out when we've the leisure," said Alleyn. "I'll come back for the things."

He kissed her and rejoined the doctor.

Rupert Bartholomew's room was two doors along the passage. Dr. Carmichael stopped. "He doesn't know," he said. "Unless, of course, someone has come up and told him."

"If he's taken Lattienzo's pill he'll be asleep."

"Should be. But it's one of the mildest sort."

Dr. Carmichael opened the door and Alleyn followed him.

Rupert was not asleep. Nor had he undressed. He was sitting upright on his bed with his arms clasped round his knees. He looked very young.

"Hello!" said Dr. Carmichael. "What's all this? You ought to be sound asleep." He looked at the bedside table with its switched-on lamp, glass of water, and the tablet lying beside it. "So you haven't taken your Lattienzo pill," he said. "Why's that?"

"I didn't want it. I want to know what's happening. All that screaming and rushing about." He looked at Alleyn. "Was it her? Bella? Was it because of me? I want to know. What have I done?"

Dr. Carmichael slid his fingers over Rupert's wrist. "You haven't done anything," he said. "Calm down."

"Then what—?"

"The rumpus," Alleyn said, "was nothing to do with you. As far as we know. Nothing. It was Maria who screamed."

An expression that in less dramatic circumstances might almost have been described as huffy appeared and faded: Rupert looked at them out of the corners of his eyes. "Then, why *did* Maria scream?" he asked.

Alleyn exchanged a glance with the doctor, who slightly nodded his head.

"Well?" Rupert demanded.

"Because," Alleyn said, "there has been a disaster. A tragedy. A death. It will be a shock to you, but as far as we can see, which admittedly is not very far, there is no reason to link it with what happened after the performance. You will have to know of it and there would be no point in holding it back."

"A *death?* Do you mean—? You can't mean—? Bella?"

"I'm afraid—yes."

"Bella?" Rupert said and sounded incredulous. "Bella? *Dead?*"

"It's hard to believe, isn't it?"

There was a long silence, broken by Rupert.

"But—why? What was it? Was it heart failure?"

"You could say," Dr. Carmichael observed with a macabre touch of the professional whimsy sometimes employed by doctors, "that all deaths are due to heart failure."

"Do you know if she had any heart trouble at all?" Alleyn asked Rupert.

"She had high blood pressure. She saw a specialist in Sydney."

"Do you know who?"

"I've forgotten. Monty will know. So will Ned Hanley."

"Was it a serious condition, did you gather?"

"She was told to—to slow down. Not get overexcited. That sort of thing." He looked at them with what seemed to be apprehension.

"Should I see her?" he mumbled.

"No," they both said quickly. He breathed out a sigh.

"I can't get hold of this," he said and shook his head slowly. "I can't get hold of it at all. I can't sort of seem to believe it."

"The best thing you can do," said Dr. Carmichael, "is to take this tablet and settle down. There's absolutely nothing else you *can* do."

"Oh. Oh, I see. Well: all right, then," he replied with a strange air of speaking at random. "But I'll put myself to bed, if you don't mind."

He took the tablet, drank the water and leaned back, staring in front of him. "Extraordinary!" he said and closed his eyes.

Alleyn and Carmichael waited for a minute or two. Rupert opened his eyes and turned off the bedside lamp. Disconcerted, they moved to the door.

"Thank you," said Rupert in the dark. "Goodnight."

When they were in the passage Carmichael said: "That was a very odd little conversation."

"It was, rather."

"You'd have almost said—well—I mean—"

"What?"

"That he was relieved. Don't get me wrong. He's had a shock—I mean that extraordinary apology for his opera, which I must say I didn't find very impressive, and his faint. His pulse is still a bit erratic. But the reaction," Carmichael repeated, "*was* odd, didn't you think?"

"People do tend to behave oddly when they hear of death. I'm sure you've found that, haven't you? In this case I rather think there *has* actually been a sense of release."

"A *release?* From what?"

"Oh," said Alleyn, "from a tricky situation. From extreme anxiety. High tension. Didn't somebody say—was it Shaw?—that after the death of even one's closest and dearest, there is always a sensation of release. And relief."

Carmichael made the noise that is written "Humph." He gave Alleyn a speculative look. "You didn't," he said, "tell him it was murder."

"No. Time enough in the morning. He may as well enjoy the benefit of the Lattienzo pill."

Dr. Carmichael said "Humph" again.

Alleyn returned to Troy, who had the camera, brush, and talc powder ready for him.

"How is that boy?" she asked. "How has he taken it?"

"On the whole, very well. Remarkably well."

"Perhaps he's run out of emotional reactions," said Troy. "He's been fully extended in that department."

"Perhaps he has. You're the wisest of downy owls and had better go to roost. I'm off, and it looks like being one of those nights."

"Oh, for Br'er Fox and Thompson and Bailey?"

"You can say that again. And oh, for you to be in your London nest thirteen thousand miles away, which sounds like the burden of a ballad," said Alleyn. "But as you're here, you'd better turn the key in your lock when you go to bed."

"*Me!*" said Troy incredulously. "Why?"

"So that I'll be obliged to wake you up," said Alleyn and left her.

He asked Bert to continue his vigil.

Dr. Carmichael said: "But I don't quite see—I mean, you've got the key."

"There may be other keys and other people may have them. If Bert sits behind that screen he can see anyone who tries to effect an entry."

"I can't imagine anyone wanting to go back. Not even her murderer."

"Can't you?" said Alleyn. "I can."

He and Dr. Carmichael went downstairs to the drawing room leaving Bert on guard.

A wan little trio of leftovers was there: Hilda Dancy, Sylvia Parry, Lattienzo. Mr. Reece, Alleyn gathered, was closeted with Ben Ruby and Hanley in the study. The drawing room had only been half-tidied of its preprandial litter when the news broke. It was tarnished with used champagne glasses, full ashtrays, and buckets of melted ice. The fire had burned down to embers, and when Alleyn came in Signor Lattienzo was gingerly dropping a small log on them.

Miss Dancy at once tackled Alleyn. Was it, she boomed, true that he was in charge? If so would he tell them exactly what had happened. Had the Sommita really been done away with? Did this mean there was a murderer at large in the house? *How* had she been done away with?

Signor Lattienzo had by this time stationed himself behind Miss Dancy in order to make deprecating faces at Alleyn.

"We have a right to be told," said the masterful Miss Dancy.

"And told you shall be," Alleyn replied. "Between one and two hours ago Madame Sommita was murdered in her bedroom. That is all that any of us knows. I have been asked by Mr. Reece to take charge until such time as the local police can be informed. I'm going to organize a search of the premises. There are routine questions that should be asked of everybody who was in the house after the last launch trip. If you would prefer to go to your rooms, please do so but with the knowledge that I may be obliged to call on you when the search is completed. I'm sure Signor Lattienzo will be pleased to escort you to your rooms."

Signor Lattienzo gave slightly incoherent assurances that he was theirs, dear ladies, to command.

"I'm staying where I am," Miss Dancy decided. "What about you, dear?"

"Yes. Yes, so am I," Sylvia Parry decided, and to Alleyn: "Does Rupert know? About Madame Sommita?"

"Dr. Carmichael and I told him."

Dr. Carmichael made diffident noises.

"It will have been a terrible shock for Rupert," said Sylvia. "For everybody, of course, but specially for Rupert. After—what happened." And with an air of defiance she added: "I think Rupert did a very brave thing. It took an awful lot of guts."

"We all know that, dear," said Miss Dancy with a kind of gloomy cosiness.

Alleyn said, "Before I go, I wonder if you'd tell me exactly what happened after Bartholomew fainted."

Their account was put together like a sort of unrehearsed duet with occasional stoppages when they disagreed about details and called upon Signor Lattienzo. It seemed that as soon as Rupert fell, Hanley, who was standing by, said, "Curtains" and closed them himself. Sylvia Parry knelt down by Rupert and loosened his collar and tie. Roberto Rodolfo said something about fresh air and fanned Rupert with his biblical skirt. The Sommita, it appeared, after letting out an abortive shriek, stifled herself with her own hand, looked frantically round the assembly, and then flung herself upon the still unconscious Rupert with such abandon that it was impossible to decide whether she was moved by remorse or fury. It was at this point that Signor Lattienzo arrived, followed in turn by Mr. Reece and Ben Ruby.

As far as Alleyn could make out, these three men lost no time in tackling the diva in a very businesslike manner, detaching her from Rupert and suggesting strongly that she go to her room. From here the narrative followed, more or less, the accounts already given by Signor Lattienzo and the doctor. Mr. Reece accompanied the Sommita out of the concert hall, which was by this time emptied of its audience, and was understood to conduct her to her room. Hanley fetched Dr. Carmichael, and Sylvia Parry fetched water. Rupert, when sufficiently recovered, was removed to his room by the doctor and Signor Lattienzo, who fetched the sleeping tablet and placed it on the bedside table. Rupert refused all offers to help him undress and get into bed, so they left him and went down to dinner. The ladies and the rest of the cast were already at table.

"After Hanley had fetched Dr. Carmichael, what did he do?" Alleyn asked.

Nobody had noticed. Miss Dancy said that he "seemed to be all over the shop" and Sylvia thought it had been he who urged them into the dining room.

On this vague note Alleyn left them.

In the hall he ran into the ubiquitous Hanley, who said that the entire staff was assembled in their sitting room awaiting instructions. Alleyn gathered that Maria had, so to put it, "stolen the show." The New Zealand members of the staff—they of the recently bankrupt luxury hotel, including the chef and housekeeper—had grown restive under recurrent onsets of Maria's hysteria, modeled, Alleyn guessed, upon those of her late employer.

The staff sitting room, which in less democratic days would have been called the servants' hall, was large, modern in design, gaily furnished, and equipped with color television, a Ping-Pong table, and any number of functional armchairs. The housekeeper, who turned out to be called, with Congrevean explicitness, Mrs. Bacon, sat apart from her staff but adjacent to Mr. Reece. She was a well-dressed, personable lady of capable appearance. Behind her was a subdued bevy of two men and three girls, the ex-hotel staff, Alleyn assumed, that she brought with her to the Lodge.

Hanley continued in his role of restless dogsbody and hovered, apparently in readiness for something unexpected to turn up, near the door.

Alleyn spoke briefly. He said he knew how shocked and horrified they all must be and assured them that he would make as few demands upon them as possible.

"I'm sure," he said, "that you all wonder if there is a connection between this appalling crime and the recent activities of the elusive cameraman." (And he wondered if Maria had noticed the photograph pinned to the body.) "You will, I daresay, be asking yourselves if yesterday's intruder, whom we failed to hunt down, could be the criminal. I'm sure your search," Alleyn said and managed to avoid a sardonic tone, "was extremely thorough. But in a case like this every possibility, however remote, should be explored. For that reason I am going to ask the men of the household to sort themselves into pairs and to search the whole of the indoor premises. I want the pairs to remain strictly together throughout the exercise. You will not go into Madame Sommita's bedroom, which is now locked. Mr. Bartholomew has already gone to bed and you need not disturb him. Just look in quietly and make sure he is there. I must ask you simply to assure yourselves that there is no intruder in the house. Open any doors behind which someone might be hiding, look under beds and behind curtains, but don't handle anything else. I am going to ask Mrs. Bacon and Mr. Hanley to supervise this operation."

He turned to Mrs. Bacon. "Perhaps we might just have a word?" he suggested.

"Certainly," she said. "In my office."

"Good." He looked around the assembled staff.

"I want you all to remain here," he said. "We won't keep you long. I'll leave Dr. Carmichael in charge."

Mrs. Bacon conducted Alleyn and Hanley to her office, which turned out to be a sitting room with a large desk in it.

She said: "I don't know whether you gentlemen would care for a drink, but I do know I would," and went to a cupboard, from which she produced a bottle of whiskey and three glasses. Alleyn didn't want a drink but thought it politic to accept. Hanley said: "Oh, yes. Oh *yes. Please.*"

Alleyn said: "I see no point in pretending that I think the prepetrator of this crime has contrived to leave the Island, nor do I think he is somewhere out there in the storm or skulking in the hangar. Mrs. Bacon, is the entire staff collected in there? Nobody missing?"

"No. I made sure of that."

"Good. I think it will be best for you two, if you will, to apportion the various areas so that all are covered without overlapping. I'm not familiar enough with the topography of the Lodge to do this. I'll cruise. But the guests will know their way about, presumably, after yesterday's abortive search."

Mrs. Bacon had watched him very steadily. He thought that this had probably been her manner in her hotel days when listening to complaints.

She said: "Am I wrong in understanding that you don't believe the murderer was on the Island yesterday? That the trespasser was not the murderer, in fact?"

Alleyn hesitated and then said: "I don't think the murderer was a trespasser, no."

Hanley said loudly: "Oh *no!* But you can't—I mean—that would mean—I mean—oh *no.*"

"It would mean," said Mrs. Bacon, still looking at Alleyn, "that Mr. Alleyn thinks Madame Sommita was murdered either by a guest or by a member of the household. That's correct, Mr. Alleyn, isn't it? By—if I can put it that way—one of us?"

"That is perfectly correct, Mrs. Bacon," said Alleyn.

CHAPTER V

Nocturne

I

THE HUNT TURNED OUT, as Alleyn had expected it would, to be a perfectly useless exercise. The couples were carefully assorted. Marco was paired with Mrs. Bacon, Ben Ruby with Dr. Carmichael, and Hanley with the chef, for whom he seemed to have an affinity. Alleyn dodged from one pair to another, turning up where he was least expected, sometimes checking a room that had already been searched, sometimes watching the reluctant activities of the investigators, always registering in detail their reactions to the exercise.

These did not vary much. Hanley was all eyes and teeth and inclined to get up little intimate arguments with the chef. Ben Ruby, smoking a cigar, instructed his partner, Dr. Carmichael, where to search, but did nothing in particular himself. Alleyn thought he seemed to be preoccupied as if confronted by a difficult crossword puzzle. Signor Lattienzo looked as if he thought the exercise was futile.

When the search was over they all returned to the staff sitting room, where, on Alleyn's request, Hilda Dancy and Sylvia Parry joined them. Nobody had anything to report. The New Zealanders, Alleyn noticed, collected in a huddle. Mrs. Bacon and the ex-hotel staff showed a joint tendency to eye the Italians. Marco attached himself to Signor Lattienzo. Maria entered weeping but in a subdued manner, having been chastened, Alleyn fancied, by Mrs. Bacon. Hanley detached himself from his chef and joined Ben Ruby.

When they were all assembled, the door opened and Mr. Reece walked in. He might have arrived to take the chair at a shareholders' meeting. Hanley was assiduous with offers of a seat and was disregarded.

Mr. Reece said to Alleyn: "Please don't let me interrupt. Do carry on."

"Thank you," Alleyn said. He told Mr. Reece of the search and its non-result and was listened to with stony attention. He then addressed the company. He said he was grateful to them for having carried out a disagreeable job and asked that if any one of them, on afterthought, should remember something that, however remotely, could be of significance, he would at once speak of it. There was no response. He then asked how many of them possessed cameras.

The question was received with concern. Glances were exchanged. There was a general shuffling of feet.

"Come on," Alleyn said. "There's no need to show the whites of your eyes over a harmless inquiry. I'll give you a lead." He raised his hand, "I've got a camera and I don't mind betting most of you have. Hands up." Mr. Reece, in the manner of seconding the motion, raised his. Seven more followed suit, one after another, until only six had not responded: three New Zealand housemen with Maria, Marco, and Hilda Dancy.

"Good," Alleyn said. "Now. I'm going to ask those of you who *do* possess a camera to tell me what the make is and if you've used it at any time during the last week and if so, what you took. Mrs. Bacon?"

The response was predictable. A cross-section of cameras, from a wildly expensive type of self-developing instrument, the property of Mr. Reece, down to low-priced popular items at the falling-off-a-log level of simplicity, belonging to Sylvia Parry and two of the maids.

Mr. Ruby's camera was another highly sophisticated and expensive version of instantaneous self-development. He had used it that very morning when he had lined up the entire houseparty with the Lodge for a background. He actually had the "picture," as he consistently called the photograph, on him and showed it to Alleyn. There was Troy between Mr. Reece, who, as usual, conveyed nothing, and Signor Lattienzo, who playfully ogled her. And there, at the center, of course, the Sommita with her arm laid in tigerish possession across the shoulders of a haunted Rupert, while Sylvia Parry, on his other side, looked straight ahead. A closer examination showed that she had taken his hand.

Alleyn himself, head and shoulders taller than his neighbors, was, he now saw with stoic distaste, being winsomely contemplated by the ubiquitous Hanley, three places removed in the back row.

Signor Lattienzo was a problem. He waved his hands and cast up his eyes. "Oh, my dear Mr. Alleyn!" he said. "Yes, I have a camera. It was presented to me by—forgive my conscious looks and mantling cheeks—a grateful pupil. Isabella, in fact. I cannot remember the name and have been unable to master its ridiculously complicated mechanism. I carry it about with me, in order to show keen."

"And you haven't used it?"

"Well," said Signor Lattienzo. "In a sense I *have* used it. Yesterday. It upsets me to remember. Isabella proposed that I take photographs of her at the bathing pool. Rather than confess my incompetence, I aimed it at her and pressed a little protuberance. It gave no persuasive click. I repeated the performance several times but nothing emerged. As to any latent result, one has grave misgivings. If there *are* any, they rest in some prenatal state in the womb of the camera. You shall play the midwife," offered Signor Lattienzo.

"Thank you. Perhaps if I could see the camera—?"

"But of course. Of course. Shall I fetch it?"

"Please do."

Signor Lattienzo bustled away, but after a considerable period, during which Alleyn finished the general camera check, he returned looking flustered.

"Alas!" he proclaimed and spread his arms.

"Have you lost your camera?" Alleyn said.

"Not to say *lost,* my dear fellow. *Mislaid.* I suspect by the swimming pool. By now, one fears, drowned."

"One does indeed."

And that being so, the round of camera owners was completed, the net result being that Mr. Reece, Ben Ruby, Hanley, and Signor Lattienzo (if he had known how to use it) all possessed cameras that could have achieved the photograph now pinned under the breast of the murdered Sommita. To these proceedings Maria had listened with a sort of smoldering resentment. At one point she flared up and reminded Marco, in vituperative Italian, that he had a camera and had not declared it. He responded with equal animosity that his camera had disappeared during the Australian tour and hinted darkly that Maria herself knew more than she was prepared to let on in that connection. As neither of them could remember the make of the camera, their dialogue was unfruitful.

Alleyn asked if Rupert Bartholomew possessed a camera. Hanley said he did and had taken photographs of the Island from the lakeshore and of the lakeshore from the Island. Nobody knew anything at all about his camera.

Alleyn wound up the proceedings, which had taken less time in performance than in description. He said that if this had been a police inquiry they would all have been asked to show their hands and roll up their sleeves and if they didn't object he would be obliged if—?

Only Maria objected, but on being called to order in no uncertain terms by Mr. Reece, offered her clawlike extremities as if she expected to be stripped to the buff. There were no signs of bloodstains on anybody, which, if one of them was guilty, supported the theory that the Sommita was dead when the photograph was skewered to her heart.

This daunting formality completed, Alleyn told them they could all go to bed and it might be as well to lock their doors. He then returned to the landing, where Bert sustained his vigil behind a large screen, across whose surface ultramodern nudes frisked busily. He had been able to keep a watch on the Sommita's bedroom door through hinged gaps between panels. The searchers to this part of the house had been Ruby and Dr. Carmichael. They had not tried the bedroom door but stood outside it for a moment or two, whispering, for all the world as if they were afraid the Sommita might overhear them.

Alleyn told Bert to remain unseen and inactive for the time being. He then unlocked the door, and he and Dr. Carmichael returned to the room.

In cases of homicide when the body has been left undisturbed, and particularly when there is an element of the grotesque or of extreme violence in its posture, there can be a strange reaction before returning to it. Might it have moved? There is something shocking about finding it just as it was, like the Sommita, still agape, still with her gargoyle tongue, still staring, still rigidly pointing upside-down on her bed. He photographed it from just inside the door.

Soon the room smelled horridly of synthetic violets as Alleyn made use of the talc powder. He then photographed the haft of the knife, a slender, spirally grooved affair with an ornate silver knob. Dr. Carmichael held the bedside lamp close to it.

"I suppose you don't know where it came from?" he asked.

"I think so. One of a pair on the wall behind the pregnant woman."

"What pregnant woman?" exclaimed the startled doctor.

"In the hall."

"Oh. That."

"There were two, crossed and held by brackets. Only one now." And after a pause during which Alleyn took three more shots: "You wouldn't know when it was removed?" Dr. Carmichael said.

"Only that it was there before the general exodus this evening."

"You're trained to notice details, of course."

Using Troy's sable brush, he spread the violet powder round the mouth, turning the silent scream into the grimace of a painted clown.

"By God, you're a cool hand," the doctor remarked.

Alleyn looked up at him and something in the look caused Dr. Carmichael to say in a hurry: "Sorry, I didn't mean—"

"I'm sure you didn't," Alleyn said. "Do you see this? Above the corners of the mouth? Under the cheekbones?"

Carmichael stooped. "Bruising," he said.

"Not hypostases?"

"I wouldn't think so. I'm not a pathologist, Alleyn."

"No. But there are well-defined differences, aren't there?"

"Precisely."

"She used very heavy makeup. Heavier than usual, of course, for the performance, and she hadn't removed it. Some sort of basic stuff topped up with a finishing cream. Then coloring. And then a final powdering. Don't those bruises, if bruises they are, look as if the makeup under the cheekbones has been disturbed? Pushed up, as it were!"

After a considerable pause, Dr. Carmichael said: "Could be. Certainly could be."

"And look at the area below the lower lip. It's not very marked, but don't you think it may become more so? What does that suggest to you?"

"Again bruising."

"Pressure against the lower teeth?"

"Yes. That. It's possible."

Alleyn went to the Sommita's dressing table, where there was an inevitable gold-mounted manicure box. He selected a slender nail file, returned to the bed, slid it between the tongue and the lower lip, exposing the inner surface.

"Bitten," he said. He extended his left hand to within half an inch of the terrible face with his thumb below one cheekbone, his fingers below the other, and the heel of his hand over the chin and mouth. He did not touch the face.

"Somebody with a larger hand than mine, I fancy," he said, "but not much. I could almost cover it."

"You're talking about asphyxia, aren't you?"

"I'm wondering about it. Yes. There are those pinpoint spots."

"Asphyxial hemorrhages. On the eyeballs."

"Yes," said Alleyn and closed his own eyes momentarily. "Can you come any nearer to a positive answer?"

"An autopsy would settle it."

"Of course," Alleyn agreed.

He had again stooped over his subject and was about to take another photograph when he checked, stooped lower, sniffed, and then straightened up.

"Will you?" he said. "It's very faint."

Dr. Carmichael stooped. "Chloroform," he said. "Faint, as you say, but unmistakable. And look here, Alleyn. There's a bruise on the throat to the right of the voice box."

"And have you noticed the wrists?"

Dr. Carmichael looked at them—at the left wrist on the end of the rigid upraised arm and at the right one on the counterpane. "Bruising," he said.

"Caused by—would you say?"

"Hands. So now what?" asked Dr. Carmichael.

"Does a tentative pattern emerge?" Alleyn suggested. "Chloroform. Asphyxia. Death. Ripping the dress. Two persons—one holding the wrists. The other using the chloroform. The stabbing coming later. If it's right, it would account for there being so little blood, wouldn't it?"

"Certainly would," Dr. Carmichael said. "And there's very, very little. I'd say that tells us there was a considerable gap between death and the stabbing. The blood had had time to sink."

"How long?"

"Don't make too much of my guesswork, will you? Perhaps as much as twenty minutes—longer even. But what a picture!" said Dr. Carmichael. "You know? Cutting the dress, ripping it open, placing the photograph over the heart, and then using the knife. I mean—it's so—so farfetched. *Why?*"

"As farfetched as a vengeful killing in a Jacobean play," Alleyn said and then: "Yes. A vengeful killing."

"Are you—are we," Carmichael asked, "not going to withdraw the weapon?"

"I'm afraid not. I've blown my top often enough when some well-meaning fool has interfered with the body. In this case I'd be the well-meaning fool."

"Oh, come. But I see your point," Carmichael said. "I suppose I'm in the same boat myself. I should go no further than making sure she's dead. And, by God, it doesn't need a professional man to do that."

"The law, in respect of bodies, is a bit odd. They belong to nobody. They are not the legal property of anyone. This can lead to muddles."

"I can imagine."

"It's all jolly fine for the lordly Reece to order me to take charge. I've no right to do so and the local police would have *every* right to cut up rough if I did."

"So would the pathologist if I butted in."

"I imagine," Alleyn said, "they won't boggle at the photographs. After all there will be—changes."

"There will indeed. This house is central-heated."

"There may be a local switch in this room. Yes. Over there where it could be reached from the bed. Off with it."

"I will," said Carmichael and switched it off.

"I wonder if we can open the windows a crack without wreaking havoc," Alleyn said. He pulled back the heavy curtains and there was the black and streaming glass. They were sash windows. He opened one and then others half an inch at the top, admitting blades of cold air and the voice of the storm.

"At least, if we can find something appropriate, we can cover her," he said and looked about the room. There was a sandalwood chest against the wall. He opened it and lifted out a folded bulk of black material. "This will do," he said. He and Carmichael opened it out, and spread it over the body. It was scented and heavy and it shone dully. The rigid arm jutted up underneath it.

"What on earth is it *for?*" Carmichael wondered.

"It's one of her black satin sheets. There are pillowcases to match in the box."

"Good God!"

"I know."

Alleyn locked the door into the bathroom, wrapped the key in his handkerchief, and pocketed it.

He and the doctor stood in the middle of the room. Already it was colder. Slivers of wind from outside stirred the marabou trimming on the Sommita's dressing gown and even fiddled with her black satin pall so that she might have been thought to move stealthily underneath it.

"No sign of the wind dropping," said Carmichael. "Or is there?"

"It's not raining quite so hard, I fancy. I wonder if the launch man's got through. Where would the nearest police station be?"

"Rivermouth, I should think. Down on the coast. About sixty miles, at a guess."

"And as, presumably, the cars are all miles away returning guests to their homes east of the ranges, and the telephone at the boatshed will be out of order, we can only hope that the unfortunate Les has set out on foot for the nearest sign of habitation. I remember that on coming here we stopped to collect the mailbag at a railway station some two miles back along the line. A very small station called Kai-kai, I think."

"That's right. With about three *whares** and a pub. He may wait till first light," said Dr. Carmichael, "before he goes anywhere."

* A *whare* is a small dwelling.

"He *did* signal 'Roger,' which of course may only have meant 'Message received and understood.' Let's leave this bloody room, shall we?"

They turned, and took two steps. Alleyn put his hand on Carmichael's arm. Something had clicked.

The door handle was turning, this way and that. A pause and then the sound of a key being inserted and engaged.

The door opened and Maria came into the room.

II

This time Maria did not launch out into histrionics. When she saw the two men she stopped, drew herself up, looked beyond them to the shrouded figure on the bed, and said in English that she had come to be of service to her mistress.

"I perform the last rites," said Maria. "This is my duty. Nobody else. It is for me."

Alleyn said: "Maria, certainly it would be for you if circumstances had been different, but this is murder and she must not be touched until permission has been given by the authorities. Neither Doctor Carmichael nor I have touched her. We have examined but we have not touched. We have covered her for dignity's sake but that is all, and so it must remain until permission is given. We can understand your wish and are sorry to prevent you. Do you understand?"

She neither replied nor looked at him. She went to a window and reached for the cord that operated it.

"No," Alleyn said. "Nothing must be touched." She made for the heavier, ornate cord belonging to the curtains. "Not that either," Alleyn said. "Nothing must be touched. And I'm afraid I must ask you to come away from the room, Maria."

"I wait. I keep *veglia.*"

"It is not permitted. I am sorry."

She said, in Italian, "It is necessary for me to pray for her soul."

"You can do so. But not here."

Now she did look at him, directly and for an uncomfortably long time. Dr. Carmichael cleared his throat.

She walked toward the door. Alleyn reached it first. He opened it, removed the key and stood aside.

"*Sozzume,*" Maria said and spat inaccurately at him. She looked and sounded like a snake. He motioned with his head to Dr. Carmichael, who followed Maria quickly to the landing. Alleyn turned off the lights in the room, left it, and locked the door. He put Maria's key in his pocket. He now had two keys to the room.

"I remain," Maria said. "All night. Here."

"That is as you wish," Alleyn said.

Beside the frisky nude-embellished screen behind which Bert still kept his vigil, there were chairs and a clever occasional table with a lamp carved in wood—an abstract with unmistakable phallic implications, the creation, Alleyn guessed, of the master whose pregnant lady dominated the hall.

"Sit down, Maria," Alleyn said. "I have something to say to you."

He moved a chair toward her. "Please," he said.

At first he thought she would refuse, but after two seconds or so of stony immobility she did sit, poker-backed, on the edge of the offered chair.

"You have seen Madame Sommita and you know she has been murdered," he said. "You wish that her murderer will be found, don't you?"

Her mouth set in a tight line and her eyes flashed. She did not speak, but if she had delivered herself of a tirade it could not have been more eloquent.

"Very well," Alleyn said. "Now then: when the storm is over and the Lake is calmer, the New Zealand police will come and they will ask many questions. Until they come, Mr. Reece has put me in charge and anything you tell me, I will tell them. Anything I ask you, I will ask for one reason only: because I hope your answer may help us to find the criminal. If your reply is of no help it will be forgotten—it will be as if you had not made it. Do you understand?"

He thought: I shall pretend she has answered. And he said: "Good. Well now. First question. Do you know what time it was when Madame Sommita came upstairs with Mr. Reece and found you waiting for her? No? It doesn't matter. The opera began at eight and they will know how long it runs."

He had a pocket diary on him and produced it. He made quite a business of opening it and flattening it on the table. He wrote in it, almost under her nose.

"Maria. Time of S's arrival in bedroom. No answer."

When he looked up he found that Maria was glaring at his notebook. He pushed it nearer and turned it toward her. "Can you see?" he asked politely.

She unclamped her mouth.

"Twenty past nine. By her clock," she said.

"Splendid. And now, Maria—by the way, I haven't got your surname, have I? Your *cognome*."

"Bennini."

"Thank you." He added it to his note. "I see you wear a wedding ring," he said. "What was your maiden name, please?"

"Why do you ask me such questions? You are impertinent."

"You prefer not to answer?" Alleyn inquired politely.

Silence.

"Ah well," he said. "When you are more composed and I hope a little recovered from the terrible shock you have sustained, will you tell me exactly what happened after she arrived with Signor Reece?"

And astonishingly, with no further ado, this creature of surprises, who a few seconds ago had called him "filth" and spat at him, embarked upon a coherent and lucid account. Maria had gone straight upstairs as soon as the curtain fell on the opera. She had performed her usual duties, putting out the glass of water and the tranquilizer that the Sommita always took after an opening night, folding her negligé over the back of a chair, and turning down the crimson counterpane. The Sommita arrived with Signor Reece. She was much displeased, Maria said, which Alleyn thought was probably the understatement of the year, and ordered Maria to leave the room. This, he gathered, was a not unusual occurrence. She also ordered Mr. Reece to leave, which *was*. He tried to soothe her, but she became enraged.

"About what?" Alleyn asked.

About something that happened after the opera. Maria had already left the audience. The Signor Bartholomew, she gathered, had insulted the diva. Signor Reece tried to calm her, Maria herself offered to massage her shoulders but was flung off. In the upshot he and Maria left and went downstairs together, Mr. Reece suggesting that Maria give the diva time to calm down and then take her a hot drink, which had been known on similar occasions to produce a favorable reaction.

Maria had followed this advice.

How long between the time when they had left the room and Maria returned to it?

About an hour, she thought.

Where was she during that time?

In the servants' quarters, where she made the hot drink. Mrs. Bacon and Bert the chauffeur were there most of the time, and others of the staff came to and fro from their duties in the dining room, where the guests were now at table. Mr. Reece had joined them. Maria sat and waited for her mistress to compose herself, as Mr. Reece had suggested, and then made the hot drink. Then she returned to the bedroom, found her mistress murdered, and raised the alarm.

"When Madame Sommita dismissed you, did she lock the door after you?"

Yes, it appeared, Maria heard the lock click. She had her own key and used it on her return.

Had anybody else a key to the room?

For the first time she boggled. Her mouth worked but she did not speak.

"Signor Reece, for instance?" Alleyn prompted.

She made the Italian negative sign with her finger.

"Who, then?"

A sly look appeared. Her eyes slid around in the direction of the passage to the right of the landing. Her hand moved to her breast.

"Do you mean Signor Bartholomew?" Alleyn asked.

"Perhaps," she said, and he saw that, very furtively, she crossed herself.

He made a note about keys in his book.

She watched him avidly.

"Maria," he said when he had finished writing, "how long have you been with Madame Sommita?"

Five years, it appeared. She had come to Australia as wardrobe mistress with an Italian opera company, and had stayed on as sewing maid at the Italian Embassy. The Signora's personal maid had displeased her and been dismissed and Signor Reece had inquired of an aide-de-camp who was a friend of his if they could tell him of anyone suitable. The Ambassador had come to the end of his term and the household staff was to be reorganized. Maria had been engaged as personal dresser and lady's maid to Isabella Sommita.

"Who do you think committed this crime?" Alleyn asked suddenly.

"The young man," she answered venomously and at once as if that was a foolish question. And then with another of her abrupt changes of key she urged, begged, demanded that she go back into the room and perform the last services for her mistress—lay her out with decency and close her eyes and pray it would not be held in wrath against her that she had died in a state of sin. "I must go. I insist," said Maria.

"That is still impossible," said Alleyn. "I'm sorry."

He saw that she was on the edge of another outburst and hoped that if she was again moved to spit at him her aim would not have improved.

"You must pull yourself together," he said. "Otherwise I shall be obliged to ask Mr. Reece to have you locked up in your own room. Be a good girl, Maria. Grieve for her. Pray for her soul but do not make scenes. They won't get you anywhere, you know."

Dr. Carmichael, who had contemplated Maria dubiously throughout, now said with professional authority: "Come along like a sensible woman. You'll make yourself unwell if you go on like this. I'll take you down and we'll see if we can find the housekeeper. Mrs. Bacon, isn't it? You'd much better go to bed, you know. Take an aspirin."

"And a hot drink?" Alleyn mildly suggested.

She looked furies at him but with the abruptness that was no longer unexpected stood up, crossed the landing, and walked quickly downstairs.

"Shall I see if I can find Mrs. Bacon and hand her over?" Dr. Carmichael offered.

"Do, like a good chap," said Alleyn. "And if Mrs. B. has vanished, take her to bed yourself."

"Choose your words," said Dr. Carmichael and set off in pursuit.

Alleyn caught him up at the head of the stairs. "I'm going back in there," he said. "I may be a little time. Join me if you will when you've brought home the Bacon. Actually I hope they're all tucked up for the night, but I'd like to know."

Dr. Carmichael ran nimbly downstairs and Alleyn returned, once more, to the bedroom.

III

He began a search. The bedroom was much more ornate than the rest of the house. No doubt, Alleyn thought, this reflected the Sommita's taste more than that of the clever young architect. The wardrobe doors, for instance were carved with elegant festoons and swags of flowers in deep relief, each depending from the central motif of a conventionalized sunflower with a sunken black center, the whole concoction being rather loudly painted and reminiscent of art nouveau.

Alleyn made a thorough search of the surfaces under the bed, of the top of her dressing table, of an escritoire, on which he found the Sommita's jewel box. This was unlocked and the contents were startling in their magnificence. The bedside table. The crimson coverlet. Nothing. Could it be under the body? Possible, he supposed, but he must not move the body.

The bathroom: all along the glass shelves, the floor, everywhere.

And yet Maria, if she was to be believed, had heard the key turned in the lock after she and Mr. Reece were kicked out. And when she returned she had used her own key. He tried to picture the Sommita, at the height, it seemed, of one of her rages, turning the key in the lock, withdrawing it, and then putting it—where? Hiding it? But why? There was no accommodation for it in the bosom of her Hebraic gown, which was now slashed down in ribbons. He uncovered the horror that was the Sommita, and with infinite caution, scarcely touching it, examined the surface of the counterpane round the body. He even slid his hand under the body. Nothing. He re-covered the body.

"When all likely places have been fruitlessly explored, begin on the unlikely and carry on into the preposterous." This was the standard practice. He attacked the drawers of the dressing table. They were kept, by Maria, no doubt, in perfect order. He patted, lifted and replaced lacy undergarments, stockings, gloves. Finally, in the bottom drawer on the left he arrived at the Sommita's collection of handbags. On the top was a gold mesh, bejeweled affair that he remembered her carrying on the evening of their arrival.

Using his handkerchief he gingerly opened it and found her key to the room lying on top of an unused handkerchief.

The bag would have to be fingerprinted, but for the moment it would be best to leave it undisturbed.

So what was to be concluded? If she had taken her bag downstairs and left it in her dressing room, then she must have taken it back to the bedroom. Mr. Reece was with her. There would have been no call for the key, for Maria was already in the room, waiting for her. She was, it must never be forgotten, in a passion, and the Sommita's passions, he would have thought, did not admit of methodical tidying away of handbags into drawers. She would have been more likely to chuck the bag at Mr. Reece's or Maria's head, but Maria had made no mention of any such gesture. She had merely repeated that when they beat their retreat they heard the key turn in the lock and that when she came back with the hot drink she used her own key.

Was it then to be supposed that, having locked herself in, the Sommita stopped raging and methodically replaced her key in the bag and the bag in the drawer? Unlikely, because she must have used the key to admit her killer and was not likely to replace it. Being, presumably dead.

Unless, of course, Maria was her killer. This conjured up a strange picture. The fanatically devoted Maria, hot drink in hand, reenters the bedroom, places the brimming cup in its saucer on the bedside table, and chloroforms her tigerish mistress, who offers no resistance, and she then produces the dagger and photograph and, having completed the jog, sets up her own brand of hullabaloo and rushes downstairs proclaiming the murder? No.

Back to the Sommita, then. What had she done after she had locked herself in? She had not undressed. She had not taken her pill. How had she spent her last minutes before she was murdered?

And what, oh what about Rupert Bartholomew?

At this point there was a tap on the door and Dr. Carmichael returned.

" 'Safely stowed,' " he said. "At least, I hope so. Mrs. Bacon was still up and ready to cope. We escorted that tiresome woman to her room, she offering no resistance. I waited outside. Mrs. B. saw her undressed, be-nightied and in bed. She gave her a couple of aspirins, made sure she took them, and came out. We didn't lock her up, by the way."

"We've really no authority to do that," said Alleyn. "I was making an idle threat."

"It seemed to work."

"I really am very grateful indeed for your help, Carmichael. I don't know how I'd manage without you."

"To tell you the truth, in a macabre sort of way, I'm enjoying myself. It's a change from general practice. What now?" asked Dr. Carmichael.

"Look here. This is important. When you went backstage to succor the wretched Bartholomew, the Sommita was still on deck, wasn't she?"

"She was indeed. Trying to manhandle the boy."

"Still in her Old Testament gear, of course?"

"Of course."

"When they persuaded her to go upstairs—Reece and Lattienzo, wasn't it?—did she take a gold handbag with her? Or did Reece take it?"

"I can't remember. I don't think so."

"It would have looked pretty silly," Alleyn said. "It wouldn't exactly team up with the white samite number. I'd have thought you'd have noticed it." He opened the drawer and showed Dr. Carmichael the bag.

"She was threshing about with her arms quite a bit," the doctor said. "No, I'm sure she hadn't got that thing in her hand. Why?" Alleyn explained.

Dr. Carmichael closed his eyes for some seconds. "No," he said at last, "I can't reconcile the available data with any plausible theory. Unless—"

"Well?"

"Well, it's a most unpleasant thought but—unless the young man—"

"There is that, of course."

"Maria is already making strong suggestions along those lines."

"Is she, by George," said Alleyn and after a pause, "But it's the Sommita's behavior and her bloody key that won't fit in. Did you see anything of our host downstairs?"

"There's a light under what I believe is his study door and voices beyond."

"Come on then. It's high time I reported. He may be able to clear things up a bit."

"I suppose so."

"Either confirm or refute la bella Maria, at least," said Alleyn. "Would you rather go to bed?"

Dr. Carmichael looked at his watch. "Good Lord," he exclaimed, "it's a quarter to twelve."

"As Iago said, 'Pleasure and action make the hours seem short.' "

"Who? Oh. Oh, yes. No, I don't want to go to bed."

"Come on then."

Again they turned off the lights and left the room. Alleyn locked the door.

Bert was on the landing.

"Was you still wanting a watch kept up," he said, "I'll take it on if you like. Only a suggestion."

"You *are* a good chap," Alleyn said. "But—"

"I appreciate you got to be careful. The way things are. But seeing you suggested it yourself before and seeing I never set eyes on one of this mob until I took the job on, I don't look much like a suspect. Please yourself."

"I accept with very many thanks. But—"

"If you was thinking I might drop off, I'd thought of that. I might, too. I could put a couple of them chairs in front of the door and doss down for the night. Just an idea," said Bert.

"It's the answer," Alleyn said warmly. "Thank you, Bert."

And he and Dr. Carmichael went downstairs to the study.

Here they found not only Mr. Reece but Signor Lattienzo, Ben Ruby, and Hanley, the secretary.

Mr. Reece, perhaps a trifle paler than usual, but he was always rather wan, sat at his trendy desk—his swivel chair turned toward the room as if he had interrupted his work to give an interview. Hanley drooped by the window curtains and had probably been looking out at the night. The other two men sat by the fire and seemed to be relieved at Alleyn's appearance. Signor Lattienzo did, in fact, exclaim: "*Ecco!* At last!" Hanley, reverting to his customary solicitude, pushed chairs forward.

"I am very glad to see you, Mr. Alleyn," said Mr. Reece in his pallid way. "Doctor!" he added with an inclination of his head toward Carmichael.

"I'm afraid we've little to report," Alleyn said. "Doctor Carmichael is very kindly helping me, but so far we haven't got beyond the preliminary stages. I'm hoping that you, sir, will be able to put us right on some points, particularly in respect of the order of events from the time Rupert Bartholomew fainted until Maria raised the alarm."

He had hoped for some differences: something that could give him a hint of a pattern or explain the seeming discrepancies in Maria's narrative. Particularly, something about keys. But no, on all points the account corresponded with Maria's.

Alleyn asked if the Sommita made much use of her bedroom key.

"Yes; I think she did, I recommended it. She has—had—there was always—a considerable amount of jewelry in her bedroom. You may say very valuable pieces. I tried to persuade her to keep it in my safe in this room, but she wouldn't do that. It was the same thing in hotels. After all, we have got a considerable staff here and it would be a temptation."

"Her jewel case in the escritoire—unlocked."

Mr. Reece clicked his tongue. "She's—she was incorrigible. The artistic temperament, I am told, though I never, I'm afraid, have known precisely what that means."

"One is never quite sure of its manifestations," said Alleyn, surprised by this unexpected turn in the conversation. Mr. Reece seemed actually to have offered something remotely suggesting a rueful twinkle.

"Well," he said, "you, no doubt, have had firsthand experience," and with a return to his elaborately cumbersome social manner. "Delightful, in your case, may I hasten to say."

"Thank you. While I think of it," Alleyn said, "do you, by any chance, remember if Madame Sommita carried a gold-meshed handbag when you took her up to her room?"

"No," said Mr. Reece, after considering it. "No, I'm sure she didn't."

"Right. About these jewels. No doubt the police will ask you later to check the contents of the box."

"Certainly. But I am not familiar with all her jewels."

Only, Alleyn thought, with the ones he gave her, I daresay.

"They are insured," Mr. Reece offered. "And Maria would be able to check them."

"Is Maria completely to be trusted?"

"Oh, certainly. Completely. Like many of her class and origin she has an uncertain temper and she can be rather a nuisance, but she was devoted to her mistress, you might say fanatically so. She has been upset," Mr. Reece added with one of his own essays in understatement.

"Oh, my dear Monty," Signor Lattienzo murmured. "Upset! So have we all been upset. 'Shattered' would be a more appropriate word." He made an uncertain gesture and took out his cigarette case.

And indeed he looked quite unlike himself, being white and, as Alleyn noticed, tremulous. "Monty, my dear," he said. "I should like a little more of your superb cognac. Is it permitted?"

"Of course, Beppo. Mr. Alleyn? Doctor? Ben?"

The secretary, with a sort of ghostly reminder of his customary readiness, hurried into action. Dr. Carmichael had a large whiskey-and-soda and Alleyn nothing.

Ben Ruby, whose face was puffed and blotched and his eyes bloodshot, hurriedly knocked back his cognac and pushed his glass forward. "What say it's one of that mob?" he demanded insecurely. "Eh? What say one of those buggers stayed behind?"

"Nonsense," said Mr. Reece.

" 'S all very fine, say 'nonsense.' "

"They were carefully chosen guests of known distinction."

"All ver' well. But what say," repeated Mr. Ruby, building to an unsteady climax, "one of your sodding guestserknownstinction was not what he bloody seemed. Eh? *What say* he was Six."

"Six?" Signor Lattienzo asked mildly. "Did you say six?"

"I said nothing of sort. I said," shouted Mr. Ruby, "*Strix.*"

"Oh, *no!*" Hanley cried out, and to Mr. Reece: "I'm sorry but honestly! There *was* the guest list. I gave one to the launch person and he was to tick off all the names as they came aboard in case anybody had been left behind. In the loo or something. I thought you couldn't be too careful in case of accidents. Well, you know, it was—I mean *is—such* a night."

"Yes, yes," Mr. Reece said wearily. "Give it a rest. You acted very properly." He turned to Alleyn. "I really can't see why it should be supposed that Strix, if he is on the premises, could have any motive for committing this crime. On the contrary, he had every reason for wishing Bella to remain alive. She was a fortune to him."

"All ver' well," Mr. Ruby sulked. "If it wasn't, then who was it? Thass the point. D'you think you know who it was? Beppo? Monty? Ned? Come on. No, you don't. See what I mean?"

"Ben," said Mr. Reece quite gently. "Don't you think you'd better go to bed?"

"You may be right. I mean to say," said Mr. Ruby, appealing to Alleyn, "I've got a hell of a lot to do. Cables. Letters. There's the U.S. concert tour. She's booked out twelve months ahead: booked solid. All those managements."

"They'll know about it soon enough," said Mr. Reece bitterly. "Once this storm dies down and the police arrive it'll be world news. Go to bed, boy. If you can use him, Ned will give you some time tomorrow." He glanced at Hanley. "See to that," he said.

"Yes, of *course,*" Hanley effused, smiling palely upon Mr. Ruby, who acknowledged the offer without enthusiasm. "Well, ta," he said. "Won't be necessary, I daresay. I can type."

He seemed to pull himself together. He finished his brandy, rose, advanced successfully upon Mr. Reece, and took his hand. "Monty," he said, "dear old boy. You know me? Anything I can do? Say the word."

"Yes, Benny," Mr. Reece said, shaking his hand. "I know. Thank you."

"There've been good times, haven't there?" Mr. Ruby said wistfully. "It wasn't all fireworks, was it? And now—!"

For the first time Mr. Reece seemed to be on the edge of losing his composure. "And now," he surprised Alleyn by saying, "she no longer casts a shadow." He clapped Mr. Ruby on the shoulder and turned away. Mr. Ruby gazed mournfully at his back for a moment or two and then moved to the door.

"Good night, all," he said. He blew his nose like a trumpet and left them.

He was heard to fall rather heavily on his way upstairs.

"He is fortunate," said Signor Lattienzo, who was swinging his untouched cognac around in the glass. "Now, for my part, the only occasions on which I take no consolation from alcohol are those of disaster. This is my third libation. The cognac is superb. Yet I know it will leave me stone-cold sober. It is very provoking."

Mr. Reece, without turning to face Alleyn, said: "Have you anything further to tell me, Mr. Alleyn?" and his voice was elderly and tired.

Alleyn told him about the Morse signals and Mr. Reece said dully that it was good news. "But I meant," he said, "about the crime itself. You will appreciate, I'm sure, how—confused and shocked—to find her—like that. It was—" He made a singular and uncharacteristic gesture as if warding off some menace. "It was so dreadful," he said.

"Of course it was. One can't imagine anything worse. Forgive me," Alleyn said, "but I don't know exactly how you learned about it. Were you prepared in any way? Did Maria—?"

"You must have heard her. I was in the drawing room and came out and she was there on the stairs, screaming. I went straight up with her. I think I made out before we went into the room and without really taking it in, that Bella was dead. Was murdered. But not—how. Beppo, here, and Ned—arrived almost at the same moment. It may sound strange but the whole thing, at the time, seemed unreal: a nightmare, you might say. It still does."

Alleyn said: "You've asked me to take over until the police come. I'm very sorry indeed to trouble you—"

"No. Please," Mr. Reece interrupted with a shaky return to his customary formality. "Please, do as you would under any other circumstances."

"You make it easy for me. First of all, you are sure, sir, are you, that after Madame Sommita ordered you and Maria to leave the bedroom you heard her turn the key in the lock?"

"Absolutely certain. May I ask why?"

"And Maria used her own key when she returned?"

"She must have done so, I presume. The door was not locked when Maria and I returned after she raised the alarm."

"And there are—how many keys to the room?"

If atmosphere can be said to tighten without a word being uttered, it did so then in Mr. Reece's study. The silence was absolute; nobody spoke, nobody moved.

"Four?" Alleyn at last suggested.

"If you know, why do you ask?" Hanley threw out.

Mr. Reece said: "That will do, Ned."

"I'm sorry," he said, cringing a little yet with a disreputable suggestion of blandishment. "Truly."

"Who has the fourth key?" Alleyn asked.

"If there is one I don't imagine it is used," said Mr. Reece.

"I think the police will want to know."

"In that case we must find out. Maria will probably know."

"Yes," Alleyn agreed. "I expect she will." He hesitated for a moment and then said, "Forgive me. The circumstances I know are almost unbelievably grotesque, but did you look closely? At what had been done? And how it had been done?"

"Oh, really, Alleyn—" Signor Lattienzo protested, but Mr. Reece held up his hand.

"No, Beppo," he said and cracked a dismal joke, "as you yourself would say: I asked for it, and now I'm getting it." And to Alleyn. "There's something under the knife. I didn't go—near. I couldn't. What is it?"

"It is a photograph. Of Madame Sommita singing."

Mr. Reece's lips formed the word "photograph" but no sound came from them.

"This is a madman," Signor Lattienzo broke out. "A homicidal maniac. It cannt be otherwise."

Hanley said: "Oh yes, *yes!*" as if there was some sort of comfort in the thought. "A madman. Of course. A lunatic."

Mr. Reece cried out so loudly that they were all startled, "No! What you tell me alters the whole picture. I have been wrong. From the beginning I have been wrong. The photograph proves it. If he had left a signed acknowledgment, it couldn't be clearer."

There was a long silence before Lattienzo said flatly: "I think you may be right."

"Right! Of course I am right."

"And if you are, Monty, my dear, this Strix was on the Island yesterday and unless he managed to escape by the launch is still on this Island tonight. And, in spite of all our zealous searching, may actually be in the house. In which case we shall indeed do wisely to lock our doors." He turned to Alleyn. "And what does the professional say to all this?" he asked.

"I think you probably correct in every respect, Signor Lattienzo," said Alleyn. "Or rather, in every respect but one."

"And what may that be?" Lattienzo asked sharply.

"You are proposing, aren't you, that Strix is the murderer? I'm inclined to think you may be mistaken there."

"And I would be interested to hear why."

"Oh," said Alleyn, "just one of those things, you know. I would find it hard to say why. Call it a hunch."

"But my dear sir—the photograph."

"Ah yes," said Alleyn. "Quite so. There is always the photograph, isn't there?"

"You choose to be mysterious."

"Do I? Not really. What I really came in for was to ask you all if you happened to notice that an Italian stiletto, if that is what it is, was missing from its bracket on the wall behind the nude sculpture. And if you did notice, when."

They stared at him. After a long pause Mr. Reece said: "You will find this extraordinary, but nevertheless it is a fact. I had not realized that was the weapon."

"Had you not?"

"I am, I think I may say, an observant man but I did not notice that the stiletto was missing and I did not recognize it"—he covered his eyes with his hands—"when I—saw it."

Hanley said: "Oh, God! Oh, how terrible."

And Lattienzo: "They were hers. You knew that of course, Monty, didn't you? Family possessions, I always understood. I remember her showing them to me and saying she would like to use one of them in *Tosca*. I said it would be much too dangerous, however cleverly she faked it. And I may add that the Scarpia wouldn't entertain the suggestion for a second. Remembering her temperament, poor darling, it was not surprising."

Mr. Reece looked up at Alleyn. His face was deadly tired and he seemed an old man.

"If you don't mind," he said, "I think I must go to my room. Unless of course there is anything else."

"Of course not." Alleyn glanced at Dr. Carmichael, who went to Mr. Reece.

"You've had about as much as you can take," he said. "Will you let me see you to your room?"

"You are very kind. No, thank you, doctor. I am perfectly all right. Only tired."

He stood up, straightened himself and walked composedly out of the room.

When he had gone, Alleyn turned to the secretary.

"Mr. Hanley," he said, "did you notice one of the stilettos was missing?"

"I'd have said so, wouldn't I, if I had?" Hanley pointed out in an aggrieved voice. "As a matter of fact, I simply loathe the things. I'm like that over knives. They make me feel sick. I expect Freud would have had something to say about it."

"No doubt," said Signor Lattienzo.

"It was her idea," Hanley went on. "She had them hung on the wall. She thought they teamed up with that marvelous pregnant female. In a way, one could see why."

"Could one?" said Signor Lattienzo and cast up his eyes.

"I would like again to ask you all," said Alleyn, "if on consideration, you can think of anyone—but *anyone*, however unlikely—who might have had some cause, however outrageous, to wish for Madame Sommita's death. Yes, Signor Lattienzo?"

"I feel impelled to say that my answer is no I can *not* think of anyone. I believe that this is a crime of passion and impulse and not a coldly calculated affair. The outrageous *grotesquerie,* the use of the photograph and of her own weapon—everything points to some—I feel inclined to say Strindbergian love-hatred of lunatic force. Strix or not, I believe you are looking for a madman, Mr. Alleyn."

IV

After that the interview began to languish and Alleyn sensed the unlikelihood of anything to the point emerging from it. He suggested that they go to bed.

"I am going to the studio," he said. "I shall be there for the next half-hour or so and if anything crops up, however slight, that seems to be of interest, I would be glad if you would report to me there. I do remind you all," he said, "that what I am trying to do is a sort of caretaker's job for the police: to see, if possible, that nothing is done inadvertently or with intention, to muddle the case for them before they arrive. Even if it were proper for me to attempt a routine police investigation, it wouldn't be possible to do so singlehanded. Is that clear?"

They muttered weary assents and got to their feet.

"Good night," said Dr. Carmichael. It was the second and last time he had spoken.

He followed Alleyn into the hall and up the stairs.

When they reached the first landing they found that Bert had put two chairs together face-to-face, hard against the door to the Sommita's room, and was lying very comfortably on this improvised couch, gently snoring.

"I'm along there," said Dr. Carmichael, pointing to the left-hand passage.

"Unless you're asleep on your feet," said Alleyn, "will you come into the studio, for a moment or two? No need, if you can't bear the thought."

"I'm well trained to eccentric hours."

"Good."

They crossed the landing and went into the studio. The great empty canvas still stood on its easel but Troy had put away her drawings. Alleyn's dispatch case had been removed from their bedroom and placed conspicuously on the model's throne with a flashlight on top of it. Good for Troy, he thought.

Yesterday, sometime after Troy had been settled in the studio, a supply of drinks had been brought in and stored in a wallside unit. Alleyn wondered if this was common practice at the Lodge wherever a room was inhabited.

He said: "I didn't have a drink down there: could you do with another?"

"I believe I could. A small one, though."

They had their drinks and lit their pipes. "I haven't dared do this before," said the doctor.

"Nor I," said Alleyn. He performed what had now become a routine exercise and drew back the curtains. The voice of the wind, which he was always to remember as a kind of leitmotiv to the action, invaded their room. The windowpane was no longer masked with water but was a black nothing with vague suggestions of violence beyond. When he leaned forward his ghost-face, cadaverous with shadows, moved toward him. He closed the curtains.

"It's not raining," he said, "but blowing great guns."

"What's called 'blowing itself out,' perhaps?"

"Hope so. But that doesn't mean the Lake will automatically go calmer."

"Unfortunately no. Everything else apart, it's bloody inconvenient," said the doctor. "I've got a medical conference opening in Auckland tomorrow. Eru Johnstone said he'd ring them up. I hope he remembers."

"Why did you stay?"

"Not from choice. I'm a travel-sickness subject. Ten minutes in that launch topped up by mile after mile in a closed bus would have been absolute hell for me and everyone else. Reece was insistent that I should stay. He wanted me to take on the Great Lady as a patient. Some notion that she was heading for a nervous crisis, it seemed."

"One would have thought it was a chronic condition," said Alleyn. "All the same I got the impression that even when she peaked, temperamentally speaking, she never went completely over the top. I'd risk a guess that she always knew jolly well what she was up to. Perhaps with one exception."

"That wretched boy?"

"Exactly."

"You'd say she'd gone overboard for him?" asked the doctor.

"I certainly got that impression," Alleyn said.

"So did I, I must say. In Sydney—"

"You'd met them before?" Alleyn exclaimed. "In Sydney?"

"Oh yes. I went over there for her season. Marvelous it was, too. I was asked to meet her at a dinner party and then to a supper Reece gave after the performance. He—they—were hospitable and kind to me for the rest of the season. Young Bartholomew was very much in evidence and she made no bones about it. I got the impression that she was—I feel inclined to say 'savagely' devoted."

"And he?"

"Oh, besotted and completely out of his depth."

"And Reece?"

"If he objected he didn't show it. I think his might be a case of collector's satisfaction. You know? He'd acquired the biggest star in the firmament."

"And was satisfied with the *fait accompli?* So 'that was that'?"

"Quite. He may even have been a bit sick of her tantrums, though I must say he gave no sign of it."

"No."

"By the way, Alleyn, I suppose it's occurred to you that I'm a candidate for your list of suspects."

"In common with everyone else in the house. Oh, yes, but you don't come very high on the list. Of course, I didn't know you'd had a previous acquaintance with her," Alleyn said coolly.

"Well, I must say!" Dr. Carmichael exclaimed.

"I felt I really needed somebody I could call upon. You and Bert seemed my safest bets. Having had, as I then supposed, no previous connection with her and no conceivable motive."

Dr. Carmichael looked fixedly at him. Alleyn pulled a long face.

"I am a lowland Scot," said the doctor, "and consequently a bit heavy-handed when it comes to jokes."

"I'll tell you when I mean to be funny."

"Thank you."

"Although, God knows, there's not much joky material going in this business."

"No, indeed."

"I suppose," said Dr. Carmichael after a companionable silence, "that you've noticed my tact? Another lowland Scottish characteristic is commonly thought to be curiosity."

"So I've always understood. Yes. I noticed. You didn't ask me if I know who dunnit."

"Do you?"

"No."

"Do you hae your suspeesions?"

"Yes. You're allowed one more."

"Am I? What shall I choose? Do you think the photographer—Strix—is on the Island?"

"Yes."

"And took—that photograph?"

"You've exceeded your allowance. But, yes. Of course. Who else?" said Alleyn.

"And murdered Isabella Sommita?"

"No."

And after that they wished each other good night. It was now thirteen minutes past one in the morning.

When Dr. Carmichael had gone Alleyn opened a note that lay on top of his dispatch case, took out an all too familiar file and settled down to read it for the seventh time.

Isabella Pepitone, known as Isabella Sommita. *Born:* ?1944, reputedly in Palermo, Sicily. Family subsequently settled in U.S.A. *Father:* Alfredo Pepitone, successful businessman U.S.A., suspected of Mafia activities but never arrested. Suspect in Rossi homicide case 1965. Victim: Bianca Rossi, female. Pepitone subsequently killed in car accident. Homicide suspected. No arrest.

Alleyn had brought his library book upstairs. There it lay near to hand —*Il Mistero da Bianca Rossi.*

Subject trained as singer. First in New York and later for three years under Beppo Lattienzo in Milan. 1965-1968, sang with small German opera companies. Subject's debut 1968 La Scala. Became celebrated. 1970-79 associated socially with Hoffman-Beilstein Group.

1977 May 10th: Self-styled "Baron" Hoffman-Beilstein, since believed to be Mr. Big behind large-scale heroin chain, cruised his yacht *Black Star* round the Bermudas. Subject was one of his guests. Visited Miami via Fort Lauderdale. First meeting with Montague V. Reece, fellow passenger.

1977 May 11th: Subject and Hoffman-Beilstein lunched at Palm Beach with Earl J. Ogden, now known to be background figure in heroin trade. He dined aboard yacht same night. Subsequently a marked increase in street sales and socially high-class markets Florida and, later, New York. F.B.I. suspects heroin brought ashore from *Black Star* at Fort Lauderdale. Interpol interested.

1977: Relations with Hoffman-Beilstein became less frequent.

1978: Relations H-B apparently terminated. Close relationship developed with Reece. Subject's circle now consists of top impeccable socialites and musical celebrities.

Written underneath these notes in the spiky, irritable hand of Alleyn's Assistant Commissioner,

For Ch. Sup. Alleyn's attn. Not much joy. Any items however insignificant will be appreciated.

Alleyn locked the file back in the case. He began to walk about the room as if he kept an obligatory watch. It would be so easy, he thought, to concoct a theory based on the meager document. How would it go?

The Sommita, born Bella Pepitone, which he thought he'd heard or read somewhere was a common Sicilian name, was reared in the United States. He remembered the unresolved Rossi case quite well. It was of the sort that turns up in books about actual crimes. The feud was said to be generations deep: a hangover from some initial murder in Sicily. It offered good material for "true crimes" collections, being particularly bloody and having a peculiar twist: in the long succession of murders the victims had always been women and the style of their putting off grisly.

The original crime, which took place in 1910 in Sicily and triggered off the feud, was said to have been the killing of a Pepitone woman in circumstances of extreme cruelty. Ever since, hideous idiocies had been perpetrated on both sides at irregular intervals in the name of this vendetta.

The macabre nature of the Sommita's demise and her family connections would certainly qualify her as a likely candidate and it must be supposed would notch up several points on the Rossi score.

Accepting, for the moment, this outrageous proposition, what, he speculated, about the M.O.? How was it all laid on? Could Strix be slotted into the pattern? Very readily, if you let your imagination off the chain. Suppose Strix was in the Rossi interest and had been hired, no doubt at an exorbitant price, to torment the victim, but not necessarily to dispatch her? Perhaps Strix was himself a member of the Rossi Family? In this mixed stew of concoctions there was one outstanding ingredient: the identity of Strix. For Alleyn it was hardly in doubt, but if he was right it followed that Strix was not the assassin. (And how readily that melodramatic word surfaced in this preposterous case.) From the conclusion of the opera until Alleyn went upstairs to write his letter, this "Strix" had been much in evidence downstairs. He had played the ubiquitous busybody. He had been present all through dinner and in the hall when the guests were milling about waiting to embark.

He had made repeated trips from house to jetty full of consoling chat, sheltering departing guests under a gigantic umbrella. He had been here, there, and everywhere but he certainly had not had time to push his way through the crowd, go upstairs, knock on the Sommita's door, be admitted, administer chloroform, asphyxiate her, wait twenty minutes, and then implant the stiletto and the photograph. And return to his duties, unruffled, in his natty evening getup.

For, in Alleyn's mind at this juncture, there were no two ways about the identity of Strix.

CHAPTER VI

Storm Continued

I

ALLEYN WROTE UP his notes. He sat at the brand-new paint table Troy would never use and worked for an hour, taking great pains to be comprehensive, detailed, succinct, and lucid, bearing in mind that the notes were destined for the New Zealand police. And the sooner he handed them over and he and Troy packed their bags, the better he would like it.

The small hours came and went and with them that drained sensation accompanied by the wakefulness that replaces an unsatisfied desire for sleep. The room, the passage outside, the landing, and the silent house beyond seemed to change their character and lead a stealthy night life of their own.

It was raining again. Giant handfuls of rice seemed to be thrown across the windowpanes. The Lodge, new as it was, jolted under the onslaught. Alleyn thought of the bathing pool, below the studio windows, and almost fancied he could hear its risen waters slapping at the house.

At a few minutes short of two o'clock he was visited by an experience Troy, ever since the early days of their marriage when he had first confided in her, called his Familiar, though truly a more accurate name might be Unfamiliar or perhaps Alter Ego. He understood that people interested in such matters were well acquainted with this state of being and that it was not at all unusual. Perhaps the E.S.P. buffs had it taped. He had never cared to ask.

The nearest he could get to it was to say that without warning he would feel as if he had moved away from his own identity and looked at himself as if at a complete stranger. He felt that if he held on outside himself, something new and very remarkable would come out of it. But he never did hang on and as suddenly as normality had gone it would return. The slightest disturbance clicked it back and he was within himself again.

As now, when he caught a faint movement that had not been there before—the sense rather than the sound—of someone in the passage outside the room.

He went to the door and opened it and was face to face with the ubiquitous and serviceable Hanley.

"Oh," said Hanley, "*so* sorry. I was just going to knock. One saw the light under your door and wondered if—you know—one might be of use."

"You're up late. Come in."

He came in, embellishing his entrance with thanks and apologies. He wore a dressing gown of Noel Coward vintage and Moroccan slippers. His hair was fluffed up into a little crest like a baby's. In the uncompromising lights of the studio it could be seen that he was not very young.

"I think," he said, "it's absolutely fantastic of you to take on all this beastliness. Honestly!"

"Oh," Alleyn said, "I'm only treading water, you know, until the proper authorities arrive."

"A prospect that doesn't exactly fill one with rapture."

"Why are you abroad so late, Mr. Hanley?"

"Couldn't you settle for 'Ned'? 'Mr. Hanley' makes one feel like an undergraduate getting gated. I'm abroad in the night because I can't sleep. I can't help seeing—everything—her. Whenever I close my eyes—there it is. If I do doze—it's there. Like those crummy old horror films. An awful face suddenly rushing at one. It might as well be one of Dracula's ladies after the full treatment." He gave a miserable giggle and then looked appalled. "I shouldn't be like this," he said. "Even though as a matter of fact, it's no more than the truth. But I mustn't bore you with my woes."

"Where is your room?"

"One flight up. Why? Oh, I see. You're wondering what brought me down here, aren't you? You'll think it very peculiar and it's not easy to explain, but actually it was that thing about being drawn towards something that gives one the horrors like edges of precipices and spiders. You know? After trying to sleep and getting nightmares, I began to think I had to make myself come down to this floor and cross the landing outside—that room. When I went up to bed I actually used the staff stairs to avoid doing that very thing and here I was under this beastly compulsion. So I did it. I hated it and I did it. And in the event there was our rather good-looking chauffeur, Bert, snoring on chairs. He must have very acute hearing, because when I crossed the landing he opened his eyes and stared at me. It was disconcerting because he didn't utter. I lost my head and said: 'Oh, hullo, Bert, it's perfectly all right. Don't get up,' and made a bolt of it into this passage and saw the light under your door. I seem to be cold. Would you think it too bold if I asked you if I might have a brandy? I didn't downstairs because I make it a rule never to unless the Boss Man offers and anyway I don't really like the stuff. But I think—tonight—"

"Yes, of course. Help yourself."

"Terrific," Hanley said. Alleyn saw him half-fill a small tumbler, take a pull at it, shudder violently, and close his eyes.

"Would you mind awfully if I turned on that radiator?" he asked. "Our central heating goes off between twelve and seven."

Alleyn turned it on. Hanley sat close to it on the edge of the throne and nursed his brandy. "That's better," he said. "I feel much better. Sweet of you to understand."

Alleyn, as far as he knew, had given no sign of having understood anything. He had been thinking that Hanley was the second distraught visitor to the studio over the past forty-eight hours and that in a way he was a sort of unconvincing parody of Rupert Bartholomew. It struck him that Hanley was making the most of his distress, almost relishing it.

"As you're feeling better," he suggested, "perhaps you won't mind putting me straight on one or two domestic matters—especially concerning the servants."

"If I can," Hanley said, readily enough.

"I hope you can. You've been with Mr. Reece for some years, haven't you?"

"Since January 1976. I was a senior secretary with the Hoffman-Beilstein Group in New York. Transferred from their Sydney offices. The Boss Man was chums with them in those days and I saw quite a lot of him. And he of me. His secretary had died and in the upshot," said Hanley, a little too casually, "I got the job." He finished his brandy. "It was all quite amicable and took place during a cruise of the Caribbean in the Hoffman yacht. I was on duty. The Boss Man was a guest. I think it was then that he found out about the Hoffman-Beilstein organization being naughty. He's absolutely Caesar's Wife himself. Well, you know what I mean. Pure as the driven snow. Incidentally, that was when he first encountered the Lady," said Hanley, and his mouth tightened. "But without any noticeable reaction. He wasn't really a lady's man."

"No?"

"Oh, no. She made all the running. And, face it, she *was* a collector's piece. It was like pulling off a big deal. As a matter of fact, in my opinion, it was—well—far from being a *grande passion*. Oh dear, there I go again. But it was, as you might say, a very aseptic relationship."

This chimed, Alleyn thought, with Dr. Carmichael's speculation.

"Yes, I see," he said lightly. "Has Mr. Reece any business relationships with Hoffman-Beilstein?"

"He pulled out. Like I said, we didn't fancy the way things shaped up. There were very funny rumors. He broke everything off after the cruise. Actually he rescued Madame—and me—at the same time. That's how it all started."

"I see. And now—about the servants."

"I suppose you mean Marco and Maria, don't you? Straight out of grand opera, the two of them. Without the voice for it, of course."

"Did they come into the household before your time?"

"Maria was with Madame, of course, at the time I made my paltry entrance. I understand the Boss Man produced her. From the Italian Embassy or somewhere rather smooth. But Marco arrived after me."

"When was that?"

"Three years ago. Third Australian tour. The Boss Man wanted a personal servant. I advertised and Marco was easily the best bet. He had marvelous references. We thought that being Italian he might understand Maria and the Lady."

"Would that be about the time when Strix began to operate?"

"About then, yes," Hanley agreed and then stared at Alleyn. "Oh, *no!*" he said. "You're not suggesting? Or are you?"

"I'm not suggesting anything. Naturally I would like to hear more about Strix. Can you give me any idea of how many times the offensive photographs appeared?"

Hanley eyed him warily. "Not precisely," he said. "There had been some on her European tour, before I joined the circus. About six, I think. I've filed them and could let you know."

"Thank you. And afterwards. After you and Marco had both arrived on the scene?"

"Now you'll be making *me* feel awkward. No, of course you won't. I don't mean that. Let me think. There was the one in Double Bay when he bounced round a corner in dark glasses with a scarf over his mouth. And the stage-door *débâcle* when he was in drag and the one in Melbourne when he came alongside in a car and shot off before they could see what he was like. *And* of course the *really* awful one on the Opera House steps. There was a rumor then that he was a blond. That's only *four!*" Hanley exclaimed. "With all the hullabaloo it seemed more like the round dozen. It certainly did the trick with Madame. The *scenes!*" He finished his brandy.

"Did Madame Sommita keep in touch with her family, do you know?"

"I don't think there is any family in Australia. I think I've heard they're all in the States. I don't know what they're called or anything, really, about them. The origins, one understood, were of the earth, earthy."

"In her circle of acquaintances, are there many—or any—Italians?"

"Well—" Hanley said warming slightly to the task. "Let's see. There are the ambassadorial ones. We always make V.I.P. noises about them, of course. And I understand there was a big Italian fan mail in Australia. We've a considerable immigrant population over there, you know."

"Did you ever hear of anybody called Rossi?"

Hanley shook his head slowly. "Not to remember."

"Or Pepitone?"

"No. What an enchanting fun-name. Is he a fan? But, honestly, I don't have anything to do with the Lady's acquaintances or correspondents or ongoings of any sort. If you want to dig into *her* affairs," said Hanley, and now a sneer was clearly to be heard, "you'd better ask the infant phenomenon, hadn't you?"

"Bartholomew?"

"Who else? He's supposed to be her secretary. Secretary! My God!"

"You don't approve of Bartholomew?"

"He's marvelous to *look* at, of course."

"Looks apart?"

"One doesn't want to be catty," said Hanley, succeeding in being so pretty well, nevertheless, "but what else is there? The opera? You heard that for yourself. And all that carry-on at the curtain call! I'm afraid I think he's a complete phony. *And* spiteful with it."

"Really? Spiteful? You surprise me."

"Well, look at him. Take, take, take. Everything she could give. But *everything*. All caught up with the opera nonsense and then when it flopped, turning round and making a public fool of himself. *And* her. I could see *right* through the high tragedy bit, don't you worry: it was an act. He blamed her for the disaster. For egging him on. He was getting back at her." Hanley had spoken rapidly in a high voice. He stopped short, swung round, and stared at Alleyn.

"I suppose," he said, "I shouldn't say these things to you. For Christ's sake don't go reading something awful into it all. It's just that I got *so* bored with the way everyone fell for the boy beautiful. *Everyone*. Even the Boss Man. Until he chickened out and said he wouldn't go on with the show. That put a different complexion on the *affaire*, didn't it? Well, on everything, really. The Boss Man was livid. Such a change!"

He stood up and carefully replaced his glass on the tray. "I'm a trifle tiddly," he said, "but quite clear in the head. Is it true or did I dream it that the British press used to call you the Handsome Sleuth? Or something like that?"

"You dreamt it," said Alleyn. "Good night."

II

At twenty to three Alleyn had finished his notes. He locked them away in his dispatch case, looked around the studio, turned out the lights, and, carrying the case, went out into the passage, locking the door behind him.

And now how quiet was the Lodge. It smelled of new carpets, of dying fires, and of the aftermath of food, champagne, and cigarettes. It was not altogether silent. There were minuscule sounds suggestive of its adjusting to the storm. As he approached the landing there were Bert's snores to be heard, rhythmic but not very loud.

Alleyn had, by now, a pretty accurate knowledge, acquired on the earlier search, of the Lodge and its sleeping quarters. The principal bedrooms and the studio were all on this floor and opened onto two passages that led off, right and left, from the landing, each taking a right-angled turn after three rooms had been passed. The guests' names were inserted in neat little slots on their doors: *à la* Versailles, thought Alleyn; they might as well have gone the whole hog while they were about it and used the discriminating *pour*. It would be "*Pour* Signor Lattienzo." But he suspected merely "Dr. Carmichael."

He crossed the landing. Bert had left the shaded table lamp on, and it softly illuminated his innocent face. As Alleyn passed him he stopped snoring and opened his eyes. They looked at each other for a second or two. Bert said "Gidday" and went back to sleep.

Alleyn entered the now dark passage on the right of the landing, passed his own bedroom door and thought how strange it was that Troy should be in there and that soon he would be able to join her. He paused for a moment and as he did so heard a door open somewhere beyond the turn of the passage.

The floor, like all floors in this padded house, was thickly carpeted, but nevertheless he felt rather than heard somebody walking toward him.

Realizing that he might be silhouetted against the dimly glowing landing, he flattened himself against the wall and slid back to where he remembered seeing a switch for the passage lights. After some groping his hand found it. He turned it on and there, almost within touching distance, was Rupert Bartholomew.

For a moment he thought Rupert would bolt. He had jerked up his hands as if to guard his face. He looked quickly behind him, hesitated, and then seemed to pull himself together.

"It's you," he whispered. "You gave me a shock."

"Wasn't Signor Lattienzo's pill any good?"

"No. I've got to get to the lavatory. I can't wait."

"There isn't one along here, you must know that."

"Oh God!" said Rupert loudly. "Lay off me, can't you?"

"Don't start anything here, you silly chap. Keep your voice down and come to the studio."

"No."

"Oh, yes, you will. Come on."

He took him by the arm.

Down the passage, back across the landing, back past Bert Smith, back into the studio. Will this night never end? Alleyn wondered, putting down his dispatch case.

"If you really want the Usual Offices," he said, "there's one next door, which you know as well as I do, and I don't mind betting there's one in your own communicating bathroom. But you *don't* want it, do you?"

"Not now."

"Where were you bound for?"

"I've told you."

"Oh, come *on.*"

"Does it matter?"

"Of course it matters, you ass. Ask yourself."

Silence.

"Well?"

"I left something. Downstairs."

"What?"

"The score."

"Of *The Alien Corn?*"

"Yes."

"Couldn't it wait till daylight? Which is not far off."

"No."

"Why?"

"I want to burn it. The score. All the parts. Everything. I woke up and kept thinking of it. There, on the hall fire, burn it, I thought."

"The fire will probably be out."

"I'll blow it together," said Rupert.

"You're making this up as you go along. Aren't you?"

"No. No. Honestly. I swear not. I want to burn it."

"And anything else?"

He caught back his breath and shook his head.

"Are you *sure* you want to burn it?"

"How many times do I have to say!"

"Very well," said Alleyn.

"Thank God."

"I'll come with you."

"*No.* I mean there's no need. I won't," said Rupert with a wan attempt at lightness, "get up to any funny business."

"Such as?"

"Anything. Nothing. I just don't want an audience. I've had enough of audiences," said Rupert and contrived a laugh.

"I'll be unobtrusive."

"You suspect me. Don't you?"

"I suspect a round half-dozen of you. Come on."

Alleyn took him by the arm.

"I've changed my mind," Rupert said and broke away.

"If you're thinking I'll go to bed and then you'll pop down by yourself, you couldn't be more mistaken. I'll sit you out."

Rupert bit his finger and stared at Alleyn. A sudden battering by the gale sent some metal object clattering across the patio down below. Still blowing great guns, thought Alleyn.

"Come along," he said. "I'm sorry I've got to be bloody-minded but you might as well take it gracefully. We don't want to do a cinematic roll down the stairs in each other's arms, do we?"

Rupert turned on his heel and walked out of the room. They went together, quickly, to the stairs and down them to the hall.

It was a descent into almost total darkness. A red glow at the far end must come from the embers of the fire, and there was a vague, scarcely perceptible luminosity filtered down from the lamp on the landing. Alleyn had put Troy's torch in his pocket and used it. Its beam dodged down the stairs ahead of them.

"There's your fire," he said. "Now, I suppose, for the sacrifice."

He guided Rupert to the back of the hall and through the double doors that opened into the concert chamber. When they were there he shut the doors and turned on the wall lamps. They stood blinking at a litter of discarded programs, the blank face of the stage curtain, the piano and the players' chairs and music stands with their sheets of manuscript. How long, Alleyn wondered, had it taken Rupert to write them out? And then on the piano, the full score. On the cover "The Alien Corn" painstakingly lettered, "by Rupert Bartholomew." And underneath: "Dedicated to Isabella Sommita."

"Never mind," Alleyn said. "This was only a beginning. Lattienzo thinks you will do better things."

"Did he say so?"

"He did indeed."

"The duet, I suppose. He did say something about the duet," Rupert admitted.

"The duet it was."

"I rewrote it."

"So he said. Greatly to its advantage."

"All the same," Rupert muttered after a pause, "I shall burn it."

"Sure?"

"Absolutely. I'm just going behind. There's a spare copy; I won't be a moment."

"Hold on," Alleyn said. "I'll light you."

"*No!* Don't bother. Please. I know where the switch is."

He made for a door in the back wall, stumbled over a music stand, and fell. While he was clambering to his feet, Alleyn ran up the apron steps and slipped through the curtains. He crossed upstage and went out by the rear exit, arriving in a back passage that ran parallel with the stage and had four doors opening off it.

Rupert was before him. The passage lights were on and a door with a silver star fixed to it was open. The reek of cosmetics flowed out of the room.

Alleyn reached the door. Rupert was in there, too late with the envelope he was trying to stuff into his pocket.

The picture he presented was stagy in the extreme. He looked like an early illustration for a Sherlock Holmes story—the young delinquent caught red-handed with the incriminating document. His eyes even started in the approved manner.

He straightened up, achieved an awful little laugh, and pushed the envelope down in his pocket.

"That doesn't look much like a spare copy of an opera," Alleyn remarked.

"It's a good-luck card I left for her. I—it seemed so ghastly, sitting there. Among the others. *'Good Luck!'* You know?"

"I'm afraid I don't. Let me see it."

"No. I can't. It's private."

"When someone has been murdered," Alleyn said, "nothing is private."

"You can't make me."

"I could, very easily," he answered and thought: And how the hell would *that* look in subsequent proceedings?

"You don't understand. It's got nothing to do with what happened. You wouldn't understand."

"Try me," Alleyn suggested and sat down.

"No."

"You know you're doing yourself no good by this," Alleyn said. "If whatever's in that envelope has no relevance it will not be brought into the picture. By behaving like this you suggest that it has. You make me wonder if your real object in coming down here was not to destroy your work but to regain possession of this card, if that's what it is."

"No. *No.* I *am* going to burn the script. I'd made up my mind."

"Both copies?"

"What? Yes. Yes, of course. I've said so."

"And where is the second copy, exactly? Not in here?"

"Another room."

"Come now," Alleyn said, not unkindly. "There is no second copy, is there? Show me what you have in your pocket."

"You'd read—all sorts of things—into it."

"I haven't got that kind of imagination. You might ask yourself, with more cause, what I am likely to read into a persistent refusal to let me see it."

He spared a thought for what he would in fact be able to do if Rupert *did* persist. With no authority to take possession forcibly, he saw himself spending the fag end of the night in Rupert's room and the coming day until such time as the police might arrive, keeping him under ludicrous surveyance. No. His best bet was to keep the whole thing in as low a key as possible and trust to luck.

"I do wish," he said, "that you'd just think sensibly about this. Weigh it up. Ask yourself what a refusal is bound to mean to you, and for God's sake cough up the bloody thing and let's go to bed for what's left of this interminable night."

He could see the hand working in the pocket and hear paper crumple. He wondered if Rupert tried, foolishly, to tear it. He sat out the silence, read messages of goodwill pinned round the Sommita's looking glass and smelled the age-old incense of the makeup bench. He even found himself, after a fashion, at home.

And there, abruptly, was Rupert, holding out the envelope. Alleyn took it. It was addressed tidily to the Sommita in what looked to be a feminine hand, and Alleyn thought had probably enclosed one of the greeting cards. It was unsealed. He drew out the enclosure: a crumpled corner, torn from a sheet of music.

He opened it. The message had been scrawled in pencil and the writing was irregular as if the paper had rested on an uneven surface.

> Soon it will all be over. If I were a Rossi I would make a better job of it. R.

Alleyn looked at the message for much longer than it took to read it. Then he returned it to the envelope and put it in his pocket.

"When did you write this?" he asked.

"After the curtain came down. I tore the paper off the score."

"And wrote it here, in her room?"

"Yes."

"Did she find you in here when she came for you?"

"I was in the doorway. I'd finished—that."

"And you allowed yourself to be dragged on?"

"Yes. I'd made up my mind what I'd say. She asked for it," said Rupert through his teeth, "and she got it."

" 'Soon it will all be over,' " Alleyn quoted. "What would be over?"

"Everything. The opera. Us. What I was going to do. You heard me, for God's sake. I told them the truth." Rupert caught his breath back and then said, "I was not planning to kill her, Mr. Alleyn. And I did not kill her."

"I didn't think that even you would have informed her in writing, however ambiguously, of your intention. Would you care to elaborate on the Rossi bit?"

"I wrote that to frighten her. She'd told me about it. One of those Italian family feuds. Mafia sort of stuff. Series of murders and the victim always a woman. She said she was in the direct line to be murdered. She really believed that. She even thought the Strix man might be one of them—the Rossis. She said she'd never spoken about it to anyone else. Something about silence."

"Omertà?"

"Yes. That was it."

"Why did she tell *you* then?"

Rupert stamped his feet and threw up his hands. "Why! Why! Because she wanted me to pity her. It was when I first told her that thing was no good and I couldn't go on with the performance. She—I think she saw that I'd changed. Seen her for what she was. It was awful. I was trapped. From then on I—well, you know, don't you, what it was like. She could still whip up—"

"Yes. All right."

"Tonight—last night—it all came to a head. I hated her for singing my opera so beautifully. Can you understand that? It was a kind of insult. As if she deliberately showed how worthless it was. She was a vulgar woman, you know. That was why she degraded me. That was what I felt after the curtain fell—degraded—and it was then I knew I hated her."

"And this was written on the spur of the moment?"

"Of course. I suppose you could say I was sort of beside myself. I can't tell you what it did to me. Standing there. Conducting, for Christ's sake. It was indecent exposure."

Alleyn said carefully: "You will realize that I must keep the paper for the time being, at least. I will write you a receipt for it."

"Do you believe what I've said?"

"That's the sort of question we're not supposed to answer. By and large—yes."

"Have you finished with me?"

"I think so. For the present."

"It's an extraordinary thing," said Rupert. "And there's no sense in it, but I feel better. Horribly tired but—yes—better."

"You'll sleep now," Alleyn said.

"I still want to get rid of that abortion."

Alleyn thought wearily that he supposed he ought to prevent this, but said he would look at the score. They switched off the backstage lights and went to the front-of-house. Alleyn sat on the apron steps and turned through the score, forcing himself to look closely at each page. All those busy little black marks that had seemed so eloquent, he supposed, until the moment of truth came to Rupert and all the strangely unreal dialogue that librettists put in the mouths of their singers. Remarks like: "What a comedy!" and "Do I dream?" and "If she were mine."

He came to the last page and found that, sure enough, the corner had been torn off. He looked at Rupert and found he was sound asleep in one of the V.I.P. chairs.

Alleyn gathered the score and separate parts together, put them beside Rupert, and touched his shoulder. He woke with a start as if tweaked by a puppeteer.

"If you are still of the same mind," Alleyn said, "it's all yours."

So Rupert went to the fireplace in the hall where the embers glowed. Papers bound solidly together are slow to burn. *The Alien Corn* merely smoldered, blackened, and curled. Rupert used an oversized pair of bellows and flames crawled round the edges. He threw on loose sheets from the individual parts and these burst at once into flame and flew up the chimney. There was a basket of kindling by the hearth. He began to heap it on the fire in haphazard industry as if to put his opera out of its misery. Soon firelight and shadows leapt about the hall. The pregnant woman looked like a smirking candidate for martyrdom. At one moment the solitary dagger on the wall flashed red. At another the doors into the concert chamber appeared momentarily, and once the stairs were caught by an erratic flare.

It was then that Alleyn saw a figure on the landing. It stood with its hands on the balustrade and its head bent, looking down into the hall. Its appearance was as brief as a thought, a fraction of a fraction of a second. The flare expired and when it fitfully reappeared, whoever it was up there had gone.

Bert? Alleyn didn't think so. It had, he felt sure, worn a dressing gown or overcoat, but beyond that there had been no impression of an individual among the seven men, any one of whom might have been abroad in the night.

At its end *The Alien Corn* achieved dramatic value. The wind howled in the chimney, blazing logs fell apart, and what was left of the score flew up and away. The last they saw of it was a floating ghost of black thread-paper with "Dedicated to Isabella Sommita" in white showing for a fraction of a second before it too disintegrated and was gone up the chimney.

Without a word Rupert turned away and walked quickly upstairs. Alleyn put a fireguard across the hearth. When he turned away he noticed, on a table, inside the front entrance, a heavy canvas bag with a padlock and chain: the mailbag. Evidently it should have gone off with the launch and in the confusion had been overlooked.

Alleyn followed Rupert upstairs. The house was now very quiet. He fancied there were longer intervals between the buffets of the storm.

When he reached the landing he was surprised to find Rupert still there and staring at the sleeping Bert.

Alleyn murmured: "You've got a key to that door, haven't you?"

"Didn't you get it?" Rupert whispered.

"I? Get it? What do you mean?"

"She said you wanted it."

"Who did?"

"Maria."

"When?"

"After you and the doctor left my room. After I'd gone to bed. She came and asked for the key."

"Did you give it to her?"

"Yes, of course. For you." Alleyn drew in his breath. "I didn't want it," Rupert whispered. "My God! Go into that room! See her! *Like that.*"

Alleyn waited for several seconds before he asked: "Like what?"

"Are you mad?" Rupert asked. "You've seen her. A nightmare."

"So *you've* seen her too?"

And then Rupert realized what he had said. He broke into a jumble of whispered expostulations and denials. Of course he hadn't seen her. Maria had told him what it was like. Maria had described it. Maria had said Alleyn had sent her for the key.

He ran out of words, made a violent gesture of dismissal, and bolted. Alleyn heard his door slam.

And at last Alleyn himself went to bed. The clock on the landing struck four as he walked down the passage to their room. When he parted the window curtains there was a faint grayness in the world outside. Troy was fast asleep.

III

Marco brought their breakfast at eight o'clock. Troy had been awake for an hour. She had woken when Alleyn came to bed and had lain quiet and waited to see if he wanted to talk, but he had touched her head lightly and in a matter of seconds was dead to the world.

It was not his habit to use a halfway interval between sleep and wake. He woke like a cat, fully and instantly, and gave Marco good morning. Marco drew the curtains and the room was flooded with pallid light. There was no rain on the windowpanes and no sound of wind.

"Clearing, is it?" Alleyn asked.

"Yes, sir. Slowly. The Lake is still very rough."

"Too rough for the launch?"

"Too much rough, sir, certainly."

He placed elaborate trays across them both and brought them extra pillows. His dark rather handsome head came close to theirs.

"It must be quite a sight—the Lake and the mountains?" Alleyn said lightly.

"Very impressive, sir."

"Your mysterious photographer should be there again with his camera."

A little muscle jumped under Marco's olive cheek.

"It is certain he has gone, sir. But, of course you are joking."

"Do you know exactly how Madame Sommita was murdered, Marco? The details?"

"Maria is talking last night but she is excitable. When she is excitable she is not reasonable. Or possible to understand. It is all," said Marco, "very dreadful, sir."

"They forgot to take the mailbag to the launch last night. Had you noticed?"

Marco knocked over the marmalade pot on Troy's tray.

"I am very sorry, madame," he said. "I am clumsy."

"It's all right," Troy said. "It hasn't spilt."

"Do you know what I think, Marco?" said Alleyn. "I think there never was a strange photographer on the Island."

"Do you, sir? Thank you, sir. Will that be all?"

"Do you have a key to the postbag?"

"It is kept in the study, sir."

"And is the bag unlocked during the time it is in the house?"

"There is a posting box in the entrance, sir. Mr. Hanley empties it into the bag when it is time for the launch man to take it."

"Too bad he overlooked it last night."

Marco, sheet-white, bowed and left the room.

"And I suppose," Troy ventured, "I pretend I didn't notice you've terrified the pants off that poor little man."

"Not such a poor little man."

"Not?"

"I'm afraid not."

"Rory," said his wife. "Under ordinary circumstances I never, *never* ask about cases. Admit."

"My darling, you are perfection in that as in all other respects. You never do."

"Very well. These circumstances are *not* ordinary and if you wish me to give my customary imitation of a violet by a mossy stone half-hidden *from* the view, you must also be prepared for me to spontaneously combust."

"Upon my word, love, I can't remember how much you do or do not know of our continuing soap opera. Let us eat our breakfasts and you ask questions the while. When, by the way, did we last meet? Not counting bed?"

"When I gave you the powder and brush in the studio. Remember?"

"Ah yes. Oh, and thank you for the dispatch case. Just what I wanted, like a Christmas present. You don't know *how* she was killed, do you?"

"Signor Lattienzo told me. Remember?"

"Ah yes. He came up to the studio, didn't he?"

"Yes. To see if I was all right. It was kind of him, really."

"Very," said Alleyn dryly.

"Don't you like him?"

"Did he tell you in detail?"

"Just that she was stabbed. At first it seemed unreal. Like more bad opera. You know his flowery way of saying things. And then, of course, when it got real—quite appalling. It's rather awful to be wallowing between silken sheets, crunching toast while we talk about it," said Troy, "but I happen to be hungry."

"You wouldn't help matters if you suddenly decided to diet."

"True."

"I think I'd better tell you the events of the night in order of occurrence. Or, no," said Alleyn. "You can read my file. While you're doing that I'll get up and see if Bert is still on duty, poor chap."

"Bert? The chauffeur?"

"That's right. I won't be long."

He gave her the file, put on his dressing gown and slippers, and went out to the landing. Bert was up and slightly disheveled. The chairs still barricaded the door.

"Gidday," he said. "Glad to see you."

"I'm sorry I've left it so late. Did you have a beastly night of it?"

"Naow. She was good. Wee bit drafty, but we mustn't grumble."

"Anything to report?"

"Maria. At four-twenty. I'm right out to it but I reckon she must of touched me because I open my eyes and there she bloody is, hanging over me with a key in her hand looking as if she's trying to nut it out how to get the door open. Brainless. I say: 'What's the big idea?' and she lets out a screech and drops the key. On me. Plonk. No trouble."

"And did you—?"

"Grab it. Kind of reflex action, really."

"You didn't give it back to her, Bert?"

Bert assumed a patient, quizzical expression and produced the key from his trouser pocket.

"Good *on* you, boy," said Alleyn, displaying what he hoped was the correct idiom and the proper show of enthusiasm. He clapped Bert on the shoulder. "What was her reaction?" he asked and wondered if he, too, ought to adopt the present tense.

"She's moanin'," said Bert.

"Moaning?"

"This is right. Complainin'. Reckonin' she'll put my pot on with the boss. Clawin' at me to get it back. Reckonin' she wants to lay out the deceased and say prayers and that lot. But never raising her voice, mind. Never once. When she sees it's no dice and when I tell her I'll hand the key over to you she spits in my face, no trouble, and beats it downstairs."

"That seems to be the Maria form. I'll take the key, Bert, and thank you very much indeed. Do you happen to know how many keys there are to the room? Four, is it?"

"That's right. To all the rooms. Weird idea."

Alleyn thought: This one, which was Rupert Bartholomew's. The ones already in my pocket, and the Sommita's in her evening bag at the bottom of her dressing-table drawer.

He said: "While I think of it. On the way over here you said something about a vet putting down Madame Sommita's dog. You said he chloroformed it before giving it the injection."

"That's correct," said Bert, looking surprised.

"Do you remember, by any chance, what happened to the bottle?"

Bert stared at him. "That's a hairy one," he said. "What happened to the bottle, eh?" He scratched his head and pulled a face. "Hold on," he said. "Yeah! That's right. He put it on a shelf in the hangar and forgot to take it away."

"And would you," said Alleyn, "know what became of it? Is it still there?"

"No, it is not. Maria come out to see if it was all O.K. about the dog. She'd been sent by the Lady. She seen the bottle. It was, you know, labeled. She reckoned it wasn't safe having it lying around. She took it off."

"Did she indeed?" said Alleyn. "Thank you, Bert."

"Be my guest."

Alleyn said: "Well, you'd better get something to eat, hadn't you?"

"I don't mind if I do," said Bert. "Seeing you," and went, in a leisurely manner, downstairs.

Alleyn returned to their bedroom. Troy was deep in the file and continued to read it while he shaved, bathed, and dressed. Occasionally she shouted an inquiry or a comment. She had just finished it and was about to get up when there was a tap on the door. Alleyn opened it and there was Mrs. Bacon, trim and competent: the very epitome of the five-star housekeeper.

"Good morning, Mr. Alleyn," said Mrs. Bacon. "I've just come up to see if Mrs. Alleyn has everything she wants. I'm afraid, in all this disturbance, she may have been neglected, and we can't have that, can we?"

Alleyn said we couldn't and Troy called out for her to come in.

When she had been assured of Troy's well-being, Mrs. Bacon told Alleyn she was glad of the opportunity to have a word with him. "There are difficulties. It's very inconvenient," she said as if the plumbing had failed them.

"I'm sure it is," he said. "If there's anything I can do—"

"It's Maria."

"Is she still cutting up rough?"

"Indeed she is." Mrs. Bacon turned to Troy. "This is all so unpleasant, Mrs. Alleyn," she apologized. "I'm sorry to bring it up!"

The Alleyns made appropriate noises.

"Of course she *is* upset," Mrs. Bacon conceded. "We understand that, don't we? But really!"

"What form is it taking now?" Alleyn asked.

"She wants to go—in there."

"Still on that lay, is she. Well, she can't."

"She—being a Catholic, of course, one should make allowances," Mrs. Bacon herself astonishingly allowed. "I hope you're not—?" she hurriedly added, turning pink. "And, of course, being a foreigner should be taken into consideration. But it's getting more than a joke. She wants to lay Madame out. I was wondering if—just to satisfy her?"

"I'm afraid not, Mrs. Bacon," Alleyn said. "The body must be left as it is until the police have seen it."

"That's what they always say in the thrillers, of course. I know that, but I thought it might be an exaggeration."

"Not in this instance, at any rate."

"She's worrying Mr. Reece about it. He's spoken to me. He's very much shocked, you can sense that, although he doesn't allow himself to show it. He told me everything must be referred to you. I think he would like to see you."

"Where is he?"

"In the study. That Italian gentleman, Mr. Lattienzo, and Mr. Ruby are with him. And then," Mrs. Bacon went on, "there are the two ladies, the singers, who stayed last night, I must say what I can to them. They'll be wondering. Really, it's almost more than one can be expected to cope with."

"Maddening for you," said Troy.

"Well, it *is*. And the staff! The two housemaids are talking themselves into hysterics and refusing to come up to this landing, and the men are not much better. I thought I could depend on Marco, but he's suddenly gone peculiar and doesn't seem to hear when he's spoken to. Upon my word," said Mrs. Bacon, "I'll be glad to see the police on the premises and I never thought I'd say *that* in my occupation."

"Can't Hanley help out?" asked Alleyn.

"Not really. They all giggle at him or did when they had a giggle left in them. I told them they were making a mistake. It's obvious what he is, of course, but that doesn't mean he's not competent. Far from it. He's very shrewd and very capable and he and I get on quite well. I really don't know," Mrs. Bacon exclaimed, "why I'm boring you like this! I must be going off at the deep end myself."

"Small wonder if you did," said Troy. "Look, don't worry about the rooms. How about you and me whipping round when they're all out of them?"

"Oh!" cried Mrs. Bacon, "I couldn't dream of it."

"Yes, you could. Or, I tell you what. I'll talk to Miss Dancy and Miss Parry and see how they feel about a bit of bedmaking. Do us all good instead of sitting round giving each other the jimjams. Wouldn't it, Rory?"

"Certainly," said Alleyn and put his arm round her.

"Are they in their rooms? I'll ring them up," Troy offered.

"If you don't mind my saying so, Mrs. Alleyn, you're a darling. Their breakfasts went up at 8:30. They'll still be in bed, eating it."

"One of them isn't," said Alleyn, who had gone to the window. "Look."

Mrs. Bacon joined him.

The prospect from their windows commanded the swimming pool on the extreme left and the hangar on the right. In the center, Lake Waihoe swept turbulently away into nothing. The mountains that rose from its far shore had been shut off by a curtain of ashen cloud. The fringes of trees that ran out into the Lake were intermittently wind-whipped. The waters tumbled about the shore, washed over the patio, and reared and collapsed into the brimming pool, which still overflowed its borders.

And down below on the bricked terrace, just clear of the water, stood

Rupert and a figure in a heavy mackintosh and sou'wester so much too big that it was difficult to identify it as Miss Sylvia Perry.

Mrs. Bacon joined Alleyn at the window. "Well," she said after a pause. "If that's what it seems to be, it's a pity it didn't develop when he was going away for days at a time for all those rehearsals."

"Where was that?"

"On the other side—at a Canterbury seaside resort. The chopper used to take him over and he stayed the night. Mr. Reece had them all put at the Carisbrooke. Luxury. Seven-star," said Mrs. Bacon. "They rehearsed in a local hall and gave concerts."

Down below, Rupert was speaking. The girl touched his arm and he took her hand in his. They remained like that for some moments. It had begun fitfully to rain again. He led her out of sight, presumably into the house.

"Nice girl," said Mrs. Bacon crisply. "Pity. Oh, well, you never know, do you?"

She made for the door.

Alleyn said: "Wait a second, Mrs. Bacon. Listen. Troy, listen."

They listened. As always when an imposed silence takes over, the background of household sounds that had passed unnoticed and the voice of the wind outside to which they had grown inattentive, declared themselves. Behind them, very distant but thinly clear, was the sound of a bell.

"Les, by Heaven!" said Alleyn. "Here. Mrs. Bacon. Have you got a bell in the house? A big bell."

"No," she said, startled.

"A gong?"

"Yes. We don't often use it."

"Bring it out on the terrace, please. Or get the men to bring it. And field glasses. I saw a pair in the hall, didn't I? But quick."

He pulled the slips off two of their pillows and ran down to the hall and out on the terrace to a point from which the jetty and boathouse could be seen across the Lake. Out here the sound of the bell was louder and echoed in the unseen hills.

It was ringing irregularly: long-spaced notes mixed with quick short-spaced ones.

"Bless his heart, he's signaling again," said Alleyn. He got out his notebook and pen and set himself to read the code. It was a shortish sequence confused by its echo and repeated after a considerable pause. The second time around, he got it. *"Police informed,"* Les signaled.

Alleyn, hoping he was a fairly conspicuous figure from the boat shed, had begun a laborious attempt at semaphoring with pillowcases when Bert and Marco, piloted by Mrs. Bacon, staggered out of the house bearing an enormous Burmese gong on a carved stand. They set it up on the terrace. Alleyn discarded his pillowcase and whacked out a booming acknowledgment. This too set up an echo.

"Received and understood thanks."

It struck him that he had created a picture worthy of Salvador Dali—a Burmese gong on an island in New Zealand, a figure beating it—pillowslips on a wet shore and on the far shore another figure, waving. And in the foreground a string of unrelated persons strung out at intervals. For, in addition to trim Mrs. Bacon, Dr. Carmichael, Hanley, Ben Ruby, Signor Lattienzo, and Mr. Reece, in that order, had come out of the house.

Mrs. Bacon gave Alleyn the binoculars. He focused them and Les, the launch man, jumped up before him. He was wearing a red woollen cap and oilskins. He wiped his nose with a mittened hand and pointed in the direction of the rustic belfry. He was going to signal again. He gesticulated, as much as to say "Hold on," and went into the belfry.

"Doyng!" said the bell. *" 'oyng, 'oyng, 'oyng,"* said the echo.

This time Alleyn got it first try. *"Launch engine crook,"* it read and was repeated. *"Launch engine crook."*

"Hell!" said Alleyn and took it out on the gong.

Mr. Reece, wearing an American sporting raincoat and pigskin gloves, was at his elbow. "What's the message?" he asked.

"Shut up," said Alleyn. "Sorry. He's at it again."

Les signaled: *"Hope temporary."*

"Bang!" Alleyn acknowledged. " 'ang, 'ang, 'ang," said the echo.

"Over and out," signaled Les.

"Bang."

Alleyn followed Les through the binoculars down to the jetty, which was swept at intervals by waves. He saw Les dodge the waves, board the launch, jouncing at its moorings, and disappear into the engine room.

He gave Mr. Reece a full account of the exchange.

"I must apologize for my incivility," he said.

Mr. Reece waved it aside. "So if the Lake becomes navigable," he said, "we are still cut off."

"He did say he hopes the trouble's temporary. And by the time he's fixed it, surely the wind will have dropped and the helicopter will become a possibility."

"The helicopter is in Canterbury. It took the piano tuner back yesterday afternoon and remained on the other side."

"Nobody loves us," said Alleyn. "Could I have a word with you, indoors?"

"Certainly. Alone?"

"It might be as well, I think."

When they went indoors Alleyn was given an illustration of Mr. Reece's gift of authority. Signor Lattienzo and Ben Ruby clearly expected to return with him to the study. Hanley hovered. Without saying a word to any of them but with something in his manner that was perfectly explicit, Mr. Reece gave them to understand that this was not to be.

Signor Lattienzo, who was rigged out in a shepherd's cape and a Tyrolese hat, said: "My dear Ben, it is not raining. Should we perhaps, for the good of our digestions, venture a modest step or two abroad? To the landing and back? What do you say?"

Mr. Ruby agreed without enthusiasm.

Mr. Reece said to Hanley: "I think the ladies have come down. Find out if there is anything we can do for them, will you? I shan't need you at present."

"Certainly, sir," said Hanley.

Dr. Carmichael returned from outside. Alleyn suggested to their host that perhaps he might join them in the study.

When they were once more seated in the huge soft leather chairs of that singularly negative apartment, Alleyn said he thought that Mr. Reece would probably like to know about the events of the previous night.

He went over them in some detail, making very little of Rupert's bonfire and quite a lot of Maria's ongoings and Bert's vigil. Mr. Reece listened with his habitual passivity. Alleyn thought it quite possible that he had gone his own rounds during the night and wondered if it was he who had looked down from the landing. It would, somehow, be in character for Mr. Reece not to mention his prowl but to allow Alleyn to give his own account of the bonfire without interruption.

Alleyn said: "I hope you managed to get some sleep last night."

"Not very much, I confess. I am not a heavy sleeper at normal times. You wanted to see me?"

"I'd better explain. I seem to be forever raising the cry that I am really, as indeed we all are, treading water until the police arrive. It's difficult to decide how far I can, with propriety, probe. The important thing has been to make sure, as far as possible, that there has been no interference at the scene of the crime. I thought perhaps you might be prepared to give me some account of Madame Sommita's background and of any events that might, however remotely, have some bearing on this appalling crime."

"I will tell you anything I can, of course."

"Please don't feel you are under any obligation to do so. Of course you are not. And if my questions are impertinent we'll make it a case of 'No comment' and, I hope, no bones broken."

Mr. Reece smiled faintly. "Very well," he said. "Agreed."

"You see, it's like this. I've been wondering, as of course we all have, if the crime ties up in any way with the Strix business and if it does whether the motive could be a longstanding affair. Based, perhaps, on some sort of enmity. Like the Macdonalds and the Campbells, for instance. Not that in this day and age they have recourse to enormities of that kind. Better perhaps to instance the Montagues and Capulets."

Mr. Reece's faint smile deepened.

He said, "You are really thinking more of the Lucianos and Costellos, aren't you?"

Alleyn thought: He's rumbled that one pretty smartly, and he said: "Yes, in a way, I am. It's the Italian background that put it into my head. The whole thing is so shockingly outlandish and—well—theatrical. I believe Madame Sommita was born a Pepitone: a Sicilian."

"You are very well informed."

"Oh," Alleyn said, "when we got your letter, asking me to come out with Troy and take a look at the Strix business, the Yard did a bit of research. It did seem a remote possibility that Strix might be acting as an agent of sorts. I was going to ask you if such an idea, or something at all like it, had ever occurred to you."

With more animation than one might have supposed him to be capable of, Mr. Reece gave a dismal little laugh and brought the palms of his hands down on the arms of his chair. He actually raised his voice.

"*Occurred to me!*" he exclaimed. "You've got, as they say, to be joking, Mr. Alleyn. How could it not have occurred to me when she herself brought it to my notice day in, day out, ever since this wretched photographer came on the scene?"

He paused and looked very hard at Alleyn, who merely replied: "She did?"

"She most certainly did. It was an obsession with her. Some family feud that had started generations ago in Sicily. She persuaded herself that it had cropped up again in Australia, of all places. She really believed she was next in line for—elimination. It was no good telling her that this guy Strix was in it for the money. She would listen, say nothing, calm down, and then when you thought you'd got somewhere simply say she *knew*. I made inquiries. I talked to the police in Australia and the U.S.A. There was not a shred of evidence to support the idea. But she couldn't be moved."

"Last night you said you were certain Strix was her murderer."

"Because of what you told me about—the photograph. That seemed to be—still seems to be—so much in character with the sort of thing she said these people do. It was as if the man had signed his work and wanted to make sure it was recognized. As if I had been wrong and she had been right—right to be terrified. That we should have had her fully guarded. That I am responsible. And this," said Mr. Reece, "is a very, very dreadful thought, Mr. Alleyn."

"It may turn out to be a mistaken thought. Tell me, how much do you know about Madame Sommita's background—her early life? Her recent associates?"

Mr. Reece clasped his large well-kept hands and tapped them against his lower teeth. He frowned and seemed to be at a loss. At last he said: "That is difficult to answer. How much do I know? In some ways a lot, in others very little. Her mother died in childbirth. She was educated at convent schools in the U.S.A., the last being in New York, where her voice was first trained. I got the impression that she saw next to nothing of her father, who lived in Chicago and died when Bella was already abroad. She was brought up by an aunt of sorts, who accompanied her to Italy and is now deceased. There used to be confused allusions to this reputed feud, but in a way they were reticent—generalizations, nothing specific. Only these—these expressions of fear. I am afraid I thought they were little more than fairytales. I knew how she exaggerated and dramatized everything."

"Did she ever mention the name Rossi?"

"Rossi? It sounds familiar. Yes, I believe she may have, but she didn't, as a matter of fact, mention names—Italian names—when she talked about this threat. She would seem as if she was going to, but if I asked her point-blank to be specific in order that I could make inquiries, she merely crossed herself and wouldn't utter. I'm afraid I found that exasperating. It confirmed me in the opinion that the whole thing was imaginary."

"Yes, I see." Alleyn put his hand in his overcoat pocket, drew out the book from the library, and handed it to Mr. Reece. "Have you ever seen this?" he asked.

He took it and turned it over distastefully.

"Not that I remember," he said. He opened it and read the title, translat-

"Well, of course I have," Mr. Reece said at once. "About him, and, as you say, about all of them. But there is no earthly reason, no conceivable motive for Marco to do anything—wrong."

"Not if Marco should happen to be Strix?" Alleyn asked.

CHAPTER VII

Strix

I

WHEN ALLEYN and Dr. Carmichael joined Troy in the studio, rifts had appeared in the rampart of clouds and, at intervals, shafts of sunlight played fitfully across Lake Waihoe and struck up patches of livid green on mountain flanks that had begun to reappear through the mist.

The landing stage was still under turbulent water. No one could have used it. There were now no signs of Les on the mainland.

"You gave Mr. Reece a bit of a shakeup," said Dr. Carmichael. "Do you think he was right when he said the idea had never entered his head?"

"What, that Marco was Strix? Who can tell? I imagine Marco has been conspicuously zealous in the anti-Strix cause. His reporting an intruder on the Island topped up with his production of the lens cap was highly convincing. Remember how you all plunged about in the undergrowth? I suppose you assisted in the search for nobody, didn't you?"

"Blast!" said Dr. Carmichael.

"Incidentally, the cap was a mistake, a fancy touch too many. It's off a mass-produced camera, probably his own, as it were, official toy and not at all the sort of job that Strix must use to get his results. Perhaps he didn't want to part with the Strix cap and hadn't quite got the nerve to produce it, or perhaps it hasn't got a cap."

"Why," asked Troy, "did he embark on all that nonsense about an intruder?"

"Well, darling, don't you think because he intended to take a 'Strix' photograph of the Sommita—his *bonne bouche*—and it seemed advisable to plant the idea that a visiting Strix was lurking in the underbrush. But the whole story of the intruder was fishy. The search party was a shocking-awful carry-on, but by virtue of sheer numbers one of you would have floundered into an intruder if he'd been there."

"And you are certain," said Dr. Carmichael, "that he is not your man?"

"He couldn't be. He was waiting in the dining room and busy in the hall until the guests left and trotting to and from the launch with an umbrella while they were leaving."

"And incidentally on the porch, with me, watching the launch after they had gone. Yes. That's right," agreed Dr. Carmichael.

"Is Mr. Reece going to tackle him about Strix?" Troy asked.

"Not yet. He says he's not fully persuaded. He prefers to leave it with me."

"And you?"

"I'm trying to make up my mind. On the whole I think it may be best to settle Strix before the police get here."

"Now?"

"Why not?"

Troy said: "Of course he knows you're onto it. After your breakfast tray remarks."

"He's got a pretty good idea of it, at least," said Alleyn and put his thumb on the bell.

"Perhaps he won't come."

"I think he will. What's the alternative? Fling himself into the billowy wave and do a Leander for the mainland?"

"Shall I disappear?" offered Dr. Carmichael.

"And I?" said Troy.

"Not unless you'd rather. After all, I'm not going to arrest him."

"Oh? Not?" they said.

"Why would I do that? For being Strix? I've no authority. Or do you think we might borrow him for being a public nuisance or perhaps for false pretenses? On my information he's never actually conned anybody. He's just dressed himself up funny-like and taken unflattering photographs. There's the forged letter in the *Watchman*, of course. That might come within the meaning of some act: I'd have to look it up. Oh, yes, and makes himself out to be a gentleman's gent, with forged references, I daresay."

"Little beast," said Troy. "Cruel little pig, tormenting her like that. And everybody thinking it a jolly joke. And the shaming thing is, it *was* rather funny."

"That's the worst of ill-doing, isn't it? It so often has its funny side. Come to think of it, I don't believe I could have stuck my job out if it wasn't so. The earliest playwrights knew all about that: their devils more often than not were clowns and their clowns were always cruel. Here we go."

There had been a tap at the door. It opened and Marco came in.

He was an unattractive shade of yellow but otherwise looked much as usual.

He said: "You rang, sir?"

"Yes," Alleyn agreed. "I rang. I've one or two questions to ask you. First, about the photograph you took yesterday afternoon through the window of the concert chamber. Did you put the print in the letter-bag?"

"I don't know what you mean, sir."

"Yes, you do. You are Strix. You got yourself into your present job with the intention of following up your activities with the camera. Stop me if I'm wrong. But on second thoughts you're more likely to stop me if I'm right, aren't you? Did you see the advertisement for a personal servant for Mr. Reece in the paper? Did it occur to you that as a member of Mr. Reece's entourage you would be able to learn a lot more about Madame Sommita's programs for the day? On some occasion when she was accompanied by Mr. Reece or when Mr. Reece was not at home and you were not required, you would be able to pop out to a room you kept for the purpose, dress yourself up like a sore thumb, startle her, and photograph her with her mouth open looking ridiculous. You would hand the result in to the press and notch up another win. It was an impudently bold decision and it worked. You gave satisfaction as a valet and came here with your employer."

Marco had assumed an air of casual insolence.

"Isn't it marvelous?" he asked of nobody in particular and shrugged elaborately.

"You took yesterday's photograph with the intention of sending it back to the *Watchman* and through them to the chain of newspapers with whom you've syndicated your productions. I know you did this. Your footprints are underneath the window. I fancy this was to be your final impertinence and that having knocked it off you would have given in your notice, claimed your money, retired to some inconspicuous retreat, and written your autobiography."

"No comment," said Marco.

"I didn't really suppose there would be. Do you know where that photograph is now? Do you, Marco?"

"I don't know anything about any ——ing photograph," said Marco, whose Italian accent had become less conspicuous and his English a good deal more idiomatic.

"It is skewered by a dagger to your victim's dead body."

"My victim! She was not my victim. Not—" He stopped.

"Not in the sense of your having murdered her, were you going to say?"

"Not in any sense. I don't," said Marco, "know what you're talking about."

"And I don't expect there'll be much trouble about finding your fingerprints on the glossy surface."

Marco's hand went to his mouth.

"Come," Alleyn said, "don't you think you're being unwise? What would you say if I told you your room will be searched?"

"Nothing!" said Marco loudly. "I would say nothing. You're welcome to search my room."

"Do you carry the camera—is it a Strassman, by the way?—on you? How about searching *you?*"

"You have no authority."

"That is unfortunately correct. See here, Marco. Just take a look at yourself. I shall tell the police what I believe to be the facts: that you are Strix, that you took the photograph now transfixed over Madame Sommita's heart, that it probably carries your fingerprints. If it does not it is no great matter. Faced by police investigation, the newspapers that bought your photographs will identify you."

"They've never seen me," Marco said quickly and then looked as if he could have killed himself.

"It was all done by correspondence, was it?"

"They've never seen me because I'm not—I've never had anything to do with them. You're putting words in my mouth."

"Your Strix activities have come to an end. The woman you tormented is dead, you've made a packet and will make more if you write a book. With illustrations. The only thing that is likely to bother you is the question of how the photograph got from your camera to the body. The best thing you can do if you're not the murderer of Isabella Sommita is help us find out who *is*. If you refuse, you remain a prime suspect."

Marco looked from Troy to Dr. Carmichael and back to Troy again. It was as if he asked for their advice. Troy turned away to the studio window.

Dr. Carmichael said: "You'd much better come across, you know. You'll do yourself no good by holding back."

There was a long silence.

"Well," said Marco at last and stopped.

"Well?" said Alleyn.

"I'm not admitting anything."

"But suppose—?" Alleyn prompted.

"Suppose, for the sake of argument, Strix took the shot you talk about. What *would* he do with it? He'd post it off to the *Watchman,* at once, wouldn't he? He'd put it in the mailbox to be taken away in the bag."

"Or," Alleyn suggested, "to avoid Mr. Hanley noticing it when he cleared the box, he might slip it directly into the mailbag while it was still unlocked and waiting in the study."

"He might do that."

"Is that what you'd say he did?"

"I don't say what he did. I don't know what he did."

"Did you know the mailbag was forgotten last night and is still on the premises?"

Marco began to look very scared. "No," he said. "Is it?"

"So if our speculation should turn out to be the truth: if you put the photograph, addressed to the *Watchman,* in the mailbag, the question is: who removed it? Who impaled it on the body? If, of course, you didn't."

"It is idiotic to persist in this lie. Why do you do it? Where for me is the motive? Suppose I were Strix? So. I kill the goose that lays the golden egg? Does it make sense? So: after all, the man who takes the photograph does not post it. He is the murderer and he leaves it on the body."

"What is your surname?"

"Smith."

"I see."

"It is *Smith,*" Marco shouted. "Why do you look like that? Why should it not be Smith? Is there a law against Smith? My father was an American."

"And your mother?"

"A Calabrian. Her name was Croce. I am Marco Croce Smith. Why?"

"Have you any Rossis in your family?"

"None. Again, why?"

"There is an enmity between the Rossis and Madame Sommita's family."

"I know nothing of it," said Marco and then burst out, "How could I have done it? When was it done? I don't even know when it was done, but all the time from when the opera is ended until Maria found her, I am on duty. You saw me. Everybody saw me. I wait at table. I attend in the hall. I go to and from the launch. I have alibis."

"That may be true. But you may also have had a collaborator."

"You are mad."

"Yes, it really is."

"What do you suppose will happen first, the telephone be reconnected, or the launch engine be got going or the police appear on the far bank or the chopper turn up?"

"Lord knows."

Troy said into the telephone, "Of *course* I understand. Don't give it another thought. We'll meet at lunchtime. Oh. Oh, I see. I'm so sorry. Yes, I think you're very wise. No, no news. Awful, isn't it?"

She hung up. "Miss Dancy has got a migraine," she said. "She sounds very Wagnerian. Well, I'd better make the best I can of the beds."

"You're not going round on your own, Troy."

"Aren't I? But why?"

"It's inadvisable."

"But, Rory, I promised Mrs. Bacon."

"To hell with Mrs. Bacon. I'll tell her it's not on. They can make their own bloody beds. I've made ours," said Alleyn. "I'd go round with you but I don't think that'd do, either."

"I'll make beds with you, Mrs. Alleyn," offered Dr. Carmichael in a sprightly manner.

"That's big of you, Carmichael," said Alleyn. "I daresay all the rooms will be locked. Mrs. Bacon will have spare keys."

"I'll find out."

Troy said: "You can pretend it's a hospital. You're the matron and I'm a hamfisted probationer. I'll just go along to our palatial suite for a moment. Rejoin you here."

When she had gone, Alleyn said: "She's hating this. You can always tell if she goes all joky. I'll be glad to get her out of it."

"If I may say so, you're a lucky man."

"You may indeed say so."

"Perhaps a brisk walk round the Island when we've done our chores."

"A splendid idea. In a way," Alleyn said, "this bed-making nonsense might turn out to be handy. I've no authority to search, of course, but you two might just keep your eyes skinned."

"Anything in particular?"

"Not a thing. But you never know. The skinned eye and a few minor liberties."

"I'll see about the keys," said Dr. Carmichael happily and bustled off.

II

Alleyn wondered if he were about to take the most dangerous decision of his investigative career. If he took this decision and failed, not only would he make an egregious ass of himself before the New Zealand police but he would effectively queer the pitch for their subsequent investigations and probably muck up any chance of an arrest. Or would he? In the event of failure was there no chance of a new move, a strategy in reserve, a surprise attack? If there was, he was damned if he knew what it could be.

He went over the arguments again: The time factor. The riddle of the keys. The photograph. The conjectural motive. The appalling conclusion. He searched for possible alternatives to each of these and could find none.

He resurrected the dusty old bit of investigative folklore: "If all explanations except one fail, then that one, however outrageous, will be the answer."

And, God knew, they were dealing with the outrageous.

So he made up his mind and, having done that, went downstairs and out into the watery sunshine for a breather.

All the guests had evidently been moved by the same impulse. They were abroad on the Island in pairs and singly. Whereas earlier in the morning Alleyn had likened those of them who had come out into the landscape to surrealistic details; now, while still wildly anachronistic, as was the house itself, in their primordial setting, they made him think of persons in a poem by Verlaine or perhaps by Edith Sitwell. Signor Lattienzo, in his Tyrolean cape and his gleaming eyeglass, stylishly strolled beside Mr. Ben Ruby, who smoked a cigar and was rigged out for the country in a brand new Harris tweed suit. Rupert Bartholomew, wan in corduroy, his hair romantically disordered, his shoulders hunched, stood by the tumbled shore and stared over the Lake. And was himself stared at, from a discreet distance, by the little Sylvia Parry with a scarlet handkerchief around her head. Even the stricken Miss Dancy had braved the elements. Wrapped up, scarfed, and felt-hatted, she paced alone up and down a gravel path in front of the house as if it were the deck of a cruiser.

To her from indoors came Mr. Reece in his custom-built outfit straight from pages headed "Rugged Elegance: For Him" in the glossiest of periodicals. He wore a peaked cap, which he raised ceremoniously to Miss Dancy, who immediately engaged him in conversation, clearly of an emotional kind. But he's used to that, thought Alleyn, and noticed how Mr.

Reece balanced Miss Dancy's elbow in his pigskin grasp as he squired her on her promenade.

He had thought they completed the number of persons in the landscape until he caught sight, out of the corner of his eye, of some movement near one of the great trees near the Lake. Ned Hanley was standing there. He wore a dark green coat and sweater and merged with his background. He seemed to survey the other figures in the picture.

One thing they all had in common, and that was a tendency to halt and stare across the Lake or shade their eyes, tip back their heads, and look eastward into the fast-thinning clouds. He had been doing this himself.

Mr. Ben Ruby spied him, waved his cigar energetically, and made toward him. Alleyn advanced and at close quarters found Mr. Ruby looking the worse for wear and self-conscious.

"Morning, old man," said Mr. Ruby. "Glad to see you. Brightening up, isn't it? Won't be long now. We hope!"

"We do indeed."

"*You* hope, anyway, I don't mind betting. Don't envy you your job. Responsibility without the proper backing, eh?"

"Something like that," said Alleyn.

"I owe you an apology, old man. Last evening. I'd had one or two drinks. You know that?"

"Well–"

"What with one thing and another–the shock and that. I was all to pieces. Know what I mean?"

"Of course."

"All the same–bad show. Very bad show," said Mr. Ruby, shaking his head and then wincing.

"Don't give it another thought."

"Christ, I feel awful," confided Mr. Ruby and threw away his cigar. "It was good brandy, too. The best. Special cognac. Wonder if this guy Marco could rustle up a corpse-reviver."

"I daresay. Or Hanley might."

Mr. Ruby made the sound that is usually written: "T'ss" and after a brief pause said in a deep voice and with enormous expression, "Bella! Bella Sommita! You can't credit it, can you? The most beautiful woman with the most gorgeous voice God ever put breath into. Gone! And how! And what the hell we're going to do about the funeral's nobody's business. I don't know of any relatives. It'd be thoroughly in character if she's left detailed instructions and bloody awkward ones at that. Pardon me, it slipped out. But it might mean cold storage to anywhere she fancied or ashes in the Adriatic." He caught himself up and gave Alleyn a hard if bloodshot stare. "I suppose it's out of order to ask if you've formed an idea?"

"It is, really. At this stage," Alleyn said, "we must wait for the police."

"Yeah? Well, here's hoping they know their stuff." He reverted to his elegiac mood. "Bella!" he apostrophized. "After all these years of taking the rough with the smooth, if you can understand me. Hell, it hurts!"

"How long an association has it been?"

"You don't measure grief by months and years," Mr. Ruby said reproachfully. "How long? Let me see? It was on her first tour of Aussie. That would be in '72. Under the Bel Canto management in association with my firm—Ben Ruby Associates. There was a disagreement with Bel Canto and we took over."

Here Mr. Ruby embarked on a long parenthesis explaining that he was a self-made man, a Sydneysider who had pulled himself up by his own boot-strings and was proud of it and how the Sommita had understood this and had herself evolved from peasant stock.

"And," said Alleyn when an opportunity presented itself, "a close personal friendship had developed with the business association?"

"This is right, old man. I reckon I understood her as well as anybody ever could. There was the famous temperament, mind, and it was a snorter while it lasted, but it never lasted long. She always sends—sent—for Maria to massage her shoulders, and that would do the trick. Back into the honied-kindness bit and everybody loving everybody."

"Mr. Ruby—have you anything to tell me that might in however far-fetched or remote a degree help to throw light on this tragedy?"

Mr. Ruby opened his arms wide and let them fall in the classic gesture of defeat.

"Nothing?" Alleyn said.

"This is what I've been asking myself ever since I woke up. When I got round, that is, to asking myself anything other than why the hell I had to down those cognacs."

"And how do you answer yourself?"

Again the gesture. "I don't," Mr. Ruby confessed. "I can't. Except—" He stopped, provokingly, and stared at Signor Lattienzo, who by now had arrived at the lakeside and contemplated the water rather, in his Tyrolean outfit, like some poet of the post-Romantic era.

"Except?" Alleyn prompted.

"Look!" Mr. Ruby invited. "Look at what's been done and *how* it's been done. Look at that. If you had to say—you, with your experience—what it reminded you of, what would it be? Come on."

"Grand opera," Alleyn said promptly.

Mr. Ruby let out a strangulated yelp and clapped him heavily on the back. "Good on you!" he cried. "Got it in one! Good on you, mate. And the Italian sort of grand opera, what's more. That funny business with the dagger and the picture! Verdi would have loved it. Particularly the picture. Can you see any of *us,* supposing he was a murderer, doing it that way? That poor kid Rupert? Ned Hanley, never mind if he's one of those? Monty? *Me? You?* Even if you'd draw the line at the props and the business. 'No,' you'd say; 'no.' Not that way. It's not in character, it's impossible, it's not—it's not—" and Mr. Ruby appeared to hunt excitedly for the *mot juste* of his argument. "It's not British," he finally pronounced and added: "Using the word in its widest sense. I'm a Commonwealth man myself."

Alleyn had to give himself a moment or two before he was able to respond to this declaration.

"What you are saying," he ventured, "in effect, is that the murderer must be one of the Italians on the premises. Is that right?"

"That," said Mr. Ruby, "is dead right."

"It narrows down the field of suspects," said Alleyn dryly.

"It certainly does," Mr. Ruby portentously agreed.

"Marco and Maria?"

"Right."

During an uncomfortable pause Mr. Ruby's rather bleary regard dwelt upon Signor Lattienzo in his windblown cape by the lakeside.

"And Signor Lattienzo, I suppose?" Alleyn suggested.

There was no reply.

"Have you," Alleyn asked, "any reason, apart from the grand opera theory, to suspect one of these three?"

Mr. Ruby seemed to be much discomforted by this question. He edged with his toe at a grassy turf. He cleared his throat and looked aggrieved.

"I knew you'd ask that," he said resentfully.

"It was natural, don't you think, that I should?"

"I suppose so. Oh, yes. Too right it was. But listen. It's a terrible thing to accuse anyone of. I know that. I wouldn't want to say anything that'd unduly influence you. You know. Cause you to—to jump to conclusions or give you the wrong impression. I wouldn't like to do that."

"I don't think it's very likely."

"No? You'd *say* that, of course. But I reckon you've done it already. I reckon like everyone else you've taken the old retainer stuff for real."

"Are you thinking of Maria?"

"Too bloody right I am, mate."

"Come on," Alleyn said. "Get it off your chest. I won't make too much of it. Wasn't Maria as devoted as one was led to suppose?"

"Like hell she was! Well, that's not correct either. She was devoted all right, but it was a flaming uncomfortable sort of devotion. Kind of dog-with-a-bone affair. Sometimes when they'd had a difference you'd have said it was more like hate. Jealous! She's eaten up with it. And when Bella was into some new 'friendship'—know what I mean?—Maria as likely as not would turn plug-ugly. She was even jealous in a weird sort of way, of the artistic triumphs. Or that's the way it looked to me."

"How did she take the friendship with Mr. Reece?"

"Monty?" A marked change came over Mr. Ruby. He glanced quickly at Alleyn as if he wondered whether he were unenlightened in some respect. He hesitated and then said quietly, "That's different again, isn't it?"

"Is it? How, 'different'?"

"Well—you know."

"But, I don't know."

"It's platonic. Couldn't be anything else."

"I see."

"Poor old Monty. Result of an illness. Cruel thing, really."

"Indeed? So Maria had no cause to resent him."

"This is right. She admires him. They do, you know. Italians. Especially his class. They admire success and prestige more than anything else. It was a very different story when young Rupert came along. Maria didn't worry about letting everyone see what she felt about *that* lot. I'd take long odds she'll be telling you the kid done—did—it. That vindictive, she is. Fair go—I wouldn't put it past her. Now."

Alleyn considered for a moment or two. Signor Lattienzo had now joined Rupert Bartholomew on the lakeside and was talking energetically and clapping him on the shoulder. Mr. Reece and Miss Dancy still paced their imaginary promenade deck and the little Sylvia Parry, perched dejectedly on a rustic seat, watched Rupert.

Alleyn said: "Was Madame Sommita tolerant of these outbursts from Maria?"

"I suppose she must have been in her own way. There were terrible scenes, of course. That was to be expected, wasn't it? Bella'd threaten Maria with the sack and Maria'd throw a fit of hysterics and then they'd both go weepy on it and we'd be back to square one with Maria standing behind Bella massaging her shoulders and swearing eternal devotion.

Italians!! My oath! But it was different, totally different—with the kid. I'd never seen her as far gone over anyone else as she was with him. Crazy about him. In at the deep end, boots and all. That's why she took it so badly when he saw the light about that little opera of his and wanted to opt out. He was dead right, of course, but Bella hadn't got any real musical judgment. Not really. You ask Beppo."

"What about Mr. Reece?"

"Tone-deaf," said Mr. Ruby.

"Really?"

"Fact. Doesn't pretend to be anything else. He was annoyed with the boy for disappointing her, of course. As far as Monty was concerned, the diva had said the opus was great, and what she said had got to be right. And then of course he didn't like the idea of throwing a disaster of a party. In a way," said Mr. Ruby, "it was the *Citizen Kane* situation with the boot on another foot. Sort of." He waited for a moment and then said: "I feel bloody sorry for that kid."

"God knows, so do I," said Alleyn.

"But he's young. He'll get over it. All the same, she'd a hell of a lot to answer for."

"Tell me. You knew her as well as anybody, didn't you? Does the name 'Rossi' ring a bell?"

"Rossi," Mr. Ruby mused. "Rossi, eh? Hang on. Wait a sec."

As if to prompt, or perhaps warn him, raucous hoots sounded from the jetty across the water, giving the intervals without the cadence of the familiar signing-off phrase "Dah dahdy dah-dah. Dah *Dah*."

Les appeared on deck and could be seen to wave his scarlet cap.

The response from the islanders was instant. They hurried into a group. Miss Dancy flourished her woollen scarf. Mr. Reece raised his arm in a Roman salute. Signor Lattienzo lifted his Tyrolese hat high above his head. Sylvia ran to Rupert and took his arm. Hanley moved out of cover and Troy, Mrs. Bacon, and Dr. Carmichael came out of the house and pointed Les out to each other from the steps. Mr. Ruby bawled out, "He's done it. Good on 'im, 'e's done it."

Alleyn took a handkerchief from his breast pocket and a spare from his overcoat. He went down to the lake edge and semaphored: "Nice Work." Les returned to the wheelhouse and sent a short toot of acknowledgment.

The islanders chattered excitedly, telling each other that the signal *must* mean the launch was mobile again, that the Lake was undoubtedly calmer, and that when the police did arrive they would be able to cross.

The hope that they themselves would all be able to leave remained unspoken.

They trooped up to the house and were shepherded in by Mr. Reece, who said, with somber playfulness, that "elevenses" were now served in the library.

Troy and Dr. Carmichael joined Alleyn. They seemed to be in good spirits. "We've finished our chores," Troy said, "and we've got something to report. Let's have a quick swallow, and join up in the studio."

"Don't make it too obvious," said Alleyn, who was aware that he was now under close though furtive observation by most of the household. He fetched two blameless tomato juices for himself and Troy. They joined Rupert and Sylvia Parry, who were standing a little apart from the others and were not looking at each other. Rupert was still white about the gills but, or so Alleyn thought, rather less distraught—indeed there was perhaps a hint of portentousness, of self-conscious gloom in his manner.

She has provided him with an audience, thought Alleyn. Let's hope she knows what she's letting herself in for.

Rupert said: "I've told Sylvia about—last night."

"So I supposed," said Alleyn.

"She thinks I was right."

"Good."

Sylvia said: "I think it took wonderful courage and artistic integrity and I do think it was right."

"That's a very proper conclusion."

"It won't be long now, will it?" Rupert asked. "Before the police come?" He pitched his voice rather high and brittle, with the sort of false airiness some actors employ when they hope to convey suppressed emotion.

"Probably not," said Alleyn.

"Of course, I'll be the prime suspect," Rupert announced.

"Rupert, *no,*" Sylvia whispered.

"My dear girl, it sticks out a mile. After my curtain performance. Motive. Opportunity. The lot. We might as well face it."

"We might as well not make public announcements about it," Troy observed.

"I'm sorry," said Rupert grandly. "No doubt I'm being silly."

"Well," Alleyn cheerfully remarked, "you said it. We didn't. Troy, hadn't we better sort out those drawings of yours?"

"O.K. Let's. I'd forgotten."

"She leaves them unfixed and tiles the floor with them," Alleyn explained. "Our cat sat on a preliminary sketch of the Prime Minister and turned it into a jungle flower. Come on, darling."

They found Dr. Carmichael already in the studio. "I didn't want Reece's 'elevenses,' " he said. And to Troy: "Have you told him?"

"I waited for you," said Troy.

They were, Alleyn thought, as pleased as Punch with themselves. "You tell him," they said simultaneously. "Ladies first," said the doctor.

"Come on," said Alleyn.

Troy inserted her thin hand in a gingerly fashion into a large pocket of her dress. Using only her finger and her thumb, she drew out something wrapped in one of Alleyn's handkerchiefs. She was in the habit of using them, as she preferred a large one and she had been known when intent on her work to confuse the handkerchief and her paint rag, with regrettable results to the handkerchief and to her face.

She carried her trophy to the paint table and placed it there. Then, with a sidelong look at her husband, she produced two clean hoghair brushes and, using them upside down in the manner of chopsticks, fiddled open the handkerchief and stood back.

Alleyn walked over, put his arm across her shoulders, and looked at what she had revealed.

A large heavy envelope, creased and burned but not so extensively that an airmail stamp and part of the address were not still in evidence. The address was typewritten.

The Edit
"The Watchma
P.O. Bo
N.S.W. 14C
Sy
Australia

"Of course," Troy said after a considerable pause, "it may be of no consequence at all, may it?"

"Suppose we have the full story?"

"Yes. All right. Here goes, then."

Their story was that they had gone some way with their housemaiding expedition when Troy decided to equip herself with a box-broom and a duster. They went downstairs in search of them and ran into Mrs. Bacon emerging from the study. She intimated that she was nearing the end of her tether. The staff, having gone through progressive stages of hysteria and suspicion, had settled for a sort of work-to-rule attitude and, with the exception of the chef, who had agreed to provide a very basic luncheon, and Marco, who was, said Mrs. Bacon, abnormally quiet but did his jobs, either sulked in their rooms or muttered together in the staff sitting room. As far as Mrs. Bacon could make out, the New Zealand ex-hotel group suspected in turn Signor Lattienzo, Marco, and Maria on the score of their being Italians and Mr. Reece, whom they cast in the role of de facto cuckold. Rupert Bartholomew was fancied as an outside chance on the score of his having turned against the Sommita. Maria had gone to earth, supposedly in her room. Chaos, Mrs. Bacon said, prevailed.

Mrs. Bacon herself had rushed round the dining and drawing rooms while Marco set out the elevenses. She had then turned her attention to the study and found to her horror that the open fireplace had not been cleaned or the fire relaid. To confirm this, she had drawn their attention to a steel ashpan she herself carried in her rubber-gloved hands.

"And that's when I saw it, Rory," Troy explained. "It was sticking up out of the ashes and I saw what's left of the address."

"And she nudged me," said Dr. Carmichael proudly, "and I saw it too."

"And he behaved *perfectly*," Troy intervened. "He said: 'Do let me take that thing and tell me where to empty it.' And Mrs. Bacon said, rather wildly: 'In the bin. In the yard,' and made feeble protestations, and at that moment we all heard the launch hooting and she became distracted. So Dr. Carmichael got hold of the ashpan. And I—well—I—got hold of the envelope and put it in my pocket amongst your handkerchief, which happened to be there."

"So it appears," Dr. Carmichael summed up, "that somebody typed a communication of some sort to the *Watchman* and stamped the envelope, which he or somebody else then chucked on the study fire, and it dropped through the grate into the ashpan when it was only half-burnt. Or doesn't it?"

"Did you get a chance to have a good look at the ashes?" asked Alleyn.

"Pretty good. In the yard. They were faintly warm. I ran them carefully into a zinc rubbish bin, already half-full. There were one or two very small fragments of heavily charred paper and some clinkers. Nothing else. I heard someone coming and cleared out. I put the ashpan back under the study grate."

Alleyn bent over the trophy. "It's a Sommita envelope," said Troy. "Isn't it?"

"Yes. Bigger than the Reece envelope, but the same paper: like the letter she wrote to the Yard."

"Why would she write to the *Watchman?*"

"We don't know that she did."

"Don't we?"

"Or if she did, whether her letter was in this envelope." He took one of Troy's brushes and used it to flip the envelope over. "It may have been stuck up," he said, "and opened before the gum dried. There's not enough left to be certain. It's big enough to take the photograph."

Dr. Carmichael blew out his cheeks and then expelled the air rather noisily. "That's a long shot, isn't it?" he said.

"Of course it is," agreed Alleyn. "Pure speculation."

"If *she* wrote it," Troy said carefully, "she dictated it. I'm sure she couldn't type, aren't you?"

"I think it's *most* unlikely. The first part of her letter to the Yard was impeccably typed and the massive postscript flamboyantly handwritten. Which suggested that she dictated the beginning or told young Rupert to concoct something she could sign, found it too moderate, and added the rest herself."

"But why," Dr. Carmichael mused, "was this thing in the study, on Reece's desk? I know! She asked that secretary of his to type it because she'd fallen out with young Bartholomew. How's that?"

"Not too bad," said Alleyn. "Possible. And where, do you suggest, is the letter? It wasn't in the envelope. And, by the way, the envelope was not visible on Reece's desk when you and I, Carmichael, visited him last night."

"Really? How d'you know?"

"Oh, my dear chap, the cop's habit of using the beady eye, I suppose. It might have been there under some odds and ends in his 'out' basket."

Troy said: "Rory, I think I know where you're heading."

"Do you, my love? Where?"

"Could Marco have slid into the study to put the photograph in the postbag, before Hanley had emptied the mailbox into it, and could he have seen the typed and addressed envelope on the desk and thought there was a marvelous opportunity to send the photograph to the *Watchman,* because nobody would question it? And so he took out her letter or whatever it was and chucked it on the fire and put the photograph in this envelope and—"

Troy, who had been going great guns, brought up short. "Blast!" she said.

"Why didn't he put it in the postbag?" asked Alleyn.

"Yes."

"Because," Dr. Carmichael staunchly declared, "he was interrupted and had to get rid of it quick. I think that's a damn' good piece of reasoning, Mrs. Alleyn."

"Perhaps," Troy said, "her letter had been left out awaiting the writer's signature and—no, that's no good."

"It's a lot of good," Alleyn said warmly. "You have turned up trumps, you two. Damn Marco. Why can't he make up his dirty little mind that his best move is to cut his losses and come clean? I'll have to try my luck with Hanley. Tricky."

He went out on the landing. Bert had resumed his guard duty and lounged back in the armchair reading a week-old sports tabloid. A homemade cigarette hung from his lower lip. He gave Alleyn the predictable sideways tip of his head.

Alleyn said: "I really oughtn't to impose on you any longer, Bert. After all, we've got the full complement of keys now and nobody's going to force the lock with the amount of traffic flowing through this house."

"I'm not fussy," said Bert, which Alleyn took to mean that he had no objections to continuing his vigil.

"Well, if you're sure," he said.

"She'll be right."

"Thank you."

The sound of voices indicated the emergence of the elevenses party. Miss Dancy, Sylvia Parry, and Rupert Bartholomew came upstairs. Rupert, with an incredulous look at Bert and a scared one at Alleyn, made off in the direction of his room. The ladies crossed the landing quickly and ascended the next flight. Mr. Reece, Ben Ruby, and Signor Lattienzo made for the study. Alleyn ran quickly downstairs in time to catch Hanley emerging from the morning room.

"Sorry to bother you," he said, "but I wonder if I might have a word. It won't take a minute."

"But of *course,*" said Hanley. "Where shall we go? Back into the library?"

"Right."

When they were there Hanley winningly urged further refreshment. Upon Alleyn's declining, he said: "Well, *I* will; just a teeny tiddler," and helped himself to a gin-and-tonic. "What can I do for you, Mr. Alleyn?" he said. "Is there any further development?"

Alleyn said: "Did you type a letter to the *Watchman* sometime before Madame Sommita's death?"

Hanley's jaw dropped and the hand holding his drink stopped halfway to his mouth. For perhaps three seconds he maintained this position and then spoke.

"Oh, Christmas!" he said. "I'd forgotten. You wouldn't credit it, would you? I'd entirely forgotten."

He made no bones about explaining himself and did so very fluently and quite without hesitation. He had indeed typed a letter from the Sommita to the *Watchman.* She had been stirred up "like a hive of bees," he said, by the episode of the supposed intruder on the Island and had decided that it was Strix who had been sent by the *Watchman* and had arrived after dark the previous night, probably by canoe, and had left unobserved by the same means, she didn't explain when. The letter which she dictated was extremely abusive and threatened the editor with a libel action. She had made a great point of Mr. Reece not being told of the letter.

"Because of course he'd have stopped all the nonsense," said Hanley. "I was to type it and take it to her to sign and then put it in the bag, all unbeknownst. She asked *me* to do it because of the row with the Wonder Boy. She gave me some of her notepaper."

"And you did it?"

"My dear! As much as my life was worth to refuse. I typed it out, calming it down the least morsel, which she didn't notice. But when she'd signed it, I bethought me that maybe when it had gone *she'd* tell the Boss Man and he'd be cross with me for doing it. So I left the letter on his desk, meaning to show it to him after the performance. I put it under some letters he had to sign."

"And the envelope?"

"The envelope? Oh, on the desk. And then, I remember, Marco came in to say I was wanted onstage to refocus a light."

"When was this?"

"When? I wouldn't know. Well—late afternoon. After tea, sometime, but well before the performance."

"Did Marco leave the study before you?"

"*Did* he? I don't know. Yes, I do. He said something about making up the fire and I left him to it."

"Did Mr. Reece see the letter, then?"

Hanley flapped his hands. "I've no notion. He's said nothing to me, but then with the catastrophe—I mean everything else goes out of one's head, doesn't it, except that nothing ever goes out of *his* head. You could ask him."

"So I could," said Alleyn. "And will."

Mr. Reece was alone in the study. He said at once in his flattest manner that he had found the letter on his desk under a couple of business communications which he was to sign in time for Hanley to send them off by the evening post. He did sign them and then read the letter.

"It was ill advised," he said, cutting the episode down to size. "She had been overexcited ever since the matter of the intruder arose. I had told her Sir Simon Marks had dealt with the *Watchman* and there would be no more trouble in that quarter. This letter was abusive in tone and would have stirred everything up again. I threw it on the fire. I intended to speak to her about it but not until after the performance when she would be less nervous and tense."

"Did you throw the envelope on the fire too?" Alleyn asked and thought: "If he says yes, bang goes sixpence and we return to square one."

"The envelope?" said Mr. Reece. "No. It was not in an envelope. I don't remember noticing one. May I ask what is the significance of all this, Chief Superintendent?"

"It's really just a matter of tidying up. The half-burnt envelope stamped and addressed to the *Watchman* was in the ashpan under the grate this morning."

"I have no recollection of seeing it," Mr. Reece said heavily. "I believe I would remember if I had seen it."

"After you burnt the letter, did you stay in the study?"

"I believe so," he said, and Alleyn thought he detected a weary note. "Or no," Mr. Reece corrected himself. "That is not right. Maria came in with a message that Bella wanted to see me. She was in the concert chamber. The flowers that I had ordered for her had not arrived and she was—distressed. I went to the concert chamber at once."

"Did Maria go with you?"

"I really don't know what Maria did, Superintendent. I fancy—no, I am not sure but I don't think she did. She may have returned there a little later. Really, I do *not* remember," said Mr. Reece and pressed his eyes with his thumb and forefinger.

"I'm sorry," Alleyn said; "I won't bother you any longer. I wouldn't have done so now, but it just might be relevant."

"It is no matter," said Mr. Reece. And then: "I much appreciate what you are doing," he said. "You will excuse me, I'm sure, if I seem ungracious."

"Good Lord, yes," said Alleyn quickly. "You should just hear some of the receptions we get."

"I suppose so," said Mr. Reece heavily. "Very likely." And then with a lugubrious attempt at brightening up, "The sun is shining continuously and the wind has almost gone down. Surely it can't be long, now, before the police arrive."

"We hope not. Tell me, have you done anything about Marco? Spoken to him? Faced him with being Strix?"

And then Mr. Reece made the most unexpected, the most remarkable statement of their conversation.

"I couldn't be bothered," he said.

III

On leaving the study, Alleyn heard sounds of activity in the dining room. The door was open, and he looked in to find Marco laying the table.

"I want a word with you," Alleyn said. "Not here. In the library. Come on."

Marco followed him there, saying nothing.

"Now, listen to me," Alleyn said. "I do not think, indeed I have never thought, that you killed Madame Sommita. You hadn't time to do it. I now think—I am almost sure—that you went into the study yesterday afternoon, intending to put the photographs you took of her, in the mailbag. You saw on the desk a stamped envelope addressed in typescript to the *Watchman*. It was unsealed and empty. This gave you a wonderful opportunity; it made everything safer and simpler. You transferred the photograph from its envelope to this envelope, sealed it down, and would have put it in the bag, but I think you were interrupted and simply dropped it back on the desk and I daresay explained your presence there by tidying the desk. Now. If this is so, all I want from you is the name of the person who interrupted you."

Marco had watched Alleyn carefully with a look, wary and hooded, that often appears on the faces of the accused when some telling piece of evidence is produced against them. Alleyn thought of it as the "dock face."

"You *have* been busy," Marco sneered. "Congratulations."

"I'm right, then?"

"Oh, yes," he said casually. "I don't know how you got there, but you're right."

"And the name?"

"You know so much, I'd have thought you'd know that."

"Well?"

"Maria," said Marco.

From somewhere in the house there came a sound, normally unexceptionable but now arresting. A door banged and shut it off.

"Telephone," Marco whispered. "It's the telephone."

"Did Maria see you? See you had the envelope in your hands? Did she?"

"I'm not sure. She might have. She could have. She's been—looking—at me. Or I thought so. Once or twice. She hasn't said anything. We haven't been friendly."

"No?"

"I went back to the study. Later. Just before the opera, and it had gone. So I supposed someone had put it in the mailbag."

There was a flurry of voices in the hall. The door swung open and Hanley came in.

"The telephone!" he cried. "Working. It's the—" He pulled up short looking at Marco. "Someone for you, Mr. Alleyn," he said.

"I'll take it upstairs. Keep the line alive."

He went into the hall. Most of the guests were collected there. He passed through them and ran upstairs to the first landing and the studio, where he found Troy and Dr. Carmichael. He took the receiver off the telephone. Hanley's voice fluted in the earpiece: "Yes. Don't hang up, will you? Mr. Alleyn's on his way. Hold the line please." And a calm reply: "Thank you, sir. I'll hold on."

"All right, Hanley," Alleyn said. "You can hang up now," and heard the receiver being cradled. "Hullo," he said. "Alleyn speaking."

"Chief Superintendent Alleyn? Inspector Hazelmere, Rivermouth Police, here. We've had a report of trouble on Waihoe Island and are informed of your being on the premises. I understand it's a homicide."

Alleyn gave him the bare bones of the case. Mr. Hazelmere repeated everything he said. He was evidently dictating. There were crackling disturbances on the line.

"So you see," Alleyn ended, "I'm a sort of minister without portfolio."

"Pardon? Oh. Oh, I get you. Yes. Very fortunate coincidence, though. For us. We'd been instructed by head office that you were in the country, of course. It'll be an unexpected honor. . . ." A crash of static obliterated the rest of this remark. ". . . temporary repair. Better be quick . . . should make it . . . chopper . . . hope . . . doctor . . ."

"There's a doctor here," Alleyn shouted. "I'd suggest a fully equipped homicide squad and a search warrant—can you hear?—and a brace and bit. Yes, that's what I said. Large. Yes, large. Observation purposes. Are you there? Hullo? Hullo?"

The line was dead.

"Well," said Troy after a pause. "This is the beginning of the end, I suppose."

"In a way the beginning of the beginning," Alleyn said wryly. "If it's done nothing else it's brought home the virtues of routine. I'm not sure if they have homicide squads in New Zealand, but whatever they do have they'll take the correct steps in the correct way and with authority. And you, my love, will fly away home with an untouched canvas." He turned to Dr. Carmichael. "I really don't know what I'd have done without you," he said.

Before Dr. Carmichael could answer there was a loud rap at the door.

"Not a dull moment," said Alleyn. "Come in!"

It was Signor Lattienzo, pale and strangely unsprightly.

"I am *de trop*," he said. "Forgive me. I thought you would be here. I find the ambiance downstairs uncomfortable. Everybody asking questions and expressing relief and wanting above all to know when they can go away. And behind it all—fear. Fear and suspicion. Not a pretty combination. And to realize that one is in much the same state oneself, after all! That I find exceedingly disagreeable."

Dr. Carmichael said to Alleyn, "They'll be wanting to know about the telephone call. Would you like me to go downstairs and tell them?"

"Do. Just say it *was* the police and they are on their way and the line's gone phut again."

"Right."

"That's a *very* nice man," said Troy when he had gone. "We never completed our bed-making. I don't suppose it matters so much now, but we ought at least to put our gear away, don't you think?"

She had managed to get behind Signor Lattienzo and pull a quick face at her husband.

"I expect you're right," he said, obediently, and she made for the door. Signor Lattienzo seemed to make an effort. He produced a rather wan replica of his more familiar manner.

"Bed-making! 'Gear'?" he exclaimed. "But I am baffled. Here is the most distinguished painter of our time, whom I have, above all things, desired to meet and she talks of bed-making as a sequence to murder."

"She's being British," said Alleyn. "If there were any bullets about, she'd bite on them. Pay no attention."

"That's right," Troy assured Signor Lattienzo. "It's a substitute for hysterics."

"If you say so," said Signor Lattienzo, and as an afterthought seized and extensively kissed Troy's hand. She cast a sheepish glance at Alleyn and withdrew.

Alleyn, who had begun to feel rather British himself, said he was glad that Signor Lattienzo had looked in. "There's something I've been wanting to ask you," he said, "but with all the excursions and alarms, I haven't got round to it."

"Me? But, of course! Anything! Though I don't imagine that I can produce electrifying tidings," said Signor Lattienzo. He sat down in the studio's most comfortable armchair and appeared to relax. "Already," he said, "I feel better," and took out his cigarette case.

"It's about Madame Sommita's background."

"Indeed?"

"She was your pupil for some three years, wasn't she, before making her debut?"

"That is so."

"You were aware, I expect, of her real name?"

"Naturally. Pepitone."

"Perhaps you helped her decide on her professional name? Sommita, which is as much as to say 'The Tops,' isn't it?"

"It was not my choice. I found it a little extravagant. She did not and she prevailed. You may say she has been fully justified."

"Indeed you may. You may also say, perhaps, that the choice was a matter of accuracy rather than of taste."

Signor Lattienzo softly clapped his hands. "That is precisely the case," he applauded.

"Maestro," Alleyn said, "I am very ignorant in these matters, but I imagine that the relationship between pedagogue and pupil is, or at least can be, very close, very intimate."

"My dear Mr. Alleyn, if you are suggesting—"

"Which I am not. Not for a moment. There can be close relationships that have no romantic overtones."

"Of course. And allow me to say that with a pupil it would be in the highest degree a mistake to allow oneself to become involved in such an attachment. And apart from all that," he added with feeling, "when the lady has the temperament of a wildcat and the appetite of a hyena, it would be sheer lunacy."

"But all the same, I expect some kind of aseptic intimacy does exist, doesn't it?"

Signor Lattienzo broke into rather shrill laughter. "'Aseptic intimacy,'" he echoed. "You are a master of the *mot juste,* my dear Mr. Alleyn. It is a pleasure to be grilled by you."

"Well then: did you learn anything about a family feud—one of those vendetta-like affairs—between the Pepitones and another Sicilian clan: the Rossis?"

Signor Lattienzo took some time in helping himself to a cigarette and lighting it. He did not look at Alleyn. "I do not concern myself with such matters," he said.

"I'm sure you don't but did *she?*"

"May I, first of all, ask you a question? Do you suspect that this appalling crime might be traced to the Pepitone-Rossi affair? I think you must do so, otherwise you would not bring it up."

"As to that," said Alleyn, "it's just a matter of avenues and stones, however unlikely. I've been told that Madame Sommita herself feared some sort of danger threatened her and that she suspected Strix of being an agent or even a member of the Rossi family. I don't have to tell you that Marco is Strix. Mr. Reece will have done that."

"Yes. But—do you think—?"

"No. He has an unbreakable alibi."

"Ah."

"I wondered if she had confided her fears to you?"

"You will know, of course, of the habit of *omertà.* It has been remorselessly, if erroneously, paraded in works of popular fiction with a *mafioso* background. I expected that she knew of her father's alleged involvement with *mafioso* elements, although great care had been taken to remove her from the milieu. I am surprised to hear that she spoke of the Rossi affair. Not to the good Monty, I am sure?"

"Not specifically. But it appears that even to him she referred repeatedly, though in the vaguest of terms, to sinister intentions behind the Strix activities."

"But otherwise—"

Signor Lattienzo stopped short and for the first time looked very hard at Alleyn. "Did she tell that unhappy young man? Is that it? I see it is. Why?"

"It seems she used it as a weapon when she realized he was trying to escape her."

"Ah! That is believable. An appeal to his pity. That I can believe. Emotional blackmail."

Signor Lattienzo got up and moved restlessly about the room. He looked out at the now sunny prospect, thrust his plump hands into his trouser pockets, took them out and examined them as if they had changed, and finally approached Alleyn and came to a halt.

"I have something to tell you," he said.

"Good."

"Evidently you are familiar with the Rossi affair."

"Not to say familiar, no. But I do remember something of the case."

Alleyn would have thought it impossible that Signor Lattienzo would ever display the smallest degree of embarrassment or loss of savoir-faire, but he appeared to do so now. He screwed in his eyeglass, stared at a distant spot somewhere to the right of Alleyn's left ear, and spoke rapidly in a high voice.

"I have a brother," he proclaimed. "Alfredo Lattienzo. He is an *avvocato,* a leading barrister, and he, in the course of his professional duties, has appeared in a number of cases where the *mafioso* element was—ah—involved. At the time of the Rossi trial, which as you will know became a *cause célèbre* in the U.S.A., he held a watching brief on behalf of the Pepitone element. It was through him, by the way, that Isabella became my pupil. But that is of no moment. He was never called upon to take a more active part but he did—ah—he did learn—ah—from, as you would say, the horse's mouth, the origin and subsequent history of the enmity between the two houses."

He paused. Alleyn thought that it would be appropriate if he said: "You interest me strangely. Pray continue your most absorbing narrative." However, he said nothing, and Signor Lattienzo continued.

"The origin," he repeated. "The event that set the whole absurdly wicked feud going. I have always thought there must have been Corsican blood somewhere in that family. The whole story smacks more of the vendetta than the *mafioso* element. My dear Alleyn, I am about to break a confidence with my brother, and one does not break confidences of this sort."

"I think I may assure that whatever you may tell me, I won't reveal the source."

"It may, after all, not seem as striking to you as it does to me. It is this. The event that gave rise to the feud so many, many years ago, was the murder of a Pepitone girl by her Rossi bridegroom. He had discovered a passionate and explicit letter from a lover. He stabbed her to the heart on their wedding night."

He stopped. He seemed to balk at some conversational hurdle.

"I see," said Alleyn.

"That is not all," said Signor Lattienzo. "That is by no means all. Pinned to the body by the stiletto that killed her was the letter. That is what I came to tell you and now I shall go."

CHAPTER VIII

The Police

I

"FROM NOW ON," Alleyn said to Dr. Carmichael, "it would be nice to maintain a masterly inactivity. I shall complete my file and hand it over, with an anxious smirk, to Inspector Hazelmere in, please God, the course of a couple of hours or less."

"Don't you feel you'd like to polish it off yourself? Having gone so far?"

"Yes, Rory," said Troy. "Don't you?"

"If Fox and Bailey and Thompson could walk in, yes, I suppose I do. That would be, as Noel Coward put it, 'an *autre paire de souliers.*' But this hamstrung solo, poking about without authority, has been damned frustrating."

"What do you suppose the chap that's coming will do first?"

"Inspect the body and the immediate environment. He can't look at my improvised dabs-and-photographs, because they are still in what Lattienzo calls the womb of the camera. He'll take more of his own."

"And then?"

"Possibly set up a search of some if not all of their rooms. I suggested he bring a warrant. And by that same token did your bed-making exercise prove fruitful? Before or after the envelope-and-ashes episode?"

"A blank," said Dr. Carmichael. "Hanley has a collection of bedside books with Wilde and Gide at the top and backstreet Marseilles at the bottom, but all with the same leitmotiv."

"And Ben Ruby," said Troy, "has an enormous scrapbook of newspaper cuttings all beautifully arranged and dated and noted and with all the rave bits in the reviews underlined. For quotation in advance publicity, I suppose. It's got the Strix photographs and captions and newspaper correspondence, indignant and supportive. Do you know there are only seven European Strix photographs, two American, and four Australian, including the retouched one in the *Watchman*? Somehow one had imagined, or I had, a hoard of them. Signor Lattienzo's got a neat little pile of letters in Italian on his desk. Mr. Reece has an enormous colored photograph framed in silver of the diva in full operatic kit—I wouldn't know which opera, except that it's not *Butterfly*. And there are framed photographs of those rather self-conscious slightly smug walking youths in the Athens Museum. He's also got a marvelous equestrian drawing in sanguine of a nude man on a stallion which I could swear is a da Vinci original. Can he be as rich as all that? I really do swear it's not a reproduction."

"I think he probably can," said Alleyn.

"What a shut-up sort of man he is," Troy mused. "I mean who would have expected it? Does he really appreciate it or has he just acquired it because it cost so much? Like the diva, one might say."

"Perhaps not quite like that," said Alleyn.

"Do you attach a lot of weight to Signor Lattienzo's observations?" asked the doctor suddenly. "I don't know what they were, of course."

"They were confidential. They cast a strongly Italian flavor over the scene. Beyond that," said Alleyn, "my lips are sealed."

"Rory," Troy asked, "are you going to see Maria again? Before the police arrive?"

"I've not quite decided. I think perhaps I might. Very briefly."

"We mustn't ask why, of course," said Carmichael.

"Oh yes, you may. By all means. If I do see her, it will be to tell her that I shall inform the police of her request to—attend to her mistress and shall ask them to accede to it. When they've finished their examination of the room, of course."

"You will?"

"That's the general idea."

"Well, then— Are you going to explain why?"

"Certainly," said Alleyn. And did.

When he had finished Troy covered her face with her hands. It was an uncharacteristic gesture. She turned away to the windows. Dr. Carmichael looked from her to Alleyn and left the studio.

"I wouldn't have had this happen," Alleyn said, "for all the world."

"Don't give it another thought," she mumbled into his sweater and helped herself to his handkerchief. "It's nothing. It's just the *fact* of that room along there. Off the landing. You know—behind the locked door. Like a Bluebeard's chamber. I can't stop thinking about it. It's kind of got me down a bit."

"I know."

"And now—Maria. Going in there. *Damn!*" said Troy and stamped. "I'd got myself all arranged not to be a burden and now look at me."

"Could it be that you've done a morsel too much self-arranging and I've done a morsel too much male chauvinism, although, I must say," Alleyn confessed, "I'm never quite sure what the ladies mean by the phrase. Have a good blow," he added as Troy was making gingerly use of his handkerchief. She obeyed noisily and said she was feeling better.

"What would Br'er Fox say to me?" she asked and answered herself. Alleyn joined in.

"'We'll have to get you in the Force, Mrs. Alleyn,'" they quoted in unison.

"And wouldn't I make a pretty hash of it if you did," said Troy.

"You've done jolly well with the half-burnt envelope. Classic stuff that and very useful. It forced Marco to come tolerably clean."

"Well, come, that's something."

"It's half an hour to lunch time. How about putting a bit of slap on your pink nose and coming for a brisk walk."

"Lunch!" said Troy, "and Mr. Reece's massive small talk. And *food!* More *food!*"

"Perhaps the cook will have cut it down to clear soup and a slice of ham. Anyway, come on."

"All right," said Troy.

So they went out of doors, where the sun shone, the dark wet trees glittered, the Lake was spangled, and the mountains were fresh, as if, it seemed, from creation's hand. The morning was alive with bird song, sounds that might have been the voice of the bush itself, its hidden waters, its coolness, its primordial detachment.

They walked round the house to the empty hangar and thence, across the landing ground, to the path through the bush and arrived at the lakeside.

"Wet earth and greenery again," said Troy. "The best smell there is."

"The Maori people had a god-hero called Maui. He went fishing, and hauled up the South Island."

"Quite recently, by the feel of it."

"Geologically it was, in fact, thrust up from the ocean bed by volcanic action. I've no idea," said Alleyn, "whether it was a slow process or a sudden commotion. It's exciting to imagine it heaving up all of a sudden with the waters pouring down the flanks of its mountains, sweeping across its plains and foaming back into the sea. But I daresay it was a matter of eons rather than minutes."

"And you say there are now lots and lots of painters, busy as bees, having a go at"—Troy waved an arm at the prospect—"all that."

"That's right. From pretty peeps to competent posters and from factual statements to solemn abstractions. You name it."

"How brave of them all."

"Only some of them think so." Alleyn took her arm. "Some have got pretty near the bones. If things had been different," he said, "would you have wanted to paint?"

"Not at once. Make charcoal scribbles, perhaps. And after a time make some more with paint. Bones," said Troy vaguely. "The anatomy of the land. Something might come of it."

"Shall we see what happens if we follow round the shore?"

"If you like. We'll either fetch up in the front of the house or get ourselves bushed. After all we *are* on an island."

"All right, smarty-pants. Come on."

A rough track followed the margin of the lake, for the most part clear of the bush but occasionally cutting through it. In places storm water poured across the path. They came to a little footbridge over a deep-voiced creek. Here the bush was dense but farther on it thinned enough to allow glimpses, surprisingly close at hand, of the west wall of the house. They were walking parallel with the path that skirted the concert chamber. The ground here was soft under their feet.

They walked in single file. Alleyn stopped short and held up his hand. He turned and laid his finger on his lips.

Ahead of them, hidden by the bush, someone was speaking.

The voice was so low, so very quiet that it was almost toneless and quite without a personality. It was impossible to catch what was said or guess at who said it.

Alleyn signaled to Troy to stay where she was and himself moved soundlessly along the path. He was drawing closer to the voice. He remembered that at a point opposite the first window of the concert chamber there was a garden seat, and he fancied the speaker might be sitting on it. He moved on and in another moment or two realized that he should be able to make out the sense of what was said and then that it was said in Italian. At first the phrases slid past incomprehensibly and then he began to tune in.

"—I have acted in this way because of what is being—hinted—suggested by you. All of you. And because when these policemen come you may try—"

Alleyn lost the next phrase or two. There were gaps as if the speaker paused for a reply and none was forthcoming. The voice was raised "*—this is why—I have anticipated—I warn you—can go further and if necessary I will. Now. How do you answer? You understand, do you not? I mean what I say? I will act as I have said? Very well. Your answer? Speak up. I cannot hear you.*"

Nor could Alleyn. There had been some sort of reply—breathy—short—incomprehensible.

"*I am waiting.*"

Into the silence that followed a bell-bird, close at hand, dropped his clear remark ending with a derisive clatter. Then followed, scarcely perceptible, a disturbance, an intrusion, nowhere—somewhere—coming closer and louder: the commonplace beat of a helicopter.

Inside the house a man shouted. Windows were thrown open.

"*Il elicottero!*" exclaimed the voice. There was a stifled response from his companion and sounds of rapid retreat.

"Here are the cops, darling!" said Alleyn.

"Rapture! Rapture! I suppose," said Troy. "Will you go and meet them?"

"It may be a case of joining in the rush, but yes, I think I'd better."

"Rory—what'll be the drill?"

"Unusual, to say the least. I suppose I introduce them to Reece unless he's already introduced himself, and when that's effected I'll hand over my file and remain on tap for questioning."

"Will you use the studio?"

"I'd prefer the study, but doubt if we'll get it. Look, my love, after lunch will you take to the studio if it's available? Or if you can't stand that anymore, our room? I know you must have *had* them both, but perhaps you might suffer them again, for a bit. Carmichael will look in and so will I, of course, but I don't know—"

"I'll be as right as rain. I might even try a few tentative notes—"

"Might you? Truly? Marvelous," he said. "I'll see you round to the front of the house."

Their path took a right turn through the bush and came out beyond the garden seat. On the gravel walk in front of the house stood Maria with her arms folded, a black shawl over her head, staring up at the helicopter, now close overhead and deafening.

"Good morning, Maria," Alleyn shouted, cheerfully. "Here are the police."

She glowered.

"I have been meaning to speak to you: when they have completed their examination, I think you'll be permitted to perform your office. I shall recommend that you are."

She stared balefully at him from under her heavy brows. Her lips formed a soundless acknowledgment: *"Grazie tante."*

Hanley came running out of the house, pulling on a jacket over his sweater.

"Oh, hul-*lo,* Mr. Alleyn," he cried. "Thank goodness. I'm the Official Welcome. The Boss Man told me to collect you and here you are. *Ben' troveto,* if that's what they say. You *will* come, won't you? I thought *he* ought to be there in person but no, he's receiving them in the library. You haven't seen the library have you, Mrs. Alleyn? My dear, *smothered* in synthetic leather. Look! That contraption's alighting! Do let us hurry."

Troy went up the front steps to the house. Signor Lattienzo was there, having apparently stepped out of the entrance. Alleyn saw him greet her with his usual exuberance. She waved.

"Mr. Alleyn, *please!"* cried the distracted Hanley and led the way at a canter.

They arrived at the clearing as the helicopter landed and were raked with the unnatural gale from its propeller. Hanley let out an exasperated screech and clutched his blond hair. The engine stopped.

In the silence that followed, Alleyn felt as if he was involved in some Stoppard-like time slip and was back suddenly in the middle of a routine job. The three men who climbed out of the helicopter wore so unmistakably the marks of their calling, townish suits on large heavily muscled bodies, felt hats, sober shirts and ties. Sharp eyes and an indescribable air of taking over. Their equipment was handed down: cases and a camera. The fourth man who followed was slight, tweedy, and preoccupied. He carried a professional bag. Police surgeon, thought Alleyn.

The largest of the men advanced to Alleyn.

"Chief Superintendent Alleyn?" the large man said. "Hazelmere. Very glad indeed to see you, sir. Meet Dr. Winslow. Detective Sergeant Franks, Detective Sergeant Barker."

Alleyn shook hands. The police all had enormous hands and excruciating grips and prolonged the ceremony with great warmth.

"I understand you've had a spot of bother," said Inspector Hazelmere.

"If I *may* butt in," Hanley said anxiously. "Inspector, Mr. Reece hopes—" and he delivered his invitation to the library.

"Very kind, I'm sure," acknowledged Hazelmere. "You'll be his secretary, sir? Mr. Hanley? Is that correct? Well now, if it's all the same to Mr. Reece, I think it might be best if we took a look at the scene of the fatality. And if the Chief Superintendent would be kind enough to accompany us, he can put us in the picture, which will save a lot of time and trouble when we see Mr. Reece."

"Oh," said Hanley. "Oh, yes. I see. Well"—he threw a troubled glance at Alleyn—"if Mr. Alleyn will—"

"Yes, of course," said Alleyn.

"Yes. Well, I'll just convey your message to Mr. Reece. I'm sure he'll understand," said Hanley uneasily.

"I suggest," said Alleyn, "that you might ask Dr. Carmichael to join us. I'm sure Dr. Winslow would be glad to see him."

"Are you? Yes. Of course."

"Thank you very much, Mr. Hanley," said Hazelmere, blandly dismissive.

Hanley hesitated for a second or two, said, "Yes, well—" again, and set off for the house.

Alleyn said: "I can't tell you how glad I am to see you. You'll understand what a tricky position I've been in. No official authority but expected to behave like everybody's idea of an infallible sleuth."

"Is that a fact, sir?" said Mr. Hazelmere. He then paid Alleyn some rather toneless compliments, fetching up with the remark that he knew nothing beyond the information conveyed by Les, the launch man, over a storm-battered telephone line, that a lady had been, as he put it, made away with and could they now view the remains and would Alleyn be kind enough to put them in the picture.

So Alleyn led them into the house and up to the first landing. He was careful, with suitable encomiums, to introduce Bert, who was laconic and removed his two armchairs from their barrier-like position before the door. Dr. Carmichael arrived and was presented, Alleyn unlocked the door, and they all went into the room.

Back to square one. Blades of cool air slicing in through the narrowly opened windows, the sense of damp curtains, dust, stale scent, and a pervasive warning of mortality, shockingly emphasized when Alleyn and Dr. Carmichael drew away the black satin sheet.

Hazelmere made an involuntary exclamation, which he converted into a clearance of the throat. Nobody spoke or moved and then Detective Sergeant Franks whispered, "Christ!" It sounded more like a prayer than an oath.

"What was the name?" Hazelmere asked.

"Of course," Alleyn said, "you don't know, do you?"

"The line was bad. I missed a lot of what the chap was saying."

"He didn't know either. We communicated by various forms of semaphore."

"Is that a fact? Fancy!"

"She was a celebrated singer. In the world class. The tops, in fact."

"*Not*," exclaimed Dr. Winslow, "Isabella Sommita? It can't be!"

"It is, you know," said Dr. Carmichael.

"You better have a look, doc," Hazelmere suggested.

"Yes. Of course."

"If you're thinking of moving her, we'll just let Sergeant Barker and Sergeant Franks in first, doc," said Hazelmere. "For photos and dabs."

Alleyn explained that he had used his own professional camera and had improvised fingerprinting tactics. "I thought it might be as well to do this in case of postmortem changes. Dr. Carmichael and I disturbed nothing and didn't touch her. I daresay the results won't be too hot and I think you'd better not depend on them. While they're doing their stuff," he said to Hazelmere, "would you like to get the picture?"

"Too right I would," said the Inspector and out came his notebook.

And so to the familiar accompaniment of clicks and flashes, Alleyn embarked on an orderly and exhaustive report, event after event as they fell out over the past three days, including the Strix-Marco element, the puzzle of the keys, and the outcome of the opera. He gave a list of the inmates and guests in the Lodge. He spoke with great clarity and care, without hesitation or repetition. Hazelmere paused, once, and looked up at him.

"Am I going too fast?" Alleyn asked.

"It's not that, sir," Hazelmere said. "It's the way you give it out. Beautiful!"

Succinct though it was, the account had taken some time. Franks and Barker had finished. They and the two doctors who had covered the body and retired to the far end of the room to consult, now collected round Alleyn, listening.

When he had finished he said: "I've made a file covering all this stuff and a certain amount of background—past history and so on. You might like to see it. I'll fetch it, shall I?"

When he had gone Dr. Winslow said: "Remarkable."

"Isn't it?" said Dr. Carmichael with a slightly proprietory air.

"You'll never hear better," Inspector Hazelmere pronounced. He addressed himself to the doctors. "What's the story, then, gentlemen?"

Dr. Winslow said he agreed with the tentative opinion formed by Alleyn and Dr. Carmichael: that on a superficial examination the appearances suggested that the deceased had been anesthetized and then asphyxiated and that the stiletto had been driven through the heart after death.

"How long after?" Hazelmere asked.

"Hard to say. After death the blood follows the law of gravity and sinks. The very scant effusion here suggested that this process was well advanced. The postmortem would be informative."

Alleyn returned with the file and suggested that Inspector Hazelmere, the two doctors, and he go to the studio leaving Sergeants Barker and Franks to extend their activities to the room and bathroom. They had taken prints from the rigid hands of the Sommita and were to look for any that disagreed with them. Particularly, Alleyn suggested, on the bottom left-hand drawer of the dressing table, the gold handbag therein, and the key in the bag. The key and the bag were to be replaced. He explained why.

"The room had evidently been thoroughly swept and dusted that morning, so anything you find will have been left later in the day. You can expect to find Maria's and possibly Mr. Reece's, but we know of nobody else who may have entered the room. The housekeeper, Mrs. Bacon, may have done so. You'll find her very cooperative."

"So it may mean getting dabs from the lot of them," said Hazelmere.

"It may, at that."

"By the way, sir. That was a very bad line we spoke on. Temporary repairs after the storm. Excuse me, but did you ask me to bring a brace and bit?"

"I did, yes."

"Yes. I thought it sounded like that."

"*Did* you bring a brace and bit, Inspector?"

"Yes. I chanced it."

"Large-sized bit?"

"Several bits. Different sizes."

"Splendid."

"Might I ask—?"

"Of course. Come along to the studio and I'll explain. But first—take a look at the fancy woodwork on the wardrobe doors."

II

The conference in the studio lasted for an hour and at its conclusion Dr. Winslow discussed plans for the removal of the body. The Lake was almost back to normal and Les had come over in the launch with the mail. "She'll be sweet as a millpond by nightfall," he reported. The police helicopter was making a second trip, bringing two uniform constables, and would take Dr. Winslow back to Rivermouth. He would arrange for a mortuary van to be sent out and the body would be taken across by launch to meet it. The autopsy would be performed as soon as the official pathologist was available: probably that night.

"And now," said Hazelmere, "I reckon we lay on this—er—experiment, don't we?"

"Only if you're quite sure you'll risk it. Always remembering that if it flops you may be in for some very nasty moments."

"I appreciate that. Look, Mr. Alleyn, if you'd been me, would you have risked it?"

"Yes," said Alleyn, "I would. I'd have told myself I was a bloody fool but I'd have risked it."

"That's good enough for me," said Hazelmere. "Let's go."

"Don't you think that perhaps Mr. Reece has been languishing rather a long time in the library?"

"You're dead right. Dear me, yes. I better go down."

But there was no need for Hazelmere to go down. The studio door opened and Mr. Reece walked in.

Alleyn thought he was probably very angry indeed.

Not that his behavior was in any way exceptionable. He did not scold and he did not shout. He stood stock-still in his own premises and waited for somebody else to perform. His mouth was tightly closed and the corners severely compressed.

With his head, metaphysically, lowered to meet an icy breeze, Alleyn explained that they had thought it best first to make an official survey and for Inspector Hazelmere, whom he introduced and who was given a stony acknowledgment, to be informed of all the circumstances before troubling Mr. Reece. Mr. Reece slightly inclined his head. Alleyn then hurriedly introduced Dr. Winslow, who was awarded a perceptibly less glacial reception.

"As you are now at liberty," Mr. Reece pronounced, "perhaps you will be good enough to come down to the library, where we will not be disturbed. I shall be glad to learn what steps you propose to take."

Hazelmere, to Alleyn's satisfaction, produced his own line of imperturbability and said blandly that the library would no doubt be very convenient. Mr. Reece, then pointedly addressing himself to Alleyn, said that luncheon had been postponed until two o'clock and would be in the nature of a cold buffet to which the guests would help themselves when so inclined. It was now one-twenty.

"In the meantime," Mr. Reece magnificently continued, "I will take it as a favor if you will extend my already deep obligation to you by joining us in the library."

Alleyn thought there would be nothing Hazelmere would enjoy less than having him, Alleyn, on the sideline, a silent observer of his investigatory techniques.

He said that he had promised to look in on Troy. He added (truthfully) that she suffered from occasional attacks of migraine and (less truthfully) that one had threatened this morning. Mr. Reece expressed wooden regrets and hoped to see him as soon as it was convenient. Alleyn felt as if they were both repeating memorized bits of dialogue from some dreary play.

Mr. Reece said: "Shall we?" to Hazelmere and led the way out of the studio. Hazelmere turned in the doorway, and Alleyn rapidly indicated that he was returning to the bedroom. The Inspector stuck up his vast thumb and followed Mr. Reece to the stairs.

Alleyn shut the door and Dr. Carmichael, who had continued his now familiar role of self-obliteration, rose up and asked if Hazelmere really meant to carry out the Plan.

"Yes, he does, and I hope to God he'll do himself no harm by it."

"Not for the want of warning."

"No. But it was I who concocted it."

"What's the first step?"

"We've got to fix Maria asking for, or being given unasked, permission to lay out the body. Hazelmere had better set it up that she'll be told when she may do it."

"Suppose she's gone off the idea?"

"That's a sickening prospect, isn't it? But we're hoping the opportunity it offers will do the trick. I'm going along now to get those two chaps onto it."

Dr. Carmichael said, "Alleyn, if you can spare a moment, would you be very kind and go over the business about the keys? I know it, but I'd like to be reminded."

"All right. There are at least four keys to the bedroom. Maria had one, which I took possession of, the Sommita another, and young Bartholomew the third. Mrs. Bacon had the fourth. When Reece and the Sommita went upstairs after the concert they found Maria waiting. If the door had been locked she had let herself in with her own key. The Sommita threw a violent temperament, gave them what for, kicked them out, and locked the door after them. They have both said individually that they distinctly heard the key turn in the lock. Maria returned later with a hot drink, let herself in with her own key, and found her mistress murdered. There was no sight anywhere on any surface or on the floor or on the body, of the Sommita's key. I found it subsequently in her evening bag neatly disposed and wrapped at the bottom of a drawer. Reece is sure she didn't have the bag when they took her upstairs. The people who fussed round her in her dressing room say she hadn't got it with her and indeed in that rig it would have been an incongruous object for her to carry—even offstage. Equally it's impossible to imagine her at the height of one of her towering rages, getting the key from wherever it was, putting it in the lock in the fraction of time between Reece or Maria, closing the door behind them and then both hearing the turn of the lock. And then meticulously getting out her evening bag, putting her key in it, and placing it in the drawer. It even was enclosed in one of those soft cloth bags women use to prevent gold mesh from catching in the fabric of things like stockings. That's the story of the keys."

"Yes. That's right. That's what I thought," said Dr. Carmichael uneasily.

"What's the matter?"

"It's just—rather an unpleasant thought."

"About the third key?"

"Yes!"

"Rupert Bartholomew had it. Maria came to his room, very late in the night, and said I'd sent her for it."

"Did she, by God!"

"He gave it to her. Bert, asleep in the chairs across the doorway, woke up to find Maria trying to stretch across him and put the key in the lock."

"She must have been dotty. What did she think she'd do? Open the door and swarm over his sleeping body?"

"Open the door, yes. It opens inwards. And chuck the key into the room. She was hell-bent on our finding it there. Close the door, which would remain unlocked: she couldn't do anything about that. And when, as is probable, Bert wakes, throw a hysterical scene with all the pious drama about praying for the soul of the Sommita and laying her out."

"Actually what did happen?"

"Bert woke up to find her generous personal equipment dangling over him. She panicked, dropped the key on him, and bolted. He collected it and gave it to me. So she is still keyless."

"Could you ever prove all these theories?"

"If the plan works."

"Maria, eh?" said Dr. Carmichael. "Well, of course, she does look—I mean to say—"

"We've got to remember," Alleyn said, "that from the time Maria and Reece left the room and went downstairs and he joined his guests for dinner, Maria was in the staff sitting room preparing the hot drink. Mrs. Bacon and Marco and others of the staff can be called to prove it."

Carmichael stared at him. "An alibi?" he said. "For Maria? That's awkward."

"In this game," Alleyn said, "one learns to be wary of assumption."

"I suppose I'm making one now. Very reluctantly."

"The boy?"

"Yes."

"Well, of course, he's the prime suspect. One can turn on all the clichés: 'lust turned to hatred,' 'humiliation,' 'breaking point'—the lot. He was supposedly in his room at the crucial time but could have slipped out, and he had his key to her room. He had motive and opportunity and he was in an extremely unstable condition."

"Do the rest of them think—?"

"Some of them do. Hanley does, or behaves and drops hints as if he does. Maria, and Marco I fancy, have been telling everyone he's the prime suspect. As I daresay the rest of the domestic staff believe, being aware, no doubt, of the changed relationship between the boy and the diva. And of course most of them witnessed the curtain speech and the fainting fit."

"What about Lattienzo?"

"Troy and I overheard the jocund maestro in the shrubbery or near it, and in far from merry pin, threatening an unseen person with an evidently damaging exposure if he or she continued to spread malicious gossip. He spoke in Italian and the chopper was approaching so I missed whole chunks of his discourse."

"Who was he talking to?"

"Somebody perfectly inaudible."

"Maria?"

"I think so. When we emerged she was handy. On the front steps watching the chopper. Lattienzo was not far off."

"I thought Lattienzo was not in his usual ebullient form when he came up here just now."

"You were right," said Alleyn and gave an account of the interview.

"The Italian element with a vengeance," said the doctor thoughtfully.

"I must go along and fix things up in that room and then hie me to the library and Mr. Reece's displeasure. Look in on Troy, like a good chap, would you, and tell her this studio's free? Do you mind? She's in our bedroom."

"I'm delighted," said the gallant doctor.

And so Alleyn returned to the Sommita's death chamber and found Sergeants Franks and Barker in dubious consultation. A brace and a selection of bits was laid out on a sheet of newspaper on the floor.

"The boss said you'd put us wise, sir," said Franks.

"Right," said Alleyn. He stood with his back to one of the exuberantly carved and painted wardrobe doors, felt behind him and bent his knees until his head was on a level with the stylized sunflower which framed it like a formalized halo. He made a funnel of his hand and looked through it at the covered body on the bed. Then he moved to the twin door and went through the same procedure.

"Yes," he said, "it'll work. It'll work all right."

He opened the doors.

The walk-in wardrobe was occupied but not crowded with dresses. He divided them and slid them on their hangers to opposite ends of the interior. He examined the inside of the doors, came out, and locked them.

He inspected the bits.

"This one will do," he said and gave it, with the brace, to Sergeant Franks. "Plumb in the middle," he said, putting his finger on the black center of the sunflower. "And slide that newspaper under to catch the litter. Very careful, now. No splintering, whatever you do. Which of you's the joiner?"

"Aw heck!" said Franks to Barker, "what about you having a go, Merv."

"I'm not fussy, thanks," said Barker, backing off.

They looked uncomfortably at Alleyn.

"Well," he said, "I asked for it and it looks as if I've bought it. If I make a fool of myself I can't blame anyone else, can I? Give it here, Franks. Oh, God, it's one of those push-me-pull-you brutes that shoot out at you when you least expect it." He thumbed a catch and the business end duly shot out. "What did I tell you? You guide it, Franks, and hold it steady. Dead center. Anyone'd think we were defusing a bomb. Come on."

"She's new, sir. Sharp as a needle and greased."

"Good."

He raised the brace and advanced it. Franks guided the point of the bit. "Dead center, sir," he said.

"Here goes, then," said Alleyn.

He made a cautious preliminary pressure. "How's that?"

"Biting, sir."

"Straight as we go, then." Alleyn pumped the brace.

A little cascade of wood dust trickled through the elaborate carving and fell on the newspaper.

"Nearly there," he grunted presently, and a few seconds later the resistance was gone and he disengaged the tool.

At the black center of the sunflower was a black hole as wide as the iris of an eye and very inconspicuous. Alleyn blew away the remnants of wood dust that were trapped in curlicues, twisted a finger in the hole, and stood back. "Not too bad," he said.

He opened the door. The hole was clean-cut.

"Now for the twin," he said and gave the companion door the same treatment.

Then he went into the wardrobe and shut the doors. The interior smelt insufferably of La Sommita's scent. He looked through one of the holes. He saw the body. Neatly framed. Underneath the black satin cover its arm, still raised in cadaveric spasm, seemed to point at him. He came out, shut and locked the wardrobe doors, and put the key in his pocket.

"It'll do," he said. "Will you two clean up? Very thoroughly? Before you do that, I think you should know why you've been called on to set this up and what we hope to achieve by it. Don't you?"

They intimated by sundry noises that they did think so and he then told them of the next steps that would be taken, the procedure to be followed, and the hoped-for outcome. "And now I think perhaps one of you might relieve poor old Bert on the landing, and I'd suggest the other reports for duty to Mr. Hazelmere, who will probably be in the library. It opens off the entrance hall. Third on the right from the front. I'm going down there now. Here's the key to this room. O.K.?"

"She'll be right, sir," said Franks and Barker together.

So Alleyn went down to the library.

It came as no surprise to find the atmosphere in that utterly neutral apartment tepid, verging on glacial. Inspector Hazelmere had his notebook at the ready. Mr. Reece sat at one of the neatly laden tables with the glaze of boredom veiling his pale regard. When Alleyn apologized for keeping him waiting, he raised his hand and let it fall as if words now failed him.

The Inspector, Alleyn thought, was not at the moment happy in his work though he put up a reasonable show of professional savoir-faire and said easily that he thought he had finished "bothering" Mr. Reece and believed he was now fully in the picture. Mr. Reece said woodenly that he was glad to hear it. An awkward silence followed, which he broke by addressing himself pointedly to Alleyn.

"Would you," he said, "be good enough to show me where you found that book? I've been wondering about it."

Alleyn led the way to the remote corner of the library and the obscure end of a top shelf. "It was here," he said, pointing to the gap. "I could only just reach it."

"I would require the steps," said Mr. Reece. He put on his massive spectacles and peered. "It's very badly lit," he said. "The architect should have noticed that."

Alleyn switched on the light.

"Thank you. I would like to see the book when you have finished with it. I suppose it has something to do with this family feud or vendetta or whatever, that she was so concerned about?"

"I would think so, yes."

"It is strange that she never showed it to me. Perhaps that is because it is written in Italian. I would have expected her to show it to me," he said heavily. "I would have expected her to feel it would give validity to her theory. I wonder how she came by it. It is very shabby. Perhaps it was second-hand."

"Did you notice the name on the flyleaf? 'M. V. Rossi'?"

"Rossi? *Rossi!*" he repeated, and stared at Alleyn. "But that was the name she *did* mention. On the rare occasions when she used a name. I recollect that she once said she wished my name did not resemble it. I thought this very farfetched but she seemed to be quite serious about it. She generally referred simply to the '*nemico*'—meaning the enemy."

"Perhaps, after all, it was not her book."

"It was certainly not *mine,*" he said flatly.

"At some time—originally, I suppose—it has been the property of the 'enemy.' One wouldn't have expected her to have acquired it."

"You certainly would not," Mr. Reece said emphatically. "Up there, was it? What sort of company was it keeping?"

Alleyn took down four of the neighboring books. One, a biography called *La Voce,* was written in Italian and seemed from cover to cover to be an unmodified rave about the Sommita. It was photographically illustrated, beginning with a portrait of a fat-legged infant, much befrilled, beringleted and beribboned, glowering on the lap, according to the caption, of "*La Zia Giulia*," and ending with La Sommita receiving a standing ovation at a royal performance of *Faust*.

"Ah, yes," said Mr. Reece. "The biography. I always intended to read it. It went into three editions. What are the others?"

One in English, one in Italian—both novels with a strong romantic interest. They were gifts to the Sommita, lavishly inscribed by admirers.

"Is the autobiography there?" asked Mr. Reece. "That meant a helluva lot to me. Yes sir. A helluva lot." This piece of information was dealt out by Mr. Reece in his customary manner: baldly as if he were citing a quotation from Wall Street. For the first time he sounded definitely American.

"I'm sure it did," Alleyn said.

"I never got round to reading it right through," Mr. Reece confessed and then seemed to brighten up a little. "After all," he pointed out, "she didn't write it herself. But it was the thought that counted."

"Quite. This seems, doesn't it, to be a corner reserved for her own books?"

"I believe I remember, now I come to think of it, her saying something about wanting someplace for her own books. She didn't appreciate the way they looked in her bedroom. Out of place."

"Do you think she would have put them up there herself?"

Mr. Reece took off his spectacles and looked at Alleyn as if he had taken leave of his senses. "Bella?" he said. "Up there? On the steps?"

"Well, no. Silly of me. I'm sorry."

"She would probably have told Maria to do it."

"Ah, apropos! I don't know," Alleyn said, "whether Mr. Hazelmere has told you?" He looked at the Inspector, who slightly shook his head. "Perhaps we should—?"

"That's so, sir," said Hazelmere. "We certainly should." He addressed himself to Mr. Reece. "I understand, sir, that Miss Maria Bennini has expressed the wish to perform the last duties and Mr. Alleyn pointed out that until the premises had been thoroughly investigatged, the *stattus*" (so Mr. Hazelmere pronounced it) "*quow* must be maintained. That is now the case. So, if it's acceptable to yourself, we will inform Miss Bennini and in due course—"

"Yes, yes. Tell her," Mr. Reece said. His voice was actually unsteady. He looked at Alleyn almost as if appealing to him. "And what then?" he asked.

Alleyn explained about the arrangements for the removal of the body.

"It will probably be at dusk or even after dark when they arrive at the lakeside," he said. "The launch will be waiting."

"I wish to be informed."

Alleyn and Hazelmere said together: "Certainly, sir."

"I will—" he hunted for the phrase. "I will see her off. It is the least I can do. If I had not brought her to this house—" He turned aside, and looked at the books without seeing them. Alleyn put them back on their shelf. "I'm not conversant with police procedure in New Zealand," Mr. Reece said. "I understand it follows the British rather than the American practice. It may be quite out of order, at this juncture, to ask whether you expect to make an arrest in the foreseeable future."

Hazelmere again glanced at Alleyn, who remained silent. "Well, sir," Hazelmere said, "it's not our practice to open up wide, like, until we are very, very sure of ourselves. I think I'm in order if I say that we hope quite soon to be in a position to take positive action."

"Is that your view, too, Chief Superintendent?"

"Yes," Alleyn said. "That's my view."

"I am very glad to hear it. You wish to see Maria, do you not? Shall I send for her?"

"If it's not putting you out, sir, we'd be much obliged," said Inspector Hazelmere, who seemed to suffer from a compulsion to keep the interview at an impossibly high-toned level.

Mr. Reece used the telephone. "Find Maria," he said, "and ask her to come to the library. Yes, at once. Very well, then, find her. Ask Mrs. Bacon to deal with it."

He replaced the receiver. "Staff coordination has gone to pieces," he said. "I asked for service and am told the person in question is sulking in her room."

A long silence followed. Mr. Reece made no effort to break it. He went to the window and looked out at the Lake. Hazelmere inspected his notes, made two alterations, and under a pretense of consulting Alleyn about them, said in a slurred undertone: "Awkward if she won't."

"Hellishly," Alleyn agreed.

Voices were raised in the hall, Hanley's sounding agitated, Mrs. Bacon's masterful. A door banged. Another voice shouted something that might have been an insult and followed it up with a raucous laugh. Marco, Alleyn thought. Hanley, all eyes and teeth, made an abrupt entrance.

"I'm terribly sorry, sir," he said. "There's been a little difficulty. *Just coming.*"

Mr. Reece glanced at him with contempt. He gave a nervous titter and withdrew only to reappear and stand, door in hand, to admit Maria in the grip of Mrs. Bacon.

"I'm extremely sorry, Mr. Reece," said Mrs. Bacon in a high voice. "Maria has been difficult."

She released her hold as if she expected her catch would bolt and when she did not, left the arena. Hanley followed her, shutting the door but not before an indignant contralto was heard in the hall: "No, this is too much. I can take no more of this," said Miss Dancy.

"You handle this one, eh?" Hazelmere murmured to Alleyn.

But Mr. Reece was already in charge.

He said: "Come here." Maria walked up to him at once and waited with her arms folded, looking at the floor.

"You are making scenes, Maria," said Mr. Reece, "and that is foolish of you: you must behave yourself. Your request is to be granted; see to it that you carry out your duty decently and with respect."

Maria intimated rapidly and in Italian that she would be a model of decorum, or words to that effect, and that she was now satisfied and grateful and might the good God bless Signor Reece.

"Very well," said Mr. Reece. "Listen to the Chief Superintendent and do as he tells you."

He nodded to Alleyn and walked out of the room.

Alleyn told Maria that she was to provide herself with whatever she needed and wait in the staff sitting room. She would not be disturbed.

"You found her. You have seen what it is like," he said. "You are sure you want to do this?"

Maria crossed herself and said vehemently that she was sure.

"Very well. Do as I have said."

There was a tap on the door and Sergeant Franks came in.

Hazelmere said: "You'll look after Miss Bennini, Franks, won't you? Anything she may require."

"Sir," said Sergeant Franks.

Maria looked as if she thought she could do without Sergeant Franks and intimated that she wished to be alone with her mistress.

"If that's what you want," said Hazelmere.

"To pray. There should be a priest."

"All that will be attended to," Hazelmere assured her. "Later on."

"When?"

"At the interment," he said flatly.

She glared at him and marched out of the room.

"All right," Hazelmere said to Franks. "Later on. Keep with it. You know what you've got to do."

"Sir," said Sergeant Franks and followed her.

"Up we go," said Alleyn.

He and Hazelmere moved into the hall and finding it empty, ran upstairs to the Sommita's bedroom.

III

It was stuffy in the wardrobe now they had locked themselves in. The smell was compounded of metallic cloth, sequins, fur, powder, scent, and of the body when it was still alive and wore the clothes and left itself on them. It was as if the Sommita had locked herself in with her apparel.

"Cripes, it's close in here," said Inspector Hazelmere.

"Put your mouth to the hole," Alleyn suggested.

"That's an idea, too," Hazelmere said and began noisily to suck air through his peephole. Alleyn followed his own advice. Thus they obliterated the two pencils of light that had given some shape to the darkness as their eyes became adjusted to it.

"Makes you think of those funny things jokers on the telly get up to," Hazelmere said. "You know. Crime serials." And after a pause. "They're taking their time, aren't they?"

Alleyn grunted. He applied his eye to his peephole. Again, suddenly confronting him, was the black satin shape on the bed: so very explicit, so eloquent of the body inside. The shrouded limb, still rigid as a yardarm, pointing under its funereal sheet—at him.

He thought: But shouldn't the rigidity be going off now? And tried to remember the rules about cadaveric spasm as opposed to rigor mortis.

"I told Franks to give us the office," said Hazelmere. "You know. Unlock the door and open it a crack and say something loud."

"Good."

"What say we open these doors, then? Just for a second or two? Sort of fan them to change the air? I suffer from hay fever," Hazelmere confessed.

"All right. But we'd better be quick about it, hadn't we? Ready?"

Their keys clicked.

"Right."

They opened the doors wide and flung them to and fro, exchanging the wardrobe air for the colder and more ominously suspect air of the room. Something fell on Alleyn's left foot.

"Bloody hell!" said Hazelmere. "I've dropped the bloody key."

"Don't move. They're coming. Here! Let me."

Alleyn collected it from the floor, pushed it in the keyhole, and shut and locked both doors. He could feel Hazelmere's bulk heaving slightly against his own arm.

They looked through their spy holes. Alleyn's was below the level of his eyes and he had to bend his knees. The bedroom door was beyond their range of sight but evidently it was open. There was the sound of something being set down, possibly on the carpet. Detective Sergeant Franks said: "There you are, then, lady. I'll leave you to it. If you want anything knock on the door. Same thing when you've finished. Knock."

And Maria: "Give me the key. I let myself out."

"Sorry, lady. That's not my orders. Don't worry. I won't run away. Just knock when you're ready. See you."

The bedroom door shut firmly. They could hear the key turn in the lock.

Alleyn could still see, framed by his spy hole, the body and beyond it a section of the dressing table.

As if by the action of a shutter in a camera they were blotted out. Maria was not two feet away and Alleyn looked into her eyes. He thought for a sickening moment that she had seen the hole in the sunflower but she was gone only to reappear by the dressing table:—stoooping—wrenching open a drawer—a bottom drawer.

Hazelmere gave him a nudge. Alleyn remembered that he commanded a slightly different and better view than his own of the bottom left-hand end of the dressing table.

But now Maria stood up and her hands were locked round a gold meshed bag. They opened it and inverted it and shook it out on the dressing table and her right hand fastened on the key that fell from it.

Hazelmere shifted but Alleyn, without moving his eye from the spy hole, reached out and touched him.

Maria now stood over the shrouded body and looked at it, one would have said, speculatively.

With an abrupt movement, more feline than human, she knelt and groped under the shroud—she scuffled deep under the body, which jolted horridly.

The black shroud slithered down the raised arm and by force of its own displaced weight slid to the floor.

And the arm dropped.

It fell across her neck. She screamed like a trapped ferret and with a grotesque and frantic movement, rolled away and scrambled to her feet.

"Now," Alleyn said.

He and Hazelmere unlocked their doors and walked out into the room.

Hazelmere said: "Maria Bennini, I arrest you on a charge—"

CHAPTER IX

Departure

I

THE SCENE MIGHT have been devised by a film director who had placed his camera on the landing and pointed it downward to take in the stairs and the hall beneath where he had placed his actors, all with upturned faces. For sound he had used only the out-of-shot Maria's screams, fading them as she was taken by the two detective sergeants to an unoccupied bedroom. This would be followed by total silence and immobility and then, Alleyn thought, the camera would probably pan from face to upturned face: from Mr. Reece halfway up the stairs, pallid and looking, if anything, scandalized, breathing hard, and to Ben Ruby, immensely perturbed and two steps lower down, to Signor Lattienzo with his eyeglass stuck in a white mask. Ned Hanley, on the lowest step, held on to the banister as if in an earthquake. Below him Miss Dancy at ground level, appropriately distraught and wringing every ounce of star quality out of it. Farther away Sylvia Parry clung to Rupert Bartholomew. And finally, in isolation Marco stood with his arms folded and wearing a faint, unpleasant smile.

Removed from all these stood Mrs. Bacon in command of her staff, who were clustered behind her. Near the door onto the porch, Les and Bert kept themselves to themselves in close proximity to the pregnant nude, whose smirk would no doubt be held in shot for a second or two, providing an enigmatic note. Finally, perhaps, the camera would dwell upon the remaining stiletto and the empty bracket where its opposite number had hung.

Alleyn supposed this company had been made aware of what was going on by Hanley and perhaps Mrs. Bacon and that the guests had been at their buffet luncheon and the staff assembled for theirs in their own region and that Maria's screams had brought them out like a fire alarm.

Mr. Reece, as ever, was authoritative. He advanced up the stairs and Inspector Hazelmere met him at the top. He, too, in his professional manner was impressive and Alleyn thought: He's going to handle this.

"Are we to know," Mr. Reece asked, at large, "what has happened?"

"I was coming to see you, sir," said Inspector Hazelmere. "If you'll excuse me for a moment"—he addressed the company at large—"I'll ask everybody at the back, there, if you please, to return to whatever you were doing before you were disturbed. For your information, we have been obliged to take Miss Maria Bennini into custody"—he hesitated for a moment—"you may say protective custody," he added. "The situation is well in hand and we'll be glad to make that clear to you as soon as possible. Thank you. Mrs.—er—"

"Bacon," Alleyn murmured.

"Mrs. Bacon—if you would be kind enough—"

Mrs. Bacon was kind enough and the set was, as it were, cleared of supernumeraries.

For what, Alleyn thought, might well be the last time, Mr. Reece issued a colorless invitation to the study and was at some pains to include Alleyn. He also said that he was sure there would be no objection to Madame's singing maestro, for whom she had a great affection, Signor Lattienzo, and their old friend and associate, Mr. Ben Ruby, being present.

"They have both been with me throughout this dreadful ordeal," Mr. Reece said drearily and added that he also wished his secretary to be present and take notes.

The Inspector controlled any surprise he may have felt at this request. His glance, which was of the sharp and bright variety, rested for a moment on Hanley before he said there was no objection. In fact, he said, it had been his intention to ask for a general discussion. Alleyn thought that if there had been a slight juggling for the position of authority, the Inspector had politely come out on top. They all proceeded solemnly to the study and the soft leather chairs in front of the unlit fireplace. It was here, Alleyn reflected, that this case had taken on one of its more eccentric characteristics.

Inspector Hazelmere did not sit down. He took up his stance upon that widely accepted throne of authority, the hearthrug. He said: "With your permission, sir, I am going to request Chief Superintendent Alleyn to set out the events leading up to this crime. By a very strange but fortunate coincidence he was here and I was not. Mr. Alleyn."

He stepped aside and made a very slight gesture, handing over the hearthrug, as it were, to Alleyn, who accordingly took his place on it. Mr.

Reece seated himself at his desk, which was an ultramodern affair, streamlined and enormous. It accommodated two people, facing each other across it. Mr. Reece signaled to Hanley, who hurried into the second and less opulent seat and produced his notebook. Alleyn got the impression that Mr. Reece highly approved of these formalities. As usual he seemed to compose himself to hear the minutes of the last meeting. He took a leather container of keys from his pocket, looked as if he were surprised to see it, and swiveled round in his chair with it dangling from his fingers.

Alleyn said: "This is a very unusual way to follow up an arrest on such a serious charge, but I think that, taking all the circumstances, which are themselves extraordinary, into consideration, it is a sensible decision. Inspector Hazelmere and I hope that in hearing this account of the case and the difficulties it presents you will help us by correcting anything I may say if you know it to be in the smallest degree mistaken. Also we do beg you, if you can add any information that will clear up a point, disprove or confirm it, you will stop me and let us all hear what it is. That is really the whole purpose of the exercise. We ask for your help."

He paused.

For a moment or two nobody spoke and then Mr. Reece cleared his throat and said he was sure they all "appreciated the situation." Signor Lattienzo, still unlike his usual ebullient self, muttered "*Naturalmente*" and waved a submissive hand.

"O.K., O.K.," Ben Ruby said impatiently. "Anything to wrap it up and get shut of it all. Far as I'm concerned, I've always thought Maria was a bit touched. Right from the start I've had this intuition and now you tell me that's the story. She did it."

Alleyn said: "If you mean she killed her mistress single-handed, we don't think she did any such thing."

Mr. Reece drew back his feet as if he was about to rise but thought better of it. He continued to swing his keys.

Signor Lattienzo let out a strong Italian expletive and Ben Ruby's jaw dropped and remained in that position without his uttering a word. Hanley said "*What!*" on a shrill note and immediately apologized.

"In that case," Mr. Reece asked flatly, "why have you arrested her?"

The others made sounds of resentful agreement.

"For impaling the dead body with the stiletto thrust through the photograph," said Alleyn.

"This is diabolical," said Signor Lattienzo. "It is disgusting."

"What possible proof can you have of it?" Mr. Reece asked. "Do you know, now positively, that Marco is Strix and took the photograph?"

"Yes. He has admitted it."

"In that case how did she obtain it?"

"She came into this room when he was putting it into an envelope addressed to the *Watchman* in typescript, on Madame Sommita's instructions, by Mr. Hanley."

"That's right—" Hanley said. "The envelope was meant for her letter to the *Watchman* when she'd signed it. I've told you—" And then, on a calmer note, "I see what you mean. Marco would have thought it would be posted without—anybody—*me*—thinking anything of it. Yes, I see."

"Instead of which we believe Maria caught sight of Marco pushing the photograph into the envelope. Her curiosity was aroused. She waited until Marco had gone, and took it out. She kept it, and made the mistake of throwing the envelope into the fire. It fell, half burnt, through the bars of the grate into the ashpan, from where we recovered it."

"If this is provable and not merely conjecture," said Mr. Reece, swinging his keys, "do you argue that at this stage she anticipated the crime?"

"If the murder was the last in a long series of retributive crimes, it would appear so. In the original case an incriminating letter was transfixed to the body."

There followed a long silence. "So she was right," said Mr. Reece heavily. "She was right to be afraid. I shall never forgive myself."

Ben Ruby said Mr. Reece didn't want to start thinking that way. "We none of us thought there was anything in it," he pleaded. "She used to dream up such funny ideas. You couldn't credit them."

Signor Lattienzo threw up his hands. "Wolf. Wolf," he said.

"I've yet to be convinced," Mr. Reece said. "I cannot believe it of Maria. I know they used to fall out occasionally, but there was nothing in that. Maria was devoted. Proof!" he said still contemplating his keys. "You have advanced no proof."

"I see I must now give some account of the puzzle of the keys."

"The keys? Whose keys?" asked Mr. Reece, swinging his own.

Alleyn suppressed a crazy impulse to reply, "The Queen's keys," in the age-old challenge of the Tower of London. He merely gave as clear an account as possible of the enigma of the Sommita's key and the impossibility of her having had time to remove it from a bag in the bottom drawer of the dressing table and lock the bedroom door in the seconds that elapsed between her kicking out Mr. Reece and Maria and their hearing it click in the lock.

Mr. Reece chewed this over and then said: "One can only suppose that at this stage her bag was not in the drawer but close at hand."

"Even so: ask yourself. She orders you out, you shut the door and immediately afterwards hear it locked: a matter of perhaps two seconds."

"It may have already been in her hand."

"Do you remember her hands during the interview?"

"They were clenched. She was angry."

"Well—it could be argued, I suppose. Just. But there is a sequel," Alleyn said. And he told them of Maria's final performance and arrest.

"I'm afraid," he ended, "that all the pious protestations, all her passionate demands to perform the last duties, were an act. She realized that she had blundered, that we would, on her own statement, expect to find her mistress's key in the room, and that she must at all costs get into the room and push it under the body, where we would find it in due course."

"What did she say when you arrested her?" Lattienzo asked.

"Nothing. She hasn't spoken except—"

"Well? Except?"

"She accused Rupert Bartholomew of murder."

Hanley let out an exclamation. Lattienzo stared at him. "You spoke, Mr. Hanley?" he said.

"No, no. Nothing. Sorry."

Ben Ruby said: "All the same, you know—well, I mean you *can't* ignore —I mean to say, there *was* that scene, wasn't there? I mean she had put him through it, no kidding. And the curtain speech and the way he acted. I mean to say, he's the only one of us who you could say had motive and opportunity—I mean—"

"My good Ben," Lattienzo said wearily, "we all know, in general terms, what you mean. But when you say 'opportunity,' what *precisely* do you mean? Opportunity to murder? But Mr. Alleyn tells us he does not as yet accuse the perpetrator of the dagger-and-photograph operation of the murder. And Mr. Alleyn convinces me, for what it's worth, that he knows what he's talking about. I would like to ask Mr. Alleyn if he links Maria, who has been arrested for the photograph abomination, with the murder and if so what that link is. Or are we to suppose that Maria, on reentering the room, hot drink in hand, discovered the dead body and was inspired to go downstairs, unobserved by the milling crowd, remove the dagger from the wall, collect the photograph from wherever she'd put it, return to the bedroom, perform her atrocity, and then raise the alarm? Is that, as dear Ben would put it, the story?"

"Not quite," said Alleyn.

"Ah!" said Lattienzo. "So I supposed."

"I didn't say we don't suspect her of murder: on the contrary. I merely said she was arrested on the charge of mutilating the body, not on a charge of murder."

"But that may follow?"

Alleyn was silent.

"Which is as much as to say," Ben Ruby said, "that you reckon it's a case of conspiracy and that Maria is half of the conspiracy and that one of us—I mean of the people in this house—was the principal. Yeah?"

"Yes."

"Charming!" said Mr. Ruby.

"Are we to hear any more?" Mr. Reece asked. "After all, apart from the modus operandi in Maria's case, we have learned nothing new, have we? As, for instance, whether you have been able to clear any of us of suspicion. Particularly the young man—Bartholomew."

"Monty, my dear," said Lattienzo, who had turned quite pale, "how right you are. And here I would like to say, with the greatest emphasis, that I resist vehemently any suggestion, open or covert, that this unfortunate boy is capable of such a crime. Mr. Alleyn, I beg you to consider! What does such a theory ask us to accept? Consider his behavior."

"Yes," Alleyn said, "consider it. He makes what amounts to a public announcement of his break with her. He puts himself into the worst possible light as a potential murderer. He even writes a threatening message on a scrap of his score. He is at particular pains to avoid laying on an alibi. He faints, is taken upstairs, recovers, and hurries along to the bedroom, where he chloroforms and asphyxiates his victim and returns to his own quarters."

Lattienzo stared at Alleyn for a second or two. The color returned to his face, he made his little crowing sound and seized Alleyn's hands. "Ah!" he cried. "You agree! You see! You see! It is impossible! It is ridiculous!"

"If I may just pipe up," Hanley said, appealing to Mr. Reece. "I mean, all this virtuous indignation on behalf of the Boy Beautiful! Very touching and all that." He shot a glance at his employer and another at Lattienzo. "One might be forgiven for drawing one's own conclusions."

"That will do," said Mr. Reece.

"Well, all right, then, sir. Enough said. But I mean—after all, one would like to be officially in the clear. I mean: take me. From the time you escorted Madame upstairs and she turned you and Maria out until Maria returned and found her—dead—I was in the dining room and hall calming down guests and talking to Les and telling you about the Lake and making a list for Les to check the guests by. I really could not," said Hanley on a rising note of hysteria, "have popped upstairs and murdered Madame and come back, as bright as a button, to speed the parting guests and tramp about with umbrellas. And anyway," he added, "I hadn't got a key."

"As far as that goes," said Ben Ruby, "*she* could have let you in and I don't mean anything nasty. Just to set the record straight."

"Thank you very much," said Hanley bitterly.

"To return to the keys," Mr. Reece said slowly, still swinging his own as if to illustrate his point. "About the third key, *her* key." He appealed to Hazelmere and Alleyn. "There must be some explanation. Some quite simple explanation. Surely."

Alleyn looked at Hazelmere, who nodded very slightly.

"There is," said Alleyn, "a *very* simple explanation. The third key was in the bag in the bottom drawer, where it had lain unmolested throughout the proceedings."

Into the silence that followed there intruded a distant pulsation: the chopper returning, thought Alleyn.

Mr. Reece said: "But when Maria and I left—we—heard the key turn in the lock. What key? You've accounted for the other two. She locked us out with her own key."

"We think not."

"But Maria heard it, too. She has said so. I don't understand this," said Mr. Reece. "Unless— But no. No, I don't understand. Why did Maria do as you say she did? Come back and try to hide the key under—? It's horrible. *Why* did she do that?"

"Because, as I've suggested, she realized we would expect to find it."

"Ah. Yes. I take the point but all the same—"

"Monty," Signor Lattienzo cried out, "for pity's sake *do* something with those accursed keys. You are lacerating my nerves."

Mr. Reece looked at him blankly. "Oh?" he said. "Am I? I'm sorry." He hesitated, examined the key by which he had suspended the others and, turning to his desk, fitted it into one of the drawers. "Is that better?" he asked and unlocked the drawer.

Ben Ruby said in a voice that was pitched above its normal register: "I don't get any of this. All I know is we better look after ourselves. And as far as our lot goes—you, Monty, and Beppo and me—we were all sitting at the dinner table from the time you left Bella alive and throwing a temperament, until Maria raised the alarm." He turned on Alleyn. "That's right, isn't it? That's correct? Come on—isn't it?"

"Not quite," said Alleyn. "When Mr. Reece and Maria left Madame Sommita she was not throwing a temperament. She was dead."

II

In the bad old days of capital punishment it used to be said that you could tell when a verdict of guilty was about to be returned. The jury always avoided looking at the accused. Alleyn was reminded now, obliquely, of this dictum. Nobody moved. Nobody spoke. Everyone looked at him and only at him.

Inspector Hazelmere cleared his throat.

The helicopter landed. So loud, it might have been on the roof or outside on the gravel. The engine shut off and the inflowing silence was intolerable.

Mr. Reece said: "More police, I assume."

Hazelmere said: "That is correct, sir."

Somebody crossed the hall, and seconds later Sergeant Franks walked past the windows.

"I think, Chief Superintendent Alleyn," said Mr. Reece, "you must be out of your mind."

Alleyn took out his notebook. Hazelmere placed himself in front of Mr. Reece. "Montague Reece," he said, "I arrest you for the murder of Isabella Sommita and I have to warn you that anything you say will be taken down in writing and may be used in evidence."

"Hanley," Mr. Reece said, "get through to my solicitors in Sydney."

Hanley said in a shaking voice: "Certainly, sir." He took up the receiver, fumbled, and dropped it on the desk. He said to Alleyn: "I suppose—is it all right? I mean—"

Hazelmere said: "It's in order."

"Do it," Mr. Reece said. And then, loudly to Hazelmere, "The accusation is grotesque. You will do yourself a great deal of harm."

Alleyn wrote this down.

Mr. Reece looked round the room as if he were seeing it for the first time. He swiveled his chair and faced his desk. Hanley, drawn back in his chair with the receiver at his ear, watched him. Alleyn took a step forward.

"Here *are* the police," Mr. Reece observed loudly.

Hazelmere, Lattienzo, and Ruby turned to look.

Beyond the windows Sergeant Franks tramped past, followed by a uniform sergeant and a constable.

"No!" Hanley screamed. *"Stop him! No!"*

There was nothing but noise in the room.

Alleyn had not prevented Mr. Reece from opening the unlocked drawer and snatching out the automatic, but he had knocked up his arm. The bullet had gone through the top of a windowpane, and two succeeding shots had lodged in the ceiling. Dust fell from the overhead lampshades.

Two helmets and three deeply concerned faces appeared at the foot of the window, slightly distorted by pressure against glass. The owners rose and could be heard thundering round the house.

Alleyn, with Mr. Reece's arms secured behind his back, said, a trifle breathlessly: "That was a very silly thing to do, Signor Rossi."

III

". . . almost the only silly thing he did," Alleyn said. "He showed extraordinary coolness and judgment throughout. His one serious slip was to say he heard the key turn in the lock. Maria set that one up, and he felt he had to fall in with it. He was good at avoiding conflicts and that's the only time he told a direct lie."

"What I *can't* understand," Troy said, "is his inviting you of all people to his party."

"Only, I think, after the Sommita, or perhaps Hanley, told him about her letter to the Yard. It was dated a week before his invitations to us. Rather than un-pick her letter, he decided to confirm it. And I'm sure he really did *want* the portrait. Afterwards it could have been, for him, the equivalent of a scalp. And as for my presence in the house, I fancy it lent what the *mafiosi* call 'elegance' to the killing."

"My God," said Signor Lattienzo, "I believe you are right."

"There was one remark he made that brought me up with a round turn," Alleyn said. "He was speaking of her death to Ben Ruby and he said, 'And now she no longer casts a shadow.' "

"But that's—isn't it—a phrase used by—?"

"The *mafiosi?* Yes. So I had discovered when I read the book in the library. It was not in Mr. Reece's usual style, was it?"

Signor Lattienzo waited for a little and then said, "I assure you, my dear Alleyn, that I have sworn to myself that I will not pester you, but I immediately break my resolution to say that I die to know how you discovered his true identity. His name. 'Rossi.' "

"Have you ever noticed that when people adopt pseudonyms they are so often impelled to retain some kind of link with their old name. Often, it is the initials, often there is some kind of assonance—Reece—Rossi. M. V. Rossi—Montague V. Reece. He actually had the nerve to tell me his Bella had confided that she wished his surname didn't remind her of the 'enemy.' The M. V. Rossi signature in the book bears quite a strong resemblance to the Reece signature, spiky letters and all. He seems to have decided very early in life to opt out of the 'family' business. It may even have been at his father's suggestion. Papa Rossi leaves a hefty swag of ill-gotten gains, which Monty Reece manipulates brilliantly and with the utmost propriety and cleanest of noses. I think it must have amused him to plant the book up there with the diva's bi- and autobiographies. The book has been instructive. The victim in the case it deals with was a Rossi girl—his sister. A paper was stabbed to her heart. She had a brother, Michele-Victor Rossi, who disappeared."

"Our Mr. Reece?"

"It's a good guess."

"And Maria?"

"The widow Bennini? Who wouldn't tell me her maiden name. I wouldn't be surprised if it turns out to have been Rossi. He is said to have picked her up at the Italian Embassy. He may even have planted her there. Obviously they were in heavy cahoots. I imagine them enjoying a good gloat over the Strix ongoings."

Signor Lattienzo said: "Was Strix in Monty's pay?"

"So far there's no proof of it. It would fit in very tidily, wouldn't it? But all this is grossly speculative stuff. At best, merely Gilbertian 'corroborative detail.' The case rests on the bedrock fact that once you accept that the crime was committed at the earlier time, which the medical opinion confirms, everything falls into place and there are no difficulties. Nobody else could have done it, not even young Bartholomew, who was being tended in his room by you and Dr. Carmichael. The rest of us were at dinner. The doctors will testify that the stab was administered an appreciable time after death."

"And—he—Monty, took Bella up to her room and—he—?"

"With Maria's help, chloroformed and stifled her. I've been told that the diva, after cutting up rough always, without fail, required Maria to massage her shoulders. Maria actually told me she offered this service and was refused, but perhaps it was Maria, ready and waiting, who seized the opportunity to grind away at Madame's shoulders and then use the chloroform while Mr. Reece, who—all inarticulate sympathy—had been holding the victim's hands, now tightened his grip and when she was insensitive went in for the kill. He then joined us in the dining room, as you will remember, and told us she was not very well. Maria meanwhile prepared the hot drink and collected the dagger and photograph."

"So that extra touch was all her own?"

"If it was, I feel sure he approved it. It was in the *mafioso* manner. It had, they would consider, style and elegance."

"That," observed Signor Lattienzo, "as Monty himself would say, figures."

Bert came into the hall. He said they were ready and opened the front doors. There, outside, was the evening. Bell-birds chimed through the bush like rain distilled into sound. The trees, blurred in mist, were wet and smelt of honeydew. The Lake was immaculate and perfectly still.

Troy said: "This landscape belongs to birds: not to men, not to animals: huge birds that have gone now, stalked about in it. Except for birds it's empty."

Bert shut the doors of the Lodge behind them.

He and Alleyn and Troy and Signor Lattienzo walked across the graveled front and down to the jetty where Les waited in the launch.

A WREATH FOR RIVERA

Contents

Cast of Characters

<table>
<tr><td colspan="2">Lord Pastern and Bagott</td></tr>
<tr><td colspan="2">Lady Pastern and Bagott</td></tr>
<tr><td colspan="2">Félicité de Suze, her daughter</td></tr>
<tr><td colspan="2">The Honourable Edward Manx, Lord Pastern's second cousin</td></tr>
<tr><td colspan="2">Carlisle Wayne, Lord Pastern's niece</td></tr>
<tr><td colspan="2">Miss Henderson, companion-secretary to Lady Pastern</td></tr>
<tr><td>Spence
Miss Parker
William
Mary
Myrtle
Hortense</td><td>domestic staff at Duke's Gate</td></tr>
<tr><td>Breezy Bellairs
Happy Hart, pianist
Sydney Skelton, tympanist
Carlos Rivera, piano-accordionist</td><td>of Breezy Bellair's Boys</td></tr>
<tr><td colspan="2">Caesar Bonn, maître de café at the Metronome</td></tr>
<tr><td colspan="2">David Hahn, his secretary</td></tr>
<tr><td colspan="2">Nigel Bathgate, of the Evening Chronicle</td></tr>
<tr><td colspan="2">Dr. Allington</td></tr>
<tr><td colspan="2">Mrs. Roderick Alleyn</td></tr>
<tr><td>Roderick Alleyn, Chief Detective-Inspector
Detective-Inspector Fox
Dr. Curtis
Detective-Sergeant Bailey, finger-print expert
Detective-Sergeant Thompson, photographer
Detective-Sergeants Gibson, Marks, Scott and Sallis
Sundry policemen, waiters, bandsmen and so on</td><td>of the Criminal Investigation Department, New Scotland Yard</td></tr>
</table>

CHAPTER I

Letters

FROM LADY PASTERN and Bagott to her niece by marriage, Miss Carlisle Wayne:

3, DUKE'S GATE
EATON PLACE
LONDON, S.W.I

MY DEAREST CARLISLE,

I am informed with that air of inconsequence which characterizes all your uncle's utterances, of your arrival in England. Welcome Home. You may be interested to learn that I have rejoined your uncle. My motive is that of expediency. Your uncle proposed to give Clochemere to the Nation and has returned to Duke's Gate, where, as you may have heard, I have been living for the last five years. During the immediate post-war period I shared its dubious amenities with members of an esoteric Central European sect. Your uncle granted them what I believe colonials would call squatters' rights, hoping no doubt to force me back upon the Cromwell Road or the society of my sister Désirée, with whom I have quarrelled since we were first able to comprehend each other's motives.

Other aliens were repatriated, but the sect remained. It will be a sufficient indication of their activities if I tell you that they caused a number of boulders to be set up in the principal reception room, that their ceremonies began at midnight and were conducted in antiphonal screams, that their dogma appeared to prohibit the use of soap and water and that they were forbidden to cut their hair. Six months ago they returned to Central Europe (I have never inquired the precise habitat) and I was left mistress of this house. I had it cleaned and prepared myself for tranquillity. Judge of my dismay! I found tranquillity intolerable. I had, it seems, acclimatized myself to nightly pandemonium. I had become accustomed to frequent encounters with persons who resembled the minor and dirtier prophets. I was unable to endure silence, and the unremarkable presence of servants. In fine, I was lonely. When one is lonely one thinks of one's mistakes. I thought of your uncle. Is one ever entirely bored by the incomprehensible? I doubt it. When I married your uncle (you will recollect that he was an attaché at your embassy in Paris and a frequent caller at my parents' house) I was already a widow. I was not, therefore, *jeune fille*. I did not demand Elysium. Equally I did not anticipate the ridiculous. It is understood that after a certain time one should not expect the impossible of one's husband. If he is tactful one remains ignorant. So much the better. One is reconciled. But your uncle is not tactful. On the contrary, had there been liaisons of the sort which I trust I have indicated, I should have immediately become aware of them. Instead of second or possibly third establishments I found myself confronted in turn by Salvation Army Citadels, by retreats for Indian yogis, by apartments devoted to the study of Voodoo; by a hundred and one ephemeral and ludicrous obsessions. Your uncle has turned with appalling virtuosity from the tenets of Christadelphians to the practice of nudism. He has perpetrated antics which, with his increasing years, have become the more intolerable. Had he been content to play the pantaloon by himself and leave me to deplore, I should have perhaps been reconciled. On the contrary he demanded my collaboration.

For example in the matter of nudism. Imagine me, a de Fouteaux, suffering a proposal that I should promenade, without costume, behind laurel hedges in The Weald of Kent. It was at this juncture and upon this provocation that I first left your uncle. I have returned at intervals only to be driven away again by further imbecilities. I have said nothing of his temper, of his passion for scenes, of his minor but distressing idiosyncrasies. These failings have, alas, become public property.

Yet, my dearest Carlisle, as I have indicated, we are together again at Duke's Gate. I decided that silence had become intolerable and that I should be forced to seek a flat. Upon this decision came a letter from your uncle. He is now interested in music and has associated himself with a band in which he performs upon the percussion instruments. He wished to use the largest of the reception rooms for practice; in short he proposed to rejoin me at Duke's Gate. I am attached to this house. Where your uncle is, there also is noise and noise has become a necessity for me. I consented.

Félicité, also, has rejoined me. I regret to say I am deeply perturbed on account of Félicité. If your uncle realized, in the smallest degree, his duty as a stepfather, he might exert some influence. On the contrary he ignores, or regards with complacency, an attachment so undesirable that I, her mother, cannot bring myself to write more explicitly of it. I can only beg, my dearest Carlisle, that you make time to visit us. Félicité has always respected your judgment. I hope most earnestly that you will come to us for the first weekend in next month. Your uncle, I believe, intends to write to you himself. I join my request to his. It will be delightful to see you again, my dearest Carlisle, and I long to talk to you.

Your affectionate aunt,
CÉCILE DE FOUTEAUX PASTERN AND BAGOTT

From Lord Pastern and Bagott to his niece Miss Carlisle Wayne:

3, DUKE'S GATE
EATON PLACE
LONDON, S.W.1

DEAR LISLE,

I hear you've come back. Your aunt tells me she's asked you to visit us. Come on the third and we'll give you some music.

Your aunt's living with me again.

Your affectionate uncle
GEORGE

From "The Helping Hand," G.P.F.'s page in *Harmony:*

DEAR G.P.F.

I am eighteen and unofficially engaged to be married. My fiancé is madly jealous and behaves in a manner that I consider more than queer and terribly alarming. I enclose details under separate cover because after all he might read this and then we *should* be in the soup. Also five shillings for a special Personal Chat letter. Please help me.

"TOOTS"

Poor Child in Distress, let me help you if I can. Remember I shall speak as a man and that is perhaps well, for the masculine mind is able to understand this strange self-torture that is clouding your fiancé's love for you and making you so unhappy. Believe me, there is only *one* way. You must be patient. You must prove your love by your candour. Do not tire of reassuring him that his suspicions are groundless. Remain tranquil. *Go on loving him.* Try a little gentle laughter but if it is unsuccessful *do not continue. Never* let him think you impatient. A thought. *There are some natures so delicate and sensitive that they must be handled like flowers. They need sun.*

They must be tended. Otherwise their spiritual growth is checked. Your Personal Chat letter will reach you to-morrow.

Footnote to G.P.F.'s page. G.P.F. will write you a very special Personal Chat if you send a stamped and addressed envelope and five shilling postal order to "Personal Chat. *Harmony*. 5 Materfamilias Lane, E.C. 2."

From Miss Carlisle Wayne to Miss Félicité de Suze:

FRIARS PARDON
BENHAM
BUCKS.

DEAR FÉE,

I've had rather a queer letter from Aunt Cile, who wants me to come on the third. What have you been up to? Love,

LISLE

From the Honourable Edward Manx to Miss Carlisle Wayne:

HARROW FLATS
SLOANE SQUARE
LONDON, S.W.1

DEAREST LISLE,

Cousin Cécile says you are invited to Duke's Gate for the weekend on Saturday the third. I shall come down to Benham in order to drive you back. Did you know she wants to marry me to Félicité? I'm really not at all keen and neither, luckily, is Fée. She's fallen in a big way for an extremely dubious number who plays a piano-accordion in Cousin George's band. I imagine there's a full-dress row in the offing *à cause,* as Cousin Cécile would say, *de* the band and particularly *de* the dubious number whose name is Carlos something. They aren't 'alf cups of tea are they? Why do you go away to foreign parts? I shall arrive at about 5 P.M. on the Saturday.

Love,
NED

From the *Monogram* gossip column:

Rumour hath it that Lord Pastern and Bagott, who is a keen exponent of boogie-woogie, will soon be heard at a certain restaurant "not a hundred miles from Piccadilly." Lord Pastern and Bagott, who, of course, married Madame de Suze, (née de Fouteaux) plays the tympani with enormous zest. His band includes such well-known exponents as Carlos Rivera and is conducted by none other than the inimitable Breezy Bellairs, both of the Metronome. By the way, I saw lovely Miss Félicité (Fée) de Suze, Lady Pastern and Bagott's daughter by her first marriage, lunching the other day at the Tarmac *à deux* with the Hon. Edward Manx, who is, of course, her second cousin on the distaff side.

From Mr. Carlos Rivera to Miss Félicité de Suze:

102 BEDFORD MANSIONS
AUSTERLY SQUARE
LONDON, S.W.1

LISTEN GLAMOROUS,

You cannot do this thing to me. I am not an English Honourable This or Lord That to sit complacent while my woman makes a fool of me. No. With me it is all or nothing. I am a scion of an ancient house. I do not permit trespassers and I am tired, I am very tired indeed, of waiting. I wait no longer. You announce immediately our engagement or—finish! It is understood? *Adios*

CARLOS DE RIVERA

Telegram from Miss Félicité de Suze to Miss Carlisle Wayne:

DARLING FOR PITY'S SAKE COME EVERYTHING TOO TRICKY AND PECULIAR HONESTLY DO COME GENUINE CRI DE COEUR TONS OF LOVE DARLING FEE.

Telegram from Miss Carlisle Wayne to Lady Pastern and Bagott:

THANK YOU SO MUCH LOVE TO COME ARRIVING ABOUT SIX SATURDAY 3RD. CARLISLE.

CHAPTER II

The Persons Assemble

I

AT PRECISELY ELEVEN O'CLOCK in the morning G.P.F. walked in at a side door of the *Harmony* offices in 5 Materfamilias Lane, E.C.2. He went at once to his own room. PRIVATE G.P.F. was written in white letters on the door. He unwound the scarf with which he was careful to protect his nose and mouth from the fog, and hung it, together with his felt hat and overcoat, on a peg behind his desk. He then assumed a green eye-shade, and shot a bolt in his door. By so doing he caused a notice, ENGAGED, to appear on the outside.

His gas fire was burning brightly and the tin saucer of water set before it to humidify the air sent up a little drift of steam. The window was blanketed outside by fog. It was as if a yellow curtain had been hung on the wrong side of the glass. The footsteps of passers-by sounded close and dead and one could hear the muffled coughs and shut-in voices of people in a narrow street on a foggy morning. G.P.F. rubbed his hands together, hummed a lively air, seated himself at his desk and switched on his green-shaded lamp. "Cosy," he thought. The light glinted on his dark glasses, which he took off and replaced with reading spectacles.

"One, two. Button your boot," sang G.P.F. in a shrill falsetto and pulled a wire basket of unopened letters toward him. "Three, four, knock on the gate," he sang facetiously and slit open the top letter. A postal order for five shillings fell out on the desk.

DEAR G.P.F. [he read],

I feel I simply must write and thank you for your *lush* Private Chat letter—which I may as well confess has rocked me to my foundations. You couldn't be more right to call yourself Guide, Philosopher and Friend, honestly you couldn't. I've thought so much about what you've told me and I can't help wondering what you're *like*. To look at and listen to, I mean. I think your voice must be rather deep ["Oh Crumbs!" G.P.F. murmured] and I'm sure you are tall. I wish—

He skipped restlessly through the next two pages and arrived at the peroration:

I've tried madly to follow your advice but my young man really is! I can't help thinking that it would be immensely energizing to talk to you. I mean really *talk*. But I suppose that's hopelessly out of bounds, so I'm having another five bob's worth of Private Chat.

G.P.F. followed the large flamboyant script and dropped the pages, one by one, into a second wire basket. Here, at last, was the end.

I suppose he would be madly jealous if he knew I had written to you like this but I just felt I had to. Your grateful

"TOOTS"

G.P.F. reached for his pad of copy, gazed for a moment in a benign absent manner at the fog-lined window and then fell to. He wrote with great fluency, sighing and muttering under his breath.

"Of course I am happy," he began, "to think that I have helped." The phrases ran out from his pencil ". . . you must still be patient . . . sure you will understand . . . anonymity . . . just think of G.P.F. as a friendly ghost . . . write again if you will . . . more than usually interested . . . best of luck and my blessing . . ." When it was finished he pinned the postal note to the top sheet and dropped the whole in a further basket which bore the legend "Personal Chat."

The next letter was written in a firm hand on good notepaper. G.P.F. contemplated it with his head on one side, whistling between his teeth.

The writer [it said] is fifty years old and has recently consented to rejoin her husband who is fifty-five. He is eccentric to the verge of lunacy but, it is understood, not actually certifiable. A domestic crisis has arisen in which he refuses to take the one course compatible with his responsibilities as a stepfather. In a word, my daughter contemplates a marriage that from every point of view but that of unbridled infatuation is disastrous. If further details are required I am prepared to supply them, but the enclosed cuttings from newspapers covering a period of sixteen years will, I believe, speak for themselves. I do not wish this communication to be published, but enclose a five-shilling postal order which I understand will cover a letter of personal advice.

I am etc.,

Cécile de Fouteaux Pastern and Bagott

G.P.F. dropped the letter delicately and turned over the sheaf of paper clippings. "Peer Sued for Kidnapping Stepdaughter," he read; "Peer Practices Nudism"; "Scene in Mayfair Courtroom"; "Lord Pastern Again"; "Lady Pastern and Bagott Seeks Divorce"; "Peer Preaches Free Love"; "Rebuke from Judge"; "Lord Pastern Now Goes Yogi"; "Boogie-Woogie Peer"; "Infinite Variety."

G.P.F. glanced through the letterpress beneath these headlines, made a small impatient sound and began to write very rapidly indeed. He was still at this employment when, glancing up at the blinded window, he saw, as if on a half-developed negative, a shoulder emerge through the fog. A face peered, a hand was pressed against the glass and then closed to tap twice. G.P.F. unlocked his door and returned to his desk. A moment later the visitor came coughing down the passage. *"Entrez!"* called G.P.F. modishly and his visitor walked into the room.

"Sorry to harry you," he said. "I thought you'd be in, this morning. It's the monthly subscription to that relief fund. Your signature to the cheque."

G.P.F. swivelled round in his chair and held out Lady Pastern's letter. His visitor took it, whistled, read it through and burst out laughing. "Well!" he said. "Well, *honestly.*"

"Press cuttings," said G.P.F. and handed them to him.

"She *must* be in a fizz! That it should come to this!"

"Damned if I know why you say that."

"I'm sorry. Of course there's no reason, but– How have you replied?"

"A stinger."

"May I see it?"

"By all means. There it is. Give me the cheque."

The visitor leant over the desk, at the same time reading the copy sheets and groping in his breast pocket for his wallet. He found a cheque and, still reading, laid it on the desk. Once he looked up quickly as if to speak but G.P.F. was bent over the cheque so he finished the letter.

"Strong," he said.

"Here's the cheque," said G.P.F.

"Thank you." He glanced at it. The signature was written in a small, fat and incredibly neat calligraphy: "G.P. Friend."

"His dottiness? No, all the other Settingers seem to be tolerably sane. No, I fancy Cousin George is a sport. A sort of monster, in the nicest sense of the word."

"That's a comfort. After all I'm his blood niece, if that's the way to put it. You're only a collateral on the distaff side."

"Is that a cheap sneer, darling?"

"I wish you'd put me wise to the current set-up. I've had some very queer letters and telegrams. What's Félicité up to? Are you going to marry her?"

"I'll be damned if I do," said Edward with some heat. "It's Cousin Cécile who thought that one up. She offered to house me at Duke's Gate when my flat was wrested from me. I was there for three weeks before I found a new one and naturally I took Fée out a bit and so on. It now appears that the invitation was all part of a deep-laid plot of Cousin Cécile's. She really is excessively French, you know. It seems that she went into a sort of state-huddle with my mama and talked about Félicité's *dot* and the desirability of the old families standing firm. It was all terrifically Proustian. My mama, who was born in the colonies and doesn't like Félicité anyway, kept her head and preserved an air of impenetrable grandeur until the last second when she suddenly remarked that she never interfered in my affairs and wouldn't mind betting I'd marry an organizing secretary in the Society for Closer Relations with Soviet Russia."

"Was Aunt Cile at all rocked?"

"She let it pass as a joke in poor taste."

"What about Fée herself?"

"She's in a great to-do about her young man. He, I don't mind telling you, is easily the nastiest job of work in an unreal sort of way that you are ever likely to encounter. He glistens from head to foot and is called Carlos Rivera."

"One mustn't be insular."

"No doubt, but wait till you see him. He goes in for jealousy in a big way and he says he's the scion of a noble Spanish-American family. I don't believe a word of it and I think Félicité has her doubts."

"Didn't you say in your letter that he played the piano-accordion?"

"At the Metronome, in Breezy Bellairs's Band. He walks out in a spotlight, and undulates. Cousin George is going to pay Breezy some fabulous sum to let him, Cousin George, play the tympani. That's how Félicité met Carlos."

"Is she really in love with him?"

"Madly, she says, but she's beginning to take a poor view of his jealousy. He can't go dancing with her himself, because of his work. If she goes to the Metronome with anyone else he looks daggers over his piano-accordion and comes across and sneers at them during the solo number. If she goes to other places he finds out from other bandsmen. They appear to be a very close corporation. Of course, being Cousin George's step-daughter, she's used to scenes, but she's getting a bit rattled nevertheless. It seems that Cousin Cécile, after her interview with my mama, asked Félicité if she thought she could love me. Fée telephoned at once to know if I was up to any nonsense and asked me to lunch with her. So we did and some fool put it in the paper. Carlos read it and went into his act with unparalleled vigour. He talked about knives and what his family do with their women when they are flighty."

"Fée *is* a donkey," said Carlisle after a pause.

"You, my dearest Lisle, are telling me."

IV

Three, Duke's Gate, Eaton Place, was a pleasant Georgian house of elegant though discreet proportions. Its front had an air of reticence which was modified by a fanlight, a couple of depressed arches and beautifully designed doors. One might have hazarded a guess that this was the town house of some tranquil wealthy family who in pre-war days had occupied it at appropriate times and punctually left it in the charge of caretakers during the late summer and the shooting seasons. A house for orderly, leisured and unremarkable people, one might have ventured.

Edward Manx dropped his cousin there, handing her luggage over to a mild elderly man-servant and reminding her that they would meet again at dinner. She entered the hall and noticed with pleasure that it was unchanged.

"Her ladyship is in the drawing-room, miss," said the butler. "Would you prefer—?"

"I'll go straight in, Spence."

"Thank you, miss. You are in the yellow room, miss. I'll have your luggage taken up."

Carlisle followed him to the drawing-room on the first floor. As they reached the landing, a terrific rumpus broke out beyond a doorway on their left.

A saxophone climbed through a series of lewd dissonances into a prolonged shriek; a whistle was blown and cymbals clashed. "A wireless, at last, Spence?" Carlisle ejaculated. "I thought they were forbidden."

"That is his lordship's band, miss. They practise in the ballroom."

"The band," Carlistle muttered. "I'd forgotten. Good heavens!"

"Miss Wayne, my lady," said Spence, in the doorway.

Lady Pastern and Bagott advanced from the far end of a long room. She was fifty and tall for a Frenchwoman. Her figure was impressive, her hair rigidly groomed, her dress admirable. She had the air of being encased in a transparent, closely fitting film that covered her head as well as her clothes and permitted no disturbance of her surface. Her voice had edge. She used the faultless diction and balanced phraseology of the foreigner who has perfect command but no love of the English language.

"My dearest Carlisle," she said crisply, and kissed her niece with precision, on both cheeks.

"Dear Aunt Cile, how nice to see you."

"It is charming of you to come."

Carlisle thought that they uttered these greetings like characters in a somewhat dated comedy, but their pleasure, nevertheless, was real. They had an affection for each other, an unexacting enjoyment of each other's company. "What I like about Aunt Cécile," she had said to Edward, "is her refusal to be rattled about anything." He had reminded her of Lady Pastern's occasional rages and Carlisle retorted that these outbursts acted like safety-valves and had probably saved her aunt many times from committing some act of physical violence upon Lord Pastern.

They sat together by the large window. Carlisle, responding punctually to the interchange of inquiries and observations which Lady Pastern introduced, allowed her gaze to dwell with pleasure on the modest cornices and well-proportioned panels; on chairs, tables and cabinets which, while they had no rigid correspondence of period, achieved an agreeable harmony born of long association. "I've always liked this room," she said presently. "I'm glad you don't change it."

"I have defended it," Lady Pastern said, "in the teeth of your uncle's most determined assaults."

"Ah," thought Carlisle, "the preliminaries are concluded. Now, we're off."

"Your uncle," Lady Pastern continued, "has, during the last sixteen years, made periodic attempts to introduce prayer-wheels, brass Buddhas, a totem-pole, and the worst excesses of the surrealists. I have withstood them all. On one occasion I reduced to molten silver an image of some Aztec deity. Your uncle purchased it in Mexico City. Apart from its repellent appearance I had every reason to believe it spurious."

"He doesn't change," Carlisle murmured.

"It would be more correct, my dear child, to say that he is constant in inconstancy." Lady Pastern made a sudden and vigorous gesture with both her hands. "He is ridiculous to contemplate," she said strongly, "and entirely impossible to live with. A madman, except in a few unimportant technicalities. He is not, alas, certifiable. If he were, I should know what to do."

"Oh, come!"

"I repeat, Carlisle, I should know what to do. Do not misunderstand me. For myself, I am resigned. I have acquired armour. I can suffer perpetual humiliation. I can shrug my shoulders at unparalleled buffooneries. But when my daughter is involved," said Lady Pastern with uplifted bust, "complaisance is out of the question. I assert myself. I give battle."

"What's Uncle George up to, exactly?"

"He is conniving, where Félicité is concerned, at disaster. I cannot hope that you are unaware of her attachment."

"Well–"

"Evidently, you are aware of it. A professional bandsman who, as no doubt you heard on your arrival, is here, now, at your uncle's invitation, in the ballroom. It is almost certain that Félicité is listening to him. An utterly impossible young man of a vulgarity–" Lady Pastern paused and her lips trembled. "I have seen them together at the theatre," she said. "He is beyond everything. One cannot begin to describe. I am desperate."

"I'm so sorry, Aunt Cile," Carlisle said uneasily.

"I knew I should have your sympathy, dearest child. I hope I shall enlist your help. Félicité admires and loves you. She will naturally make you her confidante."

"Yes, but, Aunt Cile–"

A clamour of voices broke out in some distant part of the house. "They are going," said Lady Pastern hurriedly. "It is the end of the *répétition*. In a moment your uncle and Félicité will appear. Carlisle, may I implore you–"

"I don't suppose–" Carlisle began dubiously, and at that juncture, hearing her uncle's voice on the landing, rose nervously to her feet. Lady Pastern, with a grimace of profound significance, laid her hand on her niece's arm. Carlisle felt a hysterical giggle rise in her throat. The door opened and Lord Pastern and Bagott came trippingly into the room.

CHAPTER III

Preprandial

I

HE WAS SHORT, not more than five foot seven, but so compactly built that he did not give the impression of low stature. Everything about him was dapper, though not obtrusively so; his clothes, the flower in his coat, his well-brushed hair and moustache. His eyes, light grey with pinkish rims, had a hot impertinent look, his underlip jutted out and there were clearly defined spots of local colour over his cheekbones. He came briskly into the room, bestowed a restless kiss upon his niece and confronted his wife.

"Who's dinin'?" he said.

"Ourselves, Félicité, Carlisle, of course, and Edward Manx. And I have asked Miss Henderson to join us to-night."

"Two more," said Lord Pastern. "I've asked Bellairs and Rivera."

"That is quite impossible, George," said Lady Pastern, calmly.

"Why?"

"Apart from other unanswerable considerations, there is not enough food for two extra guests."

"Tell 'em to open a tin."

"I cannot receive these persons for dinner."

Lord Pastern grinned savagely. "All right. Rivera can take Félicité to a restaurant and Bellairs can come here. Same number as before. How are you, Lisle?"

"I'm very well, Uncle George."

"Félicité will not dine out with this individual, George. I shall not permit it."

"You can't stop 'em."

"Félicité will respect my wishes."

"Don't be an ass," said Lord Pastern. "You're thirty years behind the times, m'dear. Give a gel her head and she'll find her feet." He paused, evidently delighted with this aphorism. "Way you're goin', you'll have an elopement on your hands. Comes to that, I don't see the objection."

"Are you demented, George?"

"Half the women in London'd give anything to be in Fée's boots."

"A Mexican bandsman."

"Fine, well-set-up young feller. Inoculate your old stock. That's Shakespeare, ain't it Lisle? I understand he comes of a perfectly good Spanish family. *Hidalgo,* or whatever it is," he added vaguely. "A feller of good family happens to be an artist and you go and condemn him. Sort of thing that makes you sick." He turned to his niece: "I've been thinkin' seriously of givin' up the title, Lisle."

"George!"

"About dinner, can you find something for them to eat or can't you? Speak up."

Lady Pastern's shoulders rose with a shudder. She glanced at Carlisle, who thought she detected a glint of cunning in her aunt's eye. "Very well, George," Lady Pastern said. "I shall speak to the servants. I shall speak to Dupont. Very well."

Lord Pastern darted an extremely suspicious glance at his wife and sat down. "Nice to see you, Lisle," he said. "What have you been doin' with yourself?"

"I've been in Greece, Famine Relief."

"If people understood dietetics there wouldn't be all this starvation," said Lord Pastern darkly. "Are you keen on music?"

Carlisle returned a guarded answer. Her aunt, she realized, was attempting to convey by means of a fixed stare and raised eyebrows some message of significance.

"I've taken it up, seriously," Lord Pastern continued. "Swing. Boogie-woogie. Jive. Find it keeps me up to the mark." He thumped with his heel on the carpet, beat his hands together and in a strange nasal voice intoned: " 'Shoo-shoo-shoo, baby, Bye-bye, bye Baby.' "

The door opened and Félicité de Suze came in. She was a striking young woman with large black eyes, a wide mouth and an air of being equal to anything. She cried, "Darling—you're heaven its very self," and kissed Carlisle with enthusiasm. Lord Pastern was still clapping and chanting. His stepdaughter took up the burden of his song, raised a finger and jerked rhythmically before him. They grinned at each other. "You're coming along very prettily indeed, George," she said.

Carlisle wondered what her impression would have been if she were a complete stranger. Would she, like Lady Pastern, have decided that her uncle was eccentric to the point of derangement? "No," she thought, "probably not. There's really a kind of terrifying sanity about him. He's overloaded with energy, he says exactly what he thinks and he does exactly what he wants to do. But he's an oversimplification of type, and he's got no perspective. He's never mildly interested in anything. But which of us," Carlisle reflected, "has not, at some time, longed to play the big drum?"

Félicité, with an abandon that Carlisle found unconvincing, flung herself into the sofa beside her mother. "Angel," she said richly, "don't be so *grande dame!* George and I are having fun!"

Lady Pastern disengaged herself and rose. "I must see Dupont."

"Ring for Spence," said her husband. "Why d'you want to go burrowin' about in the servants' quarters?"

Lady Pastern pointed out, with great coldness, that in the present food shortage one did not, if one wished to retain the services of one's cook, send a message at seven in the evening to the effect that there would be two extra for dinner. In any case, she added, however great her tact, Dupont would almost certainly give notice.

"He'll give us the same dinner as usual," her husband rejoined. "The Three Courses of Monsieur Dupont!"

"Extremely witty," said Lady Pastern coldly. She then withdrew.

"George!" said Félicité. "Have you won?"

"I should damn' well think so. Never heard anything so preposterous in me life. Ask a couple of people to dine and your mother behaves like Lady Macbeth. I'm going to have a bath."

When he had gone, Félicité turned to Carlisle, and made a wide helpless gesture. "Darling, *what* a life! Honestly! One prances about from moment to moment on the edge of a volcano, *never* knowing when there'll be a major eruption. I suppose you've heard all about ME."

"A certain amount."

"He's madly attractive."

"In what sort of way?"

Félicité smiled and shook her head. "My dear Lisle, he just does things for me."

"He's not by any chance a bounder?"

"He can bound like a ping-pong ball and I won't bat an eyelid. To me he's heaven; *but* just plain heaven."

"Come off it, Fée," said Carlisle. "I've heard all this before. What's the catch in it?"

Félicité looked sideways at her. "How do you mean, the catch?"

"There's always a catch in your young men, darling, when you rave like this about them."

Félicité began to walk showily about the room. She had lit a cigarette and wafted it to and fro between two fingers, nursing her right elbow in the palm of the left hand. Her manner became remote. "When English people talk about a bounder," she said, "they invariably refer to someone who has more charm and less *gaucherie* than the average Englishman."

"I couldn't disagree more; but go on."

Félicité said loftily: "Of course I knew from the first Mama would kick like the devil. *C'la va sans dire.* And I don't deny Carlos is a bit tricky. In fact, 'It's hell but it's worth it' is a fairly accurate summing-up of the situation at the moment. I'm adoring it, really—I think."

"I don't think."

"Yes, I am," said Félicité violently. "I adore a situation. I've been brought up on situations. Think of George. You know, I honestly believe I've got more in common with George than I would have had with my own father. From all accounts, Papa was excessively *rangé*."

"You'd do with a bit more orderliness yourself, old girl. In what way is Carlos tricky?"

"Well, he's just *so* jealous he's like a Spanish novel."

"I've never read a Spanish novel unless you count *Don Quixote* and I'm certain you haven't. What's he do?"

"My dear, everything. Rages and despairs and sends frightful letters by special messenger. I got a stinker this morning, *à cause de*—well, *à cause de* something that really is a bit daffy."

She halted and inhaled deeply. Carlisle remembered the confidences that Félicité had poured out in her convent days, concerning what she called her "raves." There had been the music master who had fortunately snubbed Félicité and the medical student who hadn't. There had been the brothers of the other girls and an actor whom she attempted to waylay at a charity matinée. There had been a male medium, engaged by Lord Pastern during his spiritualistic period, and a dietician—Carlisle pulled herself together and listened to the present recital. It appeared that there was a crisis: a *crise* as Félicité called it. She used far more occasional French than her mother and was fond of laying her major calamities at the door of Gallic temperament.

"—and as a matter of fact," Félicité was saying, "I hadn't so much as smirked at another *soul,* and there he was seizing me by the wrists and giving me that shattering sort of look that begins at your boots and travels up to your face and then makes the return trip. And breathing loudly, don't you know, through the nose. I don't deny that the first time was rather fun. But after he got wind of old Edward it really was, and I may say still is, beyond a joke. And now to crown everything, there's the *crise.*"

"But what crisis? You haven't said—"

For the first time Félicité looked faintly embarrassed.

"He found a letter," she said. "In my bag. Yesterday."

"You aren't going to tell me he goes fossicking in your bag? And what letter, for pity's sake? Honestly, Fée!"

"I don't expect you to understand," Félicité said grandly. "We were lunching and he hadn't got a cigarette. I was doing my face at the time and I told him to help himself to my case. The letter came out of the bag with the case."

"And he—well, never mind. *What* letter?"

"I know you're going to say I'm mad. It was a sort of rough draft of a letter I sent to somebody. It had a bit in it about Carlos. When I saw it in his hand I was pretty violently rocked. I said something like 'Hi-hi you can't read that,' and of course with Carlos that tore everything wide open. He said 'So.' "

"So what?"

"So, all by itself. He does that. He's Latin-American."

"I thought that sort of 'so' was German."

"Whatever it is I find it terrifying. I began to fluff and puff and tried to pass it off with a jolly laugh but he said that either he could trust me or he couldn't and if he could, how come I wouldn't let him read a letter? I completely lost my head and grabbed it and he began to hiss. We were in a restaurant."

"Good Lord!"

"Well, I know. Obviously he was going to react in a really big way. So in the end the only thing seemed to be to let him have the letter. So I gave it to him on condition he wouldn't read it till we got back to the car. The drive home was hideous. But hideous."

"But what was in the letter, if one may ask, and who was it written to? You are confusing, Fée."

There followed a long uneasy silence. Félicité lit another cigarette. "Come on," said Carlisle at last.

"It happened," said Félicité haughtily, "to be written to a man whom I don't actually know, asking for advice about Carlos and me. Professional advice."

"What can you mean! A clergyman! Or a lawyer?"

"I don't think so. He'd written me rather a marvellous letter and this was thanking him. Carlos, of course, thought it was for Edward. The worst bit, from Carlos's point of view, was where I said: 'I suppose he'd be madly jealous if he knew I'd written to you like this.' Carlos really got weaving after he read that. He—"

Félicité's lips trembled. She turned away and began to speak rapidly, in a high voice. "He roared and stormed and wouldn't listen to anything. It was devastating. You can't conceive what it was like. He said I was to announce our engagement at once. He said if I didn't he'd—he said he'd go off and just simply end it all— He's given me a week. I've got till next Tuesday. That's all. I've got to announce it before next Tuesday."

"And you don't want to?" Carlisle asked gently. She saw Félicité's shoulders quiver and went to her. "Is that it, Fée?"

The voice quavered and broke. Félicité drove her hands through her hair. "I don't know *what* I want," she sobbed. "Lisle, I'm in such a muddle. I'm terrified, Lisle. It's so damned awful, Lisle. I'm terrified."

II

Lady Pastern had preserved throughout the war and its exhausted aftermath an unbroken formality. Her rare dinner parties had, for this reason, acquired the air of period pieces. The more so since, by feat of superb domestic strategy, she had contrived to retain at Duke's Gate a staff of trained servants, though a depleted one. As she climbed into a long dress, six years old, Carlisle reflected that if the food shortage persisted, her aunt would soon qualify for the same class as that legendary Russian nobleman who presided with perfect equanimity at an interminable banquet of dry bread and water.

She had parted with Félicité, who was still shaking and incoherent, on the landing: "You'll see him at dinner," Félicité had said. "You'll see what I mean." And with a spurt of defiance: "And anyway, I don't care what anyone thinks. If I'm in a mess, it's a thrilling mess. And if I want to get out of it, it's not for other people's reasons. It's only because— Oh, God, what's it matter!"

Félicité had then gone into her own room and slammed the door. It was perfectly obvious, Carlisle reflected, as she finished her face and lit a cigarette, that the wretched girl was terrified and that she herself would, during the week-end, be a sort of buffer-state between Félicité, her mother and her stepfather. "And the worst of it is," Carlisle thought crossly, "I'm fond of them and will probably end by involving myself in a major row with all three at once."

She went down to the drawing-room. Finding nobody there, she wandered disconsolately across the landing and, opening a pair of magnificent double doors, looked into the ballroom.

Gilt chairs and music stands stood in a semicircle like an island in the vast bare floor. A grand piano stood in their midst. On its closed lid, with surrealistic inconsequence, were scattered a number of umbrellas and parasols. She looked more closely at them and recognized a black and white, exceedingly Parisian, affair, which ten years ago or more her aunt had flourished at Ascot. It had been an outstanding phenomenon, she remembered, in the Royal Enclosure and had been photographed. Lady Pastern had been presented with it by some Indian plenipotentiary on the occasion of her first marriage and had clung to it ever since. Its handle represented a bird and had ruby eyes. Its shaft was preposterously thin and was jointed and bound with platinum. The spring catch and the dark bronze section that held it were uncomfortably encrusted with jewels and had ruined many a pair of gloves. As a child, Félicité had occasionally been permitted to unscrew the head and the end section of the shaft, and this, for some reason, had always afforded her extreme pleasure. Carlisle picked it up, opened it, and jeering at herself for being superstitious, hurriedly shut it again. There was a pile of band parts on the piano seat and on the top of this a scribbled programme.

"Floor Show," she read. "(1) A New Way with Old Tunes. (2) Skeleton. (3) Sandra. (4) Hot Guy."

At the extreme end of the group of chairs, and a little isolated, was the paraphernalia of a dance-band tympanist—drums, rattles, a tambourine, cymbals, a wire whisk and coconut shells. Carlisle gingerly touched a pedal with her foot and jumped nervously when a pair of cymbals clashed. "It would be fun," she thought, "to sit down and have a whack at everything. What can Uncle George be like in action!"

She looked round. Her coming-out ball had been here; her parents had borrowed the house for it. Utterly remote those years before the war! Carlisle repeopled the hollow room and felt again the curious fresh gaiety of that night. She felt the cord of her programme grow flossy under the nervous pressure of her gloved fingers. She saw the names written there and read them again in the choked print of casualty lists. The cross against the supper dances had been for Edward. "I don't approve," he had said, guiding her with precision, and speaking so lightly that, as usual, she doubted his intention. "We've no business to do ourselves as well as all this." "Well, if you're not having fun—" "But I am. I am." And he had started one of their novelettes: "In the magnificent ballroom at Duke's Gate, the London house of Lord Pastern and Bagott, amid the strains of music and the scent of hot-house blooms—" And she had cut in: "Young Edward Manx swept his cousin into the vortex of the dance." "Lovely," she thought. Lovely it had been. They had had the last dance together and she had been tired yet buoyant, moving without conscious volition; *really* floating, she thought. "Good night, good night, it's been perfect." Later, as the clocks struck four, up the stairs to bed, light-headed with fatigue, drugged with gratitude to all the world for her complete happiness.

"How young," thought Carlisle, looking at the walls and floor of the ballroom, "and how remote. The Spectre of the Rose," she thought, and a phrase of music ended her recollections on a sigh.

There had been no real sequel. More balls, with the dances planned beforehand, an affair or two and letters from Edward, who was doing special articles in Russia. And then the war.

She turned away and recrossed the landing to the drawing-room.

It was still unoccupied. "If I don't talk to somebody soon," Carlisle thought, "I shall get a black dog on my back." She found a collection of illustrated papers and turned them over, thinking how strange it was that photographs of people eating, dancing, or looking at something that did not appear in the picture should command attention.

"Lady Dartmoor and Mr. Jeremy Thringle enjoyed a joke at the opening night of *Fewer and Dearer*." "Miss Penelope Santon-Clarke takes a serious view of the situation at Sandown. With her, intent on his racing card, is Captain Anthony Barr-Barr." "At the Tarmac: Miss Félicité de Suze in earnest conversation with Mr. Edward Manx." "I don't wonder," thought Carlisle, "that Aunt Cécile thinks it would be a good match," and put the paper away from her. Another magazine lay in her lap: a glossy publication with a cover illustration depicting a hilltop liberally endowed with flowers and a young man and woman of remarkable physique gazing with every expression of delight and well-being at something indistinguishable in an extremely blue sky. The title *Harmony* was streamlined across the top of the cover.

Carlisle turned the pages. Here was Edward's monthly review of the shows. Much too good, it was, mordant and penetrating, for a freak publication like this. He had told her they paid very well. Here, an article on genetics by "The Harmony Consultant," here something a bit overemotional about Famine Relief, which Carlisle, an expert in her way, skimmed through with disapproval. Next an article, "Radiant Living," which she passed by with a shudder. Then a two-page article headed "Crime Pays," which proved to be a highly flavoured but extremely outspoken and well-informed article on the drug racket. Two Latin-American business firms with extensive connections in Great Britain were boldly named. An editorial note truculently courted information backed by full protection. It also invited a libel action and promised a further article. Next came a serial by a Big Name and then, on the centre double-page with a banner headline:

THE HELPING HAND
Ask G.P.F. About It
(Guide, Philosopher, Friend)

Carlisle glanced through it. Here were letters from young women asking for advice on the conduct of their engagements and from young men seeking guidance in their choice of wives and jobs. Here was a married woman prepared, it seemed, to follow the instructions of an unknown pundit in matters of the strictest personal concern, and here a widower who requested an expert report on remarriage with someone twenty years his junior. Carlisle was about to turn the page when a sentence caught her eye:

> I am eighteen and unofficially engaged to be married. My fiancé is madly jealous and behaves . . .

She read it through to the end. The style was vividly familiar. The magazine had the look of having been frequently opened here. There was cigarette ash in the groove between the pages. Was it possible that Félicité—? But the signature: "Toots"! Could Félicité adopt a nom de plume like Toots? Could her unknown correspondent—? Carlisle lost herself in a maze of speculation from which she was aroused by some faint noise—a metallic click. She looked up. Nobody had entered the room. The sound was repeated and she realized it had come from her uncle's study, a small room that opened off the far end of the drawing-room. She saw that the door was ajar and that the lights were on in the study. She remembered that it was Lord Pastern's unalterable habit to sit in this room for half an hour before dinner, meditating upon whatever obsession at the moment enthralled him, and that he had always liked her to join him there.

She walked down the long deep carpet to the door and looked in.

Lord Pastern sat before the fire. He had a revolver in his hands and appeared to be loading it.

III

For a few moments Carlisle hesitated. Then, in a voice that struck her as being pitched too high, she said: "What *are* you up to, Uncle George?"

He started and the revolver slipped in his hands and almost fell.

"Hullo," he said. "Thought you'd forgotten me."

She crossed the room and sat opposite him. "Are you preparing for burglars?" she said.

"No." He gave her what Edward had once called one of his leery looks and added: "Although you might put it that way. I'm gettin' ready for my big moment." He jerked his hand towards a small table that stood at his elbow. Carlisle saw that a number of cartridges lay there. "Just goin' to draw the bullets," said Lord Pastern, "to make them into blanks, you know. I like to attend to things myself."

"But what is your big moment?"

"You'll see, to-night. You and Fée are to come. It ought to be a party. Who's your best young man?"

"I haven't got one."

"Why not?"

"Arst yourself."

"You're too damn' stand-offish, me gel. Wouldn't be surprised if you had one of those things—Oedipus and all that. I looked into psychology when I was interested in companionate marriage."

Lord Pastern inserted his eyeglass, went to his desk and rummaged in one of the drawers.

"What's happening to-night?"

"Special extension night at the Metronome. I'm playin'. Floor show at eleven o'clock. My first appearance in public. Breezy engaged me. Nice of him, wasn't it? You'll enjoy yourself, Lisle."

He returned with a drawer filled with a strange collection of objects—pieces of wire, a fret-saw, razor blades, candle-ends, wood-carving knives, old photographs, electrical gear, plastic wood, a number of tools and quantities of putty in greasy paper. How well Carlisle remembered that drawer. It had been a wet-day solace of her childhood visits. From its contents, Lord Pastern, who was dextrous in such matters, had concocted manikins, fly-traps and tiny ships.

"I believe," she said, "I recognize almost everything in the collection."

"Y' father gave me that revolver," Lord Pastern remarked. "It's one of a pair. He had 'em made by his gunsmith to take special target ammunition. Couldn't be bored having to reload with every shot like you do with target pistols, y'know. Cost him a packet, these did. We were always at it, he and I. He scratched his initials one day on the butt of this one. We'd had a bit of a row about differences in performance in the two guns, and shot it out. Have a look."

She picked up the revolver gingerly. "I can't see anything."

"There's a magnifying glass somewhere. Look underneath near the trigger guard."

Carlisle rummaged in the drawer and found a lens. "Yes," she said. "I can make them out now. C.D.W."

"We were crack shots. He left me the pair. The other's in the case, somewhere in that drawer."

Lord Pastern took out a pair of pliers and picked up one of the cartridges. "Well, if you haven't got a young man," he said, "we'll have Ned Manx. That'll please your aunt. No good asking anyone else for Fée. Carlos cuts up rough."

"Uncle George," Carlisle ventured as he busied himself over his task, "do you approve of Carlos? Really?"

He muttered and grunted. She caught disjointed phrases: "—take their course—own destiny—goin' the wrong way to work. He's a damn' fine piano-accordionist," he said loudly and added, more obscurely: "They'd much better leave things to me."

"What's he like?"

"You'll see him in a minute. I know what I'm about," said Lord Pastern, crimping the end of a cartridge from which he had extracted the bullet.

"Nobody else seems to. Is he jealous?"

"She's had things too much her own way. Make her sit up a bit and a good job, too."

"Aren't you making a great number of blank cartridges?" Carlisle asked idly.

"I rather like making them. You never know. I shall probably be asked to repeat my number lots of times. I like to be prepared."

He glanced up and saw the journal which Carlisle still held in her lap. "Thought you had a mind above that sort of stuff," said Lord Pastern, grinning.

"Are you a subscriber, darling?"

"Y' aunt is. It's got a lot of sound stuff in it. They're not afraid to speak their minds, b'God. See that thing on drug-runnin'? Names and everything and if they don't like it they can damn' well lump it. The police," Lord Pastern said obscurely, "are no good; pompous incompetent lot. Hidebound. Ned," he added, "does the reviews."

"Perhaps," Carlisle said lightly, "he's G.P.F., too."

"Chap's got brains," Lord Pastern grunted bewilderingly. "Hog sense in that feller."

"Uncle George," Carlisle demanded suddenly, "you don't know by any chance if Fée's ever consulted G.P.F.?"

"Wouldn't let on if I did, m'dear. Naturally."

Carlisle reddened. "No, of course you wouldn't if she'd told you in confidence. Only usually Fée can't keep anything to herself."

"Well, ask her. She might do a damn' sight worse."

Lord Pastern dropped the bullets he had extracted into the waste-paper basket and returned to his desk. "I've been doin' a bit of writin' myself," he said. "Look at this, Lisle."

He handed his niece a sheet of music manuscript. An air had been set down, with many rubbings out, it seemed, and words had been written under the appropriate notes. "This Hot Guy," Carlisle read, "does he get mean? This Hot Gunner with his accord-een. Shoots like he plays an' he tops the bill. Plays like he shoots an' he shoots to kill. Hi-de oh hi. Yip. Ho de oh do. Yip. Shoot buddy, shoot and we'll sure come clean. Hot Guy, Hot Gunner on your accord-een. Bo. Bo. Bo."

"Neat," said Lord Pastern complacently. "Ain't it?"

"It's astonishing," Carlisle murmured and was spared the necessity of further comment by the sound of voices in the drawing-room.

"That's the Boys," said Lord Pastern briskly. "Come on."

The Boys were dressed in their professional dinner suits. These were distinctive garments, the jackets being double-breasted with the famous steel pointed buttons and silver revers. The sleeves were extremely narrow and displayed a great deal of cuff. The taller of the two, a man whose rotundity was emphasized by his pallor, advanced, beaming upon his host.

"Well, well, well," he said. "Look who's here."

It was upon his companion that Carlisle fixed her attention. Memories of tango experts, of cinema near-stars with cigarette holders and particoloured shoes, of armoured women moving doggedly round dance floors in the grasp of younger men—all these memories jostled together in her brain.

"—and Mr. Rivera—" her uncle was saying. Carlisle withdrew her hand from Mr. Bellairs's encompassing grasp and it was at once bowed over by Mr. Rivera.

"Miss Wayne," said Félicité's Carlos.

He rose from his bow with grace and gave her a look of automatic homage. "So we meet, at last," he said. "I have heard so much." He had, she noticed, a very slight lisp.

Lord Pastern gave them all sherry. The two visitors made loud conversation. "That's very fine," Mr. Breezy Bellairs pronounced and pointed to a small Fragonard above the fireplace. "My God, that's beautiful, you know, Carlos. Exquisite."

"In my father's *hacienda,*" said Mr. Rivera, "there is a picture of which I am vividly reminded. This picture to which I refer is a portrait of one of my paternal ancestors. It is an original Goya." And while she was still wondering how a Fragonard could remind Mr. Rivera of a Goya, he turned to Carlisle. "You have visited the Argentine, Miss Wayne, of course?"

"No," said Carlisle.

"But you must. It would appeal to you enormously. It is a little difficult, by the way, for a visitor to see us, as it were, from the inside. The Spanish families are very exclusive."

"Oh."

"Oh, yes. An aunt of mine, Doña Isabella de Manuelos-Rivera, used to say ours was the only remaining aristocracy." He inclined towards Lord Pastern and laughed musically. "But, of course, she had not visited a certain charming house in Duke's Gate, London."

"What? I wasn't listening," said Lord Pastern. "Look here, Bellairs, about to-night—"

"To-night," Mr. Bellairs interrupted, smiling from ear to ear, "is in the bag. We'll rock them, Lord Pastern. Now, don't you worry about to-night. It's going to be wonderful. You'll be there, of course, Miss Wayne?"

"I wouldn't miss it," Carlisle murmured, wishing they were not so zealous in their attentions.

"I've got the gun fixed up," her uncle said eagerly. "Five rounds of blanks, you know. What about those umbrellas, now—"

"You are fond of music, Miss Wayne? But of course you are. You would be enchanted by the music of my own country."

"Tangos and rhumbas?" Carlisle ventured. Mr. Rivera inclined towards her. "At night," he said, "with the scent of magnolias in the air—those wonderful nights of music. You will think it strange, of course, that I should be—" he shrugged up his shoulders and lowered his voice—"performing in a dance band. Wearing these appalling clothes! Here, in London. It is terrible, isn't it?"

"I don't see why."

"I suppose," Mr. Rivera sighed, "I am what you call a snob. There are times when I find it almost unendurable. But I must not say so." He glanced at Mr. Bellairs, who was deep in conversation with his host. "A heart of gold," he whispered. "One of nature's gentlemen. I should not complain. How serious we have become," he added gaily. "We meet and in two minutes I confide in you. You are *simpática,* Miss Wayne. But of course you have been told that before."

"Never," said Carlisle firmly and was glad to see Edward Manx come in.

"Evenin', Ned," said Lord Pastern, blinking at him. "Glad to see you. Have you met—"

Carlisle heard Mr. Rivera draw in his breath with a formidable hiss. Manx, having saluted Mr. Bellairs, advanced with a pleasant smile and extended hand. "We haven't met, Rivera," he said, "but at least I'm one of your devotees at the Metronome. If anything could teach me how to dance I'm persuaded it would be your piano-accordion."

"How do you do," said Mr. Rivera, and turned his back. "As I was saying, Miss Wayne," he continued, "I believe entirely in first impressions. As soon as we were introduced—"

Carlisle looked past him at Manx, who had remained perfectly still. At the first opportunity, she walked round Mr. Rivera and joined him. Mr. Rivera moved to the fireplace, before which he stood with an air of detachment, humming under his breath. Lord Pastern instantly buttonholed him. Mr. Bellairs joined them with every manifestation of uneasy geniality. "About my number, Carlos," said Lord Pastern, "I've been tellin' Breezy—"

"Of all the filthy rude—" Manx began to mutter. Carlisle linked her arm in his and walked him away. "He's just plain frightful, Ned. Félicité must be out of her mind," she whispered hastily.

"If Cousin George thinks I'm going to stand round letting a bloody fancy-dress dago insult me—"

"For *pity's* sake don't fly into one of your rages. Laugh it off."

"Heh-heh-heh."

"That's better."

"He'll probably throw his sherry in my face. Why the devil was I asked, if he was coming. What's Cousin Cécile thinking of?"

"It's Uncle George—shut up. Here come the girls."

Lady Pastern, encased in black, entered with Félicité at her heels. She suffered the introductions with terrifying courtesy. Mr. Bellairs redoubled his geniality. Mr. Rivera had the air of a man who never blossoms but in the presence of the great.

"I am so pleased to have the honour, at last, of being presented," he said. "From Félicité I have heard so much of her mother. I feel, too, that we may have friends in common. Perhaps, Lady Pastern, you will remember an uncle of mine who had, I think, some post at our embassy in Paris, many years ago. Señor Alonso de Manuelos-Rivera."

Lady Pastern contemplated him without any change of expression. "I do not remember," she said.

"After all it was much too long ago," he rejoined gallantly. Lady Pastern glanced at him with cold astonishment and advanced upon Manx. "Dearest Edward," she said, offering her cheek, "we see you far too seldom. This is delightful."

"Thank you, Cousin Cécile. For me, too."

"I want to consult you— You will forgive us, George. I am determined to have Edward's opinion on my petit point."

"Let me alone," Manx boasted, "with petit point."

Lady Pastern put her arm through his and led him apart. Carlisle saw Félicité go to Rivera. Evidently she had herself well in hand: her greeting was prettily formal. She turned with an air of comradeship from Rivera to Bellairs and her stepfather. "Will anyone bet me," she said, "that I can't guess what you chaps have been talking about?" Mr. Bellairs was immediately very gay. "Now, Miss de Suze, that's making it just a little tough. I'm afraid you know much too much about us. Isn't that the case, Lord Pastern?" "I'm worried about those umbrellas," said Lord Pastern moodily and Bellairs and Félicité began to talk at once.

Carlisle was trying to make up her mind about Rivera and failing to do so. Was he in love with Félicité? If so was his jealousy of Ned Manx a genuine and therefore an alarming passion? Was he on the other hand a complete adventurer? Could any human being be as patently bogus as Mr. Rivera or was it within the bounds of possibility that the scions of noble Spanish-American families behaved in a manner altogether too faithful to their Hollywood opposites? Was it her fancy or had his olive-coloured cheeks turned paler as he stood and watched Félicité? Was the slight tic under his left eye, that smallest possible muscular twitch, really involuntary or, as everything else about him seemed to be, part of an impersonation along stereotyped lines? And as these speculations chased each other through her mind, Rivera himself came up to her.

"But you are so serious," he said. "I wonder why. In my country we have a proverb: a woman is serious for one of two reasons—she is about to fall in love or already she loves without success. The alternative being unthinkable, I ask myself—to whom is this lovely lady about to lose her heart?"

Carlisle thought: "I wonder if this is the line of chat that Félicité has fallen for." She said: "I'm afraid your proverb doesn't apply out of South America."

He laughed as if she had uttered some brilliant equivocation and began to protest that he knew better, indeed he did. Carlisle saw Félicité stare blankly at them and, turning quickly, surprised just such another expression on Edward Manx's face. She began to feel acutely uncomfortable. There was no getting away from Mr. Rivera. His raillery and archness mounted with indecent emphasis. He admired Carlisle's dress, her modest jewel, her hair. His lightest remark was pronounced with such a killing air that it immediately assumed the character of an impropriety. Her embarrassment at these excesses quickly gave way to irritation when she saw that while Mr. Rivera bent upon her any number of melting glances he also kept a sharp watch upon Félicité. "And I'll be damned," thought Carlisle, "if I let him get away with that little game." She chose her moment and joined her aunt, who had withdrawn Edward Manx to the other end of the room and, while she exhibited her embroidery, muttered anathemas upon her other guests. As Carlisle came up, Edward was in the middle of some kind of uneasy protestation: "—but, Cousin Cécile, I don't honestly think I can do much about it. I mean—oh, hullo Lisle. Enjoyed your Latin-American petting party?"

"Not enormously," said Carlisle, and bent over her aunt's embroidery. "It's lovely, darling," she said. "How do you do it?"

"You shall have it for an evening bag. I have been telling Edward that I fling myself on his charity, and," Lady Pastern added in a stormy undertone, "and on yours, my dearest child." She raised her needlework as if to examine it and they saw her fingers fumble aimlessly across its surface. "You see, both of you, this atrocious person. I implore you—" Her voice faltered. "Look," she whispered, "look now. Look at him."

Carlisle and Edward glanced furtively at Mr. Rivera, who was in the act of introducing a cigarette into a jade holder. He caught Carlisle's eye. He did not smile but glossed himself over with appraisement. His eyes widened. "Somewhere or other," she thought, "he has read about gentlemen who undress ladies with a glance." She heard Manx swear under his breath and noted with surprise her own gratification at this circumstance. Mr. Rivera advanced upon her.

"Oh, Lord!" Edward muttered.

"Here," said Lady Pastern loudly, "is Hendy. She is dining with us. I had forgotten."

The door at the far end of the drawing-room had opened and a woman plainly dressed came quietly in.

"Hendy!" Carlisle echoed. "I had forgotten Hendy," and went swiftly towards her.

CHAPTER IV

They Dine

I

MISS HENDERSON HAD BEEN Félicité's governess and had remained with the family after she grew up, occupying a post that was half-way between that of companion and secretary to both Félicité and her mother. Carlisle called her controller-of-the-household and knew that many a time she had literally performed the impossible task this title implied. She was a greyish-haired woman of forty-five; her appearance was tranquil but unremarkable, her voice pleasant. Carlisle, who liked her, had often wondered at her faithfulness to this turbulent household. To Lady Pastern, who regarded all persons as neatly graded types, Miss Henderson was no doubt an employee of good address and perfect manners whose presence at Duke's Gate was essential to her own peace of mind. Miss Henderson had her private room where usually she ate in solitude. Sometimes, however, she was asked to lunch or dine with the family; either because a woman guest had slipped them up, or because her employer felt it was suitable that her position should be defined by such occasional invitations. She seldom left the house and if she had any outside ties, Carlisle had never heard of them. She was perfectly adjusted to her isolation and if she was ever lonely gave no evidence of being so. Carlisle believed Miss Henderson to have more influence than anyone else with Félicité, and it struck her now as odd that Lady Pastern should not have mentioned Hendy as a possible check to Mr. Rivera. But then the family did not often remember Hendy until they actually wanted her for something. "And I myself," Carlisle thought guiltily, "although I like her so much, had forgotten to ask after her." And she made her greeting the warmer because of this omission.

"Hendy," she said, "how lovely to see you. How long is it? Four years?"

"A little over three, I think." That was like her. She was always quietly accurate.

"You look just the same," said Carlisle, nervously aware of Mr. Rivera close behind her.

Lady Pastern icily performed the introductions. Mr. Bellairs bowed and smiled expansively from the hearth-rug. Mr. Rivera, standing beside Carlisle, said: "Ah, yes, of course. Miss Henderson." And might as well have added: "The governess, I believe." Miss Henderson bowed composedly and Spence announced dinner.

They sat at a round table, a pool of candlelight in the shadowed dining-room. Carlisle found herself between her uncle and Rivera. Opposite her, between Edward and Bellairs, sat Félicité. Lady Pastern, on Rivera's right, at first suffered his conversation with awful courtesy, presumably, thought Carlisle, in order to give Edward Manx, her other neighbour, a clear run with Félicité. But as Mr. Bellairs completely ignored Miss Henderson, who was on his right, and lavished all his attention on Félicité herself, this manoeuvre was unproductive. After a few minutes Lady Pastern engaged Edward in what Carlisle felt to be an extremely ominous conversation. She caught only fragments of it as Rivera had resumed his crash tactics with herself. His was a simple technique. He merely turned his shoulder on Lady Pastern, leant so close to Carlisle that she could see the pores of his skin, looked into her eyes and, with rich insinuation, contradicted everything she said. Lord Pastern was no refuge as he had sunk into a reverie from which he roused himself from time to time only to throw disjointed remarks at no one in particular, and to attack his food with a primitive gusto which dated from his Back-to-Nature period. His table manners were defiantly and deliberately atrocious. He chewed with parted lips, glaring about him like a threatened carnivore, and as he chewed he talked. To Spence and the man who assisted him and to Miss Henderson, who accepted her isolation with her usual composure, the conversation must have come through like the dialogue in a boldly surrealistic broadcast.

". . . such a good photograph, we thought, Edward, of you and Félicité at the Tarmac. She so much enjoyed her party with you . . ."

". . . but I'm not at all musical . . ."

". . . you must not say so. You are musical. There is music in your eyes —your voice . . ."

". . . now that's quite a nifty little idea, Miss de Suze. We'll have to pull you in with the Boys . . ."

". . . so it is arranged, my dear Edward."

". . . thank you, Cousin Cécile, but . . ."

". . . you and Félicité have always done things together, haven't you? We were laughing yesterday over some old photographs. Do you remember at Clochemere . . . ?"

". . . Gee, where's my sombrero?"

". . . with this dress you should wear flowers. A cascade of orchids. Just here. Let me show you . . ."

". . . I beg your pardon, Cousin Cécile, I'm afraid I didn't hear what you said . . ."

"Uncle George, it's time you talked to me . . ."

"Eh? Sorry, Lisle, I'm wondering where my sombrero . . ."

"Lord Pastern is very kind in letting me keep you to myself. Don't turn away. Look, your handkerchief is falling."

"*Damn!*"

"Edward!"

"I beg your pardon, Cousin Cécile, I don't know what I'm thinking of."

"Carlos."

". . . in my country, Miss Wayne . . . no, I cannot tell you Miss Wayne. Car-r-r-lisle! What a strange name . . . Strange and captivating."

"Carlos!"

"Forgive me. You spoke?"

"About those umbrellas, Breezy."

"Yes, I did speak."

"A thousand pardons, I was talking to Carlisle."

"I've engaged a table for three, Fée. You and Carlisle and Ned. Don't be late."

"My music to-night shall be for you."

"I am coming also, George."

"*What!*"

"Kindly see that it is a table for four."

"*Maman!* But I thought . . ."

"You won't like it, C."

"I propose to come."

"Damn it, you'll sit and glare at me and make me nervous."

"Nonsense, George," Lady Pastern said crisply. "Be good enough to order the table."

Her husband glowered at her, seemed to contemplate giving further battle, appeared suddenly to change his mind and launched an unexpected attack at Rivera.

"About your being carried out, Carlos," he said importantly. "It seems a pity I can't be carried out too. Why can't the stretcher party come back for me?"

"Now, now, now," Mr. Bellairs interrupted in a great hurry. "We've got everything fixed, Lord Pastern, now, haven't we? The first routine. You shoot Carlos. Carlos falls. Carlos is carried out. You take the show away. Big climax. Finish. Now don't you get me bustled," he added playfully. "It's good and it's fixed. Fine. That's right, isn't it?"

"It is what has been decided," Mr. Rivera conceded grandly. "For myself, I am perhaps a little dubious. Under other circumstances I would undoubtedly insist upon the second routine. I am shot at but I do not fall. Lord Pastern misses me. The others fall. Breezy fires at Lord Pastern and nothing happens. Lord Pastern plays, faints, is removed. I finish the number. Upon this routine under other circumstances, I should insist." He executed a sort of comprehensive bow, taking in Lord Pastern, Félicité, Carlisle and Lady Pastern. "But under these exclusive and most charming circumstances, I yield. I am shot. I fall. Possibly I hurt myself. No matter."

Bellairs eyed him. "Good old Carlos," he said uneasily.

"I still don't see why I can't be carried out too," said Lord Pastern fretfully.

Carlisle heard Mr. Bellairs whisper under his breath: "For the love of Pete!" Rivera said loudly: "No, no, no, no. Unless we adopt completely the second routine, we perform the first as we rehearse. It is settled."

"Carlisle," said Lady Pastern, rising, "shall we . . . ?"

She swept her ladies into the drawing-room.

II

Félicité was puzzled, resentful and uneasy. She moved restlessly about the room, eyeing her mother and Carlisle. Lady Pastern paid no attention to her daughter. She questioned Carlisle about her experiences in Greece and received her somewhat distracted answers with perfect equanimity. Miss Henderson, who had taken up Lady Pastern's box of embroidery threads, sorted them with quiet movements of her hands and seemed to listen with interest.

Suddenly Félicité said: "I don't see much future in us all behaving as if we'd had the Archbishop of Canterbury to dinner. If you've got anything to say about Carlos, all of you, I'd be very much obliged if you'd say it."

Miss Henderson, her hands still for a moment, glanced up at Félicité and then bent again over her task. Lady Pastern, having crossed her ankles and wrists, slightly moved her shoulders and said: "I do not consider this a suitable occasion, my dear child, for any such discussion."

"Why?" Félicité demanded.

"It would make a scene, and under the circumstances," said Lady Pastern with an air of reasonableness, "there's no time for a scene."

"If you think the men are coming in, *Maman,* they are not. George has arranged to go over the programme again in the ballroom."

A servant came in and collected the coffee cups. Lady Pastern made conversation with Carlisle until the door had closed behind him.

"So I repeat," Félicité said loudly, "I want to hear, *Maman,* what you've got to say against Carlos."

Lady Pastern slightly raised her eyes and lifted her shoulders. Her daughter stamped. "Blast and hell!" she said.

"Félicité!" said Miss Henderson. It was neither a remonstrance nor a warning. The name fell like an unstressed comment. Miss Henderson held an embroidery stiletto firmly between finger and thumb and examined it placidly. Félicité made an impatient movement. "If you think," she said violently, "anybody's going to be at their best in a strange house with a hostess who looks at them as if they smelt!"

"If it comes to that, dearest child, he does smell. Of a particularly heavy kind of scent, I fancy," Lady Pastern added thoughtfully.

From the ballroom came a distant syncopated roll of drums ending in a crash of cymbals and a loud report. Carlisle jumped nervously. The stiletto fell from Miss Henderson's fingers to the carpet. Félicité, bearing witness in her agitation to the efficacy of her governess's long training, stooped and picked it up.

"It is your uncle, merely," said Lady Pastern.

"I ought to go straight out and apologize to Carlos for the hideous way he's been treated," Félicité stormed, but her voice held an overtone of uncertainty and she looked resentfully at Carlisle.

"If there are to be apologies," her mother rejoined, "it is Carlisle who should receive them. I am so sorry, Carlisle, that you should have been subjected to these—" she made a fastidious gesture—"these really insufferable attentions."

"Good Lord, Aunt C," Carlisle began in acute embarrassment and was rescued by Félicité, who burst into tears and rushed out of the room.

"I think perhaps . . . ?" said Miss Henderson, rising.

"Yes, please go to her."

But before Miss Henderson reached the door, which Félicité had left open, Rivera's voice sounded in the hall. "What is the matter?" it said distinctly and Félicité, breathless, answered, "I've got to talk to you." "But certainly, if you wish it." "In here, then." The voices faded, were heard again, indistinctly, in the study. The connecting door between the study and the drawing-room was slammed to from the far side.

"You had better leave them, I think," said Lady Pastern.

"If I go to my sitting-room, she may come to me when this is over."

"Then go," said Lady Pastern, drearily. "Thank you, Miss Henderson."

"Aunt," said Carlisle when Miss Henderson had left them, "what are you up to?"

Lady Pastern, shielding her face from the fire, said: "I have made a decision. I believe that my policy in this affair has been a mistaken one. Anticipating my inevitable opposition, Félicité has met this person in his own setting and has, as I think you would say, lost her eye. I cannot believe that when she has seen him here, and has observed his atrocious antics, his immense vulgarity, she will not come to her senses. Already, one can see, she is shaken. After all, I remind myself, she is a de Fouteaux and a de Suze. Am I not right?"

"It's an old trick, darling, you know. It doesn't always work."

"It is working, however," said Lady Pastern, setting her mouth. "She sees him, for example, beside dear Edward, to whom she has always been devoted. Of your uncle as a desirable contrast, I say nothing, but at least his clothes are unexceptionable. And though I deeply resent, dearest child, that you should have been forced, in my house, to suffer the attentions of this animal, they have assuredly impressed themselves disagreeably upon Félicité."

"Disagreeably—yes," said Carlisle, turning pink. "But look here, Aunt Cécile, he's shooting this nauseating little line with me to—well, to make Fée sit up and take notice." Lady Pastern momentarily closed her eyes. This, Carlisle remembered, was her habitual reaction to slang. "And, I'm not sure," Carlisle added, "that she hasn't fallen for it."

"She cannot be anything but disgusted."

"I wouldn't be astonished if she refuses to come to the Metronome tonight."

"That is what I hope. But I am afraid she will come. She will not give way so readily, I think." Lady Pastern rose. "Whatever happens," she said, "I shall break this affair. Do you hear me, Carlisle? I shall break it."

Beyond the door at the far end of the room, Félicité's voice rose, in a sharp crescendo, but the words were indistinguishable.

"They are quarrelling," said Lady Pastern with satisfaction.

III

As Edward Manx sat silent in his chair, glass of port and a cup of coffee before him, his thoughts moved out in widening circles from the candle-lit table. Removed from him, Bellairs and Rivera had drawn close to Lord Pastern. Bellairs's voice, loud but edgeless, uttered phrase after phrase. "Sure, that's right. Don't worry, it's in the bag. It's going to be a world-breaker. O.K., we'll run it through. Fine." Pastern fidgeted, stuttered, chuckled, complained. Rivera, leaning back in his chair, smiled, said nothing and turned his glass. Manx, who had noticed how frequently it had been refilled, wondered if he was tight.

There they sat, wreathed in cigar smoke, candle-lit, an unreal group. He saw them as three dissonant figures at the centre of an intolerable design. "Bellairs," he told himself, "is a gaiety merchant. Gaiety!" How fashionable, he reflected, the word had been before the war. Let's be gay, they had all said, and glumly embracing each other had tramped and shuffled, while men like Breezy Bellairs made their noise and did their smiling for them. They christened their children "Gay," they used the word in their drawing-room comedies and in their dismal, dismal songs. "Gaiety!" muttered the disgruntled and angry Edward. "A lovely word, but the thing itself, when enjoyed, is unnamed. There's Cousin George, who is undoubtedly a little mad, sitting, like a mouth-piece for his kind, between a jive merchant and a cad. And here's Fée anticking inside the unholy circle while Cousin Cécile solemnly gyrates against the beat. In an outer ring, I hope unwillingly, is Lisle, and here I sit, as sore as hell, on the perimeter." He glanced up and found that Rivera was looking at him, not directly but out of the corners of his eyes. "Sneering," thought Edward, "like an infernal caricature of himself."

"Buck up, Ned," Lord Pastern said, grinning at him. "We haven't had a word from you. You want takin' out of yourself. Bit of gaiety, what?"

"By all means, sir," said Edward. A white carnation had fallen out of the vase in the middle of the table. He took it up and put it in his coat. "The blameless life," he said.

Lord Pastern cackled and turned to Bellairs. "Well, Breezy, if you think it's all right, we'll order the taxis for a quarter past ten. Think you can amuse yourselves till then?" He pushed the decanter towards Bellairs.

"Sure, sure," Bellairs said. "No, thanks a lot, no more. A lovely wine, mind you, but I've got to be a good boy."

Edward slid the port on to Rivera, who, smiling a little more broadly, refilled his glass.

"I'll show you the blanks and the revolver, when we move," said Lord Pastern. "They're in the study." He glanced fretfully at Rivera, who slowly pulled his glass towards him. Lord Pastern hated to be kept waiting. "Ned, you look after Carlos, will you? D'you mind, Carlos? I want to show Breezy the blanks. Come on, Breezy."

Manx opened the door for his uncle and returned to the table. He sat down and waited for Rivera to make the first move. Spence came in, lingered for a moment and withdrew. There followed a long silence.

At last Rivera stretched out his legs and held his port to the light. "I am a man," he said, "who likes to come to the point. You are Félicité's cousin, yes?"

"No."

"No?"

"I'm related to her stepfather."

"She has spoken of you as her cousin."

"A courtesy title," said Edward.

"You are attached to her, I believe."

Edward paused for three seconds and then said, "Why not?"

"It is not at all surprising," Rivera said and drank half his port. "Carlisle also speaks of you as her cousin. Is that too a courtesy title?"

Edward pushed back his chair. "I'm afraid I don't see the point of all this," he said.

"The point? Certainly. I am a man," Rivera repeated, "who likes to come to the point. I am also a man who does not care to be cold-shouldered or to be—what is the expression?—taken down a garden path. I find my reception in this house unsympathetic. This is displeasing to me. I meet, at the same time, a lady who is not displeasing to me. Quite on the contrary. I am interested. I make a tactful inquiry. I ask, for example, what is the relationship of this lady to my host. Why not?"

"Because it's a singularly offensive question," Edward said and thought: "My God, I'm going to lose my temper."

Rivera made a convulsive movement of his hand and knocked his glass to the floor. They rose simultaneously.

"In my country," Rivera said thickly, "one does not use such expressions without a sequel."

"Be damned to your country."

Rivera gripped the back of his chair and moistened his lips. He emitted a shrill belch. Edward laughed. Rivera walked towards him, paused, and raised his hand with the tips of the thumb and middle finger daintily pressed together. He advanced his hand until it was close to Edward's nose and, without marked success, attempted to snap his fingers. "Bastard," he said cautiously. From the distant ballroom came a syncopated roll of drums ending in a crash of cymbals and deafening report.

Edward said: "Don't be a fool, Rivera."

"I laugh at you till I make myself vomit."

"Laugh yourself into a coma if you like."

Rivera laid the palm of his hand against his waist. "In my country this affair would answer itself with a knife," he said.

"Make yourself scarce or it'll answer itself with a kick in the pants," said Edward. "And if you worry Miss Wayne again I'll give you a damn' sound hiding."

"Aha!" cried Rivera. "So it is not Félicité but the cousin. It is the enchanting little Carlisle. And I am to be warned off, ha? No, no, my friend." He backed away to the door. "No, no, no, no."

"Get out."

Rivera laughed with great virtuosity and made an effective exit into the hall. He left the door open. Edward heard his voice on the next landing. "What is the matter?" and after a pause, "But certainly, if you wish it."

A door slammed.

Edward walked once round the table in an irresolute manner. He then wandered to the sideboard and drove his hands through his hair. "This is incredible," he muttered. "It's extraordinary. I never dreamt of it." He noticed that his hand was shaking and poured himself a stiff jorum of whiskey. "I suppose," he thought, "it's been there all the time and I simply didn't recognize it."

Spence and his assistant came in. "I beg your pardon, sir," said Spence. "I thought the gentlemen had left."

"It's all right, Spence. Clear, if you want to. Pay no attention to me."

"Are you not feeling well, Mr. Edward?"

"I'm all right, I think. I've had a great surprise."

"Indeed, sir? Pleasant, I trust."

"In its way, wonderful, Spence. Wonderful."

IV

"There y'are," said Lord Pastern complacently. "Five rounds and five extras. Neat, aren't they?"

"Look good to me," said Bellairs, returning him the blank cartridges. "But I wouldn't know." Lord Pastern broke open his revolver and began to fill the chamber. "We'll try 'em," he said.

"Not in here, for Pete's sake, Lord Pastern."

"In the ballroom."

"It'll rock the ladies a bit, won't it?"

"What of it?" said Lord Pastern simply. He snapped the revolver shut and gave the drawer a shove back on the desk. "I can't be bothered puttin' that thing away," he said. "You go to the ballroom. I've a job to do. I'll join you in a minute."

Obediently, Breezy left him and went into the ballroom, where he wandered about restlessly, sighing and yawning and glancing towards the door.

Presently his host came in looking preoccupied.

"Where's Carlos?" Lord Pastern demanded.

"Still in the dining-room, I think," said Bellairs with his loud laugh. "Wonderful port you've turned on for us, you know, Lord Pastern."

"Hope he can hold it. We don't want him playin' the fool with the show."

"He can hold it."

Lord Pastern clapped his revolver down on the floor near the tympani. Bellairs eyed it uneasily.

"I wanted to ask you," said Lord Pastern, sitting behind the drums, "have you spoken to Sydney Skelton?"

Bellairs smiled extensively. "Well, I just haven't got round . . ." he began. Lord Pastern cut him short. "If you don't want to tell him," he said, "I will."

"No, no!" cried Bellairs, in a hurry. "No. I don't think that'd be quite desirable, Lord Pastern, if you can understand." He looked anxiously at his host, who had turned away to the piano and with an air of restless preoccupation examined the black and white parasol. Breezy continued: "I mean to say, Syd's funny. He's very temperamental if you know what I mean. He's quite a tough guy to handle, Syd. You have to pick your moment with Syd, if you can understand."

"Don't keep on asking if I can understand things that are as simple as falling off a log," Lord Pastern rejoined irritably. "You think I'm good on the drums, you've said so."

"Sure, sure."

"You said if I'd made it my profession I'd have been as good as they come. You said any band'd be proud to have me. Right. I am going to make it my profession and I'm prepared to be your full-time tympanist. Good. Tell Skelton and let him go. Perfectly simple."

"Yes, but—"

"He'll get a job elsewhere fast enough, won't he?"

"Yes. Sure. Easy. But . . ."

"Very well, then," said Lord Pastern conclusively. He had unscrewed the handle from the parasol and was now busy with the top end of the shaft. "This comes to bits," he said. "Rather clever, what? French."

"Look!" said Bellairs winningly. He laid his soft white hand on Lord Pastern's coat. "I'm going to speak very frankly, Lord Pastern. *You* know. It's a hard old world in our game, if you under—I mean, I have to think all round a proposition like this, don't I?"

"You've said you wished you had me permanently," Lord Pastern reminded him. He spoke with a certain amount of truculence but rather absent-mindedly. He had unscrewed a small section from the top end of the parasol shaft. Breezy watched him mesmerized as he took up his revolver and, with the restless concentration of a small boy in mischief, poked this section on a short way up the muzzle, at the same time holding down with his thumb the spring catch that served to keep the parasol closed. "This," he said, "would fit."

"Hi!" Breezy said. "Is that gun loaded?"

"Of course," Lord Pastern muttered. He put down the piece of shaft and glanced up. "You said it to me and Rivera," he added. He had Hotspur's trick of reverting to the last remark but four.

"I know, I know," Bellairs gabbled, smiling to the full extent of his mouth, "but listen. I'm going to put this very crudely . . ."

"Why the hell shouldn't you!"

"Well, then. You're very keen and you're good. Sure, you're good! But, excuse my frankness, will you stay keen? That's my point, Lord Pastern. Suppose, to put it crudely, you died on it."

"I'm fifty-five and as fit as a flea."

"I mean suppose you kind of lost interest. Where," asked Mr. Bellairs passionately, "would I be then?"

"I've told you perfectly plainly . . ."

"Yes, but . . ."

"Do you call me a liar, you bloody fellow?" shouted Lord Pastern, two brilliant patches of scarlet flaming over his cheekbones. He clapped the dismembered parts of the parasol on the piano and turned on his conductor, who began to stammer.

"Now, listen, Lord Pastern . . . I–I'm nervy to-night. I'm all upset. Don't get me flustered, now."

Lord Pastern bared his teeth at him. "You're a fool," he said. "I've been watchin' you." He appeared to cogitate and come to a decision. "Ever read a magazine called *Harmony?*" he demanded.

Breezy shied violently. "Why, yes. Why–I don't know what your idea is, Lord Pastern, bringing that up."

"I've half a mind," Lord Pastern said darkly, "to write to that paper. I know a chap on the staff." He brooded for a moment, whistling between his teeth, and then barked abruptly: "If you don't speak to Skelton to-night, I'll talk to him myself."

"O.K., O.K. I'll have a wee chat with Syd. O.K."

Lord Pastern looked fixedly at him. "You'd better pull y'self together," he said. He took up his drumsticks and without more ado beat out a deafening crescendo, crashed his cymbals, and snatching up his revolver, pointed it at Bellairs and fired. The report echoed madly in the empty ballroom. The piano, the cymbals and the double-bass zoomed in protest and Bellairs, white to the lips, danced sideways.

"For crisake!" he said violently and broke into a profuse sweat.

Lord Pastern laughed delightedly and laid his revolver on the piano. "Good, isn't it?" he said. "Let's just run through the programme. First, there's 'A New Way with Old Tunes,' 'Any Ice To-day?' 'I Got Everythin',' 'The Peanut Vendor' and 'The Umbrella Man.' That's a damn' good idea of mine about the umbrellas."

Bellairs eyed the collection on the piano and nodded.

"The black and white parasol's m'wife's. She doesn't know I've taken it. You might put it together and hide it under the others, will you? We'll smuggle 'em out when she's not lookin'."

Bellairs fumbled with the umbrellas and Lord Pastern continued: "Then Skelton does his thing. I find it a bit dull, that number. And then the Sandra woman does her songs. And then," he said with an affectation of carelessness, "then you say somethin' to introduce me, don't you?"

"That's right."

"Yes. Somethin' to the effect that I happened to show you a thing I'd written, you know, and you were taken with it and that I've decided that my *métier* lies in this direction and all that. What?"

"Quite."

"I come out and we play it once through and then we swing it, and then there's the shootin', and then, by God, I go into my solo. Yes."

Lord Pastern took up his drumsticks, held them poised for a moment and appeared to go into a brief trance. "I'm still not so sure the other routine wasn't the best after all," he said.

"Listen! Listen!" Breezy began in a panic.

Lord Pastern said absently: "Now, you keep your hair on. I'm thinkin'." He appeared to think for some moments and then—ejaculating "Sombrero!"—darted out of the room.

Breezy Bellairs wiped his face with his handkerchief, sank on to the piano stool and held his head in his hands.

After a considerable interval the ballroom doors were opened and Rivera came in. Bellairs eyed him. "How's tricks, Carlos?" he asked dolefully.

"Not good." Rivera, stroking his moustache with his forefinger, walked stiffly to the piano. "I have quarrelled with Félicité."

"You asked for it, didn't you? Your little line with Miss Wayne . . ."

"It is well to show women that they are not irreplaceable. They become anxious and, in a little while, they are docile."

"Has it worked out that way?"

"Not yet, perhaps. I am angry with her." He made a florid and violent gesture. "With them all! I have been treated like a dog, I, Carlos de . . ."

"Listen," said Breezy, "I can't face a temperament from you, old boy. I'm nearly crazy with worry myself. I just can't face it. God, I wish I'd never taken the old fool on! God, I'm in a mess! Give me a cigarette, Carlos."

"I am sorry. I have none."

"I asked you to get me cigarettes," said Breezy and his voice rose shrilly.

"It was not convenient. You smoke too much."

"Go to hell."

"Everywhere," Rivera shouted, "I am treated with impertinence. Everywhere I am insulted." He advanced upon Bellairs, his head thrust forward. "I am sick of it all," he said. "I have humbled myself too much. I am a man of quick decisions. No longer shall I cheapen myself by playing in a common dance band . . ."

"Here, here, here!"

"I give you, now, my notice."

"You're under contract. Listen, old man . . ."

"I spit on your contract. No longer shall I be your little errand boy. 'Get me some cigarettes.' Bah!"

"Carlos!"

"I shall return to my own country."

"Listen old boy . . . I . . . I'll raise your screw . . ." His voice faltered.

Rivera looked at him and smiled. "Indeed? By how much? It would be by perhaps five pounds?"

"Have a heart, Carlos."

"Or if, for instance, you would care to advance me five hundred . . ."

"You're crazy! Carlos, for Pete's sake . . . Honestly, I haven't got it."

"Then," said Rivera magnificently, "you may look for another to bring you your cigarettes. For me it is . . . finish."

Breezy wailed loudly: "And where will I be? What about me?"

Rivera smiled and moved away. With an elaborate display of nonchalance, he surveyed himself in a wall-glass, fingering his tie. "You will be in a position of great discomfort, my friend," he said. "You will be unable to replace me. I am quite irreplaceable." He examined his moustache closely in the glass and caught sight of Breezy's reflection. "Don't look like that," he said, "you are extremely ugly when you look like that. Quite revolting."

"It's a breach of contract. I can . . ." Breezy wetted his lips. "There's the law," he mumbled. "I suppose . . ."

Rivera turned and faced him.

"The law?" he said. "I am obliged to you. Of course one can call upon the law, can one not? That is a wise step for a band leader to take, no doubt. I find the suggestion amusing. I shall enjoy repeating it to the ladies who smile at you so kindly, and ask you so anxiously for their favourite numbers. When I no longer play in your band their smiles will become infrequent and they will go elsewhere for their favourite numbers."

"You wouldn't do that, Carlos."

"Let me tell you, my good Breezy, that if the law is to be invoked it is I who invoke it."

"Damn and blast you," Breezy shouted in a frenzy.

"What the devil's all the row about?" asked Lord Pastern. He had entered unobserved. A wide-brimmed sombrero decorated his head, its strap supporting his double chin. "I thought I'd wear this," he said. "It goes with the shootin' don't you think? Yipee!"

V

When Rivera left her, Félicité had sat on in the study, her hands clenched between her knees, trying to bury quickly and forever the memory of the scene they had just ended. She looked aimlessly about her, at the litter of tools in the open drawer at her elbow, at the typewriter, at familiar prints, ornaments and books. Her throat was dry. She was filled with nausea and an arid hatred. She wished ardently to rid herself of all memory of Rivera and in doing so to humiliate and injure him. She was still for so long that when at last she moved, her right leg was numb and her foot pricked and tingled. As she rose stiffly and cautiously, she heard someone cross to the landing, pass the study and go into the drawing-room next door.

"I'll go up to Hendy," she thought. "I'll ask Hendy to tell them I'm not coming to the Metronome."

She went out on the landing. Somewhere on the second floor her stepfather's voice shouted: "My sombrero, you silly chap—Somebody's taken it. That's all. Somebody's collared it." Spence came through the drawing-room door, carrying an envelope on a salver.

"It's for you, miss," he said. "It was left on the hall table. I'm sure I'm very sorry it was not noticed before."

She took it. It was addressed in typescript. Across the top was printed a large "Urgent" with "by District Messenger" underneath. Félicité returned to the study and tore it open.

Three minutes later Miss Henderson's door was flung open and she, lifting her gaze from her book, saw Félicité, glowing before her.

"Hendy—Hendy, come and help me dress. Hendy, come and make me lovely. Something marvellous has happened. Hendy, darling, it's going to be a wonderful party."

CHAPTER V

A Wreath for Rivera

I

AGAINST A DEEP BLUE BACKGROUND the arm of a giant metronome kept up its inane and constant gesture. It was outlined in miniature lights, and to those patrons who had drunk enough, it left in its wake a formal ghost pattern of itself in colour. It was mounted on part of the wall overhanging the band alcove. The ingenious young man responsible for the *décor* had so designed this alcove that the band platform itself appeared as a projection from the skeleton tower of the metronome. The tip of the arm swept to and fro above the bandsmen's heads in a maddening reiterative arc, pointing them out, insisting on their noise. An inverted metronome had been considered "great fun" by the ingenious young man but it had been found advisable to switch off the mechanism from time to time and when this was done the indicator pointed downwards. Either Breezy Bellairs or a favoured soloist was careful to place himself directly beneath the light-studded pointer at its tip.

On their semicircular rostrum the seven performers of the dance band crouched, blowing, scraping and hitting at their instruments. This was the band that worked on extension nights, from dinner time to eleven o'clock, at the Metronome. It was known as the Jivesters, and was not as highly paid or as securely established as Breezy Bellairs and His Boys. But of course it was a good band, carefully selected by Caesar Boon, the manager and *maître de café,* who was also a big shareholder in the Metronome.

Caesar himself, glossy, immeasurably smart, in full control of his accurately graded cordiality, moved, with a light waggle of his hips, from the vestibule into the restaurant and surveyed his guests. He bowed roguishly as his headwaiter, with raised hand, preceded a party of five to their table. "Hullo, Caesar. Evenin'," said Lord Pastern. "Brought my family, you see."

Caesar flourished his hands. "It is a great evening for the Metronome, my lady. A gala of galas."

"No doubt," said her ladyship.

She seated her guests. She herself, with erect bust, faced the dance floor, her back to the wall. She raised her lorgnette. Caesar and the head-waiter hovered. Lord Pastern ordered hock.

"We are much too close, George," Lady Pastern shouted above the Jivesters, who had just broken out in a frenzy. And indeed their table had been crammed in alongside the band dais and hard by the tympanist. Félicité could have touched his foot. "I had it put here specially," Lord Pastern yelled. "I knew you'd want to watch me."

Carlisle, sitting between her uncle and Edward Manx, nervously clutched her evening bag and wondered if they were all perhaps a little mad. What, for instance, had come over Félicité? Why, whenever she looked at Edward, did she blush? Why did she look so often and so queerly at him, like a bewildered and—yes—a besotted schoolgirl? And why, on the landing at Duke's Gate, after a certain atrocious scene with Rivera (Carlisle closed her memory on the scene), had Ned behaved with such ferocity? And why, after all, was she, in the middle of a complicated and disagreeable crisis, so happy?

Edward Manx, seated between Félicité and Carlisle, was also bewildered. A great many things had happened to him that evening. He had had a row with Rivera in the dining-room. He had made an astonishing discovery. Later (and, unlike Carlisle, he found this recollection entirely agreeable) he had come on to the landing at the precise moment when Rivera was making a determined effort to embrace Carlisle and had hit Rivera very hard on the left ear. While they were still, all three of them, staring at each other, Félicité had appeared with a letter in her hands. She had taken one look at Edward and, going first white under her make-up and then scarlet, had fled upstairs. From that moment she had behaved in the most singular manner imaginable. She kept catching his eye and as often as this happened she smiled and blushed. Once she gave a mad little laugh. Edward shook his head and asked Lady Pastern to dance. She consented. He rose, and placing his right hand behind her iron waist walked her cautiously down the dance floor. It was formidable, dancing with Cousin Cécile.

"If anything," she said when they had reached the spot farthest away from the band, "could compensate for my humiliation in appearing at this lamentable affair, my dearest boy, it is the change your presence has wrought in Félicité."

"Really?" said Edward nervously.

"Indeed, yes. From her childhood, you have exerted a profound influence."

"Look here, Cousin Cécile—" Edward began in extreme discomfort, but at that moment the dance band, which had for some time contented itself with the emission of syncopated grunts and pants, suddenly flared up into an elaborate rumpus. Edward was silenced.

Lord Pastern put his head on one side and contemplated the band with an air of critical patronage. "They're not bad, you know," he said, "but they haven't got enough guts. Wait till you hear us, Lisle. What?"

"I know," Carlisle said encouragingly. At the moment his naïveté touched her. She was inclined to praise him as one would a child. Her eyes followed Edward, who now guided Lady Pastern gingerly past the band dais. Carlisle watched them go by and in so doing caught the eye of a man who sat at the next table. He was a monkish-looking person with a fastidious mouth and well-shaped head. A woman with short dark hair was with him. They had an air of comradeship. "They look nice," Carlisle thought. She felt suddenly uplifted and kindly disposed to all the world, and, on this impulse, turned to Félicité. She found that Félicité, also, was watching Edward and still with that doting and inexplicable attention.

"Fée," she said softly, "what's up? What's happened?" Félicité, without changing the direction of her gaze, said: "Something too shattering, darling. I'm all *bouleversée* but I'm in heaven."

Edward and Lady Pastern, after two gyrations, came to a halt by their table. She disengaged herself and resumed her seat. Edward slipped in between Carlisle and Félicité. Félicité leant towards him and drew the white carnation from his coat. "There's nobody else here with a white flower," she said softly.

"I'm very *vieux jeu* in my ways," Edward rejoined.

"Let's dance, shall we?"

"Yes, of course."

"Want to dance, C?" asked Lord Pastern.

"No thank you, George."

"Mind if Lisle and I trip a measure? It's a quarter to eleven, I'll have to go round and join the Boys in five minutes. Come on, Lisle."

You had, thought Carlisle, to keep your wits about you when you danced with Uncle George. He had a fine sense of rhythm and tremendous vigour. No stickler for the conventions, he improvised steps as the spirit moved him, merely tightening his grip upon her as an indication of further variations and eccentricities. She noticed other couples glancing at them with more animation than usually appears on the faces of British revellers.

"D'you jitter-bug?" he asked.

"No, darling."

"Pity. They think 'emselves too grand for it in this place. Sickenin' lot of snobs people are, by and large, Lisle. Did I tell you I'm seriously considerin' givin' up the title?"

He swung her round with some violence. At the far end of the room she caught a glimpse of her cousin and his partner. Ned's back was towards her. Félicité gazed into his eyes. Her hand moved farther across his shoulders. He stooped his head.

"Let's rejoin Aunt C, shall we?" said Carlisle in a flat voice.

II

Breezy Bellairs hung up his overcoat on the wall and sat down, without much show of enthusiasm, at a small table in the inner room behind the office. The tympanist, Syd Skelton, threw a pack of cards on the table and glanced at his watch. "Quarter to," he said. "Time for a brief gamble."

He dealt two poker hands. Breezy and Skelton played show poker on most nights at about this time. They would leave the Boys in their room behind the band dais and wander across to the office. They would exchange a word with Caesar or David Hahn, the secretary, in the main office, and then repair to the inner room for their game. It was an agreeable prelude to the long night's business.

"Hear you've been dining in exalted places," said Skelton acidly.

Breezy smiled automatically and with trembling hands picked up his cards. They played in a scarcely broken silence. Once or twice Skelton invited conversation, but without success.

At last he said irritably: "What's the trouble? Why the great big silence?"

Breezy fiddled with his cards and said: "I'm licked to hell, Syd."

"For the love of Mike! What's the tragedy this time?"

"Everything. I'll crack if it goes on. Honest, I'm shot to pieces."

"It's your own show. I've warned you. You look terrible."

"And how do I feel! Listen, Syd, it's this stunt to-night. It's his lordship. It's been a big mistake."

"I could have told you that, too. I did tell you."

"I know. I know. But we're booked to capacity, Syd."

"It's cheap publicity. Nothing more nor less and you know it. Pandering to a silly dope, just because he's got a title."

"He's not all that bad. As an artist."

"He's terrible," said Skelton briefly.

"I know the number's crazy and full of corn but it'll get by. It's not that, old boy, it's him. Honest, Syd, I think he's crackers." Breezy threw his cards face down on the table. "He's got me that *nervy,*" he said. "Listen, Syd, he's—he hasn't said anything to you, has he?"

"What about?"

"So he hasn't. All right. Fine. Don't take any notice if he does, old man."

Skelton leant back in his chair. "What the hell are you trying to tell me?" he demanded.

"Now don't make me nervous," Breezy implored him. "You know how nervy I get. It's just a crazy notion he's got. I'll stall him off, you bet." He paused. Skelton said ominously, "It wouldn't be anything about wanting to repeat this fiasco, would it?"

"In a way, it would, Syd. Mind, it's laughable."

"Now, you get this," Skelton said and leant across the table. "I've stood down once, to-night, to oblige you, and I don't like it and I won't do it again. What's more it's given me a kind of unpleasant feeling that I'm doing myself no good, working with an outfit that goes in for cheap sensationalism. You know me. I'm quick-tempered and I make quick decisions. There's other bands."

"Now, Syd, Syd, Syd! Take it easy," Breezy gabbled. "Forget it, old boy. I wouldn't have mentioned anything only he talked about chatting to you himself."

"By God," Skelton said, staring at him, "are you trying to tell me, by any chance, that this old so-and-so thinks he'd like my job? Have you got the flaming nerve to . . ."

"For crisake, Syd! Listen, Syd, I said it was crazy. Listen, it's going to be all right. It's not my fault, Syd. Be fair, now, it's not my fault."

"Whose fault is it then?"

"Carlos," said Breezy, lowering his voice to a whisper. "Take it easy, now. He's next door, having a drink with Caesar. It's Carlos. He's put the idea in the old bee's head. He wants to keep in with him on account the girl can't make up her mind and him wanting the old bee to encourage her. It's all Carlos, Syd. He told him he was wonderful."

Skelton said briefly what he thought of Rivera. Breezy looked nervously towards the door. "This settles it," Skelton said and rose. "I'll talk to

Carlos, by God." Breezy clawed at him. "No, Syd, not now. Not before the show. Keep your voice down, Syd, there's a pal. He's in there. You know how he is. He's thrown a temperament once to-night. Geeze," cried Breezy, springing to his feet, "I nearly forgot! He wants us to use the other routine in the new number, after all. Can you beat it? First it's this way and then it's what-have-you. He's got me so's I'm liable to give an imitation of a maestro doing two numbers at once. Gawd knows how his lordship'll take it. I got to tell the Boys. I as near as damn it forgot, I'm that nervy. Listen, you haven't heard what's really got me so worried. You know what I am. It's that gun. It's such a hell of a thing, Syd, and his lordship's made those blanks himself and, by God, I'm nervous. He's dopey enough to mix the real things up with the phony ones. They were all mucked up together in a bloody drawer, Syd, and there you are. And he really points the thing at Carlos, old boy, and fires it. Doesn't he now?"

"I wouldn't lose any sleep if he plugged him," said Skelton with violence.

"Don't talk that way, Syd," Breezy whispered irritably. "It's a hell of a situation. I hoped you'd help me, Syd."

"Why don't you have a look at the gun?"

"Me? I wouldn't know. He wouldn't let me near it. I tell you straight, I'm scared to go near him for fear I start him up bawling me out."

After a long pause, Skelton said: "Are you serious about this gun?"

"Do I look as if I was kidding?"

"It's eight minutes to eleven. We'd better go across. If I get a chance I'll ask him to show me the ammunition."

"Fine, Syd. That'd be swell," said Breezy, mopping his forehead. "It'd be marvellous. You're a pal, Syd. Come on. Let's go."

"Mind," Skelton said, "I'm not passing up the other business. I've just about had Mr. Carlos Rivera. He's going to find something out before he's much older. Come on."

They passed through the office. Rivera, who was sitting there with Caesar Bonn, disregarded them. Breezy looked timidly at him. "I'm just going to fix it with the Boys, old man," he said. "You'll enter by the end door, won't you?"

"Why not?" Rivera said acidly. "It is my usual entrance. I perform as I rehearse. Naturally."

"That's right. Naturally. Excuse my fussiness. Let's go, Syd."

Caesar rose. "It is time? Then I must felicitate our new artist."

He preceded them across the vestibule where crowds of late arrivals still streamed in. Here they encountered Félicité, Carlisle and Edward. "We're going in to wish George luck," said Félicité. "Hullo, Syd. Nice of you to let him have his fling. Come on, chaps."

They all entered the band-room, which was immediately behind the dais end of the restaurant and led into the band alcove. Here they found the Boys assembled with their instruments. Breezy held up his hand and, sweating copiously, beamed at them. "Listen, boys. Get this. We'll use the other routine, if it's all the same with the composer. Carlos doesn't feel happy about the fall. He's afraid he may hurt himself on account he's holding his instrument."

"Here!" said Lord Pastern.

"It's the way you wanted it, Lord Pastern, isn't it?" Breezy gabbled. "That's fine, isn't it? Better egzzit altogether."

"I faint and get carried out?"

"That's right. The other routine. I persuaded Carlos. Everybody happy? Swell."

The Boys began to warm up their instruments. The room was filled with slight anticipatory noises. The double-bass muttered and zoomed.

Skelton strolled over to Lord Pastern. "I had to come in and wish the new sensation all the best," he said, looking hard at him.

"Thank yer."

"A great night," Caesar Bonn murmured. "It will be long remembered."

"Would this be a loaded gun?" Skelton asked and laughed unpleasantly.

The revolver lay, together with the sombrero, near the drums. Lord Pastern took it up. Skelton raised his hands above his head. "I confess everything," he said. "*Is* it loaded?"

"With blanks."

"By cripes," said Skelton with a loud laugh, "I hope they *are* blanks."

"George made them himself," said Félicité.

Skelton lowered his right hand and held it out towards Lord Pastern, who put the revolver into it.

Breezy, at a distance, sighed heavily. Skelton broke the revolver, slipped a finger-nail behind the rim of a cartridge and drew it out.

"Very nice work, Lord Pastern," he said. He spun the cylinder, drawing out and replacing one blank after the other. "Very nice work indeed," he said.

Lord Pastern, obviously gratified, embarked on a history of the revolver, of his own prowess as a marksman, and of the circumstances under which his brother-in-law had presented the revolver to him. He pointed out the initials scratched under the butt. Skelton made a show of squinting down the barrel, snapped the revolver shut and returned the weapon to Lord Pastern. He turned away and glanced at Breezy. "O.K.," he said. "What are we waiting for?" He began to heighten the tension of his drums. "Good luck to the new act," he said and the drum throbbed.

"Thanks, Syd," said Breezy.

His fingers were in his waistcoat pocket. He looked anxiously at Skelton. He felt in one pocket after another. Sweat hung in fine beads over his eyebrows.

"What's up, boy?" said Happy Hart.

"I can't find my tablet."

He began pulling his pocket linings out. "I'm all to pieces, without it," he said. "God, I know I've got one somewhere!"

The door leading to the restaurant opened and the Jivesters came through with their instruments. They grinned at Breezy's Boys and looked sideways at Lord Pastern. The room was full of oiled heads, black figures and the strange shapes of saxophones, double-basses, piano-accordions and drums.

"We'd better make ourselves scarce, Fée," Edward said. "Come on, Lisle. Good luck, Cousin George."

"Good luck."

"Good luck."

They went out. Breezy still searched his pockets. The others watched him nervously.

"You shouldn't let yourself get this way," said Skelton. Lord Pastern pointed an accusing finger at Breezy. "Now perhaps you'll see the value of what I was tellin' you," he admonished. Breezy shot a venomous glance at him.

"For heaven's sake, boy," said Happy Hart. "We're *on!*"

"I've got to have it. I'm all shaky. I can't look. One of you . . ."

"What *is* all this!" Lord Pastern cried with extreme irritation. He darted at Breezy.

"It's only a tablet," Breezy said. "I always take one. For my nerves."

Lord Pastern said accusingly, "Tablet be damned!"

"For crisake, I *got* to have it, blast you."

"Put your hands up."

Lord Pastern began with ruthless efficiency to search Breezy. He hit him all over and turned out his pockets, allowing various objects to fall about his feet. He opened his cigarette case and wallet and explored their contents. He patted and prodded. Breezy giggled. "I'm ticklish," he said foolishly. Finally Lord Pastern jerked a handkerchief out of Breezy's breast pocket. A small white object fell from it. Breezy swooped on it, clapped his hand to his mouth and swallowed. "Thanks a lot. All set, boys? Let's go."

They went out ahead of him. The lights on the walls had been switched off. Only the pink table lamps glowed. A flood-light, hidden in the alcove ceiling, drove down its pool of amber on the gleaming dais; the restaurant was a swimming cave filled with dim faces, occasional jewels, many colours. The waiters flickered about inside it. Little drifts of cigarette smoke hung above the tables. From the restaurant, the band dais glowed romantically in its alcove. The players and their instruments looked hard and glossy. Above them the arm of the giant metronome pointed motionless at the floor. The Boys, smiling as if in great delight, seated themselves. The umbrellas, the sombrero and the tympani were carried in by waiters.

In the band-room Lord Pastern, standing beside Breezy, fiddled with his revolver, whistled under his breath and peered sideways through the door. Beyond the tympani, he could see the dimly glowing faces of his wife, his step-daughter, his niece and his cousin. Félicité's face was inclined up to Ned Manx's. Lord Pastern suddenly gave a shrill cackle of laughter.

Breezy Bellairs glanced at him in dismay, passed his hand over his head, pulled down his waistcoat, assumed his ventriloquist's doll smile and made his entrance. The Boys played him on with their signature tune. A patter of clapping filled the restaurant like a mild shower. Breezy smiled, bowed, turned and, using finicking sharp gestures that were expressly his own, conducted.

Syd Skelton bounced slightly in his seat. His foot moved against the floor, not tapping but flexing and relaxing in a constant beat against the syncopated, precise illogic of the noises he made. The four saxophonists swayed together, their faces all looking alike, expressionless because of their lips and puffed cheeks. When they had passages of rest they at once smiled. The band was playing tunes that Carlisle knew; very old tunes. They were recognizable at first and then a bedevilment known as the Breezy Bellairs Manner sent them screeching and thudding into a jungle of obscurity. "All swing bandsmen," Carlisle thought, "ought to be Negroes. There's something wrong about their not being Negroes."

Now three of them were singing. They had walked forward with long easy steps and stood with their heads close together, rocking in unison. They made ineffable grimaces. "Peea-nuts," they wailed. But they didn't let the song about peanuts, which Carlisle rather liked, speak for itself. They bedevilled and twisted and screwed it and then went beaming back to their instruments. There was another old song—"The Umbrella Man."

She had a simple taste and its quiet monotony pleased her. They did it once, quietly and monotonously. The flood-light dimmed and a brilliant spot light found the pianist. He was playing by himself and singing. That was all right, thought Carlisle. She could mildly enjoy it. But a piercing shriek cut across the naïve tune. The spot light switched to a doorway at the far end of the restaurant. Carlos Rivera stood there, his hands crawling over the keys of his piano-accordion. He advanced between the tables and mounted the dais. Breezy turned to Rivera. He hardly moved his baton. His flesh seemed to jump about on his submerged skeleton. This was his Manner. Rivera, without accompaniment, squeezed trickles, blasts and moans from his piano-accordion. He was a master of his medium. He looked straight at Carlisle, widening his eyes and bowing himself towards her. The sounds he made were frankly lewd, thought Edward Manx. It was monstrous and ridiculous that people in evening clothes should sit idly in a restaurant, mildly diverted, while Rivera directed his lascivious virtuosity at Carlisle.

Now the spot light was in the centre of the dais and only the tympanist played, while the double-bass slapped his instrument. The others moved one by one through the spot light, holding opened umbrellas and turning them like wheels. It was an old trick and they did it, Carlisle thought, sillily. They underdid it. Lady Pastern during a quieter passage said clearly: "Félicité, that is my Ascot parasol."

"Well, *Maman,* I believe it is."

"Your stepfather had no right whatsoever. It was a wedding present of great value. The handle is jewelled."

"Never mind."

"I object categorically and emphatically."

"He's having difficulty with it. Look, they've stopped turning their parasols."

The players were all back in their seats. The noise broadened and then faded out in an unanticipated wail and they were silent.

Breezy bowed and smiled and bowed. Rivera looked at Carlisle.

A young woman in a beautiful dress and with hair like blond seaweed came out of a side door and stood in the spot light, twisting a length of scarlet chiffon in her hands. She contemplated her audience as if she were a sort of willing sacrifice and began to moo very earnestly: "Yeoo knee-oo it was onlee summer lightning." Carlisle and Edward both detested her.

Next Syd Skelton and a saxophonist played a duet which was a *tour de force* of acrobatics and earned a solid round of applause.

When it was over Skelton bowed and with an expression of huffy condescension walked into the band-room.

In the ensuing pause, Breezy advanced to the edge of the dais. His smile was broad and winning. He said in a weak voice that he wanted to thank them all very very much for the wonderful reception his Boys had been given and that he had a little announcement to make. He felt sure that when he told them what was in store for them, they would agree with him that this was a very special occasion. (Lady Pastern hissed under her breath.) Some weeks ago, Breezy said, he had been privileged to hear a wonderful little performance on the tympani by a distinguished—well, he wouldn't say amateur. He had prevailed upon this remarkable performer to join with the Boys to-night and as an additional attraction the number given would be this performer's own composition. Breezy stepped back, pronounced Lord Pastern's names and title with emphasis and looked expectantly towards the door at the rear of the alcove.

Carlisle, as all other relations, distant or close, of Lord Pastern, had often suffered acute embarrassment at his hands. Tonight she had fully expected to endure again that all too familiar wave of discomfort. When, however, he came through the door and stood before them with pink cheeks and a nervous smile, she was suddenly filled with compassion. It was silly, futile and immensely touching that he should make a fool of himself in this particular way. Her heart went out to him.

He walked to the tympani, made a polite little bow and, with an anxious expression, took his seat. They saw him, with a furtive air, lay his revolver on the dais close to Félicité's chair and place his sombrero over it. Breezy pointed his baton at him and said: "Ladies and gentlemen: 'Hot Guy Hot Gunner.'" He gave the initial down-beat and they were off.

It sounded, really, much like all the other numbers they had heard that night, Carlisle thought. Lord Pastern banged, and rattled, and zinged much in the same way as Syd Skelton. The words, when the three singers came out, were no sillier than those of the other songs. The tune was rather catchy. But, "Oh," she thought, "how vulnerable he is among his tympani!"

Edward thought: "There he sits, cat's meat to any satirist who feels as I do about the social set-up. You might make a cartoon of this or a parable. A cartoon certainly. Cousin George, thumping and banging away under Breezy's baton, and in the background a stream of displaced persons. The metronome is Time . . . finger of scorn . . . making its inane gesture to society. A bit too obvious, of course," he thought, dismissing it, "false, because of its partial truth." And he turned his head to watch Carlisle.

Félicité thought: "There goes George. He has fun, anyway." Her glance strayed to Lord Pastern's sombrero. She touched Edward's knee. He bent towards her and she said in his ear: "Shall I pinch George's gun? I could. Look!" She reached out towards the edge of the dais and slipped her hand under the sombrero.

"Fée, don't!" he ejaculated.

"Do you dare me?"

He shook his head violently.

"Poor George," said Félicité, "what *would* he do?" She withdrew her hand and leant back in her chair, turning the white carnation in her fingers. "Shall I put it in my hair?" she wondered. "It would probably look silly and fall out but it might be a good idea. I wish he'd say something—just one thing—to show we understand each other. After this we can't just go on for ever, pretending."

Lady Pastern thought: "There is no end to one's capacity for humiliation. He discredits me and he discredits his class. It's the same story. There will be the same gossip, the same impertinences in the paper, the same mortification. Nevertheless," she thought, "I did well to come. I did well to suffer this torment to-night. My instinct was correct." She looked steadily at Rivera, who was advancing into the centre of the stage. "I have disposed of you," she thought triumphantly.

Lord Pastern thought: "No mistakes so far. And one, bang and two bang and one crash bang zing. One two and three with his accord-een and wait for it. This is perfectly splendid. I *am* this noise. Look out. Here he comes. Hi-de oh hi. Yip. Here he comes. It's going to work. Hot Gunner with his accord-een."

He crashed his cymbal, silenced it and leant back in his seat.

Rivera had advanced in the spot light. The rest of the band was tacit. The great motionless arm of the metronome stabbed its pointer down at his head. He seemed rapt—at once tormented and exalted. He swayed and jerked and ogled. Although he was not by any means ridiculous, he was the puppet of his own music. The performance was a protracted crescendo, and as it rocketed up to its climax he swayed backwards at a preposterous angle, his instrument raised, the pointer menacing it as it undulated across his chest. A screaming dissonance tore loose from the general din, the spot light switched abruptly to the tympani. Lord Pastern, wearing his sombrero, had risen. Advancing to within five feet of Rivera he pointed his revolver at him and fired.

The accordion blared grotesquely down a scale. Rivera sagged at the knees and fell. The accordion crashed a final chord and was silent. At the same moment as the shot was fired the tenor saxophonist played a single shrill note and sat down. Lord Pastern, apparently bewildered, looked from the recumbent Rivera to the saxophonist, paused for a second and then fired three more blanks. The pianist, the trombone, and finally the double-bass each played a note in a descending scale and each imitated a collapse.

There was a further second's pause. Lord Pastern, looking very much taken-aback, suddenly handed the revolver to Bellairs, who pointed it at him and pulled the trigger. The hammer clicked but there was no discharge. Bellairs aped disgust, shrugged his shoulders, looked at the revolver and broke it open. It discharged its shells in a little spurt. Breezy scratched his head, dropped the revolver in his pocket and made a crisp gesture with his baton hand.

"Yipes," Lord Pastern shouted. The band launched itself into a welter of noise. He darted back and flung himself at his tympani. The spot light concentrated upon him. The metronome, which had been motionless until now, suddenly, swung its long arm. Tick-tack, tick-tack, it clacked. A kaleidoscopic welter of coloured lights winked and flickered along its surface and frame. Lord Pastern went madly to work on the drums.

"Hell!" Edward ejaculated. "At this pace he'll kill himself."

Breezy Bellairs had got a large artificial wreath. Dabbing his eyes with his handkerchief he knelt by Rivera, placed the wreath on his chest and felt his heart. He bent his head, groped frantically inside the wreath and then looked up with a startled expression in the direction of the tympani, where the spot light revealed Lord Pastern in an ecstatic fury, wading into his drums. His solo lasted about eighty seconds. During this time four waiters had come in with a stretcher. Bellairs spoke to them excitedly. Rivera was carried off while the saxophones made a grotesque lugubrious sobbing and Lord Pastern, by hitting his big drum and immediately releasing the tension, produced a series of muffled groans.

The metronome clacked to a standstill, the restaurant lights went up and the audience applauded generously. Breezy, white to the lips and trembling, indicated Lord Pastern, who joined him, glistening with sweat, and bowed. Breezy said something inaudible to him and to the pianist and went out, followed by Lord Pastern. The pianist, the double-bass and the three saxophonists began to play a dance tune.

"Good old George!" cried Félicité. "I think he was superb, *Maman* darling, don't you? Ned, wasn't he heaven?"

Edward smiled at her. "He's astonishing," he said, and added: "Cousin C, do you mind if Lisle and I dance? You will, won't you, Lisle?"

Carlisle put her hand on his shoulder and they moved away. The head-waiter slid past them and stooped for a moment over a man at a table further down the room. The man rose, let his eyeglass fall and, with a preoccupied look, passed Carlisle and Edward on his way to the vestibule.

They danced in silence, companionably. At last Edward said: "What will he do next, do you suppose? Is there anything left?"

"I thought it dreadfully pathetic."

"Quintessence of foolery. Lisle, I haven't had a chance to talk to you about that business before we left. I suppose I oughtn't to have hit the fellow, considering the set-up with Fée, but really it was a bit too much. I'm sorry if I made an unnecessary scene, but I must say I enjoyed it." When she didn't answer, he said uncertainly: "Are you seriously annoyed? Lisle, you didn't by any chance . . ."

"No," she said. "No, I didn't. I may as well confess I was extremely gratified." His hand tightened on hers. "I stood," she added, "in the door of my cave and preened myself."

"Did you notice his ear? Not a cauliflower, but distinctly puffy, and a little trickle of blood. And then the unspeakable creature had the infernal nerve to goggle at you over his hurdy-gurdy."

"It's all just meant to be one in the eye for Fée."

"I'm not so sure."

"If it is, he's not having much success."

"How do you mean?" Edward asked sharply.

"Arst yerself, dearie."

"You mean Fée . . ." He stopped short and turned very red. "Lisle," he said, "about Fée . . . Something very odd has occurred. It's astonishing and, well, it's damned awkward. I can't explain but I'd like to think you understood."

Carlisle looked up at him. "You're not very lucid," she said.

"Lisle, my dear . . . Lisle, see here . . ."

They had danced round to the band dais. Carlisle said: "Our waiter's standing over there, watching us. I think he's trying to catch your eye."

"Be blowed to him."

"Yes, he is. Here he comes."

"It'll be some blasted paper on my tracks. Yes, do you want me?"

The waiter had touched Edward's arm. "Excuse me, sir. An urgent call."

"Thank you. Come with me, Lisle. Where's the telephone?"

The waiter hesitated, glanced at Carlisle and said: "If madam will excuse me, sir . . ." His voice sank to a murmur.

"Good Lord!" Edward said and took Carlisle by the elbow. "There's been some sort of trouble. Cousin George wants me to go in. I'll drop you at the table, Lisle."

"What's he up to now, for pity's sake?"

"I'll come as soon as I can. Make my excuses."

As he went out Carlisle saw, with astonishment, that he was very pale.

In the vestibule, which was almost deserted, Edward stopped the waiter. "How bad is it?" he asked. "Is he badly hurt?"

The man raised his clasped hands in front of his mouth. "They say he's dead," said the waiter.

III

Breezy Bellairs sat at the little table in the inner office where he had played poker. When Edward came through the outer office he had heard scuffling and expostulations and he had opened the door upon a violent struggle. Breezy was being lugged to his feet from a squatting position on the floor and hustled across the room. He was slack, now, and unresisting. His soft hands scratched at the surface of the table. He was dishevelled and breathless; tears ran out of his eyes, and his mouth was open. David Hahn, the secretary, stood behind him and patted his shoulder. "You shouldn't have done it, old boy," he said. "Honest. You shouldn't have done a thing like that."

"Keep off me," Breezy whispered. Caesar Bonn, wringing his hands in the conventional gesture of distress, looked past Edward into the main office. The man with the eyeglass sat at the desk there, speaking inaudibly into the telephone.

"How did it happen?" Edward asked.

"Look," Lord Pastern said.

Edward crossed the room. "You must not touch him," Caesar Bonn gabbled. "Excuse me, sir, forgive me. Dr. Allington has said at once, he must not be touched."

"I'm not going to touch him."

He bent down. Rivera lay on the floor. His long figure was stretched out tidily against the far wall. Near the feet lay the comic wreath of flowers and a little farther off, his piano-accordion. Rivera's eyes were open. His upper lip was retracted and the teeth showed. His coat was thrown open and the surface of his soft shirt was blotted with red. Near the top of the blot a short dark object stuck out ridiculously from his chest.

"What is it? It looks like a dart."

"Shut that door," Bonn whispered angrily. Hahn darted to the communicating door and shut it. Just before he did so, Edward heard the man at the telephone say: "In the office. I'll wait for you, of course."

"This will ruin us. We are ruined," said Bonn.

"They will think it an after-hours investigation, that is all," said Hahn. "If we keep our heads."

"It will all come out. I insist we are ruined."

In a voice that rose to a weak falsetto, Breezy said: "Listen boys. Listen Caesar, I didn't know it was that bad. I couldn't see. I wasn't sure. I can't be blamed for that, can I? I passed the word something was wrong to the Boys. It wouldn't have made any difference if I'd acted different, would it, Dave? They can't say anything to me, can they?"

"Take it easy, old man."

"You did right," Bonn said, vigorously. "If you had done other wise—what a scene! What a debacle! And to no purpose. No, no, it was correct."

"Yes, but look Caesar, it's terrible, the way we carried on. A cod funeral march and everything. I knew it was unlucky. I said so when he told me he wanted the other routine. All the Boys said so!" He pointed a quivering finger at Lord Pastern. "It was your big idea. You wished it on us. Look where it's landed us. What a notion, a cod funeral march!"

His mouth sagged and he began to laugh, fetching his breath in gasps and beating on the table.

"Shut up," said Lord Pastern, irritably. "You're a fool."

The door opened and the man with the eyeglass came in. "What's all this noise?" he asked. He stood over Breezy. "If you can't pull yourself together, Mr. Bellairs," he said, "we shall have to take drastic steps to make you." He glanced at Bonn. "He'd better have brandy. Can you beat up some aspirin?"

Hahn went out. Breezy sobbed and whispered.

"The police," said the man, "will be here in a moment. I shall, of course, be required to make a statement." He looked hard at Edward. "Who is this?"

"I sent for him," said Lord Pastern. "He's with my party. My cousin, Ned Manx, Dr. Allington."

"I see."

"I thought I'd like to have Ned," Lord Pastern added wistfully.

Dr. Allington turned back to Breezy and picked up his wrist. He looked sharply at him. "You're in a bit of a mess, my friend," he remarked.

"It's not my fault. Don't look at me like that. I can't be held responsible, my God."

"I don't suggest anything of the sort. Is brandy any good to you? Ah, here it is."

Hahn brought it in. "Here's the aspirin," he said. "How many?" He shook out two tablets. Breezy snatched the bottle and spilt half a dozen on the table. Dr. Allington intervened and gave him three. He gulped them down with the brandy, wiped his face over with his handkerchief, yawned and shivered.

Voices sounded in the outer office. Bonn and Hahn moved towards Breezy. Lord Pastern planted his feet apart and lightly flexed his arms. This posture was familiar to Edward. It usually meant trouble. Dr. Allington put his glass in his eye. Breezy made a faint whispering.

Somebody tapped on the door. It opened and a thick-set man with grizzled hair came in. He wore a dark overcoat, neat, hard and unsmart, and carried a bowler hat. His eyes were bright and he looked longer and more fixedly than is the common habit at those he newly encountered. His sharp impersonal glance dwelt in turn upon the men in the room and upon the body of Rivera, from which they had stepped aside. Dr. Allington moved out from the group.

"Trouble here?" said the newcomer. "Are you Dr. Allington, sir? My chaps are outside. Inspector Fox."

He walked over to the body. The doctor followed him and they stood together, looking down at it. Fox gave a slight grunt and turned back to the others. "And these gentlemen?" he said. Caesar Bonn made a dart at him and began to talk very rapidly.

"If I could just have the names," said Fox and took out his notebook. He wrote down their names, his glance resting longer on Breezy than upon the others. Breezy lay back in his chair and gaped at Fox. His dinner-jacket with its steel buttons sagged on one side. The pocket was dragged down.

"Excuse me, sir," Fox said, "are you feeling unwell?" He stooped over Breezy.

"I'm shot all to hell," Breezy whimpered.

"Well, now, if you'll just allow me . . ." He made a neat unobtrusive movement and stood up with the revolver in his large gloved hand.

Breezy gaped at it and then pointed a quivering hand at Lord Pastern. "That's not my gun," he chattered. "Don't you think it. It's his. It's his lordship's. He fired it at poor old Carlos and poor old Carlos fell down like he wasn't meant to. That's right, isn't it, chaps? Isn't it, Caesar? God, won't somebody speak up for me and tell the Inspector? His lordship handed me that gun."

"Don't you fret," Fox said comfortably. "We'll have a chat about it presently." He dropped the revolver in his pocket. His sharp glance travelled again over the group of men. "Well, thank you, gentlemen," he said and opened the door. "We'll need to trouble you a little further, Doctor, but I'll ask the others to wait in here, if you please."

They filed into the main office. Four men already waited there. Fox nodded and three of them joined him in the inner room. They carried black canes and a tripod.

"This is Dr. Curtis, Dr. Allington," said Fox. He unbuttoned his overcoat and laid his bowler on the table. "Will you two gentlemen take a look? We'll get some shots when you're ready, Thompson."

One of the men set up a tripod and camera. The doctors behaved like simultaneous comedians. They hitched up their trousers, knelt on their right knees and rested their forearms on their left thighs.

"I was supping here," said Dr. Allington. "He was dead when I got to him, which must have been about three to five minutes after this—" he jabbed a forefinger at the blotch on Rivera's shirt—"had happened. When I got here they had him where he is now. I made a superficial examination and rang the Yard."

"Nobody tried to withdraw the weapon?" said Dr. Curtis and added: "Unusual, that."

"It seems that one of them, Lord Pastern it was, said it shouldn't be touched. Some vague idea of an effusion of blood following the withdrawal. They realized almost at once that he was dead. At a guess, would you say there'd been considerable penetration of the right ventricle? I haven't touched the thing, by the way. Can't make out what it is."

"We'll take a look in a minute," said Dr. Curtis. "All right, Fox."

"All right, Thompson," said Fox.

They moved away. Their shadows momentarily blotted the wall as Thompson's lamp flashed. Whistling under his breath he manoeuvred his camera, flashed and clicked.

"O.K., Mr. Fox," he said at last.

"Dabs," said Fox. "Do what you can about the weapon, Bailey."

The finger-print expert, a thin dark man, squatted by the body.

Fox said: "I'd like to get a statement about the actual event. You can help us, there, Dr. Allington? What exactly was the set-up? I understand a gun was used against the deceased in the course of the entertainment."

He had folded his overcoat neatly over the back of his chair. He now sat down, his knees apart, his spectacles adjusted, his notebook flattened out on the table. "If I may trouble you, Doctor," he said. "In your own words, as we say."

Dr. Allington fitted his glass in position and looked apologetic. "I'm afraid I'm not going to be a success," he said. "To be quite frank, Inspector, I was more interested in my guest than in the entertainment. And, by the way, I'd like to make my apologies to her as soon as possible. She must be wondering where the devil I've got to."

"If you care to write a note, sir, we'll give it to one of the waiters."

"What? Oh, all right," said Dr. Allington fretfully. A note was taken out by Thompson. Through the opened door they caught a glimpse of a dejected group in the main office. Lord Pastern's voice, caught midway in a sentence, said shrilly: ". . . entirely the wrong way about it. Making a mess, as usual . . ." and was shut off by the door.

"Yes, Doctor?" said Fox placidly.

"Oh God, they were doing some kind of idiotic turn. We were talking and I didn't pay much attention except to say it was a pretty poor show, old Pastern making an ass of himself. This chap, here"—he looked distastefully at the body—"came out from the far end of the restaurant and made a hell of a noise on his concertina or whatever it is, and there was a terrific bang. I looked up and saw old Pastern with a gun of some sort in his hand. This chap did a fall, the conductor dropped a wreath on him and then he was carried out. About three minutes later they sent for me."

"I'll just get that down, if you please," said Fox. With raised eyebrows and breathing through his mouth, he wrote at a steady pace. "Yes," he said comfortably, "and how far, Doctor, would you say his lordship was from the deceased when he fired?"

"Quite close. I don't know. Between five and seven feet. I don't know."

"Did you notice the deceased's behaviour, sir, immediately after the shot was fired? I mean, did it strike you there was anything wrong?"

Dr. Allington looked impatiently at the door. "Strike me!" he repeated. "I wasn't struck by anything in particular. I looked up when the gun went off. I think it occurred to me that he did a very clever fall. He was a pretty ghastly-looking job of work, all hair oil and teeth."

"Would you say . . ." Fox began and was interrupted.

"I really wouldn't say anything, Inspector. I've given you my opinion from the time I examined the poor devil . . . To go any further would be unprofessional and stupid. I simply wasn't watching and therefore don't remember. You'd better find somebody who did watch and does remember."

Fox had raised his head and now looked beyond Dr. Allington to the door. His hand was poised motionless over his notebook. His jaw had dropped. Dr. Allington slewed round and was confronted with a very tall dark man in evening dress.

"I was watching," said this person, "and I think I remember. Shall I try, Inspector?"

IV

"Good Lor'!" Fox said heavily and rose. "Well, thank you, Dr. Allington," he said. "I'll have a typed statement sent round to you to-morrow. Would you be good enough to read it through and sign it if it's in order? We'll want you for the inquest, if you please."

"All right. Thanks," said Dr. Allington, making for the door, which the newcomer opened. "Thanks," he repeated. "Hope you make a better fist of it than I did, what?"

"Most unlikely, I'm afraid," the other rejoined pleasantly and closed the door after him. "You're in for a party, Fox," he said, and walked over to the body. Bailey, the finger-print expert, said, "Good evening, sir," and moved away grinning.

"*If* I may ask, sir," said Fox, "how do you come to be in on it?"

"May I not take mine ease in mine restaurant with mine wife? Shall there be no more cakes and ale? None for you, at all events, you poor chap," he said, bending over Rivera. "You haven't got the thing out yet, I see, Fox."

"It's been dabbed and photographed. It can come out."

Fox knelt down. His hand wrapped in his handkerchief closed round the object that protruded from Rivera's chest. It turned with difficulty. "Tight," he said.

"Let me look, may I?"

Fox drew back. The other knelt beside him. "But what is it?" he said. "Not an orthodox dart. There's thread at the top. It's been unscrewed from something. Black. Silver-mounted. Ebony, I fancy. Or a dark bronze. What the devil is it? Try again, Fox."

Fox tried again. He twisted. Under the wet silk the wound opened slightly. He pulled steadily. With a jerk and a slight but horrible sound, the weapon was released. Fox laid it on the floor and opened out the handkerchief. Bailey clicked his tongue.

Fox said: "Will you look at that. Good Lord, what a set-up! It's a bit of an umbrella shaft, turned into a dart or bolt."

"A black and white parasol," said his companion. Fox looked up quickly but said nothing. "Yes. There's the spring clip, you see. That's why it wouldn't come out readily. An elaborate affair, almost a museum piece. The clip's got tiny jewels in it. And, look, Fox."

He pointed a long finger. Protruding from one end was a steel, about two inches long, wide at the base and tapering sharply to a point. "It looks like some awl or a stiletto. Probably it was originally sunk in a short handle. It's been driven into one end of this bit of parasol shaft and sealed up somehow. Plastic wood, I fancy. The end of the piece of shaft, you see, was hollow. Probably the longer section of the parasol screwed into it and a knob or handle of some kind, in turn, was screwed on the opposite end." He took out his notebook and made a rapid sketch which he showed to Fox. "Like this," he said. "It'll be a freak of a parasol. French, I should think. I remember seeing them in the enclosure at Longchamps when I was a boy. The shaft's so thin that they have to put a separate section in to take the slip and groove. This is the section. But why in the name of high fantasy use a bit of parasol shaft as a sort of dagger?"

"We'll have another shot of this, Thompson." Fox rose stiffly and after a long pause said: "Where were you sitting, Mr. Alleyn?"

"Next door to the Pastern party. A few yards off the dais."

"What a bit of luck," said Fox simply.

"Don't be too sure," rejoined Chief Inspector Alleyn. He sat on the table and lit a cigarette. "This is no doubt a delicate situation, Br'er Fox. I mustn't butt in on your job, you know."

Fox made a short derisive noise. "You'll take over, sir, of course."

"I can at least make my report. I'd better warn you at the outset, I was watching that extraordinary chap Pastern most of the time. What a queer cup of tea it is, to be sure."

"I suppose," said Fox stolidly, "you'll be telling me, sir, that you were his fag at Eton."

Alleyn grinned at this jibe. "If I had been I should probably have spent the rest of my life in a lunatic asylum. No, I was going to say that I watched him to the exclusion of the others. I noticed, for instance, that he really pointed his gun—a revolver of some sort—at this man and that he stood not more than seven feet off him when he did it."

"This is more like it," Fox said and reopened his book. "You don't mind, Mr. Alleyn?" he added primly.

Alleyn said: "You're gloating over this, aren't you? Very well. They did a damn' silly turn, revolving umbrellas and parasols like a bunch of superannuated chorus girls, and I noticed that one parasol, a very pansy Frenchified affair of black and white lace, seemed to be giving trouble. The chap had to shove his hand up to hold it."

"Is that so?" Fox looked at Thompson. "You might get hold of the umbrella." Thompson went out. Bailey moved forward with an insufflator and bent over the weapon.

"I'd better describe the final turn, I suppose," said Alleyn and did so. His voice moved on quietly and slowly. Thompson returned with the black and white parasol. "This is it, sure enough, sir," he said. "A section of the shaft's gone. Look here! No clip anywhere to keep it shut." He laid it beside the dart.

"Good enough," Fox said. "Get your shots, will you."

Thompson, having taken three further photographs of the weapon, folded it in the handkerchief and put it in Fox's case. "I'll fix it up with proper protection when we're finished, Mr. Fox," he said. On a nod from Fox, he and Bailey went out with their gear.

". . . when the shot was fired," Alleyn was saying, "he had swung round, facing Lord Pastern, with his back half turned to the audience and fully turned to the conductor. He was inclined backwards at a grotesque angle, with the instrument raised. He was directly under the point of the metronome, which was motionless. After the report he swung round still further and straightened up a bit. The piano-accordion, if that's what it is, ran down the scale and let out an infernal bleat. His knees doubled and he went down on them, sat on his heels and then rolled over, fetching up on his back with his instrument between himself and the audience. At the same time one of the bandsmen aped being hit. I couldn't see Rivera clearly because the spot light had switched to old Pastern, who, after a moment's hesitation, loosed off the other rounds. Three more of the band chaps did comic staggers as if he'd hit them. Something seemed a bit out of joint here. They all looked as if they weren't sure what came next. However, Pastern gave his gun to Bellairs, who pointed it at him and pulled the trigger. The last round had been used, so there was only a click. Bellairs registered disgust, broke the revolver, pocketed it and gestured as much as to say: 'I've had it. Carry on,' and Lord Pastern then went to market in a big way and generally raised hell. He looked extraordinary. Glazed eyes, sweating, half-smiling and jerking about over his drums. An unnerving exhibition from a middle-aged peer but of course he's as mad as a March hare. Troy and I were snobbishly horrified. It was then that the metronome went into action in a blaze of winking lights. It'd been pointing straight down at Rivera before. A waiter chucked a wreath to the conductor, who knelt down by this chap Rivera and dumped it on his chest. He felt his heart and then looked closely at Rivera and bent over his body, groping inside the wreath. He turned in a startled sort of way to old Pastern. He said something to the blokes with the stretcher. The wreath hid the face and the accordion was half across the stomach. Bellairs spoke to the pianist and then to Lord Pastern, who went out with him when they finished their infernal din. I smelt trouble, saw a waiter speak to Allington and stop a chap in Lady Pastern's party. I had a long argument with myself, lost it and came out here. That's all. Have you looked at the revolver?"

"I've taken it off Bellairs. It's in my pocket." Fox put his glove on, produced the revolver and laid it on the table. "No known make," he said.

"Probably been used for target-shooting," Alleyn muttered. He laid the dart beside it. "It'd fit, Fox. Look. Had you noticed?"

"We haven't got very far."

"Of course not."

"I don't know quite what line to take about all the folk in there." Fox jerked his head in the direction of the restaurant.

"Better get names and addresses. The waiters can do it. They'll know a lot of them already. They can say it's a new police procedure on extension nights. It's our good fortune, Br'er Fox, that the public will believe any foolishness if they are told we are the authors of it. The Pastern party had better be held."

"I'll fix it," Fox said. He went out, revealing for a moment the assembly in the outer office ". . . hang about kickin' my heels all night . . ." Lord Pastern's voice protested and was shut off abruptly.

Alleyn knelt by the body and began to search it. The coat was turned back and the breast pocket had been pulled out. Four letters and a gold cigarette case had slipped down between the body and the coat. The case was half-filled and bore an inscription: "From Félicité." He searched the other pockets. A jade holder. Two handkerchiefs. A wallet with three pound-notes. He laid these objects out in a row and turned to the piano-accordion. It was a large, heavily ornamental affair. He remembered how it had glittered as Rivera swung it across his chest in that last cacophony before he fell. As Alleyn lifted it, it raised a metallic wail. He put it down hastily on the table and returned to his contemplation of the body. Fox came back. "That's all fixed up," he said.

"Good."

Alleyn stood up. "He was a startling fellow to look at," he said. "One felt one had seen him in innumerable Hollywood band features, ogling the camera man against an exotic background. We might cover him up, don't you think? The management can produce a clean table-cloth."

"The mortuary man will be outside now, Mr. Alleyn," said Fox. He glanced down at the little collection on the floor. "Much obliged, sir," he said. "Anything useful?"

"The letters are written in Spanish. Postmark. He'll have to be dusted, of course."

"I rang the Yard, Mr. Alleyn. The A.S.M.'s compliments and he'll be glad if you'll take over."

"That's a thumping great lie," said Alleyn mildly. "He's in Godalming."

"He's come back, sir, and happened to be in the office. Quite a coincidence."

"You go to hell, Fox. Damn it, I'm out with my wife."

"I sent a message in to Mrs. Alleyn. The waiter brought back a note."

Alleyn opened the folded paper and disclosed a lively drawing of a lady asleep in bed. Above her, encircled by a balloon, Alleyn and Fox crawled on all fours inspecting, through a huge lens, a nest from which protruded the head of a foal, broadly winking.

"A very stupid woman, I'm afraid, poor thing," Alleyn muttered, grinning, and showed it to Fox. "Come on," he said. "We'll take another look at the revolver and then get down to statements."

CHAPTER VI

Dope

I

ABOVE THE DOOR leading from the foyer of the Metronome to the office was a clock with chromium hands and figures. As the night wore on, the attention of those persons who were congregated there became increasingly drawn to this clock, so that when at one in the morning the long hand jumped to the hour, everyone observed it. A faint sigh, and a dreary restlessness, stirred them momentarily.

The members of the band who were assembled at the end of the foyer sat in dejected attitudes on gilded chairs that had been brought in from the restaurant. Syd Skelton's hands dangled between his knees, tapping each other flaccidly. Happy Hart was stretched back with his legs extended. The light found out patches on his trousers worn shiny by the pressure of his thighs against the under-surface of his piano. The four saxophonists sat with their heads together, but they had not spoken for some time and inertia, not interest, held them in these postures of intimacy. The double-bass, a thin man, rested his elbows on his knees and his head on his hands. Breezy Bellairs, in the centre of his Boys, fidgeted, yawned, wiped his hands over his face and bit feverishly at his nails. Near the band stood four waiters and the spot-light operator, whose interrogation had just ended, quite fruitlessly.

At the opposite end of the foyer, in a muster of easier chairs, sat Lady Pastern and her guests. Alone of the whole assembly, she held an upright posture. The muscles of her face sagged a little; its lines were clogged with powder and there were greyish marks under her eyes, but her wrists and ankles were crossed composedly, her hair was rigidly in order. On her right and left the two girls drooped in their chairs. Félicité, chain-smoking, gave her attention fitfully to the matter in hand and often took a glass from her bag and looked resentfully at herself, repainting her lips with irritable gestures.

Carlisle, absorbed as usual with detail, watched the mannerisms of her companions through an increasing haze of sleepiness and was only half aware of what they said. Ned Manx listened sharply as if he tried to memorize all that he heard. Lord Pastern was never still. He would throw himself into a chair with an air of abandon and in a moment spring from it and walk aimlessly about the room. He looked with distaste at the speaker of the moment. He grimaced and interjected. At one side, removed from the two main groups, stood Caesar Bonn and the secretary, David Hahn. These two were watchful and pallid. Out of sight, in the main office, Dr. Curtis, having seen to the removal of Rivera's body, jotted down notes for his report.

In the centre of the foyer, Inspector Fox sat at a small table with his notebook open before him and his spectacles on his nose. His feet rested side by side on the carpet and his large knees were pressed together. He contemplated his notes with raised eyebrows.

Behind Fox stood Chief Detective-Inspector Alleyn, and to him the attention of the company, in some cases fitfully, in others constantly, was drawn. He had been speaking for about a minute. Carlisle, though she tried to listen to the sense of his words, caught herself thinking how deep his voice was and how free from mannerisms his habit of speech. "A pleasant chap," she thought, and knew by the small affirmative noise Ned Manx made when Alleyn paused that he agreed with her.

". . . so you see," Alleyn was saying now, "that a certain amount of ground must be covered here and that we must ask you to stay until it *has* been covered. That can't be helped."

"Damned if I see . . ." Lord Pastern began and fetched up short. "What's your name?" he said. Alleyn told him. "I thought so," said Lord Pastern with an air of having found him out in something. "Point is: are you suggestin' I dug a dart in the chap or aren't you? Come on."

"It doesn't, at the moment, seem to be a question, as far as you are concerned, sir, of digging."

"Well, shootin' then. Don't split straws."

"One may as well," Alleyn said mildly, "be accurate."

He turned aside to Fox's case, which lay on a table. From it he took an open box containing the weapon that had killed Rivera. He held the box up, tilting it towards them.

"Will you look at this?" They looked at it. "Do any of you recognize it? Lady Pastern?"

She had made an inarticulate sound, but now she said indifferently: "It looks like part of a parasol handle."

"A black and white parasol?" Alleyn suggested and one of the saxophonists looked up quickly.

"Possibly," said Lady Pastern. "I don't know."

"Don't be an ass, C," said her husband. "Obviously it's off that French thing of yours. We borrowed it."

"You had no right whatever, George . . ."

Alleyn interrupted. "We've found that one of the parasols used in the Umbrella Man number is minus a few inches of its shaft." He glanced at the second saxophonist. "I think you had some difficulty in managing it?"

"That's right," the second saxophonist said. "You couldn't shut it properly, I noticed. There wasn't a clip or anything."

"This is it: five inches of the shaft containing the clip. Notice that spring catch. It is jewelled. Originally, of course, it kept the parasol closed. The actual handle or knob on its own piece of shaft has been engaged with the main shaft of the parasol. Can you describe it?" He looked at Lady Pastern, who said nothing. Lord Pastern said: "Of course you can, C. A damn-fool thing like a bird with emeralds for eyes. French."

"You're sure of that, sir?"

"Of course I'm sure. Damn it, I took the thing to bits when I was in the ballroom."

Fox raised his head and stared at Lord Pastern with a sort of incredulous satisfaction. Edward Manx swore under his breath, the women were rigidly horrified.

"I see," Alleyn said. "When was this?"

"After dinner. Breezy was with me. Weren't you, Breezy?"

Breezy shied violently and then nodded.

"Where did you leave the bits, sir?"

"On the piano. Last I saw of 'em."

"Why," Alleyn asked, "did you dismember the parasol?"

"For fun."

"*Mon dieu, mon dieu,*" Lady Pastern moaned.

"I knew it'd unscrew and I unscrewed it."

"Thank you," Alleyn said. "For the benefit of those of you who haven't examined the parasol closely, I'd better describe it a little more fully. Both ends of this piece of shaft are threaded, one on the outer surface to engage with the top section, the other on the inner surface to receive the main shaft of the parasol. It has been removed and the outer sections screwed together. Now look again at this weapon made from the section that has been removed. You will see that a steel tool has been introduced into this end and sunk in plastic wood. Do any of you recognize this tool? I'll hold it a little closer. It's encrusted with blood and a little difficult to see."

He saw Carlisle's fingers move on the arms of her chair. He saw Breezy rub the back of his hand across his mouth and Lord Pastern blow out his cheeks. "Rather unusual," he said, "isn't it? Wide at the base and tapering. Keen pointed. It might be an embroidery stiletto. I don't know. Do you reognize it, Lady Pastern?"

"No."

"Anybody?" Lord Pastern opened his mouth and shut it again. "Well," Alleyn murmured after a pause. He replaced the box containing the weapon and took up Lord Pastern's revolver. He turned it over in his hands.

"If that's the way you chaps go to work," said Lord Pastern, "I don't think much of it. That thing may be smothered with finger-prints, for all you know, and you go pawin' it about."

"It's been printed," Alleyn said without emphasis. He produced a pocket lens and squinted through it down the barrel. "You seem to have given it some rough usage," he said.

"No, I haven't," Lord Pastern countered instantly. "Perfect condition. Always has been."

"When did you last look down the barrel, sir?"

"Before we came here. In my study, and again in the ballroom. Why?"

"George," said Lady Pastern. "I suggest for the last time that you send for your solicitor and refuse to answer any questions until he is here."

"Yes, Cousin George," Edward murmured. "I honestly think . . ."

"My solicitor," Lord Pastern rejoined, "is a snufflin' old ass. I'm perfectly well able to look after myself, C. What's all this about my gun?"

"The barrel," Alleyn said, "is, of course, fouled. That's from the blank rounds. But under the stain left by the discharges there are some curious marks. Irregular scratches, they seem to be. We'll have it photographed but I wonder if in the meantime you can offer an explanation?"

"Here," Lord Pastern ejaculated. "Let me see."

Alleyn gave him the revolver and lens. Grimacing hideously he pointed the barrel to the light and squinted down it. He made angry noises and little puffing sounds through his lips. He examined the butt through the lens and muttered indistinguishable anathemas. Most unexpectedly, he giggled. Finally he dumped it on the table and blew loudly. "Hanky-panky," he said briefly and returned to his chair.

"I beg your pardon?"

"When I examined the gun in my study," Lord Pastern said forcibly, "it was as clean as a whistle. As clean, I repeat, as a whistle. I fired one blank from it in my own house and looked down the barrel afterwards. It was a bit fouled and that was all. All right. They y'are!"

Carlisle, Félicité, Manx and Lady Pastern stirred uneasily. "Uncle George," Carlisle said. "Please."

Lord Pastern glared at her. "Therefore," he said, "I repeat, hanky-panky. The barrel was unmarked when I brought the thing here. I ought to know. It was unmarked when I took it into the restaurant."

Lady Pastern looked steadily at her husband. "You *fool*, George," she said.

"George."

"Cousin George."

"Uncle George . . ."

The shocked voices overlapped and faded out.

Alleyn began again. "Obviously you realize the significance of all this. When I tell you that the weapon—it is, in effect, a dart or bolt, isn't it?—is half an inch shorter than the barrel of the revolver and somewhat less in diameter . . ."

"All right, all right," Lord Pastern interjected.

"I think," said Alleyn, "I should point out . . ."

"You needn't point anything out. And you," Lord Pastern added, turning on his relatives, "can all shut up. I know what you're gettin' at. The barrel was unscratched. By God, I ought to know. And what's more, I noticed when Breezy and I were in the ballroom that this bit of shaft would fit in the barrel. I pointed it out to him."

"Here, here, here!" Breezy expostulated. "I don't like the way this is going. Look here—"

"Did anyone else examine the revolver?" Alleyn interposed adroitly.

Lord Pastern pointed at Skelton. "He did," he said. "Ask him."

Skelton moved forward, wetting his lips.

"Did you look down the barrel?" Alleyn asked.

"Glanced," said Skelton reluctantly.

"Did you notice anything unusual?"

"No."

"Was the barrel quite unscarred?"

There was a long silence. "Yes," said Skelton at last.

"There y'are," said Lord Pastern.

"It would be," Skelton added brutally, "seeing his lordship hadn't put his funny weapon in it yet."

Lord Pastern uttered a short, rude and incredulous word. "Thanks," said Skelton and turned to Alleyn.

Edward Manx said: "May I butt in, Alleyn?"

"Of course."

"It's obvious that you think this thing was fired from the revolver. It's obvious, in my opinion, that you are right. How else could he have been killed? But isn't it equally obvious that the person who used the revolver could have known nothing about it? If he had wanted to shoot Rivera he could have used a bullet. If, for some extraordinary reason, he preferred a sort of rifle grenade or dart or what-not, he would surely have used something less fantastic than the affair you have just shown us. The only object in using the piece of parasol shaft, if it has in fact been so used, would have been this: the spring catch—which is jewelled, by the way—would keep the weapon fixed in the barrel and it wouldn't fall out if the revolver was pointed downwards, and the person who fired the revolver would therefore be unaware of the weapon in the barrel. You wouldn't," Edward said with great energy, "fix up an elaborate sort of thing like this unless there was a reason for it and there would be no reason if you yourself had full control of the revolver and could load it at the last moment. Only an abnormally eccentric . . ." He stopped short, floundered for a moment and then said: "That's the point I wanted to make."

"It's well taken," Alleyn said. "Thank you."

"Hi!" said Lord Pastern.

Alleyn turned to him.

"Look here," he said. "You think these scratches were made by the jewels on that spring thing. Skelton says they weren't there when he looked at the gun. If anyone was fool enough to try and shoot a feller with a thing like this, he'd fire it off first of all to see how it worked. In private. Follow me?"

"I think so, sir."

"All right, then," said Lord Pastern with a shrill cackle, "why waste time jabberin' about scratches?"

He flung himself into his chair.

"Did any of you who were there," Alleyn said, "take particular notice when Mr. Skelton examined the revolver?"

Nobody spoke. Skelton's face was very white. "Breezy watched," he said and added quickly: "I was close to Lord Pastern. I couldn't have . . . I mean . . ."

Alleyn said, "Why did you examine it, Mr. Skelton?"

Skelton wetted his lips. His eyes shifted their gaze from Lord Pastern to

Breezy Bellairs. "I—was sort of interested. Lord Pastern had fixed up the blanks himself and I thought I'd like to take a look. I'd gone in to wish him luck. I mean . . ."

"Why don't you tell him!"

Breezy was on his feet. He had been yawning and fidgeting in his chair. His face was stained with tears. He had seemed to pay little attention to what was said but rather to be in the grip of some intolerable restlessness. His interruption shocked them all by its unexpectedness. He came forward with a shambling movement and grinned at Alleyn.

"I'll tell you," he said rapidly. "Syd did it because I asked him to. He's a pal. I told him. I told him I didn't trust his lordship. I'm a nervous man where firearms are concerned. I'm a nervous man altogether if you can understand." His fingers plucked at his smiling lips. "Don't look at me like that," he said and his voice broke into shrill falsetto. "Everybody's staring as if I'd done something. Eyes. Eyes. Eyes. O God, give me a smoke!"

Alleyn held out his cigarette case. Breezy struck it out of his hand and began to sob. "Bloody sadist," he said.

"I know what's wrong with you, you silly chap," Lord Pastern said accusingly. Breezy shook a finger at him. "You *know!*" he said. "You started it. You're as good as a murderer. You *are* a murderer, by God!"

"Say that again, my good Bellairs," Lord Pastern rejoined with relish, "and I'll have you in the libel court. Action for slander, b' George."

Breezy looked wildly round the assembly. His light eyes with their enormous pupils fixed their gaze on Félicité. He pointed a trembling hand at her. "Look at that girl," he said, "doing her face and sitting up like Jackie with the man she was supposed to love lying stiff and bloody in the morgue. It's disgusting."

Caesar Bonn came forward, wringing his hands. "I can keep silent no longer," he said. "If I am ruined, I am ruined. If I do not speak, there are others who will." He looked at Lord Pastern, at Edward Manx and at Hahn.

Edward said: "It's got to come out, certainly. In common fairness."

"Certainly. Certainly."

"What," Alleyn asked, "has got to come out?"

"Please, Mr. Manx. You will speak."

"All right, Caesar. I think," Edward said slowly, turning to Alleyn, "that you should know what happened before any of you arrived. I myself had only just walked into the room. The body was where you saw it." He paused for a moment. Breezy watched him, but Manx did not look at

Breezy. "There was a sort of struggle going on," he said. "Bellairs was on the floor by Rivera and the others were pulling him off."

"Damned indecent thing," said Lord Pastern virtuously, "trying to go through the poor devil's pockets."

Breezy whimpered.

"I'd like a closer account of this, if you can give it to me. When exactly did this happen?" Alleyn asked.

Caesar and Hahn began talking at once. Alleyn stopped them. "Suppose," he said, "we trace events through the point where Mr. Rivera was carried out of the restaurant!" He began to question the four waiters who had carried Rivera. The waiters hadn't noticed anything was wrong with him. They were a bit flustered anyway because of the confusion about which routine was to be followed. There had been so many contradictory orders that in the end they just watched to see who fell down and then picked up the stretcher and carried him out. The wreath covered his chest. As they lifted him on to the stretcher, Breezy had said quickly: "He's hurt. Get him out." They had carried him straight to the office. As they put the stretcher down they heard him make a noise, a harsh rattling noise, it had been. When they looked closer they found he was dead. They fetched Caesar Bonn and Hahn and then carried the body into the inner room. Then Caesar ordered them back to the restaurant and told one of them to fetch Dr. Allington.

Lord Pastern, taking up the tale, said that while they were still on the dais, after the removal of Rivera, Breezy had gone to him and muttered urgently: "For God's sake come out. Something's happened to Carlos." The pianist, Happy Hart, said that Breezy had stopped at the piano on his way out and had told him in an aside to keep going.

Caesar took up the story. Breezy and Lord Pastern came to the inner office. Breezy was in a fearful state, saying he'd seen blood on Rivera when he put the wreath on his chest. They were still gathered round Rivera's body, laying him out tidily on the floor. Breezy kept gibbering about the blood and then he caught sight of the body and turned away to the wall, retching and scrabbling in his overcoat pockets for one of his tablets and complaining because he had none. Nobody did anything for him and he went into the lavatory off the inner office and was heard vomiting in there. When he came back he looked terrible and stood gabbling about how he felt. At this point Breezy interrupted Caesar. "I told them," he said shrilly. "I told them. It was a terrible shock to me when he fell. It was a shock to all of us, wasn't it, boys?"

"Quite near the edge of the dais," Alleyn repeated. "So that, for the sake of argument, you, Miss de Suze, or Miss Wayne, or Mr. Manx, could have reached out to the sombrero. In fact, while some of your party were dancing, anyone who was left at the table could also have done this. Do you all agree?"

Carlisle was acutely aware of the muscles of her face. She was conscious of Alleyn's gaze, impersonal and deliberate, resting on her eyes and her mouth and her hands. She remembered noticing him—how many hours ago?—when he sat at the next table. "I mustn't look at Fée or at Ned," she thought. She heard Edward move stealthily in his chair. The paper in Félicité's hand rustled. There was a sharp click and Carlisle jumped galvanically. Lady Pastern had flicked open her lorgnette and was now staring through it at Alleyn.

Manx said: "You were next to our table, I think, weren't you, Alleyn?"

"By an odd coincidence," Alleyn rejoined pleasantly.

"I think it better for us to postpone our answers."

"Do you?" Alleyn said lightly. "Why?"

"Obviously, the question about whether we could have touched this hat, or whatever it was . . ."

"You know perfectly well what it was, Ned," Lord Pastern interjected. "It was my sombrero, and the gun was under it. We've had all that."

". . . this sombrero," Edward amended, "is a question that has dangerous implications for all of us. I'd like to say that quite apart from the possibility, which we have not admitted, of any of us touching it, there is surely no possibility at all that any of us could have taken a revolver from underneath it, shoved a bit of a parasol up the barrel and replaced the gun, without anything being noticed. If you don't mind my saying so, the suggestion of any such manoeuvre is obviously ridiculous."

"Oh, I don't know," said Lord Pastern with an air of judicial impartiality. "All that switchin' about of the light and the metronome waggin' and everybody naturally watchin' me, you know. I should say, in point of fact, it was quite possible. I wouldn't have noticed, I promise you."

"George," Félicité whispered fiercely, "do you *want* to do us in?"

"I want the truth," her stepfather shouted crossly. "I was a Theosophist, once," he added.

"You are and have been and always will be an imbecile," said his wife, shutting her lorgnette.

"Well," Alleyn said and, the attention of the band, the employees of the restaurant and its guests having been diverted to this domestic interchange, swung back to him, "ridiculous or not, I shall put the question.

You are, of course, under no compulsion to answer it. Did any of you handle Lord Pastern's sombrero?"

They were silent. The waiter, who had gathered up the pieces of broken mirror, faced Alleyn with an anxious smile. "Excuse me, sir," he said.

"Yes?"

"The young lady," said the waiter, bowing towards Félicité, "did put her hand under the hat. I was the waiter for that table, sir, and I happened to notice. I hope you will excuse me, miss, but I did happen to notice."

Fox's pencil whispered over the paper.

"Thank you," said Alleyn.

Félicité cried out: "This is the absolute *end.* Suppose I said it's not true."

"I shouldn't," Alleyn said. "As Mr. Manx has pointed out, I was sitting next to your table."

"Then why ask?"

"To see if you would frankly admit that you did, in fact, put your hand under the sombrero."

"People," said Carlisle suddenly, "think twice about making frank statements all over the place when a capital crime is involved."

She looked up at Alleyn and found him smiling at her. "How right you are," he said. "That's what makes homicide cases so tiresome."

"Are we to hang about all night," Lord Pastern demanded, "while you sit gossipin'? Never saw such a damned amateur set-up in all m'life. Makes you sick."

"Let us get on by all means, sir. We haven't very much more ground to cover here. It will be necessary, I'm afraid, for us to search you before we can let you off."

"All of us?" Félicité said quickly.

They looked, with something like awe, at Lady Pastern.

"There is a wardress in the ladies' cloak-room," Alleyn said, "and a detective-sergeant in the men's. We shall also need your finger-prints, if you please. Sergeant Bailey will attend to that. Shall we set about it? Perhaps you, Lady Pastern, will go in first?"

Lady Pastern rose. Her figure, tightly encased, seemed to enlarge itself. Everybody stole uneasy glances at it. She faced her husband. "Of the many indignities you have forced upon me," she said, "this is the most intolerable. For this I shall never forgive you."

"Good Lord, C," he rejoined, "what's the matter with bein' searched?

Trouble with you is you've got a dirty mind. If you'd listened to my talks on the Body Beautiful that time in Kent . . ."

"*Silence!*" she said (in French) and swept into the ladies' cloak-room. Félicité giggled nervously.

"Anybody may search *me*," Lord Pastern said generously. "Come on." He led the way to the men's cloak-room.

Alleyn said: "Perhaps, Miss de Suze, you would like to go with your mother. It's perfectly in order, if you think she'd prefer it."

Félicité was sitting in her chair with her left hand clutching her bag and her right hand out of sight. "I expect she'd rather have a private martyrdom, Mr. Alleyn," she said.

"Suppose you go and ask her? You can get your part of the programme over when she is free."

He stood close to Félicité, smiling down at her. She said, "Oh, all right. If you like." Without enthusiasm, and with a backward glance at Manx, she followed her mother. Alleyn immediately took her chair and addressed himself to Manx and Carlisle.

"I wonder," he said, "if you can help me with one or two routine jobs that will have to be tidied up. I believe you were both at the dinner party at Lord Pastern's house—it's in Duke's Gate, isn't it?—before this show tonight."

"Yes," Edward said. "We were there."

"And the rest of the party? Bellairs and Rivera and of course Lord and Lady Pastern. Anyone else?"

"No," Carlisle said and immediately corrected herself. "I'd forgotten. Miss Henderson."

"Miss Henderson?"

"She used to be Félicité's governess and stayed on as a sort of general prop and stay to everybody."

"What is her full name?"

"I—I really don't know. Ned, have you ever heard Hendy's Christian name?"

"No," Edward said. "Never. She's simply Hendy. I should think it might be Edith. Wait a moment though," he added, "I do know. Fée told me years ago. She saw it on an electoral roll or something. It's Petronella Xantippe."

"I don't believe you."

"People so seldom have the names you expect," Alleyn murmured vaguely. "Can you give me a detailed description of your evening at

Duke's Gate? You see, as Rivera was there, the dinner party assumes a kind of importance."

Carlisle thought: "We're waiting too long. One of us ought to have replied at once."

"I want," Alleyn said at last, "if you can give it to me, an account of the whole thing. When everybody arrived. What you talked about. Whether you were all together most of the time or whether you split up, for instance, after dinner, and were in different rooms. That kind of thing."

They began to speak together and stopped short. They laughed uncomfortably, apologized and invited each other to proceed. At last Carlisle embarked alone on a colourless narrative. She had arrived at Duke's Gate at about five and had seen her aunt and uncle and Félicité. Naturally there had been a good deal of talk about the evening performance. Her uncle had been in very good spirits.

"And Lady Pastern and Miss de Suze?" Alleyn said. Carlisle replied carefully that they were in much their usual form. "And how is that?" he asked. "Cheerful? Happy family atmosphere, would you say?"

Manx said lightly: "My dear Alleyn, like most families they rub along together without—without—"

"Were you going to say 'without actually busting up'?"

"Well—well—"

"Ned," Carlisle interjected, "it's no good pretending Uncle George and Aunt Cécile represent the dead norm of British family life. Presumably, Mr. Alleyn reads the papers. If I say they were much as usual it means they were much as usual on their own lines." She turned to Alleyn. "On their own lines, Mr. Alleyn, they were perfectly normal."

"If you'll allow me to say so, Miss Wayne," Alleyn rejoined warmly, "you are evidently an extremely sensible person. May I implore you to keep it up."

"Not to the extent of letting you think a routine argument to them is matter for suspicion to you."

"They argue," Manx added, "perpetually and vehemently. It means nothing. Well, you've heard them."

"And did they, for example, argue about Lord Pastern's performance in the band?"

"Oh, yes," they said together.

"And about Bellairs or Rivera?"

"A bit," said Carlisle after a pause.

"Boogie-woogie merchants," Manx said, "are not, in the nature of things, my cousin Cécile's cups of tea. She is, as you may have noticed, a little in the *grande dame* line of business."

Alleyn leant forward in his chair and rubbed his nose. He looked, Carlisle thought, like a bookish man considering some point that had been raised in an interminable argument.

"Yes," he said at last. "That's all right, of course. One can see the obvious and rather eccentric *mise en scène*. Everything you've told me is no doubt quite true. But the devil of it is, you know, that you're going to use the palpable eccentricities as a sort of smoke screen for the more profound disturbances."

They were astonished and disconcerted. Carlisle said tentatively that she didn't understand. "Don't you?" Alleyn murmured. "Oh, well! Shall we get on with it? Bellairs has suggested an engagement between Rivera and Miss de Suze. Was there an engagement, if you please?"

"No, I don't think so. Was there, Lisle?"

Carlisle said that she didn't think so either. Nothing had been announced.

"An understanding?"

"He wanted her to marry him, I think. I mean," Carlisle amended with heightened colour, "I know he did. I don't think she was going to. I'm sure she wasn't."

"How did Lord Pastern feel about it?"

"Who can tell?" Edward muttered.

"I don't think it bothered him much one way or the other," Carlisle said. "He was too busy planning his début."

But into her memory came the figure of Lord Pastern, bent over his task of drawing bullets from cartridges, and she heard again his grunted: "much better leave things to me."

Alleyn began to lead them step by step through the evening at Duke's Gate. What had they talked about before dinner? How had the party been divided, and into which rooms? What had they themselves done and said? Carlisle found herself charged with an account of her arrival. It was easy to say that her aunt and uncle had argued about whether there should be extra guests for dinner. It was not so easy when he led her back to the likelihood of an engagement between Rivera and Félicité, asking if it had been discussed and by whom, and whether Félicité had confided in her.

"These seem impertinent questions," Alleyn said, and anticipated her attempt to suggest as much. "But, believe me, they are entirely impersonal. Irrelevant matters will be most thankfully rejected and forgotten.

We want to tidy up the field of inquiry, that's all." And then it seemed to Carlisle that evasions would be silly and wrong and she said that Félicité had been worried and unhappy about Rivera. She sensed Edward's uneasiness and added that there had been nothing in the Félicité-Rivera situation, nothing at all. "Félicité makes emotional mountains out of sentimental mole-hills," she said. "I think she enjoys it." But she knew while she said this that Félicité's outburst had been more serious than she suggested and she heard her voice lose its integrity and guessed that Alleyn heard this too. She began to be oppressed by his quiet insistence and yet her taste for detail made her a little pleased with her own accuracy, and she felt something like an artist's reluctance to slur or distort. It was easy again to recall her solitary time before dinner in the ballroom. As soon as she began to speak of it the sensation of nostalgia flashed up in her memory and she found herself telling Alleyn that her coming-out ball had been there, that the room had a host of associations for her and that she had stood there, recollecting them.

"Did you notice if the umbrellas and parasols were there?"

"Yes," she said quickly. "I did. They were there on the piano. I remembered the French parasol. It was Aunt Cile's. I remembered Félicité playing with it as a child. It takes to pieces." She caught her breath. "But you know it does that," she said.

"And it was intact then, when you saw it? No bits gone out of the shaft?"

"No, no."

"Sure?"

"Yes. I picked it up and opened it. That's supposed to be unlucky, isn't it? It was all right then."

"Good. And after this you went into the drawing-room. I know this sounds aimlessly exacting but what happened next, do you remember?"

Before she knew where she was she had told him about the magazine, *Harmony,* and there seemed no harm in repeating her notion that Félicité had written one of the letters on G.P.F.'s page. Alleyn gave no sign that this was of interest. It was Edward who, unaccountably, made a stifled ejaculation. Carlisle thought, "Have I blundered?" and hurried on to an account of her visit to her uncle's study when he drew the bullets from the cartridges. Alleyn asked casually how he had set about this and seemed to be diverted from the matter in hand, amused at Lord Pastern's neatness and dexterity.

Carlisle was accustomed to being questioned about Lord Pastern's eccentricities. She considered him fair game and normally enjoyed trying to make sharp, not unkindly little word-sketches of him for her friends. His notoriety was so gross that she had always felt it would be ridiculous to hesitate. She slipped into this habit now.

Then, the picture of the drawer, pulled out and laid on the desk at his elbow, suddenly presented itself. She felt a kind of shrinking in her midriff and stopped short.

But Alleyn had turned to Ned Manx and Ned, dryly and slowly, answered questions about his own arrival in the drawing-room. What impression did he get of Bellairs and Rivera? He hadn't spoken to them very much. Lady Pastern had taken him apart to show him her embroidery.

"*Gros point?*" Alleyn asked.

"And petit point. Like most Frenchwomen of her period, she's pretty good. I really didn't notice the others much."

The dinner party itself came next. The conversation, Ned was saying, had been fragmentary, about all sorts of things. He couldn't remember in detail.

"Miss Wayne has an observer's eye and ear," Alleyn said, turning to her. "Perhaps you can remember, can you? What did you talk about? You sat, where?"

"On Uncle George's right."

"And on your other hand?"

"Mr. Rivera."

"Can you remember what he spoke about, Miss Wayne?"

Alleyn offered his cigarette case to her. As he lit her cigarette Carlisle looked past him at Ned, who shook his head very slightly.

"I thought him rather awful, I'm afraid," she said. "He really was a bit too thick. All flowery compliments and too Spanish-grandee for anyone to swallow."

"Do you agree, Mr. Manx?"

"Oh, yes. He was quite unreal and rather ridiculous I thought."

"Offensively so, would you say?"

They did not look at each other. Edward said: "He just bounded sky-high, if you call that offensive."

"Did they speak of the performance to-night?"

"Oh, yes," Edward said. "And I must say I'm not surprised that the waiters were muddled about who they were to carry out. It struck me that both Uncle George and Rivera wanted all the fat and that neither of them could make up his mind to letting the other have the stretcher. Bellairs was clearly at the end of his professional tether about it."

Alleyn asked how long the men had stayed behind in the dining-room.

Reluctantly—too reluctantly Carlisle thought, with a rising sense of danger—Ned told them that Lord Pastern had taken Breezy away to show him the blank cartridges. "So you and Rivera were left with the port?" Alleyn said.

"Yes. Not for long."

"Can you recall the conversation?"

"There was nothing that would be any help to you."

"You never know."

"I didn't encourage conversation. He asked all sorts of questions about our various relationships to each other and I snubbed him."

"How did he take that?"

"Nobody enjoys being snubbed, I suppose, but I fancy he had a tolerably thick hide on him."

"Was there actually a quarrel?"

Edward stood up. "Look here, Alleyn," he said, "if I was in the slightest degree implicated in this business I should have followed my own advice and refused to answer any of your questions. I am not implicated. I did not monkey with the revolver. I did not bring about Rivera's death."

"And now," Carlisle thought in despair, "Ned's going to give him a sample of the family temper. O God," she thought, "please don't let him."

"Good," Alleyn said and waited.

"Very well then," Edward said grandly and sat down.

"So there was a quarrel."

"I merely," Edward shouted, "showed the man I thought he was impertinent and he walked out of the room."

"Did you speak to him again after this incident?"

Carlisle remembered a scene in the hall, the two men facing each other, Rivera with his hand clapped to his ear. What was it Ned had said to him? Something ridiculous, like a perky schoolboy. "Put that in your hurdy-gurdy and squeeze it," he had shouted with evident relish.

"I merely asked these questions," Alleyn said, "because the bloke had a thick ear, and I wondered who gave it to him. The skin's broken and I notice you wear a signet ring."

III

In the main office, Dr. Curtis contemplated Breezy Bellairs with the air of wary satisfaction. "He'll do," he said, and, stepping neatly behind Breezy's chair, he winked at Alleyn. "He must have got hold of something over and above the shot I gave him. But he'll do."

Breezy looked up at Alleyn and gave him the celebrated smile. He was pallid and sweating lightly. His expression was one of relief, of well-being. Dr. Curtis washed his syringe in a tumbler of water on the desk and then returned it to his case.

Alleyn opened the door into the foyer and nodded to Fox, who rose and joined him. Together they returned to the contemplation of Breezy.

Fox cleared his throat. "*Alors,*" he said cautiously and stopped.

"*Évidemment,*" he said, "*il y a un avancement, n'est-ce pas?*"

He paused, slightly flushed, and looked out of the corners of his eyes at Alleyn.

"*Pas grand'chose,*" Alleyn muttered. "But as Curtis says, he'll do for our purpose. You go, by the way, Br'er Fox, from strength to strength. The accent improves."

"I still don't get the practice though," Fox complained. Breezy, who was looking with complete tranquility at the opposite wall, laughed comfortably. "I feel lovely, now," he volunteered.

"He's had a pretty solid shot," Dr. Curtis said. "I don't know what he'd been up to before but it seems to have packed him up a bit. But he's all right. He can answer questions, can't you, Bellairs?"

"I'm fine," Breezy rejoined dreamily. "Box of birds."

"Well . . ." Alleyn said dubiously. Fox added in a sepulchral undertone: "*Faute de mieux.*" "Exactly," Alleyn said and, drawing up a chair, placed himself in front of Breezy.

"I'd like you to tell me something," he said. Breezy lazily withdrew his gaze from the opposite wall and Alleyn found himself staring into eyes that, because of the enormous size of their pupils, seemed mere structures and devoid of intelligence.

"Do you remember," he said, "what you did at Lord Pastern's house?"

He had to wait a long time for an answer. At last Breezy's voice, detached and remote, said: "Don't let's talk. It's nicer not talking."

"Talking's nice too, though."

Dr. Curtis walked away from Breezy and murmured to no one in particular, "Get him started and he may go on."

"It must have been fun at the dinner party," Alleyn suggested. "Did Carlos enjoy himself?"

Breezy's arm lay curved along the desk. With a luxurious sigh, he slumped further into the chair and rested his cheek on his sleeve. In a moment or two his voice began again, independently, it seemed, with no conscious volition on his part. It trailed through his scarcely moving lips in a monotone.

"I told him it was silly but that made no difference at all. 'Look,' I said, 'you're crazy!' Well, of course I was sore on account of he held back on me, not bringing me my cigarettes."

"What cigarettes?"

"He never did anything I asked him. I was so good to him. I was as good as gold. I told him. I said, 'Look,' I said, 'she won't take it from you, boy. She's as sore as hell,' I said, 'and so's he, and the other girl isn't falling so what's the point?' I knew there'd be trouble. 'And the old bastard doesn't like it,' I said. 'He pretends it doesn't mean a thing to him but that's all hooey because he just naturally wouldn't like it.' No good. No notice taken."

"When was this?" Alleyn asked.

"Off and on. Most of the time you might say. And when we were in the taxi and he said how the guy had hit him, I said: 'There you are, what was I telling you?' "

"Who hit him?"

There was a longer pause. Breezy turned his head languidly.

"Who hit Carlos, Breezy?"

"I heard you the first time. What a gang, though! The Honourable Edward Manx in serious mood while lunching at the Tarmac with Miss Félicité de Suze who is of course connected with him on the distaff side. Her stepfather is Lord Pastern and Bagott, but if you ask me it's a punctured romance. *Cherchez la femme.*"

Fox glanced up from his notes with an air of bland interest.

"The woman in this case," Alleyn said, "being . . ."

"Funny name for a girl."

"Carlisle?"

"Sounds dopey to me, but what of that? But that's the sort of thing they do. Imagine having two names. Pastern and Bagott. And I can look after both of them, don't you worry. Trying to swing one across me. What a chance! Bawling me out. Saying he'll write to this bloody paper. Him and his hot-gunning and where is he now?"

"Swing one across you?" Alleyn repeated quietly. He had pitched his voice on Breezy's level. Their voices ran into and away from each other. They seemed to the two onlookers to speak as persons in a dream, with tranquillity and secret understanding.

"He might have known," Breezy was saying, "that I wouldn't come at it but you've got to admit it was awkward. A permanent engagement. Thanks a lot. How does the chorus go?"

He laughed faintly, yawned, whispered, "Pardon me," and closed his eyes.

"He's going," Dr. Curtis said.

"Breezy," Alleyn said loudly. "*Breezy.*"

"What?"

"Did Lord Pastern want you to keep him on permanently?"

"I told you. Him and his blankety-blankety blank cartridges."

"Did he want you to sack Skelton?"

"It was all Carlos's fault," Breezy said quite loudly and on a plaintive note. "He thought it up. God, was he angry!"

"Was who angry?"

With a suggestion of cunning the voice murmured: "That's telling."

"Was it Lord Pastern?"

"Him? Don't make me laugh!"

"Syd Skelton?"

"When I told him," Breezy whispered faintly, "he looked like murder. Honest, I *was* nervy."

He rolled his face over on his arm and fell into a profound sleep. "He won't come out of that for eight hours," said Dr. Curtis.

IV

At two o'clock the cleaners came in, five middle-aged women who were admitted by the police and who walked through the foyer into the restaurant with the tools of their trade. Caesar Bonn was greatly distressed by their arrival and complained that the pressmen, who had been sent away with a meager statement that Rivera had collapsed and died, would lie in wait for these women and question them. He sent the secretary, David Hahn, after the cleaners. "They are to be silenced at all costs. At all costs, you understand." Presently the drone of vacuum-cleaners arose in the restaurant. Two of Alleyn's men had been there for some time. They now returned to the foyer and, joining the policemen on duty there, glanced impassively at its inhabitants.

Most of the Boys were asleep. They were sprawled in ungainly postures on their small chairs. Trails of ash lay on their clothes. They had crushed out their cigarette butts on empty packets, on the soles of their shoes, on match boxes, or had pitched them at the floor containers. The smell of dead butts seemed to hang over the entire room.

Lady Pastern appeared to sleep. She was inclined backwards in her armchair and her eyes were closed. Purplish shadows had appeared on her face and deep grooves ran from her nostrils to the corners of her mouth. Her cheeks sagged. She scarcely stirred when her husband, who had been silent for a considerable time, said: "Hi, Ned!"

"Yes, Cousin George?" Manx responded guardedly.

"I've got to the bottom of this."

"Indeed?"

"I know who did it."

"Really? Who?"

"I disagree entirely and emphatically with capital punishment," Lord Pastern said, puffing out his cheeks at the group of police officials. "I shall therefore keep my knowledge to myself. Let 'em muddle on. Murder's a matter for the psychiatrist, not the hangman. As for judges, they're a pack of conceited old sadists. Let 'em get on with it. They'll have no help from me. For God's sake, Fée, stop fidgetin'."

Félicité was curled up in the chair she had used earlier in the evening. From time to time she thrust her hands out of sight, exploring, it seemed, the space between the upholstered arms and seat. She did this furtively with sidelong glances at the others. Carlisle said: "What *is* it, Fée? What have you lost?" "My hanky." "Here, take mine, for pity's sake," said Lord Pastern and threw it at her.

The searching had gone forward steadily. Carlisle, who liked her privacy, had found the experience galling and unpleasant. The wardress was a straw-coloured woman with large artificial teeth and firm pale hands. She had been extremely polite and uncompromising.

Now the last man to be searched, Syd Skelton, returned from the men's cloak-room and at the same time Alleyn and Fox came out of the office. The Boys woke up. Lady Pastern opened her eyes.

Alleyn said: "As the result of these preliminary inquiries . . ." ("Preliminary!" Lord Pastern snorted.) . . . "I think we have got together enough information and may allow you to go home. I'm extremely sorry to have kept you here so long."

They were all on their feet. Alleyn raised a hand. "There's one restriction, I'm afraid. I think you'll all understand and, I hope, respect it. Those of you who were in immediate communication with Rivera or who had access to the revolver used by Lord Pastern, or who seem to us, for sufficient reasons, to be in any way concerned in the circumstances leading to

Rivera's death, will be seen home by police officers. We shall provide ourselves with search-warrants. If such action seems necessary, we shall use them."

"Of all the footlin', pettifoggin' . . ." Lord Pastern began, and was interrupted.

"Those of you who come under this heading," Alleyn said, "are Lord Pastern and the members of his party, Mr. Bellairs and Mr. Skelton. That's all, I think. Thank you, ladies and gentlemen."

"I'm damned if I'll put up with this. Look here, Alleyn . . ."

"I'm sorry, sir. I must insist, I'm afraid."

"George," said Lady Pastern. "You have tried conclusions with the law on more than one occasion and as often as you have done so you have made a fool of yourself. Come home."

Lord Pastern studied his wife with an air of detachment. "Your hairnet's loose," he pointed out, "and you're bulgin' above your waist. Comes of wearin' stays. I've always said . . ."

"I, at least," Lady Pastern said directly to Alleyn, "am prepared to accept your conditions. So, I am sure, are my daughter and my niece. Félicité! Carlisle!"

"Fox," said Alleyn.

She walked with perfect composure to the door and waited there. Fox spoke to one of the plain-clothes men, who detached himself from the group near the entrance. Félicité held out a hand towards Edward Manx. "Ned, you'll come, won't you? You'll stay with us?"

After a moment's hesitation he took her hand.

"Dearest Edward," said Lady Pastern from the door. "We should be so grateful."

"Certainly, Cousin Cécile. Of course."

Félicité still held his hand. He looked at Carlisle. "Coming?" he asked.

"Yes, of course. Good night, Mr. Alleyn," said Carlisle.

"Good night, Miss Wayne."

They went out, followed by the plain-clothes man.

"I should like to have a word with you, Mr. Skelton," Alleyn said. "The rest of you"—he turned to the Boys, the waiters and the spot-light man—"may go. You will be given notice of the inquest. Sorry to have kept you up so late. Good night."

The waiters and the electrician went at once. The band moved forward in a group. Happy Hart said: "What about Breezy?"

"He's sound asleep and will need a bit of rousing. I shall see he's taken home."

Hart shuffled his feet and looked at his hands. "I don't know what you're thinking," he said, "but he's all right. Breezy's O.K. really. I mean he's just been making the pace a bit too hot for himself as you might say. He's a very nervy type, Breezy. He suffers from insomnia. He took the stuff for his nerves. But he's all right."

"He and Rivera got on well, did they?"

Several of the Boys said quickly: "That's right. Sure. They were all right." Hart added that Breezy was very good to Carlos and gave him his big chance in London.

All the Boys agreed fervently with this statement except Skelton. He stood apart from his associates. They avoided looking at him. He was a tall darkish fellow with narrow eyes and a sharp nose. His mouth was small and thin-lipped. He stooped slightly.

"Well, if that's all," Happy Hart said uneasily, "we'll say good night."

"We've got their addresses, haven't we, Fox? Good. Thank you. Good night."

They filed out, carrying their instruments. In the old days when places like the Metronome and Quags and the Hungaria kept going up to two in the morning the Boys had worked through, sometimes going on to parties in private houses. They were Londoners who turned homewards with pale faces and blue jaws at the time when fans of water from giant hose pipes strike across Piccadilly and Whitehall. They had been among the tag-ends of the night in those times, going soberly to their beds as the first milk carts jangled. In summer-time they had undressed in the dawn to the thin stir of sparrows. They shared with taxi drivers, cloak-room attendants, waiters and commissionaires a specialized disillusionment.

Alleyn watched them go and then nodded to Fox. Fox approached Caesar Bonn and David Hahn, who lounged gloomily near the office door. "Perhaps you gentlemen wouldn't mind coming into the office," he suggested. They followed him in. Alleyn turned to Skelton. "Now, Mr. Skelton."

"What's the idea," Skelton said, "keeping me back? I've got a home, same as everybody else. Though how the hell I'm going to get there's nobody's business."

"I'm sorry. It's a nuisance for you, I know, but it can't be helped."

"I don't see why."

The office door was opened from inside. Two constables came out with Breezy Bellairs hanging between them like a cumbersome puppet. His face was lividly pale, his eyes half open. He breathed stertorously and made a complaining noise like a wretched child. Dr. Curtis followed. Bonn and Hahn watched from inside the office.

"All right?" Alleyn said.

"He'll do. We'll just get him into his coat."

They held Breezy up while Curtis, with difficulty, crammed him into his tight-fitting overcoat. During this struggle Breezy's baton fell to the floor. Hahn came forward and picked it up. "You wouldn't think," Hahn said, contemplating it sadly, "how good he was. Not to look at him now."

Dr. Curtis yawned. "These chaps'll see him into his bed," he said. "I'll be off, if you don't want me, Rory."

"Right." The dragging procession disappeared. Fox returned to the office and shut the door.

"That's a nice way," Skelton said angrily, "for a first-class band leader to be seen going home. Between a couple of flatties."

"They'll be very tactful," Alleyn rejoined. "Shall we sit down?"

Skelton said he'd sat down for so long that his bottom was numb. "Let's get cracking for God's sake. I've had it. What's the idea?"

Alleyn took out his notebook.

"The idea," he said, "is further information. I think you can give it to us. By all means let's get cracking."

"Why pick on me? I know no more than the others."

"Don't you?" Alleyn said vaguely. He glanced up. "What's your opinion of Lord Pastern as a tympanist?"

"Dire. What of it?"

"Did the others hold this opinion?"

"They knew. Naturally. It was a cheap stunt. Playing up the snob value." He thrust his hands down in his pockets and began to walk to and fro, impelled, it seemed, by resentment. Alleyn waited.

"It's when something like this turns up," Skelton announced loudly, "that you see how rotten the whole set-up really is. I'm not ashamed of my work. Why the hell should I be? It interests me. It's not easy. It takes doing and anybody that tells you there's nothing to the best type of our kind of music talks through his hat. It's got something. It's clever and there's a lot of hard thinking behind it."

"I don't know about music," Alleyn said, "but I can imagine that from the technical point of view your sort can be almost purely intellectual. Or is that nonsense?"

Skelton glowered at him. "You're not far out. A lot of the stuff we have to play is wet and corny, of course. They," he jerked his head at the empty restaurant, "like it that way. But there's other stuff that's different. If I could pick my work I'd be in an outfit that went for the real McCoy. In a country where things were run decently I'd be able to do that. I'd be able to say: 'This is what I can do and it's the best I can do,' and I'd be directed into the right channels. I'm a communist," he said loudly.

Alleyn was suddenly and vividly reminded of Lord Pastern. He said nothing and after a pause Skelton went on.

"I realize I'm working for the rottenest section of a crazy society but what can I do? It's my job and I have to take it. But this affair! Walking out and letting a dopey old dead beat of a lord make a fool of himself with my instruments, and a lot of dead beat effects added to them! Looking as if I like it! Where's my self-respect?"

"How," Alleyn asked, "did it come about?"

"Breezy worked it because . . ."

He stopped short and advanced on Alleyn. "Here!" he demanded. "What's all this in aid of? What do you want?"

"Like Lord Pastern," Alleyn said lightly, "I want the truth. Bellairs, you were saying, worked it because—of what?"

"I've told you. Snob value."

"And the others agreed?"

"They haven't any principles. Oh, yes. They took it."

"Rivera, for instance, didn't oppose the idea?"

Skelton flushed deeply. "No," he said. Alleyn saw his pockets bulge as the hidden hands clenched. "Why not?" he asked.

"Rivera was hanging his hat up to the girl. Pastern's stepdaughter. He was all out to make himself a hero with the old man."

"That made you very angry, didn't it?"

"Who says it made me angry?"

"Bellairs said so."

"Him! Another product of our so-called civilization. Look at him."

Alleyn asked him if he knew anything about Breezy's use of drugs. Skelton, caught, as it seemed, between the desire of a zealot to speak his mind and an undefined wariness, said that Breezy was the child of his age and circumstances. He was a by-product, Skelton said, of a cynical and disillusioned social set-up. The phrases fell from his lips with the precision of slogans. Alleyn listened and watched and felt his interest stirring. "We all knew," Skelton said, "that he was taking some kind of dope to keep him going. Even *he*—old Pastern. He'd nosed it out all right and I reckon he knew where it came from. You could tell. Breezy's changed a hell of a lot. He used to be a nice sort of joker in a way. Bit of a wag. Always having us on. He got off-side with that Dago for that."

"Rivera?"

"That's right. Breezy used to be crazy on practical jokes. He'd fix a silly squeaker in one of the saxes or sneak a wee bell inside the piano. Childish. He got hold of Rivera's p-a and fixed it with little bits of paper between the keys so's it wouldn't go. Only for rehearsal, of course. Rivera came out all glamour and hair oil and swung his p-a. Nothing happened. There was Breezy grinning like he'd split his face and the Boys all sniggering. You had to laugh. Rivera tore the place up: he went mad and howled out he'd quit. Breezy had a hell of a job fixing him. It was quite a party."

"Practical jokes," Alleyn said. "A curious obsession, I always think."

Skelton looked sharply at him. "Here!" he said. "You don't want to get ideas. Breezy's all right. Breezy wouldn't come at anything like this." He laughed shortly, and added with an air of disgust: "Breezy fix Rivera! Not likely."

"About this drug habit—" Alleyn began. Skelton said impatiently: "Well, there you are! It's just one of those things. I told you—we all knew. He used to go to parties on Sundays with some gang."

"Any idea who they were?"

"No, I never asked. I'm not interested. I tried to tell him he was heading for a crash. Once. He didn't like it. He's my boss and I shut up. I'd have turned it up and gone over to another band but I'm used to working with these boys and they do better stuff than most."

"You never heard where he got his drug, whatever it is?"

Skelton muttered, "I never *heard*. Naturally."

"But you formed an opinion, perhaps?"

"Perhaps."

"Going to tell me about it?"

"I want to know what you're getting at. I've got to protect myself, haven't I? I like to get things straight. You've got some notion that because I looked at Pastern's gun I might have shoved this silly umbrella what-have-you up the nuzzle. Why don't you come to the point?"

"I shall do so," Alleyn said. "I've kept you behind because of this circumstance and because you were alone with Lord Pastern for a short time after you left the platform and before he made his entrance. So far as I can see at the moment there is no connection between your possible complicity and the fact that Bellairs takes drugs. As a police officer I'm concerned with drug addicts and their source of supply. If you can help me with any information I'll be grateful. Do you know, then, where Bellairs got whatever he took?"

Skelton deliberated, his brows drawn together, his lower lip thrust out. Alleyn found himself speculating about his background. What accumulation of circumstances, ill-adjustments or misfortunes had resulted in this particular case? What would Skelton have been if his history had been otherwise? Were his views, his truculence, his suspicions, rooted in honesty or in some indefinable sense of victimization? To what lengths would they impel him? And finally Alleyn asked himself the inevitable question: could this be a killer?

Skelton wetted his lips. "The drug racket," he said, "is like any other racket in a capitalistic government. The real criminals are the bosses, the barons, the high-ups. They don't get pulled in. It's the little blokes that get caught. You have to think it out. Silly sentiment and big talk won't work. I've got no tickets on the police department in this country. A fairly efficient machine working for the wrong ideas. But drug-taking's no good from any point of view. All right. I'll co-operate this far. I'll tell you where Breezy got his dope."

"And where," said Alleyn patiently, "did Breezy get his dope?"

"From Rivera," said Skelton. "Now! From Rivera."

CHAPTER VII

Dawn

I

SKELTON HAD GONE HOME, and Caesar Bonn and David Hahn. The cleaners had retired into some remote part of the building. Only the police remained: Alleyn and Fox, Bailey, Thompson, the three men who had searched the restaurant and band-room and the uniformed constable who would remain on duty until he was relieved after daybreak. The time was now twenty minutes to three.

"Well, Foxkin," said Alleyn, "where are we? You've been very mousy and discreet. Let's have your theory. Come on."

Fox cleared his throat and placed the palms of his hands on his knees. "A very peculiar case," he said disapprovingly. "Freakish, you might say. Silly. Except for the corpse. Corpses," Mr. Fox observed with severity, "are never silly."

Detective-Sergeants Bailey and Thompson exchanged winks.

"In the first place, Mr. Alleyn," Fox continued, "I ask myself: Why do it that way? Why fire a bit of an umbrella handle from a revolver when you might fire a bullet? This applies in particular to his lordship. And yet it seems it must have been done. You can't get away from it. Nobody had a chance of stabbing the chap while he was performing, did they now?"

"Nobody."

"All right then. Now, if anybody pushed this silly weapon up the gun after Skelton examined it, they had the thing concealed about their person. Not much bigger than a fountain pen but sharp as hell. Which brings us to Bellairs, for one. If you consider Bellairs, you have to remember that his lordship seems to have searched him very thoroughly before he went out to perform."

"Moreover his lordship in the full tide of his own alleged innocence declares that the wretched Breezy didn't get a chance to pocket anything after he had been searched, or to get at the gun."

"Does he really?" said Fox. "Fancy!"

"In fact his lordship, who, I submit, is no fool, has been at peculiar pains to clear everybody but himself."

"No fool, perhaps," Fox grunted, "but would you say a bit off the plumb mentally?"

"Everybody else says so, at all events. In any case, Fox, I'll give sworn evidence that nobody stabbed Rivera before or at the time he was shot at. He was a good six feet away from everybody except Lord Pastern, who was busy with his blasted gun."

"There you are! And it wasn't planted among the music stands because they were used by the other band. And anyway none of the musicians went near his lordship's funny hat where the gun was. And being like that, I asked myself, isn't his lordship the most likely to use a silly fanciful method if he'd made up his mind to do a man in? It all points to his lordship. You can't get away from it. And yet he seems so pleased with himself and kind of unruffled. Of course you do find that attitude in homicidal mania."

"You do. What about motive?"

"Do we know what he thought of his stepdaughter keeping company with the deceased? The other young lady suggested that he didn't seem to care one way or the other but you never know. Something else may turn up. Personally, as things stand at the moment, I favor his lordship. What about you, Mr. Alleyn?"

Alleyn shook his head. "I'm stumped," he said. "Perhaps Skelton could have got the thing into the revolver when he examined it but Lord Pastern, who undoubtedly is as sharp as a needle, swears he didn't. They were alone together for a minute while Breezy made his announcement but Skelton says he didn't go near Lord Pastern, who had the gun in his pocket. It's not likely to be a lie because Pastern could deny it. You didn't hear Skelton. He's an odd chap—a truculent communist. Australian, I should say. A hard, determined thinker. Nobody's fool and completely sincere. One-track minded. There's no doubt he detested Rivera, both on general principles and because Rivera backed up Lord Pastern's appearance to-night. Skelton bitterly resented this and says so. He felt he was prostituting what he is pleased to regard as his art and conniving at something entirely against his social principles. I believe him to be fanatically sincere in this. He looked on Rivera and Lord Pastern as parasites. Rivera, by the way, supplied Breezy Bellairs with his dope, whatever it is. Curtis says cocaine, and it looks as if he found himself something to go on when he searched the body. We'll have to follow that one up, Fox."

"Dope," said Fox profoundly. "There you are! When we do get a windfall it's a dead man. Still, there may be something in his rooms to give us a lead. South America, now. That may link up with the Snowy Santos gang. They operate through South America. It'd be nice," said Mr. Fox, whose talents for some time had been concerned with the sale of illicit drugs, "it'd be lovely, in fact, to get the tabs on Snowy Santos."

"Lovely, wouldn't it?" Alleyn agreed absently. "Get on with your argument, Fox."

"Well, now, sir. Seeing Rivera wasn't meant to fall down and *did,* you can say he was struck at that moment. I know that sounds like a glimpse of the obvious, but it cuts out any idea that there was some kind of jiggery-pokery *after* he fell because nobody knew he was going to fall. And unless you feel like saying somebody threw the weapon like a dart at the same time as his lordship fired the first shot— Well," said Fox disgustedly, "that would be a fat-headed sort of notion wouldn't it? So we come back to the idea it was fired from the revolver. Which is supported by the scratches in the barrel. Mind, we'll have to get the experts going there."

"We shall, indeed."

"But saying, for the moment, that the little jewelled clip, acting as a sort of stop, did mark the barrel, we come to Skelton's statement that the scratches were not there when he examined it. And that looks like his lordship again. Look at it how you will, you get back to his lordship, you know."

"Miss de Suze," Alleyn said, rubbing his nose in vexation, "did grope under the damned sombrero. I saw her and so did Manx and so did the waiter. Manx seemed to remonstrate and she laughed and withdrew her hand. She couldn't have got the weapon in then but it shows that it was possible for anyone sitting on her chair to get at the gun. Lady Pastern was left alone at their table while the others danced."

Fox raised his eyebrows and looked puffy. "Very icy," he said. "A haughty sort of lady and with a will and temper of her own. Look how she's stood up to his lordship in the past. Very masterful."

Alleyn glanced at his old colleague and smiled. He turned to the group of waiting men. "Well, Bailey," he said, "we've about got to you. Have you found anything new?"

Bailey said morosely: "Nothing to write home about, Mr. Alleyn. No prints on this dart affair. I've packed it up with protection and can have another go at it."

"The revolver?"

"Very plain sailing, there, Mr. Alleyn. Not a chance for latents."

"That's why I risked letting him handle it."

"Yes, sir. Well now," said Bailey with a certain professional relish, "the revolver. Lord Pastern's prints on the revolver. And this band leader's. Breezy Bellairs or whatever he calls himself."

"Yes. Lord Pastern handed the gun to Breezy."

"That's right, sir. So I understand."

"Thompson," said Alleyn suddenly, "did you get a good look at Mr. Manx's left hand when you dabbed him?"

"Yes, sir. Knuckles a bit grazed. Very slight. Wears a signet ring."

"How about the band platform, Bailey?"

Bailey looked at his boots and said he'd been over the floor space round the tympani and percussion stand. There were traces of four finger tips identifiable as Miss de Suze's. No others.

"And Rivera? On the body?"

"Not much there," Bailey said, but they would probably bring up latent prints where Bellairs and the doctor had handled him. That was all, so far.

"Thank you. What about you other chaps in the restaurant and band-room? Find anything? Gibson?"

One of the plain-clothes men came forward. "Not much, sir. Nothing out of the ordinary. Cigarette butts and so on. We picked up the wads and shells and Bellairs's handkerchief, marked, on the platform."

"He mopped his unpleasant eyes with it when he did his stuff with the wreath," Alleyn muttered. "Anything else?"

"There was a cork," said Detective-Sergeant Gibson apologetically, "on the band platform. Might have been dropped by a waiter, sir."

"Not up there. Let's see it."

Gibson produced an envelope from which he shook out a smallish cork on to the table. Alleyn looked at it without touching it. "When was the band platform cleaned?"

"Polished in the early morning, Mr. Alleyn, and mopped over before the evening clients came in."

"Where exactly did you find this thing?"

"Half-way back and six feet to left of center. I've marked the place."

"Good. Not that it'll help much." Alleyn used his lens. "It's got a black mark on it." He stopped and sniffed. "Boot polish, I think. It was probably kicked about the place by bandsmen. But there's another smell. Not wine or spirit and anyway it's not that sort of cork. It's smaller and made with a narrow end and a wide top. No trade-mark. What *is* this smell? Try, Fox."

Fox's sniff was stentorian. He rose, meditated and said: "Now, what am I reminded of?" They waited. "Citronella," Fox pronounced gravely. "Or something like it."

"How about gun oil?" said Alleyn.

Fox turned and contemplated his superior with something like indignation. "Gun oil? You're not going to tell me, Mr. Alleyn, that in addition to stuffing jewelled parasol handles up a revolver somebody stopped it with a cork like a ruddy pop-gun?"

Alleyn grinned. "The case is taking liberties with your credulity, Br'er Fox." He used his lens again. "The bottom surface has been broken, I fancy. It's a forlorn hope, Bailey, but we might try for dabs."

Bailey put the cork away. Alleyn turned to the others. "I think you can pack up," he said. "I'm afraid I'll have to keep you, Thompson, and you, Bailey, with us. It's a non-stop show. Gibson, you'll pick up a search-warrant and go on to Rivera's rooms. Take someone with you. I want a complete search there. Scott and Watson are attending to Bellairs's rooms and Sallis has gone with Skelton. You'll all report back to me at the Yard at ten. Get people to relieve you when you've finished. Bellairs and Skelton will both have to be kept under observation, damn it, though I fancy that for the next eight hours Breezy won't give anybody a headache except himself. Inspector Fox and I will get extra men and attend to Duke's Gate. All right. We'll move."

In the office a telephone bell rang. Fox went in to answer it and was heard uttering words of reproach. He came out looking scandalized.

"It's that new chap we sent back with his lordship's party. Marks. And what do you suppose he's done?" Fox glared round upon his audience and slapped the palm of his hand on the table. "Silly young chump! When they get in they say they're all going to the drawing-room. 'Oh,' says Marks, 'then it's my duty, if you please, to accompany you.' The gentlemen say they want to retire first, and they go off to the downstairs cloakroom. The ladies have the same idea and they go upstairs and Sergeant Expeditious Marks tries to tear himself in halves which is nothing to what I'll do for him. And while he's exhausting himself running up and down keeping observation, what happens? One of the young ladies slips down the servants' stairs and lets herself out by the back door."

"Which one?" Alleyn asked quickly.

"Don't," said Mr. Fox with bitter scorn, "ask too much of Detective-Sergeant Marks, sir. Don't make it too tough. He wouldn't know which one. Oh, no. He comes bleating to the phone while I daresay the rest of 'em are lighting off wherever the fancy takes 'em. Sergeant ruddy Police-College Marks! What is it?"

A uniformed constable had come in from the front entrance. "I thought I'd better report, sir," he said. "I'm on duty outside. There's an incident."

"All right," said Alleyn. "What incident?"

"A taxi's pulled up some distance away, sir, and a lady got out."

"A lady?" Fox demanded so peremptorily that the constable glanced nervously at him.

"Yes, Mr. Fox. A young lady. She spoke to the driver. He's waiting. She looked round and hesitated. I was in the entrance, sir, well in the shadow, and I don't think she saw me."

"Recognize her?" Alleyn asked.

"I wouldn't be sure, sir. The clothes are different but I reckon it's one of the ladies in Lord Pastern's party."

"Have you locked the doors behind you?"

"Yes, sir."

"Unlock them and make yourself scarce. Clear out, all of you. Scatter. Step lively."

The foyer was emptied in five seconds. The doors into the office and the band-room closed noiselessly. Alleyn darted to the light switches. A single lamp was left to glow pinkly against the wall. The foyer was filled with shadow. He slipped to his knees behind a chair in the corner farthest from the light.

The clock ticked discreetly. Somewhere in a distant basement a pail clanked and a door slammed. Innumerable tiny sounds closer at hand became evident: the tap of a blind cord somewhere in the restaurant, a stealthy movement and scuffle behind the walls, an indefinable humming from the main switchboard. Alleyn smelt carpet, upholstery, disinfectant, and stale tobacco. Entrance into the foyer from outside must be effected through two sets of doors—those giving on the street and those inside made of plate glass and normally open but now swung-to. Through these he could see only a vague greyness crossed by reflections in the glass itself. The image of the one pink lamp floated midway up the right-hand pane. He fixed his gaze on this. Now, beyond the glass doors, there came a paleness. The street door had been opened.

The face appeared quite suddenly against the plate glass, obscuring the reflected lamp and distorted by pressure. One door squeaked faintly as it opened.

She stood for a moment, holding her head scarf half across her face. Then she moved forward swiftly and was down on her knees before an armchair. Her finger-nails scrabbled on its tapestry. So intent was she upon her search that she did not hear him cross the thick carpet behind her, but when he drew the envelope from his pocket it made a slight crackle. Still kneeling, she swung round, saw him and cried out sharply.

"Is this what you are hunting for, Miss Wayne?" Alleyn asked.

II

He crossed over to the wall and switched up the lights. Without moving, Carlisle watched him. When he returned he still held the envelope. She put her hand to her burning face and said unsteadily: "You think I'm up to no good, I suppose. I suppose you want an explanation."

"I should be glad of an answer to my question. Is this what you want?"

He held the envelope up, but did not give it to her. She looked at it doubtfully. "I don't know—I don't think—"

"The envelope is mine. I'll tell you what it contains. A letter that had been thrust down between the seat and the arm of the chair you have been exploring."

"Yes," Carlisle said. "Yes. That's it. May I have it, please?"

"Do sit down," Alleyn rejoined. "We'd better clear this up, don't you think?"

He waited while she rose. After a moment's hesitation, she sat in the chair.

"You won't believe me, of course," she said, "but that letter—I suppose you have read it, haven't you—has nothing whatever to do with this awful business to-night. Nothing in the wide world. It's entirely personal and rather important."

"Have you even read it?" he asked. "Can you repeat the contents? I should like you to do that, if you will."

"But—not absolutely correctly—I mean—"

"Approximately."

"It—it's got an important message. It concerns someone—I can't tell you in so many words—"

"And yet it's so important that you return here at three o'clock in the morning to try and find it." He paused but Carlisle said nothing. "Why," he said, "didn't Miss de Suze come and collect her own correspondence?"

"Oh dear!" she said. "This is difficult."

"Well, for pity's sake keep up your reputation and be honest about it."

"I am being honest, damn you!" said Carlisle with spirit. "The letter's a private affair and—and—extremely confidential. Félicité doesn't want anyone to see it. I don't know exactly what's in it."

"She funked coming back herself?"

"She's a bit shattered. Everyone is."

"I'd like you to see what the letter's about," said Alleyn after a pause. She began to protest. Very patiently he repeated his usual argument. When someone had been killed the nicer points of behaviour had to be disregarded. He had to prove to his own satisfaction that the letter was immaterial and then he would forget it. "You remember," he said, "this letter dropped out of her bag. Did you notice how she snatched it away from me? I see you did. Did you notice what she did after I said you would all be searched? She shoved her hand down between the seat and arm of the chair. Then she went off to be searched and I sat in the chair. When she came back she spent a miserable half-hour fishing for the letter and trying to look as if she wasn't. All right."

He drew the letter from the envelope and spread it out before her. "It's been finger-printed," he said, "but without any marked success. Too much rubbing against good solid chair-cover. Will you read it or—"

"Oh, all right," Carlisle said angrily.

The letter was typed on a sheet of plain notepaper. There was no address and no date.

> My Dear [Carlisle read]: Your loveliness is my undoing. Because of it I break my deepest promise to myself and to others. We are closer than you have ever dreamed. I wear a white flower in my coat to-night. It is yours. But as you value our future happiness, make not the slightest sign—even to me. Destroy this note, my love, but keep my love. G.P.F.

Carlisle raised her head, met Alleyn's gaze and avoided it quickly. "A white flower," she whispered. "G.P.F.? *G.P.F.?* I don't believe it."

"Mr. Edward Manx had a white carnation in his coat, I think."

"I won't discuss this letter with you," she said strongly. "I should never have read it. I won't discuss it. Let me take it back to her. It's nothing to do with this other thing. Nothing. Give it to me."

Alleyn said, "You must know I can't do that. Think for a moment. There was some attachment, a strong attachment of one kind or another, between Rivera and your cousin—your step-cousin. After Rivera is murdered, she is at elaborate pains to conceal this letter, loses it, and is so anxious to retrieve it that she persuades you to return here in an attempt to recover it. How can I disregard such a sequence of events?"

"But you don't know Fée! She's always in and out of tight corners over her young men. It's nothing. You don't understand."

"Well," he said, looking good-humouredly at her, "help me to understand. I'll drive you home. You can tell me on the way. Fox."

Fox came out of the office. Carlisle listened to Alleyn giving his instructions. The other men appeared from the cloak-room, held a brief indistinguishable conversation with Fox and went out through the main entrance. Alleyn and Fox collected their belongings and put on their coats. Carlisle stood up. Alleyn returned the letter to its envelope and put it in his pocket. She felt tears stinging under her eyelids. She tried to speak and produced only an indeterminate sound.

"What is it?" he said, glancing at her.

"It can't be true," she stammered. "I won't believe it. I won't."

"What? That Edward Manx wrote this letter?"

"He couldn't. He couldn't write like that to her."

"No?" Alleyn said casually. "You think not? But she's quite good-looking, isn't she? Quite attractive, don't you think?"

"It's not that. It's not that at all. It's the letter itself. He couldn't write like that. It's so bogus."

"Have you ever noticed love-letters that are read out in court and published in the papers? Don't they sound pretty bogus? Yet some of them have been written by extremely intelligent people. Shall we go?"

It was cold out in the street. A motionless pallor stood behind the rigid silhouette of roofs. "Dawn's left hand," Alleyn said to nobody in particular and shivered. Carlisle's taxi had gone but a large police car waited. A second man sat beside the driver. Fox opened the door and Carlisle got in. The two men followed. "We'll call at the Yard," Alleyn said.

She felt boxed-up in the corner of the seat and was conscious of the impersonal pressure of Alleyn's arm and shoulder. Mr. Fox, on the farther side, was a bulky man. She turned and saw Alleyn's head silhouetted against the bluish window. An odd notion came into her head. "If Fée happens to calm down and take a good look at him," she thought, "it'll be all up with G.P.F. and the memory of Carlos and everybody." And with that her heart gave a leaden thump or two. "Oh, Ned," she thought, "how you *could!*" She tried to face the full implication of the letter but almost at once shied away from it. "I'm miserable," she thought, "I'm unhappier than I've been for years and years."

"What," Alleyn's voice said close beside her, "I wonder, is the precise interpretation of the initials 'G.P.F.'? They seem to ring some bell in my atrocious memory but I haven't got there yet. Why, do you imagine, G.P.F.?" She didn't answer and after a moment he went on. "Wait a bit, though. Didn't you say something about a magazine you were reading before you visited Lord Pastern in his study? *Harmony?* Was that it?" He turned his head to look at her and she nodded. "And the editor of the tell-it-all-to-auntie page calls himself Guide, Philosopher and Friend? How does he sign his recipes for radiant living?"

Carlisle mumbled: "Like that."

"And you had wondered if Miss de Suze had written to him," Alleyn said tranquilly. "Yes. Now, does this get us anywhere, do you imagine?"

She made a non-committal sound. Unhappy recollections forced themselves upon her. Recollections of Félicité's story about a correspondence with someone she had never met who had written her a "marvellous" letter. Of Rivera reading her answer to this letter and making a scene about it. Of Ned Manx's article in *Harmony*. Of Félicité's behaviour after they all met to go to the Metronome. Of her taking the flower from Ned's coat. And of his stooping his head to listen to her as they danced together.

"Was Mr. Manx," Alleyn's voice asked, close beside her, "wearing his white carnation when he arrived for dinner?"

"No," she said, too loudly. "No. Not till afterwards. There were white carnations on the table at dinner."

"Perhaps it was one of them."

"Then," she said quickly, "it doesn't fit. The letter must have been written before he ever saw the carnation. It doesn't fit. She said the letter came by district messenger. Ned wouldn't have known."

"By district messenger, did she? We'll have to check that. Perhaps we'll find the envelope. Would you say," Alleyn continued, "that he seemed to be very much attached to her?"

(Edward had said: "About Fée. Something very odd has occurred. I can't explain but I'd like to think you understand.")

"Strongly attracted, would you think?" Alleyn said.

"I don't know. I don't know what to think."

"Do they see much of each other?"

"I don't know. He—he stayed at Duke's Gate while he was flat hunting."

"Perhaps an attachment developed then. What do you think?"

She shook her head. Alleyn waited. Carlisle now found his unstressed persistence intolerable. She felt her moorings go and was adrift in the darkness. A wretchedness of spirit that she was unable to control or understand took possession of her. "I won't talk about it," she stammered, "it's none of my business. I can't go on like this. Let me go, please. Please let me go."

"Of course," Alleyn said. "I'll take you home."

III

When they arrived at Duke's Gate, dawn was so far established that the houses with their blind windows and locked doors were clearly distinguishable in a wan half-light.

The familiar street, emerging from night, had an air of emaciation and secrecy, Carlisle thought, and she was vaguely relieved when milk bottles jingled up a side alley breaking across the blank emptiness. "Have you got a key?" Alleyn said. He and Fox and the man from the front seat waited while she groped in her bag. As she opened the door a second car drew up and four men got out. The men from the front seat joined them. She thought: "This makes us all seem very important. This is an important case. A case of murder."

In the old days she had come back from parties once or twice with Ned Manx at this hour. The indefinable house-smell made itself felt as they entered. She turned on a lamp and it was light in the silent hall. She saw herself reflected in the inner glass doors, her face stained with tears. Alleyn came in first. Standing there, in evening dress, with his hat in his hand, he might have been seeing her home, about to wish her good-bye. The other men followed quickly. "What happens now?" she wondered. "Will he let me go now? What are they going to do?"

Alleyn had drawn a paper from his pocket. "This is a search-warrant," he said. "I don't want to hunt Lord Pastern out of his bed. It will do I think, if—"

He broke off, moved quickly to the shadowed staircase and up half-a-dozen steps. Fox and the other men stood quiet inside the doors. A little French clock in the stair well ticked flurriedly. Upstairs on the first floor a door was flung open. A faint reflected light shone on Alleyn's face. A voice, unmistakably Lord Pastern's, said loudly: "I don't give a damn how upset you are. You can have kittens if you like but you don't go to bed till I've got my time-table worked out. Sit down."

With a faint grin Alleyn moved upstairs and Carlisle, after a moment's hesitation, followed him.

They were all in the drawing-room. Lady Pastern, still in evening dress and now very grey about the eyes and mouth, sat in a chair near the door. Félicité, who had changed into a housecoat and reduced her make-up, looked frail and lovely. Edward had evidently been sitting near her and had risen on Alleyn's entrance. Lord Pastern, with his coat off and his sleeves turned up, sat at a table in the middle of the room. Sheets of paper lay before him and he had a pencil between his teeth. A little removed from this group, her hands folded in the lap of her woollen dressing gown and her grey hair neatly braided down her back, sat Miss Henderson. A plain-clothes officer stood inside the door. Carlisle knew all about him. He was the man who had escorted them home: hours ago, it seemed, in another age. She had given him the slip when she returned to the Metronome and now wondered, for the first time, how dim a view the police would take of this manoeuvre. The man looked awkwardly at Alleyn, who seemed about to speak to him as Carlisle entered, but stood aside to let her pass. Edward came quickly towards her. "Where have you been?" he said angrily. "What's the matter? I—" He looked into her face. "Lisle," he said. "What is it?"

Lord Pastern glanced up. "Hello," he said. "Where the devil did you get to, Lisle? I want you. Sit down."

"It's like a scene from a play," she thought. "All of them sitting about exhausted, in a grand drawing-room. The third act of a thriller." She caught the eye of the plain-clothes officer, who was looking at her with distaste.

"I'm sorry," she said, "I'm afraid I just walked out by the back door."

"I realize that, miss," he said.

"We can't be in two places at once, can we?" Carlisle added brightly. She was trying to avoid Félicité. Félicité was looking at her anxiously, obviously, with inquiring eyebrows.

Lord Pastern said briskly: "Glad you've come, Alleyn, though I must say you've taken your time about it. I've been doin' your job for you. Sit down."

Lady Pastern's voice, sepulchral with fatigue, said: "May I suggest, George, that as in all probability this gentleman is about to arrest you, your choice of phrase is inappropriate."

"That's a damn tiresome sort of thing to say, C," her husband rejoined. "Gets you nowhere. What you want," he continued, darting his pencil at Alleyn, "is a time-table. You want to know what we were all doin' with ourselves before we went to the Metronome. System. All right. I've worked it out for you." He slapped the paper before him. "It's incomplete without Breezy's evidence, of course, but we can get that to-morrow. Lisle, there are one or two things I want from you. Come here."

Carlisle stood behind him and looked at Alleyn. His face was politely attentive, his eyes were on Lord Pastern's notes. In her turn and in response to an impatient tattoo of the pencil, she too looked at them.

She saw a sort of table, drawn up with ruled lines. Across the top, one each at the head of nine columns, she read their names: her own, Lady Pastern's, Félicité's, Edward's, Lord Pastern's, Bellairs's, Rivera's, Miss Henderson's, and Spence's. Down the left-hand side, Lord Pastern had written a series of times, beginning at 8:45 and ending at 19:30. These were ruled off horizontally and in the spaces thus formed, under each name, were notes as to the owner's whereabouts. Thus, at "9:15 approx" it appeared that she and Lady Pastern had been in the drawing-room, Miss Henderson on her way upstairs, Félicité in the study, Rivera in the hall, Lord Pastern and Breezy Bellairs in the ballroom, and Spence in the servants' quarters.

"The times," Lord Pastern explained importantly, "are mostly only approximate. We know some of them for certain but not all. Thing is, it shows you the groupin'. Who was with who and who was alone. Method. Here y'are, Lisle. Go over it carefully and check up your entries."

He flung himself back in his chair and ruffled his hair. He reeked of complacency. Carlisle took up the pencil and found that her hand trembled. Exhaustion had suddenly overwhelmed her. She was nauseated and fuddled with fatigue. Lord Pastern's time-table swam before her. She heard her voice saying, "I think you've got it right," and felt a hand under her arm. It was Alleyn's. "Sit down," he said from an enormous distance. She was sitting down and Ned, close beside her, was making some sort of angry protest. She leant forward, propping her head on her hands. Presently it cleared and she listened, with an extraordinary sense of detachment, to what Alleyn was now saying.

". . . very helpful, thank you. And now, I'm sure, you'll all be glad to get to bed. We shall be here during what's left of the night—hardly anything, I'm afraid, but we shan't disturb you."

They were on their feet. Carlisle, feeling very sick, wondered what would happen if she got to hers. She looked at the others through her fingers and thought that there was something a little wrong, a little misshapen, about all of them. Her aunt, for instance. Why had she not seen before that Lady Pastern's body was too long and her head too big? It was so. And surely Félicité was fantastically narrow. Her skeleton must be all wrong: a tiny pelvis with the hip-bones jutting out from it like rocks.

Carlisle's eyes, behind their sheltering fingers, turned to Lord Pastern and she thought how monstrous it was that his forehead should overhang the rest of his face—a blind over a shop window; that his monkey's cheeks should bunch themselves up when he was angry. Even Hendy: Hendy's throat was like some bird's and now that her hair was braided one saw that it was thin on top. Her scalp showed. They were caricatures, really, all of them. Subtly off-pitch: instruments very slightly out of tune. And Ned? He was behind her, but if she turned to look at him, what, in the perceptiveness born of nervous exhaustion, would she see? Were not his eyes black and small? Didn't his mouth, when it smiled, twist and show canine teeth a little too long? But she would not look at Ned.

And now, thought the bemused Carlisle, here was Uncle George at it again. "I've no intention of goin' to bed. People sleep too much. No need for it: look at the mystics. Workin' from this time-table I can show you . . ."

"That's extremely kind of you, sir." Alleyn's voice was clear and pleasant. "But I think not. We have to get through our routine jobs. They're dreary beyond words and we're best left to ourselves while we do them."

"Routine," shouted Lord Pastern. "Official synonym for inefficiency. Things are straightened out for you by someone who takes the trouble to use his head and what do you do? Tell him to go to bed while you gallop about his house makin' lists like a bumbailiff. Be damned if I'll go to bed. Now!"

"Oh, God!" Carlisle thought desperately. "How's he going to cope with this?" She felt the pressure of a hand on her shoulder and heard Ned's voice.

"May I suggest that whatever Cousin George decides to do there's no reason why the rest of us should keep a watch of supererogation."

"None at all," Alleyn said.

"Carlisle, my dear," Lady Pastern murmured as if she were giving the signal to rise from a dinner party. "Shall we?"

Carlisle stood up. Edward was close by and it seemed to her that he still looked angry. "Are you all right?" he asked.

"Perfectly," she said. "I don't know what possessed me. I got a bit run-down in Greece and I suppose—" Her voice died. She was thinking of the long flight of stairs up to her room.

"My dearest child," her aunt said, "I shall never forgive myself that you have been subjected to this ordeal."

"But she's wondering," Carlisle thought, "what I've been up to. They're all wondering."

"Perhaps some wine," her aunt continued, "or whiskey. It is useless to suggest, George, that you . . ."

"I'll get it," Edward said quickly.

But Miss Henderson had already gone and now returned with a glass in her hand. As she took it from her, Carlisle smelt Hendy's particular smell of soap and talcum powder. "Like a baby," she thought and drank. The almost neat whiskey made her shudder convulsively. "Hendy!" she gasped. "You do pack a punch. I'm all right. Really. It's you, Aunt Cécile, who should be given corpse revivers."

Lady Pastern closed her eyes momentarily upon this vulgarism. Félicité, who had been perfectly silent ever since Alleyn and Carlisle came in, said: "I'd like a drink, Ned. Let's have a pub crawl in the dining-room, shall we?"

"The decanter's here if you want it, dear." Miss Henderson also spoke for the first time.

"In that case," Edward said, "if it's all right by you, Alleyn, I'll take myself off."

"We've got your address, haven't we? Right."

"Good-bye, Cousin Cile. If there's anything I can do . . ." Ned stood in the doorway. Carlisle did not look at him. "Good-bye, Lisle," he said. "Good-bye, Fée."

Félicité moved swiftly to him and with an abrupt compulsive movement put her arm round his neck and kissed him. He stood for a moment with his head stooped and his hand on her arm. Then he was gone.

Beneath the heavy mask of exhaustion that her aunt wore, Carlisle saw a faint glimmer of gratification. "Come, my children," Lady Pastern said, almost briskly. "Bed." She swept them past Alleyn, who opened the door for them. As Carlisle turned, with the others, to mount the stairs, she heard Lord Pastern.

"Here I am," he shouted, "and here I stick. You don't turf me off to bed or anywhere else, short of arresting me."

"I'm not, at the moment, proposing to do that," Alleyn said distinctly, "though I think, sir, I should warn you . . ."

The door shut off the remainder of his sentence.

IV

Alleyn shut the door on the retiring ladies and looked thoughtfully at Lord Pastern. "I think," he repeated, "I should warn you that if you do decide, against my advice, to stay with us, what you do and say will be noted and the notes may be used. . . ."

"Oh, fiddle-faddle!" Lord Pastern interrupted shrilly. "All this rigmarole. I didn't do it and you can't prove I did. Get on with your precious routine and don't twaddle so."

Alleyn looked at him with a sort of astonishment. "You bloody little old fellow," he thought. Lord Pastern blinked and smirked and bunched up his cheeks.

"All right, sir," Alleyn said. "But you're going to be given the customary warning, twaddle or not, and what's more I'll have a witness to it."

He crossed the landing, opened the ballroom door, said: "Fox, can you give me a moment?" and returned to the drawing-room, where he waited in silence until Inspector Fox came in. He then said: "Fox, I've asked Lord Pastern to go to bed and he refuses. I want you to witness this. I warn him that from now onwards his words and behaviour will be noted and that the notes may later on be used in evidence. It's a nuisance, of course, but short of taking a much more drastic step, I don't see what else can be done about it. Have the extra men turned up?"

Fox, looking with marked disapproval at Lord Pastern, said that they had.

"Tell them to keep observation, will you? Thank you, Fox, I'll carry on here."

"Thank you, Mr. Alleyn," said Fox. "I'll get on with it in the study then."

He turned to the door. Lord Pastern said: "Hi! Where're you goin'? What're you up to?"

"If you'll excuse me for passing the remark, my lord," said Fox severely, "you're acting very foolishly. Very ill-advised and foolish, what you're doing, if I may say so." He went out.

"Great ham-fisted ass of a chap," Lord Pastern remarked.

"On the contrary, sir," Alleyn rejoined with perfect politeness, "an extremely efficient officer and should have had his promotion long ago."

He left Lord Pastern, walked to the centre of the long drawing-room and surveyed it for some minutes with his hands in his pockets. A clock on the landing struck five. Alleyn began a closer inspection of the room. He traversed it slowly, moving across and across it and examining any object that lay in his path. Lord Pastern watched him and sighed and groaned audibly. Presently Alleyn came to a chair beside which stood an occasional table. On the table was an embroidery frame, and a work-box of elaborate and elegant design. He opened the lid delicately and stooped to examine the contents. Here, neatly disposed, were innumerable skeins of embroidery silks. The box was fitted with every kind of tool, each in its appointed slot: needle-cases, scissors, bodkins, a thimble, an ivory measure, a tape in a cloisonné case, stilettoes held in their places by silken sheaths. One slot was untenanted. Alleyn sat down and began, with scrupulous care, to explore the box.

"Pity you didn't bring your sewin'," said Lord Pastern, "isn't it?"

Alleyn took out his notebook, glanced at his watch and wrote briefly.

"I'd thank you," Lord Pastern added, "to keep your hands out of m' wife's property." He attempted to repress a yawn, shed a tear over the effort and barked suddenly: "Where's your search-warrant, b' God?"

Alleyn completed another note, rose and exhibited his warrant. "Tscha!" said Lord Pastern.

Alleyn had turned to examine Lady Pastern's embroidery. It was stretched over a frame and was almost completed. A riot of cupids in postures of extreme insouciance circled about a fabulous nosegay. The work was exquisite. He gave a slight appreciative chuckle which Lord Pastern instantly parodied. Alleyn resumed his search. He moved steadily on at a snail's pace. Half an hour crawled by. Presently an odd little noise disturbed him. He glanced up. Lord Pastern, still on his feet, was swaying dangerously. His eyes were glazed and horrible and his mouth was open. He had snored.

Alleyn tiptoed to the door at the far end of the room, opened it and slipped into the study. He heard a sort of roaring noise behind him, shut the door and, finding a key in the lock, turned it.

Inspector Fox, in his shirt-sleeves, was examining the contents of an open drawer on the top of the desk. Laid out in front of him were a tube of plastic wood, an empty bottle marked "gun oil," with no cork in it, and a white ivory handle into which some tool had once fitted.

V

Fox laid a broad finger on the desk beside these exhibits, not so much for an index as to establish their presence and significance. Alleyn nodded and crossed quickly to the door that gave on the landing. He locked it and waited near it with his head cocked. "Here he comes," he said.

There was a patter of feet outside. The handle of the door was turned and then rattled angrily. A distant voice said: "I'm sorry, my lord, but I'm afraid that room's under inspection just now."

"Who the hell d'you think you are?"

"Sergeant Marks, my lord."

"Then let me tell you . . ."

The voices faded out.

"He won't get into the ballroom either," said Fox, "unless he tries a knock-up with Sergeant Whitelaw."

"How about the dining-room?"

"They've finished there, Mr. Alleyn."

"Anything?"

"Wine had been spilt on the carpet. Port, I'd say. And there's a bit of a mark on the table near the centre flower bowl as if a drop or two of water had laid there. White carnations in the bowl. Nothing else. The tables had been cleared, of course."

Alleyn looked at the collection on the desk. "Where did you beat this lot up, Foxkin?"

"In this drawer which was pulled out and left on top of the desk like it is now. Half a junk shop in it, isn't there, sir? These articles were lying on the surface of the other mess."

"Bailey had a go at it?"

"Yes. No prints on any of 'em," said Fox. "Which is funny."

"How about the typewriter?"

"We've printed it. Only his lordship's dabs and they're very fresh."

"No cap on the plastic wood tube."

"It was on the floor."

Alleyn examined the tube. "It's set hard, of course, at the open end but not very deep. Tube's three-quarters full."

"There are crumbs of plastic wood in the drawer and on the desk and the carpet."

Alleyn said absently, "Are there, by Gum!" and turned his attention to the small white handle. "Exhibit B," he said. "Know what it is, Fox?"

"I can make a healthy guess, I fancy, Mr. Alleyn."

"It's the fellow of a number of gadgets in a very elegant French work-box in the drawing-room. Crochet hooks, scissors and so on. They're fixed inside the lid, in slots. One slot's empty."

"This is just a handle, you'll notice, sir."

"Yes. Do you think it ought to have an embroidery stiletto fitted in the hollow end?"

"It's what I reckoned."

"I think you're right."

Fox opened his bag and took out a narrow cardboard box. In this, secured and protected by strings, was the dart. The jewels in the spring clip, tiny emeralds and brilliants, glittered cheerfully. Only a narrow platinum band near the top and the stiletto itself were dulled with Rivera's blood.

"Bailey'll have a go for latent prints," Fox said.

"Yes, of course. We can't disturb it. Later on it can be dismembered, but on looks, Fox, we've got something."

Alleyn held the ivory handle beside the stiletto. "I'll swear they belong," he said, and put it down. "Here's exhibit C. An empty gun-oil bottle. Where's that cork?"

Fox produced it. "It fits," he said, "I've tried. It fits and it has the same stink. Though why the hell it should turn up on the bandstand . . ."

"Ah me," Alleyn said. "Why the hell indeed. Well, look what turns up in your particular fancy's very own drawer in his very own study! Could anything be more helpful?"

Fox shifted bulkily in his chair and contemplated his superior officer for some moments. "I know it seems funny," he said at last. "Leaving evidence all over the place: making no attempt to clear himself, piling up a case against himself, you might say. But then he *is* funny. Would you say he was not responsible within the meaning of the act?"

"I'm never sure what is the precise meaning of the infernal act. Responsible. Not responsible. Who's to mark a crucial division in the stream of human behaviour running down from something we are pleased to call sanity into raving lunacy? Where's the point at which a human being ceases to be a responsible being? Oh, I know the definitions, and I know we do our best with them, but it seems to me it's here, over this business of the pathology of behaviour, that any system of corrective and coercive law shows at its dimmest. Is this decidedly rum peer so far south in the latitude of behaviour that he would publicly murder a man by a ridiculously elaborate method that points directly to himself, and then, in effect, do everything in his power to get himself arrested? There have been cases of the sort, but is this going to be one of them?"

"Well, sir," said Fox stolidly, "I must say I think it is. It's early days yet, but as far as we've got I think it looks like it. This gentleman's previous record and his general run of behaviour point to a mental set-up that, without going beyond the ordinary view, is eccentric. Everyone knows he's funny."

"Yes. Everyone. Everyone knows," Alleyn agreed. "Everyone would say: 'It's in character. It's just like him!' "

With as near an approach to exasperation as Alleyn had ever heard from him, Fox said: "All right, Mr. Alleyn, then. I know what you're getting at. But who could have planted it on him? Tell me that. Do you believe any of the party at the table could have got at the revolver when it was under the sombrero and shoved this silly dart or bolt or what-have-you up it? Do you think Bellairs could have planted the bolt and picked it up after his lordship searched him? Where could he have planted it? In a bare band-room with nothing in it but musical instruments and other men? And how could he have got it into the revolver when his lordship had the revolver on his person and swears to it that it never left him? Skelton. Skelton handled the gun while a roomful of people watched him do it. Could Skelton have palmed this thing up the barrel? The idea's laughable. Well, then."

"All right, old thing," Alleyn said. "Let's get on with it. The servants will be about soon. How far have you got in here?"

"Not much further than what you've seen, sir. The drawer was a daisy. The bullets he extracted when he made his dummies are in the waste-paper basket there."

"Carlisle Wayne watched him at that. How about the ballroom?"

"Bailey and Thompson are in there."

"Oh, well. Let's have another look at Lord Pastern's revolver, Fox."

Fox lifted it from his bag and laid it on the desk. Alleyn sat down and produced his lens.

"There's a very nice lens here, in his lordship's drawer," Fox remarked. Alleyn grunted. He was looking into the mouth of the barrel.

"We'll get a photomicrograph of this," he muttered. "Two longish scratches and some scrabbles." He gave the revolver to Fox, who was sitting in the chair which, nine hours earlier, Carlisle had occupied. Like Carlisle, Fox used Lord Pastern's lens.

"Did you notice," Alleyn said, "that when I gave the thing to that old freak to look at, it was the underside of the butt near the trigger guard that seemed to interest him. I can't find anything there. The maker's plate's on the heel. What was he up to, do you suppose?"

"God knows," Fox grunted crossly. He was sniffing at the muzzle.

"You look like an old maid with smelling salts," Alleyn observed.

"So I may, sir, but I don't smell anything except gun oil."

"I know. That's another thing. Listen."

In some distant part of the house there was movement. A door slammed, shutters were thrown back and a window opened.

"The servants are stirring," Alleyn said. "We'll seal this room, leave a man to watch it and come back to it later on. Let's collect everything we've picked up, find out what the others have got and catch three hours' sleep. Yard at ten o'clock, don't forget. Come on."

But he himself did not move. Fox looked dubiously at him and began to pack away the revolver, the plastic wood, the empty bottle and the ivory handle.

"No, blast it," Alleyn said, "I'll work through. Take those things, Fox, and dispatch them off to the experts. Fix up adequate relief for surveillance here, and away you go. I'll see you at ten. What's the matter?"

"I'd as soon stay, Mr. Alleyn."

"I know all about that. Zealous young officer. Away you go."

Fox passed his hand over his short grizzled hair and said: "I keep very fit, really. Make a point of never thinking about the retiring age. Well, thank you very much, Mr. Alleyn."

"I might have another dig at the witnesses."

"The party upstairs won't wake before ten."

"I'll stir 'em up if I need 'em. Why should they have all the fun? I want to ring up my wife. Good morning to you, Mr. Fox."

Fox unlocked the door on to the landing and turned the handle. The door flew inwards, striking his shoulder. He stepped back with an oath and Lord Pastern's body fell across his feet.

VI

It remained there for perhaps three seconds. Its eyes were open and glared furiously. Fox bent over it and the mouth also opened.

"What the hell d'you think you're doing'?" Lord Pastern demanded.

He rolled over neatly and got to his feet. His jaw and cheeks glistened with a sort of hoar-frost, his eyes were bloodshot and his evening dress disordered. A window on the landing shed the cruel light of early morning upon him and he looked ghastly in it. His manner, however, had lost little if its native aggressiveness. "What are you starin' at?" he added.

"We might fairly ask you," Alleyn rejoined, "what you were up to, sitting, it appears, on the landing with your back to the door."

"I dozed off. Pretty state of affairs when a man's kept out of his own rooms at five o'clock in the morning."

"All right, Fox," Alleyn said wearily, "you get along."

"Very well, sir," said Fox. "Good morning, my lord." He side-stepped Lord Pastern and went out, leaving the door ajar. Alleyn heard him admonishing Sergeant Marks on the landing: "What sort of surveillance do you call this?" "I was only told to keep observation, Mr. Fox. His lordship fell asleep as soon as he touched the floor. I thought he might as well be there as anywhere." Fox growled majestically and passed out of hearing.

Alleyn shut the study door and went to the window. "We haven't finished in this room," he said, "but I think I may disturb it so far."

He drew back the curtains and opened the window. It was now quite light outside. A fresh breeze came in through the window, emphasizing, before it dismissed them, the dense enclosed odors of carpet, leather and stale smoke. The study looked inhospitable and unkempt. The desk lamp still shed a raffish yellowness on the litter that surrounded it. Alleyn turned from the window to face Lord Pastern and found him rummaging with quick inquisitive fingers in the open drawer on the desk.

"I wonder if I can show you what you're hunting for," Alleyn said. He opened Fox's bag and then took out his notebook. "Don't touch anything please, but will you look in that case?"

He did look, but impatiently, and, as far as Alleyn could see, without any particular surprise.

"Where'd you find that?" Lord Pastern demanded, pointing a not very steady finger at the ivory handle.

"In the drawer. Can you identify it?"

"I might be able to," he muttered.

Alleyn pointed to the weapon. "The stiletto that's been sunk in the end with plastic wood might have belonged to this ivory handle. We shall try it. If it fits, it came originally from Lady Pastern's work-box in the drawing-room."

"So you say," said Lord Pastern insultingly. Alleyn made a note.

"Can you tell me if this stiletto was in your drawer here, sir? Before last night?"

Lord Pastern was eyeing the revolver. He thrust out his underlip, shot a glance at Alleyn, and darted his hand towards it.

"All right," Alleyn said, "you may touch it, but please answer my question about the stiletto."

"How should I know?" he said indifferently. "I don't know." Without removing it from the case, he tipped the revolver over and, snatching up his lens, peered at the underside of the butt. He gave a shrill cackle of laughter.

"What did you expect to see?" Alleyn asked casually.

"Hoity-toity," Lord Pastern rejoined. "*Wouldn't* you like to know!"

He stared at Alleyn. His bloodshot eyes twinkled insolently. "It's devilish amusin'," he said. "Look at it whatever way you like, it's damn funny."

He dropped into an armchair, and with an air of gloating relish rubbed his hands together.

Alleyn shut down the lid of Fox's case and succeeded in snatching back his temper. He stood in front of Lord Pastern and deliberately looked into his eyes. Lord Pastern immediately shut them very tight and bunched up his cheeks.

"I'm sleepy," he said.

"Listen to me," Alleyn said. "Have you any idea at all of the personal danger you are in? Do you know the consequences of withholding or refusing crucial information when a capital crime has been committed? It's my duty to tell you that you are under grave suspicion. You've had the formal warning. Confronted with the body of a man whom, one assumes, you were supposed to hold in some sort of regard, you've conducted yourself appallingly. I must tell you, sir, that if you continue in this silly affectation of frivolity, I shall ask you to come to Scotland Yard where you will be questioned and, if necessary, detained."

He waited. Lord Pastern's face had gradually relaxed during this speech. His mouth now pouted and expelled a puff of air that blew his moustache out. He was, apparently, asleep again.

Alleyn contemplated him for some moments. He then seated himself at the desk in a position that enabled him to keep Lord Pastern in sight. After a moment's cogitation, he pulled the typewriter towards him, took Félicité's letter from his pocket, found a sheet of paper and began to make a copy.

At the first rattle of the keys Lord Pastern's eyes opened, met Alleyn's gaze and shut again. He mumbled something indistinguishable and snored with greater emphasis. Alleyn completed his copy and laid it beside the original. They had been typed on the same machine.

On the floor, beside the chair Carlisle had used on the previous night, lay the magazine *Harmony*. He took it up and ruffled the pages. A dozen or more flopped over and then the binding opened a little. He was confronted with G.P.F.'s page and noticed, as Carlisle had noticed, the cigarette ash in the groove. He read the letter signed "Toots," turned a few more pages and came upon the anti-drug-racket article and a dramatic review signed by Edward Manx. He once more confronted that preposterous figure in the armchair.

"Lord Pastern," he said loudly, "wake up. Wake up."

Lord Pastern jerked galvanically, made a tasting noise with his tongue and lips and uttered a nightmarish sound.

"A-a-ah?"

"Come now, you're awake. Answer me this," said Alleyn and thrust the copy of *Harmony* under his nose. "How long have you known that Edward Manx was G.P.F.?"

CHAPTER VIII

Morning

I

LORD PASTERN BLINKED OWLISHLY at the paper, swung round in his chair and eyed the desk. The letter and the copy lay conspicuously beside the typewriter.

"Yes," Alleyn said, "that's how I know. Will you give me an explanation of all this?"

Lord Pastern leant forward and, resting his forearm on his knees, seemed to stare at his clasped hands. When he spoke his voice was subdued and muffled.

"No," he said, "I'll be damned if I do. I'll answer no questions. Find out for yourself. I'm for bed."

He pulled himself out of the chair and squared his shoulders. The air of truculence was still there but Alleyn thought it overlaid a kind of indecision. With the nearest approach to civility that he had yet exhibited he added: "I'm within my rights, aren't I?"

"Certainly," Alleyn said at once. "Your refusal will be noted. That's all. If you change your mind about sending for your solicitor, we shall be glad to call him in. In the meantime, I'm afraid, sir, I shall have to place you under very close observation."

"D'you mean some damn bobby's goin' to follow me about like a bulkin' great poodle?"

"If you care to put it that way. It's no use, I imagine, for me to repeat any warnings about your own most equivocal position."

"None whatever." He went to the door and stood with his back to Alleyn, holding the knob and leaning heavily on it. "Get them to give you breakfast," he said without looking round and went slowly out and up the stairs. Alleyn called his thanks after him and nodded to Marks, who was on the landing. Marks followed Lord Pastern upstairs.

Alleyn returned to the study, shut the window, had a last look round, packed Fox's bag, removed it to the landing and finally locked and sealed the door. Marks had been replaced on the landing by another plain-clothes man. "Hullo, Jimson," Alleyn said. "Just come on?"

"Yes, sir. Relieving."

"Have you seen any of the staff?"

"A maid came upstairs just now, Mr. Alleyn. Mr. Fox left instructions they were to be kept off this floor so I sent her down again. She seemed very much put about."

"She would," Alleyn said. "All right. Tactful as you can, you know, but don't miss anything."

"Very good, sir."

He crossed the landing and entered the ballroom where he found Thompson and Bailey packing up. Alleyn looked at the group of chairs round the grand piano and at a sheet of note paper Bailey had collected. On it was pencilled the band programme for the previous night. Bailey pointed out the light coating of dust on the piano top and showed Alleyn where they had found clear traces of the revolver and the parasol and umbrellas. It was odd, Bailey and Thompson thought, but it appeared that quantities of dust had fallen after these objects had rested in this place. Not so very odd, Alleyn suggested, as Lord Pastern had, on his own statement, fired off a blank round in the ballroom and that would probably have brought down quite a lot of dust from the charming but ornately moulded ceiling. "Happy hunting ground," he muttered. "Whose are the prints round these traces of the parasol section and knob? Don't tell me," he added wearily. "His lordship's?"

"That's right," Thompson and Bailey said together. "His lordship's and Breezy's." Alleyn saw them go and then came out and sealed the ballroom doors.

He returned to the drawing-room, collected Lady Pastern's work-box, debated with himself about locking this room up too and decided against it. He then left all his gear under the eye of the officer on the landing and went down to the ground floor. It was now six o'clock.

The dining-room was already prepared for breakfast. The bowl of white carnations, he noticed, had been removed to a side table. As he halted before a portrait of some former Settinger who bore a mild resemblance to Lord Pastern, he heard a distant mingling of voices beyond the service door. The servants, he thought, having their first snack. He pushed open the door, found himself in a servery with a further door which led, it appeared, into the servants' hall. The best of all early morning smells, that of freshly brewed coffee, was clearly discernible. He was about to go forward when a voice, loud, dogged and perceptibly anxious, said very slowly:

"Parlez, monsieur, je vous en prie, plus lentement, et peut-être je vous er—er—comprendrerai—No, blast it, as you were, *je vous pouverai*—"

Alleyn pushed open the door and discovered Mr. Fox, seated cosily before a steaming cup of coffee, flanked by Spence and a bevy of attentive ladies and *vis-à-vis* a dark imposing personage in full chef's regalia.

There was only a fractional pause while Alleyn surveyed this tableau. Fox then rose.

"Perhaps you'd like a cup of coffee, Mr. Alleyn," he suggested and, addressing the chef, added carefully: *"C'est Monsieur—er—le chef-inspecteur Alleyn, Monsieur*. Mr. Alleyn, this is Miss Parker, the housekeeper, and Mademoiselle Hortense. And these girls are Mary and Myrtle. This is Mr. Spence and this is Monsieur Dupont and the young chap over there is William. Well!" concluded Fox, beaming upon the company, "this is what I call cosy."

Alleyn took the chair placed for him by William and stared fixedly at his subordinate. Fox responded with a bland smile. "I was just leaving, sir," he said, "when I happened to run into Mr. Spence. I knew you'd want to inform these good people of our little contretemps so here, in point of fact, I am."

"Fancy," said Alleyn.

Fox's technique on the working side of the green baize doors was legendary at the Yard. This was the first time Alleyn had witnessed it in action. But even now, he realized, the fine bloom of the exotic was rubbed off and it was his own entrance which had destroyed it. The atmosphere of conviviality had stiffened. Spence had risen, the maids hovered uneasily on the edges of their chairs. He did his best and it was a good best, but evidently Fox, who was an innocent snob, had been bragging about him and they all called him "sir."

"Well," he said cheerfully, "if Mr. Fox has been on this job there'll be no need for me to bother any of you. This is the best coffee I've drunk for years."

"I am gratified," said Monsieur Dupont in fluent English. "At present, of course, one cannot obtain the fresh bean as readily as one desires."

Mademoiselle Hortense said, "Naturally," and the others made small affirmative noises.

"I suppose," Fox said genially, "his lordship's very particular about his coffee. Particular about everything, I daresay?" he added, invitingly.

William, the footman, laughed sardonically and was checked by a glance from Spence. Fox prattled on. It would be her ladyship, of course, who was particular about coffee, being of Mademoiselle Hortense's and Monsieur Dupont's delightful nationality. He attempted this compliment in French, got bogged down and told Alleyn that Monsieur Dupont had been giving him a lesson. Mr. Alleyn, he informed the company, spoke French like a native. Looking up, Alleyn found Spence gazing at him with an expression of anxiety.

"I'm afraid this is a great nuisance for all of you," Alleyn said.

"It's not that, sir," Spence rejoined slowly, "it does put us all about very much, I can't deny. Not being able to get things done in the usual way—"

"I'm sure," Miss Parker intervened, "I don't know what her ladyship's going to say about the first floor. Leaving everything. It's very awkward."

"Exactly. But the worrying thing," Spence went on, "is not knowing what it's all about. Having the police in, sir, and everything. Just because the party from this house happens to be present when this Mr. Rivera passes away in a restaurant."

"Quite so," said Miss Parker.

"The circumstances," Alleyn said carefully, "are extraordinary. I don't know if Inspector Fox has told you—"

Fox said that he had been anxious not to distress the ladies. Alleyn, who thought that the ladies looked as if they were half-dead with curiosity, agreed that Fox had shown great delicacy but added that it would have to come out sometime. "Mr. Rivera," he said, "was killed."

They stirred attentively. Myrtle, the younger of the maids, ejaculated, "Murdered?" clapped her hands over her mouth and suppressed a nervous giggle. Alleyn said it looked very much like it and added that he hoped they would all cooperate as far as they were able in helping to clear the ground. He had known, before he met it, what their response would be. People were all very much alike when it came to homicide cases. They wanted to be removed to a comfortable distance where curiosity could be assuaged, prestige maintained and personal responsibility dissolved. With working people this wish was deepened by a heritage of insecurity and the necessity to maintain caste. They were filled with a kind of generic anxiety: at once disturbed by an indefinite threat and stimulated by a crude and potent assault on their imagination.

"It's a matter," he said, "of clearing innocent people, of tidying them up. I'm sure you will be glad to help us in this, if you can."

He produced Lord Pastern's time-table, spread it out before Spence and told them who had compiled it.

"If you can help us check these times, any of you, we shall be very grateful," he said.

Spence put on his spectacles and with an air of slight embarrassment began to read the time-table. The others, at Alleyn's suggestion, collected round him, not altogether unwillingly.

"It's a bit elaborate, isn't it?" Alleyn said. "Let's see if it can be simplified at all. You see that between half-past eight and nine the ladies left the dining-room and went to the drawing-room. So we get the two groups in the two rooms. Can any of you add to or confirm that?"

Spence could. It was a quarter to nine when the ladies went to the drawing-room. When he came away from serving their coffee he passed Lord Pastern and Mr. Bellairs on the landing. They went into his lordship's study. Spence continued on through the dining-room, paused there to see that William had served coffee to the gentlemen and noticed that Mr. Manx and Mr. Rivera were still sitting over their wine. He then went into the servants' hall where a few minutes later he heard the nine o'clock news on the wireless.

"So now," Alleyn said, "we have three groups. The ladies in the drawing-room, his lordship and Mr. Bellairs in the study, and Mr. Manx and Mr. Rivera in the dining-room. Can anyone tell us when the next move came and who made it?"

Spence remembered coming back into the dining-room and finding Mr. Manx there alone. His reticence at this point became more marked, but Alleyn got from him the news that Edward Manx had helped himself to a stiff whiskey. He asked casually if there was anything about his manner which was at all remarkable, and got the surprising answer that Mr. Edward seemed to be very pleased and said he'd had a wonderful surprise.

"And now," Alleyn said, "Mr. Rivera has broken away from the other groups. Where has he gone? Mr. Manx is in the dining-room, his lordship and Mr. Bellairs in the study, the ladies in the drawing-room, and where is Mr. Rivera?"

He looked round the group of faces with their guarded unwilling expressions until he saw William, and in William's eye he caught a zealous glint. William, he thought, with any luck read detective magazines and spent his day-dreams sleuthing. "Got an idea?" he asked.

"Well, sir," William said, glancing at Spence, "if you'll excuse me, I think his lordship and Mr. Bellairs have parted company where you've got to. I was tidying the hall, sir, and I heard the other gentleman, Mr. Bellairs, come out of the study. I glanced up at the landing, like. And I heard his lordship call out he'd join him in a minute and I saw the gentleman go into the ballroom. I went and got the coffee tray from the drawing-room, sir. The ladies were all there. I put it down on the landing and was going to set the study to rights, when I heard the typewriter in there. His lordship doesn't like being disturbed when he's typing, sir, so I took the tray by the staff stairs to the kitchen and after a few minutes came back. And his lordship must have gone into the ballroom while I was downstairs because I could hear him talking very loud to Mr. Bellairs, sir."

"What about, do you remember?"

William glanced again at Spence and said: "Well, sir, it was something about his lordship telling somebody something if Mr. Bellairs didn't want to. And then there was a terrible loud noise. Drums. And a report like a gun. They all heard it down here in the hall, sir."

Alleyn looked at the listening staff. Miss Parker said coldly that his lordship was no doubt practising, as if Lord Pastern were in the habit of loosing firearms indoors and there were nothing at all remarkable in the circumstances. Alleyn felt that both she and Spence were on the edge of giving William a piece of their minds and he hurried on.

"What did you do next?" he asked William.

He had been, it appeared, somewhat shattered by the report, but had remembered his duties. "I crossed the landing, sir, thinking I'd get on with the study, but Miss de Suze came out of the drawing-room. And then—well, the murdered gentleman, he came from the dining-room and they met and she said she wanted to speak to him alone and they went into the study."

"Sure of that?"

Yes, it appeared that William was perfectly certain. He had lingered, evidently, at the end of the landing. He even remembered that Miss de Suze had something in her hand. He wasn't sure what it was. Something bright, it might have been, he said doubtfully. After she and the gentleman had gone into the study and shut the door, Miss Henderson had come out of the drawing-room and gone upstairs.

Alleyn said: "Now, that's a great help. You see it corresponds exactly so far with his lordship's time-table. I'll just check it over, Fox, if you . . ."

Fox took the tip neatly and while Alleyn affected to study Lord Pastern's notes continued what he liked to call the painless extraction method with William. It must, he said, have been awkward for William. You couldn't go barging in on a *tête-à-tête*, could you, and yet a chap liked to get his job done. Life, said Fox, was funny when you came to think of it. Here was this poor young lady happily engaged in conversation with—well, he supposed he wasn't giving any secrets away if he said with her fiancé, and little did she think that in a couple of hours or so he would be lying dead. Miss Parker and the maids were visibly moved by this. William turned extremely red in the face and shuffled his feet. "She'll treasure every word of that last talk, I'll be bound," said Fox. "Every word of it." He looked inquiringly at William, who, after a longish pause, blurted out very loudly: "I wouldn't go so far as to say that, Mr. Fox."

"That'll do, Will," said Spence quietly but Fox's voice overrode him. "Is that so?" Fox inquired blandly. "You wouldn't? Why not?"

"Because," William announced boldly, "they was at it hammer-and-tongs."

"Will!"

William turned on his superior. "I ought to tell the truth, didn't I, Mr. Spence? To the police?"

"You ought to mind your own business," said Miss Parker with some emphasis and Spence murmured his agreement.

"All right then," William said, huffily. "I'm sure I don't want to push myself in where I'm not welcome."

Fox was extremely genial and complimented William on his natural powers of observation and Miss Parker and Spence upon their loyalty and discretion. He suggested, without exactly stating as much and keeping well on the safe side of police procedure, that any statements anybody offered would, by some mysterious alchemy, free all concerned of any breath of suspicion. In a minute or two he had discovered that sharp-eared William, still hovering on the landing, had seen Rivera go into the ballroom and had overheard most of his quarrel with Breezy Bellairs. To this account Spence and Miss Parker raised no objections and it was tolerably obvious that they had already heard it. It became clear that Mademoiselle Hortense was stifling with repressed information. But she had her eye on Alleyn and it was to him that she addressed herself. She had that particular knack, that peculiar talent commanded by so many of her countrywomen, of making evident, without the slightest emphasis, her awareness of her own attractions and those of the man to whom she was speaking. Alleyn, she seemed to assume, would understand perfectly that she was the confidante of Mademoiselle. Monsieur Dupont, who had remained aloof, now assumed an air of gloomy acquiescence. It was understood, he said, that the relationship between a personal maid and her mistress was one of delicacy and confidence.

"About *l'affaire Rivera . . .*" suggested Fox, doggedly Gallic.

Hortense lifted her shoulders and rocked her head slightly. She addressed herself to Alleyn. Undoubtedly this Monsieur Rivera had been passionately attached. That was evident. And Mademoiselle had responded, being extremely impressionable. But an engagement? Not precisely. He had urged it. There had been scenes. Reconciliations. Further scenes. But last night! She suddenly executed a complicated and vivid gesture with her right hand as if she wrote something off on the air. And against the unuttered but almost tangible disapproval of the English servants, Hortense, with a darting incisiveness, said: "Last night everything was ended. But irrevocably *ended.*"

II

It appeared that at twenty to ten Hortense was summoned to Lady Pastern's bedroom, where she prepared her for the road, putting her into a cloak, and adding, Alleyn supposed, some kind of super-gloss to that already immaculate surface. Hortense kept an eye on the time as the car was ordered for ten-thirty and Lady Pastern liked to have leisure. About ten minutes late Miss Henderson had come in with the news that Félicité was extremely excited and wished to make an elaborate change in her *toilette.* She herself was sent to Félicité's room.

"And conceive the scene, Monsieur!" said Hortense, breaking into her native tongue. "The room in complete disarray and Mademoiselle in *déshabillé.* There must be a completely new *toilette,* you understand. Everything, from the foundation, is it not? And while I dress her she relates the whole story. With Monsieur Rivera it is as if it had never been. There has been a formidable quarrel. She had dismissed him forever and in the meantime a letter has arrived in romantic circumstances. It is a letter from a journalistic gentleman she has never seen but with whom she has corresponded frequently. He is about to reveal himself. He declares his passionate attachment. Yet secrecy must be observed. And for myself," Hortense added with conscious rectitude, "I would never, never have allowed myself to repeat one syllable of this matter if it had not become my duty to assure Monsieur that as far as Mademoiselle is concerned, she had no further interest in Monsieur Rivera and was happily released from him and that this is not therefore a *crime passionel.*"

"I see," Alleyn said. "Yes, perfectly. It is understood."

Hortense gave him a soubrettish glance and a hard smile.

"And do you know," he said, "who this person was? The letter-writer?"

Félicité, it appeared, had shown her the letter. And as the party was leaving for the Metronome, Hortense had run downstairs with Lady Pastern's vinaigrette and had seen (with what emotion!) Monsieur Edward Manx wearing a white flower in his coat. All was revealed! And how great, Hortense had reflected as Spence closed the front door on their departure, how overwhelming would be the joy of her ladyship, who had always desired this union! Hortense had been quite unable to conceal her own gratification and had sung for pure joy as she rejoined her colleagues in the servants' hall. Her colleagues, with the exception of Monsieur Dupont, now cast black glances at her and refrained from comment.

Alleyn checked over the events related by Hortense and found that they corresponded as nearly as necessary with the group movements suggested by Lord Pastern's notes. From the nucleus of persons, further individuals had broken away. Manx had been alone in the drawing-room. Lady Pastern had been alone in her room until Hortense arrived. Hortense herself, and William, had cruised about the house and so had Spence. Alleyn was about to lay down his pencil when he remembered Miss Henderson. She had gone to her room earlyish in the evening and had presumably stayed there until after being visited by Félicité; she herself reported this incident to Lady Pastern. It was odd, he thought, that he should have forgotten Miss Henderson.

But there were still a good many threads to be caught up and introduced into the texture. He referred again to Lord Pastern's notes. At 9:26, the notes declared specifically, Lord Pastern, then in the ballroom, had suddenly recollected the sombrero which he desired to wear in his own number. He had glanced at his watch, perhaps, and taken alarm. The note merely said, "9:26. Self. Ballroom. Sombrero. Search for. All over house. William. Spence. Etc."

Questioned on this matter the servants willingly recalled the characteristic hullabaloo that had been raised in this search. It set in immediately after the last event related by William. Félicité and Rivera were in the study, Miss Henderson was on her way upstairs and William himself was hovering on the landing, when Lord Pastern shot out of the ballroom, shouting: "Where's my sombrero?" In no time the hunt was in full cry. Spence, William and Lord Pastern scattered in various directions. The sombrero was finally discovered by Miss Henderson (she was no doubt the "etc." of the notes) in a cupboard on the top landing. Lord Pastern appeared with the thing on his head and re-entered the ballroom in triumph. During this uproar, Spence, questing in the hall, had found a letter on the table addressed to Miss de Suze.

Here the narrative was interrupted by a dignified passage-of-arms between Spence, William and the parlour-maid, Mary. Mr. Spence, William said resentfully, had torn a strip off him for not taking the letter in to Miss Félicité as soon as it came. William had denied knowledge of the letter and had not opened the door to any district messenger. Nor had Mary. Nor had anyone else. Spence obviously considered that someone was lying. Alleyn asked if any of them had seen the envelope. Hortense, needlessly dramatic, cried out that she had tidied an envelope up from the floor of Mademoiselle's bedroom. Fox held a smothered colloquy about rubbish bins with William, who made an excited exit and returned, flushed with modest triumph, to lay a crushed and stained envelope on the table before Alleyn. Alleyn recognized the eccentricities of Lord Pastern's typewriter and pocketed the envelope.

"It's my belief, Mr. Spence," William announced boldly, "that there never was a district messenger."

Leaving them no time to digest this theory, Alleyn continued with the business of checking Lord Pastern's time-table. Spence, still very anxious, said that having discovered the letter on the hall table he had come upstairs and taken it into the drawing-room, where he found only his mistress, Miss Wayne, and Mr. Manx, who, he thought, had not long arrived there from the dining-room. On returning to the landing Spence encountered Miss de Suze, coming out of the study, and gave her the letter. Sounds of the sombrero hunt reached him from upstairs. He was about to join it when a cry of triumph from Lord Pastern reassured him, and he returned to the servants' quarters. He had noticed the time: 9:45.

"And at that time," Alleyn said, "Lady Pastern and Miss Wayne are about to leave Mr. Manx alone in the drawing-room and go upstairs. Miss de Suze and Miss Henderson are already in their rooms and Lord Pastern is about to descend, wearing his sombrero. Mr. Bellairs and Mr. Rivera are in the ballroom. We have forty-five minutes to go before the party leaves for the Metronome. What happens next?"

But he had struck a blank. Apart from Hortense's previous account of her visits to the ladies upstairs there was little to be learned from the servants. They had kept to their own quarters until, a few minutes before the departure for the Metronome, Spence and William had gone into the hall, assisted the gentlemen into their overcoats, given them their hats and gloves and seen them into their cars.

"Who," Alleyn asked, "helped Mr. Rivera into his coat?"

William had done this.

"Did you notice anything about him? Anything at all out of the ordinary, however slight?"

William said sharply: "The gentleman had a—well, a funny ear, sir. Red and bleeding a bit. A cauliflower ear, as you might say."

"Had you noticed this earlier in the evening? When you leant over his chair, serving him, at dinner, for instance?"

"No, sir. It was all right then, sir."

"Sure?"

"Swear to it," said William crisply.

"You think carefully, Will, before you make statements," Spence said uneasily.

"I know I'm right, Mr. Spence."

"How do you imagine he came by this injury?" Alleyn asked. William grinned, pure Cockney. "Well, sir, if you'll excuse the expression, I'd say somebody had handed the gentleman a four-penny one."

"Who, at a guess?"

William rejoined promptly: "Seeing he was holding his right hand, tender-like, in his left and seeing the way the murdered gentleman looked at him so fierce, I'd say it was Mr. Edward Manx, sir."

Hortense broke into a spate of excited and gratified comment. Monsieur Dupont made a wide, conclusive gesture and exclaimed: "Perfectly! It explains itself!" Mary and Myrtle ejaculated incoherently while Spence and Miss Parker, on a single impulse, rose and shouted awfully: "That WILL DO, William."

Alleyn and Fox left them, still greatly excited, and retraced their steps to the downstairs hall.

"What have we got out of that little party," Alleyn grunted, "beyond confirmation of old Pastern's time-table up to half an hour before they all left the house?"

"Damn all, sir. And what does that teach us?" Fox grumbled. "Only that every man Jack of them was alone at some time or other and might have got hold of the parasol handle, taken it to the study, fixed this silly little stiletto affair in the end with plastic wood and then done Gawd-knows-what. Every man Jack of 'em."

"And every woman Jill?"

"I suppose so. Wait a bit, though."

Alleyn gave him the time-table and his own notes. They had moved into the entrance lobby, closing the inner glass doors behind them. "Mull it over in the car," Alleyn said, "I think there's a bit more to be got out of it, Fox. Come on."

But as Alleyn was about to open the front door Fox gave a sort of grunt and he turned back to see Félicité de Suze on the stairs. She was dressed for the day and in the dim light of the hall looked pale and exhausted. For a moment they stared at each other through the glass panel and then tentatively, uncertainly, she made an incomplete gesture with one hand. Alleyn swore under his breath and re-entered the hall.

"Do you want to speak to me?" he said. "You're up very early."

"I couldn't sleep."

"I'm sorry," he said formally.

"I think I do want to speak to you."

Alleyn nodded to Fox, who re-entered the hall.

"Alone," said Félicité.

"Inspector Fox is acting with me in this case."

She glanced discontentedly at Fox. "All the same . . ." she said, and then as Alleyn made no answer: "Oh, well!"

She was on the third step from the foot of the stairs, standing there boldly, aware of the picture she made. "Lisle told me," she said, "about you and the letter. Getting it from her, I mean. I suppose you take rather a dim view of my sending Lisle to do my dirty work, don't you?"

"It doesn't matter."

"I was all *bouleversée*. I know it was rather awful letting her go, but I think in a way she quite enjoyed it." He noticed that her upper lip was fuller than the under one and that when she smiled it curved richly. "Darling Lisle," she said, "doesn't have much fun and she's so madly interested always in other people's little flutters." She watched Alleyn out of the corners of her eyes and added: "We're all devoted to her."

"What do you want to ask me, Miss de Suze?"

"Please may I have the letter back? Please!"

"In due course," he said. "Certainly."

"Not now?"

"I'm afraid not now."

"That's rather a bore," said Félicité. "I suppose I'd better come clean in a big way."

"If it's relevant to the matter in hand," Alleyn agreed. "I am only concerned with the death of Mr. Carlos Rivera."

She leant back against the bannister, stretching her arms along it and looking downwards, arranging herself for him to look at. "I'd suggest we went somewhere where we could sit down," she said, "but here seems to be the only place where there's no lurking minor detective."

"Let it be here, then."

"You are not," Félicité said, "making this very easy."

"I'm sorry. I shall be glad to hear what you have to say but to tell the truth, there's a heavy day's work in front of us."

They stood there, disliking each other. Alleyn thought: "She's going to be one of the tricky ones. She may have nothing to say; I know the signs but I can't be sure of them." And Félicité thought: "I didn't really notice him last night. If he'd known what Carlos was like he'd have despised me. He's taller than Ned. I'd like him to be on my side thinking how courageous and young and attractive I am. Younger than Lisle, for instance, with two men in love with me. I wonder what sort of women he likes. I suppose I'm frightened."

She slid down into a sitting position on the stairs and clasped her hands about her knees; young and a bit boyish, a touch of the *gamine.*

"It's about this wretched letter. Well, not wretched at all, really, because it's from a chap I'm very fond of. You've read it, of course."

"I'm afraid so."

"My dear, I don't *mind.* Only, as you've seen, it's by way of being number one secrecy and I'll feel a bit low if it all comes popping out, particularly as it's got utterly *no* connection with your little game. It just couldn't be less relevant."

"Good."

"But I suppose I've got to prove that, haven't I?"

"It would be an excellent move if you can."

"Here we go, then," said Félicité.

Alleyn listened wearily, pinning his attention down to the recital, shutting out the thought of time sliding away, and of his wife, who would soon wake and look to see if he was there. Félicité told him that she had corresponded with G.P.F. of *Harmony* and that his advice had been too marvellously understanding and that she had felt an urge like the kick of a mule to meet him, but that although his replies had grown more and more come-to-ish he had insisted that his identity must remain hidden. "All Cupid-and-Psyche-ish only definitely less rewarding," she said. And then the letter had arrived and Edward Manx had appeared with a white flower in his coat and suddenly, after never having gone much for old Ned, she had felt astronomically uplifted. Because, after all, it was rather bracing, wasn't it, to think that all the time Ned was G.P.F. and writing these really gorgeous things and falling for one like a drayload of bricks? Here Félicité paused and then added rather hurriedly and with an air of hauteur: "You'll understand that by this time poor Carlos had, from my point of view, become comparatively a dim figure. I mean, to be as bald as an egg about it, he just faded out. I mean it couldn't have mattered less about Carlos because clearly I wasn't his cup of tea and we'd both gone tepid on it and I knew he wouldn't mind. You do see what I mean about that, don't you?"

"Are you trying to tell me that you and Rivera had parted as friends?"

Félicité shook her head vaguely and raised her eyebrows. "Even that makes it sound too important," she said. "It all just came peacefully unstuck."

"And there was no quarrel, for instance when you and he were in the study between a quarter and half-past nine? Or later, between Mr. Manx and Mr. Rivera?"

There was a long pause. Félicité bent forward and jerked at the strap of her shoe. "What in the world," she said indistinctly, "put these quaint little notions into your head?"

"Are they completely false?"

"*I* know," she said loudly and cheerfully. She looked up into his face. "You've been gossiping with the servants." She appealed to Fox. "Hasn't he?" she demanded playfully.

"I'm sure I couldn't say, Miss de Suze," said Fox blandly.

"How you could!" she accused Alleyn. "Which of them was it? Was it Hortense? My poor Mr. Alleyn, you don't know Hortense. She's the world's most accomplished liar! She just can't help herself, poor thing. It's pathological."

"So there was no quarrel?" Alleyn said. "Between any of you?"

"My dear, haven't I told you!"

"Then why," he asked, "did Mr. Manx punch Mr. Rivera over the ear?"

Félicité's eyes and mouth opened. Then she hunched her shoulders and caught the tip of her tongue between her teeth. He could have sworn she was astonished and in a moment it was evident that she was gratified.

"No!" she said. "Honestly? Ned did? Well, I must say I call that a handsome tribute. When did it happen? Before we went down to the Met? After dinner? When?"

Alleyn looked steadily at her. "I thought," he said, "that perhaps you could tell me that."

"I? But I promise you . . ."

"Had he got a trickle of blood on his ear when you talked to him in the study? On the occasion, you know, when you say there was no quarrel?"

"Let me think," said Félicité, and rested her head on her crossed arms. But the movement was not swift enough. He had seen the blank look of panic in her eyes. "No," her voice, muffled by her arms, said slowly, "no, I'm sure . . ."

There was some change of light above, where the stairs ran up to the first landing. He looked up. Carlisle Wayne stood there in the shadow. Her figure and posture still retained the effect of movement, as if while she came downstairs she had suddenly been held in suspension as the action of a motion picture may be suspended to give emphasis to a specific movement. Over Félicité's bent head, Alleyn with a slight movement of his hand arrested Carlisle's descent. Félicité had begun to speak again.

"After all," she was saying, "one is a bit uplifted. It's not every day in the week that people give other people cauliflower ears for love of one's bright eyes." She raised her face and looked at him. "How naughty of Ned, but how sweet of him. Darling Ned!"

"No, really!" said Carlisle strongly. "This is too much!"

Félicité, with a stifled cry, was on her feet.

Alleyn said: "Hullo, Miss Wayne. Good morning to you. Have you any theory about why Mr. Manx gave Rivera a clip over the ear? He did give him a clip, you know. Why?"

"If you must know," Carlisle said in a high voice, "it was because Rivera kissed me when we met on the landing."

"Good Lord!" Alleyn ejaculated. "Why didn't you say so before? Kissed *you*, did he? Did you like it?"

"Don't be a *bloody* fool!" Carlisle shouted and bolted upstairs.

"I must say," Félicité said, "I call that rather poor of darling Lisle."

"If you'll excuse us," Alleyn said. He and Fox left her staring thoughtfully at her finger-nails.

III

"A shave," Alleyn said in the car, "a bath and, with luck, two hours' sleep. I'll take it out at home. We'll send the stuff on to the experts. What about you, Fox? Troy will be delighted to fix you up."

"Thank you very much, sir, but I wouldn't think of troubling Mrs. Alleyn. There's a little place—"

"Be damned to your little place. I've had enough insubordination from you, my lad. To hell with you. You're coming to us."

Fox accepted this singular invitation in the spirit in which it was made. He took out his spectacles, Alleyn's notebook and Lord Pastern's timetable. Alleyn dragged his palm across his jaw, shuddered, yawned and closed his eyes. "A hideous curse on this case," he murmured and appeared to sleep. Fox began to whisper to himself. The car slipped down Cliveden Place, into Grosvenor Place, into Hyde Park Corner. "'T, 't, 't," Fox whispered over the time-table.

"You sound," Alleyn said without opening his eyes, "like Dr. Johnson on his way to Streatham. Can you crack your joints, Foxkin?"

"I see what you mean about this ruddy time-table."

"What *did* I mean? Split me and sink me if I know what I meant."

"Well, sir, our customer, whoever he or she may be—and you know my views on the point—had to be in the ballroom to pick up the bit of umbrella shaft, in the drawing-room to collect the stiletto and alone in the study to fix the stiletto in the bit of umbrella shaft with plastic wood."

"You'll be coming round the mountain when you come."

"It *is* a bit of a mountain and that's a fact. According to what the young lady, Miss Wayne, I mean, told you, sir, this perishing parasol was all right before dinner when she was in the ballroom and handled it, and according to her, his lordship was in the study drawing the bullets out of the cartridges. If that's correct he didn't get a chance to play the fool with the parasol before dinner. What's more it fits in with his lordship's own statement, which Bellairs can speak to if he ever wakes up, that he took the parasol to bits on the piano *after* dinner. For fun."

"Quite."

"All right. Now where does this get us? If the time-table's correct, his lordship was never alone in the study after that."

"And the only time he was alone at all, moreover, he was up and down the house, bellowing like a bull for his sombrero."

"Doesn't that look like establishing an alibi?" Fox demanded.

"It looks a bit like the original alibi itself, Br'er Fox."

"He might have carried the tube of plastic wood round in his pocket."

"So he might. Together with the bit of parasol and the stiletto, pausing in mid-bellow to fix the job."

"Gah! How about him just taking the stuff to his pocket to the Metronome and fixing everything there?"

"Oh Lord! When? How?"

"Lavatory?" Fox suggested hopefully.

"And when did he put the weapon in the gun? Skelton looked down the barrel just before they started playing, don't forget."

The car had stopped in a traffic jam in Piccadilly. Fox contemplated the Green Park with disapproval, Alleyn still kept his eyes shut. Big Ben struck seven.

"By Gum!" Fox said, bringing his palm down on his knee. "By Gum, how about this? How about his lordship in his damn-your-eyes fashion fitting the weapon into the gun while he sat there behind his drums? In front of everybody, while one of the other turns was on? It's amazing what you can do when you brazen it out. What's that yarn they're always quoting, sir? I've got it. *The Purloined Letter.* Proving that if you make a thing obvious enough nobody notices it?"

Alleyn opened one eye. "*The Purloined Letter,*" he said. He opened the other eye. "Fox, my cabbage, my rare edition, my *objet d'art,* my own especial bit of *bijouterie,* be damned if I don't think you've caught an idea. Come on. Let's further think of this."

They talked intensively until the car pulled up, in a *cul-de-sac* off Coventry Street, before Alleyn's flat.

Early sunlight streamed into the little entrance hall. Beneath a Benozzo Gozzoli, a company of dahlias, paper-white in a blue bowl, cast translucent shadows on a white parchment wall. Alleyn looked about him contentedly.

"Troy's under orders not to get up till eight," he said. "You take first whack at the bath, Fox, while I have a word with her. Use my razor. Wait a bit." He disappeared and returned with towels. "There'll be something to eat at half-past nine," he said. "The visitors' room's all yours, Fox. Sleep well."

"Very kind, I'm sure," said Fox. "May I send my compliments to Mrs. Alleyn, sir?"

"She'll be delighted to receive them. See you later."

Troy was awake in her white room, sitting up with her head aureoled in short locks of hair. "Like a faun," Alleyn said, "or a bronze dahlia. Are you well this morning?"

"Bouncing, thanks. And you?"

"As you see. Unhousel'd, unanel'd and un-everything that's civilized."

"A poor state of affairs," said Troy. "You look like the gentleman in that twenty-foot canvas in the Luxembourg. Boiled shirt in dents and gazing out over Paris through lush curtains. I think it's called 'The Hopeless Dawn'! His floozy is still asleep on an elephantine bed, you remember."

"I don't remember. Talking of floozies, oughtn't you to be asleep yourself?"

"God bless my soul!" Troy complained. "I haven't been bitten by the tsetse fly. It's getting on for nine hours since I went to bed, damn it."

"O.K. O.K."

"What's happened, Rory?"

"One of the kind we don't fancy."

"Oh, no."

"You'll hear about it anyway, so I may as well tell you. It's that florid number we saw playing the piano-accordion, the one with the teeth and hair."

"You don't mean—"

"Somebody pinked him with a sort of dagger made out of a bit of a parasol and a needlework stiletto."

"Catch!"

He explained at some length.

"Well but . . ." Troy stared at her husband. "When have you got to be at the Yard?"

"Ten."

"All right. You've got two hours and time for breakfast. Good morning, darling."

"Fox is in the bathroom. I know I'm not fit for a lady's bed chamber."

"Who said?"

"If you didn't, nobody." He put his arm across her and stooped his head. "Troy," he said, "may I ask Fox this morning?"

"If you want to, my dearest."

"I think I might. How much, at a rough guess, would you say I loved you?"

"*Words* fail me," said Troy, imitating the late Harry Tate.

"And me."

"There's Mr. Fox coming out of the bathroom. Away with you."

"I suppose so. Good morning, Mrs. Quiverful."

On his way to the bathroom Alleyn looked in upon Fox. He found him lying on the visitors' room bed, without his jacket but incredibly neat; his hair damp, his jaw gleaming, his shirt stretched tight over his thick pectoral muscles. His eyes were closed but he opened them as Alleyn looked in.

"I'll call you at half-past nine," Alleyn said. "Did you know you were going to be a godfather Br'er Fox?" And as Fox's eyes widened he shut the door and went whistling to the bathroom.

CHAPTER IX

The Yard

I

AT TEN-THIRTY in the Chief-Inspector's room at New Scotland Yard, routine procedure following a case of homicide was efficiently established.

Alleyn sat at his desk taking reports from Detective-Sergeants Gibson, Watson, Scott and Sallis. Mr. Fox, with that air of good-humour crossed with severity which was his habitual reaction to reports following observation, listened critically to his juniors, each of whom held his official notebook. Six men going soberly about their day's work. Earlier that morning, in other parts of London, Captain Entwhistle, an expert on ballistics, had fitted a dart made from a piece of a parasol into a revolver and had fired it into a bag of sand; Mr. Carrick, a government analyst, had submitted a small cork to various tests for certain oils; and Sir Grantly Morton, the famous pathologist, assisted by Curtis, had opened Carlos Rivera's thorax, and, with the greatest delicacy, removed his heart.

"All right," Alleyn said. "Get yourselves chairs and smoke if you want to. This is liable to be a session."

When they were settled, he pointed the stem of his pipe at a heavy-jawed, straw-coloured detective-sergeant with a habitually startled expression. "You searched the deceased's rooms, didn't you Gibson? Let's take you first."

Gibson thumbed his notebook open, contemplating it in apparent astonishment, and embarked on a high-pitched recital.

"The deceased man, Carlos Rivera," he said, *"lived at 102 Bedford Mansions, Austerly Square S.W.1. Service flats. Rental £500 a year."*

"Why don't we all play piano-accordions?" Fox asked of nobody in particular.

"At 3 A.M. on the morning of June 1st," Gibson continued in a shrillish voice, *"having obtained a search-warrant, I effected entrance to above*

premises by means of a key on a ring removed from the body of the deceased. The flat consists of an entrance lobby, six-by-eight feet, a sitting-room, twelve-by-fourteen feet, and a bedroom nine-by-eleven feet. Furnishings. Sitting-room: Carpet, purple, thick. Curtains, full length, purple satin."

"Stay me with flagons!" Alleyn muttered. "Purple."

"You might call it morve, Mr. Alleyn."

"Well, go on."

"Couch, upholstered green velvet, three armchairs ditto, dining table, six dining chairs, open fireplace. Walls painted fawn. Cushions: Seven. Green and purple satin." He glanced at Alleyn. "I beg pardon, Mr. Alleyn? Anything wrong?"

"Nothing. Nothing. Go on."

"Bookcase. Fourteen books. Foreign. Recognized four as on police lists. Pictures: four."

"What were *they* like?" Fox asked.

"Never you mind, you dirty old man," said Alleyn.

"Two were nude studies, Mr. Fox, what you might call heavy pin-ups. The others were a bit more so. *Cigarette boxes: four. Cigarettes, commercial product. Have taken one from each box. Wall safe. Combination lock but found note of number in deceased's pocket-book. Contents–"*

"Half a minute," Alleyn said. "Have all the flats got these safes?"

"I ascertained from inquiries, sir, that deceased had his installed."

"Right. Go on."

"Contents. I removed a number of papers, two ledgers or account-books and a locked cash-box containing three hundred pounds in notes of low denomination, and thirteen shillings in silver." Here Gibson paused of his own accord.

"There now!" said Fox. "Now we *may* be on to something."

"I left a note of the contents of the safe in the safe and I locked the safe," said Gibson, on a note of uncertainty, induced perhaps by misgivings about his prose style. "Shall I produce the contents now, sir, or go on to the bedroom?"

"I doubt if I can take the bedroom," Alleyn said. "But go on."

"It was done up in black, sir. Black satin."

"Do you put all this in your notes?" Fox demanded suddenly. "All this about colours and satin?"

"They tell us to be thorough, Mr. Fox."

"There's a medium to all things," Fox pronounced somberly. "I beg pardon, Mr. Alleyn."

"Not at all, Br'er Fox. The bedroom, Gibson."

But there wasn't anything much to the purpose in Gibson's meticulous account of Rivera's bedroom unless the revelation that he wore black satin pyjamas with embroidered initials could be called, as Alleyn suggested, damning and conclusive evidence as to character. Gibson produced the spoil of the wall safe and they examined it. Alleyn took the ledgers and Fox the bundle of correspondence. For some time there was silence, broken only by the whisper of papers.

Presently, however, Fox brought his palm down on his knee and Alleyn, without looking up, said: "Hullo?"

"Peculiar," Fox grunted. "Listen to this, sir."

"Go ahead."

> How tender [Mr. Fox began] is the first burgeoning of love! How delicate the tiny bud, how easily cut with frost! Touch it with gentle fingers, dear lad, lest its fragrance be lost to you forever.

"Cor'!" whispered Detective-Sergeant Scott.

> You say [Mr. Fox continued] that she is changeable. So is a day in spring. Be patient. Wait for the wee petals to unfold. If you would care for a very special, etc.

Fox removed his spectacles and contemplated his superior.

"What do you mean by your 'etc.,' Fox? Why don't you go on?"

"That's what it says. Etc. Then it stops. Look."

He flattened a piece of creased blue letter paper out on the desk before Alleyn. It was covered with typing, closely spaced. The Duke's Gate address was stamped on the top.

Alleyn said, "What's that you're holding back?"

Fox laid his second exhibit before him. It was a press-cutting and printed on paper of the kind used in the more exotic magazines. Alleyn read aloud:

> Dear G.P.F.: I am engaged to a young lady who at times is very affectionate and then again goes cold on me. It's not halitosis because I asked her and she said it wasn't and wished I wouldn't harp on about it. I am twenty-two, five-foot-eleven in my socks and well built. I drag down £550 per annum. I am an A grade motor-mechanic and I have prospects of a rise. She reckons she loves me and yet she acts like this. What should be my attitude? Spark-plug.

"I should advise a damn' good hiding," Alleyn said. "Poor old Spark-plug."

"Go on, sir. Read the answer."

Alleyn continued:

> Dear Spark-plug: Yours is not as unusual a problem as perhaps you, in your distress of mind, incline to believe. How tender is the first burgeoning—!

"Yes, here we go again. Yes. All right, Fox. You've found, apparently, a bit of the rough draft and the finished article. The draft, typed on Duke's Gate letter-paper, looks as if it had been crumpled up in somebody's pocket, doesn't it? Half a minute."

He opened his own file and in a moment the letter Félicité had dropped from her bag at the Metronome had been placed beside the other. Alleyn bent over them. "It's a pot-shot, of course," he said, "but I'm ready to bet it's the same machine. The *s* out of alignment. All the usual indications."

"Where does this lead us?" Fox asked. Gibson, looking gratified, cleared his throat. Alleyn said: "It leads us into a bit of a tangle. The letter to Miss de Suze was typed on the machine in Lord Pastern's study on the paper he uses for that purpose. The machine carried his dabs only. I took a chance and asked him, point-blank, how long he'd known that Edward Manx was G.P.F. He wouldn't answer but I'll swear I rocked him. I'll undertake he typed the letter after he saw Manx put a white carnation in his coat, marked the envelope, 'By District Messenger' and put it on the hall table where it was discovered by the butler. All right. Now, not so long ago, Manx stayed at Duke's Gate for three weeks and I suppose it's reasonable to assume that he may have used the typewriter and the blue letter-paper in the study when he was jotting down notes for his nauseating little G.P.F. numbers in *Harmony*. So this draft may have been typed by Manx. But, as far as we know, Manx met Rivera for the first time last night and incidentally dotted him what William pleasingly called a fourpenny one, because Rivera kissed, *not* Miss de Suze but Miss Wayne. Now, if we're right so far, how and when the hell did Rivera get hold of Manx's rough draft of this sickening G.P.F. stuff? Not last night because we've got it from Rivera's safe, and he didn't go back to his rooms. Answer me that, Fox."

"Gawd knows."

"We don't, at all events. And if we find out, is it going to tie up with Rivera's murder? Well, press on, chaps, press on."

He returned to the ledger and Fox to the bundle of papers. Presently Alleyn said: "Isn't it extraordinary how business-like they are?"

"Who's that, Mr. Alleyn?"

"Why, blackmailers to be sure. Mr. Rivera was a man of parts, Fox. Piano-accordions, drug-running, blackmail. Almost a pity we've got to nab his murderer. He was ripe for bumping off, was Mr. Rivera. This is a neatly kept record of moneys and goods received and disbursed. On the third of February, for instance, we have an entry. 'Cash. £150, 3rd installment. S.F.F.' A week later, a cryptic note on the debit side: '6 doz. per S.S., £360,' followed by a series of credits: 'J.C.M. £10,' 'B.B. £100,' and so on. These entries are in a group by themselves. He's totted them up and balanced the whole thing, showing a profit of £200 on the original outlay of £360."

"That'll be his dope racket, by Gum. 'S.S.' did you say, Mr. Alleyn? By Gum, I wonder if he *is* in with the Snowy Santos bunch."

"And B.B. on the paying side. B.B. is quite a profitable number on the paying side."

"Breezy Bellairs?"

"I shouldn't wonder. It looks to me, Fox, as if Rivera was a medium high-up in the drug racket. He was one of the boys we don't catch easily. It's long odds he never passed the stuff out direct to the small consumer. With the exception, no doubt, of the wretched Bellairs. No, I fancy Rivera's business was confined to his purple satin parlour. At the smallest sign of our getting anywhere near him, he'd have burnt his books and, if necessary, returned to his native *hacienda* or what-have-you."

"Or got in first by laying information against the small man. That's the line they take as often as not."

"Yes, indeed. As often as not. What else have you got in your lucky dip, Br'er Fox?"

"Letters," said Fox. "A sealed package. And the cash."

"Anything that chimes in with his bookkeeping. I wonder?"

"Wait a bit, sir. I wouldn't be surprised. Wait a bit."

They hadn't long to wait. The too familiar raw material of the blackmailer's trade was soon laid out on Alleyn's desk: the dingy, colourless letters, paid for again and again yet never redeemed, the discoloured clippings from dead newspapers, one or two desperate appeals for mercy, the inexorable entries on the credit side. Alleyn's fingers seemed to tarnish as he handled them but Fox rubbed his hands.

"This is something like," Fox said, and after a minute or two: "Look at this, Mr. Alleyn."

It was a letter signed "Félicité" and was some four months old. Alleyn read it through and handed it back to Fox, who said: "It establishes the relationship."

"Apparently."

"Funny," said Fox. "You'd have thought from the look of him, even when he was dead, that any girl in her senses would have picked him for what he was. There are two other letters. Much the same kind of thing."

"Yes."

"Yes. Well now," said Fox slowly. "Leaving the young lady aside for the moment, where, if anywhere, does this get us with his lordship?"

"Not very far, I fancy. Unless you find something revealing a hitherto unsuspected irregularity in his lordship's past, and he doesn't strike me as one to hide his riotings."

"All the same, sir, there may be something. What about his lordship encouraging this affair with his stepdaughter? Doesn't that look as if Rivera had a hold on him?"

"It might," Alleyn agreed, "if his lordship was anybody but his lordship. But it might. So last night, having decided to liquidate Rivera, he types this letter purporting to come from G.P.F. with the idea of throwing the all-too-impressionable Miss de Suze in Edward Manx's arms!"

"There you are!"

"How does Lord Pastern known Manx is G.P.F.? And if Rivera used this G.P.F. copy to blackmail Manx it wasn't a very hot instrument for his purpose, being typed. Anybody at Duke's Gate might have typed it. He would have to find it on Manx and try a bluff. And he hadn't met Manx. All right. For purposes of your argument we needn't pursue that one at the moment. All right. It fits. In a way. Only . . . only . . ." He rubbed his nose. "I'm sorry, Fox, but I can't reconcile the flavor of Pastern and Manx with all this. A most untenable argument, I know. I won't try to justify it. What's in that box?"

Fox had already opened it and shoved it across the desk. "It'll be the stuff itself," he said. "A nice little haul, Gibson."

The box contained neat small packages, securely sealed, and, in a separate carton, a number of cigarettes.

"That'll be it," Alleyn agreed. "He wasn't the direct receiver, evidently. This will have come in by the usual damned labyrinth." He glanced up at Detective-Sergeant Scott, a young officer. "You haven't worked on any of these cases, I think, Scott. This is probably cocaine or heroin, and has no doubt travelled long distances in bogus false teeth, fat men's navels, dummy hearing aids, phony bayonet fitments for electric light bulbs and God knows what else. As Mr. Fox says, Gibson, it's a nice little haul. We'll leave Rivera for the moment, I think." He turned to Scott and Watson. "Let's hear how you got on with Breezy Bellairs."

Breezy, it appeared, lived in a furnished flat in Pikestaff Row, off Ebury Street. To this address Scott and Watson had conveyed him, and with some difficulty put him to bed. Once there, he had slept stertorously through the rest of the night. They had combed out the flat, which, unlike Rivera's, was slovenly and disordered. It looked, they said, as if Breezy had had a frantic search for something. The pockets of his suits had been pulled out, the drawers of his furniture disembowelled and the contents left where they lay. The only thing in the flat that was at all orderly was Breezy's pile of band parts. Scott and Watson had sorted out a bundle of correspondence consisting of bills, dunning reminders, and his fan mail, which turned out to be largish. At the back of a small bedside cupboard they had found a hypodermic syringe which they produced and a number of torn and empty packages which were of the same sort as those found in Rivera's safe. "Almost too easy," said Mr. Fox with the liveliest satisfaction. "We knew it already, of course, through Skelton, but here's positive proof Rivera supplied Bellairs with his dope. By Gum," he added deeply, "I'd like to get this line on the dope-racket followed in to one of the high-ups. Now, I wonder. Breezy'll be looking for his stuff and won't know where to find it. He'll be very upset. I ask myself if Breezy won't be in the mood to talk."

"You'd better remind yourself of your police code, old boy."

"It'll be the same story," Fox muttered. "Breezy won't know how Rivera got it. He won't know."

"He hasn't been long on the injection method," Alleyn said. "Curtis had a look for needle marks and didn't find so very many."

"He'll be fretting for it, though," said Fox, and after a moment's pondering: "Oh, well. It's a homicide we're after."

Nothing more of interest had been found in Breezy's flat and Alleyn turned to the last of the men. "How did you get on with Skelton, Sallis?"

"Well, sir," said Sallis, in a loud public-school voice, "he didn't like me much to begin with. I picked up a search-warrant on the way and he took a very poor view of that. However, we talked sociology for the rest of the journey and I offered to lend him *The Yogi and the Commissar,* which bent the barriers a little. He's Australian by birth, and I've been out there so that helped to establish a more matey attitude."

"Get on with your report now," Fox said austerely. "Don't meander. Mr. Alleyn isn't concerned to know how much Syd Skelton loves you."

"I'm sorry, sir."

"Use your notes and get on with it," Fox counselled.

Sallis opened his notebook and got on with it. Beyond a quantity of communistic literature there was little out of the ordinary to be found in Skelton's rooms, which were in the Pimlico Road. Alleyn gathered that Sallis had conducted his search during a lively exchange of ideas and could imagine Skelton's guarded response to Sallis's pinkish, facile and consciously ironical observations. Finally, Skelton, in spite of himself, had gone to sleep in his chair and Sallis then turned his attention stealthily to a table which was used as a desk.

"I'd noticed that he seemed rather uneasy about this table, sir. He stood by it when we first came in and shuffled the papers about. I had the feeling there was something there that he wanted to destroy. When he was safely off, I went through the stuff on the table and I found this. I don't know if it's much cop, really, sir, but here it is."

He gave a sheet of paper to Alleyn, who opened it up. It was an unfinished letter to Rivera, threatening him with exposure if he continued to supply Breezy Bellairs with drugs.

II

The other men had gone and Alleyn invited Fox to embark upon what he was in the habit of calling "a hag." This involved the ruthless taking-to-pieces of the case and a fresh attempt to put the bits together in their true pattern. They had been engaged upon this business for about half an hour when the telephone rang. Fox answered it and announced with a tolerant smile that Mr. Nigel Bathgate would like to speak to Mr. Alleyn.

"I was expecting this," Alleyn said. "Tell him that for once in a blue moon I want to see him. Where is he?"

"Down below."

"Hail him up."

Fox said sedately: "The Chief would like to see you, Mr. Bathgate," and in a few moments Nigel Bathgate of the *Evening Chronicle* appeared, looking mildly astonished.

"I must say," he said, shaking hands, "that this is uncommonly civil of you, Alleyn. Have you run out of invectives or do you at last realize where the brains lie?"

"If you think I asked you up with the idea of feeding you with banner headlines you're woefully mistaken. Sit down."

"Willingly. How are you, Mr. Fox?"

"Nicely, thank you, sir. And you?"

Alleyn said: "Now, you attend to me. Can you tell me anything about a monthly called *Harmony?*"

"What sort of things? Have you been confiding in G.P.F., Alleyn?"

"I want to know who he is."

"Has this got anything to do with the Rivera case?"

"Yes, it has."

"I'll make a bargain with you. I want a nice meaty bit of stuff straight from the Yard's mouth. All about old Pastern and how you happened to be there and the shattered romance . . ."

"Who've you been talking to?"

"Charwomen, night porters, chaps in the band. And I ran into Ned Manx, a quarter of an hour ago."

"What had he got to say for himself?"

"He hung out on me, blast him. Wouldn't utter. And he's not on a daily, either. Unco-operative twerp."

"You might remember he's the chief suspect's cousin."

"Then there's no doubt about it being old Pastern?"

"I didn't say so and you won't suggest it."

"Well, hell, give me a story."

"About this paper. *Do* you know G.P.F.? Come on?"

Nigel lit a cigarette and settled down. "I don't know him," he said. "And I don't know anyone who does. He's a chap called G. P. Friend, I'm told, and he's supposed to own the show. If he does, he's on to a damn useful thing. It's a mystery, that paper. It breaks all the rules and rings the bell. It first came out about two years ago with a great fanfare of trumpets. They bought out the old *Triple Mirror,* you know, and took over the plant and the paper and in less than no time trebled the sales. God knows why. The thing's a freak. It mixes sound criticism with girly-girly chat and runs top-price serials alongside shorts that would bring a blush to the cheeks of *Peg's Weekly*. They tell me it's G.P.F.'s page that does the trick. And look at it! That particular racket blew out before the war and yet he gets by with it. I'm told the personal letters at five bob a time are a gold mine in themselves. He's said to have an uncanny knack of hitting on the things all these women want him to say. The types that write in are amazing. All the smarties. Nobody ever sees him. He doesn't get about with the boys and the chaps who free-lance for the rag never get past a sub who's always very bland and entirely uncommunicative. There you are. That's all I can tell you about G.P.F."

"Ever heard what he looks like?"

"No. There's a legend he wears old clothes and dark glasses. They say he's got a lock on his office door and never sees anybody on account he doesn't want to be recognized. It's all part of an act. Publicity. They play it up in the paper itself—'Nobody knows who G.P.F. is.' "

"What would you think if I told you he was Edward Manx?"

"Manx! You're not serious."

"Is it so incredible?"

Nigel raised his eyebrows. "On the face of it, yes. Manx is a reputable and very able specialist. He's done some pretty solid stuff. Leftish and fairly authoritative. He's a coming man. He'd turn sick in his stomach at the sight of G.P.F., I'd have thought."

"He does their dramatic reviews."

"Yes, I know, but that's where they're freakish. Manx has got a sort of damn-your-eyes view about theatre. It's one of his things. He wants state ownership and he'll scoop up any chance to plug it. And I imagine their anti-vice parties wouldn't be unpleasing to Manx. He wouldn't go much for the style, which is tough and coloured, but he'd like the policy. They give battle in a big way, you know. Names all over the place and a general invitation to come on and sue us for libel and see how you like it. Quite his cup of tea. Yes, I imagine *Harmony* runs Manx to give the paper *cachet* and Manx writes for *Harmony* to get at their public. They pay. Top prices." Nigel paused and then said sharply: "But Manx as G.P.F.! That's different. Have you actually good reason to suspect it? Are you on to something?"

"The case is fluffy with doubts at the moment."

"The Rivera case? It ties up with that?"

"Off the record, it does."

"By God," said Nigel profoundly, "if Ned Manx spews up that page it explains the secrecy! By God, it does."

"We'll have to ask him," Alleyn said. "But I'd have liked to have a little more to go on. Still, we can muscle in. Where's the *Harmony* office?"

"Five Materfamilias Lane. The old *Triple Mirror* place."

"When does this blasted rag make its appearance? It's a monthly, isn't it?"

"Let's see. It's the twenty-seventh today. It comes out in the first week of the month. They'll be going to press any time now."

"So G.P.F.'s likely to be on tap at the office?"

"You'd think so. Are you going to burst in on Manx with a brace of manacles?"

"Never you mind."

"Come on," Nigel said. "What do I get for all this?"

Alleyn gave him a brief account of Rivera's death and a lively description of Lord Pastern's performance in the band.

"As far as it goes, it's good," Nigel said, "but I could get as much from the waiters."

"Not if Caesar Bonn knows anything about it."

"Are you going to pull old Pastern in?"

"Not just yet. You write your stuff and send it along to me."

"It's pretty!" Nigel said. "It's as pretty as paint. Pastern's good at any time but like this he's marvellous. May I use your typewriter?"

"For ten minutes."

Nigel retired with the machine to a table at the far end of the room. "I can say you were there, of course," he said hurriedly.

"I'll be damned if you can."

"Come, come, Alleyn, be big about this thing."

"I know you. If we don't ring the bell you'll print some revolting photograph of me looking like a half-wit. Caption: 'Chief Inspector who watched crime but doesn't know whodunit.' "

Nigel grinned. "And would that be a story, and won't that be the day! Still, as it stands, it's pretty hot. Here we go, chaps." He began to rattle the keys.

Alleyn said: "There's one thing, Fox, that's sticking out of this mess like a road sign and I can't read it. Why did that perishing old mountebank look at the gun and then laugh himself sick? Here! Wait a moment. Who was in the study with him when he concocted his dummies and loaded his gun? It's a thin chance but it might yield something." He pulled the telephone towards him. "We'll talk once more to Miss Carlisle Wayne."

III

Carlisle was in her room when the call came through and she took it there, sitting on her bed and staring aimlessly at a flower print on the wall. A hammer knocked at her ribs and her throat constricted. In some remote part of her mind she thought: "As if I was in love, instead of frightened sick."

The unusually deep and clear voice said: "Is that you, Miss Wayne? I'm sorry to bother you again so soon but I'd like to have another word with you."

"Yes," said Carlisle. "Would you? Yes."

"I can come to Duke's Gate or, if you would rather, can see you here at the Yard." Carlisle didn't answer at once and he said: "Which would suit you best?"

"I—I think—I'll come to your office."

"It might be easier. Thank you so much. Can you come at once?"

"Yes. Yes, I can, of course."

"Splendid." He gave her explicit instructions about which entrance to use and where to ask for him. "Is that clear? I shall see you in about twenty minutes then."

"In about twenty minutes," she repeated and her voice cracked into an absurd cheerful note as if she were gaily making a date with him. "Right-ho," she said and thought with horror: "But I never say 'right-ho.' He'll think I'm demented."

"Mr. Alleyn," she said loudly.

"Yes? Hullo?"

"I'm sorry I made such an ass of myself this morning. I don't know what happened. I seem to have gone extremely peculiar."

"Never mind," said the deep voice easily.

"Well—all right. Thank you. I'll come straight away."

He gave a small, polite, not unfriendly sound and she hung up the receiver.

"Booking a date with the attractive Inspector, darling?" said Félicité from the door.

At the first sound of her voice Carlisle's body had jerked and she had cried out sharply.

"You *are* jumpy," Félicité said, coming nearer.

"I didn't know you were there."

"Obviously."

Carlisle opened her wardrobe. "He wants to see me. Lord knows why."

"So you're popping off to the Yard. Exciting for you."

"Marvellous, isn't it," Carlisle said, trying to make her voice ironical. Félicité watched her change into a suit. "Your face wants a little attention," she said.

"I know." She went to the dressing-table. "Not that it matters."

When she looked in the glass she saw Félicité's face behind her shoulder. "Stupidly unfriendly," she thought, dabbing at her nose.

"You know, darling," Félicité said, "I'm drawn to the conclusion you're a dark horse."

"Oh Fée!" she said impatiently.

"Well, you appear to have done quite a little act with my late best young man, last night, and here you are having a sly assignation with the dynamic Inspector."

"He probably wants to know what kind of toothpaste we all use."

"Personally," said Félicité, "I always considered you were potty about Ned."

Carlisle's hand shook as she pressed powder into the tear stains under her eyes.

"You *are* in a state, aren't you," said Félicité.

Carlisle turned on her. "Fée, for pity's sake come off it. As if things weren't bad enough without your starting these monstrous hares. You *must* have seen that I couldn't endure your poor wretched incredibly phony young man. You *must* see that Mr. Alleyn's summons to Scotland Yard has merely frightened seven bells out of me. How you *can!*"

"What about Ned?"

Carlisle picked up her bag and gloves. "If Ned writes the monstrous bilge you've fallen for in *Harmony* I never want to speak to him again," she said violently. "For the love of Mike pipe down and let me go and be grilled."

But she was not to leave without further incident. On the first floor landing she encountered Miss Henderson. After her early morning scene with Alleyn on the stairs, Carlisle had returned to her room and remained there, fighting down the storm of illogical weeping that had so suddenly overtaken her. So she had not met Miss Henderson until now.

"Hendy!" she cried out. "What's the matter?"

"Good morning, Carlisle. The matter, dear?"

"I thought you looked—I'm sorry. I expect we all look a bit odd. Are you hunting for something?"

"I've dropped my little silver pencil somewhere. It can't be here," she said as Carlisle began vaguely to look. "Are you going out?"

"Mr. Alleyn wants me to call and see him."

"Why?" Miss Henderson asked sharply.

"I don't know. Hendy, isn't this awful, this business? And to make matters worse I've had a sort of row with Fée."

The light on the first landing was always rather strange, Carlisle told herself, a cold reflected light coming from a distant window making people look greenish. It must be that because Miss Henderson answered her quite tranquilly and with her usual lack of emphasis. "Why, of all mornings, did you two want to have a row?"

"I suppose we're both scratchy. I told her I thought the unfortunate Rivera was ghastly and she thinks I'm shaking my curls at Mr. Alleyn. It was too stupid for words."

"I should think so, indeed."

"I'd better go!"

Carlisle touched her lightly on the arm and crossed to the stairs. She hesitated there, without turning to face Miss Henderson, who had not moved. "What is it?" Miss Henderson said. "Have you forgotten something?"

"No. Hendy, you know, don't you, about the fantastic thing they say killed him? The piece of parasol with an embroidery stiletto in the end?"

"Yes."

"Do you remember—I know this is ridiculous—but do you remember, last night, when there was that devastating bang from the ballroom? Do you remember you and Aunt Cile and Fée and I were in the drawing-room and you were sorting Aunt Cile's work-box?"

"Was I?"

"Yes. And you jumped at the bang and dropped something?"

"Did I?"

"And Fée picked it up."

"Did she?"

"Hendy, was it an embroidery stiletto?"

"I remember nothing about it. Nothing at all."

"I didn't notice where she put it. I wondered if you had noticed."

"If it was something from the work-box, I expect she put it back. Won't you be late, Carlisle?"

"Yes," Carlisle said without turning. "Yes, I'll go."

She heard Miss Henderson walk away into the drawing-room. The door closed gently and Carlisle went downstairs. There was a man in a dark suit in the hall. He got up when he saw her and said: "Excuse me, miss, but are you Miss Wayne?"

"Yes, I am."

"Thank you, Miss Wayne."

He opened the glass doors for her and then the front door. Carlisle went quickly past him and out into the sunshine. She was quite unaware of the man who stepped out from the corner a little way down Duke's Gate and who, glancing impatiently at his watch, waited at the bus stop and journeyed with her to Scotland Yard. "Keep observation on the whole damn boiling," Alleyn had said irritably at six o'clock that morning. "We don't know *what* we want."

She followed a constable, who looked oddly domesticated without his helmet, down a linoleumed corridor to the Chief Inspector's room. She thought: "They invite people to come and make statements. It means something. Suppose they suspect me. Suppose they've found out some little thing that makes them think I've done it." Her imagination galloped wildly. Suppose, when she went into the room, Alleyn said: "I'm afraid this is serious. Carlisle Loveday Wayne, I arrest you for the murder of Carlos Rivera and I warn you . . ." They would telephone for any clothes she wanted. Hendy, perhaps, would pack a suitcase. Perhaps, secretly, they would all be a little lightened, almost pleasurably worried, because they would no longer be in fear for themselves. Perhaps Ned would come to see her.

"In here, if you please, miss," the constable was saying with his hand on the door-knob.

Alleyn rose quickly from his desk and came towards her "Punctilious," she thought. "He's got nice manners. Are his manners like this when he's going to arrest people?"

"I'm so sorry," he was saying. "This must be a nuisance for you."

The solid grizzled detective was behind him. Fox. That was Inspector Fox. He had pulled up a chair for her and she sat in it, facing Alleyn. "With the light on my face," she thought, "that's what they do."

Fox moved away and sat behind a second desk. She could see his head and shoulders but his hands were hidden from her.

"You'll think my object in asking you to come very aimless, I expect," Alleyn said, "and my first question will no doubt strike you as being completely potty. However, here it is. You told us last night that you were with Lord Pastern when he made the dummies and loaded the revolver."

"Yes."

"Well, now did anything happen, particularly in respect of the revolver, that struck you both as being at all comic?"

Carlisle gaped at him. "Comic!"

"I told you it was a potty question," he said.

"If you mean did we take one look at the revolver and then shake with uncontrollable laughter, we didn't."

"No," he said. "I was afraid not."

"The mood was sentimental if anything. The revolver was one of a pair given to Uncle George by my father and he told me so."

"You were familiar with it then?"

"Not in the least. My father died ten years ago and when he lived was not in the habit of showing me his armoury. He and Uncle George were both crack shots, I believe. Uncle George told me my father had the revolvers made for target shooting."

"You looked at the gun last night? Closely?"

"Yes—because—" Beset by nervous and unreasoned caution, she hesitated.

"Because?"

"My father's initials are scratched on it. Uncle George told me to look for them."

There was a long pause. "Yes, I see," Alleyn said.

She found she had twisted her gloves tightly together and doubled them over. She felt a kind of impatience with herself and abruptly smoothed them out.

"It was one of a pair," Alleyn said. "Did you look at both of them?"

"No. The other was in a case in the drawer on his desk. I just saw it there. I noticed it because the drawer was under my nose, almost, and Uncle George kept putting the extra dummies, if that's what you call them, into it."

"Ah, yes. I saw them there."

"He made a lot more than he wanted in case," her voice faltered, "in case he was asked to do his turn again sometime."

"I see."

"Is that all?" she said.

"As you've been kind enough to come," Alleyn said with a smile, "perhaps we should think up something more."

"You needn't bother, thank you."

He smiled more broadly. "Fée was doing her stuff for him on the stairs this morning," Carlisle thought. "Was she actually showing the go-ahead signal or was she merely trying to stall him off?"

"It's about the steel end in this eccentric weapon. The bolt or dart," Alleyn said, and her attention snapped taut again. "We are almost certain that it's the business end of an embroidery stiletto from the work-box in the drawing-room. We found the discarded handle. I wonder if by any chance you remember when you last noticed the stiletto. If, of course, you happen to have noticed it."

"So this is it," she thought. "The revolver was nothing, it was a red herring. He's really got me here to talk about the stiletto."

She said: "I don't think the work-box was open when I was in the drawing-room before dinner. At any rate I didn't notice it."

"I remember you told me that Lady Pastern showed you and Manx her petit point. That *was* when you were all in the drawing-room before dinner, wasn't it? We found the petit point, by the way, beside the workbox."

"Therefore," she thought, "Aunt Cile or Ned or I might have taken the stiletto." She repeated: "I'm sure the box wasn't open."

She had tried not to think beyond that one time, that one safe time about which she could quickly speak the truth.

"And after dinner?" Alleyn said casually.

She saw again the small gleaming tool drop from Miss Henderson's fingers when the report sounded in the ballroom. She saw Félicité automatically stoop and pick it up and a second later burst into tears and run furiously from the room. She heard her loud voice on the landing: "I've got to speak to you," and Rivera's: "But certainly, if you wish it."

"After dinner?" she repeated flatly.

"You were in the drawing-room then. Before the men came in. Perhaps Lady Pastern took up her work. Did you, at any time, see the box open or notice the stiletto?"

How quick was thought? As quick as people said? Was her hesitation fatally long? Here she moved, on the brink of speech. She could hear the irrevocable denial, and yet she had not made it. And suppose he had already spoken to Félicité about the stiletto? "What am I looking like?" she thought in a panic. "I'm looking like a liar already."

"Can you remember?" he asked. So she had waited too long.

"I—don't think I can." Now, she had said it. Somehow it wasn't quite as shaming to lie about remembering as about the fact itself. If things went wrong she could say afterwards: "Yes, I remember, now, but I had forgotten. It had no significance for me at the time."

"You don't *think* you can." She had nothing to say but he went on almost at once: "Miss Wayne, will you please try to look squarely at this business. Will you try to pretend that it's an affair that you have read about and in which you have no personal concern. Not easy. But try. Suppose, then, a group of complete strangers was concerned in Rivera's death and suppose one of them, not knowing much about it, unable to see the factual wood for the emotional trees, was asked a question to which she knew the answer. Perhaps the answer seems to implicate her. Perhaps it seems to implicate someone she is fond of. She doesn't in the least know, it may be, what the implications are but she refuses to take the responsibility of telling the truth about one detail that may fit in with the whole truth. She won't, in fact, speak the truth if by doing so she's remotely responsible for bringing an extraordinarily callous murderer to book. So she lies. At once she finds that it doesn't end there. She must get other people to tell corroborative lies. She finds herself, in effect, whizzing down a dangerous slope with her car out of control, steering round some obstacles, crashing into others, doing irreparable damage and landing herself and possibly other innocent people in disaster. You think I'm overstating her case perhaps. Believe me, I've seen it happen very often."

"Why do you say all this to me?"

"I'll tell you why. You said just now that you didn't remember noticing the stiletto at any time after dinner. Before you made this statement you hesitated. Your hands closed on your gloves and suddenly twisted them. Your hands behaved with violence and yet they trembled. After you had spoken they continued to have a sort of independent life of their own. Your left hand kneaded the gloves and your right hand moved rather aimlessly across your neck and over your face. You blushed deeply and stared very fixedly at the top of my head. You presented me, in fact, with Example A from any handbook on behaviour of the lying witness. You were a glowing demonstration of the bad liar. And now, if all this is nonsense, you can tell counsel for the defence how I bullied you and he will treat me to as nasty a time as his talents suggest when I'm called to give evidence. Now I come to think of it, he'll be very unpleasant indeed. So however, will prosecuting counsel if you stick to your lapse of memory."

Carlisle said angrily: "My hands feel like feet. I'm going to sit on them. You don't play fair."

"My God," Alleyn said, "this isn't a game! It's murder."

"He was atrocious. He was much nastier than anyone else in the house."

"He may have been the nastiest job of work in Christendom. He was murdered and you're dealing with the police. This is not a threat but it's a warning: We've only just started—a great deal more evidence may come our way. You were not alone in the drawing-room after dinner."

She thought: "But Hendy won't tell and neither will Aunt Cile." But William came in sometime, about then. Suppose he saw Fée on the landing? Suppose he noticed the stiletto in her hand? And then she remembered the next time she had seen Félicité. Félicité had been on the top of the world, in ecstasy because of the letter from G.P.F. She had changed into her most gala dress and her eyes were shining. She had already discarded Rivera as easily as she had discarded all her previous young men. It was fantastic to tell lies for Félicité. There was something futile about this scene with Alleyn. She had made a fool of herself for nothing.

He had taken an envelope from a drawer of his desk and now opened it and shook it contents out before her. She saw a small shining object with a sharp end.

"Do you recognize it?" he asked.

"The stiletto."

"You say that because we've been talking about the stiletto. It's not a bit like it really. Look again."

She leant over it. "Why," she said, "it's a—a pencil."

"Do you know whose pencil?"

She hesitated. "I think it's Hendy's. She wears it on a chain like an old-fashioned charm. She always wears it. She was hunting for it on the landing this morning."

"This is it. Here are her initials. P.X.H. Very tiny. You almost need a magnifying glass. Like the initials you saw on the revolver. The ring at the end was probably softish silver and the gap in it may have opened with the weight of the pencil. I found the pencil in the work-box. Does Miss Henderson ever use Lady Pastern's work-box?"

This at least was plain sailing. "Yes. She tidies it very often for Aunt Cile." And immediately Carlisle thought: "I'm no good at this. Here it comes again."

"Was she tidying the box last night? After dinner?"

"Yes," Carlisle said flatly. "Oh, yes. Yes."

"Did you notice, particularly? When exactly was it?"

"Before the men came in. Well, only Ned came in actually. Uncle George and the other two were in the ballroom."

"Lord Pastern and Bellairs were at this time in the ballroom, and Rivera and Manx in the dining-room. According to the time-table." He opened a file on his desk.

"I only know that Fée had gone when Ned came in."

"She had joined Rivera in the study by then. But to return to this incident in the drawing-room. Can you describe the scene with the work-box? What were you talking about?"

Félicité had been defending Rivera. She had been on edge, in one of her moods. Carlisle had thought: "She's *had* Rivera but she won't own up." And Hendy, listening, had moved her fingers about inside the work-box. There was the stiletto in Hendy's fingers and, dangling from her neck, the pencil on its chain.

"They were talking about Rivera. Félicité considered he'd been snubbed a bit and was cross about it."

"At about this time Lord Pastern must have fired off his gun in the ballroom," Alleyn muttered. He had spread the time-table out on his desk. He glanced up at her. His glance, she noticed, was never vague or indirect, as other people's might be. It had the effect of immediately collecting your attention. "Do you remember that?" he said.

"Oh, yes."

"It must have startled you, surely?"

What were her hands doing now? She was holding the side of her neck again.

"How did you all react to what must have been an infernal racket? What for instance did Miss Henderson do? Do you remember?"

Her lips parted dryly. She closed them again, pressing them together.

"I think you do remember," he said. "What did she do?"

Carlisle said loudly. "She let the lid of the box drop. Perhaps the pencil was caught and pulled off the chain."

"Was anything in her hands?"

"The stiletto," she said, feeling the words grind out.

"Good. And then?"

"She dropped it."

Perhaps that would satisfy him. It fell to the carpet. Anyone might have picked it up. Anyone, she thought desperately. Perhaps he will think a servant might have picked it up. Or even Breezy Bellairs, much later.

"Did Miss Henderson pick it up?"

"No."

"Did anyone?"

She said nothing.

"You? Lady Pastern? No. Miss de Suze?"

She said nothing.

"And a little while afterwards, a very little while, she went out of the room. Because it was immediately after the report that William saw her go into the study with Rivera. He noticed that she had something shiny in her hand."

"She didn't even know she had it. She picked it up automatically. I expect she just put it down in the study and forgot all about it."

"We found the ivory handle there," Alleyn said, and Fox made a slight gratified sound in his throat.

"But you mustn't think there was any significance in all this."

"We're glad to know how and when the stiletto got into the study, at least."

"Yes," she said, "I suppose so. Yes."

Someone tapped on the door. The bare-headed constable came in with a package and an envelope. He laid them on the desk. "From Captain Entwhistle, sir. You asked to have them as soon as they came in."

He went out without looking at Carlisle.

"Oh, yes," Alleyn said. "The report on the revolver, Fox. Good. Miss Wayne, before you go, I'll ask you to have a look at the revolver. It'll be one more identification check."

She waited while Inspector Fox came out from behind his desk and unwrapped the parcel. It contained two separate packages. She knew the smaller one must be the dart and wondered if Rivera's blood was still encrusted on the stiletto. Fox opened the larger package and came to her with the revolver.

"Will you look at it?" Alleyn said. "You may handle it. I would like your formal identification."

Carlisle turned the heavy revolver in her hands. There was a strong light in the room. She bent her head and they waited. She looked up, bewildered. Alleyn gave her his pocket lens. There was a long silence.

"Well, Miss Wayne?"

"But . . . But it's extraordinary. I can't identify it. There are no initials. This isn't the same revolver."

CHAPTER X

The Stiletto, the Revolver and His Lordship

I

"AND WHAT," ALLEYN ASKED when Carlisle had left them, "is the betting on the favourite now, Br'er Fox?"

"By Gum," Fox said, "you always tell us that when a homicide case is full of fancy touches it's not going to give much trouble. Do you stick to that, sir?"

"I'll be surprised if this turns out to be the exception but I must say it looks like it at the moment. However, the latest development does at least cast another ray of light on your playmate. Do you remember how the old devil turned the gun over when we first let him see it at the Metronome? D'you remember how he took another look at it in the study and then had an attack of the dry grins and when I asked him what he expected to see had the infernal nerve to come back at me with: 'Hoity-toity'—yes, 'Hoity-toity—wouldn't you like to know?' "

"Ugh!"

"He'd realized all along, of course, that this wasn't the weapon he loaded in the study and took down to the Metronome. Yes," Alleyn added as Fox opened his mouth, "and don't forget he showed Skelton the gun a few minutes before it was fired. Miss Wayne says he pointed out the initials to Skelton."

"*That* looks suspicious in itself," Fox said instantly. "Why go to the trouble of pointing out initials to two people? He was getting something fixed up for himself. So's he could turn round and say: 'That's not the gun I fired.' "

"Then why didn't he say so at once?"

"Gawd knows."

"If you ask me he was sitting pretty, watching us make fools of ourselves."

Fox jabbed his finger at the revolver. "If this isn't the original weapon," he demanded, "what the hell is it? It's the one this projectile-dart-bolt or what-have-you was fired from because it's got the scratches in the barrel. That means someone had this second gun all ready loaded with the dart and ammunition and substituted it for the original weapon. Here! What's the report say, Mr. Alleyn?"

Alleyn was reading the report. "Entwhistle," he said, "has had a ballistic orgy over the thing. The scratches could have been made by the brilliants in the parasol clip. In his opinion they were so made. He's sending photomicrographs to prove it. He's fired the bolt—let's stick to calling this hybrid a bolt, shall we?—from another gun with an identical bore and it is 'somewhat similarly scratched,' which is a vile phrase. He pointed out that wavering, irregular scars were made when the bolt was shoved up the barrel. The spring clip was pressed back with the thumb while it was being inserted and then sprang out once it was inside the barrel, thus preventing the bolt from falling out if the weapon was pointed downwards. The bolt was turned slightly as it was shoved home. The second scar was made by the ejection of the bolt, the clip retaining its pressure while being expelled. He says that the scars in the revolver we submitted don't extend quite as deep up the barrel as those made by the bolt which he fired from his own gun, but he considers that they were made by the same kind of procedure and the same bolt. At a distance of four feet, the projectile shoots true. Over long distances there are 'progressive divergences' caused by the weight of the clip on one side or by air resistance. Entwhistle says he's very puzzled by the fouling from the bore which is quite unlike anything in his experience. He removed it and sent it along for analysis. The analyst finds that the fouling consists of particles of carbon and of various hydrocarbons including members of the paraffin series, apparently condensed from vapour."

"Funny."

"That's all."

"All right," Fox said heavily. "All right. That looks fair enough. The bolt that plugged Rivera *was* shot out of this weapon. This weapon is not the one his lordship showed Miss Wayne and Syd Skelton. But unless you entertain the idea of somebody shooting off another gun at the same instant, this is the one that killed Rivera. You accept that, sir?"

"I'll take it as a working premise. With reservations and remembering our conversation in the car."

"All right. Well, after Skelton examined the gun with the initials, did his lordship get a chance to substitute this one and fire it off? Could he have had this one on him all the time?"

"Hob-nobbing, cheek by jowl, with a dozen or so people at close quarters? I should say definitely not. And, he didn't know Skelton would ask to see the gun. And what did he do with the first gun afterwards? We searched him, remember."

"Planted it? Anyway, where is it?"

"Somewhere at the Metronome if we're on the right track and we've searched the Metronome. But go on."

"Well, sir, if his lordship didn't change the gun, who did?"

"His stepdaughter could have done it. Or any other member of his party. They were close to the sombrero, remember. They got up to dance and moved round between the table and the edge of the dais. Lady Pastern was alone at the table for some time. I didn't see her move but I wasn't watching her, of course. All the ladies had largish evening bags. The catch in that theory, Br'er Fox, is that they wouldn't have known they were going to be within reach of the sombrero and it's odds on they didn't know he was going to put his perishing gun under his sombrero, anyway."

Fox bit at his short grizzled moustache, planted the palms of his hands on his knees and appeared to go into a short trance. He interrupted it to mutter: "Skelton, now. Syd Skelton. Could Syd Skelton have worked the substitution? You're going to remind me they were all watching him, but were they watching all that closely? Syd Skelton."

"Go on, Fox."

"Syd Skelton's on his own, in a manner of speaking. He left the band platform before his lordship came on for his turn. Syd walked out. Suppose he had substituted this gun for the other with the initials. Suppose he walked right out and dropped the other one down the first grating he came to? Syd knew he was going to get the chance, didn't he?"

"How, when and where did he convert the bit of parasol shaft and stiletto into the bolt and put it up the barrel of the second revolver? Where did he get his ammunition? And when did he get the gun? *He* wasn't at Duke's Gate."

"Yes," Fox said heavily, "that's awkward. I wonder if you could get round that one. Well, leave it for the time being. Who else have we got? Breezy. From the substitution angle, can we do anything about Breezy?"

"He didn't get alongside Pastern, on either of their statements, from the time Skelton looked at the gun until after Rivera was killed. They were alone together in the band-room before Breezy made his entrance but Pastern, with his usual passionate industry in clearing other people, says Breezy didn't go near him. And Pastern had his gun in his hip pocket, remember."

Fox returned to his trance.

"I think," Alleyn said, "it's going to be one of those affairs where the whittling away of impossibilities leaves one face to face with a mere improbability which, as you would say, *faute de mieux*, one is forced to accept. And I think, so far, Fox, we haven't found my improbable notion an impossibility. At least it has the virtue of putting the fancy touches in a more credible light."

"We'll never make a case of it, I reckon, if it does turn out to be the answer."

"And we'll never make a case of it if we pull in his lordship and base the charge on the assumption that he substituted this gun for the one he loaded and says he fired. Skelton's put up by the defence and swears he examined the thing at his own request and saw the initials and that this is not the same weapon. Counsel points out that three minutes later Lord Pastern goes on for his turn."

Fox snarled quietly to himself and presently broke out: "We call this blasted thing a bolt. Be damned if I don't think we'll get round to calling it a dart. Be damned if I'm not beginning to wonder if it was used like one. Thrown at the chap from close by. After all it's not impossible."

"Who by? Breezy?"

"No," Fox said slowly. "No. Not Breezy. His lordship cleared Breezy in advance by searching him. Would you swear Breezy didn't pick anything up from anywhere after he came out to conduct?"

"I believe I would. He walked rapidly through the open door and down an alleyway between the musicians. He stood in a spot light a good six feet or more away from anything, conducting like a great jerking jelly-fish. They all say he couldn't have picked anything up after Pastern searched him, and in any case I would certainly swear he didn't put his hands near his pockets and that up to the time Rivera fell he was conducting with both hands and that none of his extraordinary antics in the least resembled dart-throwing. I was watching him. They rather fascinated me, those antics. And if you want any more, Br'er Fox, Rivera had his back turned to Breezy when he fell."

"All right. His lordship then. His lordship was facing Rivera. Close to him. *Blast.* Unless he's ambidextrous, how'd he fire off a gun and throw a dart all in a split second? This is getting me nowhere. Who else, then?"

"Do you fancy Lady Pastern as a dart queen?"

Fox chuckled. "That *would* be the day, sir, wouldn't it? But how about Mr. Manx? We've got a motive for Manx. Rivera had proof that Manx wrote these sissy articles in *Harmony*. Manx doesn't want that known. Blackmail," said Fox without much conviction.

"Foxkin," Alleyn said, "let there be a truce to these barren speculations. May I remind you that up to the time he fell Rivera was raising hell with a piano-accordion?"

Fox said, after another long pause: "You know I like this case. It's got something. Yes. And may I remind *you*, sir, that he wasn't meant to fall? None of them expected him to fall. Therefore he fell because somebody planted a bloody little steel embroidery gadget on a parasol handle in his heart before he fell. So where, if you don't object to the inquiry, Mr. Alleyn, do we go from here?"

"I think," Alleyn said, "that you institute a search for the missing gun and I pay a call on Miss Petronella Xantippe Henderson." He got up and fetched his hat. "And I think, moreover," he added, "that we've been making a couple of perishing fools of ourselves."

"About the dart?" Fox demanded. "Or the gun?"

"About *Harmony*. Think this one over while I call on Miss Henderson and then tell me what you make of it."

Five minutes later he went out, leaving Fox in a concentrated trance.

II

Miss Henderson received him in her room. It had the curiously separate, not quite congenial air that seems to be the characteristic of sitting-rooms that are permanently occupied by solitary women in other people's houses. There were photographs: of Félicité, as a child, as a schoolgirl and in her presentation dress; one intimidating portrait of Lady Pastern and one, enlarged, it would seem, from a snapshot, of Lord Pastern in knickerbockers and shooting boots, with a gun under his arm, a spaniel at his heels, a large house at his back and an expression of impertinence on his face. Above the desk hung a group of women undergraduates clad in the tube-like brevity of the nineteen-twenties. A portion of Lady Margaret Hall loomed in the background.

Miss Henderson was dressed with scrupulous neatness, in a dark suit that faintly resembled a uniform or habit. She received Alleyn with perfect composure. He looked at her hair, greyish, quietly fashionable in its controlled grooming, at her eyes, which were pale, and at her mouth, which was unexpectedly full.

"Well, Miss Henderson," he said, "I wonder if you will be able to throw any light on this very obscure business."

"I'm afraid it's most unlikely," she said tranquilly.

"You never know. There's one point, at least, where I hope you will help us. You were present at last night's party in this house, both before and after dinner, and you were in the drawing-room when Lord Pastern, with the help of all the people concerned, worked out and wrote down the time-table which he afterwards gave to me."

"Yes," she agreed after he had waited for a second or two.

"Would you say that as far as your personal observations and recollections cover them, the movements set down in the time-table are accurate?"

"Oh yes," she said at once, "I think so. But of course they don't go very far—my recollections. I was the last to arrive in the drawing-room, you know, before dinner and the first to leave after dinner."

"Not quite the first, according to the time-table, surely?"

She drew her brows together as if perturbed at the suggestion of inaccuracy. "Not?" she said.

"The time-table puts Miss de Suze's exit from the drawing-room a second or two before yours."

"How stupid of me. Félicité did go out first, but I followed almost at once. I forgot for the moment."

"You were all agreed on this point last night, when Lord Pastern compiled his time-table?"

"Yes. Perfectly."

"Do you remember that just before this there was a great rumpus in the ballroom? It startled you and you dropped a little stiletto on the carpet. You were tidying Lady Pastern's work-box at the time. Do you remember?"

He had thought at first that she used no more make-up than a little powder but he saw now that the faint warmth of her cheeks was artificial. The colour became isolated as the skin beneath and about it bleached. Her voice was quite even and clear.

"It was certainly rather an alarming noise," she said.

"Do you remember, too, that Miss de Suze picked up the stiletto? I expect she meant to return it to you or to the box but she was rather put out just then. She was annoyed, wasn't she, by the, as she considered, uncordial reception given to her fiancé?"

"He was not her fiancé. They were not engaged."

"Not officially, I know."

"Not officially. There was no engagement."

"I see. In any case, do you remember that instead of replacing the stiletto, she still had it in her hand when, a moment later, she left the room?"

"I'm afraid I didn't notice."

"What did you do?"

"Do?"

"At that moment. You had been tidying the box. It was exquisitely neat when we found it this morning. Was it on your knees? The table was a little too far from your chair for you to have used it, I think."

"Then," she said, with her first hint of impatience, "the box was on my knees."

"So that was how the miniature silver pencil you wear on a chain came to be in the box?"

Her hands went to the bosom of her suit, fingering it. "Yes. I suppose so. Yes. I didn't realize . . . Was that where it was?"

"Perhaps you dropped the lid and caught the pencil, dragging it off the chain."

"Yes," she repeated. "Yes. I suppose so. Yes, I remember I did do that."

"Then why did you hunt for it this morning on the landing?"

"I had forgotten about catching it in the box," she said rapidly.

"Not," Alleyn murmured apologetically, "a frightfully good memory."

"These are trivial things that you ask me to remember. In this house we are none of us, at the moment, concerned with trivial things."

"Are you not? Then, I suggest that you searched the landing, not for your trinket, which you say was a trivial thing, but for something that you knew could not be in the work-box because you had seen Miss de Suze take it out with her when she left the drawing-room in a rage. The needlework stiletto."

"But, Inspector Alleyn, I told you I didn't notice anything of the sort."

"Then what were you looking for?"

"You have apparently been told. My pencil."

"A trivial thing but your own? Here it is."

He opened his hand, showing her the pencil. She made no movement and he dropped it in her lap. "You don't seem to me," he remarked casually, "to be an unobservant woman."

"If that's a compliment," she said, "thank you."

"Did you see Miss de Suze again, after she left the drawing-room with the stiletto in her hand and after she had quarreled with Rivera when they were alone together in the study?"

"Why do you say they quarrelled?"

"I have it on pretty good authority."

"Carlisle?" she said sharply.

"No. But if you cross-examine a policeman about this sort of job, you know, he's not likely to be very communicative."

"One of the servants, I suppose," she said, dismissing it and him without emphasis. He asked her again if she had seen Félicité later that evening and after watching him for a moment she said that she had. Félicité had come to this room and had been in the happiest possible mood. "Excited?" he suggested and she replied that Félicité had been pleasurably excited. She was glad to be going out with her cousin, Edward Manx, to whom she was attached and was looking forward to the performance at the Metronome.

"After this encounter you went to Lady Pastern's room, didn't you? Lady Pastern's maid was with her. She was dismissed, but not before she had heard you say that Miss de Suze was very much excited and that you wanted to have a word with her mother about this."

"Again, the servants."

"Anybody," Alleyn said, "who is prepared to speak the truth. A man has been murdered."

"I have spoken nothing but the truth." Her lips trembled and she pressed them together.

"Good. Let's go on with it then, shall we?"

"There's nothing at all that I can tell you. Nothing at all."

"But at least you can tell me about the family. You understand, don't you, that my job, at the moment, is not so much finding the guilty person as clearing persons who may have been associated with Rivera but are innocent of his murder. That may, indeed it does, take in certain members of the household, the detailed as well as the general set-up. Now, in your position . . ."

"My position!" she muttered, with a sort of repressed contempt. Almost inaudibly she added: "What do you know of my position!"

Alleyn said pleasantly: "I've heard you're called the Controller of the Household." She didn't answer and he went on: "In any case it has been a long association and I suppose, in many ways, an intimate one. With Miss de Suze, for instance. You have brought her up, really, haven't you?"

"Why do you keep speaking about Félicité? This has nothing to do with Félicité." She got up, and stood with her back towards him, changing the position of an ornament on the mantelpiece. He could see her carefully kept and very white hand steady itself on the edge of the shelf. "I'm afraid I'm not behaving very well, am I?" she murmured. "But I find your insistence rather trying."

"Is that because, at the moment, it's directed at Miss de Suze and the stiletto?"

"Naturally, I'm uneasy. It's disturbing to feel that she will be in the smallest degree involved." She leant her head against her hand. From where he stood, behind her, she looked like a woman who had come to rest for a moment and fallen into an idle speculation. Her voice came to him remotely from beyond her stooped shoulders as if her mouth were against her hand. "I suppose she simply left it in the study. She didn't even realize she had it in her hand. It was not in her hand when she came upstairs. It had no importance for her at all." She turned and faced him. "I shall tell you something," she said. "I don't want to. I'd made up my mind I'd have no hand in this. It's distasteful to me. But I see now that I must tell you."

"Right."

"It's this. Before dinner last night and during dinner, I had opportunity to watch those—those two men."

"Rivera and Bellairs?"

"Yes. They were extraordinary creatures and I suppose in a sort of way I was interested."

"Naturally. In Rivera at all events."

"I don't know what servants' gossip you have been listening to, Inspector Alleyn."

"Miss Henderson, I've heard enough from Miss de Suze herself to tell me that there was an understanding between them."

"I watched those two men," she said exactly as if he hadn't spoken. "And I saw at once there was bad blood between them. They looked at each other—I can't describe it—with enmity. They were both, of course, incredibly common and blatant. They scarcely spoke to each other but during dinner, over and over again, I saw the other one, the conductor, eyeing him. He talked a great deal to Félicité and to Lord Pastern but he listened to . . ."

"To Rivera?" Alleyn prompted. She seemed to be incapable of pronouncing his name.

"Yes. He listened to him as if he resented every word he spoke. That would have been natural enough from any of us."

"Was Rivera so offensive?"

An expression of eagerness appeared on her face. Here was something, at last, about which she was ready to speak.

"Offensive?" she said. "He was beyond everything. He sat next to Carlisle and even she was nonplussed. Evidently she attracted him. It was perfectly revolting."

Alleyn thought distastefully: "Now what's behind all this? Resentment? At Carlisle rather than Félicité attracting the atrocious Rivera? Or righteous indignation? Or what?"

She had raised her head. Her arm still rested on the mantelpiece and she had stretched out her hand to a framed photograph of Félicité in presentation dress. He moved slightly and saw that her eyes were fixed on the photograph. Félicité's eyes, under her triple plumage, stared back with the glazed distaste (so suggestive of the unwitting influence of Mr. John Gielgud) that characterizes the modish photograph. Miss Henderson began to speak again and it was as if she addressed herself to the photograph. "Of course, Félicité didn't mind in the least. It was nothing to her. A relief, no doubt. Anything rather than suffer his odious attentions. But it was clear to me that the other creature and he had quarrelled. It was quite obvious."

"But if they hardly spoke to each other how could . . . ?"

"I've told you. It was the way the other person, Bellairs, looked at him. He watched him perpetually."

Alleyn now stood before her. They made a formal conversation piece with the length of the mantelpiece between them. He said: "Miss Henderson, who was beside you at the dinner table?"

"I sat next to Lord Pastern. On his left."

"And on your left?"

She made a fastidious movement with her shoulders. "Mr. Bellairs."

"Do you remember what he talked to you about?"

Her mouth twisted. "I don't remember that he spoke to me at all," she said. "He had evidently realized that I was a person of no importance. He devoted himself to Félicité, who was on his other side. He gave me his shoulder."

Her voice faded out almost before she had uttered the last word as if, too late, she had tried to stop herself.

"If he gave you his shoulder," Alleyn said, "how did it come about that you could see this inimical fixed stare of his?"

The photograph of Félicité crashed on the hearth. Miss Henderson cried out and knelt. "How clumsy of me," she whispered.

"Let me do it. You may cut your fingers."

"No," she said sharply, "don't touch it."

She began to pick the slivers of glass from the frame and drop them in the grate. "There's a looking-glass on the wall of the dining-room," she said. "I could see him in that." And in a flat voice that had lost all its urgency she repeated: "He watched him perpetually."

"Yes," Alleyn said, "I remember the looking-glass. I accept that."

"Thank you," she said ironically.

"One more question. Did you go into the ballroom at any time after dinner?"

She looked up at him warily and after a moment said: "I believe I did. Yes. I did."

"When?"

"Félicité had lost her cigarette case. It was when they were changing and she called out from her room. She had been in the ballroom during the afternoon and thought she might have left it there."

"Had she done so?"

"Yes. It was on the piano. Under some music."

"What else was on the piano?"

"A bundle of parasols."

"Anything else?"

"No," she said. "Nothing."

"Or on the chairs or floor?"

"Nothing."

"Are you sure?"

"Perfectly sure," she said and dropped a piece of glass with a little tinkle in the grate.

"Well," Alleyn said, "if I can't help you, perhaps I'd better take myself off."

She seemed to examine the photograph. She peered at it as if to make certain there were no flaws or scratches on Félicité's image. "Very well," she said and stood up, holding the face of the photograph against her flattish chest. "I'm sorry if I haven't told you the kind of things you want to be told. The truth is so seldom what one really wants to hear, is it? But perhaps you don't think I have told you the truth."

"I think I am nearer to it than I was before I visited you."

He left her, with the broken photograph still pressed against the bosom of her dark suit. On the landing he encountered Hortense. Her ladyship, Hortense said, smiling knowledgeably at him, would be glad to see him before he left. She was in her boudoir.

III

It was a small, delicately appointed room on the same floor. Lady Pastern rose from her desk, a pretty Empire affair, as he came in. She was firmly encased in her morning dress. Her hair was rigid, her hands ringed. A thin film of make-up had been carefully spread over the folds and shadows of her face. She looked ghastly but completely in order.

"It is so good of you to spare me a moment," she said and held out her hand. This was unexpected. Evidently she considered that her change of manner required an explanation and, without wasting time, she let him have it.

"I did not realize last night," she said concisely, "that you must be the younger son of an old friend of my father's. You are Sir George Alleyn's son, are you not?"

Alleyn bowed. This, he thought, is going to be tiresome.

"Your father," she said, "was a frequent visitor at my parents' house in the Faubourg St.-Germain. He was in those days, an attaché, I think, at your embassy in Paris." Her voice faded and an extraordinary look came over her face. He was unable to interpret it.

"What is it, Lady Pastern?" he asked.

"Nothing. I was reminded, for a moment, of a former conversation. We were speaking of your father. I remember that he and your mother called upon one occasion, bringing their two boys with them. Perhaps you do not recollect the visit."

"It is extremely kind of you to do so."

"I had understood that you were to be entered in the British Diplomatic Service."

"I was entirely unsuited for it, I'm afraid."

"Of course," she said with a sort of creaking graciousness, "young men after the first war began to find their vocation in unconventional fields. One understands and accepts these changes, doesn't one?"

"Since I am here as a policeman," Alleyn said politely, "I hope so."

Lady Pastern examined him with that complete lack of reticence which is often the characteristic of royal personages. It occurred to him that she herself would also have shaped up well, in an intimidating way, as a policewoman.

"It is a relief to me," she announced, after a pause, "that we are in your

should like you to understand that it's not based on guesswork. May we sit down?"

She sat down abruptly. He saw, and was bewildered to see, that she was trembling. He told her about the letter Félicité had received and showed her the copy he had made. He reminded her of the white flower in Manx's coat and of Félicité's change of manner after she had seen it. He said that Félicité believed Manx to be G.P.F. and had admitted as much. He said they had discovered original drafts of articles that had subsequently appeared on G.P.F.'s page and that these drafts had been typed on the machine in the study. He reminded her that Manx had stayed at Duke's Gate for three weeks. Throughout this recital she sat bolt upright, pressing her lips together and staring, inexplicably, at the top right-hand drawer of her desk. In some incomprehensible fashion he was dealing her blow after shrewd blow, but he kept on and finished the whole story. "So you see, don't you," he ended, "that, at least, it's a probability?"

"Have you asked him?" she said pallidly. "What does he say?"

"I have not asked him yet. I shall do so. Of course, the whole question of his identity with G.P.F. may be irrelevant as far as this case is concerned."

"Irrelevant!" she ejaculated as if the suggestion were wildly insane. She was looking again at her desk. Every muscle of her face was controlled but tears now began to form in her eyes and trickle over her cheeks.

"I'm sorry," Alleyn said, "that you find this distressing."

"It distresses me," she said, "because I find it is true. I am in some confusion of mind. If there is nothing more . . ."

He got up at once. "There's nothing more," he said. "Goodbye, Lady Pastern."

She recalled him before he reached the door. "One moment."

"Yes?"

"Let me assure you, Mr. Alleyn," she said, pressing her handkerchief against her cheek, "that my foolishness is entirely unimportant. It is a personal matter. What you have told me is quite irrelevant to this affair. It is of no consequence whatever, in fact." She drew in her breath with a sound that quivered between a sigh and a sob. "As for the identity of the person who has perpetrated this outrage—I mean the murder not the journalism—I am persuaded it was one of his own kind. Yes, certainly," she said more vigorously, "one of his own kind. You may rest assured of that." And finding himself dismissed, he left her.

IV

As Alleyn approached the first landing on his way down he was surprised to hear the ballroom piano. It was being played somewhat unhandily and the strains were those of hotly syncopated music taken at a funeral pace. Detective-Sergeant Jimson was on duty on the landing. Alleyn jerked his head at the ballroom doors, which were ajar. "Who's that playing?" he asked. "Is it Lord Pastern? Who the devil opened that room?"

Jimson, looking embarrassed and scandalized, replied that he thought it must be Lord Pastern. His manner was so odd that Alleyn walked past him and pushed open the double doors. Inspector Fox was discovered seated at the piano with his spectacles on his nose. He was inclined forward tensely, and followed with concentration a sheet of music in manuscript. Facing him, across the piano, was Lord Pastern, who, as Alleyn entered, beat angrily, but rhythmically, upon the lid and shouted: "No, no, my good ass, not a bit like it. N'yah—*yo.* Bo bo bo. Again." He looked up and saw Alleyn. "Here!" he said. "Can you play?"

Fox rose, without embarrassment, and removed his spectacles.

"Where have you come from?" Alleyn demanded.

"I had a little matter to report, sir, and as you were engaged for the moment I've been waiting in here. His lordship was looking for someone to try over a piece he's composing but I'm afraid . . ."

"I'll have to get one of these women," Lord Pastern cut in impatiently. "Where's Fée? This chap's no good."

"I haven't sat down to the piano since I was a lad," said Fox mildly.

Lord Pastern made for the door but Alleyn intercepted him. "One moment, sir," he said.

"It's no good worryin' me with any more questions," Lord Pastern snapped at him. "I'm busy."

"Unless you'd prefer to come to the Yard, you'll answer this one, if you please. When did you first realize that the revolver we produced after Rivera was killed was not the one you loaded in the study and carried on to the band platform?"

Lord Pastern smirked at him. "Nosed that out for yourselves, have you?" he remarked. "Fascinatin', the way our police work."

"I still want to know when you made this discovery."

"About eight hours before you did."

"As soon as you were shown the substitute and noticed there were no initials?"

"Who told you about initials? Here!" Lord Pastern said with some excitement. "Have you found my other gun?"

"Where do you suggest we look for it?"

"If I knew where it was, my good fathead, I'd have got it for meself. I value that gun, by God!"

"You handed over the weapon you fired at Rivera to Breezy Bellairs," Fox said suddenly. "Was it that one, my lord? The one with the initials? The one you loaded in this house? The one that's missing?"

Lord Pastern swore loudly. "What d'you think I am?" he shouted. "A bloody juggler? Of course it was."

"And Bellairs walked straight into the office with you and I took it off him a few minutes later and it *wasn't* the same gun. That won't wash, my lord," said Fox, "if you'll excuse my saying so. It won't wash."

"In that case," Lord Pastern said rudely, "you can put up with it dirty." Alleyn made a slight, irritated sound and Lord Pastern instantly turned on him. "What are *you* snufflin' about?" he demanded and before Alleyn could answer he renewed his attack on Fox. "Why don't you ask Breezy about it?" he said. "I should have thought even *you'd* have got at Breezy."

"Are you suggesting, my lord, that Bellairs might have worked the substitution after the murder was committed?"

"I'm not suggestin' anything."

"In which case," Fox continued imperturbably, "perhaps you'll tell me how Rivera was killed?"

Lord Pastern gave a short bark of laughter. "No, really," he said, "it's beyond belief how bone-headed you are."

Fox said: "May I press this point a little further, Mr. Alleyn?"

From behind Lord Pastern, Alleyn returned Fox's inquiring glance with a dubious one. "Certainly, Fox," he said.

"I'd like to ask his lordship if he'd be prepared to swear an oath that the weapon he handed Bellairs after the fatality was the one that is missing."

"Well, Lord Pastern," Alleyn said, "will you answer Mr. Fox?"

"How many times am I to tell you I won't answer any of your tom-fool questions? I gave you a time-table, and that's all the help you get from me."

For a moment the three men were silent: Fox by the piano, Alleyn near the door and Lord Pastern midway between them like a truculent Pekinese—an animal, it occurred to Alleyn, he closely resembled.

"Don't forget, my lord," Fox said, "that last night you stated yourself that anybody could have got at the revolver while it was under the sombrero. Anybody, you remarked, for all you'd have noticed."

"What of it?" he said, bunching his cheeks.

"There's this about it, my lord. It's a tenable theory that one of the party at your own table could have substituted the second gun, loaded with the bolt, and that you could have fired it at Rivera without knowing anything about the substitution."

"That cat won't jump," Lord Pastern said, "and you know it. I didn't tell anybody I was going to put the gun under my sombrero. Not a soul."

"Well, my lord," Fox said, "we can make inquiries about that."

"You can inquire till you're blue in the face and much good may it do you."

"Look here, my lord," Fox burst out, "do you *want* us to arrest you?"

"Not sure I don't. It'd be enough to make a cat laugh." He thrust his hands in his trouser pockets, walked round Fox, eyeing him, and fetched up in front of Alleyn. "Skelton," he said, "saw the gun. He handled it just before he went on, and when he came out while I waited for my entrance he handled it again. While Breezy did the speech about me, it was."

"Why did he handle it this second time?" Alleyn asked.

"I was a bit excited. Nervy work, hangin' about for your entrance. I was takin' a last look at it and I dropped it and he picked it up and squinted down the barrel in a damn-your-eyes supercilious sort of way. Professional jealousy."

"Why didn't you mention this before, my lord?" Fox demanded and was ignored. Lord Pastern grinned savagely at Alleyn. "Well," he said with gloating relish, "what about this arrest? I'll come quietly."

Alleyn said: "You know, I do wish that for once in a blue moon you'd behave yourself."

For the first time, he thought, Lord Pastern was giving him his full attention. He was suddenly quiet and wary. He eyed Alleyn with something of the air of a small boy who is not sure if he can bluff his way out of a misdemeanour.

"You really are making the most infernal nuisance of yourself, sir," Alleyn went on, "and, if you will allow me, the most appalling ass of yourself into the bargain."

"See here, Alleyn," Lord Pastern said with a not entirely convincing return to his former truculence, "I'm damned if I'll take this. I know what I'm up to."

"Then have the grace to suppose we know what we're up to, too. After all, sir, you're not the only one to remember that Rivera played the piano-accordion."

For a moment, Lord Pastern stood quite still with his jaw dropped and his eyebrows half-way up his forehead. He then said rapidly: "I'm late. Goin' to m'club," and incontinently bolted from the room.

CHAPTER XI

Episodes in Two Flats and an Office

I

"WELL, MR. ALLEYN," said Fox, "that settles it, in my mind. It's going to turn out the way you said. Cut loose the trimmings and you come to the—well, the *corpus delicti* as you might say."

They were sitting in a police car outside the house in Duke's Gate. Both of them looked past the driver, and through the wind-screen, at a jaunty and briskly moving figure, its hat a little to one side and swinging its walking stick.

"There he goes," Fox said, "as cock-sure and perky as you please, and there goes our chap after him. Say what you like, Mr. Alleyn, the art of tailing your man isn't what it was in the service. These young fellows think they signed on for the sole purpose of tearing about the place with the Flying Squad." And having delivered himself of his customary grumble, Fox, still contemplating the diminishing figure of Lord Pastern, added: "Where do we go from here, sir?"

"Before we go anywhere you'll be good enough to explain why your duties led you back to Duke's Gate and, more particularly, to playing that old antic's boogie-woogie on the piano."

Fox smiled in a stately manner. "Well, sir," he said, "as to what brought me, it was a bit of stale information, and another bit that's not so stale. Skelton rang up after you left, to say he had inspected his lordship's revolver the second time and was sorry he hadn't mentioned it last night. He said that he and our Mr. Eton-and-Oxford Detective-Sergeant Sallis got into a discussion about the *petite bourgeoisie* or something and it went out of his head. I thought it better not to ring you at Duke's Gate. Extension wires all over the shop in that house. So, as it seemed to settle the question about which gun his lordship took on the platform with him, I thought I'd pop along and tell you."

"And Pastern saved you the trouble."

"Quite so. And as to the piano, there was his lordship saying he'd been inspired, so to speak, with a new composition and wanted someone to try it over. He was making a great to-do over the ballroom being sealed. Our chaps have finished in there so there seemed no harm in obliging him. I thought it might establish friendly relations," Fox added sadly, "but I can't say it did in the end. Shall we tell this chap where we're going, sir?"

Alleyn said: "We'll call at the Metronome, then we'll have a look at Breezy and see how the poor swine's shaping up this morning. Then we'll have a very brief snack, Br'er Fox, and when that's over it'll be time to visit G.P.F. in his den. If he's there, blast him."

"Ah, by the way," Fox said, as they moved off, "that's the other bit of information. Mr. Bathgate rang the Yard and said he'd got hold of someone who writes regularly for this paper *Harmony* and it seems that Mr. Friend is generally supposed to be in the office on the afternoon and evening of the last Sunday in the month, on account of the paper going to press the following week. This gentleman told Mr. Bathgate that nobody on the regular staff except the editor ever sees Mr. Friend. The story is he deals direct with the proprietors of the paper but popular opinion in Fleet Street reckons he owns the show himself. They reckon the secrecy business is nothing but a build-up."

"Silly enough to be incredible," Alleyn muttered. "But we're knee-deep in imbecility. I suppose we can take it. All the same, I fancy we'll turn up a better reason for Mr. Friend's elaborate incognito before this interminable Sunday is out."

Fox said, with an air of quiet satisfaction: "I fancy we shall, sir. Mr. Bathgate's done quite a nice little job for us. It seems he pressed this friend of his a bit further and got him on to the subject of Mr. Manx's special articles for the paper and it came out that Mr. Manx is often in their office."

"Discussing his special articles. Picking up his galley sheets or whatever they do."

"Better than that, Mr. Alleyn. This gentleman told Mr. Bathgate that Mr. Manx has been noticed coming out of G.P.F.'s room on several occasions, one of them being a Sunday afternoon."

"Oh."

"Fits, doesn't it?"

"Like a glove. Good for Bathgate. We'll ask him to meet us at the *Har-*

mony offices. This being the last Sunday in the month, Br'er Fox, we'll see what we can see. But first—the Metronome."

II

When Carlisle left the Yard, it was with a feeling of astonishment and aimless boredom. So it wasn't Uncle George's revolver after all. So there had been an intricate muddle that someone would have to unravel. Alleyn would unravel it and then someone else would be arrested and she ought to be alarmed and agitated because of this. Perhaps, in the hinterland of her emotions, alarm and agitation were already established and waited to pounce, but in the meantime she was only drearily miserable and tired. She was pestered by all sorts of minor considerations. The thought of returning to Duke's Gate and trying to cope with the situation there was intolerable. It wasn't so much the idea that Uncle George or Aunt Cile or Fée might have murdered Carlos Rivera that Carlisle found appalling: it was the prospect of their several personalities forcing themselves upon her own; their demands upon her attention and courtesy. She had a private misery, a galling unhappiness, and she wanted to be alone with it.

While she walked irresolutely towards the nearest bus stop, she remembered that not far from here, in a *cul-de-sac* called Coster's Row, was Edward Manx's flat. If she walked to Duke's Gate she would pass the entry into this blind street. She was persuaded that she did not want to see Edward, that an encounter would, indeed, be unbearable; yet, aimlessly, she began to walk on. Church-going people returning home with an air of circumspection made a pattering sound in the empty streets. Groups of sparrows flustered and pecked. The day was mildly sunny. The Yard man, detailed to keep observation on Carlisle, threaded his way through a trickle of pedestrians and recalled the Sunday dinners of his boyhood. Beef, he thought, Yorkshire pudding, gravy, and afterwards a heavy hour or so in the front room. Carlisle gave him no trouble at all but he was hungry.

He saw her hesitate at the corner of Coster's Row and himself halted to light a cigarette. She glanced along the file of house fronts and then, at a more rapid pace, crossed the end of the row and continued on her way. At the same time a dark young man came out of a house six doors down Coster's Row and descended the steps in time to catch a glimpse of her. He shouted, "Lisle!" and waved his arm. She hurried on, and once past the corner, out of his sight, broke into a run. "Hi, Lisle!" he shouted.

"Lisle!" and loped after her. The Yard man watched him go by, turn the corner and overtake her. She spun round at the touch of his hand on her arm and they stood face to face.

A third man who had come out from some doorway further up the *cul-de-sac* walked briskly down the path on the same side as the Yard man. They greeted each other like old friends and shook hands. The Yard man offered cigarettes and lit a match.

"How's it going, Bob?" he said softly. "That your bird?"

"That's him. Who's the lady?"

"Mine," said the first, whose back was turned to Carlisle.

"Not bad," his colleague muttered, glancing at her.

"I'd just as soon it was my dinner, though."

"Argument?"

"Looks like it."

"Keeping their voices down."

Their movements were slight and casual: acquaintances pausing for a rather aimless chat.

"What's the betting?" said the first.

"They'll separate. I never have the luck."

"You're wrong, though."

"Going back to his place?"

"Looks like it."

"I'll toss you for it."

"O.K." The other pulled his clenched hand out of his pocket. "Your squeak," he said.

"Heads."

"It's tails."

"I never get the luck."

"I'll ring in then and get something to eat. Relieve you in half an hour, Bob."

They shook hands again heartily as Carlisle and Edward Manx, walking glumly towards them, turned into Coster's Row.

Carlisle had seen Edward Manx out of the corner of her eye as she crossed the end of the *cul-de-sac.* Unreasoned panic took hold of her. She lengthened her stride, made a show of looking at her watch and, when he called her name, broke into a run. Her heart pounded and her mouth was dry. She had the sensation of a fugitive in a dream. She was the pursued and, since even in her sudden alarm she was confusedly aware of something in herself that frightened her, she was also the pursuer. This nightmarish conviction was intensified by the sound of his feet clattering after her and of his voice, completely familiar but angry, calling her to stop.

Her feet were leaden, he was overtaking her quite easily. Her anticipation of his seizing her from behind was so vivid that when his hand actually closed on her arm it was something of a relief. He jerked her round to face him and she was glad to feel angry.

"What the hell do you think you're doing?" he said breathlessly.

"That's my business," she panted, and added defiantly, "I'm late. I'll be late for lunch. Aunt Cile will be furious."

"Don't be an ass, Lisle. You ran when you saw me. You heard me call out and you kept on running. What the devil d'you mean by it?"

His heavy eyebrows were drawn together and his lower lip jutted out.

"Please let me go, Ned," she said. "I really am late."

"That's utterly childish and you know it. I'm getting to the bottom of this. Come back to the flat. I want to talk to you."

"Aunt Cile . . ."

"Oh for God's sake! I'll ring Duke's Gate and say you're lunching here."

"No."

For a moment he looked furious. He still held her arm and his fingers bit into it, hurting her. Then he said more gently: "You can't expect me to let a thing like this pass—it's a monstrous state of affairs. I must know what's gone wrong. Last night, after we got back from the Metronome, I could tell there was something. Please, Lisle. Don't let's stand here snarling at each other. Come back to the flat."

"I'd rather not. Honestly. I know I'm behaving queerly."

He had slipped the palm of his hand inside her arm, pressing it against him. His hand was gentler now but she couldn't escape it. He began to speak persuasively and she remembered how, even when they were children, she had never been able to resist his persuasiveness. "You will, Lisle, won't you? Don't be queer, I can't bear all this peculiarity. Come along."

She looked helplessly at the two men on the opposite corner, thinking vaguely that she had seen one of them before. "I wish I knew him," she thought. "I wish I could stop and speak to him."

They turned into Coster's Row. "There's some food in the flat. It's quite a nice flat. I want you to see it. We'll have lunch together, shan't we? I'm sorry I was churlish, Lisle."

His key clicked in the lock of the blue door. They were in a small lobby. "It's a basement flat," he said, "but not at all bad. There's even a garden. Down those stairs."

"You go first," she said. She actually wondered if that would give her a chance to bolt and if she would have the nerve to do it. He looked fixedly at her.

"I don't believe I trust you," he said lightly. "On you go."

He followed close on her heels down the steep stairs and took her arm again as he reached past her and unlocked the second door. "Here we are," he said, pushing it open. He gave her a little shove forward.

It was a large, low-ceilinged room, whitewashed and oak-beamed. French windows opened on a little yard with potted flowers and plane-trees in tubs. The furniture was modern; steel chairs with rubber-foam upholstery, a carefully planned desk, a divan bed with a scarlet cover. A rigorous still-life hung above the fireplace, the only picture in the room. The bookshelves looked as if they had been stocked completely from a Left Book Shop. It was a scrupulously tidy room.

"The oaken beams are strict stockbroker's Tudor," he was saying. "Completely functionless, of course, and pretty revolting. Otherwise not so bad, do you think? Sit down while I find a drink."

She sat on the divan and only half listened to him. His belated pretence that, after all, this was a pleasant and casual encounter did nothing to reassure her. He was still angry. She took the drink he brought and found her hand was shaking so much she couldn't carry the glass to her lips. The drink spilled. She bent her head down and took a quick gulp at it, hoping this would steady her. She rubbed furtively with her handkerchief at the splashes on the cover and knew, without looking, that he watched her.

"Shall we go in, boots and all, or wait till after lunch?" he said.

"There's nothing to talk about. I'm sorry to be such an ass but after all it was a bit of a night. I suppose murder doesn't suit me."

"Oh, no," he said, "that won't do. You don't bolt like a rabbit at the sight of me because somebody killed a piano-accordionist." And after a long pause, he added, smoothly, "Unless by any chance, you think I killed him. Do you?"

"Don't be a dolt," she said, and by some fortuitous mischance, an accident quite beyond her control and unrelated to any recognizable impulse, her answer sounded unconvincing and too violent. It was the last question she had expected from him.

"Well, at least I'm glad of that," he said. He sat on the table near to her. She did not look up at him but straight before her at his left hand, lying easily across his knee. "Come on," he said, "what have I done? There *is* something I've done. What is it?"

She thought: "I'll have to tell him something—part of it. Not the real thing itself but the other bit that doesn't matter so much." She began to search for an approach, a line to take, some kind of credible presentation, but she was deadly tired and she astonished herself by saying abruptly and loud: "I've found out about G.P.F."

His hand moved swiftly, out of her range of sight. She looked up expecting to be confronted by his anger or astonishment but he had turned aside, skewing round to put his glass down on the table behind him.

"Have you?" he said. "That's awkward, isn't it?" He moved quickly away from her and across the room to a wall cupboard which he opened. With his back turned to her he said: "Who told you? Did Cousin George?"

"No," she said, wearily surprised. "No. I saw the letter."

"Which letter?" he asked, groping in the cupboard.

"The one to Félicité."

"Oh," said Manx slowly. "That one." He turned round. He had a packet of cigarettes in his hand and came towards her holding it out. She shook her head and he lit one himself with steady hands. "How did you come to see it?" he said.

"It was lost. It—I—oh, what *does* it matter! The whole thing was perfectly clear. Need we go on?"

"I still don't see why this discovery should inspire you to sprint like an athlete at the sight of me."

"I don't think I know myself."

"What were you doing last night?" he demanded suddenly. "Where did you go after we got back to Duke's Gate? Why did you turn up again with Alleyn? What were you up to?"

It was impossible to tell him that Félicité had lost the letter. That would lead at once to his discovering that Alleyn had read it: worse than that, it would lead inevitably to the admittance, perhaps the discussion, of his new attitude towards Félicité. "He might," she thought, "tell me, pointblank, that he is in love with Fée and I'm in no shape to jump the hurdle."

So she said: "It doesn't matter what I was up to. I can't tell you. In a way it would be a breach of confidence."

"Was it something to do with this G.P.F. business?" Manx said sharply, and after a pause, "You haven't told anybody about this discovery, have you?"

She hadn't told Alleyn. He had found out for himself. Miserably she shook her head. He stooped over her. "You mustn't tell anybody, Lisle. That's important. You realize how important, don't you?"

Isolated sentences of an indescribable archness flashed up in her memory of that abominable page. "You don't need to tell me that," she said, looking away from his intent and frowning eyes, and suddenly burst out: "It's such ghastly stuff, Ned. That magazine. It's like one of our novelettes gone hay-wire. How you could!"

"My articles are all right," he said, and after a pause: "So that's it, is it. You *are* a purist, aren't you?"

She clasped her hands together and fixed her gaze on them. "I must tell you," she said, "that if, in some hellish, muddled way, entirely beyond my comprehension, this G.P.F. business has anything to do with Rivera's death . . ."

"Well?"

"I mean, if it's going to—I mean—"

"You mean that if Alleyn asks you point-blank about it, you'll tell him?"

"Yes," she said.

"I see."

Carlisle's head ached. She had been unable to face her breakfast and the drink he had given her had taken effect. Their confused antagonism, the sense of being trapped in this alien room, her personal misery: all these circumstances were joined in a haze of uncertainty. The whole scene had become unreal and unendurable. When he put his hands on her shoulders and said loudly: "There's more to it than this. Come on. What is it?" she seemed to hear him from a great distance. His hands were bearing down hard. "I *will* know," he was saying.

At the far end of the room a telephone bell began to ring. She watched him go to it and take the receiver off. His voice changed its quality and became the easy friendly voice she had known for so long.

"Hullo? Hullo, Fée darling. I'm terribly sorry, I should have rung up. They kept Lisle for hours grilling her at the Yard. Yes; I ran into her and she asked me to telephone and say she was so late she'd try for a meal somewhere at hand, so I asked her to have one with me. Please tell Cousin Cécile it's entirely my fault and not hers. I promised to ring for her." He looked at Carlisle over the telephone. "She's perfectly all right," he said. "I'm looking after her."

III

If any painter, a surrealist for choice, attempted to set the figure of a working detective officer against an appropriate and composite background, he would turn his attention to rooms overlaid with films of dust, to objects suspended in unaccustomed dinginess, to ash-trays and tablecloths, unemptied waste bins, tables littered with powder, dirty glasses, disordered chairs, stale food, and garments that retained an unfresh smell of disuse.

When Alleyn and Fox entered the Metronome at twelve-thirty on this Sunday morning, it smelt of Saturday night. The restaurant, serveries and kitchens had been cleaned but the vestibule and offices were untouched and upon them the aftermath of festivity lay like a thin pall of dust. Three men in shirt-sleeves greeted Alleyn with that tinge of gloomy satisfaction which marks an unsuccessful search.

"No luck?" Alleyn said.

"No luck yet, sir."

"There's the passage that runs through from the foyer and behind the offices to the back premises," said Fox. "That's the way the deceased must have gone to make his entrance from the far end of the restaurant."

"We've been along there, Mr. Fox."

"Plumbing?"

"Not yet, Mr. Alleyn."

"I'd try that next." Alleyn pointed through the two open doors of Caesar Bonn's office into the inner room. "Begin there," he said.

He went alone into the restaurant. The table he and Troy had sat at was the second on the right. The chairs were turned up on its surface. He replaced one of them and seated himself. "For twenty years," he thought, "I have trained my memory and trained it rigorously. This is the first time I have been my own witness in a case of this sort. Am I any good or am I rotten?"

Sitting alone there, he re-created his scene, beginning with small things: the white cloth, the objects on the table, Troy's long hand close to his own and just within his orbit of vision. He waited until these details were firm in his memory and then reached out a little further. At the next table, her back towards him, sat Félicité de Suze in a red dress. She turned a white carnation in her fingers and looked sidelong at the man beside her. He was between Alleyn and the lamp on their table. His profile was rimmed with light. His head was turned towards the band dais. On his right, more clearly visible, more brilliantly lit, was Carlisle Wayne. In order to watch the performance she had swung round with her back half-turned to the table. Her hair curved back from her temples. There was a look of compassion and bewilderment in her face. Beyond Carlisle, with her back to the wall, a heavy shape almost obscured by the others, sat

Lady Pastern. As they moved he could see in turn her stony coiffure, her important shoulders, the rigid silhouette of her bust; but never her face.

Raised about them, close to them, a figure gestured wildly among the tympani. This was a vivid picture because it was contained by a pool of light. Lord Pastern's baldish head darted and bobbed. Metallic high lights flashed among his instruments. The spot light shifted and there in the centre of the stage was Rivera, bent backwards, hugging his piano-accordion to his chest. Eyes, teeth, and steel and mother-of-pearl ornament glittered. The arm of the metronome pointed fixedly at his chest. Behind, half-shadowed, a plump hand jerked up and down, beating the air with its miniature baton. A wide smile glistened in a moon face. Now Lord Pastern faced Rivera on the perimeter of the light pool. His revolver pointed at the contorted figure, flashed, and Rivera fell. Then the further shots and comic falls and then . . . In the deserted restaurant Alleyn brought his hands down sharply on the table. It had been then, and not until then, that the lights began their infernal blinking. They popped in and out down the length of the metronome and about its frame, in and out, red green, blue, green red. Then, and not until then, had the arm swung away from the prostrate figure and, with the rest of that winking stuttering bedazzlement, gone into action.

Alleyn got up and mounted the bandstand. He stood on the spot where Rivera had fallen. The skeleton tower of the metronome framed him. The reverse side of this structure revealed its electrical equipment. He looked up at the pointer of the giant arm which was suspended directly above his head. It was a hollow steel or plastic casting studded with miniature lights and for a moment reminded him fantastically of the jewelled dart. To the right of the band-room door and hidden from the audience by the piano, a small switchboard was sunk in the wall. Happy Hart, they had told Alleyn, was in charge of the lights. From where he sat at the piano and from where he fell to the floor he could reach out to the switches. Alleyn did so, now, pulling down the one marked "Motor." A hidden whirring sound prefaced the first loud *clack*. The giant downward-pointing arm swept semicircularly across, back, across and back to its own ratchet-like accompaniment. He switched on the lights and stood for a moment, an incongruous figure, motionless at the core of his kaleidoscopic setting. The point of the arm, flashing its lights, swept within four inches of his head and away and back and away again. "If you watched the damn' thing for long enough I believe it'd mesmerize you," he thought and turned off the switches.

Back in the offices he found Mr. Fox in severe control of two plumbers who were removing their jackets in the lavatory.

"If we can't find anything fishing with wires, Mr. Alleyn," Fox said, "it'll be a case of taking down the whole job."

"I don't hold out ecstatic hopes," Alleyn said, "but get on with it."

One of the plumbers pulled the chain and contemplated the ensuing phenomena.

"Well?" said Fox.

"I wouldn't say she was a sweetly running job," the plumber diagnosed, "and yet again she *works* if you can understand me." He raised a finger, and glanced at his mate.

"Trap trouble?" ventured his mate.

"Ar."

"We'll leave you to it," Alleyn said and withdrew Fox into the office. "Fox," he said, "let's remind ourselves of the key pieces in this jig-saw atrocity. What are they?"

Fox said promptly: "The set-up at Duke's Gate. The drug racket. *Harmony*. The substitution. The piano-accordion. The nature of the weapon."

"Add one more. The metronome was motionless when Rivera played. It started its blasted tick-tack stuff after he fell and after the other rounds had been fired."

"I get you, sir. Yes," said Fox, placidly, "there's that too. Add the metronome."

"Now, let's mug over the rest of the material and see where we are."

Sitting in Caesar Bonn's stale office, they sorted, discarded, correlated and dissociated the fragments of the case. Their voices droned on to the intermittent accompaniment of plumbers' aquatics. After twenty minutes Fox shut his notebook, removed his spectacles and looked steadily at his superior officer.

"It amounts to this," he said. "Setting aside a handful of insignificant details, we're short of only one piece." He poised his hand, palm down, over the table. "If we can lay hold of that and if, when we've got it, it fits —well, our little picture's complete."

"If," Alleyn said, "and when."

The door of the inner office opened and the senior plumber entered. With an air of false modesty he extended a naked arm and bleached hand. On the palm of the hand dripped a revolver. "Would this," he asked glumly, "be what you was wanting?"

IV

Dr. Curtis waited for them outside the main entrance to Breezy flat.

"Sorry to drag you out, Curtis," Alleyn said, "but we may need your opinion about his fitness to make a statement. This is Fox's party. He's the drug baron."

"How do you expect he'll be, Doctor?" Fox asked.

Dr. Curtis stared at his shoes and said guardedly: "Heavy hang-over. Shaky. Depressed. May be resentful. May be placatory. Can't tell."

"Suppose he decides to talk, is it likely to be truthful?"

"Not very. They usually lie."

Fox said: "What's the line to take? Tough or coaxing?"

"Use your own judgement."

"You might tip us the wink, though, Doctor."

"Well," said Curtis, "let's take a look at him."

The flats were of the more dubious modern kind, and brandished chromium steel almost in the Breezy Bellairs Manner—showily and without significance. Alleyn, Fox and Curtis approached the flat by way of a rococo lift and a tunnel-like passage. Fox pressed a bell and a plain-clothes officer answered the door. When he saw them he snibbed back the lock and closed the door behind him.

"How is he?" Alleyn asked.

"Awake, sir. Quiet enough, but restless."

"Said anything?" Fox asked. "To make sense, I mean."

"Nothing much, Mr. Fox. Very worried about the deceased, he seems to be. Says he doesn't know what he's going to do without him."

"*That* makes sense at all events," Fox grunted. "Shall we go in, sir?"

It was an expensive and rather characterless flat, only remarkable for its high content of framed and signed photographs and its considerable disorder. Breezy, wearing a dressing gown of unbelievable sumptuousness, sat in a deep chair into which he seemed to shrink a little further as they came in. His face was the colour of an uncooked fowl and as flabby. As soon as he saw Dr. Curtis he raised a lamentable wail.

"Doc," he whined, "I'm all shot to heaps. Doc, for petesake take a look at me and tell them."

Curtis picked up his wrist.

"Listen," Breezy implored him, "you know a sick man when you see one—listen—"

"Don't talk."

Breezy pulled at his lower lip, blinked at Alleyn and with the inconsequence of a ventriloquist's doll flashed his celebrated smile.

"Excuse us," he said.

Curtis tested his reflexes, turned up his eyelid and looked at his tongue.

"You're a bit of a mess," he said, "but there's no reason why you shouldn't answer any questions these gentlemen like to put to you." He glanced at Fox. "He's quite able to take in the usual warning," he said.

Fox administered it and drew up a chair, facing Breezy, who shot out a quavering finger at Alleyn.

"What's the idea," he said, "shooing this chap on to me? What's wrong with talking to me yourself?"

"Inspector Fox," Alleyn said, "is concerned with investigations about the illicit drug trade. He wants some information from you."

He turned away and Fox went into action.

"Well, now, Mr. Bellairs," Fox said, "I think it's only fair to tell you what we've ascertained so far. Save quite a bit of time, won't it?"

"I can't tell you a thing. I don't know a thing."

"We're aware that you're in the unfortunate position," Fox said, "of having formed the taste for one of these drugs. Gets a real hold on you, doesn't it, that sort of thing?"

Breezy said: "It's only because I'm overworked. Give me a break and I'll cut it out. I swear I will. But gradually. You have to make it gradual. That's right, isn't it, Doc?"

"I believe," Fox said comfortably, "that's the case. That's what I understand. Now, about the supply. We've learnt on good authority that the deceased, in this instance, was the source of supply. Would you care to add anything to that statement, Mr. Bellairs?"

"Was it the old bee told you?" Breezy demanded. "I bet it was the old bee. Or Syd. Syd knew. Syd's had it in for me. Dirty bolshevik! Was it Syd Skelton?"

Fox said that the information had come from more than one source and asked how Lord Pastern knew Rivera had provided the drugs. Breezy replied that Lord Pastern nosed out all sorts of things. He refused to be drawn further.

"I understand," Fox went on, "that his lordship tackled you in the matter last evening."

Breezy at once became hysterical. "He'd ruin me! That's what he'd do. Look! Whatever happens don't let him do it. He's crazy enough to do it. Honest. Honest he is."

"Do what?"

"Like what he said. Write to that bloody paper about me."

"*Harmony?*" Fox asked, at a venture. "Would that be the paper?"

"That's right. He said he knew someone—God, he's got a thing about it. You know—the stuff. Damn and blast him," Breezy screamed out, "he'll kill me. He killed Carlos and now what'll *I* do, where'll I get it? Everybody watching and spying and I don't *know*. Carlos never told me. I don't *know*."

"Never told you?" Fox said peacefully. "Fancy that now! Never let on how he got it! And I bet he made it pretty hot when it came to paying up. Um?"

"God, you're telling *me!*"

"And no reduction made, for instance, if you helped him out?"

Breezy shrank back in his chair. "I don't know anything about that. I don't get you at all."

"Well, I mean to say," Fox explained, "there'd be opportunities, wouldn't there? Ladies, or it might be their partners, asking the band leader for a special number. A note changes hands and it might be a tip or it might be payment in advance, and the goods delivered next time. We've come across instances. I wondered if he got you to oblige him. You don't have to say anything if you don't want to, mind. We've the names and addresses of all the guests last night and we've got our records. People that are known to like it, you know. So I won't press it. Don't let it worry you. But I thought that he might have had some arrangement with you. Out of gratitude as you might put it—"

"Gratitude!" Breezy laughed shrilly. "You think you know too much," he said profoundly, and drew in his breath. He was short of breath and had broken into a sallow profuse sweat. "I don't know what I'll do without Carlos," he whispered. "Someone'll have to help me. It's all the old bee's fault. Him and the girl. If I could just have a smoke—" He appealed to Dr. Curtis. "Not a prick. I know you won't give me a prick. Just one little smoke. I don't usually in the mornings but this is exceptional, Doc. Doc, couldn't you—"

"You'll have to hang on a bit longer," Dr. Curtis said, not unkindly. "Wait a bit. We won't let it go longer than you can manage. Hang on."

Suddenly and inanely Breezy yawned, a face-splitting yawn that bared his gums and showed his coated tongue. He rubbed his arms and neck. "I keep feeling as if there's something under my skin. Worms or something," he said fretfully.

"About the weapon," Fox began. Breezy leant forward, his hands on his knees, aping Fox. "About the weapon?" he mimicked savagely. "You mind your business about the weapon. Coming here tormenting a chap. Whose gun was it? Whose bloody sunshade was it? Whose bloody stepdaughter was it? Whose bloody business is it? Get out!" He threw himself back in the chair, panting. "Get out. I'm within my rights. Get out."

"Why not?" Fox agreed. "We'll leave you to yourself. Unless Mr. Alleyn . . . ?"

"No," Alleyn said.

Dr. Curtis turned at the door. "Who's your doctor, Breezy?" he asked.

"I haven't got a doctor," Breezy whispered. "Nothing ever used to be wrong with me. Not a thing."

"We'll find someone to look after you."

"Can't *you*? Can't you look after me, Doc?"

"Well," Dr. Curtis said. "I might."

"Come on," said Alleyn and they went out.

V

One end of Materfamilias Lane had suffered a bomb and virtually disappeared but the other stood intact, a narrow City street with ancient buildings, a watery smell, dark entries and impenitent charm.

The *Harmony* offices were in a tall building at a corner where Materfamilias Lane dived downhill and a *cul-de-sac* called Journeyman's Steps led off to the right. Both were deserted on this Sunday afternoon. Alleyn's and Fox's feet rang loudly on the pavement as they walked down Materfamilias Lane. Before they reached the corner they came upon Nigel Bathgate standing in the arched entry to a brewer's yard.

"In me," Nigel said, "you see the detective's ready-reckoner and pocket guide to the City."

"I hope you're right. What have you got for us?"

"His room's on the ground floor with the window on this street. The nearest entrance is round the corner. If he's there the door to his office'll be latched on the inside with an 'Engaged' notice displayed. He locks himself in."

"He's there," Alleyn said.

"How d'you know?"

"He's been tailed. Our man rang through from a call box and he should be back on the job by now."

"Up the side street if he's got the gumption," Fox muttered. "Look out, sir!"

"Softly does it," Alleyn murmured.

Nigel found himself neatly removed to the far end of the archway, engulfed in Fox's embrace and withdrawn into a recess. Alleyn seemed to arrive there at the same time.

"'You cry mum and I'll cry budget'!" Alleyn whispered. Someone was walking briskly down Materfamilias Lane. The approaching footsteps echoed in the archway as Edward Manx went by in the sunlight.

They leant motionless against the dark stone and clearly heard the bang of a door.

"Your sleuth-hound," Nigel pointed out with some relish, "would appear to be at fault. Whom, do you suppose, he's been shadowing? Obviously, not Manx."

"Obviously," Alleyn said, and Fox mumbled obscurely.

"Why are we waiting?" Nigel asked fretfully.

"Give him five minutes," Alleyn said. "Let him settle down."

"Am I coming in with you?"

"Do you want to?"

"Certainly. One merely," Nigel said, "rather wishes that one hadn't met him before."

"May be a bit of trouble, you know," Fox speculated.

"Extremely probable," Alleyn agreed.

A bevy of sparrows flustered and squabbled out in the sunny street, an eddy of dust rose inconsequently and somewhere, out of sight, halliards rattled against an untenanted flagpole.

"Dull," Fox said, "doing your beat in the City of a Sunday afternoon. I had six months of it as a young chap. Catch yourself wondering why the blazes you were there and so on."

"Hideous," Alleyn said.

"I used to carry my *Police Code and Procedure* on me and try to memorize six pages a day. I was," Fox said simply, "an ambitious young chap in those days."

Nigel glanced at his watch and lit a cigarette.

The minutes dragged by. A clock struck three and was followed by an untidy conclave of other clocks, overlapping each other. Alleyn walked to the end of the archway and looked up and down Materfamilias Lane.

"We may as well get under way," he said. He glanced again up the street and made a sign with his hand. Fox and Nigel followed him. A man in a dark suit came down the foot-path. Alleyn spoke to him briefly and then led the way to the corner. The man remained in the archway.

They walked quickly by the window, which was uncurtained and had the legend HARMONY painted across it, and turned into the *cul-de-sac.* There was a side door with a brass plate beside it. Alleyn turned the handle and the door opened. Fox and Nigel followed him into a dingy passage which evidently led back into a main corridor. On their right, scarcely discernible in the sudden twilight, was a door. The word ENGAGED painted in white, showed clearly. From beyond it they heard the rattle of a typewriter.

Alleyn knocked. The rattle stopped short and a chair scraped on boards. Someone walked towards the door and a voice, Edward Manx's, said: "Hullo? Who is it?"

"Police," Alleyn said.

In the stillness they looked speculatively at each other. Alleyn poised his knuckles at the door, waited, and said: "May we have a word with you, Mr. Manx?"

After a second's silence the voice said: "One moment. I'll come out."

Alleyn glanced at Fox who moved in beside him. The word ENGAGED shot out of sight noisily and was replaced by PRIVATE G.P.F. A latch clicked and the door opened inwards. Manx stood there with one hand on the jamb and the other on the door. There was a wooden screen behind him.

Fox's boot moved over the threshold.

"I'll come out," Manx repeated.

"On the contrary, we'll come in, if you please," Alleyn said.

Without any particular display of force or even brusqueness, but with great efficiency, they went past him and round the screen. He looked for a second at Nigel and seemed not to recognize him. Then he followed them and Nigel unobtrusively followed him.

There was a green-shaded lamp on a desk at which a figure was seated with its back towards them. As Nigel entered, the swivel-chair creaked and spun around. Dingily dressed and wearing a green eye-shade, Lord Pastern faced them with bunched cheeks.

CHAPTER XII

G.P.F.

I

HE MADE A HIGH-PITCHED snarling noise as they closed round him and reached out his hand towards an inkpot on the desk.

Fox said: "Now, my lord, don't you do anything you'll be sorry for," and moved the inkpot.

Lord Pastern sunk his head with a rapid movement between his shoulders. From behind them, Edward Manx said: "I don't know why you've done this, Alleyn. It'll get you no further."

Lord Pastern said: "Shut up, Ned," and glared at Alleyn. "I'll have you kicked out of the force," he said. "Kicked out, by God!" And after a silence: "You don't get a word from me. Not a syllable."

Alleyn pulled up a chair and sat down, facing him. "That will suit us very well," he said. "You are going to listen, and I advise you to do so with as good a grace as you can muster. When you've heard what I've got to say you may read the statement I've brought with me. You can sign it, alter it, dictate another or refuse to do any of these things. But in the meantime, Lord Pastern, you are going to listen."

Lord Pastern folded his arms tightly across his chest, rested his chin on his tie and screwed up his eyes. Alleyn took a folded typescript from his breast pocket, opened it and crossed his knees.

"This statement was prepared," he said, "on the assumption that you are the man who calls himself G. P. Friend and writes the articles signed G.P.F. in *Harmony*. It is a statement of what we believe to be fact and doesn't concern itself overmuch with motive. I, however, will deal rather more fully with motive. In launching this paper and in writing these articles, you found it necessary to observe complete anonymity. Your reputation as probably the most quarrelsome man in England, your loudly publicized domestic rows, and your notorious eccentricities would make an appearance in the rôle of Guide, Philosopher and Friend a fantastically bad joke. We presume, therefore, that through a reliable agent, you deposited adequate security in a convenient bank with the specimen signature of G. P. Friend as the negotiating instrument. You then set up the legend of your own anonymity and launched yourself in the rôle of oracle. With huge success."

Lord Pastern did not stir but a film of complacency overspread his face.

"This success," Alleyn went on, "it must always be remembered, depends entirely upon the preservation of your anonymity. Once let *Harmony's* devotees learn the G.P.F. is none other than the notoriously unharmonious peer whose public quarrels have been the punctual refuge of the penny-press during the silly season—once let that be known and G.P.F. is sunk, and Lord Pastern loses a fortune. All right. Everything goes along swimmingly. You do a lot of your journalism at Duke's Gate, no doubt, but you also make regular visits to this office wearing dark glasses, the rather shabby hat and scarf which are hanging on the wall there, and the old jacket you have on at this moment. You work behind locked doors and Mr. Edward Manx is possibly your only confidant. You enjoy yourself enormously and make a great deal of money. So, perhaps, in his degree, does Mr. Manx."

Manx said: "I've no shares in the paper if that's what you mean. My articles are paid for at the usual rate."

"Shut up, Ned," said his cousin automatically.

"The paper," Alleyn continued, "is run on eccentric but profitable lines. It explodes bombs. It exposes rackets. It mingles soft-soap and cyanide. In particular it features an extremely efficient and daringly personal attack on the drug racket. It employs experts, it makes accusations, it defies and invites prosecution. Its information is accurate and if it occasionally frustrates its own professed aims by warning criminals before the police are in a position to arrest them, it is far too much inflated with crusader's zeal and rising sales to worry its head about *that.*"

"Look here, Alleyn . . ." Manx began angrily, and simultaneously Lord Pastern shouted: "What the hell do you think you're getting at!"

"One moment," Alleyn said. Manx thrust his hands in his pockets and began to move about the room. "Better to hear this out, after all," he muttered.

"Much better," Alleyn agreed. "I'll go on. Everything prospered in the *Harmony* set-up until you, Lord Pastern, discovered an urge to exploit your talents as a tympanist and allied yourself with Breezy Bellairs and His Boys. Almost immediately there were difficulties. First: your stepdaughter, for whom I think you have a great affection, became attracted by Carlos Rivera, the piano-accordionist in the band. You are an observant man; for a supreme egoist, surprisingly so. At some time of your association with the Boys, I don't know precisely when, you became aware that Breezy Bellairs was taking drugs and, more important, that Carlos Rivera was supplying them. Through your association with *Harmony*, you are well up in the methods of drug distribution and you are far too sharp not to realize that the usual pattern was being followed. Bellairs was in a position to act as a minor distributing agent. He was introduced to the drug, acquired a habit for it, was forced to hand it out to clients at the Metronome and as a reward was given as much as Rivera thought was good for him at the usual exorbitant rate."

Alleyn looked curiously at Lord Pastern, who, at that moment, met his eye and blinked twice.

"It's an odd situation," Alleyn said, "isn't it? Here we have a man of eclectic, violent and short-lived enthusiasms suddenly confronted with a situation where his two reigning passions and his one enduring attachment are brought into violent opposition."

He turned to Manx, who had stopped still and was looking fixedly at him.

"A situation of great possibilities from your professional point of view, I should imagine," Alleyn said. "The stepdaughter whom Lord Pastern loves falls for Rivera who is engaged in an infamous trade which Lord Pastern is zealous in fighting. At the same time Rivera's dupe is the conductor of the band in which Lord Pastern burns to perform. As a final twist in an already tricky situation, Rivera has discovered, perhaps amongst Lord Pastern's music during a band rehearsal, some rough drafts for G.P.F.'s page, typed on Duke's Gate letter-paper. He is using them, no doubt, to force on his engagement to Miss de Suze. 'Either support my suit or—' For Rivera, in addition to running a drug racket, is an accomplished blackmailer. How is Lord Pastern to play the drums, break the engagement, preserve his anonymity as G.P.F. and explode the drug racket?"

"You can't possibly," Manx said, "have proof of a quarter of this. It's the most brazen guesswork."

"A certain amount of guesswork. But we have enough information and hard fact to carry us some way. I think that between you, you are going to fill out the rest."

Manx laughed shortly. "What a hope!" he said.

"Well," Alleyn murmured, "let us go on and see. Lord Pastern's inspiration comes out of a clear sky while he is working on his copy of G.P.F.'s page in *Harmony*. Among the letters in his basket seeking guidance, philosophy and friendship is one from his stepdaughter." He stopped short. "I wonder," he said, "if at some time or other there is also one from his wife? Asking perhaps for advice in her marital problems."

Manx looked quickly at Lord Pastern and away again.

"It might explain," Alleyn said thoughtfully, "why Lady Pastern is so vehement in her disapproval of *Harmony*. If she *did* write to G.P.F., I imagine the answer was one of the five-shilling Private Chat letters and extremely displeasing to her."

Lord Pastern gave a short bark of laughter and shot a glance at his cousin.

"However," Alleyn went on, "we are concerned, at this point, with the fact that Miss de Suze does write for guidance. Out of this coincidence, an idea is born. He answers the letter. She replies. The correspondence goes on, becoming, as Miss de Suze put it to me, more and more come-to-ish. Lord Pastern is an adept. He stages (again I quote Miss de Suze) a sort of Cupid-and-Psyche act at one remove. She asks if they may meet. He replies ardently but refuses. He has all the fun of watching her throughout in his own character. Meanwhile he appears to Rivera to be supporting his suit. But the ice gets thinner and thinner and his figure-skating increasingly hazardous. Moreover, here he is with a golden opportunity for a major journalistic scoop. He could expose Bellairs, represent himself as a brilliant investigator who has worked on his own in the band and now hands the whole story over to *Harmony*. And yet—and yet—there are those captivating drums, those entrancing cymbals, those stimulating wire whisks. There is his own composition. There is his début. He skates on precariously but with exhilaration. He fiddles with the idea of weaning Bellairs from his vice and frightens him into fits by threatening to supplant Syd Skelton. He—"

"Did you," Lord Pastern interrupted, "go to that police school or whatever it is? Hendon?"

"No," Alleyn said. "I didn't."

"Well, get on, get on," he snapped.

"We come to the night of the début and of the great inspiration. Lady Pastern quite obviously desires a marriage between her daughter and Mr. Edward Manx."

Manx made an expostulatory sound. Alleyn waited for a moment. "Look here, Alleyn," Manx said, "you can at least observe some kind of decency. I object most strongly—" He glared at Nigel Bathgate.

"I'm afraid you'll have to lump it," Alleyn said mildly. Nigel said: "I'm sorry, Manx. I'll clear out if you like, but I'll hear it all, in any case."

Manx turned on his heel, walked over to the window and stood there with his back to them.

"Lord Pastern," Alleyn continued, "seems to have shared this hope. And now, having built up a spurious but ardent mystery round G.P.F., he gets his big idea. Perhaps he notices Mr. Manx's instant dislike of Rivera and perhaps he supposes this dislike to arise from an attachment to his stepdaughter. At all events he sees Mr. Manx put a white carnation in his coat, he goes off to his study and he types a romantic note to Miss de Suze in which G.P.F. reveals himself as the wearer of a white carnation. The note swears her to secrecy. Miss de Suze, coming straight from a violent quarrel with Rivera, sees the white flower in Mr. Manx's jacket and reacts according to plan."

Manx said, "Oh, my *God!*" and drummed with his fingers on the window-pane.

"The one thing that seems to have escaped Lord Pastern's notice," Alleyn said, "is the fact that Mr. Manx is enormously attracted, not by Miss de Suze, but by Miss Carlisle Wayne."

"Hell!" said Lord Pastern sharply and slewed round in his swivel-chair. "Hi!" he shouted. "Ned."

"For pity's sake," Manx said impatiently, "let's forget it. It couldn't matter less." He caught his breath. "In the context," he added.

Lord Pastern contemplated his cousin's back with extreme severity and then directed his attention once more upon Alleyn. "Well?" he said.

"Well," Alleyn repeated, "so much for the great inspiration. But your activity hasn't exhausted itself. There is a scene with Bellairs in the ballroom, overheard by your footman and in part related to me by the wretched Breezy himself. During this scene you suggest yourself as a successor to Syd Skelton, and tick Bellairs off about his drug habit. You go so far, I think, as to talk about writing to *Harmony*. The idea, at this stage, would appear to be a comprehensive one. You will frighten Breezy into giving up cocaine, expose Rivera and keep on with the band. It was during this interview that you behaved in a rather strange manner. You unscrewed the end section of Lady Pastern's parasol, removed the knob and absent-mindedly pushed the bit of shaft a little way up the muzzle of your revolver, holding down the spring clip as you did so. You found that it fitted like a miniature ram-rod or bolt. Or, if you like, a rifle grenade."

"*I* told you that meself."

"Exactly. Your policy throughout has been to pile up evidence against yourself. A sane man, and we are presuming you sane, doesn't do that sort of thing unless he believes he has an extra trick or two in hand, some conclusive bits of evidence that must clear him. It was obvious that you thought you could produce some such evidence and you took great glee in exhibiting the devastating frankness of complete innocence. Another form of figure-skating on thin ice. You would let us blunder about making clowns of ourselves, and, when the sport palled or the ice began to crack, you would, if you'll excuse the mixed metaphor, plank down the extra tricks."

A web of thread-like veins started out on Lord Pastern's blanched cheek-bones. He brushed up his moustache and, finding his hand shook, looked quickly at it and thrust it inside the breast of his coat.

"It seemed best," Alleyn said, "to let you go your own gait and see how far it would take you. You wanted us to believe that Mr. Manx was G.P.F.; there was nothing to be gained, we thought, and there might be something lost in letting you see we recognized the equal possibility of your being G.P.F. yourself. This became a probability when the drafts of copy turned up amongst Rivera's blackmailing material. Because Rivera had never met Manx but was closely associated with you."

Alleyn glanced up at his colleague. "It was Inspector Fox," he said, "who first pointed out that you had every chance, during the performance, while the spot light was on somebody else, to load the revolver with the fantastic bolt. All right. But there remained your first trump card—the substituted weapon; the apparently irrefutable evidence that the gun we recovered from Breezy was not the one you brought down to the Metronome. But when we found the original weapon in the lavatory beyond the inner office that difficulty, too, fell into place in the general design. We had got as far as abundant motive and damning circumstance. Opportunity began to appear."

Alleyn stood up and with him Lord Pastern, who pointed a quivering finger at him.

"You bloody fool!" he said, drawing his lips back from his teeth. "You can't arrest me—you—"

"I believe I could arrest you," Alleyn rejoined, "but not for murder. Your second trump card is unfortunately valid. You didn't kill Rivera because Rivera was not killed by the revolver."

He looked at Manx. "And now," he said, "we come to you."

II

Edward Manx turned from the window and walked towards Alleyn with his hands in his pockets. "All right," he said. "You come to me. What have you nosed out about me?"

"This and that," Alleyn rejoined. "On the face of it there's the evidence that you quarrelled with Rivera and clipped him over the ear. Nosing, as you would put it, beneath the surface, there's your association with *Harmony*. You, and perhaps you alone, knew that Lord Pastern was G.P.F. If he told you Rivera was blackmailing him—"

"He didn't tell me."

"—and if, in addition, you knew Rivera was a drug merchant—" Alleyn waited for a moment but Manx said nothing—"why then, remembering your expressed loathing of this abominable trade, something very like a motive began to appear."

"Oh, nonsense," Manx said lightly. "I don't go about devising quaint deaths for everyone I happen to think a cad or a bad lot."

"One never knows. There have been cases. And you could have changed the revolvers."

"You've just told us that he wasn't killed by the revolver."

"Nevertheless the substitution was made by his murderer."

Manx laughed acidly. "I give up," he said and threw out his hands. "Get on with it."

"The weapon that killed Rivera couldn't have been fired from the revolver because at the time Lord Pastern pulled the trigger, Rivera had his piano-accordion across his chest and the piano-accordion is uninjured."

"I could have told you that," said Lord Pastern, rallying.

"It was a patently bogus affair, in any case. How, for instance, could Lord Pastern be sure of shooting Rivera with such a footling tool? A stiletto in the end of a bit of stick? If he missed by a fraction of an inch Rivera might not die instantly and might not die at all. No. You have to be sure of getting the right spot and getting it good and proper, with a bare bodkin."

Manx lit a cigarette with unsteady hands. "Then in that case I can't for the life of me see—" he stopped—"whodunit," he said, "and how."

"Since it's obvious Rivera wasn't hurt when he fell," Alleyn said, "he was stabbed after he fell."

"But he wasn't meant to fall. They'd altered the routine. We've had that till we're sick of the sound of it."

"It will be our contention that Rivera did not know that the routine had been altered."

"Bosh!" Lord Pastern shouted so unexpectedly that they all jumped. "He wanted it changed. I didn't. It was Carlos wanted it."

"We'll take that point a bit later," Alleyn said. "We're considering how, and when, he was killed. Do you remember the timing of the giant metronome? It was motionless, wasn't it, right up to the moment when Rivera fell; motionless and pointing straight down at him. As he leant backwards its steel tip was poised rather menacingly, straight at his heart."

"Oh, for pity's sake!" Manx said disgustedly. "Are you going to tell us somebody dropped the bolt out of the metronome?"

"No. I'm trying to dismiss the fancy touches, not add to them. Immediately after Rivera fell, the arm of the metronome went into action. Coloured lights winked and popped in and out along its entire surface and that of the surrounding tower frame. It swung to and fro with a rhythmic clack. The whole effect, of course carefully planned, was dazzling and unexpected. One's attention was drawn away from the prostrate figure and what actually happened during the next ten seconds or so was quite lost on the audience. To distract attention still further from the central figure, a spot light played on the tympani where Lord Pastern could be seen in terrific action. But what seemed to happen during those ten confusing seconds?"

He waited again and then said: "Of course you remember, both of you. A waiter threw Breezy a comic wreath of flowers. He knelt down and, pretending to weep, using his handkerchief, opened Rivera's coat and felt for his heart. He felt for his heart."

III

Lord Pastern said: "You're wrong, Alleyn, you're wrong. I searched him. I'll swear he had nothing on him then and I'll swear he didn't get a chance to pick anything up. Where the devil was the weapon? You're wrong. I searched him."

"As he intended you to do. Yes. Did you notice his baton while you searched him?"

"I told you, damn it. He held it above his head. Good God!" Lord Pastern added, and again, "Good God!"

"A short black rod. The pointed steel was held in his palm, protected by the cork out of an empty gun-oil bottle in your desk. Fox reminded me this morning of Poe's story *The Purloined Letter*. Show a thing boldly to unsuspecting observers and they will think it's what they expect it to be. Breezy conducted your programme last night with a piece of parasol handle and a stiletto. You saw the steel mounting glinting as usual at the tip of an ebony rod. The stiletto was concealed in his palm. It really was quite like his baton. Probably that gave him the idea when he handled the dismembered parasol in the ballroom. I think you asked him, didn't you, to put it together."

"Why the hell," Lord Pastern demanded, "didn't you tell us this straight away? Tormentin' people. It's a damn' scandal. I'll take you up on this, Alleyn, by God I will."

"Did you," Alleyn asked mildly, "go out of your way to confide in us? Or did you willfully and dangerously play a silly lone hand? I think I may be forgiven, sir, for giving you a taste of your own tactics. I wish I could believe it had shaken you a bit: but that, I'm afraid, is too much to hope for." Lord Pastern swore extensively, but Manx said, with a grin: "You know, Cousin George, I rather think we bought it. We've hindered the police in the execution of their duty."

"Serve 'em damn well right."

"I'm still sceptical," Manx said. "Where's your motive? Why should he kill the man who supplied him with his dope?"

"One of the servants at Duke's Gate overheard a quarrel between Bellairs and Rivera when they were together in the ballroom. Breezy asked Rivera for cigarettes—drugged cigarettes, of course—and Rivera refused to give him any. He intimated that their association was ended and talked about writing to *Harmony*. Fox will tell you that sort of thing's quite a common gambit when these people fall out."

"Oh, yes," Fox said. "They do it, you know. Rivera would have a cast-iron story ready to protect himself and get in first with the information. We'd pick Breezy up and be no further on. We might suspect Rivera but we wouldn't get on to anything. Not a thing."

"Because," Lord Pastern pointed out, "you're too thick-headed to get your man when he's screamin' for arrest under your great noses. That's why. Where's your initiative? Where's your push and drive? Why can't you—" he gestured wildly—"stir things up? Make a dust?"

"Well, my lord," said Fox placidly, "we can safely leave that kind of thing to papers like *Harmony*, can't we?"

Manx muttered: "But to kill him—no, I can't see it. And to think all that nonsense up in an hour—"

"He's a drug addict," Alleyn said. "He's been drawing near the end of his tether for some time, I fancy, with Rivera looming up bigger and bigger as his evil genius. It's a common characteristic for the addict to develop an intense hatred of the purveyor upon whom he is so slavishly dependent. This person becomes a sort of Mephistopheles-symbol for the addict. When the purveyor is also a blackmailer and, for good measure, in a position where he can terrify his victim by threats of withdrawal, you get an excruciating twist to the screw. I fancy the picture of you, Lord Pastern, firing pointblank at Rivera had begun to fascinate Bellairs long before he saw you fit the section into the barrel of the gun. I believe he had already played with the idea of fooling round with the ammunition. You added fuel to his fire."

"That be damned—" Lord Pastern began to shout, but Alleyn went on steadily.

"Breezy," he said, "was in an ugly state. He was frantic for cocaine, nervous about his show, terrified of what Lord Pastern would do. Don't forget, sir, you, too, had threatened him with exposure. He planned for a right-and-left coup. You were to hang, you know, for the murder. He has always had a passion for practical jokes."

Manx gave a snort of nervous laughter. Lord Pastern said nothing.

"But," Alleyn went on, "it was all too technicolour to be credible. His red herrings were more like red whales. The whole set-up has the characteristic unreason and fantastic logic of the addict. A Coleridge creates Kubla Khan but a Breezy Bellairs creates a surrealistic dagger made of a parasol handle and a needlework stiletto. An Edgar Allan Poe writes 'The Pit and the Pendulum' but a Breezy Bellairs steals a revolver and makes little scratches in the muzzle with the stiletto; he smokes it with a candle-end and puts it in his overcoat pocket. Stung to an intolerable activity by his unsatisfied lust for cocaine he plans grotesquely but with frantic precision. He may crack at any moment, lose interest or break down, but for a crucial period he goes to work like a demon. Everything falls into place. He tells the band, but *not* Rivera, that the other routine will be followed. Rivera has gone to the end of the restaurant to make his entrance. He persuades Skelton to look at Lord Pastern's revolver at the last minute. He causes himself to be searched, holding his dagger over his head, trembling with strangled laughter. He conducts. He kills. He finds Rivera's heart, and with his hands protected by a handkerchief and hidden from the audience by a comic wreath, he digs his stiletto in and grinds it round.

He shows distress. He goes to the room where the body lies and shows greater distress. He changes the carefully scarred revolver in his overcoat pocket with the one Lord Pastern fired. He goes into the lavatory and makes loud retching noises while he disposes of Lord Pastern's unscarred gun. He returns and, being now at the end of his course, frantically searches the body and probably finds the dope he needs so badly. He collapses. That, as we see it, is the case against Breezy Bellairs."

"Poor dope," Manx said. "If you're right."

"Poor dope. Oh, yes," Alleyn said. "Poor dope."

Nigel Bathgate murmured: "Nobody else could have done it."

Lord Pastern glared at him but said nothing.

"Nobody," Fox said.

"But you'll never get a conviction, Alleyn."

"That," Alleyn said, "may be. It won't ruin our lives if we don't."

"How young," Lord Pastern demanded suddenly, "does a feller have to be to get into detection?"

"If you'll excuse me, Alleyn," Edward Manx said hurriedly, "I think I'll be off."

"Where are you goin', Ned?"

"To see Lisle, Cousin George. We lunched," he explained, "at cross-purposes. I thought she meant she knew it was you. I thought she meant the letter was the one Fée got from *Harmony*. But I see now: she thought it was me."

"What the hell are you talkin' about?"

"It doesn't matter. Good-bye."

"Hi, wait a minute. I'll come with you." They went out into the deserted sunlight, Lord Pastern locking the door behind him.

"I'll be off too, Alleyn," said Nigel as they stood watching the two figures, one lean and loose-jointed, the other stocky and dapper, walk briskly away up Materfamilias Lane. "Unless—what are you going to do?"

"Have you got the warrant, Fox?"

"Yes, Mr. Alleyn."

"Come on, then."

"The Judges' Rules," Fox said, "may be enlightened but there are times when they give you the pip. I suppose you don't agree with that, Mr. Alleyn."

"They keep you and me in our place, Br'er Fox, and I fancy that's a good thing."

"If we could confront him," Fox burst out. "If we could break him down."

"Under pressure he might make a hysterical confession. It might not be true. That would appear to be the idea behind the Judges' Rules."

Fox muttered unprintably.

Nigel Bathgate said: "Where are we heading?"

"We'll call on him," Alleyn grunted. "And with any luck we'll find he already has a visitor. Caesar Bonn of the Metronome."

"How d'you know?"

"Information received," said Fox. "He made an arrangement over the telephone."

"And so, what do you do about it?"

"We pull Bellairs in, Mr. Bathgate, for receiving and distributing drugs."

"Fox," said Alleyn, "thinks there's a case against him. Through the customers."

"Once he's inside," Fox speculated dismally, "he *may* talk. In spite of the Usual Caution. Judges' Rules!"

"He's a glutton for limelight," Alleyn said unexpectedly.

"So what?" Nigel demanded.

"Nothing. I don't know. He may break out somewhere. Here we go."

It was rather dark in the tunnel-like passage that led to Breezy's flat. Nobody was about but a plain-clothes man on duty at the far end: a black figure against a mean window. Walking silently on the heavy carpet, they came up to him. He made a movement of his head, murmured something that ended with the phrase, "hammer and tongs."

"Good," Alleyn said and nodded. The man stealthily opened the door into Breezy's flat.

They moved into an entrance lobby where they found a second man with a notebook pressed against the wall and a pencil poised over it. The four silent men almost filled the cramped lobby.

In the living-room beyond, Caesar Bonn was quarrelling with Breezy Bellairs.

"Publicity!" Caesar was saying. "But of what a character! No, no! I am sorry. I regret this with all my heart. For me as for you it is a disaster."

"Listen, Caesar, you're all wrong. My public won't let me down. They'd *want* to see me." The voice rose steeply. "They *love* me," Breezy cried out, and after a pause: "You bloody swine, they *love* me."

"I must go."

"All right. You'll see. I'll ring Carmarelli. Carmarelli's been trying to get me for years. Or the Lotus Tree. They'll be fighting for me. And your bloody clientele'll follow me. They'll eat us. I'll ring Stein. There's not a restaurateur in town—"

"One moment," Caesar was closer to the door. "To spare you discomfiture I feel I must warn you. Already I have discussed this matter with these gentlemen. An informal meeting. We are all agreed. It will not be possible for you to appear at any first-class restaurant or club."

They heard a falsetto whining. Caesar's voice intervened. "Believe me," he said, "when I say I mean this kindly. After all, we are old friends. Take my advice. Retire. You can afford to do so, no doubt." He gave a nervous giggle. Breezy had whispered. Evidently they were close together on the other side of the door. "No, no!" Caesar said loudly. "I can do nothing about it. Nothing! Nothing!"

Breezy screamed out abruptly: "I'll ruin you!" and the pencil skidded across the plain-clothes officer's notebook.

"You have ruined yourself," Caesar gabbled. "You will keep silence. Understand me: there must be complete silence. For you there is no more spot light. You are finished. *Keep off!*" There was a scuffle, and a stifled ejaculation. Something thudded heavily against the door and slid down its surface. "There, now!" Caesar panted. He sounded scandalized and breathlessly triumphant. Unexpectedly, after a brief pause, he went on in a reflective voice: "No, truly, you are too stupid. This decides me. I am resolved. I inform the police of your activities. You will make a foolish appearance in court. Everyone will laugh a little and forget you. You will go to gaol or perhaps to a clinic. If you are of good behaviour you may, in a year or so, be permitted to conduct a little band."

"*Christ!* Tell them, then! Tell them!" Beyond the door Breezy stumbled to his feet. His voice broke into falsetto. "But it's me that'll tell the tale, me! If I go to the dock, by God, I'll wipe the grins off all your bloody faces. You haven't heard anything yet. Try any funny business with ME! Finished! By God, I've only just started. You're all going to hear how I slit up a bloody Dago's heart for him."

"This is it," Alleyn said, and opened the door.

DEATH AND THE DANCING FOOTMAN

Contents

Cast of Characters

Jonathan Royal, of Highfold Manor, Cloudyfold, Dorset
Caper, his butler
Aubrey Mandrake, born Stanley Footling, Poetic Dramatist
Sandra Compline, of Penfelton Manor
William Compline, her elder son
Nicholas Compline, her younger son
Chloris Wynne, William's fiancée
Dr. Francis Hart, a plastic surgeon
Madame Elise Lisse, beauty specialist, of the Studio Lisse
Lady Hersey Amblington, Jonathan's distant cousin, beauty specialist of the Salon Hersey
Thomas, a dancing footman
Mrs. Pouting, Jonathan's housekeeper
James Bewling, an outside hand at Highfold
Thomas Bewling, his brother
Roderick Alleyn, Chief Detective-Inspector, C.I., New Scotland Yard
Agatha Troy Alleyn, his wife
Walter Copeland, Rector of Winton St. Giles
Dinah Copeland, his daughter
Fox, Detective-Inspector, C.I., New Scotland Yard
Detective-Sergeant Thompson, a photographic expert
Detective-Sergeant Bailey, a finger-print expert
A housemaid
Superintendent Blandish, of the Great Chipping Constabulary

CHAPTER I

Project

I

ON THE AFTERNOON of a Thursday early in 1940 Jonathan Royal sat in his library at Highfold Manor. Although daylight was almost gone, curtains were not yet drawn across the windows, and Jonathan Royal could see the ghosts of trees moving in agitation against torn clouds and a dim sequence of fading hills. The north wind, blowing strongly across an upland known as Cloudyfold, was only partly turned by Highfold woods. It soughed about the weathered corners of the old house and fumbled in the chimneys. A branch, heavy with snow, tapped vaguely at one of the library windows. Jonathan Royal sat motionless beside his fire. Half of his chubby face and figure flickered in and out of shadow, and when a log fell in two and set up a brighter blaze, it showed that Jonathan was faintly smiling. Presently he stirred slightly and beat his plump hands lightly upon his knees, a discreetly ecstatic gesture. A door opened admitting a flood of yellow light, not very brilliant, and a figure that paused with its hand on the door-knob.

"Hullo," said Jonathan Royal. "That you, Caper?"

"Yes, sir."

"Lighting-up time?"

"Five o'clock, sir. It's a dark afternoon."

"Ah," said Jonathan, suddenly rubbing his hands together, "that's the stuff to give the troops."

"I beg your pardon, sir?"

"That's the stuff to give the troops, Caper. An expression borrowed from a former cataclysm. I did not intend you to take it literally. It's the stuff to give my particular little troop. You may draw the curtains."

Caper adjusted Jonathan's patent black-out screens and drew the curtains. Jonathan stretched out a hand and switched on a table lamp at his elbow. Fire and lamplight were now reflected in the glass doors that protected his books, in the dark surfaces of his desk, in his leather saddle-back chairs, in his own spectacles, and in the dome of his bald pate. With a quick movement he brought his hands together on his belly and began to revolve his thumbs one over the other, sleekly.

"Mr. Mandrake rang up, sir, from Winton St. Giles Rectory. He will be here at 5:30."

"Good," said Jonathan.

"Will you take tea now, sir, or wait for Mr. Mandrake?"

"Now. He'll have had it. Has the mail come?"

"Yes, sir. I was just—"

"Well, let's have it," said Jonathan eagerly. "Let's have it."

When the butler had gone, Jonathan gave himself a little secret hug with his elbows and, continuing to revolve his thumbs, broke into a thin falsetto, singing:—

"Il était une bergère,
Qui ron-ton-ton, petit pat-a-plan."

He moved his big head from side to side, in time with his tune and, owing to a trick of the firelight on his thick-lensed glasses, he seemed to have large white eyes that gleamed like those of the dead drummer in the Ingoldsby Legends. Caper returned with his letters. He snatched them up and turned them over with deft pernickety movements and at last uttered a little ejaculation. Five letters were set aside and the sixth opened and unfolded. He held it level with his nose but almost at arm's length. It contained only six lines of writing, but they seemed to give Jonathan the greatest satisfaction. He tossed the letter gaily on the fire and took up the thin tenor of his song. Ten minutes later when Caper brought in his tea he was still singing but he interrupted himself to say:—

"Mr. Nicholas Compline is definitely coming tomorrow. He may have the green visitors' room. Tell Mrs. Pouting, will you?"

"Yes, sir. Excuse me, sir, but that makes eight guests for the week-end?"

"Yes. Yes, eight." Jonathan ticked them off on his plump fingers. "Mrs. Compline. Mr. Nicholas and Mr. William Compline. Dr. Francis Hart. Madame Lisse. Miss Wynne. Lady Hersey Amblington, and Mr. Mandrake. Eight. Mr. Mandrake tonight, the rest for dinner tomorrow. We'll have the Heidsieck '28 tomorrow, Caper, and the Courvoisier."

"Very good, sir."

"I am particularly anxious about the dinner tomorrow, Caper. Much depends upon it. There must be a warmth, a feeling of festivity, of anticipation, of—I go so far—of positive luxury. Large fires in the bedrooms. I've ordered flowers. Your department, now. Always very satisfactory, don't think there's an implied criticism, but tomorrow—" He opened his arms wide—"Whoosh! Something quite extra. Know what I mean? I've told Mrs. Pouting. She's got everything going, I know. But your department . . . Ginger up that new feller and the maids. Follow me?"

"Certainly, sir."

"Yes. The party—" Jonathan paused, hugged his sides with his elbows and uttered a thin cackle of laughter. "The party may be a little sticky at first. I regard it as an experiment."

"I hope everything will be quite satisfactory, sir."

"Quite satisfactory," Jonathan repeated. "Yes. Sure of it. Is that a car? Have a look."

Jonathan turned off his table lamp. Caper went to the windows and drew aside their heavy curtains. The sound of wind and sleet filled the room.

"It's difficult to say, sir, with the noise outside, but—yes, sir, there are the head-lamps. I fancy it's coming up the inner drive, sir."

"Mr. Mandrake, no doubt. Show him in here, and you can take away these tea things. Too excited for 'em. Here he is."

Caper closed the curtains and went out with the tea things. Jonathan switched on his lamp. He heard the new footman cross the hall and open the great front door.

"It's beginning," thought Jonathan, hugging himself. "This is the overture. We're off."

II

Mr. Aubrey Mandrake was a poetic dramatist and his real name was Stanley Footling. He was in the habit of telling himself, for he was not without humour, that if it had been a little worse—if, for instance, it had been Albert Muggins—he would have clung to it, for there would have been a kind of distinction in such a name. Seeing it set out in the programme, under the title of his "Saxophone in Tarlatan," the public would have enclosed it in mental inverted commas. But they would not perform this delicate imaginary feat for a Stanley Footling. So he became Aubrey Mandrake, influenced in his choice by such names as Sebastian Melmoth, Aubrey Beardsley, and Peter Warlock. In changing his name he had given himself a curious psychological set-back, for in a short time he grew to identify himself so closely with his new name that the memory of the old one became intolerable, and the barest suspicion that some new acquaintance had discovered his origin threw him into a state of acute uneasiness, made still more unendurable by the circumstance of his despising himself bitterly for this weakness. At first his works had chimed with his name, for he wrote of Sin and the Occult, but, as his by no means inconsiderable talent developed, he found his subject in matters at once stranger and less colourful. He wrote, in lines of incalculable variety, of the passion of a pattern-cutter for a headless bust, of a saxophonist who could not perform to his full ability unless his instrument was decked out in tarlatan frills, of a lavatory attendant who became a gentleman of the bed-chamber (this piece was performed only by the smaller experimental theatre clubs) and of a chartered accountant who turned out to be a reincarnation of Thais. He was successful. The post-surrealists wrangled over him, the highest critics discovering in his verse a revitalizing influence on an effete language, and the Philistines were able to enjoy the fun. He was the possessor of a comfortable private income derived from his mother's boarding-house in Dulwich and the fruit of his father's ingenuity—a patent suspender-clip. In appearance he was tall, dark, and suitably cadaverous; in manner, somewhat sardonic; in his mode of dressing, correct, for he had long since passed the stage when unusual cravats and strange shirts seemed to be a necessity for his æsthetic development. He was lame, and extremely sensitive about the deformed foot which caused this disability. He wore a heavy boot on his left foot and always tried as far as possible to hide it under the chair on which he was sitting. His acquaintance with Jonathan Royal was some five years old. Late in the nineteen-thirties, Jonathan had backed one of Mandrake's plays; and though it had not made a fortune for either of them it had unexpectedly paid its way and had established their liking for one another. Mandrake's latest play, "Bad Black-out" (finished since the outbreak of war but, as far as the uninstructed could judge, and in spite of its title, not about the war), was soon to go into rehearsal with an untried company of young enthusiasts. He had spent two days at the Winton St. Giles Rectory with his leading lady and her father, and Jonathan had asked him to come on to Highfold for the week-end.

His entrance into Jonathan's library was effective, for he had motored over Cloudyfold bare-headed with the driving window open, and the north wind had tossed his hair into elf-locks. He usually did the tossing himself.

He advanced upon Jonathan with his hand outstretched, and an air of gay hardihood.

"An incredible night," he said. "Harpies and warlocks abroad. Most stimulating."

"I trust," said Jonathan, shaking his hand and blinking up at him, "that it hasn't stimulated your Muse. I cannot allow her to claim you this evening, Aubrey."

"Oh God!" said Mandrake. He always made this ejaculation when invited to speak of his writing. It seemed to imply desperate æsthetic pangs.

"Because," Jonathan continued, "I intend to claim your full attention, my dear Aubrey. Our customary positions are reversed. For to-night—yes, and for to-morrow and the next day—I shall be the creator, and you the audience." Mandrake darted an apprehensive glance at his host.

"No, no, no," Jonathan cried, steering him to the fireside, "don't look so alarmed. I've written no painful middle-age *belles-lettres,* nor do I contemplate my memoirs. Nothing of the sort."

Mandrake sat opposite his host by the fire. Jonathan rubbed his hands together and suddenly hugged them between his knees. "Nothing of the sort," he repeated.

"You look very demure," said Mandrake. "What are you plotting?"

"Plotting! That's the word! My dear, I am up to my ears in conspiracy!" He leant forward and tapped Mandrake on the knee. "Come now," said Jonathan, "tell me this. What do you think are my interests?"

Mandrake looked fixedly at him. "Your *interests?*" he repeated.

"Yes. What sort of fellow do you think I am? It is not only women, you know, who are interested in the impressions they make on their friends. Or *is* there something unexpectedly feminine in my curiosity? Never mind. Indulge me so far. Come, now."

"You skip from one query to another. Your interests, I should hazard, lie between your books, your estate, and—well—I imagine you are interested in what journalists are pleased to call human contacts."

"Good," said Jonathan. "Excellent. Human contacts. Go on."

"As for the sort of fellow you may be," Mandrake continued, "upon my word, I don't know. From my point of view a very pleasant fellow. You understand things, the things that seem to me to be important. You have never asked me, for instance, why I don't write about real people. I regard that avoidance as conclusive."

"Would you say, now, that I had a sense of the dramatic?"

"What is the dramatic? Is it merely a sense of theatre, or is it an appreciation of æsthetic climax in the extroverted sense?"

"I don't know what that means," said Jonathan impatiently. "And I'm dashed if I think you do."

"Words," said Mandrake. "Words, words, words." But he looked rather put out.

"Well, damn it, it doesn't matter two ha'p'th of pins. I maintain that I have a sense of drama in the ordinary unclassy sense. My sense of drama, whether you like it or not, attracts me to your own work. I don't say I understand it, but for me it's got *something*. It jerks me out of my ordinary reactions to ordinary theatrical experiences. So I like it."

"That's as good a reason as most."

"All right. But wait a bit. In me, my dear Aubrey, you see the unsatisfied and inarticulate artist. Temperament and no art. That's me. Or so I thought, until I got my Idea. I've tried writing and I've tried painting. The results have on the whole been pitiable—at the best negligible. Music—out of the question. And all the time, here I was, an elderly fogey plagued with the desire to create. Most of all have I hankered after drama, and at first I thought my association with you, a delightful affair from my point of view, I assure you, would do the trick; I would taste, at second hand as it were, the pleasures of creative art. But no, the itch persisted and I was in danger of becoming a disgruntled restless fellow, a nuisance to myself, and a bore to other people."

"Never that," murmured Mandrake, lighting a cigarette.

"It would have been the next stage, I assure you. It threatened. And then, in what I cannot but consider an inspired moment, my dear Aubrey, I got my Idea."

With a crisp movement Jonathan seized his glasses by their nose-piece and plucked them from his face. His eyes were black and extremely bright.

"My Idea," he repeated. "One Wednesday morning four weeks ago, as I was staring out of my window here and wondering how the devil I should spend the day, it suddenly came to me. It came to me that if I was a ninny with ink and paper, and brush and canvas, and all the rest of it, if I couldn't express so much as a how-d'ye-do with a stave of music, there was one medium that I had never tried."

"And what could that wonderful medium be?"

"Flesh and blood."

"What!"

"Flesh and blood!"

"You are *not*—" said Mandrake—"I implore you to say you are *not* going in for social welfare."

"Wait a bit. It came to me that human beings could, with a little judicious arrangement, be as carefully 'composed' as the figures in a picture. One had only to restrict them a little, confine them within the decent boundaries of a suitable canvas, and they would make a pattern. It seemed to me that given the limitations of an imposed stage, some of my acquaintances would at once begin to unfold an exciting drama; that, so restricted, their conversation would begin to follow as enthralling a design as that of a fugue. Of course the right—how shall I put it?—the right ingredients must be selected, and this was where I came in. I would set my palette with human colours, and the picture would paint itself. I would summon my characters to the theatre of my own house, and the drama would unfold itself."

"Pirandello," Mandrake began, "has become quite—"

"But this is *not* Pirandello," Jonathan interrupted in a great hurry. "No. In this instance we shall see not six characters in search of an author, but an author who has deliberately summoned seven characters to do his work for him."

"Then you mean to write, after all."

"Not I. I merely select. As for writing," said Jonathan, "that's where you come in. I make you a present of what I cannot but feel is a golden opportunity."

Mandrake stirred uneasily. "I wish I knew what you were up to," he said.

"My dear fellow, I'm telling you. Listen. A month ago I decided to make this experiment. I decided to invite seven suitably chosen characters for a winter week-end here at Highfold, and I spent a perfectly delightful morning compiling the list. My characters must, I decided, be as far as possible antagonistic to each other."

"Oh God!"

"Not antagonistic each one to the other seven, but there must at least be some sort of emotional or intellectual tension running like a connecting thread between them. Now, a very little thought showed me that I had not far to seek. Here, in my own corner of Dorset, here in the village and county undercurrents, still running high in spite of the war, I found my seven characters. And since I must have an audience, and an intelligent audience, I invited an eighth guest—yourself."

"If you expect me to break into a pæan of enraptured gratitude—"

"Not just yet, perhaps. Patience. Now, in order to savour the full bouquet of the experiment, you must be made happily familiar with the *dramatis personæ*. And to that end," said Jonathan cosily, "I propose that we ring for sherry."

III

"I propose," said Jonathan, filling his companion's glass, "to abandon similes drawn from painting or music and to stick to a figure that we can both appreciate. I shall introduce my characters in terms of dramatic art, and, as far as I can guess, in the order of their appearance. You look a little anxious."

"Then my looks," Mandrake rejoined, "do scant justice to my feelings. I feel terrified."

Jonathan uttered his little cackle of laughter. "Who can tell?" he said. "You may have good cause. You shall judge of that when I have finished. The first characters to make their unconscious entrances on our stage are a mother and two sons. Mrs. Sandra Compline, William Compline, and Nicholas Compline. The lady is a widow and lives at Penfelton, a charming house some four miles to the western side of Cloudyfold village. She is the *grande dame* of our cast. The Complines are an old Dorset family and have been neighbours of ours for many generations. Her husband was my own contemporary. A rackety handsome fellow, he was, more popular perhaps with women than with men, but he had his own set in London and a very fast set I fancy it was. I don't know where he met his wife, but I'm afraid it was an ill-omened encounter for her, poor thing. She was a pretty creature and I suppose he fell in love with her looks. His attachment didn't last as long as her beauty, and that faded pretty fast under the sort of treatment she had to put up with. When they'd been married about eight years and had these two sons, a ghastly thing happened to Sandra Compline. She went to stay abroad somewhere and, I suppose with the idea of winning him back, she had something done to her face. It was more than twenty years ago and I daresay these fellows weren't as good at their job as they are nowadays. Lord knows what the chap she consulted did with Sandra Compline's face. I've heard it said (you may imagine how people talked) that he bolstered it up with wax and that the wax slipped. Whatever happened, it was quite disastrous. Poor thing," said Jonathan, shaking his head while the lamplight glinted on his glasses, "she was a most distressing sight. Quite lopsided, you know, and worst of all there was a sort of comical look. For a long time she wouldn't go out or receive anyone. He began to ask his own friends to Penfelton, and a very dubious lot they were. We saw nothing of the Complines in those days, but local gossip was terrific. She used to hunt, wearing a thick veil and going so recklessly that people said she wanted to kill herself. Ironically, though, it was her husband who came a cropper. Fell with his horse and broke his neck. What d'you think of that?"

"Eh?" said Mandrake, rather startled by this sudden demand. "Why, my dear Jonathan, it's quite marvelous. Devastatingly Edwardian. Gloriously county! Another instance of truth being much more theatrical than fiction, and a warning to all dramatists to avoid it."

"Well, well," said Jonathan. "I daresay. Let's get on. Sandra was left with her two small sons, William and Nicholas. After a little she seemed to take heart of grace. She began to go about a bit; this house was the first she visited. The boys had their friends for the holidays, and all that, and life became more normal over at Penfelton. The elder boy, William, was a quiet sort of chap, rather plain on the whole, not a great deal to say for himself; grave, humdrum fellow. Well enough liked, but the type that—Well, you can never remember whether he was, or was not, at a party. That sort of fellow, do you know?"

"Poor William," said Mandrake unexpectedly.

"What? Oh yes, yes, but I haven't quite conveyed William to you. The truth is," said Jonathan, rubbing his nose, "that William's a bit of a teaser. He's devoted to his mother. I think he remembers her as she was before the tragedy. He was seven when she came back and I've heard that although he was strangely self-possessed when he saw her, he was found by their old nurse in a sort of hysterical frenzy, remarkable in such a really rather commonplace small boy. He *is* quiet and humdrum, certainly, but for all that there's something not quite—Well, he's a little *odd.* He's usually rather silent but when he does talk his statements are inclined to be unexpected. He seems to say more or less the first thing that comes into his head and that's a sufficiently unusual trait, you'll agree."

"Yes."

"Yes. Odd. Nothing wrong, really, of course, and he's done very well so far in this war. He's a good lad. But sometimes I wonder . . . However, you shall judge of William for yourself. I want you to do that."

"You don't really like him, do you?" asked Mandrake suddenly.

Jonathan blinked. "What can have put that notion into your head?" he said mildly. He darted a glance at Mandrake. "You mustn't become *too* subtle, Aubrey. William is merely rather difficult to describe. That is all. But Nicholas!" Jonathan continued, "Nicholas was his father over again. Damned good-looking young blade, with charm and gaiety and dash and all the rest of it. Complete egoist, bit of a showman, and born with an eye for a lovely lady. So they grew up, and so they are to-day. William's thirty-two and Nick's twenty-nine. William (I stress this point) is concentrated upon his mother, morbidly so, I think, but that's by the way. Gives up his holidays for no better reason than that she's going to be alone. Watches after her like an old Nanny. He's on leave just now, and of course rushed home to her. Nick's the opposite, plays her up for all she's worth, never lets her know when he's coming or what he's up to. Uses Penfelton like a hotel and his mother like the proprietress. You can guess which of these boys is the mother's favourite."

"Nicholas," said Mandrake. "Of course, Nicholas."

"Of course," said Jonathan, and if he felt any disappointment he did not show it. "She dotes on Nicholas and takes William for granted. She's spoilt Nicholas quite hopelessly from the day he was born. William went off to prep-school and Eton; Nick, if you please, was pronounced delicate, and led a series of tutors a fine dance until his mother decided he was old enough for the Grand Tour and sent him off with a bear-leader like some young Regency lordling. If she could have cut William out of the entail I promise you she'd have done it. As it is she can do nothing. William comes in for the whole packet, and Nick, like the hero of Victorian romance, must fend for himself. This, I believe, his mother fiercely resents. When war came, she moved heaven and earth to find a safe job for Nicholas and took it in her stride when William's regiment went to the front. Nick has got some departmental job in Great Chipping. Looks very smart in uniform, and his duties seem to take him up to London pretty often. William, at the moment, as I have told you, is spending his leave with his Mama. The brothers haven't met for some time."

"Do they get on well?"

"No. Remember the necessary element of antagonism, Aubrey. It appears, splendidly to the fore, in the Compline family. William is engaged to Nicholas' ex-fiancée."

"Really? Well done, William."

"I need scarcely tell you that the lady is the next of my characters, the ingénue in fact. She will arrive with William and his Mama, who detests her."

"Honestly, my dear Jonathan—"

"She is a Miss Chloris Wynne. One of the white-haired kind."

"A platinum blonde?"

"The colour of a light Chablis, and done up in plaster-like sausages. She resembles the chorus of my youth. I'm told that nowadays the chorus looks like the county. I find her appearance startling and her conversation difficult, but I have watched her with interest and I have formed the opinion that she is a very neat example of the woman scorned."

"Did Nicholas scorn her?"

"Nicholas wished to marry her, but being in the habit of eating his cake in enormous mouthfuls, and keeping it, he did not allow his engagement to Miss Chloris to cramp his style as an accomplished philanderer. He continued to philander with the fifth item in our cast of characters—Madame Lisse."

"Oh God!"

"More in anger than in sorrow, if Sandra Compline is to be believed, Miss Chloris broke off her engagement to Nicholas. After an interval so short that one suspects she acted on the ricochet, she accepted William who had previously courted her and been cut out by his brother. My private opinion is that when William returns to the front, Nicholas is quite capable of recapturing the lady, and what's more I think she and William both know it. Nicholas and William had quarrelled in the best tradition of rival brothers and, as I say, have not met since the second engagement. I need not tell you that Mrs. Compline and William and his betrothed do not know I have invited Nicholas, nor does Nicholas know I have invited them. He knows, however, that Madame Lisse will be here. That, of course, is why he has accepted."

"Go on," said Mandrake, driving his fingers through his hair.

"Madame Lisse, the ambiguous and alluring woman of our cast, is an Austrian beauty specialist. I don't suppose Lisse is her real name. She was among the earliest of the refugees, obtained naturalization papers, and established a salon at Great Chipping. She had letters to the Jerninghams at Pen Cuckoo, and to one or two other people in the county. Dinah Copeland at the rectory rather took her up. So, as you have gathered, did Nicholas Compline. She is markedly a dasher. Dark auburn hair, magnolia complexion, and eyes—whew! Very quiet and composed, but undoubtedly a dasher. Everybody got rather excited about Madame Lisse—everybody, that is, with the exception of my distant cousin Lady Hersey Amblington, who will arrive for dinner tomorrow evening."

The spectacles glinted in Mandrake's direction but he merely waved his hands.

"Hersey," said Jonathan, "as you may know, is also a beauty specialist. She took it up when her husband died and left her almost penniless. She did the thing thoroughly and, being a courageous and capable creature, made a success of it. The mysteries of what I believe is called 'beauty culture' are as a sealed book to me but I understand that all the best complexions and coiffures of Great Chipping and the surrounding districts were, until the arrival of Madame Lisse, Hersey's particular property. Madame Lisse immediately began to knock spots out of Hersey. Not, as Hersey explained, that she now has fewer customers, but that they are not quite so smart. The smart clientele has, with the exception of a faithful few, gone over to the enemy. Hersey considers that Madame used unscrupulous methods and always alludes to her as 'the Pirate.' You haven't met my distant cousin, Hersey?"

"No."

"No. She has her own somewhat direct methods of warfare, and I understand that she called on Madame Lisse with the intention of giving her fits. I'm afraid Hersey came off rather the worse in this encounter. Hersey is an old friend of the Complines and, as you may imagine, was not at all delighted by Nicholas' attentions to her rival. So you see she is linked up in an extremely satisfactory manner to both sides. I have really been extraordinarily fortunate," said Jonathan, rubbing his hands. "Nothing could be neater. And Dr. Hart fills out the cast to perfection. The 'heavy,' I think, is the professional term for his part."

"Dr. . . . ?"

"Hart. The seventh and last character. He, too, is of foreign extraction, though he became a naturalized Briton sometime after the last war. I fancy he is a Viennese, though whether I deduce this conclusion subconsciously from his profession I cannot tell you." Jonathan chuckled again and finished his sherry.

"What, in heaven's name, is his profession?"

"My dear Aubrey," said Jonathan, "he is a plastic surgeon. A beauty specialist *par excellence*. The male of the species."

IV

"It seems to me," said Mandrake, "that you have invited stark murder to your house. Frankly, I can imagine nothing more terrifying than the prospect of this week-end. What do you propose to do with them?"

"Let them enact their drama."

"It will more probably resemble some disastrous vaudeville show."

"With myself as *compère*. Quite possibly."

"My dear Jonathan, you will have no performance. The actors will either sulk in their dressing-rooms or leave the theatre."

"That is where we come in."

"We! I assure you—"

"It is where I come in, then. May I, without exhibiting too much complacency, claim that if I have a talent it lies in the direction of hospitality?"

"Certainly. You are a wonderful host."

"Thank you," said Jonathan, beaming at his guest. "It delights me to hear you say so. Now, in this party, I have set myself, I freely admit, a stiff task."

"I'm glad you realize it," said Mandrake. "The list of opposites is positively ghastly. I don't know if I have altogether followed you, but it appears that you hope to reconcile a rejected lover both to his successor and to his late love; a business woman to her detested rival; a ruined beauty to an exponent of the profession that made an effigy of her face, and a mother to a prospective daughter-in-law who has rejected her favourite son for his brother."

"There is another permutation that you have not yet heard. Local gossip rings with rumours of some secret understanding between Dr. Hart and Madame Lisse. It appears that Madame recommends Dr. Hart's surgery to those of her clients who have passed the stage when Lisse creams and all the rest of it can improve their aging faces."

"A business arrangement."

"Something more than that if Hersey—a prejudiced witness, certainly—is to be believed. Hersey's spies tell her that Dr. Hart has been observed leaving Madame Lisse's flat at a most compromising hour; that he presented to an exciting degree the mien of a clandestine lover, his hat drawn over his brows, his cloak (he wears a cloak) pulled about his face. They say that he has been observed to scowl most formidably at the mention of Nicholas Compline."

"Oh, no," said Mandrake, "it's really a little too much. I boggle at the cloak."

"It's a Tyrolean cloak with a hood, a most useful garment. Rain-proof. He has presented me with one. I wear it frequently. You shall see it tomorrow."

"What's he like, this face-lifter?"

"A smoothish fellow. I find him amusing. He plays very good bridge."

"We are *not* going to play bridge?"

"No. No; that, I feel, would be asking for trouble. We *are* going to play a round game, however."

"Oh God!"

"You will enjoy it. A stimulating game. I hope that it will go far towards burying our little armoury of hatchets. Imagine what fun, Aubrey, if on Monday morning they all go gaily away, full of the milk of human kindness."

"You're seeing yourself in the detestable role of uplifter. I've got it! This is not Pirandello, nor is it vaudeville. Far from it. But it *is*," cried Mandrake with an air of intense disgust, "it *is* 'The Passing of the Third Floor Back.' "

Jonathan rose and stood warming his hands at the fire. He was a small man, very upright, with a long trunk and short legs. Mandrake, staring at him, wondered if it was some trick of firelight that lent a faintly malicious tinge to Jonathan's smile; if it was merely his thick-lensed glasses that gave him that air of uncanny blankness.

"Ah, well," said Jonathan, "a peacemaker. Why not? You would like to see your room, Aubrey. The blue room, as usual, of course. It is no longer raining. I propose to take a look at the night before going up to change. Will you accompany me?"

"Very well."

They went out, crossing a wide hall to the entrance. The wind had fallen and, as Jonathan opened his great outer doors, the quiet of an upland county at dusk entered the house and the smell of earth, still only lightly covered with snow. They walked out on the wide platform in front of Highfold. Far beneath them Cloudyfold village showed dimly through tree-tops and beyond it the few scattered houses down in the Vale, four miles away. In the southern skies the stars were out, but northward above Cloudyfold Top there was a well of blackness. And as Jonathan and his guest turned towards the north they received the sensation of an icy hand laid on their faces.

"That's a deathly cold air," said Mandrake.

"It's from the north," said Jonathan, "and still smells of snow. Splendid! Let us go in."

CHAPTER II

Assembly

I

ON THE FOLLOWING DAY Mandrake observed his host to be in a high state of excitement. In spite of his finicky mannerisms and his somewhat old-maidish pedantry, it would never have occurred to his worst enemy to call Jonathan effeminate. Nevertheless he had many small talents that are unusual in a man. He took a passionate interest in the appointments of his house. He arranged flowers to perfection and on the arrival of three boxes from a florist in Great Chipping, darted at them like a delighted ant. Mandrake was sent to the Highfold glass-houses for tuberoses and gardenias. Jonathan, looking odd in one of his housekeeper's aprons, buried himself in the flower-room. He intended, he said, to reproduce bouquets from the French prints in the boudoir. Mandrake, whose floral tastes ran austerely to dead flowers, limped off to the library and thought about his new play, which was to represent twelve aspects of one character, all speaking together.

The morning was still and extremely cold. During the night there had been another light fall of snow. The sky was leaden and the countryside seemed to wait ominously for some portent from the north. Jonathan remarked several times, and with extraordinary glee, that they were in for a severe storm. Fires were lit in all the guest rooms and from the Highfold chimneys rose columns of smoke, lighter in tone than the clouds they seemed to support. Somewhere up on Cloudyfold a farmer was moving his sheep and the drowsy sound of their slow progress seemed uncannily near. So dark was the sky that the passage of the hours was seen only in a stealthy alteration of shadows. Jonathan and Mandrake lunched by lamp-light. Mandrake said that he felt the house to be alive with anticipation, but whether of a storm without or within he was unable to decide. "It's a grisly day," said Mandrake.

"I shall telephone Sandra Compline and suggest that she bring her party for tea," said Jonathan. "It will begin to snow again before six o'clock, I believe. What do you think of the house, Aubrey? How does it feel?"

"Expectant and luxurious."

"Good. Excellent. You have finished? Let us make a little tour of the rooms, shall we? Dear me, it's a long time since I looked forward so much to a party."

They made their tour. In the great drawing-room, seldom used by Jonathan, cedar-wood fires blazed at each end. Mrs. Pouting and two maids put glazed French covers on the armchairs and the *bergère* sofas.

"Summer-time uniforms," said Jonathan, "but they chime with the flowers and are gay. Admire my flowers, Aubrey. Don't they look pleasant against the linen-fold walls? Quite a tone-poem, I consider."

"And when seven furious faces are added," said Mandrake, "the harmony will be complete."

"You can't frighten me. The faces will be all smiles in less than no time, you may depend on it. And, after all, even if they are not to be reconciled, I shall not complain. My play will be less pretty but more exciting."

"Aren't you afraid that they will simply refuse to stay under the same roof with each other?"

"They will at least stay tonight; and tomorrow, I hope, will be so inclement that the weather alone will turn the balance."

"Your courage is amazing. Suppose they all sulk in separate rooms?"

"They won't. I won't let 'em. Confess now, Aubrey, aren't you a little amused, a little stimulated?"

Mandrake grinned. "I feel all the more disagreeable sensations of first-night nerves, but—all right, I'll admit to a violent interest."

Jonathan laughed delightedly and took his arm. "You must see the bedrooms and the 'boudoir' and the little smoking-room. I've allowed myself some rather childish touches but they may amuse you. Elementary symbolism. Character as expressed by vegetation. As the florists' advertisements would have it, I have 'said it with flowers.' "

"Said what?"

"What I think of everyone."

They crossed the hall to the left of the front door and entered the room that Jonathan liked to call the "boudoir"—an Adam sitting-room painted a light green and hung with French brocades, whose pert garlands were repeated in nosegays which Jonathan had set in the window, and upon a spinet and a writing-desk.

"Here," said Jonathan, "I hope the ladies will foregather to write, gossip and knit. Miss Chloris, I should explain, is a W.R.E.N., not yet called up, but filling the interim with an endless succession of indomitable socks. My distant cousin Hersey is also a vigorous knitter. I feel sure poor Sandra is hard at work on some repellent comfort."

"And Madame Lisse?"

"The picture of Madame in close co-operation with strands of khaki wool is one which could be envisaged only by a surrealist. No doubt you will find yourself able to encompass it. Come along."

The "boudoir" opened into the small smoking-room, where Jonathan permitted a telephone and a radio set, but which, he explained, had in other respects remained unaltered since his father died. Here were leather chairs, a collection of sporting prints flanked by a collection of weapons and by fading groups of Jonathan and his Cambridge friends in the curious photographic postures of the nineties. Above the mantelpiece hung a trout-rod, complete with cast and fly.

"Sweet-scented tobacco plants, you see," said Jonathan, "in pots. A trifle obvious, but I couldn't resist them. Now the library."

The library opened out of the smoking-room. It had an air of being the most used room in the house, and indeed it was here that Jonathan could generally be found amid a company of books that bore witness to generations of rather freakish taste and to the money by which such taste could be gratified. Jonathan had added lavishly to the collection. His books ranged oddly from translations of Turkish and Persian verse to the works of the most inscrutable of the moderns and text-books on criminology and police detection. He had a magpie taste in reading, but it was steadied by a constancy of devotion to the Elizabethans.

"Here," he said, "I was troubled by an embarrassment of riches. A Shakespearian nosegay seemed a little *vieux jeu,* but on the other hand it had the advantage of being easily recognized. I was tempted by Leigh Hunt's conceit of 'saying all one feels and thinks in clever daffodils and pinks; in puns of tulips and in phrases, charming for their truth, of daisies.' Unfortunately the glass-houses were not equal to Leigh Hunt in midwinter, but here, you see, is the great Doctor's ensign of supreme command, the myrtle; and here, after all, is most of poor Ophelia's rather dreary little collection. The sombre note predominates. But upstairs I have let myself go again. A riot of snowdrops for Chloris (you take the allusion to William Stone's charming conceit?), tuberoses and even some orchids for Madame Lisse, and so on."

"And for Mrs. Compline?"

"A delightful arrangement of immortelles."

"Aren't you rather cruel?"

"Dear me, I don't think so," said Jonathan, with a curious glance at his guest. "I hope you admire the really superb cactus on your window-sill, Aubrey. John Nash might pause before it, I believe, and begin to plan some wonderful arrangement of greys and elusive greens. And now I must telephone to Sandra Compline and after that to Dr. Hart. I am making the bold move of suggesting he drive Madame Lisse. Hersey has her own car. Will you excuse me?"

"One moment. What flowers have you put in your own room?"

"Honesty," said Jonathan.

II

Mrs. Compline, her son William, and his fiancée Chloris Wynne, arrived by car at four o'clock. Mandrake discovered himself to be in almost as high a state of excitement as his host. He was unable to decide whether Jonathan's party would prove to be disastrous, amusing, or merely a bore, but the anticipation, at least, was enthralling. He had formed a very precise mental picture of each of the guests. William Compline, he decided, would present the most interesting subject-matter. The exaggerated filial devotion, hinted at by Jonathan, brought him into the sphere of Mandrake's literary interest. And muttering "mother-fixation" to himself, he wondered if indeed he should find in William the starting point for a new dramatic poem. Poetically, Mrs. Compline's disfigurement might best be conveyed by a terrible mask, seen in the background of William's spoken thoughts. "Perhaps in the final scene," thought Mandrake, "I should let them turn into the semblance of animals. Or would that be a little banal?" For not the least of a modern poetic dramatist's problems lies in the distressing truth that where all is strange nothing escapes the imputation of banality. But in William Compline with his dullish appearance, his devotion to his mother, his dubious triumph over his brother, Mandrake hoped to find matter for his art. He was actually picturing an opening scene in which William, standing between his mother and his fiancée, appeared against a sky composed of cubes of greenish light, when the drawing-room door opened and Caper announced them.

They were, of course, less striking than the images that had grown so rapidly in Mandrake's imagination. He had seen Mrs. Compline as a figure in a sombre robe, and here she was in Harris tweeds. He had envisaged a black cowl, and he saw a countrified hat with a trout-fly in the band. But her face, less fantastic than his image, was perhaps more distressing. It looked as if its maker had given it two or three vicious tweaks. Her eyes, large and lack-lustre, retained something of their original beauty, her nose was short and straight, but the left corner of her mouth dropped and her left cheek fell into a sort of pocket, so that she looked as though she had hurriedly stowed a large mouthful into one side of her face. She had the exaggeratedly dolorous expression of a clown. As Jonathan had told him, there was a cruelly comic look. When Jonathan introduced them, Mandrake was illogically surprised at her composure. She had a cold, dry voice.

Miss Chloris Wynne was about twenty-three, and very, very pretty. Her light gold hair was pulled back from her forehead and moulded into cusps, so rigidly placed that they might have been made of any material rather than hair. Her eyes were wide apart and beautifully made-up, her mouth was large and scarlet, and her skin flawless. She was rather tall, and moved in a leisurely fashion, looking gravely about her. She was followed by William Compline.

In William, Mandrake saw what he had hoped to see—the commonplace faintly touched by a hint of something that was disturbing. He was in uniform and looked perfectly tidy but not quite smart. He was fair and should have been good-looking, but the lines of his features were blunted and missed distinction. He was like an unsuccessful drawing of a fine subject. There was an air of uneasiness about him and he had not been long in the room before Mandrake saw that whenever he turned to look at his fiancée, which was very often, he first darted a glance at his mother, who never returned it. Mrs. Compline talked easily and with the air of an old friend to Jonathan, who continually drew the others into their conversation. Jonathan was in grand form. "A nice start," thought Mandrake, "with plenty in reserve." And he turned to Miss Wynne with the uneasy feeling that she had said something directly to him.

". . . I didn't in the least understand it, of course," Miss Wynne was saying, "but it completely unnerved me and that's always rather fun."

"Ah," thought Mandrake, "one of my plays."

"Of course," Miss Wynne continued, "I don't know if you were thinking, when you wrote it, what I was thinking when I saw it; but if you were, I'm surprised you got past the Lord Chamberlain."

"The Lord Chamberlain," said Mandrake, "is afraid of me and for a similar reason. He doesn't know whether it's my dirty mind or his, so he says nothing."

"Ah," cried Jonathan, "is Miss Wynne a devotee, Aubrey?"

"A devotee of what?" asked Mrs. Compline in her exhausted voice.

"Of Aubrey's plays. The Unicorn is to reopen with Aubrey's new play in March, Sandra, if all goes well. You must come to the first night. It's called 'Bad Black-out' and is enormously exciting."

"A war play?" asked Mrs. Compline. It was a question that for some reason infuriated Mandrake, but he answered with alarming politeness that it was not a war play but an experiment in two-dimensional formulism. Mrs. Compline looked at him blankly and turned to Jonathan.

"What does that mean?" asked William. He stared at Mandrake with an expression of offended incredulity. "Two-dimensional? That means flat, doesn't it?"

Mandrake heard Miss Wynne give an impatient sigh and guessed at a certain persistency in William.

"Does it mean that the characters will be sort of unphotographic?" she asked.

"Exactly."

"Yes," said William heavily, "but *two-dimensional*. I don't quite see—"

Mandrake felt a terrible apprehension of boredom but Jonathan cut in neatly with an amusing account of his own apprenticeship as an audience to modern drama, and William listened with his mouth not quite closed and an anxious expression in his eyes. When the others laughed at Jonathan's facetiæ, William looked baffled. Mandrake could see him forming with his lips the offending syllables "two-dimensional."

"I suppose," he said suddenly, "it's not what you say but the way you say it that you think matters. Do your plays have plots?"

"They have themes."

"What's the difference?"

"My darling old Bill," said Miss Wynne, "you mustn't browbeat famous authors."

William turned to her and his smile made him almost handsome. "Mustn't you?" he said. "But if you do a thing, you like talking about it. I like talking about the things I do. I mean the things I did before there was a war."

It suddenly occurred to Mandrake that he did not know what William's occupation was. "What do you do?" he asked.

"Well," said William, astonishingly, "I paint pictures."

Mrs. Compline marched firmly into the conversation. "William," she said, "has Penfelton to look after in peacetime. At present, of course, we have our old bailiff, who manages very well. My younger son, Nicholas, is a soldier. Have you heard, Jonathan, that he did *not* pass his medical for active service? It was a very bitter blow to him. At the moment he is stationed at Great Chipping but he longs so much to be with his regiment in France. Of *course,*" she added. And Mandrake saw her glance at the built-up shoe on his club-foot.

"But you're on leave from the front, aren't you?" he asked William.

"Oh, yes," said William.

"My son Nicholas—" Mrs. Compline became quite animated as she spoke of Nicholas. She talked about him at great length, and Mandrake wondered if he only imagined there was a sort of defiance in her insistence on this awkward theme. He saw that Miss Wynne had turned pink and William crimson. Jonathan drew the spate of maternal eulogy upon himself. Mandrake asked Miss Wynne and William if they thought it was going to snow again, and all three walked over to the long windows to look at darkening hills and vale. Naked trees half lost their form in that fading light and rose from the earth as if they were its breath, already frozen.

"Rather menacing," said Mandrake, "isn't it?"

"Menacing?" William repeated. "It's very beautiful. All black and white and grey. I don't believe in seeing colour into things. One should paint them the first colour they seem when one looks at them. Yes, I suppose it is what you'd call menacing. Black and grey and white."

"What is your medium?" Mandrake asked, and wondered why everybody looked uncomfortable when William spoke of his painting.

"*Very* thick oil paint," said William gravely.

"Do you know Agatha Troy?"

"I know her pictures, of course."

"She and her husband are staying with the Copelands at Winton St. Giles near Little Chipping. I came on from there. She's painting the Rector."

"Do you mean Roderick Alleyn?" asked Miss Wynne. "Isn't he her husband? How exciting to be in a house-party with the handsome Inspector. What's he like?"

"Oh," said Mandrake, "quite agreeable."

They had turned away from the windows but a sound from outside drew them back again. Only the last turn of the drive as it came out of the Highfold woods could be seen from the drawing-room windows.

"That's a car," said William. "It sounds like—" He stopped short.

"Is anyone else coming?" asked Miss Wynne sharply, and caught her breath.

She and William stared through the windows. A long and powerful-looking open car, painted white, was streaking up the last rise in the drive.

"But," stammered William, very red in the face, "that's—that's—"

"Ah!" said Jonathan from behind them. "Didn't you know? A pleasant surprise for you. Nicholas is to be one of our party."

III

Nicholas Compline was an extremely striking version of his brother. In figure, height, and colouring they were alike. Their features were not dissimilar, but the suggestion of fumbled drawing in William was absent in Nicholas. William was clean-shaven but Nicholas wore a fine blond moustache. Nicholas had a presence. His uniform became him almost too well. He glittered a little. His breeches were superb. His face was not unlike a less dissipated version of the best-known portrait of Charles II, though the lines from nose to mouth were not so dominant, and the pouches under the eyes had only just begun to form.

His entrance into the drawing-room at Highfold must have been a test of his assurance. Undoubtedly it was dramatic. He came in, smiling, missed his brother and Miss Wynne, who were still in the window, shook hands with Jonathan, was introduced to Mandrake, and, on seeing his mother, looked surprised but greeted her charmingly. Jonathan, who had him by the elbow, turned him towards the windows.

There was no difficult silence because Jonathan talked briskly but there was, to a degree, a feeling of tension. For a moment Mandrake wondered if Nicholas Compline would turn on his heel and walk out, but after checking, with Jonathan's hand still at his elbow, he merely stood stock-still and looked from William to Chloris Wynne. His face was as pale as his brother's was red and there was a kind of startled sneer about his lips. It was Miss Wynne who saved the situation. She unclenched her hands and gave Nicholas a coster's salute, touching her forehead and spreading out her palm towards him. Mandrake guessed that this serio-comic gesture was foreign to her, and applauded her courage.

"Oi," said Miss Wynne.

"Oi, oi," said Nicholas, and returned her salute. He looked at William and said in a flat voice, "Quite a family party."

His mother held out her hand to him. He moved swiftly towards her and sat on the arm of her chair. Mandrake saw adoration in her eyes and mentally rubbed his hands together. "The mother-fixation," he thought, "is *not* going to let me down." And he began to warn himself against the influence of Eugene O'Neill. William and his Chloris remained in the window. Jonathan, after a bird-like glance at them, embarked on a comfortable three-cornered chat with Mrs. Compline and Nicholas. Mandrake, sitting in the shadow, found himself free to watch the lovers, and again he gloated. At first William and Chloris stared out through the windows and spoke in undertones. She pointed to something outside, but Mandrake felt certain the gesture was a bluff and that they were discussing hurriedly the arrival of Nicholas. Presently he observed a small incident that he thought curious and illuminating. It was a sort of dumb show, an interplay of looks subdued to the exigencies of polite behaviour, a quartette of glances. William had turned from the window and was staring at his mother. She had been talking with an air that almost approached gaiety to Nicholas. She looked into his face and a smile, painful in its intensity, lifted the drooping corners of her mouth. Nicholas' laugh was louder than the conversation seemed to warrant and Mandrake saw that he was looking over his mother's head full at Chloris Wynne. Mandrake read a certain insolence in this open-eyed direct stare of Nicholas. He turned to see how the lady took it and found that she returned it with interest. They looked steadfastly and inimically into each other's eyes. Nicholas laughed again and William, as if warned by this sound, turned from his sombre contemplation of his mother and stared first at Nicholas and then at Miss Wynne. Neither of them paid the smallest attention to him but Mandrake thought that Nicholas was very well aware of his brother. He thought Nicholas, in some way that was clearly perceived by the other two, was deliberately baiting William. Jonathan's voice broke across this little pantomime.

". . . a long time," Jonathan was saying, "since I treated myself to one of my own parties, and I don't mind confessing that I look forward enormously to this one."

Miss Wynne joined the group round the fire and William followed her.

"Is this the party?" she asked, "or are we only the beginning?"

"The most important beginning, Miss Chloris, without which the end would be nothing."

"Who else have you got, Jonathan?" asked Nicholas, with his eyes still on Miss Wynne.

"Well, now, I don't know that I shall tell you, Nick. Or shall I? It's always rather fun, don't you think," Jonathan said, turning his glance towards Mrs. Compline, "to let people meet without giving them any preconceived ideas about each other? However, you know one of my guests so well that it doesn't matter if I anticipate her arrival. Hersey Amblington."

"Old Hersey's coming, is she?" said Nicholas, and he looked a little disconcerted.

"Don't be too ruthless with your adjectives, Nick," said Jonathan mildly. "Hersey is ten years my junior."

"You're ageless, Jonathan."

"Charming of you, but I'm afraid people only begin to compliment one on one's youth when it is gone. But Hersey, to me, really does seem scarcely any older than she was in the days when I danced with her. She still dances, I believe."

"It will be nice to see Hersey," said Mrs. Compline.

"I don't think I know a Hersey, do I?" This was the first time Chloris had spoken directly to Mrs. Compline. She was answered by Nicholas.

"She's a flame of Jonathan's," Nicholas said. "Lady Hersey Amblington."

"She's my third cousin," said Jonathan, sedately. "We are all rather attached to her."

"Oh," said Nicholas, always to Chloris. "She's a divine creature. I adore her."

Chloris began to talk to William.

Mandrake thought that if anybody tried to bury any hatchets in the Compline armoury it would not be William. He decided that William was neither as vague nor as amiable as he seemed. Conversation went along briskly under Jonathan's leadership with Mandrake himself as an able second, but it had a sort of substratum that was faintly antagonistic. When, inevitably, it turned to the war, William, with deceptive simplicity, related a story about an incident on patrol when a private soldier uttered some comic blasphemy on the subject of cushy jobs on the home front. Mrs. Compline immediately told Jonathan how few hours of sleep Nicholas managed to get and how hard he was worked. Nicholas himself spoke of pulling strings in order to get a transfer to active service. He had, he said, seen an important personage. "Unfortunately, though, I struck a bad moment. The gentleman was very liverish. I understand," said Nicholas with one of his bright stares at Chloris, "that he has been crossed in love."

"No reason, surely," said Chloris, "why he shouldn't behave himself with comparative strangers."

Nicholas gave her the shadow of an ironical bow.

Jonathan began an account of his own activities as chairman of the local evacuation committee and made such a droll affair of it that with every phrase his listeners' guardedness seemed to relax. Mandrake, who had a certain astringent humour of his own, followed with a description of a member of the chorus who found himself in an ultra-modern play. Tea was announced and was carried through on the same cheerful note of comedy. "Good Lord," Mandrake thought, "if he should bring it off after all!" He caught Jonathan's eye and detected a glint of triumph.

After tea Jonathan proposed a brisk walk and Mandrake, knowing his host shared his own loathing for this sort of exercise, grinned to himself. Jonathan was not going to risk another session in the drawing-room. With any luck there would be more arrivals while they were out and a new set of encounters would take place in the propitious atmosphere of sherry and cocktails. When they assembled in the hall Jonathan appeared in a sage-green Tyrolese cape. He looked a quaint enough figure—but Chloris Wynne, who had evidently decided to like her host, cried out in admiration, and Mandrake, who had decided to like Chloris Wynne, echoed her. At the last moment Jonathan remembered an important telephone message and asked Mandrake to see the walking party off. He flung his cape over Nicholas' shoulders. It hung from his shoulder straps in heavy folds and turned him into a Ruritanian figure.

"Magnificent, Nick," said Jonathan, and Mandrake saw that Mrs. Compline and Chloris agreed with him. The cloak neatly emphasized the touch of bravura that seemed an essential ingredient of Nicholas' character. They went out of doors into the cold twilight of late afternoon.

IV

"But," said Dr. Hart in German, "it is an intolerable position for me—for *me*, do you understand?"

"Don't be ridiculous," said Madame Lisse in English. "And please, Francis, do not speak in German. It is a habit of which you should break yourself."

"Why should I not speak in German? I am a naturalized Austrian. Everybody knows that I am a naturalized Austrian and that I detest and abhor the Nazi regime with which we—*we* British—are in conflict."

"Nevertheless, the language is unpopular."

"Very well, very well. I now speak in English. In plain English, I tell you that if you continue your affair with this Nicholas Compline I shall take the strongest possible steps to—"

"To do what? . . . You are driving too fast."

"To put an end to it."

"How will you do that?" asked Madame Lisse, settling down into her furs with an air of secret enjoyment.

"By taking you up to London next week."

"With what object? . . . Here is Winton. I beg that you do not drive so fast."

"On our return," said Dr. Hart, shifting his foot to the brake, "we shall announce our marriage. It will have taken place quietly in London."

"Are you demented? Have we not discussed it already a thousand times? You know very well that it would injure your practice. A woman hideous with wrinkles comes to me. I see that I can do nothing, cannot even pretend to do anything. I suggest plastic surgery. She asks me if I can recommend a surgeon. I mention two or three, of whom you are one. I give instances of your success, you are here in Great Chipping, the others are abroad or in London. She goes to you. But—can I say to my client, with the same air of detached assurance, 'Certainly. Go to my husband. He is marvellous!'? And can you, my friend, whose cry has been the utter uselessness of massage, the robbery of foolish women by beauty specialists, the fatuity of creams and lotions—can you produce as your wife Elise Lisse of the Studio Lisse, beauty specialist *par excellence?* The good Lady Hersey Amblington would have something to say to that, I promise you, and by no means to our advantage."

"Then give up your business."

"And halve my income, in effect *our* income? And besides, I enjoy my work. It has amused me to win my little victories over the good Lady Hersey. The Studio Lisse is a growing concern, my friend, and I propose to remain at the head of it."

Dr. Hart accelerated again as his car mounted the steep road that climbed from the Vale of Pen Cuckoo up to Cloudyfold.

"Do you see the roofs of the large house up in those trees?" he asked suddenly.

"That is Pen Cuckoo. It is shut up at present. What of it?"

"And you know why it is shut up? I shall remind you. Two years ago it housed a homicidal lunatic, and her relatives have not returned since her trial."

Madame Lisse turned to look at her escort. She saw a sharp profile, a heavy chin, light grey eyes, and a complexion of extreme though healthy pallor.

"Well," she murmured. "Again, what of it?"

"You have heard of the case, of course. She is said to have murdered her rival in love. They were both somewhere between forty-five and fifty-five. The dangerous age in both sexes. I am myself fifty-two years of age."

"What conclusion am I supposed to draw?" asked Madame Lisse tranquilly.

"You are to suppose," Dr. Hart rejoined, "that persons of a certain age can go to extremes when the safety of their—shall I call it love-life?—is in jeopardy."

"But my dear Francis, this is superb. Am I to believe that you will lie in ambush for Nicholas Compline? What weapon shall you choose? Does he wear his sword? I believe that it is not extremely sharp, but one supposes that he could defend himself."

"Are you in love with him?"

"If I answer No, you will not believe me. If I answer Yes, you will lose your temper."

"Nevertheless," said Dr. Hart calmly, "I should like an answer."

"Nicholas will be at Highfold. You may observe us and find out."

There followed a long silence. The road turned sharply and came out on the height known as Cloudyfold. For a short distance it followed the snow-covered ridge of the hills. On their right, Madame Lisse and Dr. Hart looked down on the frozen woods of Pen Cuckoo, on cold lanes, on slow columns of chimney-smoke and, more distantly, towards a long dark mass that was the town of Great Chipping. On their left the powdered hills fell away smoothly into the Vale of Cloudyfold. Under clouds that hung like a pall from horizon to horizon, the scattered cottages of Dorset stone looked almost black, while their roofs glistened with a stealthy reflected light. A single flake of snow appeared on the windscreen and slid downwards.

"Very well," said Dr. Hart loudly, "I shall see."

Madame Lisse drew a gloved hand from under the rug and with one finger touched Dr. Hart lightly behind his ear. "I am really devoted to you," she said.

He pulled her hand down, brushing the glove aside with his lips.

"You know my temperament," he said. "It is a mistake to play the fool with me."

"Suppose I am only playing the fool with Nicholas Compline?"

"Well," he said again, "I shall see."

V

Through the office window of the Salon Cyclamen, Hersey Amblington watched two of her clients walk off down the street with small steps and certain pert movements of their sterns. They paused outside the hated windows of the Studio Lisse, hesitated for a moment, and then disappeared through the entrance.

"Going to buy Lisse Foundation Cream," thought Hersey. "So that's why they wouldn't have a facial!" She turned back into her office and was met by the familiar drone of driers, by the familiar smells of hot hair, setting lotion, and the sachets used in permanent waving, and by the familiar high-pitched indiscretions of clients in conversation with assistants.

". . . long after the milk. I look like death warmed up and what I feel is nobody's business."

". . . much better after a facial, Moddam. Aye always think a facial is marvellous, what it does for you."

". . . can't remember his name so of course I shall never see them again."

"Common woman," thought Hersey. "All my clients are common women. Damn that Lisse. Blasted pirate."

She looked at her watch. Four o'clock. She'd make a tour of the cubicles and then leave the place to her second-in-command. "If it wasn't for my snob-value," she thought grimly, "I'd be living on the Pirate's overflow." She peered into the looking-glass over her desk and automatically touched her circlet of curls. "Greyer and greyer," said Hersey, "but I'll be shot if I dye them," and she scowled dispassionately at her face. "Too wholesome by half, my girl, and a fat lot of good 'Hersey's Skin Food' is to your middle-aged charms. Oh, well."

She made her tour through her cubicles. With her assistants she had little professional cross-talk dialogues, calculated to persuade her clients that the improvement in their appearance was phenomenal. With the clients themselves she sympathized, soothed, and encouraged. She refused an invitation to dinner from the Facial and listened to a complaint from a Permanent Wave. When she returned to the office she found her second-in-command at the telephone.

"Would Madam care to make another appointment? No? Very good."

"Who's that?" asked Hersey wearily.

"Mrs. Ainsley's maid, to say she wouldn't be coming for her weekly facial to-morrow. The girls say they've seen her coming out of the Studio Lisse."

"May she grow a beard!" muttered Hersey, and grinned at her second-in-command. "To hell with her, anyway. How's the appointment book?"

"Oh, we're full enough. Booked up for three days. But they're not as smart as they used to be."

"Who cares! I'm going now, Jane. If you should want me to-morrow, I'll be at my cousin Jonathan Royal's. Highfold, you know."

"Yes, Lady Hersey. It looks as if the Lisse was going away for the week-end. I saw her come out of the shop about half an hour ago and get into Dr. Hart's car. I wonder if there's anything in those stories. She had quite a big suitcase."

"I wish she'd have a pantechnicon," said Hersey. "I'm sick of the sound of the wretched woman's name. She may live in sin all over Dorset as long as she doesn't include Highfold in the tour."

The second-in-command laughed. "*That's* not very likely, Lady Hersey, is it?"

"No, thank the Lord. Good-bye, Jane."

CHAPTER III

Contact

I

"NOT VERY PROPITIOUS WEATHER for looking at a bathing-pool," said Mandrake, "but I insist on showing it to you."

He had sent the guests off at a round pace to go through Highfold Wood, where the rides were heavy with sodden leaves, down to Jonathan's model farm and back up a steep lane to the north side of the house, where he limped out to meet them. Here they came on a wide terrace. Beneath them, at the foot of a flight of paved steps flanked by bay trees, was a large concrete swimming-pool set in smooth lawns and overlooked by a charming eighteenth-century pavilion, now trimmed, like a Christmas card, with snow. The floor of the pool had been painted a vivid blue, but now the water was wrinkled and, in the twilight of late afternoon, reflected only a broken pattern of repellent steely greys flecked by dead leaves. Mandrake explained that the pavilion had once been an aviary but that Jonathan had done it up in keeping with its Empire style and that when summer came he meant to hold *fêtes galantes* down there by his new swimming-pool. It would look very Rex Whistlerish, Mandrake said, and would have just the right air of formalized gaiety.

"At the moment," said Chloris, "it has an air of formalized desolation, but I see what you mean."

"Wouldn't you like to come for a nice bracing plunge with me, Chloris, before breakfast to-morrow?" asked Nicholas. "Do say Yes."

"No, thank you," said Chloris.

"It would have been awkward for you," said William, "if Chloris *had* said Yes." It was the first remark William had addressed directly to his brother.

"Not at all," rejoined Nicholas, and he made his stiff little bow to Chloris.

"I'd bet ten pounds," William said to nobody in particular, "that nothing on earth would have got him into that water before or after breakfast."

"Would you?" asked Nicholas. "I take you. You've lost."

Mrs. Compline instantly protested. She reminded Nicholas of the state of his heart. William grinned derisively, staring at Chloris; repeated that the bet was on. The absurd conversation began to take an unpleasant edge. Mandrake felt an icy touch on his cheek, and drew attention to a desultory scatter of snowflakes.

"If that was our brisk walk," said Chloris, "I consider we've had it. Let's go in."

"Is it a bet?" Nicholas asked his brother.

"Oh, yes," said William. "You may have to break the ice, but it's a bet."

To the accompaniment of a lively torrent of disapprobation from Mrs. Compline they walked towards the house. Mandrake's interest in William mounted with each turn of the situation. William was as full of surprises as a lucky-bag. His sudden proposal of this ridiculous wager was as unexpected as the attitude which he now adopted. He looked hang-dog and frightened. He hung back and said something to his mother, who set that tragically distorted mouth and did not answer. William gave her a look strangely compounded of malice and nervousness and strode after Chloris, who was walking with Mandrake. Nicholas had joined them and Mandrake felt sure that Chloris was very much aware of him. When William suddenly took her arm she started and seemed to draw back. They returned to the accompaniment of an irritating rattle of conversation from Nicholas.

As soon as they came out on the platform before the house, they found that someone else had arrived. Nicholas' car had been driven away and in its place stood a very smart three-seater from which servants were taking very smart suit-cases.

"That's not Hersey Amblington's car," said Mrs. Compline.

"No," said Nicholas. And he added loudly: "Look here, what's Jonathan up to?"

"What do you mean, darling?" asked his mother quickly.

"Nothing," said Nicholas. "But I think I recognize the car." He hung back as the others went into the house, and waited for Mandrake. He still wore Jonathan's cape over his uniform and it occurred to Mandrake that since Nicholas allowed himself this irregularity he must be very well aware of its effectiveness. He put his hand on Mandrake's arm. The others went into the house.

"I say," he said, "*is* Jonathan up to anything?"

"How do you mean?" asked Mandrake, wondering what the devil Jonathan would wish him to reply.

"Well, it seems to me this is a queerly assorted house-party."

"Is it? I'm a complete stranger to all the other guests, you know."

"When did you get here?"

"Last night."

"Well, hasn't Jonathan said anything? About the other guests, I mean?"

"He was very pleased with his party," said Mandrake carefully. "He's longing for it to be an enormous success."

"Is he, my God!" said Nicholas. He turned on his heel and walked into the house.

Mrs. Compline and Chloris went up to their rooms; the three men left their overcoats in a downstairs cloak-room where they noticed the twin of Jonathan's cape. When they came back into the hall they could hear voices in the library. As if by common consent they all paused. There were three voices—Jonathan's, a masculine voice that held a foreign suggestion in its level inflections, and a deep contralto.

"I thought as much," said Nicholas, and laughed unpleasantly.

"What's up?" William asked Mandrake.

"Nothing, so far as I know."

"Come on," said Nicholas. "What are we waiting for? Let's go in."

He led the way into the library.

Jonathan and his new arrivals stood before a roaring fire. The man had his back turned to the door, but the woman was facing it with an air of placid anticipation. Her face was strongly lit by a wall lamp and Mandrake's immediate reaction to it was a sort of astonishment that Jonathan could have forgotten to say how spectacular she was. In Mandrake's world women were either sophisticated and sleek or hideous and erratic. "Artificiality," he was in the habit of saying, "is a fundamental in all women with whom one falls in love, and to so exquisite an extreme has artifice been carried that it sometimes apes nature with considerable success." This subtlety of grooming appeared in Madame Lisse. Her hair was straight and from a central parting was drawn back and gathered into a knot at the nape of her neck. It lay close to her head like a black satin cap with blue high-lights. Her face was an oval, beautifully pale; her lashes needed no cosmetic to darken them; her mouth alone proclaimed her art, for it was sharply painted a dark red. Her dress was extremely simple, but in it her body seemed to be gloved rather than clothed. She was not very young, not as young as Chloris Wynne, not perhaps as pretty as Chloris Wynne either, but she had to the last degree the quality that Mandrake, though he knew very little French, spoke of and even thought of as "*soignée.*" And, in her own vein, she was exceedingly beautiful.

"Madame Lisse," Jonathan was saying, "you know Nicholas, don't you? May I introduce his brother; and Mr. Aubrey Mandrake? Hart, do you know . . ." Jonathan's introductions faded gently away.

Dr. Hart's bow was extremely formal. He was a pale dark man with a compact paunch and firm white hands. He was clad in the defiant tweeds of a firmly naturalized ex-Central-European. Mandrake gathered from his manner that either he had not met Nicholas Compline and didn't wish to do so, or else that he had met him and had taken a firm resolve never to do so again. Nicholas, for his part, acknowledged the introduction by looking at a point some distance beyond Dr. Hart's left ear, and by uttering the words "How do you do?" as if they were a malediction. Madame Lisse's greeting to Nicholas was coloured by that particular blend of composure and awareness with which Austrian women make Englishmen feel dangerous and delighted. With something of the same air, but without a certain delicate underlining, she held out her hand to William and to Mandrake. Mandrake remembered that Nicholas had known Madame Lisse was coming to the party and saw him take up a proprietary position beside her. "He's going to brazen it out," thought Mandrake. "He's going to show us the sort of dog he is with the ladies, by Heaven."

Mandrake was right. Nicholas, with a sort of defiant showmanship, devoted himself to Madame Lisse. He stood beside her in an attitude reminiscent of a Victorian military fashion-plate, one leg straight and one flexed. Occasionally he placed one hand on the back of her chair, while the other went to his blond moustache. Whenever Dr. Hart glared at them, which he did repeatedly, Nicholas bent towards Madame Lisse and uttered a loud and unconvincing laugh calculated, Mandrake supposed, to show Dr. Hart how vastly Nicholas and Madame Lisse entertained each other. Madame was the sort of woman whose natural habitat was the centre of a group of men and, with the utmost tranquillity, she dominated the conversation and even, in spite of Nicholas, contrived to instill into it an air of genuine gaiety. In this she was ably supported by Jonathan and by Mandrake himself. Even William, who watched his brother pretty closely, responded in his own odd fashion to Madame's charm. He asked her abruptly if anybody had ever painted her portrait. On learning that this had never been done he started to mutter to himself, and Nicholas looked irritated. Madame Lisse began to talk to Mandrake about his plays, Jonathan chimed in, and once again the situation was saved. It was upon a conversation piece, with Madame Lisse very much in the centre of vision, that Mrs. Compline and Chloris made their entrances. Mandrake thought that Mrs. Compline could not be aware of the affair between Nicholas and Madame Lisse, so composedly did she acknowledge the introduction. But if this was the case, what reason had Chloris given for the broken engagement with Nicholas? "Is it not impossible that everybody but his mother should be aware of *l'affaire Lisse?*" Mandrake speculated. "Perhaps she sees him as a sort of irresistible young god, choosing where he will, and, without resentment, accepts Madame as a votaress." There was no doubt about Chloris' reaction. Mandrake saw her stiffen and go very still when Jonathan pronounced Madame Lisse's name. For perhaps a full second neither of the women spoke and then, for all the world as if they responded to some inaudible cue, Chloris and Madame Lisse were extremely gracious to each other. "So they're going to take *that* line," thought Mandrake, and wondered if Jonathan shared his feelings of relief. He felt less comfortable when he saw Mrs. Compline's reaction to Dr. Hart. She murmured the conventional greeting, looked casually and then fixedly into his face, and turned so deadly white that for a moment Mandrake actually wondered if she would faint. But she did not faint. She turned away and sat in a chair farthest removed from the light. With the effect of entering on a cue, Caper brought in sherry and champagne cocktails.

II

The cocktails, though they did not perform miracles, helped considerably. Dr. Hart in particular became more sociable. He continued to avoid Nicholas but attached himself to Chloris Wynne and to William. Jonathan talked to Mrs. Compline; Mandrake and Nicholas to Madame Lisse. Nicholas still kept up his irritating performance—now, apparently, for the benefit of Chloris. Whenever Madame Lisse spoke he bent towards her and, whether her remark was grave or gay, he broke out into an exhibition of merriment calculated, Mandrake felt certain, to arouse in Chloris the pangs proper to the woman scorned. If she suffered this reaction she gave no more evidence of her distress than might be discovered in an occasional thoughtful glance at Nicholas, and it seemed to Mandrake that if she reacted at all to the performance, it was pleasurably. She listened attentively to Dr. Hart, who became voluble and bland. Chloris had asked if anyone had heard the latest wireless news. Hart instantly embarked on a description of his own reaction to radio. "I cannot endure it. It touches some nerve. It creates a most disagreeable—an unendurable—*frisson.* I read my papers and that is enough. I am informed. I assure you that I have twice changed my flat because of the intolerable persecution of neighbouring radios. Strange, is it not? There must be some psychological explanation."

"Jonathan shares your dislike," said Mandrake. "He has been persuaded to install a wireless next door in the smoking-room, but I don't believe he ever listens to it."

"My respect for my host grows with everything I hear of him," said Dr. Hart. He became expansive, enlarged upon his love of nature and spoke of holidays in the Austrian Tyrol.

"When it was still Austria," said Dr. Hart. "Have you ever visited Kaprun, Miss Wynne? How charming it was at Kaprun in those days! From there one could drive up the Gross-Glockner, one could climb into the mountains above that pleasant *Weinstube* in the ravine, and on Sunday mornings one went into Zell-am-see. Music in the central square. The cafés! And the shops where one might secure the best shoes in the world!"

"And the best cloaks," said Chloris with a smile.

"*Hein?* Ah, you have seen the cloak I have presented to our host."

"Nicholas," said Chloris, "wore it when we went for a walk just now."

Dr. Hart's eyelids, which in their colour and texture a little resembled those of a lizard, half closed over his rather prominent eyes. "Indeed," he said.

"I hope," said Jonathan, "that you visited my swimming-pool on your walk."

"Nicholas is going to bathe in it to-morrow," said William, "or hand over ten pounds to me."

"Nonsense, William," said his mother. "I won't have it. Jonathan, please forbid these stupid boys to go on with this nonsense." Her voice, coming out of the dark corner where she sat, sounded unexpectedly loud. Dr. Hart turned his head and peered into the shadow. When Chloris said something to him it appeared for a moment that he had not heard her. If, however, he had been startled by Mrs. Compline's voice he quickly recovered himself. Mandrake thought that he finished his cocktail rather rapidly and noticed that when he accepted another it was with an unsteady hand. "*That's* odd," thought Mandrake. "He's the more upset of the two, it appears, and yet they've never met before. Unless—but no! that would be too much. I'm letting the possibilities of the situation run away with me."

"Lady Hersey Amblington, sir," said Caper in the doorway.

Mandrake's first impression of Hersey Amblington was characteristic of the sort of man his talents had led him to become. As Stanley Footling of Dulwich, he would have been a little in awe of Hersey. As Aubrey Mandrake of the Unicorn Theatre, he told himself she was distressingly wholesome. Hersey's face, in spite of its delicate make-up, wore an out-of-doors look, and she did not pluck her dark brows, those two straight bars that guarded her blue eyes. She wore Harris tweed and looked, thought Mandrake, as though she would be tiresome about dogs. A hearty woman, he decided, and he did not wonder that Madame Lisse had lured away Hersey's smartest clients.

Jonathan hurried forward to greet his cousin. They kissed. Mandrake felt certain that Jonathan delayed the embrace long enough to whisper a warning in Lady Hersey's ear. He saw the tweed shoulders stiffen. With large, beautifully shaped hands, she put Jonathan away from her and looked into his face. Mandrake, who was nearer to them than the rest of the party, distinctly heard her say: "Jo, what are you up to?" and caught Jonathan's reply: "Come and see." He took her by the elbow and led her towards the group by the fire.

"You know Madame Lisse, Hersey, don't you?"

"Yes," said Hersey, after a short pause. "How do you do?"

"And Dr. Hart?"

"How do you do? Sandra, darling, how nice to see you," said Hersey, turning her back on Dr. Hart and Madame Lisse and kissing Mrs. Compline. Her face was hidden from Mandrake, but he saw that her ears and the back of her neck were scarlet.

"You haven't kissed me, Hersey," said Nicholas.

"I don't intend to. How many weeks have you been stationed in Great Chipping and never a glimpse have I had of you? William, my dear, I didn't know you had actually reached home again. How well you look."

"I feel quite well thank you, Hersey," said William gravely. "You've met Chloris, haven't you?"

"Not yet, but I'm delighted to do so, and to congratulate you both," said Hersey, shaking hands with Chloris.

"And Mr. Aubrey Mandrake," said Jonathan, bringing Hersey a drink.

"How do you do. Jonathan told me I should meet you. I've got a subject for you."

"Oh God," thought Mandrake, "she's going to be funny about my plays."

"It's about a false hairdresser who strangles his rival with three feet of dyed hair," Hersey continued. "He's a male hairdresser, you know, and he wears a helmet made of tin waving clamps and no clothes at all. Perhaps it would be better as a ballet."

Mandrake laughed politely. "A beguiling theme," he said.

"I'm glad you like it. It's not properly worked out yet, but of course his mother had long hair and when he was an infant he saw his father lugging her about the room by her pigtail, and it gave him convulsions because he hated his father and was in love with his mother, and so he grew up into a hairdresser and worked off his complexes on his customers. And I must say," Hersey added, "I wish I could follow his example."

"Do you dislike your clients, Lady Hersey?" asked Madame Lisse. "I do not find in myself any antipathy to my clients. Many of them have become my good friends."

"You must be able to form friendships very quickly," said Hersey sweetly.

"Of course," Madame Lisse continued, "it depends very much upon the class of one's clientele."

"And possibly," Hersey returned, "upon one's own class, don't you think?" And then, as if ashamed of herself, she turned again to Mrs. Compline.

"I suppose," said William's voice close to Mandrake, "that Hersey was making a joke about her subject, wasn't she?"

"Yes," Mandrake said hurriedly, for he was startled, "yes, of course."

"Well, but it *might* be a good idea, mightn't it? I mean, people do write about those things. There's that long play, I saw it in London about four years ago, where the brother and sister find out about their mother and all that. Some people thought that play was a bit thick, but I didn't think so. I thought there was a lot of reality in it. I don't see why plays shouldn't say what people feel in the same way as pictures ought to. Not what they do. What they do in their thoughts."

"That is my own contention," said Mandrake, who was beginning to feel more than a little curious about William's pictures. William gave a rather vapid laugh and rubbed his hands together. "There you are, you see," he said. He looked round the circle of Jonathan's guests, and lowered his voice. "Jonathan has played a trick on all of us," he said unexpectedly. Mandrake did not answer, and William went on: "Perhaps you planned it together."

"No, no. This party is entirely Jonathan's."

"I'll bet it is. Jonathan is doing in the ordinary way what he does in his thoughts. If you wrote a play of him what would it be like?"

"I really don't know," said Mandrake hurriedly.

"Don't you? If I painted his picture I should make him egg-shaped with quite a merry smile, and a scorpion round his head. And then, you know, for eyes he would have the sort of windows you can't see through. Clouded glass."

In Mandrake's circles this sort of thing was more or less a commonplace. "You are a surrealist, then?" he murmured.

"Have you ever noticed," William continued, placidly, "that Jonathan's eyes are quite blank? Impenetrable," he added, and a phrase from *Alice Through the Looking-Glass* jigged into Mandrake's thoughts.

"It's his thick glasses," he said.

"Oh," said William, "is that it? Has he told you about us? Nicholas and Chloris and me? And of course, Madame Lisse?" To Mandrake's intense relief William did not pause for an answer. "I expect he has," he said. "He likes talking about people and of course he would want somebody for an audience. I'm quite glad to meet Madame Lisse, and I must say it doesn't surprise me about her and Nicholas. I should like to make a picture of her. Wait a moment, I'm just going to get another drink. My third," added William, with the air of chalking up a score.

Mandrake had had one drink and was of the opinion that Jonathan's champagne cocktails were generously laced with brandy. He wondered if in this circumstance lay the explanation of William's astonishing candour. The rest of the party had already responded to the drinks, and the general conversation was now fluent and noisy. William returned, carrying his glass with extreme care.

"Of course," he said, "you will understand that Chloris and I haven't seen Nicholas since we got engaged. I went to the front the day after it was announced, and Nicholas has been conducting the war in Great Chipping ever since. But if Jonathan thinks his party is going to make any difference . . ." William broke off and drank a third of his cocktail. "What was I saying?" he asked.

"Any difference," Mandrake prompted.

"Oh, yes. If Jonathan, *or* Nicholas for that matter, imagine I'm going to lose my temper, they are wrong."

"But surely if Jonathan has any ulterior motive," Mandrake ventured, "it is entirely pacific. A reconciliation . . ."

"Oh, no," said William, "*that* wouldn't be at all amusing." He looked sideways at Mandrake. "Besides," he said, "Jonathan doesn't like me much, you know."

This chimed so precisely with Mandrake's earlier impression that he gave William a startled glance. "Doesn't he?" he asked helplessly.

"No. He wanted me to marry a niece of his. She was a poor relation and he was very fond of her. We were sort of engaged but I didn't really like her so very much, I found, so I sort of sloped off. He doesn't forget things, you know." William smiled vaguely. "She died," he said. "She went rather queer in the head, I think. It was very sad, really."

Mandrake found nothing to say, and William returned to his theme. "But I shan't do anything to Nicholas," he said. "Let him cool his ardour in the swimming-pool. After all, I've won, you know. Haven't I?"

"He *is* tight," thought Mandrake, and he said with imbecile cheerfulness: "I hope so." William finished his drink. "So do I," he said doubtfully. He looked across to the fireplace where Nicholas, standing by Madame Lisse's chair, stared at Chloris Wynne.

"But he always *will* try," said William, "to eat his cake and keep it."

III

Madame Lisse fastened three of Jonathan's orchids in the bosom of her wine-coloured dress, and contemplated herself in the looking glass. She saw a Renaissance picture smoothly painted on a fine panel—black, magnolia, and mulberry surfaces, all were sleek and richly glowing. Behind this magnificence, in shadow, was reflected the door of her room, and while she still stared at her image this door opened slowly.

"What is it, Francis?" asked Madame Lisse without turning her head.

Dr. Hart closed the door and in a moment his figure stood behind hers in the long glass.

"It was unwise to come in," she said, speaking very quietly. "That woman has the room next to yours and Mrs. Compline is on the other side of this one. Why have you not changed? You will be late."

"I must speak to you. I cannot remain in this house, Elise. I must find some excuse to leave immediately."

She turned and looked fixedly at him.

"What is it now, Francis? Surely you cannot be disturbed *à cause de* Nicholas Compline. I assure you . . ."

"It is not solely on his account. Although . . ."

"What, then?"

"His mother's!"

"His *mother's!*" she repeated blankly. "That unfortunate woman? Have you ever seen a more disastrous face? What do you mean? I wondered if perhaps Mr. Royal had thought that by inviting her he might do you a service."

"A service," Dr. Hart repeated. "A *service! Gott im Himmel!*"

"Could you not do something?"

"What you have seen," said Dr. Hart, "I did."

"*You!* Francis, she was not . . . ?"

"It was in my early days. In Vienna. It was the Schmitt-Lipmann treatment—paraffin wax. We have long ago abandoned it, but at that time it was widely practised. In this case—as you see."

"But her name. Surely you remembered her name?"

"She did not give her own name. Very often they do not. She called herself Mrs. Nicholas after her accursed son, I suppose. Afterwards of course she made a great scene. I attempted adjustments, but in those days I was less experienced, the practice of plastic surgery was in its infancy. I could do nothing. When I came to England my greatest dread was that I might one day encounter this Mrs. Nicholas." Dr. Hart uttered a sort of laugh. "I believe my first suspicions of that young man arose from the associations connected with his name."

"Obviously, she did not recognize you."

"How do you know?"

"Her manner was perfectly calm. How long ago was this affair?"

"About twenty-five years."

"And you were young Doktor Franz Hartz of Vienna? Did you not wear a beard and moustaches then? Yes. And you were slim in those days. Of course she did not recognize you."

"Franz Hartz and Francis Hart, it is not such a difference. They all know I am a naturalized Austrian and a plastic surgeon. I cannot face it. I shall speak, now, to Royal. I shall say I must return urgently to a case—"

"—And by this behaviour invite her suspicion. Nonsense, my friend. You will remain and make yourself charming to Mrs. Compline and, if she now suspects, she will say to herself: 'I was mistaken. He could never have faced me.' Come now," said Madame Lisse, drawing his face down to hers, "you will keep your head, Francis, and perhaps to-morrow, who knows, you will have played your part so admirably, that we shall change places."

"What do you mean?"

Madame Lisse laughed softly. "I may be jealous of Mrs. Compline," she said. "No, no, you are disarranging my hair. Go and change and forget your anxiety."

Dr. Hart moved to the door and paused. "Elise," he said, "suppose this was planned."

"What do you mean?"

"Suppose Jonathan Royal knew. Suppose he deliberately brought about this encounter."

"What next! Why in the world should he do such a thing?"

"There is something mischievous about him."

"Nonsense," she said. "Go and change."

IV

"Hersey, I want to speak to you."

From inside the voluminous folds of the dress she was hauling over her head Hersey said: "Sandra, darling, do come in. I'm longing for a gossip with you. Wait a jiffy. Sit down." She tugged at the dress and her head, firmly tied up in a strong net, came out at the top. For a moment she stood and stared at her friend. That face, so painfully suggestive of an image in some distorting mirror, was the colour of parchment. The lips held their enforced travesty of a smile but they trembled and the large eyes were blurred by tears.

"Sandra, my dear, what is it?" cried Hersey.

"I can't stay here. I want you to help me. I've got to get away from this house."

"Sandra! But why?" Hersey knelt by Mrs. Compline. "You're not thinking of the gossip about Nick and the Pirate, blast her eyes?"

"What gossip? I don't know what you mean. What about Nicholas?"

"It doesn't matter. Nothing. Tell me what's happened." Hersey took Mrs. Compline's hands between her own and, feeling them writhe together in her grasp, was visited by an idea that the distress which Mrs. Compline's face was incapable of expressing had flowed into these struggling hands. "What happened?" Hersey repeated.

"Hersey, that man, Jonathan's new friend, I can't meet him again."

"Aubrey Mandrake?"

"No, no. The other."

"Dr. Hart?"

"I can't meet him."

"But why?"

"Don't look at me. I know it's foolish of me, Hersey, but I can't tell you if you look at me. Please go on dressing and let me tell you."

Hersey returned to the dressing-table and presently Mrs. Compline began to speak. The thin exhausted voice, now well-controlled, lent no colour to the story of despoiled beauty. It trailed dispassionately through her husband's infidelities, her own despair, her journey to Vienna, and her return. And Hersey, while she listened, absently made up her own face, took off her net, and arranged her hair. When it was over she turned towards Mrs. Compline but came no nearer to her.

"But can you be sure?" she said.

"It was his voice. When I heard of him first, practising in Great Chipping, I wondered. I said so to Deacon, my maid. She was with me that time in Vienna."

"It was over twenty years ago, Sandra. And his name—"

"He must have changed it when he became naturalized."

"Does he look at all as he did then?"

"No. He has changed very much."

"Then—"

"I am not positive, but I am almost positive. I can't face it, Hersey, can I?"

"I think you can," said Hersey, "and I think you will."

V

Jonathan stood in front of a blazing fire in the drawing-room. Brocaded curtains hung motionless before the windows, the room glowed with reflected light and, but for the cheerful hiss and crackle of burning logs, was silent. The night outside was silent, too, but every now and then Jonathan heard a momentary sighing as if the very person of the north wind explored the outer walls of Highfold. Presently one of the shutters knocked softly at its frame and then the brocaded curtains stirred a little, and Jonathan looked up expectantly. A door at the far end of the room opened and Hersey Amblington came in.

"Hersey, how magnificent! You have dressed to please me, I believe. I have a passion for dull green and furs. Charming of you, my dear."

"You won't think me so charming when you hear what I've got to say," Hersey rejoined. "I've got a bone to pick with you, Jo."

"What an alarming phrase that is," said Jonathan. "Will you have a drink?"

"No, thank you. Sandra Compline has been threatening to go home."

"Indeed? That's vexing. I hope you dissuaded her?"

"Yes, I did."

"Splendid. I'm so grateful. It would have quite spoiled my party."

"I told her not to give you the satisfaction of knowing you had scored."

"Now that really *is* unfair," cried Jonathan.

"No, it's not. Look here, did you know about Sandra and your whey-faced boy-friend?"

"Mandrake?"

"Now, Jo, none of that nonsense. Sandra confides in her maid, and she tells me the maid is bosom friends with your Mrs. Pouting. You've listened to servants' gossip, Jo. You've heard that Sandra thought this Hart man might be the Dr. Hartz who made that appalling mess of her face."

"I only wondered. It would be an intriguing coincidence."

"I'm ashamed of you, and I'm furious with you on my own account. Forcing me to be civil to that blasted German."

"Is she a German?"

"Whatever she is, she's a dirty fighter. I've heard on excellent authority she's started a rumour that my Magnolia Food Base grows beards. But never mind about that. I can look after myself."

"Darling Hersey! If only you had allowed me to perform that delightful office!"

"It's the cruel trick you've played on Sandra that horrifies me. You've always been the same, Jo. You've a passion for intrigue wedded to an unholy curiosity. You lay your plans and when they work out and people are hurt or angry, nobody is more sorry or surprised than you. It's a sort of blind patch in your character."

"Was that why you refused me, Hersey, all those years ago?"

Hersey caught her breath and for a moment was silent.

"Not that I agree with you, you know," said Jonathan. "One of my objectives is a lavish burial of hatchets. I hope great things of this week-end."

"Do you expect the Compline brothers to become reconciled because you have given Nicholas an opportunity to do his barn-yard strut before Chloris Wynne? Do you suppose Hart, who is obviously in love with the Pirate, will welcome the same performance with her, or that the Pirate and I will wander up and down your house with our arms round each other's waists, or that Sandra Compline will invite Hart to have another cut at her face? You're not a fool, Jo."

"I *had* hoped for your co-operation," said Jonathan wistfully.

"*Mine!*"

"Well, darling, to a certain extent I've had it. You made a marvellous recovery from your own encounter with Madame Lisse, and you tell me you've persuaded Sandra to stay."

"Only because I felt it was better for her to face it."

"Don't you think it may be better for all of us to face our secret bogey-man? Hersey, I've collected a group of people each one of whom is in a great or small degree hag-ridden by a fear. Even Aubrey Mandrake has his little bogey-man."

"The poetic dramatist? What have you nosed out from his past?"

"Do you really want to know?"

"No," said Hersey, turning pink.

"You are sitting beside him at dinner. Say in these exact words that you understand he has given up footling, and see what sort of response you get."

"Why should I use this loathsome phrase to Mr. Mandrake?"

"Why, simply because, although you won't admit it, darling, you have your share of the family failing—curiosity."

"I *don't* admit it. And I won't do it."

Jonathan chuckled. "It is an amusing notion. I shall make the same suggestion to Nicholas. I believe it would appeal to him. To return to our cast of characters: Each of them—Sandra Compline to an extreme degree—has pushed his or her fear into a cupboard. Chloris is afraid of her old attraction to Nicholas, William is afraid of Nicholas' fascination for Chloris and for his mother, Hart is afraid of Nicholas' fascination for Madame Lisse, Sandra is afraid of a terrible incident in her past, Madame Lisse, though I must say she does not reveal her fear, is perhaps a little afraid of both Hart and Nicholas. You, my dearest, fear the future. If Nicholas has a fear it is that he may lose prestige, and that is a terrible fear."

"And you, Jo?"

"I am the *compère.* Part of my business is to unlock the cupboards and show the fears to be less terrible in the light of day."

"And you have no bogey-man of your own?"

"Oh, yes, I have," said Jonathan, and the light gleamed on his spectacles. "His name is Boredom."

"And therein am I answered," said Hersey.

CHAPTER IV

Threat

I

WHILE HE WAS DRESSING, Mandrake had wondered how Jonathan would place his party at dinner. He actually tried to work out, on several sheets of Highfold note-paper, a plan that would keep apart the most bitterly antagonistic of the guests. He found the task beyond him. The warring elements could be separated, but any such arrangement seemed only to emphasize friendships that were in themselves infuriating to one or another of the guests. It did not enter his head that Jonathan, with reckless bravado, would choose the most aggravating and provocative arrangement possible. But this was what he did. The long dining-table had been replaced by a round one. Madame Lisse sat between Jonathan and Nicholas, Chloris between Nicholas and William. Sandra Compline was on Jonathan's right and had Dr. Hart for her other partner. Hersey Amblington was next to Dr. Hart and Mandrake himself, the odd man, sat between Hersey and William. From the moment when they found their places it was obvious to Mandrake that the success of the dinner-party was most endangered by Mrs. Compline and Dr. Hart. These two had been the last to arrive, Mrs. Compline appearing after Caper had announced dinner. Both were extremely pale and, when they found their place-cards, seemed to flinch all over: "Like agitated horses," thought Mandrake. When they were all seated, Dr. Hart darted a strange glance across the table at Madame Lisse. She looked steadily at him for a moment. Jonathan was talking to Mrs. Compline; Dr. Hart, with an obvious effort, turned to Hersey Amblington. Nicholas, who had the air of a professional diner-out, embarked upon a series of phrases directed equally, Mandrake thought, at Madame Lisse and Chloris Wynne. They were empty little phrases, but Nicholas delivered them with many inclinations of his head, this way and that, with archly masculine glances, punctual shouts of laughter, and frequent movements of his hand to his blond moustache. "In the nineties," Mandrake thought, "Nicholas would have been known as a 'masher.' There is no modern word to describe his gallantries." They were successful gallantries, however, for both Chloris and Madame Lisse began to look alert and sleek. William preserved a mulish silence and Dr. Hart, while he spoke to Hersey, glanced from time to time at Madame Lisse.

Evidently Jonathan had chosen a round table with the object of keeping the conversation general and in this project he was successful. However angry Hersey may have been with her cousin, she must have decided to pull her weight in the role of hostess for which he had obviously cast her. Mandrake, Madame Lisse, and Nicholas all did their share, and presently there appeared a kind of gaiety at the table. "It's merely going to turn into a party that is precariously successful in the teeth of extraordinary obstacles," Mandrake told himself. "We have made a fuss about nothing." But this opinion was checked when he saw Dr. Hart stare at Nicholas; when, on turning to William, he found him engaged in what appeared to be some whispered expostulation with Chloris; and when, turning away in discomfort, he saw Mrs. Compline, with shaking hands, hide an infinitesimal helping under her knife and fork. He emptied his glass and gave his attention to Hersey Amblington who seemed to be talking about him to Jonathan.

"Mr. Mandrake sniffs at my suggestion," Hersey was saying. "Don't you, Mr. Mandrake?"

"Do I?" Mandrake rejoined uneasily. "What suggestion, Lady Hersey?"

"There! He hasn't even heard me, Jo. Why, the suggestion I made before dinner, for a surrealist play."

Before Mandrake could find an answer Nicholas Compline suddenly struck into the conversation.

"You mustn't be flippant with Mr. Mandrake, Hersey," he said. "He's looking very austere. I'm sure he's long ago given up footling."

Mandrake experienced the sensation of a violent descent in some abandoned lift. His inside seemed to turn over and the tips of his fingers went cold. "God!" he thought. "They know! In a moment they will speak playfully of Dulwich." And he sat with his fork held in suspended animation, halfway to his mouth. "This atrocious woman," he thought, "this atrocious woman! This loathsome grinning young man!" He turned to Hersey and found her staring at him with an expression that he interpreted as knowing. Mandrake shied away and looking wildly round the table, encountered the thick-lensed glasses of his host. Jonathan's lips were pursed and in the faint creases at the corners of his mouth Mandrake read complacency and amusement. "So that's it," thought Mandrake furiously. "He knows and he's told them. It's the sort of thing that would delight him. My vulnerable spot. He's having a tweak at it and he and his cousin and his bloody friend will laugh delicately and tell each other they were very naughty with poor Mr. Stanley Footling." But Jonathan was speaking to him, gently carrying forward the theme of Hersey's suggestion for a play.

"I have noticed, Aubrey, that the layman is always eager to provide the artist with ideas. Do you imagine, Hersey darling, that Aubrey is a sort of æsthetic scavenger?"

"But mine was such a *good* idea."

"You must excuse her, Aubrey. No sense of proportion, I'm afraid, poor woman."

"Mr. Mandrake *does* excuse me," said Hersey, and her smile held such a warmth of friendliness that it dispelled Mandrake's panic. "I was mistaken," he thought, "another false alarm. Why must I be so absurdly sensitive? Other people have changed their names without experiencing these terrors." The relief was so great that for a time he was lost in it and heard only the gradual quieting of his own heartbeats. But presently he became aware of a lull in the general conversation. They had reached dessert. Jonathan's voice alone was heard speaking and Mandrake thought that he must have been speaking for some little time.

II

"No one person," Jonathan was saying, "is the same individual to more than one other person. That is to say the reality of individuals is not absolute. Each individual has as many exterior realities as the number of encounters he makes."

"Ah," said Dr. Hart, "this is a pet theory of my own. The actual 'he' is known to nobody."

"Does the actual 'he' even exist?" Jonathan returned. "May it not be argued that 'he' has no intrinsic reality since different selfs arise out of a conglomeration of selfs to meet different events?"

"I don't see what you mean," said William, with his air of worried bafflement.

"Nor do I, William," said Hersey. "One knows how people will react to certain events, Jo. We say: 'Oh So-and-so is no good when it comes to such-and-such a situation!' "

"My contention is that this is exactly what we do *not* know."

"But Mr. Royal," cried Chloris, "we *do* know. We know, for instance, that some people will refuse to listen to gossip."

"We know," said Nicholas, "that one man will keep his head in a crisis where another will go jitterbug. This war—"

"Oh, don't let's talk about this war," said Chloris.

"There are some men in my company—" William began, but Jonathan raised his hand and William stopped short.

"Well, I concede," said Jonathan, "that the same 'he' may make so many appearances that we may gamble on his turning up under certain circumstances, but I contend that it *is* a gamble and that though under these familiar circumstances we may agree on the probability of certain reactions, we should quarrel about theoretical behaviour under some unforeseen, hitherto unexperienced circumstances."

"For example?" asked Madame Lisse.

"Parachute invasion—" began William, but his mother said quickly: "No, William, not the war." It was the first time since dinner that Mandrake had heard her speak without being addressed.

"I agree," said Jonathan, "let us not draw our examples from the war. Let us suppose that—what shall I say—"

"That the Archangel Gabriel popped down the chimney," suggested Hersey, "and blasted his trump in your ear."

"Or that Jonathan told us," said Nicholas, "that this was a Borgia party and the champagne was lethal and we had but twelve minutes to live."

"*Not* the Barrie touch, I implore you," said Mandrake, rallying a little.

"Or," said Jonathan, peering into the shadows beyond the candle-lit table, "that my new footman, who is not present at the moment, suddenly developed homicidal mania and was possessed of a lethal weapon. Let us, at any rate, suppose ourselves shut up with some great and impending menace." He paused, and for a moment complete silence fell upon the company.

The new footman returned. He and Caper moved round the table again. "So he's keeping the champagne going," thought Mandrake, "in case the women won't have brandy or liqueurs. Caper's being very judicious. Nobody's tight unless it's William or Hart. I'm not sure of them. Everybody else is nicely thank you."

"Well," said Jonathan, "under some such disastrous circumstance, how does each of you believe I would behave? Come now, I assure you I shan't cavil at the strictest censure. Sandra, what do you think I would do?"

Mrs. Compline raised her disfigured face. "What you would do?" she repeated. "I think you would talk, Jonathan." And for the first time that evening there was a burst of spontaneous laughter. Jonathan uttered his high-pitched giggle.

"*Touché*," he said. "And you, Madame Lisse?"

"I believe that for perhaps the first time in your life you would lose your temper, Mr. Royal."

"Nick?"

"I don't know. I think—"

"Come on, now, Nick. You can't insult me. Fill Mr. Compline's glass, Caper. Now, Nick?"

"I think you might be rather flattened out."

"I don't agree," said Chloris, quickly. "I think he'd take us all in hand and tell us what to do."

"William?"

"What? Oh, ring up the police, I suppose," said William, and he added in a vague mumble only heard by Mandrake: "Or you might go mad, of course."

"I believe he would enjoy himself," said Mandrake, quickly.

"I agree," said Hersey, to Mandrake's surprise.

"And Dr. Hart?"

"In a measure, I too agree. I think that you would be enormously interested in the behaviour of your guests."

"You see?" said Jonathan in high glee. "Am I not right? So many Jonathan Royals. Now shall we go further? Shall we agree to discuss our impressions of each other, and to keep our tempers as we do so? Come now."

"How clever of Jonathan," thought Mandrake, sipping his brandy. "Nothing interests people so much as the discussion of their own characters. His invitation may be dangerous, but at least it will make them talk." And talk they did. Mrs. Compline believed that Nicholas would suffer from extreme sensibility but would show courage and resource. Nicholas, prompted, as Mandrake considered, by a subconscious memory of protective motherhood, thought his mother would console and shelter. William, while agreeing with Nicholas about their mother, hinted that Nicholas himself would shift his responsibilities. Chloris Wynne, rather defiantly, supported William. She suggested that William himself would show up very well in a crisis and her glance at Nicholas and at Mrs. Compline seemed to say that they would resent his qualities. Mandrake, nursing his brandy glass, presently felt his brain clear miraculously. He would speak to these people in rhythmic, perfectly chosen phrases and what he said would be of enormous importance. He heard his own voice telling them that Nicholas, in the event of a crisis, would treat them to a display of pyrotechnics, and that two women would applaud him and one man deride. "But the third woman," said Mandrake solemnly, as he stared at Madame Lisse, "must remain a shadowed figure. I shall write a play about her. Dear me, I am afraid I must be a little drunk." He looked anxiously round, only to discover that nobody had been listening to him, and he suddenly realized that he had made his marvellous speech in a whisper. This discovery sobered him. He decided to take no more of Jonathan's brandy.

III

Jonathan did not keep the men long in the dining-room and Mandrake, who had taken stock of himself and had decided that he would do very well if he was careful, considered that his host had judged the drinks nicely as far as he and the Complines were concerned but that in the case of Dr. Hart, Jonathan had been over-generous. Dr. Hart was extremely pale, there were dents in his nostrils and a smile on his lips. He was silent and fixed his gaze, which seemed a little out of focus, on Nicholas Compline. Nicholas was noisily cheerful. He moved his chair up to William's and subjected his brother to a kind of banter that made Mandrake shudder and caused William to become silent and gloomy. Jonathan caught Mandrake's eye and suggested that they should move to the drawing-room.

"By all means," said Nicholas. "Here's old Bill as silent as the grave, Jonathan, longing for his love. And Dr. Hart not much better, though whether it's from the same cause or not, we mustn't ask."

"You are right," said Dr. Hart thickly. "It would not be amusing to ask such a question."

"Come along, come along," said Jonathan quickly, and opened the door. Mandrake hurriedly joined him and William followed. At the door Mandrake turned and looked back. Nicholas was still in his chair. His hands rested on the table, he leant back and smiled at Dr. Hart who had risen and was leaning heavily forward. Mandrake was irresistibly reminded of an Edwardian problem picture. It was a subject for the Honourable John Collier. There was the array of glasses, each with its highlight and reflection, there was the gloss of mahogany, of boiled shirt-front, of brass buttons. There was Dr. Hart's face so violently expressive of some conjectural emotion, and Nicholas', flushed, and wearing a sneer that dated perfectly with the Honourable John's period; all this unctuously lit by the candles on Jonathan's table. "The title," thought Mandrake, "would be 'The Insult.'"

"Come along, Nick," said Jonathan, and when it appeared that Nicholas had not heard him, he murmured in an undertone: "You and William go on, Aubrey. We'll follow."

So Mandrake and William did not hear what Nicholas and Dr. Hart had to say to each other.

IV

Mandrake had suspected that if Jonathan failed it would be from too passionate attention to detail. He feared that Jonathan's party would die of over-planning. Having an intense dislike of parlour games, he thought gloomily of sharpened pencils and pads of paper neatly set out by the new footman. In this he misjudged his host. Jonathan introduced his game with a tolerable air of spontaneity. He related an anecdote of another party at which the game of Charter had been played. Jonathan had found himself with a collection of six letters and one blank. When the next letter was called it chimed perfectly with his six, but the resulting word was one of such gross impropriety that even Jonathan hesitated to use it. A duchess of formidable rigidity had been present. "I encountered her eye. The glare of a basilisk, I assure you. I could not venture. But the amusing point of the story," said Jonathan, "is that I am persuaded her own letters had fallen in the same order. We played for threepenny points and she loathes losing her money. I hinted at my own dilemma and saw an answering glint. She was in an agony."

"But what is the game?" asked Mandrake, knowing that somebody was meant to ask this question.

"My dear Aubrey, have you never played Charter? It is entirely *vieux jeu* nowadays, but I still confess to a passion for it."

"It's simply a crossword game," said Hersey. "You are each given the empty crossword form and the letters are called one by one from a pack of cards. The players put each letter as it is read out into a square of the diagram. This goes on until the form is full. The longest list of complete words wins."

"You score by the length of the words," said Chloris. "Seven-letter words get fifteen points, three-letter words two points, and so on. You may not make any alterations, of course."

"It sounds entertaining," said Mandrake with a sinking heart.

"Shall we?" asked Jonathan, peering at his guests. "What does everybody think? Shall we?"

His guests, prompted by champagne and brandy to desire, vaguely, success rather than disaster, cried out that they were all for the game, and the party moved to the smoking-room. Here, Jonathan, with a convincing display of uncertainty, hunted in a drawer where Mandrake had seen him secrete the printed blocks of diagrams and the requisite number of pencils. Soon they were sitting in a semicircle round the fire with their pencils poised and with expressions of indignant bewilderment on their faces. Jonathan turned up the first card:

"X," he said; "X for Xerxes."

"Oh, *can't* we have another?" cried Madame Lisse. "There aren't any— Oh no, wait a moment. I see."

"K for King."

Mandrake, finding himself rather apt at the game, began to enjoy it. With the last letter he completed his long word, "EXTRACT," and with an air of false modesty handed his Charter to Chloris Wynne, his next-door neighbour, to mark. He himself took William's Charter and was embarrassed to find it in a state of the strangest confusion. William had either failed to understand the game, or else had got left so far behind that he could not catch up with the letters. Many of the spaces were blank and in the left-hand corner William had made a singular little drawing of a strutting rooster with a face that certainly bore a strong resemblance to his brother Nicholas.

"Anyway," said William looking complacently at Mandrake, "the drawing is quite nice. Don't you think so?"

Mandrake was saved from making a reply by Nicholas who at that moment uttered a sharp ejaculation.

"What's up, Nick?" asked Jonathan.

Nicholas had turned quite pale. In his left hand he held two of the Charter forms. He separated them and crushed one into a wad in his right hand.

"Have I made a mistake?" asked Dr. Hart softly.

"You've given me two forms," said Nicholas.

"Stupid of me. I must have torn them off the block at the same time."

"They have both been used."

"No doubt I forgot to remove an old form and tore them off together."

Nicholas looked at him. "No doubt," he said.

"You can see which is the correct form by my long word. It is 'THREATS.'"

"I have not missed it," said Nicholas, and turned to speak to Madame Lisse.

V

Mandrake went to his room at midnight. Before switching on his light he pulled aside the curtains and partly opened the window. He saw that at last the snow had come. Fleets of small ghosts drove steeply forward from darkness into the region beyond the window-panes, where they became visible in the firelight. Some of them, meeting the panes, slid down their surface and lost their strangeness in the cessation of their flight. Though the room was perfectly silent, this swift enlargement of oncoming snowflakes beyond the windows suggested to Mandrake a vast nocturnal whispering. He suddenly remembered the black-out and closed the window. He let fall the curtain, switched on the light, and turned to stir his fire. He was accustomed to later hours and felt disinclined for sleep. His thoughts were busy with memories of the evening. He was filled with a nagging curiosity about the second Charter form which had caused Nicholas Compline to turn pale and to look so strangely at Dr. Hart. He could see Nicholas' hand, thrusting the crumpled form down between the seat and the arm of his chair. "Perhaps it is still there," Mandrake thought. "Without a doubt it is still there. Why should it have upset him so much? I shall never go to sleep. It is useless to undress and get into bed." And the prospect of the books Jonathan had chosen so carefully for his bedside filled him with dismay. At last he changed into pyjamas and dressing-gown, visited the adjoining bathroom, and noticed that there was no light under the door from the bathroom into William's bedroom at the further side. "So William is not astir." He returned to his room, opened the door into the passage, and was met by the indifferent quiet of a sleeping house. Mandrake left his own door open and stole along the passage as far as the stairhead. In the wall above the stairs was a niche from which a great brass Buddha, indestructible memorial to Jonathan's Anglo-Indian grandfather, leered peacefully at Mandrake. He paused here, thinking. "A few steps down to the landing, then the lower flight to the hall. The smoking-room door is almost opposite the foot of the stairs." Nicholas had sat in the fourth chair from the end. Why should he not go down and satisfy himself about the crumpled form? If by any chance someone was in the smoking-room, he could get himself a book from the library next door and return. There was no shame in looking at a discarded paper from a round game.

He limped softly to the head of the stairs. Here, in the diffused light, he found a switch and turned it on. A wall-lamp halfway down the first flight came to life. Mandrake descended the stairs. The walls sighed to his footfall, and near the bottom one of the steps creaked so loudly that he started and then stood rigid, his heart beating hard against his ribs. "This is how burglars and illicit lovers feel," thought Mandrake, "but why on earth should I?" Yet he stole cat-footed across the hall, pushed open the smoking-room door with his finger-tips, and waited long in the dark before he groped for the light-switch and snapped it down.

There stood the nine armchairs in a semicircle before a dying fire. They had an air of being in dumb conclave and in their irregular positions were strangely eloquent of their late occupants. There was Nicholas Compline's chair, drawn close to Madame Lisse's and turned away contemptuously from Dr. Hart's saddle-back. Mandrake actually fetched a book from a sporting collection in a revolving case before he moved to Nicholas' chair, before his fingers explored the crack between the arm and the seat. The paper was crushed into a tight wad. He smoothed it out on the arm of the chair and read the five words that had been firmly pencilled in the diagram.

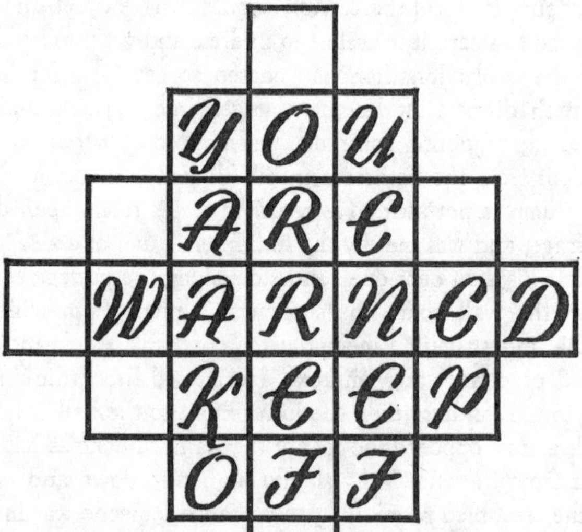

The fire settled down with a small clink of dead embers, and Mandrake, smiling incredulously, stared at the scrap of paper in his hand. It crossed his mind that perhaps he was the victim of an elaborate joke, that Jonathan had primed his guests, had invented their antipathies, and now waited maliciously for Mandrake himself to come to him, agog with his latest find. "But that won't wash," he thought. "Jonathan could not have guessed I would return to find the paper. Nicholas *DID* change colour when he saw it. I must presume that Hart *DID* write this message and hand it to Nicholas with the other. He must have been crazy with fury to allow himself such a ridiculous gesture. Can he suppose that Nicholas will be frightened off the lady? No, it's too absurd."

But, as if in answer to his speculations, Mandrake heard a voice speaking behind him: "I tell you, Jonathan, he means trouble. I'd better get out."

For a moment Mandrake stood like a stone, imagining that Jonathan and Nicholas had entered the smoking-room behind his back. Then he turned, found the room still empty, and realized that Nicholas had spoken from beyond the door into the library, and for the first time noticed that this door was not quite shut. He was still speaking, his voice raised hysterically.

"It will be better if I clear out, now. A pretty sort of party it'll be! The fellow's insane with jealousy. For her sake—don't you see—for her sake—"

The voice paused, and Mandrake heard a low murmur from Jonathan, interrupted violently by Nicholas.

"I don't give a damn what they think." Evidently Jonathan persisted, because in a moment Nicholas said: "Yes, of course I see that, but I can say . . ." His voice dropped, and the next few sentences were half lost. ". . . It's not that. . . . I don't see why . . . urgent call from headquarters . . . Good Lord, of course not! . . . Miserable, fat little squirt, I've cut him out and he can't take it." Another pause, and then: "I don't mind if *YOU* don't. It was more on your account than . . . But I've told you about the letter, Jonathan . . . not at first. . . . Well, if you think . . . Very well, I'll stay." And for the first time Mandrake caught Jonathan's words: "I'm sure it's better, Nick. Can't turn tail, you know. Good night." "Good night," said Nicholas, none too graciously, and Mandrake heard the door from the library to the hall open and close. Then from the next room came Jonathan's reedy tenor:—

"Il était une bergère,
Qui ron-ton-ton, petit pat-a-plan."

Mandrake stuck out his chin, crossed the smoking-room and entered the library by the communicating door.

"Jonathan," he said, "I've been eavesdropping."

VI

Jonathan was sitting in a chair before the fire. His short legs were drawn up, knees to chin, and he hugged his shins like some plump and exultant kobold. He turned his spectacles towards Mandrake and, by that familiar trick of light, the thick lenses obscured his eyes and glinted like two moons.

"I've been eavesdropping," Mandrake repeated.

"My dear Aubrey, come in, come in. Eavesdropping? Nonsense. You heard our friend Nicholas? Good! I was coming to your room to relate the whole story. A diverting complication."

"I only heard a little of what he said. I'd come down to the smoking-room." He saw Jonathan's spectacles turned on the book he still held in his hand. "Not really to fetch a book," said Mandrake.

"No? One would seek a book in the library, one supposes. But I am glad my choice for your room was not ill-judged."

"I wanted to see this."

Like a small boy in disgrace Mandrake extended his right hand and opened it, disclosing the crumpled form.

"Ah," said Jonathan.

"You have seen it?"

"Nick told me about it. I wondered if anyone else would share my own curiosity. May I have it? Ah—Thank you. Sit down, Aubrey." Mandrake sat down, tortured by the suspicion that Jonathan was laughing at him.

"You see," said Mandrake, "that I am badly inoculated with your virus. I simply could not go to bed without knowing what was on that form."

"Nor I, I assure you. I was about to look for it myself. As perhaps you heard, Nick is in a great tig. It seems that before coming here he had had letters from Hart warning him off the lady. According to Nick, Hart is quite mad for love of her and consumed by an agonizing jealousy."

"Poor swine," said Mandrake.

"What? Oh, yes. Very strange and uncomfortable. I must confess that I believe Nick is right. Did you notice the little scene after dinner?"

"You may remember that you gave me to understand very definitely that my cue was to withdraw rapidly."

"So I did. Well, there wasn't much in it. He merely glared at Nick across the table and said something in German which neither of us understood."

"You'll be telling me next he's a fifth columnist," said Mandrake.

"Not at all. He gives himself away much too readily. But I fancy he has frightened Nick. I have observed, my dear Aubrey, that of the two Complines, William catches your attention more than Nicholas. I have known them all their lives and I suggest that you turn your eyes on Nicholas. Nicholas is rapidly becoming the—not perhaps the *jeune premier*—but the central character of our drama. In Nicholas we see the vain man, frightened. The male flirt who finds an agreeable stimulant in another man's jealousy and suddenly realizes that he has roused the very devil in his rival. Would you believe it, Nicholas wanted to leave tonight? He advanced all sorts of social and gallant reasons, consideration for me, for the lady, for the success of the party; but the truth is Nick had a jitterbug and wanted to make off."

"How did you prevent him?"

"I?" Jonathan pursed his lips. "I have usually been able to manage Nicholas. I let him see I understood his real motive. He was afraid I would make a pleasing little anecdote of his flight. His vanity won. He will remain."

"But what does he think Hart will do?"

"He used the word 'murderous.' "

There was a long silence. At last Mandrake said: "Jonathan, I think you should have let Nicholas Compline go."

"But why?"

"Because I agree with him. I have watched Hart to-night. He did look murderous."

"Gorgeous!" Jonathan exclaimed, and hugged his hands between his knees.

"Honestly, I think he means trouble. He's at the end of his tether."

"You don't think he'll go for Nick with a dinner knife?"

"I don't think he's responsible for his behaviour."

"He was a little tipsy, you know."

"So was Compline. While the champagne and brandy worked he rather enjoyed baiting Hart. Now, evidently, he's not so sure. Nor am I."

"You disappoint me, Aubrey. Our æsthetic experiment is working beautifully and your only response—"

"Oh, I'm absorbingly interested. If *YOU* don't mind—after all, it's your house."

"Exactly. And my responsibility. I assembled the cast and, my dear fellow, I offered you a seat in the stalls. The play is going too well for me to stop it at the close of the first act. It falls very prettily on Nick's exit and I fancy the last thing we hear, before the curtain blots out the scene, is a sharp click."

"What?"

"Nicholas Compline turning the key in his bedroom door."

"I hope to God you're right," said Mandrake.

CHAPTER V

Attempt

I

THE NEXT MORNING Mandrake woke at the rattle of curtain rings to find his room penetrated by an unearthly light and knew that Highfold was under snow. A heavy fall, the maid said. There were patches of clear sky, but the local prophets said they'd have another storm before evening. She rekindled his fire and left him to stare at his tea-tray and to remember that, not so many years ago, Mr. Stanley Footling, in the attic room of his mother's boarding-house in Dulwich, had enjoyed none of these amenities. Stanley Footling always showed a tendency to return at the hour of waking and this morning Mandrake asked himself for the hundredth time why he could not admit his metamorphosis with an honest gaiety; why he should suffer the miseries of unconfessed snobbery. He could find no answer and, tired of his thoughts, decided to rise early.

When he went downstairs he found William Compline alone at the breakfast table.

"Hullo," said William. "Good morning. Jolly day for Nick's bath, isn't it?"

"What?"

"Nick's bath in the pool. Have you forgotten the bet?"

"I should think *he* had."

"I shall remind him."

"Well," said Mandrake, "personally I should pay a good deal more than ten pounds to get out of it."

"Yes, but you're not my brother Nicholas. He'll do it."

"But," said Mandrake uncomfortably, "hasn't he got something wrong with his heart? I mean—"

"It won't hurt him. The pool's not frozen. I've been to look. He can't swim, you know, so he'll just have to pop in at the shallow end and duck." William gave a little crow of laughter.

"I'd call it off, if I were you."

"Yes," said William, "but you're not me. I'll remind him of it, all right." And on this slightly ominous note they continued their breakfast in silence. Hersey Amblington and Chloris Wynne came in together, followed by Jonathan, who appeared to be in the best of spirits.

"We shall have a little sunshine, I believe," said Jonathan. "It may not last long, so doubtless the hardier members of the party will choose to make the most of it."

"I don't propose to build a snow-man, Jonathan, if that's what you're driving at," said Hersey.

"Don't you, Hersey?" said William. "I rather thought I might. After Nick's bath, you know. Have you heard about Nick's bath?"

"Your mother told me. You're not going to hold him to it, William?"

"He needn't if he doesn't want to."

"Bill," said Chloris, "*don't* remind him of it. Your mother—"

"She won't get up for ages," said William, "and I don't suppose there'll be any need to remind Nick. After all, it *was* a bet."

"I think you're behaving rather badly," said Chloris uncertainly. William stared at her.

"Are you afraid he'll get a little cold in his nose?" he asked, and added: "I was up to my waist in snow and slush in France not so long ago."

"I know, darling, but—"

"Here *is* Nick," said William placidly. His brother came in and paused at the door.

"Good morning," said William. "We were just talking about the bet. They all seem to think I ought to let you off."

"Not at all," said Nicholas. "You've lost your tenner."

"*There!*" said William, "I said you'd do it. You mustn't get that lovely uniform wet, Nick. Jonathan will lend you a bathing suit, I expect. Or you could borrow my uniform. It's been up to—" Mandrake, Chloris, Hersey and Jonathan all began to speak at once and William, smiling gently, fetched himself another cup of coffee. Nicholas turned away to the sideboard. Mandrake had half expected Jonathan to interfere but he merely remarked on the hardihood of the modern young man and drew a somewhat tiresome analogy from the exploits of ancient Greeks. Nicholas suddenly developed a sort of gaiety that set Mandrake's teeth on edge, so falsely did it ring.

"Shall you come and watch me, Chloris?" asked Nicholas, seating himself beside her.

"I don't approve of your doing it."

"Oh, Chloris! Are you angry with me? I can't bear it. Tell me you're not angry with me. I'm doing it all for your sake. I must have an audience. Won't you be my audience?"

"Don't be a fool," said Chloris. But, damn it, thought Mandrake, she's preening herself all the same. Dr. Hart arrived and was very formal with his greetings. He looked ghastly and breakfasted on black coffee and toast. Nicholas threw him a glance curiously compounded of malice and nervousness and began to talk still more loudly to Chloris Wynne of his bet with William. Hersey, who had evidently got sick of Nicholas, suddenly said she thought it was time he cut the cackle and got to the 'osses.

"But everybody isn't here," said William. "Madame Lisse isn't here."

"Divine creature!" exclaimed Nicholas affectedly, and showed the whites of his eyes at Dr. Hart. "She's in bed."

"How do you know?" asked William, against the combined mental opposition of the rest of the party.

"I've investigated. I looked in to say good morning on my way down."

Dr. Hart put down his cup with a clatter and walked quickly out of the room.

"You are a damned fool, Nick," said Hersey softly.

"It's starting to snow again," said William. "You'd better hurry up with your bath."

II

Mandrake thought that no wager had ever fallen as inauspiciously as this one. Even Jonathan seemed uneasy and when they drifted into the library made a half-hearted attempt to dissuade Nicholas. Lady Hersey said flatly that she thought the whole affair extremely boring and silly; Chloris Wynne at first attempted an air of jolly house-party waggishness, but a little later Mandrake overheard her urging William to call off the bet. Mrs. Compline somehow got wind of the project and sent down a message forbidding it, but this was followed by a message from Madame Lisse saying that she would watch from her bedroom window. Mandrake tried to get up a party to play Badminton in the barn, but nobody really listened to him. An atmosphere of bathos hung over them like a pall and through it William remained complacent and Nicholas embarrassingly flamboyant.

Finally, it was resolved by the Complines that Nicholas should go down to the pavilion, change there into a bathing suit and, as William put it, go off at the shallow end. William was to watch the performance and Nicholas, rather offensively, insisted upon a second witness. Neither Hersey nor Chloris seemed able to make up her mind whether she would go down to the pool. Jonathan had gone out saying something about Dr. Hart. It appeared that Mandrake would be obliged to witness Nicholas' ridiculous antics and, muttering to himself, he followed him into the hall.

The rest of the party had disappeared. Nicholas stood brushing up his moustache and, eying Mandrake with an air half mischievous, half defiant. "Well," he said, "this is a pretty damn-fool sort of caper, isn't it?"

"To be frank," said Mandrake, "I think it is. It's snowing like hell again. Don't you rather feel the bet's fallen flat?"

"I'll be damned if I let Bill take that tenner off me. Are you coming?"

"I'll go up and get my coat," said Mandrake unwillingly.

"Take one out of the cloak-room here. I'm going to. The Tyrolese cape."

"Jonathan's?"

"Or Hart's!" Nicholas grinned. "Hart's mantle may as well fall across my shoulders, what? I'll go down now and change in that bloody pavilion. You follow. Bill's running down from the west door when he's given me time to undress."

Nicholas went into the cloak-room and reappeared wearing one Tyrolese cape and carrying another. "Here you are," he said, throwing it at Mandrake. "Don't be long."

He pulled the hood of his cape over his head and went out through the front doors. For a moment Mandrake saw him, a fantastic figure caught in a flurry of snow. Then Nicholas lowered his head to the wind and ran out of sight.

Mandrake's club-foot prevented him from running. It was some distance from the front of the house to the pool and he remembered that the west door opened directly on a path that led to the terrace above the pool. He decided that, like William, he would go down that way. He would go at once, before William started. He loathed people to check their steps to his painful limp. Imitating Nicholas, he pulled the hood of the second cape over his head and made his way along a side passage to the west door and, as he opened it, heard somebody call after him from the house. He ignored the call and, filled with disgust at the whole situation, slammed the door behind him and limped out into the storm.

The north wind drove against him, flattening the cloak against his right side and billowing it out on his left. He felt snow on his eyelids and lips and pulled the hood further over his brows so that he could see only the ground before him. As he limped forward, snow squeaked under his steps.

It closed over his sound foot above the rim of his shoe. The path was still defined and he followed it to the edge of the terrace. Below him lay the pool and the pavilion. The water was a black hole in a white field but the pavilion resembled a light-hearted decoration, so well did the snow become it. Mandrake was tempted to watch from the terrace but the wind was so violent there that he changed his mind and crept awkwardly down the long flight of steps, thinking to himself that it would be just like this party if he slipped and broke his good leg. At last he reached the rounded embankment that curved sharply above the pool, hiding the surface of the water from anybody who did not climb its steps. Mandrake reached the top of this bank with difficulty and descended the far side to the paved kerb, now covered in snow. He glanced at the pavilion and saw Nicholas wave from one of the windows. Mandrake walked to the deep end of the pool where there was a diving platform and stood huddled in his cloak, watching fleets of snow die on the black surface of the water. He looked back towards the terrace steps but the embankment hid the bottom flight. There was nobody on the top flight. Perhaps, after all, none of the others would come. "Damn!" said Mandrake. "Damn Nicholas, damn William, and damn Jonathan for his filthy party. I've never been so bored or cold or angry in my life before." He staggered a little against a sudden gust of wind and snow.

The next moment something drove hard against his shoulders. He took a gigantic stride forward into nothingness and was torn from head to foot with the appalling shock of icy water.

III

The fabric of the cape was in his eyes and mouth and clamped about his arms and legs. The cold cut him with terrible knives of pain. As he sank he thought: "This is disgusting. This is really bad. A terrible thing has happened to me." Water rushed in at his nose and ears. His heavy boot pulled at his leg. His arms fought the cape and after a timeless interval it rose above his head, free of his face, and he saw a green prison about him. Then, with frozen limbs, he struggled and fought; and at last, feeling the bottom of the pool, struck at it with his feet and rose into the folds of the cape. His lungs were bursting, his body dying of cold. His hands wrenched at the fastening about his throat and broke it, his arms fought off the nightmare cape, and after an age of suffocating despair, he reached the surface. He drew a retching gasp and swallowed air. For a moment he felt and saw snow and heard, quite close by, a voice. As he sank again, something slapped the water above his head. "But I can swim a little," he thought, as wheels clashed and whirred behind his brain, and he made frog-like gestures with his arms and legs. Immediately the fingers of his right hand touched something smooth that slipped away from them. He made a more determined effort and, after three violent strokes, again reached the surface. As he gasped and opened his eyes, he was confronted by a scarlet face, beaked, on the end of a long scarlet neck. He flung his arms round this neck, fell backwards and was half-suffocated with another in-drawn jet of water. Then he found himself lying on the pond, choking into the face of a monstrous bird. Again he heard voices, but they now sounded unreal and very far away.

"Are you all right? Kick. Kick out. You're coming this way."

"But that is *my* cloak."

"Kick, Aubrey, kick."

He kicked and, after an æon of time, floated into the view of five faces, upside down with their mouths open. His head struck against hardness.

"The rail. There's a rail here. Get hold of it."

"You're all right, now. Here!"

He was drawn up. His arms scraped against stone. He was lying on the edge of the pool clasping an inflated India-rubber bird to his bosom. He was turned so that his face hung over the edge of the pond. His jaws had developed an independent life of their own and his teeth chattered like castanets. His skin, too, leapt and jerked over the surface of his frozen muscles. When he tried to speak he made strange ugly noises. Acrid water trickled from his nostrils over his lips and chin.

"How the devil did it happen?" somebody—William—was asking.

"The edge is horribly slippery," said Chloris Wynne. "I nearly fell in myself."

"I didn't fall," Mandrake mouthed out with great difficulty. "I was pushed." Nicholas Compline burst into a shout of laughter and Mandrake wondered dimly if he could make a quick grab at his ankle and overturn him into the pool. It was borne in on Mandrake that Nicholas was wearing bathing drawers under his cape.

"Did he fall or was he pushed?" shouted Nicholas.

"Shut up, Nicholas." That was Chloris Wynne.

"My dear fellow," Jonathan made a series of little dabs at Mandrake, "you must come up at once. My coat. Take my coat. Ah, yours too, William, that's better. Help him up, now. A hot toddy and a blazing fire, eh Hart? There never was anything more unfortunate. Come now."

Mandrake was suddenly torn by a violent retching. "Disgusting," he thought, "*disgusting!*"

"That will be better," said a voice. Dr. Hart's! "We should get him up quickly. Can you walk, Mr. Mandrake?"

"Yes."

"Your arm across my shoulders. So. Come, now."

"I'll just get into my clothes," said Nicholas.

"Perhaps, Mr. Compline, as you are in bathing dress, you will be good enough to retrieve my cape."

"Sorry, I can't swim."

"We'll fish it out somehow," said Chloris. "Take Mr. Mandrake in."

Jonathan, William and Dr. Hart took him back. Over the embankment, up the terrace steps, through a mess of footprints left by the others. The heavy boot on his club-foot dragged and hit against snow and sodden turf. Halfway up he was sick again. Jonathan ran ahead and, when at last they reached the house, could be heard shouting out orders to the servants. "Hot-water bottles. All you can find. His bath—quickly. Brandy, Caper. The fire in his room. What are you doing, all of you! God bless my soul, Mrs. Pouting, here's Mr. Mandrake, half-drowned."

If only his teeth would stop chattering he would enjoy being in bed, watching flames mount in the fireplace, feeling the toddy set up a little system of warmth inside him. The hot bath had thawed his body, the hot bottles lay snug against his legs. Jonathan again held the glass to his lips.

"What happened?" asked Mandrake.

"After you fell, you mean? Nick looked out from the window of his dressing-room. He saw you and ran out. He can't swim, you know, but he snatched up the inflated pelican—there are several in the pavilion—and threw it into the pool. By that time I fancy William and Hart were there. They arrived before Miss Wynne and myself. It appears that William had stripped off his overcoat and was going after you when you seized the improvised lifebuoy. When we arrived your arms were wreathed about its neck and you were fighting your way to the side. My dear Aubrey, I can't tell you how distressed I am. Another sip, now, do."

"Jonathan, somebody came behind me and thrust me forward."

"But, my dear fellow—"

"I tell you they did. I can still feel the impact of their hands. I did *not* slip. Good God, Jonathan, I'm not romancing! I tell you I was deliberately thrown into that water."

"Nicholas saw nobody," said Jonathan uncomfortably. He primmed his lips and gave a little cough.

"When did he look out?" Mandrake said. "I know he saw me when I first got there. But afterwards?"

"Well—the first thing he saw was your cape—Dr. Hart's cape, unhappily—on the surface of the water."

"Exactly. Whoever pushed me in had by that time hidden himself. He had only to dodge over the embankment and duck down."

"But we should have seen him," said Jonathan.

"Hart and William Compline were already there when you arrived?"

"Yes, but—"

"Did they go down together to the pond?"

"I—no, I think not. Hart left by the front door and came by the other path, past the pavilion. William came by the west door."

"Which of them arrived first? Thank God I've stopped chattering."

"I don't know. I persuaded Hart to go out. I managed to calm him down after that *most* unfortunate passage with Nicholas at breakfast. I don't quite know how I managed it, but I did. I suggested he should go out for a—for a sort of breather, do you know—and I suppose he followed the path to the pavilion and was arrested by Nicholas' shout for help. I myself heard Nicholas as I went to the west door. I overtook Miss Wynne, who was already on the terrace. When I reached the edge of the terrace, Hart and the two Complines were all by the pond. My dear Aubrey, I shall tire you if I go on at this rate. Finish your drink and try to go to sleep."

"I don't in the least want to go to sleep, Jonathan. Somebody has just tried to drown me and I do not find the experience conducive to slumber."

"No?" murmured Jonathan unhappily.

"No. And don't, I implore you, look as though I was mentally unhinged."

"Well, you *have* had a shock. You may even have a slight fever. I don't want to alarm you—"

"If you try to fob me off, I shall certainly run a frightful temperature. At the moment I assure you I am perfectly normal, and I tell you, Jonathan, somebody tried to drown me in your loathsome pond. I confess I should like to know who it was."

"A thoughtless piece of foolery, perhaps," mumbled Jonathan. Mandrake suddenly pointed a trembling finger at the mound in the bed-clothes made by his left foot.

"Does anyone but a moron play that sort of prank on a cripple?" he asked savagely.

"Oh, my dear fellow, I know, but—"

"Madame Lisse!" Mandrake cried. "She was to watch from her window. She must have seen."

"You can't see that end of the pool from her window," said Jonathan, quickly. "It's hidden by the yew tree on the terrace."

"How do you know?"

"I do know. Yesterday, when I did her flowers, I noticed. I assure you."

Mandrake looked at him. "Then whoever did it," he said, "must have also known that she could not see him. Or else—"

There was a tap on the door.

"Come in," cried Jonathan in a loud voice. "Come in."

IV

It was Nicholas Compline. "Look here," he said. "I hope you don't mind my butting in. I had to see Jonathan. Are you all right?"

"Thanks to you," said Mandrake, "I believe I am."

"Look here, I'm damn' sorry I laughed."

"It was infuriating, but I can't quarrel with you. As we say in the provinces, you quite literally gave me the bird. Not the first time I have been so honoured, but certainly the first time I have welcomed it with both arms."

"Jonathan," said Nicholas, "you realize the significance of this business?"

"The significance, Nick?"

"It was done deliberately."

"Just what I've been trying to tell Jonathan, Compline. My God, I was literally hurled into that water. I'm sorry to dwell on a tiresome subject, but somebody tried to drown me."

"No, they didn't."

"What!"

"They tried to drown *me*."

"Here," shouted Mandrake, "what the hell d'you mean?"

"Jonathan," said Nicholas, "we'd better tell him about me and Hart."

"Oh, that," said Mandrake. "I know all about that."

"May I ask how?"

"Need we go into it?"

"My dear Nick," began Jonathan in a great hurry, "Mandrake noticed all was not well between you. The scene at the dinner table. The game of Charter. He asked me if I—if I—"

"Well, never mind," Nicholas interrupted impatiently. "You know he's been threatening me? All right. Now, let me tell you that as I went down to the pond I glanced up at the front of the house. You know the window on the first floor above the front door?"

"Yes," said Jonathan.

"All right. He was watching me through that window."

"But, my dear Nick—"

"He was watching me. He saw me go down wearing that cape. He didn't see Mandrake go down wearing the other cape, because Mandrake went out at the west door. Don't interrupt me, Jonathan, this is serious. When Mandrake was shoved overboard, he was standing up to his hocks in snow on the kerb of the pool, with that embankment hiding his legs from anybody that came up from behind. You had the hood pulled over your head, I suppose, Mandrake?"

"Yes."

"Yes. Well, it was Hart shoved you overboard, and Hart thought he was doing me in, by God."

"But Nick, we must keep our heads and not rush impetuously into conclusions—"

"See here," said Nicholas, always to Mandrake. "Had anybody in this party reason to wish you any harm?"

"I'd never met one of them in my life before. Except Jonathan, of course."

"And I can assure you, my dear Aubrey, that I entertain only the kindest—"

"Of course."

"Well, then!" said Nicholas.

"I believe you're right," cried Mandrake.

The door opened and Dr. Hart came in.

Nicholas, who had been sitting on the edge of the bed, sprang up and walked out of the room. Jonathan uttered a series of little consolatory noises and moved to the window. Hart went to the bed and laid his fingers on Mandrake's wrist.

"You are better?" he said. "That is right. It will be well to remain in bed to-day, perhaps. There has been a little shock." He looked placidly at Mandrake and repeated: "Just a little shock."

"Yes," said Mandrake. Hart turned to Jonathan. "If I might speak to you, Mr. Royal."

"To me?" Jonathan gave a little start. "Yes, of course. Here?"

"I was about to suggest—somewhere else. But perhaps . . . I remember,

Mr. Mandrake, that as we brought you to the house, you declared repeatedly that you had been deliberately pushed into this swimming-pool."

Mandrake looked at the large pale face, surely more pale than ever since its owner began to speak, and thought: "This may be the face of a potential murderer." Aloud, he said: "I am quite convinced of it."

"Then perhaps it would be well to set your mind at ease on this matter. No attempt was made wittingly upon you, Mr. Mandrake."

"How do you know?"

"It was a case of mistaken identity."

"Good God!" said Jonathan with violence. Dr. Hart tapped the palm of one hand with the fingers of the other. "The person who made this attack," he said, "believed that he was making it upon me."

V

Mandrake's first reaction to this announcement was a hysterical impulse to burst out laughing. He looked at Jonathan, who stood with his back to the light, and wondered if he only imagined that an expression of mingled relief and astonishment had appeared for a moment on his host's face. Then he heard his voice, pedantic and high-pitched as usual.

"But my dear Dr. Hart," Jonathan said, "what can have put such a strange notion into your head?"

"The fact that there is, among your guests, a man who wishes most ardently for my death."

"Surely not," said Jonathan, making a little purse of his lips.

"Surely, yes. I had not intended to go so far. I merely wished to reassure Mr. Mandrake. Perhaps if we withdrew?"

"For pity's sake," Mandrake ejaculated, "don't withdraw. I'm all right. I want to get this thing straight. After all," he added peevishly, "it *was* me in the pond."

"True," said Jonathan.

"And I think I should tell you, Dr. Hart, that as I came down the steps, Compline saw me through the pavilion window and waved. He must have recognized me."

"It was snowing very heavily. Your face, no doubt, was in shadow, hidden by the hood of my cape."

"I hope you got your cape," said Jonathan anxiously.

"Thank you, yes. There must be a considerable amount of weed in your pond. It is to me quite evident, Mandrake, that Compline mistook you for myself. He came out of the pavilion and ran quickly up behind you, giving you a sharp thrust on the shoulder-blades."

"It *was* a sharp thrust on the shoulder-blades. But you forget that there is one thing about me that is quite distinctive." Mandrake spoke rapidly with an air of jeering at himself. "I am lame. I wear a heavy boot. I use a stick. You can't mistake a man with a club-foot, Dr. Hart."

"Your foot was hidden. One does not walk evenly in snow and I assure you that while I, as a medical man, would not make such a mistake, Compline, glancing out through heavy sheets of falling snow, might easily do so."

"I don't agree with you. And didn't Compline see you looking from an upper window as he went to the pond? He could hardly imagine you would spirit yourself down there as quickly as that."

"Why not? I could have done so. A matter of a few moments. In actual fact I did go down a few minutes later. Mr. Royal saw me leave."

"Is it altogether wise to stress that point, do you think?"

"I do not understand you, Mr. Mandrake."

Jonathan began to talk very quickly, stuttering a little and making sharp gestures with both hands.

"And, my dear Hart, even if, as you suggest, anyone could mistake Mandrake for yourself; even supposing, and I cannot suppose it, that anyone could entertain the idea of thrusting you into that water, surely, *surely* it would be preposterous to suggest that it was with any—any—ah—murderous intent. Can you not swim, my dear doctor?"

"Yes, but—"

"Very well, then. I myself cannot help thinking that Mandrake is mistaken, that a sudden gust of wind caught him—"

"No, Jonathan."

"—or that at the worst it was a stupid and dangerous practical joke."

"A *joke!*" shouted Dr. Hart. "A JOKE!" Mandrake suppressed a nervous giggle. Hart stared sombrely at him, and then turned to Jonathan. "And yet I do not know," he said heavily. "Perhaps with an Englishman it is possible. Perhaps he did not mean to kill me. Perhaps he wished to make me a foolish figure, shivering, dripping stagnant water, my teeth chattering—Yes, I can accept that possibility. He recognized the Tyrolese cape and thought—"

"Wait a moment," Mandrake interrupted, "before we go any further I must put you right about the cape. It is impossible that Nicholas Compline should have thought you were inside your own Tyrolese cape."

"And why?"

"Because he himself gave it to me to wear to the pond."

Dr. Hart was silent. He looked from Mandrake to Jonathan, and those little dents appeared in his nostrils. "You are protecting him," he said.

"I assure you I am speaking the truth."

"There is one explanation that seems to have occurred to nobody." Jonathan raised his hands to his spectacles and adjusted them slightly. "I myself wear a Tyrolese cape, your own gift, my dear Hart, and a delightful one. Is it not at least possible that somebody may have thought it would be amusing to watch me flounder in my own ornamental pool?"

"But who the hell?" Mandrake objected.

"It might be argued," said Jonathan, smiling modestly, "almost every member of my house-party."

VI

When they had left him alone, Mandrake surrendered himself to a curious state of being, engendered by exhaustion, brandy, speculation, and drowsiness. His thoughts floated in a kind of hinterland between sleep and wakefulness. At times they were sharply defined, at times nebulous and disconnected, but always they circled about the events leading to his plunge into the swimming-pool. At last he dozed off into a fitful sleep from which he was roused, as it seemed, by a single clear inspiration. "I must see William Compline," he heard himself say. "Must see William Compline." He was staring at the ridge of snow that had begun to mount from the sill up the window-pane, when his door moved slightly and Chloris Wynne's beautifully groomed head appeared in the opening.

"Come in."

"I thought you might be asleep. I called to enquire."

"The report is favourable. Sit down and have a cigarette. I haven't the remotest idea of the time."

"Nearly lunch-time."

"Really? What are you all doing?"

"I've known house-parties to go with a greater swing. Nicholas is sulking by the radio in the smoking-room. Lady Hersey and Mr. Royal seem to be having a quarrel next door in the library, and when I tried the boudoir on the other side of the smoking-room I ran into Dr. Hart and Madame Lisse, both quite green in the face and obviously at the peak of an argument. My ex-future-mother-in-law has developed a bad cold and I have had a snorter of a row with William."

"Here!" said Mandrake. "What *is* all this?"

"I ticked him off for harping on about the bet with Nicholas, and then he said some pretty offensive things about Nicholas and me, and I said he was insane, and he huffed and puffed and broke off our engagement. I don't know why I tell you all this, unless it's to get in first with the news bulletin."

"It's all very exciting, of course, but I consider the human interest really centres about me."

"Because you fell in the pool?"

"Because I was pushed in."

"That's what we're quarreling about, actually. So many people seem to think it was all a mistake."

"The fact remains, I was pushed in."

"Oh, they've stopped saying it was an *accident*. But each of the men seems to think you were mistaken for him."

"Does William think that?"

"No. William confines himself to saying he wishes it had been Nicholas. He's made Nicholas pay him the ten pounds."

"I suppose," said Mandrake, "*you* didn't push me in?"

"No, honestly I didn't. When I got to the top of the steps William and Nicholas and Dr. Hart were all down by the pool, screaming instructions to you. I got a frightful shock. I thought you were Mr. Royal drowning in his own baroque waters."

"Why?"

"I don't know. Oh, because of the cloak, I suppose. It was floating about like a large water-lily leaf, and I said to myself: 'Crikey, that's Jonathan Royal.' "

Mandrake sat up in bed and bent his most austere gaze upon Miss Wynne. "How did you feel," he asked, "when you knew it was I?"

"Well, when Mr. Royal came up behind me, I knew it was thee, if that's the right grammar. And then I saw you clinging to that bathing bird and your hair was over your face like seaweed and your tie was round at the back of your neck, and so on and—" her voice quivered slightly, "and I was terribly sorry," she said.

"No doubt I was a ludicrous figure. Look here, from what you tell me it seems that you were the last to arrive."

"No, Mr. Royal came after me. He'd been round at the front of the house, I think. He overtook me on the steps."

"Will you tell me something? Please try to remember. Did you notice the footprints on the terrace and the steps?"

"I *say,*" said Miss Wynne, "are we going to do a bit of 'teckery'? Footprints in the snow!"

"Do leave off being gay and amusing, I implore you, and try to remember the footprints. There would be mine of course."

"Yes. I noticed yours. I mean I—"

"You saw the marks of my club-foot. You needn't be so delicate about it."

"You needn't be so insufferably on the defensive," said Chloris with spirit, and immediately added: "Oh, gosh, I'm so sorry. At least let there not be a quarrel up here by your bed of sickness. Yes, I saw your footprints, and I think I saw—no, I can't remember except that there were others. William's, of course."

"Any coming back to the house?"

"No, I'm sure not. But—"

"Yes?"

"Well, you're wondering, aren't you, if somebody could have gone down and shoved you overboard and then come back up the steps and then sort of pretended they were going down for the first time? I'd thought of that. You see, as I went down I stepped in your footprints because it was easier going. Anybody else might have done that. It was snowing so hard nobody would have noticed the steps within the steps."

"Hart came by a different path from the front of the house, William came down the terrace steps, then you, then Jonathan. I don't think William would have had time unless he came hard on my heels. I'd only just got there when it happened. Nicholas didn't do it because he gave me the cloak and therefore couldn't have mistaken me for anyone else. I believe Nicholas is right. I believe Hart did it. He saw Nicholas, wearing his cloak, go by the front way, and followed him. Then he skulked round the corner of the pavilion, saw a figure in a cloak standing on the kerb, darted out through the snow and did his abominable stuff. Then he darted back and reappeared, all surprise and consternation, when he heard Nicholas yell. By that time William was coming down the steps, no doubt, and you, followed by Jonathan, were leaving the house. Hart's our man."

"Yes, but *why?*"

"My dear girl—"

"All right, all right. Because of Madame Lisse. We only met last night and you talk as if I were a congenital idiot."

"There's nothing like attempted murder to bring people together."

"Nicholas *is* a fool."

"You ought to know. I thought you still seemed to get a flutter out of him."

"Now *that,*" said Chloris warmly, "I do consider an absolutely insufferable remark."

"It's insufferable because it happens to be true. Nicholas Compline is the sort of person that all females get self-conscious about and all males instinctively wish to award a kick in the pants."

"Barn-yard jealousy."

"You know," said Mandrake, "you've got more penetration than I first gave you credit for. All the same," he said, after a long pause, "there's one little thing that doesn't quite fit in with my theory. It doesn't exactly contradict it, but it doesn't fit in."

"Well, don't mumble about it. Or aren't you going to tell me?"

"When they brought me back up those unspeakable steps, I was sick."

"You don't need to tell me that. I was looking after you."

"I'm damned if I know how I came to notice them, but I did notice them. At the top of the terrace, leading out from the house, coming round from the front door and stopping short at the edge of the terrace. You didn't see them when you went down. Neither did I. Which proves—"

"Do you mind," Chloris interrupted, "breaking the thread of your narrative just for a second? Surrealism may be marvellous in poetic drama but it's not so good in simple conversation. What didn't we see going down that you saw coming back, sick and all as you were?"

"A row of footprints in the snow coming out from the house as far as the top of the terrace and turning back again."

"Oh."

"They were small footprints."

CHAPTER VI

Flight

I

THE AFTERNOON WAS REMARKABLE for an increasing heaviness in the snowfall, the state of Mandrake's feelings, and the behaviour of William Compline. Snow mounted from the window-sill in a tapering shroud, light diminished stealthily in Mandrake's bedroom while he felt too relaxed and too idle to stretch out his hand to the bedside lamp. Yet though his body was fatigued, his brain was active and concerned itself briskly with the problem of his immersion and with speculations on the subject of Chloris Wynne's strange relations with the Compline brothers. He was convinced that she was not in love with William but less sure that she did not still hanker after Nicholas. Mandrake wondered testily how a young woman who did not try the eyes, and was by no means a ninny, could possibly degrade her intelligence by falling for the brummagem charms of Nicholas Compline. "A popinjay," he muttered, "a stock figure of dubious gallantry." And he pronounced the noise usually associated with the word "Pshaw." He had arrived at this point when he received a visit from William and Lady Hersey.

"We hear you're better," Hersey said. "Everybody's being quite frightful downstairs and William and I thought we'd like a little first-hand information, so we've come to call. They're all saying you think somebody tried to drown you. William's afraid you might suspect him, so I've brought him up to come clean."

"Do you suspect me?" asked William anxiously. "Because I didn't, you know."

"I don't in the least suspect you. Why should I? We've had no difference of opinion."

"Well, they seem to think I might have mistaken you for Nicholas."

"Who suspects this?"

"My mama, principally. Because I stuck to the bet, you see. So I thought I'd like to explain that when I got there you were already in the pool."

"Was Hart there?"

"No. No, he turned up a minute or so later."

"Did you notice the footprints on the terrace steps?"

"Yes, rather," said William, unexpectedly. "They were your footsteps. I noticed them because one was bigger than the other."

"William!" Hersey murmured.

"Well, Hersey, he'd know about that, wouldn't he? And then, you know, Chloris and Jonathan arrived."

"Perhaps you'd like my alibi, Mr. Mandrake," said Hersey. "It's not an alibi at all, I'm afraid. I sat in the smoking-room and listened to the wireless. The first intimation I had about your adventure was provided by Jonathan who came in shouting for restoratives. I *could* tell you about the wireless programme, I think."

Hersey went to the window and looked out. When she spoke again her voice fell oddly on the silence of the room. "It's snowing like mad," she said. "Has it struck either of you that in all probability, whether we like it or not, we are shut up together in this house with no chance of escape?"

"Dr. Hart wanted to go after lunch," William said. "I heard him say so to Jonathan. But Jonathan said they've had word that you can't get over Cloudyfold, and anyway there's a drift inside the front gates. Jonathan seemed pleased about that."

"He would be." Hersey turned and rested her hands behind her on the sill. Her figure appeared almost black against the hurried silence of the storm beyond the window. "Mr. Mandrake," she said, "you know my cousin quite well, don't you?"

"I've known him for five years."

"But that doesn't say you know him well," she said quickly. "You arrived before all of us. He was up to something, wasn't he? No, that's not a fair question. You needn't answer. I know he was up to something. But whatever his scheme was, it didn't involve you unless—Yes, William, that must be it, of course: Mr. Mandrake was to be the audience."

"I don't like performing for Jonathan," William said. "I never have."

"Nor do I, and what's more I won't. The Pirate can register fatal woman in heaps all over the house, but she won't get a rise out of me."

"I suppose I *have* performed, Hersey. Chloris and I broke off our engagement before lunch."

"I thought something had happened. Why?"

William hunched his shoulders and drove his hands into his trousers' pockets. "She ticked me off about the bet," he said, "and I ticked her off about Nicholas, so what have you?"

"Well, William my dear, I'm sorry; but honestly, *is* she quite your cup of tea?" Hersey confronted Mandrake. "What do you think?" she demanded abruptly. He was not very much taken aback. For some reason that he had never been able to understand, Mandrake was a man in whom his fellow-creatures confided. He was by no means obviously sympathetic and he seldom asked for confidences but, perhaps because of these very ommissions, they came his way. Sometimes he wondered if his lameness had something to do with it. People were inclined to regard a lame man as an isolated being, set apart by his disability as a priest is set apart by his profession. He usually enjoyed hearing strange confessions and was surprised therefore at discovering in himself a reluctance to receive William's explanations of his quarrel with Chloris Wynne. He was profoundly glad that the engagement was broken and quite determined to make no suggestions about mending it.

"You must remember," he said, "that we met for the first time last night."

Hersey fixed him with a bright blue eye. "How guarded!" she said. "William, I believe Mr. Mandrake has—"

"Since we are being so frank," Mandrake interrupted in a great hurry, "I should like to know whether you believe somebody pushed me into that loathsome pond, and if so, who."

"Nick says it was Hart," said Hersey. "He's gone and thrown his mother into a fever by telling her Hart has tried to drown him. He's behaving like a peevish child."

"Mightn't you have been blown in?" William asked vaguely.

"Does a gust of wind hit you so hard on the shoulder-blades that you can feel the bruises afterwards? Damn it, I *know*. They're my shoulder-blades."

"So they are," Hersey agreed, "and I for one think it was Dr. Hart. After all, we know he was gibbering with rage at Nicholas, and it seems he saw Nicholas go down wearing a cape. I don't suppose he meant to drown him. He simply couldn't resist the temptation. I rather sympathize. Nicholas has bounded like a tennis ball, I consider, from the time he got here."

"But Hart must have known Nick couldn't swim," said William. "He kept explaining that was why he wouldn't go in at the deep end."

"True. Well, perhaps he meant to drown him."

"What does Madame Lisse say about it?" Mandrake asked.

"The Pirate?" Hersey helped herself to a cigarette. "My dear Mr. Mandrake, she doesn't say anything about it. She dressed herself up in what I happen to know is a Chanel model at fifty guineas, and came down for lunch looking like an orchid at a church bazaar. Nicholas and William and Dr. Hart curvet and goggle whenever they look at her."

"Well, you know, Hersey, she is rather exciting," said William.

"Does Jonathan goggle?"

"No," said Hersey. "He looks at her as he looks at all the rest of us—speculatively, from behind those damned glasses."

"I've always wanted," William observed, "to see a really good specimen of the *femme fatale*." Hersey snorted and then said immediately: "Oh, I grant you her looks. She's got a marvellous skin; thick and close, you can't beat 'em."

"And then there's her figure, of course."

"Yes, William, yes. I suppose you and your girl didn't by any chance quarrel over the Pirate?"

"Oh, no. Chloris isn't jealous. Not of me, at any rate. It is I," said William, "who am jealous. Of course you know, don't you, that Chloris broke her engagement to Nick because of Madame Lisse?"

"Is Madame at all in love with your brother, do you suppose?" Mandrake asked.

"I don't know," said William, "but I think Chloris is."

"Rot!" said Hersey. Mandrake suddenly felt abysmally depressed. William walked to the fireplace and stood with his back to them and his head bent. He stirred the fire rather violently with his heel, and through the splutter and rattle of coals they heard his voice.

". . . I think I'm glad. It's always been the same . . . *You* know, Hersey: second-best. For a little while I diddled myself into thinking I'd cut him out. I thought I'd show them. My mother knew. At first she was furious but pretty soon she saw it was me that was the mug as usual. My mother thinks it's all as it should be, Nick having strings of lovely ladies falling for him—*le roi s'amuse* sort of idea. By God!" said William with sudden violence, "it's not such fun having a brother like Nick. By God, I wish Hart *had* shoved him in the pond."

"William, don't."

"Why not? Why shouldn't I say for once what I think of my lovely little brother? D'you suppose I'd blame Hart, if he was after Nicholas? Not I. If I'd thought of it myself, be damned if I wouldn't have done it."

"Stop!" Hersey cried out. "Stop! Something appalling is happening to all of us. We're saying things we'll regret for the rest of our lives."

"We're merely speaking the truth."

"It's the sort that shouldn't be spoken. It's a beastly lopsided exaggerated truth. We're behaving like a collection of neurotic freaks." Hersey moved to the window. "Look at the snow," she said, "it's heavier than ever. There's a load on the trees; they're beginning to droop their branches. It's creeping up the sides of the house, and up the window-panes. Soon you'll hardly be able to see out of your window, Mr. Mandrake. What are we going to do, shut up in the house together, hating each other? What are we going to do?"

II

At half-past four that afternoon, Nicholas Compline suddenly announced in a high voice that he must get back to his headquarters at Great Chipping. He sought out Jonathan and, with small regard for plausibility, informed him that he had received an urgent summons by telephone.

"Strange!" said Jonathan, smiling. "Caper tells me that the telephone is out of commission. The lines are down."

"The order came through some time ago."

"I'm afraid you can't go, Nick. There's a six-foot drift in Deep Bottom at the end of the drive, and it'll be worse up on Cloudyfold."

"I can walk over Cloudyfold to Chipping and get a car there."

"Twelve miles!"

"I can't help that," said Nicholas loudly.

"You'll never do it, Nick. It'll be dark in an hour. I can't allow you to try. It's a soft fall. Perhaps to-morrow, if there's a frost during the night—"

"I'm going, Jonathan. You used to have a pair of Canadian snow-shoes, usen't you? May I borrow them? Do you know where they are?"

"I gave them away years ago," said Jonathan blandly.

"Well, I'm going."

Jonathan hurried up to Mandrake's room with his piece of news. Mandrake had dressed and was sitting by his fire. He still felt extremely shaky and bemused and stared owlishly at Jonathan, who plunged straight into his story.

"He's quite determined, Aubrey. Perhaps I had better remember that after all I didn't give away the snow-shoes. And yet, even with snow-shoes he will certainly lose his way in the dark or smother in a drift. Isn't it too tiresome?" Jonathan seemed to be more genuinely upset by this turn of events than by anything else that had happened since his party assembled.

"It will ruin everything," he muttered, and when Mandrake asked him if he meant that the death of Nicholas Compline from exposure would ruin everything, he replied testily: "No, no, his *departure*. The central figure! The whole action centres round him. I couldn't be more disappointed."

"Honestly, Jonathan, I begin to think you are suffering from some terrible form of insanity. The *idée fixe*. People may drown in your ornamental waters or perish in your snow-drifts, and all you can think of is your hell-inspired party." Jonathan hastened to protest but in a moment or two he was looking wistfully out of the window and declaring that surely even Nicholas could not be so great a fool as to attempt the walk over Cloudyfold in such a storm. As if in answer to this speech there came a tap on the door and Nicholas himself walked in. He wore his heavy khaki waterproof and carried his cap. He was rather white about the mouth.

"I'm off, Jonathan," he said.

"Nick, my dear fellow—I implore—"

"Orders is orders. There's a war on. Will you let me leave my luggage? I'll collect the car as soon as possible."

"Do I understand," said Mandrake, "that you are walking over Cloudyfold?"

"Needs must."

"Nick, have you considered your mother?"

"I'm not telling my mother I'm going. She's resting. I'll leave a note for her. Good-bye, Mandrake. I'm sorry you had the role of my stand-in forced upon you. If it's any satisfaction you may be quite certain that in a very short space of time I shall be just as wet and possibly a good deal colder than you were."

"If you persist, I shall come as far as Deep Bottom with you," said Jonathan, wretchedly. "We'll have some of the men with shovels, and so on."

"Please don't bother, Jonathan. Your men can hardly shovel a path all the way over Cloudyfold."

"Now listen to me," said Jonathan. "I've talked to my bailiff who came in just now, and he tells me that what you propose is out of the question. I told him you were determined, and he's sending two of our men—"

"I'm sorry, Jonathan. I've made up my mind. I'm off. Don't come down. Good-bye."

But before Nicholas got to the door, it burst open and William, scarlet in the face, strode in and confronted his brother.

"What the hell's this nonsense I hear about you going?" he demanded.

"I don't know what you've heard, but I'm going. I've got orders to report at—"

"Orders my foot! You've got the wind up and you're doing a bolt. You're so damn' frightened, you'd rather die in a snow-drift than face the music here. You're not going."

"Unusual solicitude!" Nicholas said, and the lines from his nostrils to the corners of his mouth deepened.

"Don't imagine I care what happens to you," said William, and his voice broke into a higher key. He used the clumsy vehement gestures of a man who, unaccustomed to violence of speech or action, suddenly finds himself consumed with rage. He presented a painful and embarrassing spectacle. "You could drown yourself and welcome, if it weren't for Mother. D'you want to kill her? You'll stay here and behave yourself, my bloody little Lothario."

"Oh, shut up, you fool," said Nicholas and made for the door.

"No you don't!" William said, and lurched forward. His brother's elbow caught him a jolt in the chest and the next moment Nicholas had gone.

"William!" said Jonathan sharply. "Stay where you are."

"If anything happens to him, who do you suppose she'll blame for it? For the rest of her life his damned dead sneer will tell her that but for me . . . *He's not going.*"

"You can't stop him, you know," said Mandrake.

"*Can't* I! Jonathan, please stand aside."

"Just a moment, William." Jonathan's voice had taken an unaccustomed edge. He stood, an unheroic but somehow rather menacing figure, with his plump fingers on the doorknob and his back against the door. "I cannot have you fighting with your brother up and down my house. He is determined to go and you can't stop him. I am following him to the first drift in the drive. I am quite convinced that he will not get through it and I do not propose to let him come to any grief. I shall take a couple of men with me. If you can behave yourself you had better accompany us." Jonathan touched his spectacles delicately with his left hand. "Depend upon it," he said, "your brother will not leave Highfold to-night."

III

Mandrake's bedroom windows overlooked the last sweep of the drive as it passed the east wing of Highfold and turned into the wide sweep in front of the house. Through the white-leopard mottling on his window-pane he saw Nicholas Compline, head down, trudge heavily through the snow and out of sight. A few moments later, Jonathan and William appeared, followed at some distance by two men carrying long-handled shovels. "Nicholas must have delayed a little, after he left here," Mandrake thought. "Why? To say good-bye to Madame Lisse? Or to Chloris?" And at the thought of a final interview between Nicholas and Chloris Wynne he experienced an unaccustomed and detestable sensation, as if his heart sank with horrid speed into some unfathomable limbo. He looked after the trudging figures until they passed beyond the range of his window, and then suddenly decided that he could no longer endure his own company but would go downstairs in search of Chloris Wynne.

"The difference," Jonathan observed, "between a walk in an ordinary storm and a walk in a snow-storm is the difference between unpleasant noise and even more unpleasant silence. One can hear nothing but the squeak of snow under one's feet. I'm glad you decided to come, William."

"It's not for love of dear little Nicholas, I promise you," William muttered.

"Well, well, well," said Jonathan equitably.

They plodded on, walking in Nicholas' steps. Presently Highfold Wood enclosed them in a strange twilight where shadow was made negative by reflected whiteness and where the stems of trees seemed comfortless and forgotten in their naked blackness. Here there was less snow and they mended their pace, following the drive on its twisting course downhill. At first they passed between tall banks and heard the multiple voices of tiny runnels of water, then they came out into open spaces where the snow lay thick over Jonathan's park. It stretched away before their eyes in curves of unbroken pallor and William muttered: "White, grey, and black. I don't think I could paint it." When they entered the lower wood, still going downhill, they saw Nicholas, not far ahead, and Jonathan called to him a shrill "Hello!" that set up an echo among the frozen trees. Nicholas turned and stood motionless, waiting for them to overtake him. With that air of self-consciousness inseparable from such approaches, they made their way towards him, the two farm-hands still some distance behind.

"My dear Nick," Jonathan panted, "you should have waited a little. I told you I'd see you as far as the first obstacle. See here, I've brought two of the men. They know more about the state of affairs than I do. My head shepherd and his brother. You remember James and Thomas Bewling?"

"Yes, of course," said Nicholas. "Sorry you've both been dragged out on my account."

"If there is a way through Deep Bottom," said Jonathan, "the Bewlings will find it for you. Eh, Thomas?"

The older of the two men touched his cap and moved nearer. "I do believe, sir," he said, "that without us goes at it hammer and tongs with these yurr shovels for an hour or so, they bain't *no* way over Deep Bottom."

"There, you see Nick, and in an hour or so it'll be dark."

"At least I can try," said Nicholas stiffly.

Jonathan looked helplessly at William, who was watching his brother through half-closed eyes. "Well," said Jonathan on a sudden spurt of temper, "it's beginning to snow quite abominably hard. Shall we go on?"

"Look here," William said, "you go back, Jonathan. I don't see why you should be in this. Nor you two Bewlings. Give me your shovel, Thomas."

"I've said I'll go alone, and I'm perfectly ready to do so," said Nicholas sulkily.

"Oh, damn!" said Jonathan. "Come on."

As they moved off downhill, the snow began to fall even more heavily.

Deep Bottom was at the foot of a considerable slope beyond the wood and was really a miniature ravine, extending for some two miles inside Jonathan's demesnes. It was crossed by the avenue which dipped and rose sharply to flatten out on the far side with a level stretch of some two hundred yards, ending at the entrance gates. As they approached it the north wind, from which they had hitherto been protected, drove full in their faces with a flurry of snow. Thomas Bewling began a long roaring explanation: "She comes down yurr proper blustracious like, sir. What with being druv be the wind and what with being piled up be the natural forces of gravitation, like, she slips and she slides in this-yurr bottom till she's so thick as you'd be surprised to see. Look thurr, sir. You'd tell me there was nothing but a little tiddly bit of a slant down'ill, but contrariwise. She's deceptive. She's a-laying out so smooth and sleek enough to trap you into trying 'er, but she's deep enough and soft enough to smother the lot on us. You won't get round her and you won't make t'other side, Mr. Nicholas, as well you ought to know being bred to these parts."

Nicholas looked from one to another of the four faces and without a word turned and walked on. Half a dozen strides brought him up to his knees in snow. He uttered a curious inarticulate cry and plunged forward. The next second he was floundering in a drift, spread-eagled and half-buried.

"And over he goes," William observed, mildly. "Come on."

He and the two Bewlings joined hands and by dint of extending the shovel handle brought Nicholas out of his predicament. He had fallen face first into the drift and presented a ridiculous figure. His fine moustache was clotted with snow, his cap was askew, and his nose was running.

"Quite the little snow-man," said William. "Ups-a-daisy."

Nicholas wiped his face with his gloved hands. It was blotched with cold. His lips seemed stiff and he rubbed them before he spoke.

"Very well," Nicholas whispered at last. "I give up. I'll come back. But, by God, I tell you both I'd have been safer crossing Cloudyfold in the dark than spending another night at Highfold."

IV

"Francis," said Madame Lisse, "we may not be alone together again this evening. I cannot endure this ridiculous and uncomfortable state of affairs any longer. Why do Nicholas and William Compline and the Wynne girl all avoid you? Why, when I speak of Mr. Mandrake's accident, do they look at their feet and mumble of other things? Where have they all gone? I have sat by this fire enduring the conversation of Mrs. Compline and the compliments of our host until I am ready to scream, but even that ordeal was preferable to suffering your extraordinary gloom. Where is Nicholas Compline?"

Dr. Hart stood inside the "boudoir" door, which he had closed behind him. In his face was reflected the twilight of the snowbound world outside. This strange half-light revealed a slight tic in his upper lip, a tic that suggested an independent life in one of the small muscles of his face. It was as if a moth fluttered under his skin. He raised his hand and pressed a finger on his lip, and over the top of his hand he looked at Madame Lisse.

"Why do you not answer me? Where is Nicholas?"

"Gone."

"Gone? Where?"

Without shifting his gaze from her face, Hart made a movement with his head as much as to say: "Out there." Madame Lisse stirred uneasily. "Don't look at me like that," she said. "Come here, Francis."

He came and stood before her with his hands clasped over his waistcoat and his head inclined forward attentively. There was nothing in his pose to suggest anger but she moved back in her chair almost as if she were afraid he would strike her.

"Ever since we came here," said Hart, "he has taken pains to insult me by his attentions to you. Your heads together, secret jokes, and then a glance at me to make sure I have not missed it. Last night after dinner he deliberately baited me. Well, now he is gone, and immediately I enter the room, you, YOU, ask for him."

"Must there be another of these scenes? Can you not understand that Nicholas is simply a type? It is as natural to him to pay these little attentions as it is for him to draw breath."

"And as natural for you to receive them? Well, you will not receive them again perhaps."

"What do you mean?"

"Look out there. It has been snowing all day. In a little while it will be dark and your friend will be on those hills we crossed yesterday. Do not try to seem unconcerned. Your lips are shaking."

"Why has he gone?"

"He is afraid."

"Francis," cried Madame Lisse, "what have you done? Have you threatened him? I see that you have and that they all know. This is why they are avoiding us. You fool, Francis. When these people go away from here they will lunch and dine on this story. You will be a figure of fun and what woman will choose to have a pantaloon with a violent temper to operate on her face? And my name, *mine,* will be linked with yours. The Amblington woman will see to it that I look as ridiculous as you."

"Do you love this Compline?"

"I have grown very tired of telling you I do not."

"And I am tired of hearing your lies. His behaviour is an admission."

"What has he done? What are you trying to suggest?"

"He mistook Mandrake for me. He tried to drown me."

"What nonsense is this! I have heard the account of the accident. Nicholas saw Mr. Mandrake through the pavilion window and recognized him. Nicholas told me that he recognized Mandrake and that Mandrake himself realizes that he was recognized."

"Then you have seen Compline. When did you see him?"

"Soon after the affair at the swimming-pool."

"You did not appear until nearly lunch-time. He came to your room. You had forbidden me and you received him. Is that true? Is it?"

"Cannot you see—" Madame Lisse began, but he silenced her with a vehement gesture and, stooping until his face was close to hers, began to arraign her in a sort of falsetto whisper. She leant away from him, pressing her shoulders and head into the back of her chair. The movement suggested distaste rather than fear, and all the time that he was speaking her eyes looked over his shoulder from the door to the windows. Once she raised her hand as if to silence him but he seized her wrist and held it, and she said nothing.

". . . you said I should see for myself, and *lieber Gott* have I not seen? I have seen enough and I tell you this. He was wise to go when he did. Another night and day of his insolence would have broken my endurance. It is well for him that he has gone."

He was staring into her face and saw her eyes widen. He still had her by the wrist but with her free hand she pointed to the window. He turned and looked out.

He was in time to see Jonathan Royal and William Compline trudge past laboriously in the snow. And three yards behind them, sullen and bedraggled, trailed Nicholas Compline.

V

Hersey Amblington, Mrs. Compline, Chloris Wynne and Aubrey Mandrake were in the library. They knew that Dr. Hart and Madame Lisse were in the "boudoir," separated from them by the small smoking-room. They knew, too, that Jonathan and William had gone with Nicholas on the first stage of his preposterous journey. Hersey was anxious to have a private talk with Sandra Compline, Mandrake was anxious to have a private talk with Chloris Wynne; but neither Mandrake nor Hersey could summon up the initiative to make a move. A pall of inertia hung over them all and they spoke, with an embarrassing lack of conviction, about Nicholas' summons to his headquarters in Great Chipping. Mrs. Compline was in obvious distress and Hersey kept assuring her that if the road was unsafe Jonathan would bring Nicholas back.

"Jonathan shouldn't have let him go, Hersey. It was very naughty of him. I'm extremely displeased with William for letting Nicholas go. He should never have allowed it."

"William did his best to dissuade him," said Mandrake drily.

"He should have come and told me, Mr. Mandrake. He should have used his authority. He is the elder of my sons." She turned to Hersey. "It's always been the same. I've always said that Nicholas should have been the elder."

"I don't agree," said Chloris quickly.

"No," Mrs. Compline said. "I did not suppose you would." And Mandrake, who had thought that Mrs. Compline's face could express nothing but its own distortion, felt a thrill of alarm when he saw her look at Chloris.

"I speak without prejudice," said Chloris, and two spots of colour started up in her cheeks. "William and I have broken off our engagement."

For a moment there was silence and Mandrake saw that Mrs. Compline had forgotten his existence. She continued to stare at Chloris and a shadow of a smile, painful and acrid, tugged at her distorted mouth. "I am afraid you are too late," she said.

"I don't understand."

"My son Nicholas—"

"This has nothing whatever to do with Nicholas."

"Hersey," Mrs. Compline said, "I am terribly worried about Nicholas. Surely Jonathan will bring him back. How long have they been gone?"

"It has nothing whatever to do with Nicholas," Chloris said loudly.

Mrs. Compline stood up. "Hersey, I simply cannot sit here any longer. I'm going to see if they're coming."

"You can't, Sandra. It's snowing harder than ever. There's no need to worry, they're all together."

"I'm going out on the drive. I haven't stirred from the house all day. I'm stifled."

Hersey threw up her hands and said: "All right. I'll come with you. I'll get our coats. Wait for me, darling."

"I'll wait in the hall. Thank you, Hersey."

When they had gone, Mandrake said to Chloris: "For God's sake, let's go next door and listen to the news. After this party, the war will come as a mild and pleasurable change."

They moved into the smoking-room. Mrs. Compline crossed the hall and entered the drawing-room, where she stood peering through the windows for her son, Nicholas. Hersey Amblington went upstairs. First she got her own raincoat and then she went to Mrs. Compline's room to fetch hers. She opened the wardrobe doors and stretched out her hand to a heavy tweed coat. For a moment she stood stockstill, her fingers touching the shoulders of the coat.

It was soaking wet.

And through her head ran the echo of Sandra Compline's voice: "I haven't stirred from the house all day."

VI

In the days that followed that week-end Mandrake was to trace interminably the sequence of events that in retrospect seemed to point so unmistakably towards the terrible conclusion. He was to decide that not the least extraordinary of these events had been his own attitude towards Chloris Wynne. Chloris was not Mandrake's type. If, in the midst of threats, mysteries, and mounting terrors, he had to embark upon some form of dalliance, it should surely have been with Madame Lisse. Madame was the sort of woman to whom Aubrey Mandrake almost automatically paid attention. She was dark, sophisticated, and—his own expression—immeasurably *soignée*. She was exactly Aubrey Mandrake's cup of tea. Chloris was not. Aubrey Mandrake was invariably bored by pert blondes. But—and here lay the reason for his curious behaviour—Stanley Footling adored them. At the sight of Chloris' shining honey-coloured loops of hair and impertinent blue eyes, the old Footling was roused in Mandrake. Bloomsbury died in him and Dulwich stirred ingenuously. He was only too well aware that in himself was being enacted a threadbare theme, a kind of burlesque, hopelessly out of date, on Jekyll and Hyde. It had happened before but never with such violence, and he told himself that there must be something extra special in Chloris so to rouse the offending Footling that Mandrake scarcely resented the experience.

He followed her into the smoking-room and tuned in the wireless to the war news which, in those now almost forgotten days, largely consisted of a series of French assurances that there was nothing to report. Chloris and Mandrake listened for a little while and then he switched off the radio, leant forward, and kissed her.

"Ah!" said Chloris. "The indoor sport idea, I see."

"Are you in love with Nicholas Compline?"

"I might say: 'What the hell's that got to do with you?' "

"Abstract curiosity."

"With rather un-abstract accompaniments."

"When I first saw you I thought you were a little nit-wit."

Chloris knelt on the hearthrug and poked the fire. "So I am," she said, "when it comes to your sort of language. I'm quite smartish but I'm not at all clever. I put up a bluff but you'd despise me no end if you knew me better."

She smiled at him. He felt his mouth go dry and with a sensation of blank panic he heard his own voice, distorted by embarrassment, utter the terrible phrase.

"My real name," said Mandrake, "is Stanley Footling."

"Oh, my dear, I'm so sorry," said Chloris. He knew that for a moment, when she recovered from her astonishment, she had nearly laughed.

"STAN-LEY FOOT-LING," he repeated, separating the destestable syllables as if each was an offence against decency.

"Sickening for you. But after all you've changed it, haven't you?"

"I've never told anyone else. In a squalid sort of way it's a compliment."

"Thank you. But lots of people must know, all the same."

"No. All my friendships occurred after I changed it. I got a hideous fright last night at dinner."

Chloris looked up quickly. "Why, I remember! I noticed. You went all sort of haywire for a moment. It was something Nicholas said, something about—"

"My having given up footling."

"Oh Lord!" said Chloris.

"Go on—laugh. It's screamingly funny, isn't it?"

"Well, it *is* rather funny," Chloris agreed. "But it's easily seen that you don't get much of a laugh out of it. I can't quite understand why. There are plenty of names just as funny as Footling."

"I'll tell you why. I can't brazen it out because it's got no background. If we were the Footlings of Fifeshire, or even the Footlings of Furniture Polish, I might stomach it. I'm a miserable snob. Even as I speak to you I'm horrified to hear how I give myself away by the very content of what I'm saying. I'm committing the only really unforgivable offence. I'm being embarrassing."

"It seems to me you've merely gone Edwardian. You're all out of focus. You say you're a snob. All right. So are we all in our degree, they say."

"But don't you see it's the *degree* I'm so ashamed of. Intellectual snob I may be; I don't care if I am. But to develop a really bad social inferiority complex—it's so degrading."

"It seems a bit silly, certainly. And anyway I don't see, accepting your snobbery, what you've got to worry about. If it's smartness you're after, isn't it smart to be obscure nowadays? Look at the prizefighters. Everybody's bosoms with them."

"That's from *your* point of view. *De haut en bas*. I want to be the *haut,* not the *bas,"* Mandrake mumbled.

"Well, intellectually you are." Chloris shifted her position and faced him squarely, looking up, her pale hair taking a richness from the fire. "I say," she said, "Mr. Royal knows all about it, doesn't he? About your name?"

"No. *Why?*"

"Well, I thought last night . . . I mean after Nicholas dropped that brick, I sort of felt there was something funny and I noticed that he and Lady Hersey and Mr. Royal looked at each other."

"By God, he put them up to it! I wondered at the time. By God, if he did that I'll pay him for it!"

"For the love of Heaven, why did I go and say that? I thought you and I were going to remain moderately normal. Nobody else is. Do snap out of being all Freudian over Footling. Who cares if you're called Footling? And anyway I must say I think 'Aubrey Mandrake' is a bit thick. Let's talk about something else."

The invitation was not immediately accepted, and in the silence that followed they heard Hersey Amblington come downstairs into the hall and call Mrs. Compline:—

"Sandra! Where are you? Sandra!" They heard an answering voice and in a moment or two the front doors slammed.

Mandrake limped about the room inwardly cursing Jonathan Royal, Chloris Wynne, and himself. Most of all, himself. Why had he given himself away to this girl who did not even trouble to simulate sympathy, who did not find even so much as a pleasing tang of irony in his absurd story, who felt merely a vague and passing interest, a faint insensitive amusement? He realized abruptly that it was because she made so little of it that he wanted to tell her. An attitude of sympathetic understanding would have aggravated his own morbid speculations. She had made little of his ridiculous obsession, and for the first time in his life, quite suddenly, he saw it as a needless emotional extravaganza.

"You're perfectly right, of course," he said. "Let's talk about something else."

"You needn't think I'll shrink from you on account of your name, and I won't tell anyone else."

"Not even Nicholas Compline?"

"Certainly not Nicholas Compline. At the moment I never want to see a Compline again. You needn't think you're the only one to feel sick at yourself. What about me and the Complines? Getting engaged to William on the rebound from Nicholas."

"And continuing to fall for Nicholas' line of stuff?"

"Yes. All right! I'll admit it. Up to an hour ago I knew Nicholas was faithless, horrid-idle, a philanderer, a he-flirt—all those things, and not many brains into the bargain. But as you say, I fell for his line of stuff. Why? I don't know. Haven't you ever fallen for a little bit of stuff? Of course you have. But when *we* do it, you hold up your hands and marvel."

Through Mandrake's mind floated the thought that not so long ago he had considered himself in much the same light in relation to Chloris. He began to feel ashamed of himself.

"What *does* attract one to somebody like Nicholas?" Chloris continued. "I don't know. He's got 'It,' as they say. Something in his physical make-up. And yet I've often gone all prickly and irritated over his physical tricks. He does silly things with his hands and he's got a tiresome laugh. His idea of what's funny is too drearily all on one subject. He's a bit of a cat, too, and bone from the eyes up if you try to talk about anything that's not quite in his language. And yet one more or less went through one's paces for him; played up to his barn-door antics. Why?"

"Until an hour ago, you said."

"Yes. I met him in the hall when he was going. He was in a blue funk. That tore it. I suppose the barn-door hero loses his grip when he loses his nerve. Anyway, I'm cured of Nicholas."

"Good."

"You know, I'm quite certain that Dr. Hart *did* think you were Nicholas and shoved you in the pond. I think Nicholas was right about that. We ought to be making no end of a hullabaloo, staying in the same house with a would-be murderer, and all we do is let down our back hair and talk about our own complexes. I suppose it'll be like that in the air raids."

"Nicholas was making a hullabaloo, anyway."

"Yes. I'm afraid he's a complete coward. If he'd brazened it out and stayed I daresay I shouldn't have been cured, but he scuttled away and that wrecked it. I wonder if the Lisse feels the same."

"Poor Nicholas," said Mandrake. "But I'm glad he didn't stay."

"WHAT'S THAT?"

Chloris scrambled to her feet. She and Mandrake stood stock-still gaping at each other. The hall was noisy with voices, Mrs. Compline scolding, Jonathan explaining, Hersey Amblington asking questions. It went on for some seconds and then Mandrake limped to the door and threw it open.

Outside in the hall was a group of five: Jonathan, Mrs. Compline, Hersey, William, and, standing apart, bedraggled, patched with snow, white-faced and furtive, Nicholas. Mandrake turned and stared at Chloris.

"So now, what?" he asked.

CHAPTER VII

Booby-Trap

I

WITH THE RETURN of Nicholas the house-party entered upon a new phase. From then onwards little attempt was made by anybody to pretend there was nothing wrong with Jonathan Royal's week-end. Jonathan himself, after a half-hearted effort to treat the episode as a mere inconvenient delay, fluttered his hands, surveyed the apprehensive faces of his guests, and watched them break away into small groups. Nicholas muttered something about a bath and change and followed his mother upstairs. Dr. Hart and Madame Lisse, who had come out of the boudoir on the arrival of the outdoors' party, returned to it; Mandrake and Chloris returned to the smoking-room. The others trailed upstairs to change.

Darkness came with no abatement of the storm. A belated pilot of the Coastal Command, who had flown off his map, battled over Cloudyfold through a driving misery of snow and, for a fraction of time, passed through the smoke from Jonathan's chimneys. Peering down, he discerned the vague shapes of roofs and pictured the warmth and joviality of some cheerful week-end party. Just about cocktail-time, he thought—and was gone over the rim of Cloudyfold.

It was cocktail-time down at Highfold. Jonathan ordered the drinks to be served in the drawing-room. Mandrake joined him there. He was filled with a strange lassitude—the carry-over, he supposed, from half-drowning. His thoughts clouded and cleared alternately. He was glad of the cocktail Jonathan brought him.

"After all," Jonathan said as they waited, "we've got to meet at dinner, so we may as well assemble here. What am I to do with them, Aubrey?"

"If you can prevent them from getting at each other's throats, you will have worked wonders. Jonathan, I insist on your telling me. Who do you suppose tried to drown me, and who do you suppose they thought I was?"

"It's an interesting point. I must confess, Aubrey, that I am now persuaded that an attack *was* made."

"Thank you. If you had felt—"

"I know, I know. I agree that you could not have been mistaken. I also agree that whoever made the attempt believed it to be made upon someone other than yourself. Now, let us, perfectly cold-bloodedly, examine the possibilities. You wore a cloak, and for this reason might have been taken for Nicholas, for Hart, or for myself. If you were mistaken for Nicholas then we must suppose that the assailant was Hart, who resents his attentions to Madame Lisse and who threatened him, or William who resents his attentions to Miss Chloris, or possibly Miss Chloris herself, whose feelings for Nicholas—"

"Don't be preposterous!"

"Eh? Ah well, I don't press it. If you were mistaken for Hart, then, as far as motive goes, the assailant might have been Nick himself—"

"Nicholas knew Hart was indoors. He saw him looking out of the bedroom window."

"He might have supposed Hart had hurried down by the shorter route."

"But I swear Nicholas recognized me through the pavilion window, and over and above all that, he knew I had the cloak."

"I agree that Nicholas is unlikely. I am examining motive only. Who else had motive, supposing you were thought to be Hart?"

"Madame Lisse?"

"There, we cannot tell. What are their relations? Could Madame have risen from her bed and picked her way down to the pavilion without being seen by anybody? And why, after all, should she do so? She, at least, could not have known anyone was going down singly or otherwise."

"She might have seen me from her window."

"In which case she would have realized that you were yourself, and not Hart. No, I think we may dismiss Madame as a suspect. There remains Sandra Compline."

"Good God, why Mrs. Compline?"

Jonathan blinked and uttered an apologetic titter. "A little point which I could not expect you to appreciate. My housekeeper, the excellent Pouting, is a sworn crony of Sandra's maid. It seems that when Hart first arrived in our part of the world, this maid, who was with Sandra at the time of the catastrophe in Vienna, thought she recognized him. She said nothing to her mistress, but she confided her news to Pouting. And I, in my turn, did a little gleaning. The Viennese surgeon was a Doktor Franz Hartz, I learnt, and I knew that Hart, when he changed his nationality also changed his name. The temptation was too great for me, Aubrey. I brought them together."

"It was a poisonous thing to do."

"You think so? Perhaps you are right. I am quite ashamed of myself," said Jonathan, touching his spectacles.

"There's one thing I'd rather like to hear from you, Jonathan. How did you find out my name was Stanley Footling?" Mandrake watched his host and saw him give a little inward start.

"My dear fellow!" Jonathan murmured.

"It's only a point of curiosity. I should be amused to know."

A pink flush mounted from Jonathan's chin up into his bald pate. "I really forget. It was so long ago. In the early days of our delightful association. Somebody connected with your threatre. I quite forget."

"Ah, yes," said Mandrake. "And is Lady Hersey in the joke?"

"No. No, I assure you. Word of honour."

"What about Nicholas Compline? He knows. You've told him."

"Well, I—I—really Aubrey—I—"

"You put him up to saying what he did at dinner."

"But without any intention of hurting you, Aubrey. I had no idea your secret—"

"You asked me the other night what sort of man I considered you to be. I didn't know then, and I'm damned if I know now."

The light flickered on Jonathan's spectacles. "In a sense," he said, "you might call me an unqualified practitioner."

"Of what?"

"The fashionable pursuit, my dear Aubrey. Psychology."

II

Madame Lisse dressed early that evening, and got rid of the maid Mrs. Pouting had sent to help her. She sat by her fire listening intently. She heard a delicate sound as if someone tapped with his finger-nails at her door. She turned her head quickly but did not rise. The door opened and Nicholas Compline came in.

"Nicholas! Are you certain . . . ?"

"Quite certain. He's in his bath. I listened outside the door."

He stooped swiftly and kissed her. "I had to see you," he said.

"What has happened? He's furious."

"You needn't tell me that. I suppose you realize that he tried to kill me this morning. They won't listen to me. Elise, I can't put up with this any longer. Why can't we—"

"You know very well. I cannot risk it. A scandal would ruin me. He would make scenes. God knows what he would not do. You should have gone away."

"Damn it, I did my best. Did you want me to do myself in? I tell you I *couldn't* get away. I assure you I don't enjoy the prospect of another attack."

"Quiet! Are you mad, to make such a noise. What is the matter with you? You've had too much to drink."

"I came in half-dead with cold," he said. "Do you suppose he'll have another go at me? Pleasant, isn't it, waiting?"

She looked at him attentively.

"I cannot believe he would go to such lengths, and yet one can find no other explanation. You must be careful, Nicholas. Devote yourself again to the Wynne child. You deliberately baited Francis by your behaviour. I warned you. You should have refused the invitation; it was madness to come here."

"I wanted to see you. God, Elise, you seem to forget that I love you."

"I do not forget. But we must be careful."

"Careful! Listen here. For the last time will you make a clean break? We could meet in London. You could write and—"

"I have told you, Nicholas. It is impossible. How could I continue my work? And when this war ends, my friend, what then? How should we live?"

"I could find something—" He broke off and looked fixedly at her. "You're very mercenary, Elise, aren't you?"

"All my life I have had to fight. I have known the sort of poverty that you have never dreamed of. I will not endure such poverty again, no, nor anything approaching it. Why can you not be content? I love you. I give you a great deal, do I not?"

He stooped down to her and behind them, on the firewall, their fire-shadows joined and moved only with the movement of the fire itself. From this embrace Nicholas was the first to draw back. His shadow started from hers and in the silence of the room his whisper sounded vehemently:—

"What's that?"

"What do you mean?"

"Ssh!"

He stepped back quickly towards a screen near her bed. It was the serio-comic movement of a surprised lover in some Restoration play, and it made a foolish figure of Nicholas. Madame Lisse looked at him and in response to his gesture moved to the door, where she stood listening, her eyes on Nicholas. After a moment she motioned him to stand farther aside and with a shamefaced look he slipped behind the screen. He heard that the door was opened and closed again and then her voice recalled him.

"There is nobody."

"I swear I heard somebody at that door," Nicholas whispered.

"There is nobody there. You had better go."

He crossed to the door and paused, staring at her, half hang-dog, half glowering. Nicholas did not cut a brave figure at that moment but Madame Lisse joined her hands behind his neck and drew his face down to hers. There was an urgency, a certain rich possessiveness in her gesture.

"Be careful," she whispered. "Do go, now."

"At least *you* believe he means trouble. *You* know it's he that's at the back of this."

"Yes."

"I feel as if he's behind every damn door in the place. It's a filthy feeling."

"You must go."

He looked full in her face, and a moment later slipped through the door and was gone.

Madame Lisse seemed to hesitate for a moment and then she too went to the door. She opened it a very little and looked through the crack after Nicholas. Suddenly she flung the door wide open and screamed. Immediately afterwards came the sound of a thud, a thud so heavy that she felt its vibration and heard a little glass tree on her mantelpiece set up a faint tinkle. And a second later she heard the shocking sound of a man screaming. It was Nicholas.

III

Mandrake and Jonathan heard the thud. The drawing-room chandelier set up a little chime and immediately afterwards, muffled and far away, came the sound of a falsetto scream. With no more preface than a startled exclamation, Jonathan ran from the room. Mandrake, swinging his heavy boot, followed at a painful shamble. As he toiled up the stairs, the quick thump of his heart reminded him of his nocturnal prowl. He reached the guest-wing passage and saw, halfway down it, the assembled house-party, some in dressing-gowns, some in evening clothes. They were gathered in

Nicholas' doorway: William, Chloris, Dr. Hart, Madame Lisse, and Hersey Amblington. From inside the room came the sound of Mrs. Compline's voice, agitated and emphatic, punctuated by little ejaculations from Jonathan and violent interjections from Nicholas himself. As he came to the doorway, Mandrake was dimly aware of some difference in the appearance of the passage. Without pausing to analyze this sensation he joined the group in the doorway. William, who was scarlet in the face, grabbed his arms. "By gum!" said William. "It's true after all. Somebody's after Nick, and by gum, they've nearly got him."

"Bill, *don't!*" cried Chloris, and Hersey said fiercely, "Shut up, William."

"No, but isn't it extraordinary, Mandrake? He didn't want to come back, you know. He said—"

"What's happened?"

"Look."

William stepped aside and Mandrake saw into the room.

Nicholas sat in an armchair nursing his left arm. He was deadly pale and kept turning his head to look first at Jonathan and then at his mother, who knelt beside him. Between this group and the door, lying on its back on the carpet and leering blandly at the ceiling, was an obese brass figure, and when Mandrake saw it he knew what it was he had missed from the passage. It was the Buddha that had watched him from its niche when he stole downstairs in the night.

". . . It all seemed to happen at once," Nicholas was saying shakily. "I went to push open the door—it wasn't quite shut—and it felt as if someone was resisting me on the other side. I gave it a harder shove and it opened so quickly that I sort of jumped back. I suppose that saved me because at the same time I felt a hell of a great thud on my arm, and Elise screamed."

From down the passage Madame Lisse said: "I saw something fall from the door and I screamed out to him."

"A booby-trap," said William. "It was a booby-trap, Mandrake. Balanced on the top of the door. We used to do it with buckets of water when we were kids. It *would* have killed him, you know. Only of course its dead weight dragged on the door and when it overbalanced the door shot open. That's what made him jump back."

"His arm's broken," said Mrs. Compline. "Darling, your arm's broken."

"I don't think so. It was a glancing blow. It's damn' sore, but by God it might have been my head. Well, Jonathan, what have you to say? Was I right to try and clear out?" Nicholas raised his uninjured arm and pointed to the crowded doorway. "One of them's saying to himself, 'Third time, lucky.' Do you realize that, Jonathan?"

Jonathan said something that sounded like "God forbid." Mrs. Compline began again:—

"Let me look at your arm, darling. Nicky, my dear, let me see it."

"I can't move it. Look out, Mother, that hurts."

"Perhaps you would like me—" Dr. Hart came through the door and advanced upon Nicholas.

"No, thank you, Hart," said Nicholas. "You've done enough. Keep off."

Dr. Hart stopped short, and then, as though growing slowly conscious of the silence that had fallen upon his fellow guests, he turned and looked from one face to another. When he spoke it was so softly that only a certain increase in foreign inflexions, in the level stressing of his words, gave any hint of his agitation.

"This has become too much," he said. "Is it not enough that I should be insulted, that Mr. Compline should insult me, I say, from the time that I have arrived in this house? Is that not enough to bear without this last, this fantastic accusation? I know well what you have been saying against me. You have whispered among yourselves that it was I who attacked Mr. Mandrake, thinking he was Compline, I who, goaded by open enmity as well as by secret antagonism, have plotted to injure, to murder Compline. I tell you now that I am not guilty of these outrages. If, as Compline suggests, anything further is attempted against him, it will not be by my agency. That I am his enemy I do not deny, but I tell him now that somewhere amongst us he has another and a more deadly enemy. Let him remember this." He glanced at Nicholas' injured arm. Nicholas made a quick movement. "I do not think your arm is fractured," said Dr. Hart. "You had better let someone look at it. If the skin is broken it will need a dressing, and perhaps a sling. Mrs. Compline will be able to attend to it, I think." He walked out of the room.

Mrs. Compline drew back the sleeve of Nicholas' dressing-gown. His forearm was swollen and discoloured. A sort of blind gash ran laterally across its upper surface. He turned his hand from side to side, wincing at the pain. "Well," said William, "it seems he's right about that, Nick. It can't be broken."

"It's bloody sore, Bill," said Nicholas, and Mandrake was astounded to see an almost friendly glance pass between these extraordinary brothers. William came forward and stooped down, looking at the arm. "We could do with a first-aid kit," he said, and Jonathan bustled away muttering that Mrs. Pouting was fully equipped.

"It's Hart all right," said William. He turned to contemplate Madame Lisse, who still waited with Chloris and Mandrake in the passage. "Yes," William repeated with an air of thoughtfulness, "it's Hart. I think he's probably mad, you know."

"William," said his mother, "what are you saying? You have been keeping something from me, both of you. *What do you know about this man?*"

"It doesn't matter, Mother," said Nicholas impatiently.

"It does matter, I *will* know. What have you found out about him?"

"Sandra," cried Hersey Amblington, "don't. It's not that. Don't, Sandra."

"Nicky, my dear! You know! You've guessed." Mrs. Compline's eyes seemed to Mandrake to be living fires in her dead face. She, like Nicholas, looked at Madame Lisse. "I *see,*" she said. "You know too. You've told my son. Then it is true."

"I don't know what you're talking about, Mother," said Nicholas querulously.

"Nor I," said Madame Lisse, and her voice was shriller than Mandrake could have imagined it. "This is ridiculous. I have said nothing."

"Hersey," said Mrs. Compline, "do you see what has happened?" She put her arms round Nicholas' neck and her hand, with agonized possessiveness, caressed his shoulder. "Nicky has found out and threatened to expose him. He has tried to kill Nicholas."

"Look here," William demanded, "what *is* all this?"

"It's a complete and miserable muddle," said Hersey sharply, "and it's certainly not for publication. Mr. Mandrake, do you mind . . . ?"

Mandrake muttered, "Of course," turned away and shut the door, leaving himself, Chloris Wynne, and Madame Lisse alone in the passage.

"This woman is evidently insane," said Madame Lisse. "What mystery is this she is making? What am I supposed to have told Nicholas Compline?"

Mandrake, conscious of a violent and illogical distaste for Madame Lisse, said loudly: "Mrs. Compline thinks you have told her son that Dr. Hart is the surgeon who operated on her face."

He heard Chloris catch her breath, and whisper: "No, no, it's impossible. It's too fantastic." He heard his own voice trying to explain that Jonathan was responsible. He was conscious, in himself, of a sort of affinity with Mrs. Compline, an affinity born of disfigurement. He wanted to explain to Chloris that there was nothing in the world as bad as a hideous deformity. Through this confusion of emotions and thoughts, he was aware of Madame Lisse watching him very closely, of the closed door at his back, of the murmur of Mrs. Compline's voice beyond it in Nicholas' room where, Mandrake supposed, her sons listened to the story of Dr. Franz Hartz of Vienna. The truth is, Mandrake was suffering from a crisis of nerves. His experience of the morning, his confession to Chloris, the sense of impending disaster that, like some grotesque in a dream, half comic, half menacing, seemed to advance upon Nicholas—all these circumstances had scraped at his nerves and wrought upon his imagination. When Jonathan came hurrying along the passage with a first-aid outfit in his hands, Mandrake saw him as a shifty fellow as cold-blooded as a carp. When Madame Lisse began to protest that she knew nothing of Dr. Hart's past, that Mrs. Compline was insane, that she herself could endure no longer to be shut up at Highfold, Mandrake was conscious only of a sort of wonder that this cool woman should suddenly become agitated. He felt Chloris take him by the elbow and heard her say: "Let's go downstairs." He was steadied by her touch and eager to obey it. Before they moved away, the door opened and William came stumbling out, followed by Jonathan.

"Wait a bit, Bill," Jonathan cried. "*Wait* a bit."

"The bloody swine," William said. "Oh God, the bloody swine." He went blindly past them and they heard him run downstairs. Jonathan remained in the doorway. Behind him, Mandrake saw Hersey Amblington with her arms about Mrs. Compline, who was sobbing. Nicholas, very pale, stood, looking on.

"It's *most* unfortunate," Jonathan said. He shut the door delicately. "Poor Sandra has convinced William that there has been a conspiracy against her. That Hart has made a story of the catastrophe for Madame Lisse, that—Oh, you're there, Madame. Forgive me, I hadn't noticed. It's all *too* distressing, Aubrey. Now William's in a frightful tantrum and won't listen to reason. Nicholas assures us he knew nothing of the past but he might as well speak to the wind. We're in the very devil of a mess, it's snowing harder than ever, and what in Heaven's name am I to do?"

A loud and ominous booming sound welled up through the house. Caper, finding no one to whom he could announce dinner, had fallen upon an enormous gong and beaten it. Jonathan uttered a mad little giggle.

"Well," he said, "shall we dine?"

IV

The memory of that night's dinner party was to be a strange one for Mandrake. It was to have the intermittent vividness and the unreality of a dream. Certain incidents he would never forget, others were lost the next day. At times his faculty of observation seemed abnormally acute and he observed, exactly, inflexions of voices, precise choice of words, details, of posture. At other times he was lost in a sensation of anxiety, an intolerable anticipation of calamity, and at these moments he was blind and deaf to his surroundings.

Only six of the party appeared for dinner. Madame Lisse, Mrs. Compline, and Dr. Hart had all excused themselves. Dr. Hart was understood to be in the "boudoir," where he had gone after his speech in his own defence and where, apparently at Jonathan's suggestion, he was to remain, during his waking hours, for the rest of his stay at Highfold. Mandrake wondered what Jonathan had told the servants. The party at dinner was therefore composed of the less antagonistic elements. Even the broken engagement of William and Chloris seemed a minor dissonance, quite overshadowed by the growing uneasiness of the guests. Nicholas, Mandrake decided, was now in a state of barely suppressed nerves. His injured arm was not in a sling but evidently gave him a good deal of pain and he made a clumsy business of cutting up his food, finally allowing Hersey Amblington to help him. He had come down with Hersey, and something in their manner suggested that this arrangement was not accidental. "And really," Mandrake thought, "it would be better not to leave Nicholas alone. Nothing can happen to him if somebody is always at his side." Mandrake was now positive that it was Hart who had made the attacks upon Nicholas and himself and he found that the others shared this view and discussed it openly. His clearest recollection of the dinner party was to be of a moment when William, who had been silent until now, leant forward, his hands gripping the edge of the table, and said: "What's the law about attempted murder?" Jonathan glanced nervously at the servants, and Mandrake saw Hersey Amblington nudge William. "Oh, damn," William muttered, and was silent again. As soon as they were alone, he returned to the attack. He was extraordinarily inarticulate and blundered about from one accusation to another, returning always to the ruin of his mother's beauty. "The man who did that would do anything," seemed to be the burden of his song. "The Œdipus complex with a vengeance," thought Mandrake, but he was still too bemused and shaken to crystallize his attention upon William, and listened through a haze of weary lassitude. It was useless for Nicholas to say that he had never heard the name of his mother's plastic surgeon. "Hart must have thought you knew," William said. "He thought that Mother had told you."

"Rot, Bill," said Nicholas. "You're barking up the wrong tree. *It's because of Elise Lisse.* The fellow's off his head with jealousy."

"I'm older than you," William roared out with startling irrelevancy. "I remember what she was like. She was beautiful. I remember the day she came back. We went to the station to meet her. She had a veil on, a thick veil. And when I kissed her she didn't lift it up and I felt her face through the veil and it was stiff."

"Don't, Bill," Hersey said.

"You heard what she said—what Mother herself said. She said up there in your room: 'Nicky's found out. He's afraid Nicky will expose him.' God, *I'll* expose him. He's gone to earth, has he? I'm damn well going to lug him out and—"

"William!" Jonathan's voice exploded sharply, and Mandrake roused himself to listen. "William, you will be good enough to pull yourself together. Whether you choose to do your mother an appalling wrong by reviving for public discussion a tragedy that is twenty years old, is your affair. I do not attempt to advise you. But this is my house and I am very much your senior. I must ask you to attend to me."

He paused, but William said nothing, and, after a moment, Jonathan cleared his throat and touched his spectacles. Mandrake thought dimly: "Good Heavens, he's going to make another of his speeches."

"Until this evening," Jonathan said, "I refused to believe that among my guests there could be one—ah—individual, who had planned, who still plans a murderous assault upon a fellow guest. I argued that the catastrophe at the swimming pool was the result of a mischievous, rather than a malicious attack. I even imagined that it was possible poor Aubrey had been mistaken for myself." Here Jonathan blinked behind his spectacles and the trace of a smirk appeared on his lips. He smoothed it away with his plump hand and went on very gravely. "This second attempt upon Nicholas has convinced me. If that idol, which I may say I have always rather disliked, had fallen, as without a shadow of doubt it was intended to fall, upon his head, it would have killed him. There is no doubt at all, my dear Nick, it would have killed you."

"Thank you, Jonathan," said Nicholas with a kind of sneer, "I think I realize that."

"Well, now, you know," Jonathan continued, "this sort of thing is pretty bad. It's preposterous. It's like some damn pinchbeck story-book."

"Jo," Hersey Amblington interjected suddenly, "you really can't keep us all waiting while you grizzle about the æsthetic poverty of your own show. We're all agreed it's a rotten show, but at least it has the makings of a tragedy. What are you getting at? Do you think Dr. Hart's out for Nick's blood?"

"I am forced to come to that conclusion," said Jonathan primly. "Who else are we to suspect? Not one of ourselves, surely. I am not breaking confidence, I hope, Nick, when I say that Hart has threatened you, and threatened you repeatedly."

"We've heard all about that," Hersey grunted.

"Ah—yes. So I supposed. Well, now, I am a devotee of crime fiction. I have even dabbled in quite solemn works on the detection of crime. I don't pretend to the smallest degree of proficiency, but I *have* ventured to carry out a little investigation. Nicholas tells me that ten minutes before he so nearly became the victim of that atrocious booby-trap, he left his room and—ah—visited that of Madame Lisse."

"Oh Lord!" Hersey muttered, and Mandrake thought he heard Chloris utter a small contemptuous sound.

"This was, of course, a reckless and foolish proceeding," said Jonathan. "However, it has this merit—it frees Madame Lisse from any imputation of guilt. Because Nick, when he left his room, opened and shut the door with impunity, and was talking to Madame Lisse until he returned to sustain the injury to his arm. Nick tells me he heard the clock on the landing strike the half-hour as he walked down the passage to Madame's room. I had glanced at the drawing-room clock not more than a minute before the crash and it was then twenty to eight. The two clocks are exactly synchronized. As the trap could not have been set until after Nick left his room, that gives us ten minutes for our field of enquiry. Now, at the time of the accident, Aubrey and I were both in the drawing-room. I found him there when I came down and actually heard him go downstairs some little time before that. I am therefore able to provide Aubrey with an alibi and I hope he will vouch for me. Now, can any of you do as much for each other?"

"I can for Sandra," said Hersey, "and I imagine she can for me. I was in her room talking to her when Nick yelled, and I'm sure I'd been there longer than ten minutes. I remember quite well that when I passed Nick's door it was half open and the light on. I saw him beyond the door in his room and called out something."

"I remember that," said Nicholas. "I left the room a very short time afterwards."

"So there was no Buddha on the top of the door *then,*" said Jonathan. "I am persuaded that apart from Nick having gone out in safety, proving that the trap was laid later than this, we might rest assured that if the room light was on the trap had not been set. One would be almost certain to see the dark shape on the top of the door if the light was on. I have found out, by dint of cautious enquiries, that there were no servants upstairs at that time. It appears that those members of my staff who were not with Caper, in the dining-room, were listening to the wireless in the servants' hall. Now you see, I have done quite well, haven't I, with my amateur detection? Let me see. We have found alibis for Sandra, Hersey, Madame Lisse, Aubrey and, I hope, myself. What do you think, Aubrey?"

"Eh? Oh, I think it was more than ten minutes before the thud that you came downstairs," Mandrake said.

"Well now, Miss Chloris," said Jonathan, with a little bend in her direction. "What about you?"

"When it happened I was in my room. I'd had a bath and was dressing. I don't think I can prove I didn't go out of my room before that. But I didn't leave it after I went upstairs except to go into the bathroom next door. When I heard the crash and Nicholas cried out, I put on my dressing-gown and ran into the passage."

Mandrake was roused by a sharp sensation of panic. "What does that thing weigh?" he asked. "The Buddha thing?"

"It's heavy," said Jonathan. "It's solid brass. About twenty pounds, I should say."

"Do you think Miss Wynne could raise an object weighing twenty pounds above her head and balance it on the top of a door?"

"Nobody's going to worry about whether she could or couldn't," said Nicholas impatiently. "She didn't."

"Quite so," said Mandrake.

"Well," said Chloris mildly, "that's true enough."

"Nobody's asked me for my alibi," said William. "I think it's rather feeble, all this, because, I mean, we know that Hart did it."

"But the point is—" Jonathan began.

"I was in the smoking-room," said William ruthlessly, "listening to the wireless. I suddenly realized I was a bit late and started to go upstairs. I was just about up when Nick let out that screech. I heard you come down, Jonathan, about ten minutes earlier. You spoke to Caper in the hall about drinks at dinner and I heard you. But that proves nothing, of course. Oh, wait a bit, though. I could tell you what the news was. There's been a reconnaissance flight over—"

"Oh, what the hell's it matter?" said Nicholas. "What's the good of talking like little detective fans? I'm sorry to be rude, but while you're all trying to bail each other out, our charming beauty specialist is probably thinking up a new death trap on the third-time-lucky principle."

"But to try anything else, when he knows perfectly well we suspect him!" Hersey exclaimed. "It'd be the action of a madman."

"He is a madman," said Nicholas.

"I say," said William. "Has anybody done anything about that Buddha? I mean, it's probably smothered in his finger-prints. If we're going to give him in charge . . ."

"But are we going to give him in charge?" asked Hersey uneasily.

"I will," said William. "If Nick doesn't, I will."

"I don't think you can. It's not your business."

"Why not?" William demanded. Jonathan cut in hurriedly, asking William if he proposed to make his mother's tragedy into front-page publicity. The conversation became fantastic. William showed a tendency to shout and Nicholas to sulk. Chloris turned upon Mandrake a face so eloquent of misery and alarm that he instantly took her hand and found more reality in the touch of her fingers, moving restlessly in his grasp, than in anything else that was happening. Jonathan began to explain that he had locked the Buddha away in his room. He reminded them of the nature of the trap. When Nicholas had returned to his room he had found the door not quite closed. The room was in darkness, as he had left it. He had pushed at the door with his left hand. The door had resisted him, and then given way suddenly. At the same instant his arm had been struck and Madame Lisse had screamed. He had cried out and stumbled into the room.

Nicholas irritably confirmed this description and cut in to say he had seen Dr. Hart go into the bathroom adjoining Nicholas' room, and had heard him turn on the taps. "Of course he simply dodged out when he knew I had gone. He was spying on me, I suppose, through the crack of the door. His room's only about fourteen feet away from mine on the opposite side of the passage."

Mandrake, nervously tightening his grip on Chloris' hand, thought with a sort of unreal precision of the guest wing. Mrs. Compline in the front corner room, then Madame Lisse, a cupboard, and Mandrake himself, all in a row, with a bathroom; then William; and then Hart in the corner room at the back, and another bathroom around the corner. Hersey Amblington in the converted nursery beyond. On the other side of the passage overlooking the central court round which the old Jacobean house was built, were Nicholas' room, opposite William's, and then a bathroom and an unoccupied room. Nicholas' room was diagonally opposed to Hart's. Hart could easily have spied on Nicholas, and Mandrake pictured him turning on the bath taps and then perhaps opening the door to return to his room for something and seeing Nicholas stealing down the passage towards Madame Lisse's door. He pictured Hart as the traditional figure of the suspicious lover, his compact paunch curving above the girdle of his dressing-gown. "He clutched a sponge-bag to his breast, and his eye was glued to the crevice," Mandrake decided. Perhaps he saw Nicholas tap discreetly at Madame Lisse's door or scratch with his finger-nail. Perhaps Nicholas slipped in without ceremony. And then, what? Mandrake wondered. A quick sprint down the passage to the niche? A lopsided shuffle back to Nicholas' room? Did Dr. Hart carry the Buddha under the folds of his dressing-gown? Did he turn on the light in Nicholas' room and climb on the chair? Was his somewhat unremarkable face distorted with fury as he performed these curious exercises? No. Try as he might, Mandrake could not picture Hart and the Buddha without investing the whole affair with an improper air of *opéra bouffe*. He was roused from his reverie by Chloris' withdrawing her hand and by William's saying in a loud voice: "You know, this is exactly like a thriller, except for one thing."

"What do you mean, William?" asked Jonathan crossly.

"In a thriller," William explained, "there's always a corpse and he can't give evidence. But here," and he pointed his finger at his brother, "you might say we have the corpse with us. That's the difference."

"Let us go to the library," said Jonathan.

CHAPTER VIII

Third Time Lucky

I

HERSEY AMBLINGTON AND CHLORIS did not stay long with the party in the library. They went upstairs to visit, severally, Mrs. Compline and Madame Lisse. Jonathan had suggested this move to Hersey.

"I'll go and see how Sandra's getting on, with the greatest of pleasure," Hersey said. "I was going to do so in any case. But I must say, Jo, I don't think the Pirate would welcome my solicitude. What's supposed to be the matter with her?"

"A sick headache," said Jonathan. "The migraine."

"Well, the sight of me won't improve it. Damn the woman, what business has *she* to throw a migraine?"

"Naturally," Nicholas said, "she's upset."

"Why? Because she's afraid her face-lifting friend will make another pass at you? Or because she's all shocked and horrified that we should suspect him? Which?"

Nicholas looked furious but made no rejoinder.

"Would I be any use?" asked Chloris. "I don't mind casting an eye at her."

"Good girl," said Hersey. "Come on." And they went upstairs together.

Hersey found Mrs. Compline sitting by her fire still wearing the dress into which she had changed for dinner.

"I ought to have come down, Hersey. It's *too* cowardly and difficult of me to hide like this. But I couldn't face it. Now that they all know! Imagine how they would avoid looking at me. I thought I had become hardened to it. For twenty years I've drilled myself, and now, when this happens, I am as raw as I was on the day I first let Nicholas look at me. Hersey, if you had seen him that day! He was only a tiny boy, but he—I thought he would never come to me again. He looked at me as though I was a stranger. It took so long to get him back."

"And William?" Hersey asked, abruptly.

"William? Oh, he was older, of course, and not so sensitive. He seemed very shocked for a moment and then he began to talk as if nothing had happened. I've never understood William. Nicky was just a baby, of course. He asked me what had happened to my pretty face. William never spoke of it. After a little while I think Nicky forgot I had ever had a pretty face."

"And William, it seems, never forgot."

"He was older."

"I think he's more sensitive."

"You don't understand Nicky. I see it all so plainly. He has got to know this Madame Lisse and of course she has thrown herself at his head. Women have always done that with Nicky. I've seen it over and over again."

"He doesn't exactly discourage them, Sandra."

"He *is* naughty, I know," admitted Mrs. Compline, dotingly. "He always tells me all about them. We have such laughs together sometimes. Evidently there was something between Madame Lisse and—that man. And then when she met Nicholas, of course, she lost her heart to him. I've been thinking it out. That man must have recognized me. His own handiwork! Twenty years haven't changed it much. I suppose he was horrified and rushed to her with the story. She, hoping to establish a deeper bond between herself and Nicky, told him all about it."

"Now, Sandra, Nicholas himself denies this."

"Of course he does, darling," said Mrs. Compline rapidly. "That's what I've been trying to explain—you don't understand him. He wanted to spare me. It was for *my* sake he threatened this man. It's because of what Hartz did to *me*. But to spare me he let it be thought that it was some ridiculous affair over this woman."

"That seems very far-fetched to me," said Hersey bluntly.

A dull flush mounted in Mrs. Compline's face. "Why," she said, "the woman is on her knees to him already. He has no cause to trouble himself about this Madame Lisse. It's Dr. Hart who's troubling himself."

"But why?"

"Because he has found out that Nicholas knows his real identity and is afraid of exposure. Hersey, I've made William promise that he won't leave Nicholas. I want you to do something for me. I want you to send them both up here. I'm terrified for Nicky."

"But if, as you seem to think, Hart's afraid of exposure, there wouldn't be any point in his attacking Nick. He'd have to polish off the lot of us. We all know, now."

But Hersey was up against an inflexible determination, and she saw that Sandra Compline would accept no explanation that did not show Nicholas in a heroic light. Nicholas must be upheld as the pink of courtesy, the wooed but never the wooer, the son who placed his mother above all women—a cross between a Hollywood ace and a filial Galahad. She argued no more but tried to convince Mrs. Compline that, however dangerously Hart might have threatened Nicholas, he would attempt no more assaults since he now realized that they all suspected him. She left, promising to send the two sons to their mother, and returned to the library.

II

Chloris found Madame Lisse extremely difficult. For one thing she made not the smallest effort to conceal her boredom when, after tapping at the door, Chloris came into her room. It was impossible to escape the inference that she had expected someone else. When she saw Chloris, in some subtle way she sagged. "As if," thought Chloris, "she unhooked her mental stays." She was in bed, most decoratively. There was a general impression of masses of tawny lace from which Madame Lisse emerged in pallor and smoothness. "She *is* lovely," thought Chloris, "but I believe she's bad-tempered." Aloud she said: "I just looked in to see if there was anything I could do for you."

"How kind," said Madame Lisse in an exhausted voice. "There is nothing, thank you."

"Have you got aspirin and everything?"

"I cannot take aspirin, unfortunately."

"Then I can't be of any use?"

Madame pressed the tips of her wonderfully manicured fingers against her shaded eyelids. "Too kind," she said. "No, thank you. It will pass. In time, it will pass. It is an affliction of the nerves, you understand."

"Beastly for you. I'm afraid," said Chloris after a pause, "your nerves had a bit of a jolt. We're all feeling rather temperamental at the moment."

"Where is—What is everybody doing?" Madame Lisse asked with a certain freshening of her voice.

"Well, Lady Hersey's talking to Mrs. Compline, who's pretty poorly, too, it seems. Mr. Royal and Aubrey Mandrake are in the library, and William and Nicholas are next door in the smoking-room, holding a sort of family council or something. Dr. Hart's in the 'boudoir,' I believe." Chloris hesitated, wondering if it was possible for her to establish some sort of understanding with this woman who made her feel so gauche and so uncertain of herself. It seemed to her that if any one member of the house-party fully comprehended the preposterous situation, that person must be Madame Lisse. Indeed she might be regarded as a sort of liaison officer between Nicholas and Dr. Hart. Surely, *surely,* Chloris thought, she must know for certain if Hart is after Nicholas, and if so, why. Is she lying there, sleeking herself on being a successful *femme fatale?* I believe she really *is* in a funk. And taking a deep breath, Chloris thought, "I'll ask her." With a sensation of panic she heard her own voice:—

"Madame Lisse, please forgive me for asking you, but honestly things are so desperate with all of us eying each other and nobody really knowing what they're talking about, it would be a ghastly sort of relief to know the worst, so I thought I'd just ask you."

"You thought you would just ask me what, Miss Wynne?"

"It sounds so bogus when you say it out loud."

"I can hardly be expected to understand you unless you say it out loud."

"Well, then: Is Dr. Hart trying to kill Nicholas Compline?"

Madame Lisse did not answer immediately, and for a second or two the room was quite silent. Chloris felt the palms of her hands go damp and a sensation of panic mounted in her brain. She thought: "This is frightful. My nerve must be going." And then suddenly: "I wish Aubrey were here."

When Madame Lisse spoke her voice was clear and very cold: "I know nothing whatever about it."

"But—"

"Nothing, do you hear me? Nothing."

And with a gesture whose violence shocked Chloris, she gripped the lace at her bosom. "How dare you look at me like that?" cried Madame Lisse. "Leave me alone. Go out of this room. I know nothing, I tell you. Nothing. Nothing. Nothing."

III

Jonathan struck his plump hands together and uttered a little wail of despair. "It's all very well to sit there and tell me something must be done, but what can I *do?* We've no proof. Nicholas had better go to bed and lock his door. I shall tell Nicholas to go to bed and lock his door."

"I'm not worrying so much about Nicholas," said Mandrake. "He'll look after himself. I've no opinion at all of Nicholas. He hasn't got the nerve of a louse. It's William I'm thinking about. William's dangerous, Jonathan. He's out for blood. I don't think Hart'll get Nicholas, but, by God, I believe unless you do something about it, William will get Hart."

"But why, why, why!"

"Jonathan, you pride yourself on your astuteness don't you? Can't you understand what's happened to William? Didn't you see his face when they were up there in Nicholas' room? When their mother told them that Hart was responsible for her disfigurement? Why, you yourself told me that when he was a child the disfigurement made an indelible impression on him. You have always recognized the intensity of his absorption in his mother. You've seen how readily he's adopted her extraordinary explanation of Hart's attacks on Nicholas. You've seen how he's abandoned all his private rows with Nicholas and come out strong in his defence. Can't you see that psychologically he's all of a piece? I tell you, the pent-up repressions of a lifetime have come out for an airing. William's dangerous."

"Freudian mumbo-jumbo," said Jonathan uneasily.

"It may be, but I don't think you can risk ignoring the possibilities."

"What am I to do?" Jonathan repeated angrily. "Lock up the Complines? Lock up Hart? Come, my dear Aubrey!"

"I think that at least you should have it out with Hart. Tell him flatly that we all think he's the author of these attacks. See what sort of a defence he can make. Then tackle William. You shut him up pretty successfully a little while ago, but there he is in the next room with Nicholas, who's no doubt busily engaged in churning it all up again."

"You've suddenly become wonderfully purposeful, Aubrey. At dinner I thought you seemed half in a trance."

"The look in William's eye has effectually roused me."

"And the touch of Miss Wynne's hand, perhaps?" Jonathan tittered.

"Perhaps. Are you going to tackle Hart?"

"What an odious expression that is. 'Tackle.' Very well, but you must come with me."

"As you please," said Mandrake. They moved towards the door. It opened and Chloris came in. "What's the matter?" Mandrake ejaculated.

"Nothing. At least, I've been talking to Madame Lisse. I suddenly felt I couldn't stand it. So I asked her, flat out, if she knew what Dr. Hart was up to. She turned all venomous and sort of spat at me. I've got a jitterbug. This house gets more and more noiseless every hour. Out there the snow's piling up thicker and thicker. I'm sorry," said Chloris, turning to Jonathan, "but it's suffocating, isn't it, to be shut up with something that threatens and doesn't come off? It's as if something's fumbling about the passages, setting silly, dangerous booby-traps—something mad and dangerous. Do you know, I keep wishing there'd be an air raid. That's pretty feeble-minded, isn't it?"

"Here," said Mandrake, "you sit down by the fire. What the devil do you mean by talking jitterbugs? We look towards you for a spot of brave young memsahib. Do your stuff, woman."

"I'm all right," said Chloris. "I'm sorry. I'm all right. Where were you off to, you two?"

Mandrake explained, while Jonathan fussed round Chloris, glad, so Mandrake fancied, of an excuse to postpone the interview with Dr. Hart. He threw a quantity of logs on the fire, hurried away to the dining-room, and returned with the decanter of port. He insisted on Chloris' taking a glass, helped himself and, as an afterthought, Mandrake. Hersey came in and reported her interview with Mrs. Compline. She uttered a phrase that Mandrake had begun to dread. "I looked out through the west door. It's snowing harder than ever." Jonathan showed an inclination to settle down to a chat but Mandrake said firmly that they might now leave Hersey and Chloris together. He waited for Jonathan, who gulped down his port, sighed, and got slowly to his feet. In the smoking-room next door the drone of the voices of William and Nicholas in conversation rose to some slight and amicable climax, ending in a light laugh from Nicholas. Perhaps, after all, thought Mandrake, he is making William see sense. Better not to disturb them. And he led the reluctant Jonathan, by way of the hall, into the green boudoir.

When he saw Dr. Hart the fancy crossed Mandrake's mind that Highfold was full of solitary figures crouched over fires. The door had opened silently and for a moment Hart was not aware of his visitors. He sat on the edge of an armchair, leaning forward, his arms resting upon his thighs, his hands dangling together between his knees. His head, a little sunken and inclined forward, was in shadow, but the firelight found those hands, whose whiteness, whose firm full flesh and square finger-tips, were expressive of their profession. "They've got a look of prestige," thought Mandrake, and he repeated to himself, "professional hands."

Jonathan shut the door and the hands closed like traps as Dr. Hart turned and sprang to his feet.

"Oh—er—hullo, Hart," began Jonathan, unpromisingly. "We—ah—we thought perhaps we might have a little conference."

Hart did not answer, but he turned his head and stared at Mandrake.

"I've asked Aubrey to come with me," said Jonathan, quickly, "because, you see, he's one of the—the victims, and because, as a complete stranger to all of you, ["A complete stranger to Chloris?" thought Mandrake] we can't possibly suspect him of any complicity."

"Complicity?" Hart said, still staring at Mandrake. "No. No, I suppose you are right."

"Now," said Jonathan, more firmly and with a certain briskness. "Let us sit down, shall we, and discuss this affair sensibly?"

"I have said all that I have to say. I made no attack upon Mr. Mandrake, and I made no attack upon Nicholas Compline. That I am at enmity with Compline, I admit. He has insulted me, and I do not care for insults. If it were possible I should refuse to stay in the same house with him. It is not possible but I can at least refuse to meet him. I do so. I take advantage of your offer to remain here or in my room until I am able to leave."

"Now, my dear Hart, this really won't do." Jonathan drew up two chairs to the fire and, obeying a movement of his hand, Mandrake sat in one while Jonathan himself took the other. Hart remained standing, his hands clasped behind his back.

"It won't do, you know," Jonathan repeated. "This last affair, this balancing of a Buddha, this preposterous and malicious trap, could have been planned and executed with one object only, the object of doing a fatal injury to Nicholas Compline. I have made tolerably exhaustive enquiries and I find that, motive apart, it is extremely improbable that any of my guests, excepting yourself, had an opportunity to set the second trap for Nicholas Compline. I tell you this at the outset, Dr. Hart, because I feel certain that if you can advance some proof of your—your innocence, you will now wish to do so." Jonathan struck the arms of his chair lightly with the palms of his hands. Mandrake thought: "He's not doing so badly, after all." He looked at Jonathan because he found himself unable to look at Dr. Hart and, on a flash of irrelevant thinking, he remembered that a barrister had once told him that if the members of a returning jury studiously averted their eyes from the prisoner, you could depend upon it that their verdict would be "Guilty."

"I do not know when this trap is supposed to have been set," said Dr. Hart.

"Can you tell us what you were doing during the fifteen or twenty minutes before Nicholas Compline cried out?"

Dr. Hart lifted his chin, drew down his brows and glared at the ceiling. "He's rather like Mussolini," thought Mandrake, stealing a glance at him.

"When Compline returned with you and with his brother," said Hart, "I was in this room. I went to that door and saw you in the hall. I then returned and continued a conversation with Madame Lisse, who left the room some time before I did. I remained here until it was time to dress. I went upstairs at a quarter-past seven, and immediately entered my room. Perhaps it was ten minutes later that I entered the bathroom next to my bedroom. I bathed and returned directly to my room. I had almost completed my dressing when I heard Compline scream like a woman. I heard voices in the passage. I put on my dinner jacket and went out into the passage where I found all of you grouped about the doorway to his room."

"Yes," said Jonathan. "Quite so. And between the time of your leaving this room and the discovery of the injury to Nicholas Compline, did you see any other member of the party or any of the servants?"

"No."

"Dr. Hart, do you agree that before you came here you wrote certain letters—I'm afraid I must call them threatening letters—to Nicholas Compline?"

"I cannot submit to these intolerable questions," said Hart breathlessly. "You have my assurance that I have made no attack."

"If you won't answer me, you may find yourself questioned by a person of greater authority. You oblige me to press you still further. Do you know where Nicholas Compline was when the trap was set for him?"

Hart's upper lip twitched as if a moth fluttered under the skin. Twice, he made as if to speak. At the third effort he uttered some sort of noise—a kind of moan. Mandrake felt acutely embarrassed, but Jonathan cocked his head like a bird, and it seemed to Mandrake that he was beginning to enjoy himself again. "Well, Dr. Hart?" he murmured.

"I do not know where he was. I saw nobody."

"He tells us that he was talking to Madame Lisse, in her room. . . . What did you say?"

Hart had again uttered that inarticulate sound. He wetted his lips and after a moment said loudly: "I did not know where he was."

Jonathan's fingers had been at his waistcoat pocket. He now withdrew them and with an abrupt movement held out a square of paper. Mandrake saw that it was the Charter form which he had found on the previous night in Nicholas' chair. He had time to think: "It seems more like a week ago," as he read again the words that had seemed so preposterous: "*You are warned. Keep off.*"

"Well, Dr. Hart," said Jonathan, "have you seen this paper before?"

"Never," Hart cried out shrilly. "Never!"

"Are you sure? Take it in your hand and examine it."

"I will not touch it. This is a trap. Of what do you accuse me?"

Jonathan, still holding the paper, crossed to a writing-desk in the window. Mandrake and Hart watched him peer into a drawer and finally take out a sheet of note-paper. He turned towards Hart. In his right hand he held the Charter form, in his left the sheet of note-paper.

"This is your acceptance of my invitation for the week-end," said Jonathan. "After the Charter form came into my hands," he smiled at Mandrake, "I bethought me of this note. I compared them and I came to an interesting conclusion. Your letters are characteristically formed, my dear doctor. You use a script, and it retains its Continental character. The slanting leg of the German 'K' is unusually prolonged. Here we have a 'K' in 'kind invitation.' I am looking at the note. Turning to the Charter form, we find that the letters are in script and the 'K' of 'Keep' has a slanting leg that is prolonged through the square beneath it. Now, you sat next to Nicholas on his right hand. You passed your forms to him for scoring. Instead of receiving one form from you he received two: the legitimate Charter, which curiously enough contained the word 'threats,' and this somewhat childish but, in the circumstances, quite significant warning, which you tell us you have never seen before. Now, you know, that simply won't do."

"I did not write it. It—I must have torn two sheets off together. They were stuck together at the top. Someone else had written on the bottom form."

"Ridiculous!" said Jonathan very sharply. He thrust the two papers into his pocket and moved away. When he spoke again, it was with a return to his usual air of pedantry. "No, really Dr. Hart, that will *not* do. I myself gave out the forms. Nobody could have foretold to whom I would hand this particular block. You are not suggesting, I hope, that a member of the party, by some sleight-of-hand trick, took your block of forms out of your fingers, wrote on the lower form, and returned it without attracting your attention?"

"I suggest nothing. I know nothing about it. I did not write it. Perhaps Compline himself wrote it in order to discredit me. He is capable of anything—of anything. *Ach Gott!*" cried Dr. Hart, "I can endure this no longer. I must ask you to leave me. I must insist that you leave me alone." He clasped his hands together and raised them to his eyes. "I am most unhappy," he said. "I am in great trouble. You do not understand, you are not of my race. I tell you that these accusations mean nothing to me—

nothing. I am torn by the most terrible of all emotions and I cannot fight against it. I am near breaking-point. I entreat you to leave me alone."

"Very well," said Jonathan and, rather to Mandrake's surprise, he walked to the door. "But I warn you," he said, "if anything should happen to Nicholas Compline, you, and only you, will immediately fall under the gravest suspicion. I firmly believe you tried to kill Nicholas. If there is one more threat, one more suspicious move upon your part, Dr. Hart, I shall take it upon myself to place you under arrest." He made a quick deft movement and the next moment Mandrake saw that in his right hand Jonathan held a very small pistol. "A few moments ago," said Jonathan, "I removed this little weapon from my desk. I am armed, Dr. Hart, and I shall see to it that Nicholas Compline, also, is armed. I wish you good night."

IV

Mandrake did not follow Jonathan from the room. Something had happened to him. He had succumbed to an irresistible feeling of pity for Dr. Hart. He had not ceased to believe that Hart was responsible for the attacks on Nicholas; on the contrary he was more than ever convinced that he was their author. But something in Hart's attitude, in his air of isolation, in the very feebleness of his efforts to defend himself, had touched Mandrake's sympathetic nerve. He saw Hart as a man who had been driven hopelessly off his normal course by the wind of an overwhelming jealousy. The old phrase 'Madly in love' occurred to him, and he thought Hart was indeed the victim of an insane passion. He found in himself a burning anxiety to prevent any further attack, not so much for Nicholas Compline's sake as for Hart's. It would be terrible, he thought, if Hart was to kill Nicholas and then, by this dreadful consummation of his passion, be brought to his right mind, to a full realization of the futility of what he had done. He felt that he must try and find something to say to this plump figure of tragedy, something that might reach out to him and rouse him, as some actual sound will penetrate and dispel a nightmare. Hart had turned away when Jonathan had shut the door, and had flung himself into a chair by the fire and covered his face with his hands. After a moment's hesitation Mandrake crossed to him and touched him lightly on the shoulder. He started, looked up, and said: "I thought you had gone."

"I shall go in a moment. I have stayed because I want to wake you."

"To wake me? How often have I repeated to myself that most futile of all phrases 'If only it was a dream.' If only I could be certain, *certain*. Then it would not be so bad."

Mandrake thought: "He *is* going to talk to me." He took the chair opposite to Dr. Hart and lit a cigarette. "If only you could be certain?" he repeated.

"That it is all lies, that he is her lover, that she has betrayed me. But when she denies I cannot help half believing her. I wish so much to believe. And then I see a look of boredom in her eyes, a look of weariness, of contempt. And with that comes the memory of the glances I have surprised between them, and although I know that with each denial, each scene, I injure myself still further, immediately I begin to make new scenes, demand fresh denials. I am caught in the toils of hell. I am so weary of it, yet I cannot be done with it."

"Why did you come here?"

"To prove to myself, one way or the other. To know the worst. She told me he was to be here and said quite lightly: 'Watch us and find out. It is nothing.' And then when I saw him, with all the airs of proprietorship, of complacent ownership, *laughing* at me! Do you know what should have been done in my country, if anyone insulted me as this man has insulted me? We should have met and it would have been decided once and for all. I should have killed Nicholas Compline."

"In England," said Mandrake, "we find it difficult to believe that in other countries duelling is still regarded as a satisfactory means of settling a difference. A successful duellist would be regarded as a murderer."

"In any case," said Hart, "he would not consent. He is a poltroon as well as a popinjay."

Mandrake thought: "Such glorious words!" Aloud he said: "He has some cause to be nervous, don't you think?"

"Yet, in spite of his terror," Hart continued, beating his clenched hands against his forehead, "in spite of his terror, he goes to her room. He waits until he hears me in the bathroom and then he goes to her. This morning he was in her room. I trapped her into admitting it. And now, a few minutes after she leaves me, after she has seen my agony, she keeps another assignation."

"But you know, in this country we are not conventional. I mean, we wander about into each other's rooms. I mean, Chloris Wynne and Lady Hersey, for example, both came and saw me. One thinks nothing of it. The modern Englishwoman . . ."

"In these matters she is not an Englishwoman, and I, Mr. Mandrake, am not an Englishman. We are naturalized, but we do not change our ideas of what is *convenable*. For what reason should she admit him, for what innocent reason? No, it is useless to torture myself further. She has betrayed me."

"Look here, it's none of my business but, if you are so certain, why not make a clean break? Why take a course that must lead to disaster? Let them go their ways. Things can never be as they were. Why ruin your career,"—Mandrake stammered over his series of conventional phrases,—"and jeopardize your own life over Nicholas Compline? Is he worth it? And, after all, is she worth it? Let her go. You could never be happy with her, now. Even if she married you—"

"*Married* me!" cried Hart. "*Married me!* She has been my wife for five years."

V

Mandrake stayed with Hart for a time, hearing a story in which the themes of Madame Lisse's business instinct, her husband's enslavement, and Nicholas Compline's perfidy were strangely interwoven. Madame, it seemed, had decided that their respective professions, though allied, were in a public sense incompatible. "She felt that as my wife she could not recommend me to her clients. I have always expressed considerable scepticism about the efficacy of face massage and creams. I have even published a short treatise on the subject. She said that to announce our marriage would be to embarrass my prestige with my clientele." His voice went on and on in a breathless hurry. He seemed unable to stop. Always he returned to Nicholas Compline and with each return he rekindled his own fury against Nicholas. The sudden outpouring of a long-suppressed emotion is supposed to bring relief, but Dr. Hart did not appear to take comfort from his self-revelation. He looked wretchedly ill and his nervous distress mounted with his recital. "He really is *not* responsible," Mandrake thought; "I've done no good at all. I'd better clear out." He could think of no suitable speech with which to end the conversation. Ridiculous phrases occurred to him ("Now, you *won't* kill Nicholas, *will* you?") and he wished with all his heart that he could rid himself of the notion that in some way Dr. Hart was making an appeal to him. He pulled himself to his feet. Dr. Hart, his finger pressed against that twitching lip of his, looked up desolately. At that moment, beyond the communicating door into the smoking-room, Nicholas Compline uttered a laugh loud enough to reach the ears of Dr. Hart and Mandrake. Hart sprang to his feet and for a moment Mandrake thought that he would actually make a blackguard rush into the smoking-room and go for his tormentor. Mandrake grabbed at his arm. They heard Nicholas' voice say "All right" so clearly that he must have crossed the room. There was a discordant burst of static and distorted music from the wireless, just inside the door. Hart cried out for all the world as if he had been struck, tore himself away from Mandrake and flung open the door into the smoking-room.

"GOTT IM HIMMEL," he screamed out, "must I be tortured by that devilish, that intolerable noise? TURN IT OFF. I INSIST THAT YOU TURN IT OFF!"

Nicholas appeared in the doorway. "You go to hell," he said pleasantly. "If I choose to listen to the wireless I'll bloody well listen to it." He slammed the door in Hart's face. Mandrake stumbled between Hart and the door. With a string of expletives that rather astonished himself, he shouted out instructions to Nicholas to switch off the radio, which was now roaring "Roll out the barrel . . ." It stopped abruptly, and William was heard to say: "Pipe down, for God's sake." Nicholas said: "Oh *all* right. Go to bed, Bill." Mandrake and Hart stared at each other for some seconds without speaking.

"Dr. Hart," said Mandrake, at last, "if you cannot give me your assurance that you will either go to your own room or remain in this one, I shall—I shall lock you in."

Hart sank back into his chair. "I shall do nothing," he said. "What can I do?" And to Mandrake's unbounded dismay he uttered a loud sob and buried his face in his hands.

"Oh, *God!*" thought Mandrake, "this is too much." He tried to form soothing phrases, but was dismayed by their inadequacy and finally ran out of words. For a moment he watched Dr. Hart, who was now fetching his breath in shuddering gasps and beating his hands on the arms of his chair. Mandrake remembered Jonathan's treatment for Chloris. He went to the dining-room, found a decanter of whiskey, poured out a stiff nip, and returned with it to the boudoir.

"Try this," he said. Hart motioned to him to leave it beside him. Seeing he could do no more, Mandrake prepared to leave. As an afterthought he turned at the door. "May I give you one word of advice?" he said. "Keep clear of both the Complines." And he limped away to the library.

Here he found Jonathan with Hersey Amblington and Chloris. It seemed quite natural to Mandrake to go at once to Chloris and sit on the arm of her chair, it seemed enchantingly natural that she should look up at him with pleasure.

"Well," she said, "any good?"

"None. He's in an awful state. What about the brothers Compline? We could hear snatches of their crosstalk act in there."

"Lady Hersey's been in to see them."

"And I may say," said Hersey, "that I got a surprise. Nick's pulled himself together, it seems, and is doing his best to let a little sense into poor old William."

"He has also been doing his best to drive Dr. Hart into an ecstasy of hatred by not quite tuning in at full volume to a particularly distressing rendering of 'The Beer Barrel Polka,'" said Mandrake, and described the incident. "Possibly this was an essential step in the soothing of William."

"It must have happened after I left," said Hersey.

"I wonder you didn't hear us yelling at each other from here."

"This room is practically sound-proof," said Jonathan.

"It must be. How is Nicholas getting on with William, Lady Hersey?"

"He's not made a great deal of headway but at least he's trying. They're supposed to go and see their mother, but they don't seem to be very keen on the idea. They said they particularly want to be left to themselves. What do we do now, Mr. Mandrake?"

"It's nearly ten o'clock," said Mandrake. "I'm damned if I know what we do. What do you think, Jonathan?"

Jonathan waved his hands and said nothing.

"Well," Mandrake said, "I suppose we see Nicholas to his room when he wants to go to bed. Do we lock William in *his* room or what?"

"I think we shut up Dr. Hart," said Hersey. "Then William can't get at Dr. Hart and Dr. Hart can't get at Nicholas. Or am I confused?"

"They may not fancy being locked up," Chloris pointed out. "Honestly, it's *too* difficult."

"Jo," said Hersey suddenly, "do you remember the conversation at dinner last night? When we said what we thought everybody would do in a crisis? It seems we were all wrong about each other. We agreed that you, for instance, would talk. You've not uttered a word since you came into this room. Somebody said Mr. Mandrake would be the impractical member of the party and here he is showing the most superb efficiency. Chloris—I hope you don't mind me calling you Chloris—suggested that Bill would turn up trumps, while his mother was all for Nicholas. Hopelessly incorrect! It looks as if you were right, Jo. We know nothing about each other."

"Jonathan was eloquent in the boudoir," said Mandrake listlessly.

They made disjointed conversation until Nicholas, wearing a dubious expression, came out of the smoking-room. He grimaced at the others and shut the door.

"How goes it?" Hersey asked. "Thumbs up?"

Nicholas, with exaggerated emphasis, mimed "Thumbs down."

"It's all right," said Jonathan impatiently. "He can't hear."

"He's still pretty bloody-minded," said Nicholas, throwing himself into a chair. "He's left off threatening to beat up the Doctor, thank God, but he's gone into a huddle over the fire and does *not* exactly manifest the party spirit. You know how he used to go as a kid, Hersey. All thunderous."

"Black Bill?" said Hersey. "I remember. Couldn't you do anything?"

"I've been kicked out," said Nicholas with a sheepish grin. "Hart's gone to bed, I fancy. We heard him snap off the light. So perhaps Bill might work his black dog off on the wireless."

"This is a shocking state of affairs," cried Jonathan. "I suppose we'd better leave him to himself, um?"

"Well, he's not so hot when he's like this. He'll get over it. I think I've persuaded him to keep away from Hart."

"You *think!*"

"I tell you Hart's gone upstairs. Possibly," said Nicholas, showing the whites of his eyes, "he's thought up a really fool-proof way of bumping me off."

"My dear Nick, we shall go up with you. I cannot believe, when he knows what we suspect, and I may say in the face of the little speech I made him, that he will attempt—but of course," added Jonathan in a fluster, "we must take every precaution. Your door, now . . ."

"Make no mistake," said Nicholas grimly. "I shall lock my door."

There was a short pause, broken by Hersey. "I simply can't believe it," she said abruptly. "It's so preposterous it just isn't true. All of us sitting round like a house-party in a play, waiting for frightfulness. And that booby-trap! A brass Buddha! No, it's *too* much. To-morrow, Dr. Hart will apologize to all of us and say he's sorry his sense of fun carried him too far, and he'll explain that in the Austrian Tyrol they all half-kill each other out of sheer *joie de vivre,* and we'll say we're sorry we didn't take it in the spirit in which it was meant."

"A murderous spirit," Jonathan muttered. "No, no, Hersey. We've got to face it. The attack on Nicholas was deliberately planned to injure him."

"Well, what are we going to *do?*"

"At least we could hear the war news," said Mandrake. "It might work as a sort of counter-irritant."

"We'd better not disturb William," said Jonathan quickly.

"I daresay he'll turn it on in a minute," Nicholas said, wearily. "He's keen on the news. Shall I ask him?"

"No, no," said Jonathan. "Leave him alone. It's not quite time yet. Would you like a drink, my dear Nick?"

"To be quite frank, Jonathan, I'd adore a very very large drink."

"You shall have it. Would you ring? The bell's beside you. No, you needn't trouble. I hear them coming."

A jingle of glasses sounded in the hall and the new footman came in with a tray. For the few seconds that he was in the room Chloris and Hersey made a brave effort at conversation. When he had gone Jonathan poured out the drinks. "What about William?" he asked. "Shall we . . . ? Will you ask him?"

Nicholas opened the study door and stuck his head round it. "Coming in for a drink, Bill? Not? All right, old thing, but would you mind switching on the wireless? It's just about time for the news and we'd like to hear it. Thanks."

They all waited awkwardly. Nicholas glanced over his shoulder and winked. The study wireless came to life.

"Hands, knees, and boomps-a-daisy," sang the wireless, robustly.

"Oh God!" said Mandrake automatically, but he felt an illogical sense of relief.

"Can you stick it for a minute or two?" asked Nicholas. "It's almost news-time. I'll leave the door open."

"Hands, knees, and boomps-a-daisy . . ."

"I think," said Jonathan, at the third repetition of the piece, "that I'll just make certain Dr. Hart is *not* in the 'boudoir.'" He got up. At the same moment the dance band ended triumphantly: *"Turn to your partner and bow-wow-wow."*

"Here's the news," said Hersey.

Jonathan, after listening to the opening announcement, went out into the hall. The others heard the recital of a laconic French bulletin and a statement that heavy snow was falling in the Maginot Line sector. The announcer's voice went on and on, but Mandrake found himself unable to listen to it. He was visited by a feeling of nervous depression, a sort of miserable impatience. "I can't sit here much longer," he thought. Presently Jonathan returned and, in answer to their glances, nodded his head. "No light in there," he said. He poured himself out a second drink. "He's feeling the strain, too," thought Mandrake.

"I wish old Bill'd come in," said Nicholas suddenly.

"He's better left alone," said Jonathan.

"Shall I take him in a drink?" Hersey suggested. "He can but throw it in my face. I *will*. Pour him out a whiskey, Jo."

Jonathan hesitated. She swept him aside, poured out a good three fingers of whiskey, splashed in the soda, and marched off with it into the smoking-room.

"It is learned in London tonight," said the announcer, *"that Mr. Cedric Hepbody, the well-known authority on Polish folk-music, is a prisoner in Warsaw. At the end of this bulletin you will hear a short recorded talk made by Mr. Hepbody last year on the subject of folk-music in its relation and reaction to primitive behaviourism. And now . . ."*

Hersey was standing in the doorway. Mandrake saw her first and an icy sensation of panic closed like a hand about his heart. The red leather screen at her back threw her figure into bold relief. The others turned their heads, saw her, and, as if on a common impulse, rose at once to their feet. They watched her lips moving in her sheep-white face. She mouthed at them and turned back into the smoking-room. The announcer's voice was cut off into silence.

"Jo," Hersey said. "Jo, come here."

Jonathan's fingers pulled at his lips. He did not move.

"Jo."

Jonathan crossed the library and went into the smoking-room. There was another long silence. Nobody moved or spoke. At last Hersey came round the screen.

"Mr. Mandrake," she said, "will you go in to Jonathan?"

Without a word Mandrake went into the smoking-room. The heavy door with its rows of book-shelves shut behind him.

It was then that Nicholas cried out: "My God, what's happened?"

Hersey went to him and took his hands in hers. "Nick," she said, "he's killed William."

CHAPTER IX

Alibi

I

WILLIAM WAS SITTING in a low chair beside the wireless. He was bent double. His face was between his knees and his hands were close to his shoes. His posture suggested an exaggerated scrutiny of the carpet. If Mandrake had walked in casually he might have thought at first glance that William was staring at some small object that lay between his feet. The cleft in the back of his head looked like some ugly mistake, preposterous rather than ghastly, the kind of thing one could not believe. Mandrake had taken in this much before he looked at Jonathan, who stood with his back against the door into the "boudoir." He was wiping his hands on his handkerchief. Mandrake heard a tiny spat of sound. A little red star appeared on the toe of William's left shoe.

"Aubrey, look at this."

"Is he . . . ? Are you sure . . . ?"

"Good God, *look* at him."

Mandrake had no wish to look at William but he limped over to the chair. Has anyone measured the flight of thought? In a timeless flash it can embrace a hundred images, and compass a multitude of ideas. In the second that passed before Mandrake stooped over William Compline, he was visited by a confused spiral of impressions and memories. He thought of William's oddities, of how he himself had never seen any of William's paintings, of how William's mouth might now be open and full of spilling blood. He thought, in a deeper layer of consciousness, of Chloris, who must have been kissed by William, of Dr. Hart's hands, of phrases in detective novels, of the fact that he might have to give his own name if he was called as a witness. The name of Roderick Alleyn was woven in his thoughts and over all of them rested an image of deep snow. He knelt by William and touched his right hand. It moved a little, flaccidly, under the pressure of his fingers, and that shocked him deeply. Something hit the back of his own hand and he saw a little red star like the one on William's shoe. He wiped it off with a violent movement. He stooped lower and looked up into William's face and that was terrible because the eyes as well as the mouth were wide open. Then Mandrake rose to his feet and looked at the back of William's head and felt abominably sick. He drew away with an involuntary sideways lurch and his club-foot struck against something on the floor. It lay in shadow and he had to stoop again to see it. It was a flattish spatulate object that narrowed to a short handle. He heard Jonathan's voice babbling behind him:—

"It hung on the wall there, you know. I showed it to you. It came from New Zealand. I told you. It's called a *mere.** I told you. It's made of stone."

"I remember," said Mandrake.

When he turned to speak to Jonathan he found that Nicholas had come into the room.

"Nick," said Jonathan, "my dear Nick."

"He's not dead," Nicholas said. "He can't be dead."

He thrust Jonathan from him and went to his brother. He put his hands on William's head, and made as if to raise it.

"Don't," said Mandrake. "I wouldn't. Not yet."

"You must be mad. Why haven't you tried . . . ? Leaving him! You must be mad." He raised William's head, saw his face, and uttered a deep retching sound. The head sagged forward again loosely as he released it. He began to repeat William's name—"Bill, Bill, Bill"—and walked distractedly about the room, making strange uneloquent gestures.

"What are we to do?" asked Jonathan, and Mandrake repeated to himself: "What are we to do?"

Aloud he said: "We can't do anything. We ought to get the police. A doctor. We can't do anything."

"Where's Hart?" Nicholas demanded suddenly. *"Where is he?"*

He stumbled to the door beyond Jonathan, fumbled with the key and flung it open. The green "boudoir" was in darkness and the fire there had sunk to a dead glow.

"By God, yes, where is he?" cried Mandrake.

Nicholas turned to the door into the hall and on a common impulse Mandrake and Jonathan intercepted him. "Clear out of my way," shouted Nicholas.

"Wait a minute, for Heaven's sake, Compline," said Mandrake.

"Wait a minute!"

* Pronounced "Merry."

"We're up against a madman. He may be lying in wait for you. Think, man."

He had Nicholas by the arm and he felt him slacken. He thought he saw something of the old nervousness come into his eyes.

"Aubrey's right, Nick," Jonathan was gabbling. "We've got to keep our heads, my dear fellow. We've got to lay a plan of campaign. We can't rush blindly at our fences. No, no. There's—there's your mother to think of, Nick. Your mother must be told, you know."

Nicholas wrenched himself free from Mandrake, turned away to the fireplace and flung himself into a chair. "For Christ's sake leave me alone," he said. Mandrake and Jonathan left him alone and whispered together.

"Look here," Mandrake said, "I suggest we lock up this room and go next door where we can talk. Are those two women all right in there? Better not leave them. We'll go back into the library, then." He turned to Nicholas. "I'm terribly sorry, Compline, but I don't think we ought to—to make any changes here just yet. Jonathan, are there keys in all these doors? Yes, I see."

The door into the "boudoir" was locked. He withdrew the key, locked the door into the hall, and gave both keys to Jonathan. As he crossed the room to open the library door he felt a slight prick in the sole of his normal foot and, in one layer of his conscious thoughts, cursed his shoemaker. They shepherded Nicholas back into the library. Mandrake found that, behind its rows of dummy books, the door into the library also had a lock.

They found Hersey and Chloris sitting together by the fire. Mandrake saw that Chloris had been crying. "I'm out of this," he thought, "I can't try to help." And, unrecognized by himself, a pang of jealousy shook him, jealousy of William who, by getting himself murdered, had won tears from Chloris.

Mandrake, for the first time, noticed that Jonathan was as white as a ghost. He kept opening and closing his lips, his fingers went continually to his glasses and he repeatedly gave a dry nervous cough. "I daresay I look pretty ghastly myself," thought Mandrake. Jonathan, for all his agitation, had assumed a certain air of authority. He sat down by Hersey and took her hand.

"Now, my dears," he began, and though his voice shook, his phrases held their old touch of pedantry, "I know you will be very sensible and brave. This is a most dreadful calamity, and I feel that I am myself, in a measure, responsible for it. That is an appalling burden to carry upon one's conscience but at the moment I dare not let myself consider it.

There is an immediate problem and we must deal with it as best we may. There is no doubt at all, I am afraid, that it is Dr. Hart who has killed William, and in my mind there is no doubt that he is insane. First of all, then, I want you both to promise me that you will not separate, and also that when we leave you alone together you will lock this door after us and not unlock it until one of us returns."

"But he's not going for either of us," said Hersey. "He's got nothing against us, surely."

"What had he against William?"

"William had quite a lot against *him,*" said Hersey.

"It must have been the radio," Mandrake said to Nicholas. "He nearly went for you when you turned it on."

Nicholas said: "I told him to go to hell and locked the door in his face." He leant his arms on the mantelpiece and beat his skull with his fists.

"You *locked* the door?" Mandrake repeated.

"He looked like barging in. I was sick of it all. Going for me. Screaming out his orders to me! I wanted to shut him up."

"I remember now. I heard you lock it. He must have gone out into the hall, and then into the smoking-room through the hall door."

"I suppose so," said Nicholas, and drove his fingers through his hair.

"Look here," Mandrake said slowly, "this makes a difference."

"If it does," Jonathan interrupted him, "we can hear what it is later, Aubrey. Nick, my dear chap, I think you must see your mother. And we" —he looked at Mandrake—"must find Hart." They made a plan of action. The men were to search the house together, leaving the two women in the library with the doors locked on the inside. Nicholas said that his service automatic was in his room. They decided to go upstairs at once and get it. "Bill had his," Nicholas said, and Jonathan said they would take it for Mandrake.

Hersey offered to go with Nicholas to his mother, and Chloris insisted that she would be all right left by herself in the library. "She's a good gallant girl," thought Mandrake, "and I'm in love with her." He gave her shoulder a pat and thought how out of character his behaviour was.

"Come on," said Hersey.

The library door shut behind them and they heard Chloris turn the key in the lock. The hall was quiet, a dim hollow place with a dying fire and shadows like the mouths of caverns. Bleached walls faded like smoke up into darkness; curtains, half seen, hung rigidly in the entrance. Pieces of furniture stood about with a deadly air of expectancy.

Jonathan's hand reached out and a great chandelier flooded the hall with light. The party of four moved to the stairs. Mandrake saw Jonathan take out his pistol. He led the way upstairs and switched on the wall lamps. Hersey and Nicholas followed him and Mandrake, lifting his club-foot more quickly than he was wont to do, brought up the rear. The nail in his right shoe still pricked him and he was dimly irritated by this slight discomfort. Up the first flight was the half-way landing, where the stairs divided into two narrower flights, of which they took the one that turned to their left. They went up to the top landing, where the grandfather clock ticked loudly. Here they paused. Hersey took Nicholas' arm. He squared his shoulders and with a gesture that for all its nervousness was a sort of parody of his old swagger, brushed up his moustache and went off with her to his mother's room. Mandrake and Jonathan turned to the right and walked softly down the passage.

They found Nicholas' automatic where he had told them to look for it, in a drawer of his dressing-table. William's, Nicholas had said, was in his room, beside a rucksack containing his painting materials.

"His room's next door to Hart's," whispered Jonathan. "If he's there, he'll hear us go in. What shall we do?"

"We can't leave stray automatics lying about, Jonathan. Not with a homicidal lunatic at large."

"Come on, then."

William's room was opposite his brother's. Mandrake stood on guard in the passage while Jonathan, looking extraordinarily furtive, opened the door by inches and crept in. There was no light under Hart's door. Was he there behind it, listening, waiting? Mandrake stared at it, half expecting it to open. Jonathan came back carrying a second automatic. He led the way into Mandrake's room.

"If he's in there, he's in the dark," said Mandrake.

"Quiet! You take this, Aubrey. Nicholas should have had his," whispered Jonathan. "He should have come here first."

"Are they loaded? I couldn't know less about them."

Jonathan examined the two automatics. "I think so. I myself—" His voice faded away and Mandrake caught only odd words: ". . . last resort . . . most undesirable . . ." He looked anxiously at Mandrake. "The safety catches are on, I think, but be careful, Aubrey. We must not fire, of course, unless something really desperate happens. Let him see we are armed. Wait one moment."

"What is it?"

A curious smile twisted Jonathan's lips. "It occurs to me," he whispered, "that we are at great pains to defend ourselves, Nicholas, and three of the ladies. We have quite overlooked the fourth."

"But—do you think? Good Heavens, Jonathan—"

"We can do nothing there. It is an abstract point. Are you ready? Let us go, then."

Outside Hart's door they paused. William's automatic sagged heavily in the pocket of Mandrake's dinner jacket. Nicholas' automatic was in his right hand. His heart thumped uncomfortably and he thought: This is *not* my sort of stuff. I'm hating this.

The latch clicked as Jonathan turned the handle. If it's locked, thought Mandrake, do we break it in, or what?

It was not locked. Jonathan pushed the door open quietly, slipped through, and switched on the light. The room was orderly and rather stuffy. Dr. Hart's trousers were hung over the back of a chair, his underclothes were folded across the seat, his shoes neatly disposed upon the floor. These details caught Mandrake's eye before he saw the bed which contained Dr. Hart himself.

II

Apparently he was fast asleep. He lay on his back, his mouth was open, his face patched with red, and his eyes not quite shut. The whites just showed under the lashes and that gave him so ghastly a look that for a fraction of a second Mandrake's nerves leapt to a conclusion that was at once dispelled by the sound of stertorous breathing.

Jonathan shut the door. He and Mandrake eyed each other and then, upon a common impulse, approached closer to the sleeping beauty-doctor. Mandrake was conscious of a great reluctance to waken Hart, a profound abhorrence of the scene that must follow the awakening. His imagination called up a picture of terrified expostulations, or, still worse, of a complete breakdown and confession. He found himself unable to look at Hart, his glance wandered from Jonathan's pistol to the bedside table where it was arrested by a small chemist's jar, half full of a white crystalline powder, and by a used tumbler, stained with white sediment. "Veronal?" wondered Mandrake, who had once used it himself. "If it is I didn't know it made you look so repellent. He must have taken a big dose."

How big a dose Dr. Hart had taken appeared only when Jonathan tried to wake him.

Under other circumstances Jonathan would have cut a comic figure.

First, keeping his own pistol pointed at the sleeping Doctor, he called his name. There was no response and Jonathan repeated his effort, raising his voice, finally to a cracked falsetto. "Hart, Dr. Hart! Wake up!"

Hart stirred, uttered an uncouth sound, and began to snore again. With an incoherent exclamation, Jonathan pocketed his pistol and advanced upon the bed.

"Look out," said Mandrake, "he may be foxing."

"Nonsense!" said Jonathan crisply. He shook Hart by the shoulder and: "Never heard of such a thing," said Jonathan, furiously. "Dr. Hart! Wake up."

"A-a-ah? *Was haben sie . . .*" The prominent eyes opened and stared into Jonathan's. The voice trailed away, the eyes became bored and closed again. There followed a slightly ridiculous scene, Jonathan scolding and shaking Hart, Hart mumbling and sagging off into a doze. Finally Jonathan, his face pink with vexation, dipped a towel in the water jug and slapped the Doctor's cheeks with it. This did the trick. Hart shuddered and shook his head. When he spoke again his voice was normal.

"Well," said Dr. Hart, "what in Heaven's name is all this? What now? May I not sleep, even? What now?"

He touched his head and saw Mandrake. "What are you doing with that thing in your hand?" he demanded. "Do not point at me. It is a firearm. What has happened?" Mandrake fidgeted uneasily with the automatic and curled the toes of his right foot in an attempt to avoid that pestilent shoe-nail. Hart rubbed the back of his hand across his mouth and shook his head vigorously.

Jonathan said: "We are armed because we have come to speak with a murderer."

Hart uttered a sound of exasperation. "Mr. Royal," he said, "how often am I to explain that I know nothing about it? Am I to be awakened at intervals during the night to tell you that I was in my bath?"

"What, again!" Mandrake ejaculated.

"Again? *Again!*" shouted Hart. "I do not know what you mean by *again*. I was in my bath at the time it was done. I know nothing. I did not sleep all last night. For weeks I have been suffering from insomnia, and tonight I have taken a soporific. If I do not sleep I shall go mad. Leave me alone."

"There is the body of a murdered man downstairs, Dr. Hart," said Mandrake. "I think you must stay awake a little longer to answer for it."

Hart sat up in bed. His pyjama jacket was unbuttoned and the smooth whiteness of his torso made a singularly disagreeable impression on Mandrake. Hart was fully awake, now; on his guard, and sharply attentive.

"Murdered?" he repeated, and to Mandrake's astonishment he smiled. "I see. So he has done it after all. I did not think he would go so far."

"What the devil are you talking about?" Jonathan demanded.

"He is killed, you say? Then I am speaking of his brother. I guessed that the brother set that trap. A booby-trap you call it, do you not? He betrayed himself when he reminded them of the tricks they played in their childhood. It was obvious the lady still loved her first choice. He was attractive to women." He paused and rubbed his lips again. Jonathan and Mandrake found nothing to say. "How was it done?" asked Hart.

Jonathan suddenly began to stutter. Mandrake saw that he was beside himself with rage. He cut in loudly before Jonathan had uttered a coherent phrase:—

"Wait a moment, Jonathan." Mandrake limped nearer to the bed. "He was killed," he said, "by a blow on the head from a stone club that hung with other weapons on the wall of the smoking-room. He was bending over the wireless. His murderer must have crept up behind him. No, Jonathan, wait a minute, please. A short while before he was killed, Dr. Hart, we were all in the library, and we heard him turn on the radio. You will remember that the smoking-room is between the library and the green sitting-room, called 'boudoir'—the room that you were in, alone. You will remember that it communicates with both these rooms and with the hall. With the exception of Mr. Royal, who did not enter either of the other two rooms, none of us left the library after we heard the wireless until Lady Hersey went in and found him there—murdered."

The uneven patches of red in Hart's cheeks were blotted out by a uniform and extreme pallor.

"This is infamous," he whispered. "You suggest that I—I killed him." With a movement of his hand, Mandrake checked a further outburst from Jonathan.

"I could not," said Hart. "The door was locked."

"How do you know?"

"After you had gone, I tried it. He had turned that intolerable thing on again. I could not endure it. I admit—I admit I tried it. When I found it locked I—I controlled myself. I decided to leave that room of torture. I came up here and to bed. The door was locked, I tell you."

"The door from the hall into the smoking-room was not locked."

"I did not do it. There must be some proof. It is the brother. The brother hated him as much as I. It is a pathological case. I am a medical man. I have seen it. He had stolen the mother's love and the girl still adored him."

"Dr. Hart," said Mandrake, "it is not Nicholas Compline who is dead. It is his brother, William."

In the silence that followed Mandrake heard a door, some distance down the passage, open and close. He heard voices, a footfall, somebody coughing.

"*William*," repeated Hart, and his hands moved across his chest, fumbling with his pyjama coat. "*William* Compline? It cannot be William. It *cannot*."

III

They did not have a great deal of trouble with Dr. Hart after that. He seemed at first to be completely bewildered and (the word leapt unbidden into Mandrake's thoughts) disgusted. Mandrake found himself quite unable to make up his mind whether Hart was bluffing, whether his air of confusion, his refusal to take alarm, and his obstinate denials were false or genuine. He seemed at once to be less panic-stricken and more helpless than he was when he believed, or feigned to believe, that the victim was Nicholas. He also seemed to be profoundly astonished. After a few minutes, however, he roused himself and appeared to consider his own position. He gave them quite a clear account of his own movements, from the time Mandrake left him alone in the green "boudoir," until he fell asleep. He said that he had taken some minutes to recover from his breakdown in Mandrake's presence. He was fully roused by tentative noises from the wireless, not loud but furtive. He found these sounds as intolerable to his raw nerves as the defiant blasts that preceded them. They must have affected Hart, Mandrake thought, in much the same way as he himself was affected by stealthy groping in chocolate boxes at a play. The intermittent noises continued, snatches of German and French, scraps of music, muffled bursts of static. Hart imagined Nicholas Compline turning the dial control and grinning to himself. At last the maddened doctor had rushed to the communicating door and found it locked. He had not, he seemed to suggest, meant to do more than expostulate with Nicholas, turn off the wireless at the wall switch and leave the room. However, the locked door checked him. He merely shouted a final curse at Nicholas and decided to fly from torment. He switched off the lights in the "boudoir," and went upstairs. As he crossed the hall to the foot of the stairs, he passed the new footman with his tray of glasses. He said the man saw him come out of the "boudoir" and that Hart was about half-way up the first flight when the man returned from the smoking-room and moved about the hall. He was still in the hall, locking up, when Hart reached the half-way landing and turned off to the left-hand flight. "He will tell you," said Hart, "that I did not enter the smoking-room."

"You could very easily have finished your work in the smoking-room before the man came," Jonathan said, icily. "You could have returned to the 'boudoir' and come out when you heard the man crossing the hall."

Mandrake, by a really supreme effort of self-control, held his tongue. He wanted with all his soul to cry out: "No! Don't you *see,* don't you *see* . . ." He knew Jonathan was wrong, off the track altogether. He was amazed at Jonathan's blindness. Yet, because he felt certain that somewhere, beyond his own reach, lay the answer to Hart's statement, he said nothing. Better, he thought, to wait until he had that answer.

"His skull is fractured, you say." Hart's voice, more composed than it had been since their last interview, roused Mandrake to listen. "Very well, then. You must lock up the room. The weapon must not be touched. It may have the assassin's finger-prints. The door into the hall must be examined by the police. A medical practitioner must be found. Naturally I cannot act in the matter. My own position . . ."

"You!" Jonathan ejaculated. "Great merciful Heavens, sir—"

Again Mandrake interrupted. "Dr. Hart," he asked, "suppose the rest of the party agreed, would you be prepared, in the presence of witnesses, to look at the body of William Compline?"

"Certainly," said Hart promptly. "If you wish, I will do so, though it can serve no purpose. In view of your preposterous accusations, I will not prejudice myself by making an examination, but I am perfectly ready to look. But I repeat you must immediately procure a medical man and communicate with the police."

"Have you forgotten that we're isolated?" And repeating the phrase which he had learned to dread, Mandrake added: "It's snowing harder than ever."

"This is most awkward," said Hart primly.

Jonathan burst incontinently into a tirade of abuse. Mandrake had never, until that day, seen him put out of countenance, and it was a strange and disagreeable experience to hear his voice grow shrill and his speech incoherent. His face was scarlet, his small mouth pouted and trembled, and behind those blind glasses of his Mandrake caught distorted glimpses of congested eyeballs. Without a trace of his usual precision he poured out a stream of accusations. "In my house," he kept repeating, "in my house." He ordered Hart to admit his guilt, he predicted what would happen to him. In the same breath he reminded him of Mrs. Compline's ruined beauty, of his threats to Nicholas, and of Mandrake's immersion. His outburst had the curious effect of steadying Hart. It was as though that house could hold only one hysterical middle-aged man at a time. Finally Jonathan flung himself into a chair, took out his handkerchief, saw a dark stain upon it, and with singular violence hurled it from him. He looked at Mandrake and perhaps he read astonishment and distaste in Mandrake's face, for when he spoke again it was with something of his old manner.

"You must forgive me, Aubrey. I'm exceedingly upset. Known that boy all his life. His mother's one of my oldest friends. I beg of you, Aubrey, to tell me what we should do."

Mandrake said: "I think, if Dr. Hart consents, we should leave him and lock the door after us."

"If I did not consent," said Hart, "you would still do so. One thing I shall ask of you. Will you arrange that someone, Lady Hersey perhaps, explains my present dilemma to my wife? If you permit I should like to speak to her."

"His wife? *His wife!*"

"Yes, yes, Jonathan," said Mandrake. "Madame Lisse is Madame Hart. We can't go into it now. Do you agree to these suggestions?"

Jonathan waved his hands and, taking this as an assent, Mandrake went to the bedside table and picked up the chemist's jar. "I'll take charge of this, I think," he said. "Is it veronal?"

"I most strongly object, Mr. Mandrake."

"I thought you would. Coming, Jonathan?"

He dropped the jar in his pocket and led the way to the door. He stood aside, allowing Jonathan to go out before him. He removed the key from inside the door. The last thing he saw before closing the door was Dr. Hart, his hands on his chest, staring after him. Then he stepped back over the threshold, pulled-to the door and locked it.

"Jonathan," he said, "somewhere or another we've gone incredibly wrong. Let's find Nicholas. We've got to talk."

IV

Nicholas, wearing an expression that reminded Mandrake of a nervous colt, stood at the end of the passage outside his mother's door. He hurried to meet them.

"Well," he whispered, "for God's sake, what's happened? What's wrong?"

"At the moment, nothing," said Mandrake.

"But I heard Jonathan shouting. Hart's in his room, then? Why have you left him?"

"He's locked up. Come downstairs, Compline. We've got to talk."

"I'm deadly tired," said Nicholas suddenly. And indeed he looked exhausted. "It was pretty ghastly, telling my Mama, you know."

"How is she?" asked Jonathan, taking Nicholas' arm. They moved towards the stairs.

"Hersey's with her. She's all to blazes, to be quite frank. She's got it into her head that it all hangs on—you know. What he did to her face. She thinks it's because of what Bill said about it. I couldn't do anything much. Of course she's—God, it sounds a rotten thing to say but you know how things are—she's—in a sort of way—glad it's not me. That makes me feel pretty foul as you may imagine. I'd better tell Hersey it's safe for her to come out when she wants to."

He put his head in at his mother's door and gave this message. They went downstairs to the library. Chloris was sitting very upright in her chair with her hands pressed together in her lap.

"All right?" Mandrake asked.

"Me? Yes. All right. It's nice to see you again. What's happened?"

Jonathan gave Chloris and Nicholas an account of the interview. It was an accurate narrative until he came to Hart's story. Then his indignation seemed to get the better of him and, abandoning Hart's statement altogether, Jonathan talked excitedly of preposterous evasions, trumped-up alibis, and intolerable hardihood. Seeing that Chloris and Nicholas grew more and more anxious and bewildered, Mandrake waited until Jonathan had exhausted his store of phrases and then cut in with an explicit account of Hart's movements according to himself.

"A monstrous conglomeration of lies!" Jonathan fumed.

"I don't think we can altogether dismiss them, Jonathan. I take it that we none of us doubt his guilt, but I'm afraid it's not going to be easy to get over that business of his meeting the footman—supposing, of course, that the man confirms Hart's story. There must *be* an explanation, of course, but—"

"My good Aubrey," cried Jonathan, "of course there's an explanation. When he encountered Thomas—that's the fellow's name, Thomas—it was all over. That's your explanation."

"Yes, but it isn't, you know. Because it was after Thomas came in with the drinks that we heard William turn up the wireless."

There was a rather stony silence, broken by Jonathan. "Then he came downstairs and slipped into the smoking-room."

"But he says Thomas stayed in the hall."

"*He says, he says.* The answer is that he waited in the shadows on the stairs until Thomas left the hall."

"Do you remember," Mandrake asked the other two, "the sequence of events? You, Compline, came out of the smoking-room leaving your brother—where?"

"He was over by the fire, I think. He wouldn't talk much but I remember he did say he was damned if Hart was going to stop him getting the news. It wasn't quite time for it. I'd heard Hart switch off the light in the 'boudoir' and I said he'd evidently gone, so it'd be all right. I didn't want to hear the damn' news myself and I'd told you I'd pipe down, so I came away."

"Exactly. As I remember you came in and shut the door. Later, when you opened it and called out to him about the news, could you see him?"

"No. The screen hid him. But he grunted something and I heard him cross the room."

"Right. And a moment later he turned on the wireless."

"I maintain," said Jonathan, "that it was Hart we heard in there. Hart had murdered him, and when he heard Nick ask for the news he turned it on and got out of the room."

"By that time Hart, according to himself, had met Thomas coming with the tray, had got some way up the stairs, and had seen Thomas re-enter the hall. It was only a matter of a minute or two after Thomas left that Lady Hersey went into the smoking-room. Does that give Hart time to return and do—what he did?"

"It was longer than that," said Jonathan, "the news had run for some minutes before Hersey went in."

"But . . ." Chloris made a sudden movement.

"Yes?" asked Mandrake.

"I suppose it's no good, but a wireless does take a little time to warm up. Could Dr. Hart have switched it on, after—after he'd—after it was over, and then hurried out of the room so that it would sound like Bill tuning in? Do you see what I mean?"

"By Heaven!" Nicholas said, "I believe she's got it."

"No," said Mandrake slowly, "no, I'm afraid not. The wireless was still warm. It was only a few minutes since it had been switched off. Even when they're cold they don't take longer than fifteen to twenty seconds, I fancy. For that idea to work, Hart would have had to switch it on before Thomas came in with the drinks and we didn't hear the thing until after Thomas left. And what's more it gives a still smaller margin of time for the actual crime. It would have to be done after you, Compline, left your brother, and before Thomas appeared with the glasses. Remember he had to leave the 'boudoir' by the door into the hall, enter the smoking-room by *its* door into the hall, seize his weapon, steal up—I'm sorry, but we've got to think of these things, haven't we?—do what he did, turn on the radio, return to the 'boudoir' and come out of it again in time for Thomas to see him."

"It takes much longer to describe these things than to do them," said Jonathan.

"No," said Chloris, "I think Aubrey's right, Mr. Royal. It doesn't seem to fit."

"My dear child, you can't possibly tell."

"What do you think, Nicholas?" This was the first time Chloris had spoken to Nicholas. He shook his head and pressed the palms of his hands against his eyes.

"I'm sorry," he said, "but I'm no good. Just about all in."

Mandrake suppressed a feeling of irritation. He found Nicholas in sorrow as difficult to stomach as Nicholas in good form. He realized that his impatience was unkind and his feeling of incredulity, unjust. Nicholas *was* upset. He was white and distraught, and it would have been strange if he had not been so affected. Mandrake realized with dismay that his own annoyance arose not from Nicholas' behaviour but from the compassionate glance that Chloris had given him. "Good Heavens," Mandrake thought, "I'm a pretty sort of fellow!" And to make amends to his conscience he joined Chloris and Jonathan in urging Nicholas to go to bed. Hersey Amblington came in.

"Your mother's a little calmer, Nick," she said. "But I'm afraid she's not likely to sleep. Jonathan, are there any aspirins in this house? I haven't got any."

"I—I really don't know. I never use them. I can ask the servants. Unless any of you . . . ?"

Nobody had any aspirins. Mandrake remembered Dr. Hart's veronal and groped in his pocket.

"There's this," he said. "Hart had taken as much or more than was good for him and I removed it. It's got the correct dosage on the label. It's a veronal preparation, I think, and is evidently a proprietary sample of sorts. The kind of thing they send out to doctors. Would it do?"

"It couldn't hurt, could it? She could try a small dose. I'll see, anyway."

Hersey went away and returned in a few minutes to say that she had given Mrs. Compline half the amount prescribed. Nicholas offered to go up to his mother, but Hersey said she thought it better not to disturb her.

"She locked her door after me," Hersey said. "She's quite safe and I hope she'll soon be asleep."

Hersey asked for an account of the interview with Hart and Mandrake gave it to her. She listened in silence to the story of Thomas and the encounter in the hall.

"What about the Pirate?" she asked suddenly. "Is she enjoying her beauty-sleep under a good dollop of her own skin food, or does she know what's happened?"

"If you mean Madame Lisse," said Nicholas with a return to his old air of sulkiness, "I've told her. She's frightfully upset."

"That's just too bad," said Hersey.

"She's Hart's wife," said Mandrake drearily. "Haven't we told you?"

"What?"

"Don't ask me why it was a secret. Something to do with face-lifting. It's all too fantastically involved. Perhaps you knew, Compline?"

"I didn't know. I don't believe it," said Nicholas dully, and nothing, Mandrake thought, could have shown more clearly the shock of William's death than the amazing apathy with which this news was received. They discussed it half-heartedly and soon returned to the old theme.

"What I can't understand," said Chloris, "is *why* he did it. I know Bill had talked wildly about exposing him, but after all *we* knew about the Vienna business too. He couldn't hope to frighten us into silence."

"I think he's mad," said Nicholas. "I think it was simply that last outburst of anger at the wireless that sent him off at the deep end. I think he probably went into the room with the idea of screaming out at Bill as he had already screamed at me. And I think he had a sort of hysterical crisis and grabbed the nearest weapon and—" He caught his breath in a sort of sob and for the first time Mandrake felt genuinely sorry for him. "That's what I think," said Nicholas, "and you can imagine what it feels like. I'd deliberately goaded him with the wireless. You heard me, Mandrake." He looked from one to another of his listeners. "How could I know? I suppose it was a silly thing to do, a rotten thing to do, if you like, but he'd been pretty foul with his threats and his booby-traps. It was me he was after, wasn't it? How could I know he'd take it out on old Bill? How could I know?"

"Don't, Nick," said Hersey. "You couldn't know."

Mandrake said: "You needn't blame yourself. You've got it wrong. Don't you see, all of you? He came in at the hall door. William was sitting with his back to the door, bending over the radio. All Hart could see from there was the back of his tunic and the nape of his neck. A few minutes before, he had heard you, Compline, tell him, face to face, that you were going to use the radio if you wanted to. A few seconds later both Hart and I heard you say: 'Oh, *all* right. Go to bed, Bill.' There, when he entered the room, was a man in uniform bending over the controls. The only light in the room was over by the fireplace. Don't you understand, all of you? When he struck at William Compline he thought he was attacking his brother."

V

"Aubrey, my dear fellow," said Jonathan. "I believe you are right. I am sure you are right. It is quite masterly. An admirable piece of reasoning."

"It doesn't get us over the hurdle, though," said Mandrake. "He's been too clever for us. You'll have to talk to that man, Jonathan. If he saw Hart go upstairs and remained in the hall for any length of time afterwards, Hart's got an alibi that we're going to have a devilish job to break. What's the time?"

"Five past eleven," said Chloris.

"They won't be in bed, yet, will they? You'd better send for him, Jo," said Hersey.

Jonathan fidgeted and made little doubtful sounds.

"My dear Jo, you'll have to tell the servants sometime."

"I'll go and speak to them in the servants' hall."

"I wouldn't," said Hersey. "I'd ring and speak to them here. I think we ought to be together when you talk to Thomas. After all," said Hersey, "I suppose if we can't break Dr. Hart's alibi, we're all under suspicion."

"My dear girl, that's utterly preposterous. Please remember we were all together in this room when William produced the war news on the wireless. Or, which I think more likely, when Hart produced it."

"No," said Mandrake. "We've tried that. It won't work. Jonathan, you went into the hall after the news began. Was Thomas there, then?"

"No," shouted Jonathan, angrily, "of course he wasn't. The hall was empty and there was no light in the 'boudoir.' I crossed the hall and went into the downstairs cloak-room. When I returned it was still empty."

"Then perhaps his story about Thomas—"

"For Heaven's sake," cried Hersey, "let's ask Thomas."

After a good deal of demurring, Jonathan finally rang the bell. Caper answered it and accepted the news of sudden death and homicide with an aplomb which Mandrake had imagined to be at the command only of family servants in somewhat dated comedies. Caper said "Indeed, sir?" some five or six times with nicely varied inflexions. He then went in search of Thomas, who presently appeared, wearing the air of one who had crammed himself hastily into his coat. He was a pale young man with damp waves in his hair. Evidently he had been primed by Caper, for he was not quite able to conceal a certain air of avidity. He answered Jonathan's questions promptly and sensibly. Yes, he had met Dr. Hart in the hall as he brought the tray. Dr. Hart came out of the "boudoir" as Thomas walked up the passage and into the rear of the hall. He was quite positive it was the "boudoir." He had noticed that the lights were out. He had noticed light coming from under the door into the smoking-room. Before Thomas entered the library Dr. Hart had reached the stairs and he turned on the wall switch belonging to the stair lamps. When Thomas came out of the library Dr. Hart had reached the visitors'-room flight. Thomas stayed in the hall. He locked the front doors, made up the fire and tidied the tables. In answer to a question from Mandrake, he said that he heard music from the radio in the smoking-room.

"What sort of music?" asked Mandrake.

"Beg pardon, sir?"

"Did you recognize the music?"

"Boomps-a-Daisy, sir," said Thomas unhappily.

"Well, go on, go on," said Jonathan. "You went away then, I suppose."

"No, sir."

"What the devil did you do with yourself, hanging about the hall?" demanded Jonathan, who was beginning to look extremely uneasy.

"Well, sir, excuse me, sir, I—I . . ."

"You *what?*"

"I went through the movements, sir. 'Hands, knees,' in time to the music, sir. I don't know why, I'm sure, sir. It just came over me. Only for a minute, like, because the music only lasted a very short time, sir, and then it was turned off."

"Cavorting about the hall like a buck-rabbit!" said Jonathan.

"I'm sure I'm very sorry, sir."

For a moment Jonathan seemed to be extraordinarily put out by this confession of animal spirits on the part of Thomas, but suddenly he made one of his quick pounces and cried out triumphantly: "Aha! So you were dancing, Thomas, were you? An abrupt attack of *joie de vivre?* And why not? Why not? You were intent upon it, I daresay. Turning this way and that, eh? I suppose it would take you right across the hall. I'm not very familiar with the dance, I must confess, but I imagine it's pretty lively, what?"

"Yes, sir. Rather lively, sir."

"Rather lively," repeated Jonathan. "Quite so. You'd be so taken up with it, I daresay, that you wouldn't notice if somebody came into the hall, um?"

"Beg pardon, sir, but nobody came into the hall, sir. The music stopped and the news started and I went back to the servants' sitting-room, sir, but nobody came into the hall while I was there."

"But, my good Thomas, I—I put it to you. I put it to you that while you were clapping your hands and slapping your knees and all the rest of it, it would have been perfectly easy for someone to cross the hall unnoticed. Come now!"

"Look here, Thomas," said Mandrake. "Let's put it this way: Somebody *did* come downstairs while you were in the hall. This person came downstairs and went into the smoking-room. Don't you remember?"

"I'm very sorry, sir, to contradict you," said Thomas, turning a deep plum-colour, "but I assure you they didn't. They couldn't of. I was close by the smoking-room door, sir, and facing the stairs. What I mean to say, I just 'eard, *heard* the tune, sir, and, I'm sure I don't know why, I did a couple of hands, knees, and boomps; well, for the fun of it, like."

"Thomas," Mandrake said, "suppose you were in a court of law and were asked to swear on the Bible that nobody was in the hall from the time you came out of the library until the time you went back to your own quarters. What about it?"

"I'd swear, sir."

"There's nothing to be gained by going on with this, Aubrey," said Jonathan. "Thank you, Thomas."

"Thank you, sir," said Thomas, and retired.

"There's only one explanation," said Nicholas. "He must have come back after that chap went back to his quarters."

"All the way downstairs and across the hall?" said Mandrake. "I suppose it's possible. In that case he avoided running into Jonathan and did the whole thing while that short news bulletin was being read. It was all over, and he'd bolted, when Lady Hersey went into the smoking-room and turned off the radio. It's a close call."

He bent down and slipped a finger inside his shoe. "Damn!" he said. "Does anyone mind if I take off my shoe? I've got a nail sticking into my foot."

He took off the shoe and noticed how they all glanced at his sound foot and away again quickly. He groped inside the shoe. "There it is," he muttered, "a damn' great spike of a thing."

"But there's something in the sole of your shoe," said Chloris. "Look."

Mandrake turned the shoe over. "It's a drawing-pin," he said.

"There's *some* explanation," said Nicholas with a real note of despair in his voice. "He's upstairs there, lying in his bed, by God, and laughing at us. Somehow or other he worked it. During the news. It must have been then. Somehow or other. When I think about it, I'm sure it was Bill who worked the wireless. I know you'll say it was easy for anybody to grunt and cross the room, but somehow, I can't explain why, I believe it was Bill—it sort of *felt* like Bill."

"Ssh!" said Hersey suddenly. "Listen!"

They stared at her. Her hand was raised and her head tilted. Into the profound silence that fell upon them came a wide vague drumming. The shutters of the library windows creaked. As they listened, the room was filled with that enveloping outside noise.

"It's beginning to rain," said Jonathan.

CHAPTER X

Journey

I

THEY HAD EXHAUSTED THEMSELVES arguing about the gap in Hart's story. They had said the same things over and over again. They longed to go to bed and yet were held prisoner in their chairs by a dreadful lassitude. They kept telling Nicholas to go to bed and he kept saying that he would go. They spoke in low voices to a vague background of drumming rain. Mandrake felt as if it was William himself who kept them there; William who, behind locked doors, now suffered the indignities of death. He could not help but think of that figure in the chair. Suppose, with those stealthy changes, William's body were to move? Suppose they were to hear, above the murmur of rain, a dull thud in the room next door? Nicholas too must have been visited by some such thoughts, for he said: "I can't bear to think of him—can't we—can't we?" And Mandrake had to explain again that they must not move William.

"Do you think," he asked Jonathan, "that with this rain the roads will be passable in the morning? What about the telephone? Is there any chance that the lines will be fixed up?"

There was a telephone in the library and from time to time they had tried it, knowing each time that it was useless. "If the roads are anything like passable," Mandrake said, "I'll drive into Chipping in the morning."

"You?" said Nicholas.

"Why not? My club-foot doesn't prevent me from driving a car, you know," said Mandrake. This was one of the speeches, born of his deformity, which he sometimes blurted out and always regretted.

"I didn't mean that," said Nicholas. "I'm sorry."

"Why shouldn't I go?" asked Mandrake, looking from one to another. "Even if we can't break Hart's alibi, I suppose none of you will suspect me. After all, I *was* shoved in the pond."

"I keep forgetting that complication," said Jonathan.

"I don't," Mandrake rejoined warmly.

"We ought none of us to forget it," said Chloris. "It's the beginning of the whole thing. If *only* you'd gone on looking out of the pavilion window, Nicholas!"

"I know. But I was half undressed and hellish cold. I just saw it was Mandrake and answered his wave. If only I had looked out again!"

"I've not the least doubt about what you'd have seen," Mandrake rejoined. "You'd have seen that infamous little man come up in a flurry of snow from behind the pavilion, and you'd have seen him launch a sort of flying tackle at my back."

"I've made a complete hash of everything," Nicholas burst out. "You're all being very nice about it, I know, but the facts stare you in the eye, don't they? I know what you're thinking. You're thinking that if I hadn't baited Hart this would never have happened. Well, let him get on with it, by God. He's messed it up three times, hasn't he? Let him have another pot at me. I shan't duck."

"Nick," said Hersey, "don't show off, my dear. Are we never to register dislike of anyone for fear they'll go off and murder our near relations? Don't be an ass, my dear old thing. Since we are being candid, let's put it this way. Dr. Hart was crossed in love and he couldn't take it. You did the crossing. I don't say I approve of your tactics, and, as I daresay you've noticed, I don't admire your choice. But for pity's sake don't go all broken-with-remorse on us. You've got your mother to think of."

"If anybody other than Hart is to blame," said Jonathan, "very clearly it is I."

"Now, Jo," said Hersey, roundly, "none of that from you. You've been a very silly little man, trying to re-arrange people's lives for them. This is what you get for it and no doubt it'll be a lesson to you. But it's no good putting on that face about it. We must be practical. We've got a man whom we all believe to be a murderer, locked up in his room, and as we don't seem to be very good at bringing it home to him the best thing we can do is to accept Mr. Mandrake's offer and to hope that in the morning he will be able to reach a telephone and find us a policeman."

"Hersey, my dear," said Jonathan with a little bob in her direction, "you are perfectly right. Nick and I must bow to your ruling. If Aubrey can and will go, why then go he shall."

"I thought," said Mandrake, "that I'd try to reach the rectory at Winton St. Giles. You see, there's rather a super sort of policeman staying there, and as I know him . . ."

"Roderick Alleyn?" Chloris cried out. "Why, of course!"

"I thought I'd put the whole thing before him. I thought that when I got upstairs I'd write it all down, everything I can remember from the time I got here. I don't know what the regulations are but, if I show what I've written to Alleyn, at least if *he* can't do anything he'll advise *me* what to do."

"I think we should see your notes, Aubrey."

"Of course, Jonathan. I hope you'll be able to add to them. It seems to me that when you write things out they have a way of falling into place. Perhaps when we read our notes we may see a still wider gap in Hart's alibi. I think we should concentrate on the time Jonathan was in the downstairs cloak-room and the moment or two after Jonathan returned and before Lady Hersey went into the smoking-room. I think we shall find that the gaps are there all right. If we don't, perhaps Alleyn will."

"I'm afraid I don't believe he will," said Chloris slowly. She reached out her hand and touched Mandrake's arm. "Don't think I'm crabbing your idea. It's a grand idea. But somehow, I can't tell you how I hate to say it, somehow I don't believe we will find a big enough gap. I don't think there is one."

"I won't have that," said Jonathan loudly, "there's plenty of time. There must be."

He stood up and the others rose with him. At last they were going to bed. With dragging steps and heavy yawns they moved uncertainly about the room. The men had a last drink. Desultory suggestions were made. Nicholas, with a return of nervousness which contrasted strangely with his recent mood of heroic despondency, started an argument about leaving Hart's door unguarded. Hart might try to break out, he said. Mandrake pointed out that if they kept their own doors locked it wouldn't much matter if he did. He, as much as they, was a prisoner in the house. "Anyway," added Mandrake, "we're not going to sleep through a door-smashing incident, I suppose. Here's your automatic, by the way, Compline." And for the life of him Mandrake couldn't resist adding: "You may feel more comfortable if you have it at your bedside." Nicholas took it quite meekly.

"Well," he said in a small desolate voice, "I may as well go up, I suppose." He looked towards the locked door into the smoking-room and Mandrake saw his rather prominent eyes dilate. "He offered to swap rooms with me," said Nicholas. "Decent of him, wasn't it? In case Hart tried anything during the night, you know. Of course, I wouldn't have let him. I'm glad we sort of got together a bit this evening." He looked at his hands and then vaguely up at Jonathan. "Well, good night," said Nicholas.

"We'll come up with you, Nick," said Hersey, and linked her arm in his.

"Will you? Oh, thank you, Hersey."

"Of course we shall," said Chloris. "Come on, Nick."

Jonathan and Mandrake followed, and as Mandrake, weary to death, limped up those stairs for the last time on that fatal day, he thought, and detested himself for so thinking: "He *would* go up between the two women. I bet he's got hold of Chloris' hand." Jonathan said good night on the half-way landing and turned off to his own wing. Only then did it occur to Mandrake that since his flare-up with Hart, Jonathan had been unusually quiet. "And no wonder," he thought. "They can say what they like but after all if he hadn't thrown his fool party . . ."

They went with Nicholas to his room. Moved by an obscure mixture of contrition and genuine sympathy, Mandrake shook hands with him and instantly regretted it when Nicholas, with tears in his eyes, kissed the two women and said in a broken voice: "Bless you. I'll be all right. Good night."

"Good night," said Hersey in the passage and stomped off to her room.

"Good night," said Chloris to Mandrake, and then rather defiantly: "Well, I *am* sorry for him."

"Good night," said Mandrake; "so am I."

"You do look tired. We've all forgotten about your horrid plunge. You won't tackle those notes tonight?"

"I think so. While it's still seething, don't you know?"

"Well, don't treat the subject surrealistically or we'll none of us be able to contradict you. You ought not to have had all these games thrust upon you. Are you all right?"

"Perfectly all right," said Mandrake. "But I approve of you feeling sorry for me."

So Chloris gave him a kiss, and in a state of bewildered satisfaction he went to his room.

II

It was one o'clock when he laid down his pen and read through his notes. At the end he had written a summary in which he attempted to marshal the salient facts of the three assaults. He re-read this summary twice.

1. *The incident of the Charter form.* Hart wrote the message; because he, and only he, handed his papers on to Nicholas. The letters resemble

those in his note to Jonathan. The incident followed his picking a quarrel with Nicholas after dinner. N.B. Get an account of quarrel from Jonathan, who was the only witness.

2. *The incident by the pond.* Motive apart, Nicholas didn't shove me over because he recognized me through the window and in any case knew I was wearing the cape. Besides, he saved my life by throwing in the inflated bird. William didn't because he arrived at about the same time as Nicholas and had come down the terrace steps. Nicholas saw him come. Chloris didn't because she didn't. Jonathan arrived after Chloris, catching her up when she was nearly there. He had seen Hart leave by the front drive. Hart arrived by a path that comes out behind the pavilion. I had my back turned to him. He had seen Nicholas, wearing a cape that is the double of mine. I had the hood over my head. N.B. Who was the woman who came out of the house as far as the terrace? (Footprints in snow.) She may have seen who threw me overboard. If so, why hasn't she spoken? Her prints were close to the others. A small foot. Could she have gone down the steps inside my footprints? Madame Lisse's window overlooks the terrace. Hart habitually wears a cape.

3. *The booby-trap.* Hart is the only member of the party who hasn't an alibi. Jonathan's alibi depends on me. I can't remember exactly how long he was in the drawing-room before the crash; but anyway why should Jonathan want to kill Nicholas? Hart must have set the booby-trap.

4. *The murder.* On re-reading these notes I find that Madame Lisse, Lady Hersey and Mrs. Compline have not got alibis. Madame Lisse and Mrs. Compline could have come downstairs and entered the smoking-room by the "boudoir." But if either of them did it how did she leave? Thomas was in the hall when William turned on the radio, and remained there until the news. I suppose the Lisse or Mrs. Compline might have actually hidden in the room and slipped out when Lady Hersey came to fetch Jonathan, but it seems more likely that they could have managed to dodge both Thomas and Jonathan. Mrs. Compline is out of it. No motive. Madame Lisse had no motive in killing Nicholas, so if she did it she recognized William and her motive there. . . .

At this point Mandrake, remembering that the others would read his summary, lost his nerve and scored out the next three lines and the preceding words from "No motive" onwards. He then read on:—

Nicholas didn't do it because at some time *after* he left the smoking-room, the wireless was switched on. This must have been done by William or conceivably by his murderer. We didn't see him, although the door was open. The screen hid him. But someone did cross the room and turn on the wireless.

Lady Hersey went in with the drink and of course, theoretically, could have killed William, and then come and called Jonathan. No motive.

Hart came out of the "boudoir," and was seen by Thomas as he brought the drinks. When Thomas re-appeared, a few seconds later, Hart was on the stairs. No time to go back and kill William in the interim. He didn't return before the news because Thomas remained in the hall until then and because William turned on "Boomps-a-Daisy" after Hart had gone. If Hart killed William it was after Thomas left the hall. Could he have done it in the time and still have avoided meeting Jonathan?

Jonathan himself left the library after the news began and returned before Hersey took in the drink. He says he crossed the hall to and from the cloak-room, and saw nobody. Could Hart have dodged him? Possible.

This seems to be the only explanation.

Here the summary came abruptly to an end. Mandrake sat very still for perhaps a minute. Then he took out his cigarette case, put it down unopened, and reached again for his pen. He added six words to his summary:—

Could Hart have set another booby-trap?

When he lifted his hand he saw that he had left a small red stain on the paper. He had washed his hands as soon as he came upstairs but his mind jumped, with a spasm of nausea, to the memory of the red star that had fallen from William's mouth. Then he remembered that when he took out his cigarette case he had felt a prick and there, sure enough, on the tip of his middle finger, was a little red globule. He felt again in his pocket and found the drawing-pin that had penetrated the sole of his shoe. He put it on the paper before him. Across the back of the drawing-pin was a dry white ridge.

He heard William's voice speaking gravely in the drawing-room: "*Very* thick oil paint."

He put the drawing-pin in a match-box and locked the box in his attaché-case, together with the Charter form which he had got from Jonathan.

Then he went to bed.

III

It was some time before he slept. Several times he came to the borderland where conscious thought mingles fantastically with the images of the subconscious. At these moments he saw a Maori *mere,* like Damocles' sword, suspended above his head by a hair which was fixed to the ceiling by an old drawing-pin. "It *might* hold," said William, speaking indistinctly because his mouth was full of blood. "It *might* hold, you know. I use *very* thick oil paint." He couldn't move because the folds of the Tyrolese cape were wrapped round his limbs. A rubber bird, wearing a god-like leer, bobbed its scarlet beak at him.

"It's snowing harder than ever," said the bird, and at that precise moment Hart cut the hair with a scalpel. "*Down* she comes, by Jupiter," they all shouted; but Chloris, with excellent intentions, kicked him between the shoulder-blades and he fell with a sickening jolt back into his bed and woke again to hear the rain driving against the window-pane.

At last, however, he fell into a true sleep—and was among the first of the seven living guests to do so. Dr. Hart was the very first. Long before the others came upstairs to bed, Dr. Hart's dose of proprietary soporific had restored his interrupted oblivion; and now his mouth was open, his breathing deep and stertorous.

His wife was not so fortunate. She heard them all come upstairs, she heard them wish each other good night, she heard door after door close softly and imagined key after key turning with a click as each door was shut. Sitting upright in bed in her fine nightgown, she listened to the rain and made plans for her own security.

Hersey Amblington, too, was wakeful. She kept her bedside lamp alight and absent-mindedly slapped "Hersey's Skin Food" into her face with a patent celluloid patter. As she did this, she tried distractedly to order her thoughts away from the memory of a figure in an armchair, from a head that was broken like an egg, and from a wireless cabinet that screamed "Boomps-a-Daisy." She thought of herself twenty years ago, afraid to tell her cousin Jonathan that she would marry him. She thought of her business rival and wondered quite shamelessly if, with the arrest of Hart, Madame Lisse would carry her piratical trade elsewhere. Finally, hoping to set up a sort of counter-irritant in horror, she thought about her own age. But the figure in the chair was persistent and Hersey was afraid to go to sleep.

Chloris was not much afraid. She had not seen William. But she was extremely bewildered over several discoveries that she had made about herself. The most upsetting of these was the discovery that she now felt nothing but a vague pity for Nicholas and an acute pity for William. She had never pretended to herself that she was madly in love with William, but she had believed herself to be very fond of him. It was Nicholas who had held her in the grip of a helpless attraction; it was from this bondage that she had torn herself on a climax of misery. She believed that when Nicholas had become aware of his brother's determined courtship he had set himself to cut William out. Having succeeded very easily in this project, he had tired of her; and, in the meantime, he had met Elise Lisse. She thought of the letter in which she had broken off her engagement to Nicholas and, with shame, of the new engagement to his brother; of how every look, every word that was exchanged between them, for her held only one significance, its effect upon Nicholas; of the miserable satisfaction she had known when Nicholas showed his resentment, of the exultation she had felt when, again, he began to show off his paces before her. And now it was all over. She had cried a little out of pity for William and from the shock to her nerves, and she had seen Nicholas once and for all as a silly fellow and a bit of a coward. A phrase came into her thoughts: "So that's all about the Complines." With an extraordinary lightening of her spirits she now allowed herself to think of Aubrey Mandrake. "Of Mr. Stanley Footling," she corrected herself. "It ought to be funny. Poor Mr. Stanley Footling turning as white as paper and letting me in on the ground floor. It isn't funny. I can't make a good story of it. It's infinitely touching and it doesn't matter to me, only to him." And she thought: "Did I take the right line about it?"

She had gone to her room determined to break Dr. Hart's alibi, but a whole hour had passed and not once had she thought of Dr. Hart.

Jonathan Royal clasped his hot-water bag to his midriff and stared before him into the darkness. If the top strata of his thoughts had been written down they would have read something like this: "It's an infernal bore about Thomas but there must be some way out of it. Aubrey is going to be tiresome, I can see. He's half inclined to believe Hart. *Damn* Thomas. There must be some way. An ingenious turn, now. My thoughts are going round in circles. I must concentrate. What will Aubrey write in his notes? I must read them carefully. Can't be too careful. This fellow Alleyn. What will he make of it? Why, there's motive, the two attempts, *our* alibis —he can't come to any other conclusion. *Damn* Thomas."

Nicholas tossed and turned in the bed his brother had offered to take. He was unaccustomed to consecutive or ordered thinking, and across his mind drifted an endless procession of dissociated images and ideas. He saw himself and William as children. He saw William going back to school at the end of his holidays—Nicholas and his tutor had gone in the car to the station. There was Bill's face, pressed against the window-pane as the train went out. He heard Bill's adolescent voice breaking comically into falsetto: "She'd like it to be you at Penfelton and me anywhere else. But I'm the eldest. You can't alter that. Mother will never forgive me for it." He saw Chloris the first time she came to Penfelton as William's guest for a house-party. "Mother, will you ask Chloris Wynne? She's my girl, Nick. No poaching." And lastly he saw Elise Lisse, and heard his own voice: "I never knew it could be like this. I never knew."

Sandra Compline laid down her pen. She enclosed the paper in an envelope and wrote a single word of direction. Outside on the landing, the grandfather clock struck two. She wrapped her dressing-gown more closely round her. The fire was almost dead and she was bitterly cold. The moment had come for her to get into bed. The bed-clothes were disordered. She straightened them carefully and then glanced round the room, which was quite impersonal and, but for the garments she had worn during the day, very neat. She folded them and put them away, shivering a little as she did so. She caught sight of her face in the glass and paused before it to touch her hair. On an impulse she leant forward and stared at the reflection. Next, she moved to the bedside table and for some minutes her hands were busy there. At last she got into bed, disposed the sheet carefully, and drew up the counterpane. Then she stretched out her hand to the bedside table.

IV

It was an isolated storm that visited Cloudyfold that night. Over the greater part of Dorset the snow lay undisturbed, but here in the uplands it was drilled with rain and all through the night hills and trees suffered a series of changes. In the depths of Jonathan's woods, branches, released from their burden of snow, jerked sharply upwards. From beneath battlements of snow, streams of water began to move and there were secret downward shiftings of white masses. With the diminution of snow the natural contours of the earth slowly returned. Towards dawn, in places where there had been smooth depressions, sharp furrows began to take form, and these were sunken lanes. In Deep Bottom beneath the sound of rain was the sound of running water.

The guests, when at last they slept, were sometimes troubled in their dreams by strange noises on the roofs and eaves of the house where masses of snow became dislodged and slid into gutters and hollows. The drive, and the road from Highfold down into Cloudyfold Village and up into the hills, began to find themselves. So heavy was the downpouring of rain that by dawn the countryside was dappled with streaks of heavy greys and patches of green. When Mandrake woke at eight o'clock his windows were blinded with rain and, through the rain, he saw the tops of evergreen trees, no longer burdened with snow.

He breakfasted alone with Jonathan who told him that already he had seen some of the outdoor staff. His bailiff had ridden up from his own cottage on horseback and had gone out again on a round of inspection. Jonathan had told him of the tragedy. He had offered to ride over Cloudyfold. It meant twelve miles at a walking pace, supposing he did get through.

"If I stick," said Mandrake, "he can try. If I'm not back in three hours, Jonathan, he had better try. What sort of mess is the drive, did he say?" The Bewlings, it seemed, had been down to the front gates and reported that the drive was "a masterpiece of muck" but not, they thought, impassable. You could get over Cloudyfold on a horse, no doubt, but a car would never do it.

"How about the road down to the village?" asked Mandrake.

"That's in better case, I understand."

"Then if I got through Deep Bottom I could drive down to Cloudyfold Village and telephone from there to the rectory at Winton St. Giles?"

"The lines may be down between the village and Winton. They go over the hills. I think it most probable that they are down. As far as the Bewlings went they found nothing the matter with my own line."

"Can't I get to Winton St. Giles by way of the village?"

"A venture that is comparable to Chesterton's journey to Birmingham by way of Beachy Head, my dear Aubrey. Let me see. You would have to take the main road east, turn to your right at Pen Gidding, skirt Cloudyfold hills and—but Heaven knows what state those roads would be in. From Pen Gidding there are only the merest country lanes."

"I can but try."

"I don't like it."

"Jonathan," said Mandrake, "do you like the idea of leaving William Compline's body in your smoking-room for very much longer?"

"Oh, my dear fellow, no! No, of course not. This is horrible, a nightmare. I shall never recover from this week-end, never."

"Do you think one of the Bewling brothers could come with me? If I did come to a standstill it would be helpful to have someone, and if I don't, he could direct me."

"Of course, of course. If you must go." Jonathan brightened a little and began to make plans. "You must take a flask of brandy, my dear boy. James Bewling shall go with you. Chains, now. You will need chains on your wheels, won't you?"

"There's not by any chance a police station at Cloudyfold Village?"

"Good gracious, no. The merest hamlet. No, the nearest constable, I fancy, is at Chipping, and that's beyond Winton St. Giles."

"At any rate," said Mandrake, "I think I'd better see Alleyn first. I only hope he'll consent to run the whole show and come back with me but I suppose I shall run into an entanglement of red tape if I suggest such a thing."

"Dear me, I suppose so. I scarcely know which prospect is more distasteful—the Chipping constabulary or your terrifying acquaintance."

"He's a pleasant fellow."

"Very possibly. Perhaps I had better send for old James Bewling before he plunges out-of-doors again."

Jonathan rang the bell, which was answered by Thomas—who was unable to conceal entirely an air of covert excitement. He said that the Bewlings were still in the house, and in a minute or two James appeared, very conscious of his boots.

"Now, James," said Jonathan, "Mr. Mandrake and I want your advice and assistance. Dry your legs at the fire and never mind about your boots. Listen."

He unfolded Mandrake's project. James listened with his mouth not quite shut, his eyes fixed upon some object at the far end of the room, and his brows drawn together in a formidable scowl.

"Now, do you think it is possible?" Jonathan demanded.

"Ah," said James. "Matter of twenty mile it be, that road. Going widdershins like, you see, sir. She'll be fair enough so furr as village and a good piece below. It's when she do turn in and up, if you take my meaning, sir, as us'll run into muck and as like as not, slips, and as like as not if there bean't no slips there'll be drifts."

"Then you *don't* think it possible, James?"

"With corpses stiffening on the premises, sir, all things be possible to a man with a desperate powerful idea egging him on."

"My opinion exactly, Bewling," said Mandrake. "Will you come with me?"

"That I will, sir," said James. "When shall us start?"

"Now, if you will. As soon as possible." And as he spoke these words Mandrake was moved by a great desire for this venture. Soon he would meet Chloris again, and to that meeting he looked forward steadily and ardently, but in the meantime he must be free of Highfold for a space. He must set out in driving rain on a difficult task. It would be with bad roads and ill weather that he must reckon for the next hour or so, not with the complexities of human conduct. His eagerness for these encounters was so foreign to his normal way of thinking that he felt a sort of astonishment at himself. "But I don't like leaving her here. Shall I wait until she appears and suggest that she comes with us? Perhaps she would not care to come. Perhaps I have embarrassed her with my dreary confidences. She might be afraid I'd go all Footling at her on the drive." He began to horrify himself with the notion that Chloris thought of him as underbred and overvehement, a man whom she would have to shake off before he became a nuisance. He went upstairs determined that he would not succumb to the temptation of asking her to go with him, met her on the top landing, and immediately asked her.

"Of course I'll come," said Chloris.

"It may be quite frightful. We may break down completely."

"At least we'll be out of all this. I won't be five minutes."

"You'll want layers of coats," cried Mandrake. "I'll get hold of old James Bewling and we'll have the car round at the front door as soon as he's found me some chains."

He went joyfully to his own room, put on an extra sweater, a muffler and his raincoat. He snatched up the attaché-case containing his notes, the drawing-pin and the Charter form. He remembered suddenly that the others were to have gone over the notes before he took them to Alleyn. Well, if they wanted to do that they should have got up earlier. He couldn't wait about half the morning. They would have plenty of chances to argue over his account when he came back with Alleyn. Now, for the car.

But before he went out-of-doors he found Jonathan and nerved himself to make a request. The thought of revisiting the smoking-room was horrible, but he had promised himself that he would do so. He half hoped Jonathan would refuse, but he did not. "I won't come with you, that's all. Don't ask it. Here are the keys. You may keep them. I simply can *not* accompany you."

"I shan't touch anything. Please wait by the door."

He was only a few minutes in that room. They had thrown a white sheet over the chair and what was in it. He tried not to look at that, but he was shaken when he came out and said goodbye, quietly, to Jonathan.

He went out by the west door and walked round the back of the house to the garages. The whole world seemed to be alive with the sound of rain and wind. Much of the snow lying in exposed places had gone, everywhere it was pocked and crenellated. From the eaves of Highfold, it hung in strange forms that changed continually and tapered into falling water.

Using his stick vigorously, Mandrake reached the garages to find James Bewling, assisted by his brother, engaged in fitting chains to the car-wheels. They seemed to Mandrake to be incredibly slow about this. The chains were improvised arrangements and one set kept slipping. At last, however, they were ready and he prepared to drive out.

"They'll hold now, sartin sure. Lucky we had 'em," said James. "Us'll need 'em up-along, never fear. Now then, sir, if you be agreeable I reckon car's ready to start. Us've filled her up with petrol and water and there's hauly-chains and sacks in the back."

"Come on then," said Mandrake.

James climbed in the back. As they left the garage his brother bawled at them: "If 'er skiddles, rush 'er up." He drove round to the front doors and found Chloris there. The collar of her heavy coat was turned up and she had a gay scarf tied round her head so that he saw her face as a triangle. It was a very white triangle and her eyes looked horror-stricken. As soon as she saw the car she stumbled down the steps and, leaning against the wind, ran round to the passenger's door. Before he could get it open she was struggling with the handle and in a moment had scrambled in beside him.

"What now?" asked Mandrake.

"I'd better tell you before we start, but Mr. Royal says we're to go anyway. Another ghastliness. Mrs. Compline. She's tried to kill herself."

V

Mandrake turned with his hands on the driving-wheel and gazed at her. James Bewling cleared his throat stertorously.

"Please start," said Chloris and without a word Mandrake engaged his first gear. To the sound of slapping chains, driving wind and rain, and with a cold engine, they moved across the wide sweep and round the west side of the house.

"She did it herself," said Chloris. "One of the maids went up with her breakfast and found the door locked. The housekeeper thought she ought not to be disturbed but the maid had seen lamplight under the door when she went up with early tea. So they told Mr. Royal. It seemed queer, you see, for the lamps to be going after it was light. In the end they decided to knock. It was just after you went out. They knocked and knocked and she didn't answer. By that time Nicholas was there and in an awful state. He insisted on Mr. Royal forcing the door. She'd left a note for him—for Nicholas. There's been a frightful scene, it seems, because Mr. Royal said Nicholas should give the note to somebody. He won't let Nicholas keep it, but he hasn't read it himself. I don't know what was in the note. Only Nick knows. She's unconscious. They think she's dying."

"But—how?"

"The rest of that sleeping draught and all the aspirins she'd got. She'd told Lady Hersey she had no aspirins. I suppose she wanted to get as much as possible. You'd feel sorry for Nicholas if you could see him now."

"Yes," said Mandrake sombrely. "Yes, I do feel sorry for Nicholas, now."

"He's gone to pieces. No more showing-off for poor old Nick," said Chloris with a catch in her voice. "There couldn't be any doubt at all that it was suicide, and he agreed that Dr. Hart should be asked to see her. Pretty queer, wasn't it? They all agree that he murdered Bill, and yet there he was working at artificial respiration, and snapping out orders with everybody running round obeying them. I think the world's gone mad or something. He's given me a list of things we're to get at the chemists in Chipping. It's not far beyond Winton St. Giles. I could take the car on if you like while you see Mr. Alleyn. And the police surgeon. We've got to try and find him, but the important thing is to get back as quickly as possible."

"Does Hart think . . . ?"

"I'm sure he thinks it's pretty hopeless. I wasn't in the room. I waited by the door for orders. I heard him say something about two hundred grains of veronal alone. He was barking out questions to Lady Hersey. How much had she given? How dared she give it? If it wasn't so frightful it'd be funny. She's in a pretty ghastly state herself. She feels she's responsible."

"I took the stuff away from Hart," said Mandrake. "God, that's a touch of irony for you! I was afraid he might try something on himself."

"You needn't go all remorseful," said Chloris quickly. "Dr. Hart said the aspirin alone would have been disastrous. I heard him say that to Lady Hersey."

They had reached the woods where the drive ran between steep banks. Here the surface, no longer gravelled, was soft, laced with runnels of water and littered with broken twigs and with clods of earth that had been carried away from the banks. In one place there was a miniature landslide across their route. Mandrake drove hard at it in second gear, and felt his back wheels spin and then grip on the chains.

"That's a taste of what we may expect in Deep Bottom, I suppose," he called to James Bewling.

" 'Twill be watter down-along, I reckon, sir."

"If we stick . . ." Chloris began.

"If we stick, my dear, they can damn' well produce a farm animal to lug us out on the far side."

"It's dogged as does it," said Chloris.

Beyond Highfold Wood the drive, where it crossed the exposed parklands, was furrowed and broken by pot-holes. James Bewling remarked that he and Thomas had been telling the master for a matter of ten years that he did ought to lay down a load of metal. The rain drove full on the wind-screen, checking the wiper, splaying out in serrated circles and finding its way in above the dashboard. The thrust of the wind made the car fight against Mandrake's steering. He drove cautiously towards the edge of Deep Bottom, peering through the blear of water. He recognized in himself an exhilaration, and this discovery astonished him, for he had always thought that he loathed discomfort.

Snow still lay in Deep Bottom. When they reached the lip of the hollow and looked down, they saw the drive disappear under it and rise again on the far side like a muddy ribbon.

"She be gone down a tidy piece," said James. "Not above two foot now, I reckon, but happen thurr'll be watter underneath. Happen us'd do better with sack over radiator, sir."

Mandrake pulled up and James plunged out with his sack. Mandrake stumbled after him. He didn't want to sit in the car while James fixed up the sack. He wanted to be knowledgeable and active. He tied the sacking over the radiator cap, using his handkerchief to bind it. He looked critically at the way James had tied the corners of the sack. Swinging his heavy boot briskly he came back to the car, smiling through the rain at Chloris. The warmth in her returning glance delighted him and he innocently supposed that it was inspired by his activity. It was the glance, he told himself, of the female, approving, dependent, and even clinging. He would never know that Chloris was deeply touched, not because she saw him as a protector, but because suddenly she read his thoughts. And from that moment, in her wisdom, she let herself be minded by Mandrake.

The car began its crawl down into Deep Bottom.

"For a tidy ten yurr and more," said James Bewling in the back seat, "my wold brother Thomas and me been telling master as 'ow'ee did oughter put a dinky li'l bridge across this-yurr bottom. Last winter 'er was in a muck with raging torrents and floods. Winter afore, 'er fruz. Winter afore that, 'er caved in sudden." Here the car lurched in and out of a pot-hole and James was thrown about in the back seat. "Winter afore that, 'er flooded again. Bean't no proper entrance to gentleman's 'state, us tells 'un. Ay, and us tells bailiff tu. Pull over to your right, sir, by this-yurr puddlesome corner, or us'll sink to our bottoms."

The front wheels plunged deep into a welter of slush. The back wheels churned, gripped, skidded and gripped again. Now they were into the snow with James Bewling roaring: "To tha right and rush 'er up." The bonnet dipped abruptly and a welter of snow spurted over the windscreen. Mandrake leant out of the driving window and took the whipping rain full in his eyes. "Keep 'er going, sir," yelled James.

"I'm in a blasted hole or something. Come *up*."

The car moved bodily to the left, churned, crept forward in a series of jerks and stopped. "Doan't stop in-gine fur Lawk's sake," James implored and was out and up to his knees. He disappeared in the rear of the car.

"What's he doing?" asked Mandrake. "He's on your side."

Chloris looked out on her side. "I can only see his stern. He seems to be stuffing something under the back wheel. Now, he's waving. He wants you to go on."

Mandrake engaged his bottom gear, pulled out his choke a fraction, and tried. The car gripped somewhere, wallowed forward and stuck again. James returned for his shovel and set to work in front of the bonnet.

Mandrake got out, leaving instructions with Chloris to keep the engine going. The noise of the storm met him like a physical blow and the drive of rain on his face numbed it. He struggled round to the front of the car and found James shovelling with a will in three feet of snow. Mandrake wore heavy driving-gloves, and set to work with his hands. In the centre the snow was still frozen but at the bottom it had turned to slush and the earth beneath was soft and muddy. The front wheels had jammed in a cross-gut which, as they cleared it, began to fill with water. James roared out something that Mandrake could not understand, thrust his shovel into his hands, and plunged away behind the car. Mandrake toiled on, looking up, once, to see Chloris' face pressed anxiously against the windscreen. He grinned, waved his hand and fell to again with a will. James had returned, dragging two great boughs after him. They broke them up as best they could, filled in the gut with smaller branches and thrust the remaining pieces in front of the rear wheels.

The inside of the car seemed a different world, a world that smelt of petrol, upholstery, cigarettes and something that both Mandrake and Chloris secretly realized was peculiar to James Bewling, an aftermath of oilskin, elderly man, and agricultural activities. Mandrake slammed the door, sounded his horn as a warning to James, and speeded up his engine.

"Now then, you old besom," Mandrake apostrophized his car, "up with you." With a great crackling of branches, an ominous sinking and a violent lurch, they went forward and up, with James's voice, raised to an elderly screech, sounding like a banshee in the storm. The chains bit into firmer ground. They were going uphill.

"That's the first hurdle over, I fancy," said Mandrake. "We'll wait for James at the top."

In the rectory at Winton St. Giles, Chief Detective-Inspector Alleyn put his head round the study door and said to his wife: "I've been looking out of the top windows at the summit of Cloudyfold. I wouldn't be surprised if it's raining over there. What do you say, Rector?"

The Reverend Walter Copeland turned his head to look out of the window. The lady behind the large canvas muttered to herself and laid down her brushes.

"Rain?" echoed the Rector. "It's still freezing down here. Upon my word, though, I believe you're right. Yes, yes, undoubtedly it's pouring up round Highfold. Very odd."

"Very odd indeed," said Mrs. Alleyn grimly.

"My angel," said her husband. "I apologize in fourteen different positions. Rector, for pity's sake resume your pose."

With a nervous start the Rector turned from the window, clasped his hands, tilted his fine head and stared obediently at the top left-hand corner of the canvas.

"Is that right?"

"Yes, thank you," said the lady. Her thin face, wearing a streak of green paint across the nose, looked round the side of the canvas at her husband.

"I suppose," she said with a surprising air of diffidence, "you wouldn't like to read to us."

"Yes, I would," said Alleyn. He came in and shut the door.

"Now, that's really delightful," said Mr. Copeland. "I hope I'm not a bad parish priest," he added, "but it *is* rather pleasant to know that there can be no more services today—Dinah and I had matins all to ourselves, you know—and that for once the weather is *so* bad that nobody is likely to come and visit me."

"If I were on duty," said Alleyn, looking along the bookshelves, "I should never dare to make those observations."

"Why not?"

"Because if I did, as sure as fate I'd be called out into the snow, like a melodrama heroine, to a particularly disagreeable case. However," said Alleyn, taking down a copy of *Northanger Abbey,* "I'm not on duty, thank the Lord. Shall we have Miss Austen?"

"This yurr be Pen Gidding," said James Bewling. "Just to right, sir. We'm half-way theer. A nasty stretch she'll be, round those-thurr hills, and by the looks of her thurr's bin no rain hereabouts."

"What's the time?" asked Chloris.

Mandrake held out his wrist. "Have a look."

She pushed up his cuff. "Ten past eleven."

"With any luck we'll be ringing the rectory doorbell before noon."

CHAPTER XI

Alleyn

I

"NICHOLAS," SAID MADAME LISSE, "come here to me."

He had been staring through the windows of the green sitting-room at the rain, which still came down like a multitude of rods, piercing all that remained of snow on the drive, filling the house with a melancholy insistence of sound. After she had spoken, though not immediately, he turned from the window and slowly crossed the room.

"Well?" he asked. "Well, Elise?"

She reached out her hand to him, touching his wrist, compelling him with her fingers to come nearer to her. "I am deeply grieved for you. You know that?" she said.

He took the hand and rubbed it between his two palms as if he hoped to get some warmth from it. "If she goes," he said, "I've no one else, no one at all but you." He stood beside her, still moving her fingers between his hands and peering at her oddly, almost as if he saw her for the first time. "I don't understand," he said. "I don't understand."

Madame Lisse pulled him down to the footstool beside her chair. He yielded quite obediently.

"We have got to think, to plan, to decide," said Madame Lisse. "I am, as I have said, deeply grieved for you. If she does not live it will be a great loss, of course. Your mother having always favoured you, one is much puzzled that she should despair to extremity at the death of your brother. For myself I believe her action should rather be attributed to a morbid dread of publicity about the misfortune to her beauty." Madame Lisse touched her hair with the tips of her fingers. "The loss of beauty is a sufficient tragedy, but to that she had become resigned. Your brother's threat to expose Francis, as well as the shock she sustained on recognizing Francis, no doubt unhinged her. It is very sad." She looked down at the top of his head. It was a speculative and even a calculating glance. "Of course," she said, "I have not seen her letter." Nicholas' whole body seemed to writhe. "I can't talk about it," he muttered.

"Mr. Royal has taken it?"

"Yes. In case—he said . . ."

"That was quite sensible, of course."

"Elise, did you know it was Hart who did it—to her—in Vienna?"

"He told me on Friday night that he had recognized her."

"My God, why didn't you tell me?"

"Why should I? I was already terrified of the situation between you. Why should I add to your antagonism? No, my one desire was to suppress it, my one terror that she should recognize him and that we should be ruined." She clenched her hands and beat the arms of her chair. "And now what am I to do! It will all come out. That he is my husband. That you are my lover. He will say terrible things when they arrest him. He will bring me down in his own ruin."

"I swear you won't suffer." Nicholas pressed his face against her knees and began to mutter feverish endearments and reassurances. "Elise . . . when it's over—it seems frightful to speak of it . . . everything different now . . . Elise . . . alone together. *Elise.*"

She stopped him at last, pressing her hands on his head.

"Very well," she said. "When it's all over. Very well."

II

Dr. Hart leant back on his heels, looked at the prostrate figure on the mattress, bent forward again and slapped the discoloured and distorted face. The eyes remained not quite closed, the head jerked flaccidly. He uttered a disconsolate grunt, turned the figure on its face again, and placed his hands over the ribs. Sweat was pouring down his own face and arms.

"Let me go on," said Hersey. "I know what to do."

He continued three or four times with the movements of artificial respiration and then said suddenly: "Very well. Thank you. I have a cramp."

Hersey knelt on the floor.

"It is so long," said Hart, "since I was in general practice. Twenty-three years. I cannot remember my poisons. The stomach should be emptied, that is certain. If only they can return soon from the chemist. If only they can find the police surgeon!"

"Is there any improvement?" asked Jonathan.

Hart raised his shoulders and arms and let them fall.

"Oh dear, oh dear!" cried Jonathan and wrung his hands. "What possessed her?"

"I cannot understand it. It is the other son to whom she gave her devotion."

Hersey raised her head for a moment to give Dr. Hart a very direct stare. "Do not stop or hesitate," he said at once, "steady rhythmic movements are essential. . . . Where is the other son now?"

"Nicholas is downstairs," Hersey grunted. "We thought it better to keep him out of this. All things considered."

"Perhaps you are right." He knelt again, close to Sandra Compline's head, and stooped down. "Where is that woman? That Pouting, who was to prepare the emetic and find me a tube. She is too long coming."

"I'll see," said Jonathan, and hurried out of the room.

For a time Hersey worked on in silence. Then Hart took the patient's pulse and respiration. Jonathan came panting back with a tray covered by a napkin. Hart looked at the contents. "A poor substitute," he said. "We can but try it. It will be better, perhaps, if you leave us, Mr. Royal."

"Very well." Jonathan walked to the door, where he turned and spoke in a high voice. "We are trusting you, Dr. Hart, because we have no alternative. You will remember, if you please, that you are virtually under arrest."

"Ah! ah!" Hart muttered. "Go away. Don't be silly. Go away."

"*Honestly!*" said Hersey, and then: "You'd better go, Jo."

Jonathan went, but no farther than the passage, where he paced up and down for some ten minutes. It is a peculiarity of some people to sing when they are agitated or annoyed. Jonathan was one of these. As, with mincing steps, he moved about his guest-wing passage, he hummed breathily: "*Il était une bergère . . .*" and beat time with his finger-tips on the back of his hand. Past the niche in the wall where the brass Buddha had stood, as far as the grandfather clock and back down the whole length of the passage, he trotted, with closed doors on each side of him and his figure passing in and out of shadows. Once, he broke off his sentry-go to enter Hart's room, where he stood at the window, tapping the pane, breathily humming, staring at the rain. But in a moment or two he was back and down the passage, pausing to listen outside Mrs. Compline's door and then on again to the grandfather clock. Hersey found him at this employment when she came out. She took his arm and fell into step with him.

"Well, Jo," said Hersey, and her voice was not very steady, "I'm afraid we're not doing much good. At the moment nothing's worked."

"Hersey, she *must* recover, I—I can't believe—what's happening to us, Hersey? What's happening?"

"Oh, well," said Hersey, "it'll be worse in the air raids. Dr. Hart's doing his best, Jo."

"But *is* he? Is he? A murderer, Hersey. A murderer, to stand between our dear old friend Sandra and death! What an incredible—what a frightful situation!"

Hersey stood stock-still. Her hand closed nervously on Jonathan's arm and she drew in a long breath. "I don't believe he is a murderer," she said.

Jonathan pulled his arm away as violently as if she'd pinched it.

"My dear girl," he said loudly, "don't be a fool. Great Heaven . . . !" He checked himself. "I'm sorry, my dear. I was discourteous. You will forgive me. But to suggest that Hart, *Hart,* who has scarcely attempted to conceal his guilt—"

"That's not true, Jo. I mean, if he did it, he managed to provide himself with an alibi that none of us can easily break."

"Nonsense, Hersey. *We have* broken it. He committed his crime after William had turned on the news, or else he himself turned it on and waited his chance to dart out of the room."

"Yes, I know. Why didn't you run into him?"

"Because he took very good care to avoid me."

"He seems to have done a tidy lot of dodging," said Hersey dubiously. Jonathan uttered an exasperated noise.

"What has come over you, Hersey? You agreed that he had done it. Of course he did it. Of course he killed William. Killed him brutally and deliberately, believing him to be his brother. Aubrey has made that much clear."

"I don't believe he did it," Hersey repeated, and added shakily: "After all it's not an easy thing to say. I don't enjoy facing the implication. But I—"

"Don't say it again," whispered Jonathan, and took her by the wrists. "Who else? Who else? What has come over you?"

"It's seeing him in there, working over Sandra. Why, I believe he'd even forgotten he was accused until you reminded him just now. It's the one or two things that he's said while I've been in there. I don't think he was saying them to me so much as to himself. I believe he's got an idea that if he can save Sandra, it'll atone, in a queer sort of way, for what he did to her beauty."

"Good God, what rubbish is this? He wants to save her because he thinks he'll impress us, as it seems he has impressed you, with his personal integrity. Of course he doesn't want Sandra to die."

"If he was guilty of murdering her son? That's not good reasoning, Jo. Sandra would be one of the most damaging witnesses against him."

"You must be demented," Jonathan said breathlessly, and stood looking at her and biting his fingers. "What does all this matter? I suppose you agree that whoever set the booby-trap committed the murder? Only Hart could have set the booby-trap. But I'll not argue with you, Hersey. You're distracted, poor girl, distracted, as we all are."

"No," said Hersey. "No, Jo, it's not that."

"Then God knows what it is," cried Jonathan, and turned away.

"I think I heard him," said Hersey. "I must go back."

In a moment she had gone and Jonathan was left to stare at the closed door of Sandra Compline's room.

III

"Only five more miles to go," said Mandrake. "If the snow's frozen hard all the way I believe we'll do it."

They were in a narrow lane. The car churned, squeaked, and skidded through snow that packed down under the wheels, mounted in a hard mass between the front bumpers and the radiator, and clogged the axles. Their eyes were wearied with whiteness, Mandrake's arms and back ached abominably, James Bewling had developed a distressing tendency to suck his teeth.

"Queer though it may seem in these surroundings," said Mandrake, "the engine's getting hot. I've been in bottom gear for the last two miles. Chloris, be an angel and light me a cigarette."

"Downhill now, sir, every foot of her," said James.

"That may or may not be an unmixed blessing. Why the *hell* is she sidling like this? What's happened to the chains? Never mind. On we go."

Chloris lit a cigarette and put it between his lips. "You're doing grand, dearie," she said in Cockney.

"I've been trying to sort things out a little for a quick news bulletin when we get there, always adding the proviso, *if* we get there. What's best to do? Shall I, while you push on to the chemist, tell Alleyn in a few badly chosen words, as few as possible, what's happened; and shall we implore him to come back at once, reading my notes on the way?"

"I suppose so. Perhaps he'll insist on our going on to Great Chipping for the local experts. Perhaps he won't play."

"It's a poisonous distance to Great Chipping. He can ring up. Surely the lines won't be down all over this incredibly primitive landscape. We *must* get back with the things from the chemist." The rear of the car moved uncannily sideways. "She's curtseying again. Damn, that's a bad one. *Damn.*"

They were nearly into the hedgerow. Mandrake threw out his clutch and rammed on the brake. "I'm going to have a look at those chains."

"Don't 'ee stir, sir," said James. "I'll see."

He got out. Chloris leant forward and covered her face with her hands.

"Hullo," said Mandrake. "Eye-strain?" She didn't answer but some small movement of her shoulders prompted him to put his arm about them and then he felt her trembling. "I'm so sorry," he said, "so terribly sorry. Darling Chloris, I implore you not to cry."

"I won't. I'm not going to. It's not what you think, not sorrow. Though I am terribly sorry. It must be shock or something. I've been so miserable and ashamed about the Complines. I've so wanted to be rid of them. And now—look how it's happened. It was foul of me to get engaged to Bill on the rebound. That's what it was, no denying it. And I knew all the time what I was up to. Don't be nice to me, I feel like a sweep."

"I can't be as nice as I'd like to because here, alas, comes Mr. Bewling. Blow your nose, my sweet. There'll always be an England where there's a muddy lane, a hoarding by a cowslip field, and curates in the rain. Well, James, what have you discovered?"

"Pesky chain on off hind-wheel's carried away, sir. Which is why she's been skittering and skiddling the last mile or so."

"No doubt. Well, get in, James, get in, and I'll see if I can waddle out of the hedgerow. On mature consideration, perhaps you'd better watch me."

James hovered over the now familiar process of churning wheels, short jerks and final recoveries. He stood within view of Mandrake and made violent gyratory movements with his hands, while an enormous drop swung from the tip of his nose.

"I have never responded in the smallest degree to rustic charm," said Mandrake. "All dialects are alike to me. James seems to me to be an extremely unconvincing piece of *genre*. What does he mean by these ridiculous gestures?"

"He means you're backing us into the other ditch," said Chloris, blowing her nose. "Oh, do be careful. Don't you see, he's steering an imaginary wheel."

"His antics are revolting. Moreover he smells. There, you unspeakable old grotesque, is that right?"

James, capering in the snow and unable to hear any of this, innocently nodded and grinned.

"I think you're beastly about him," said Chloris, "he's *very* kind."

"Well, he can get in again. Here he comes. Are you all right, James? Have a cigarette."

"No, thankee, sir," said James, breathing hard. "I've never smoked one of they since I was so high as yer elber. A pipe's my fancy, sir, and that be too powerful a piece of work for the lady."

"Not a bit, James," said Chloris. "Do have a pipe. You've earned it."

James thanked her and soon the inside of the car smelt of nothing but his pipe. For some little time they lurched down the lane in silence but presently Mandrake leant his head towards Chloris and said in a low voice: "I hope you won't mind my mentioning it, but I never expected to lose my heart to a blonde. The darker the better hitherto, I assure you. Not pitch-black, of course. White faces and black heads have been my undoing."

"If you're trying to cheer me up," Chloris rejoined, "you've hit on an unfortunate theme. I went ashen for Nicholas and I certainly can't revoke for you."

"There!" cried Mandrake triumphantly. "I should have known my instinct was not at fault. You idiot, darling, why did you? Oh, all right, all right. What's the time?"

"It's five minutes to twelve. We shan't be there by midday, after all."

"We shan't be much later, I swear. I wonder—Have you ever known anyone who took an overdose of a sleeping-draught?"

"Never. But we had something about them in my home-nursing course. I've been trying to remember. I think they're all barbitones, and I think the lecturer said that people who took too much sank into a coma and might keep on like that for hours or even days. You had to try and get rid of the poison and rouse them. I—I think it's terribly important that we should be quick. Dr. Hart said so. Aubrey, we've got so much to say when we get there and so little time for saying it!"

"I've tried to get it down to some sort of coherent form."

"When you made your notes did you think of anything new, anything that would help to explain about William?"

Mandrake did not answer immediately. They had reached a stretch of road where the snow was less thick and was frozen hard. They had left the Cloudyfold hills behind and to their right, and had come into a level stretch between downlands and within sight of scattered cottages, each with its banner of smoke, the only signals of warmth in that cold countryside. Hedges broke through the snow, like fringes of black coral in an immobile sea. There was no wind down here and the trees, lined with snow, made frozen gestures against a sky of lead. Mandrake was visited by the notion that his car was a little world which clung precariously to its power of movement and he felt as if he himself fought, not against snow and mud, but against immobility. He wrenched his thoughts round to Chloris' question.

"If you open that attaché-case you'll find the notes," he said. "Would you get them out? I don't know if you can read in this state of upheaval. Try."

Chloris managed to read the notes. They crept on with occasional wallowings in softer snow, and presently James Bewling said that the next turn in the road would bring them within sight of the spire of Winton St. Giles parish church, and Mandrake himself began to recognize the countryside and distant groups of trees that he had passed on his way from Winton to Cloudyfold. That was on Thursday. And, as he arrived at this point, through the open driving window came the faintest echo of a bell.

"Good Lord!" he thought, "it's Sunday. Suppose they're all in church. James," he called out, "what time is morning service at St. Giles?"

"Ah. Rector do set most store by early service," James rejoined. "She be at eight. T'others at half-past ten. Reckon he'll have it to hisself this morning."

"That's all right, then. But what's that bell?"

"Rector do ring bell at noon."

"The Angelus," said Mandrake. Chloris looked up from her papers and for a little while they listened to that distant clear-cold voice.

"They're friends of yours, aren't they?" said Chloris.

"The Copelands? Yes. Dinah's beginning to be quite a good actress. She's going to play in my new thing, if the *Blitzkrieg* doesn't beat us to it. I suppose it won't seem odd to you, but for at least twelve hours I haven't thought about my play. What do you make of the notes?"

"There are some things I didn't know about, but not many." Chloris caught her breath. "You say at the end: 'Could Hart have set a second booby-trap?' Do you mean could he have done something with that frightful weapon that would make it fall on . . . ? Is that what you mean?"

"Yes. I can't get any further though. I can't think of anything."

"A *Busman's Honeymoon*-ish sort of contraption? But there are no hanging flower-pots at Highfold."

"Well, if you can think of anything! I must tell you I went into the room before we left. I looked all round, trying to see if some little thing was out of order in the arrangement of the room, unusual in any way. I—didn't enjoy it. I couldn't see anything remotely suggestive of booby-traps. The ceiling's a high one. Anyway, how could Hart have dangled a stone weapon from the ceiling?"

As soon as these words had fallen from his lips, Mandrake experienced a strange foreknowledge of how they would be answered. So vivid was this impression that when Chloris did speak, it was to him exactly as though she echoed his thoughts.

"Are you so certain," she said, "that it must be Dr. Hart?"

And he heard his own voice answer, as if it spoke to a given cue: "I thought I was. Aren't you?" She didn't reply and a moment later he said with an air of conviction: "It must be. Who else?" And as she still kept silence: "Who else?"

"Nobody, I suppose. Nobody, of course."

"If it was anybody else the original booby-trap goes unexplained. We know that only Hart could have set it. Don't we?"

"I suppose so. Although, reading your notes, mightn't it be just possible that one of the alibis . . . ? It's your evidence."

"I know what you mean, but it's beyond all bounds incredible. Why? Not a motive in the wide world! Besides, I can't believe it. It's monstrous."

"Yes, I know. Well then, what about a second booby-trap? The detective stories tell you to look for the unusual, don't they?"

"I don't read them," said Mandrake with some slight return to his professional manner. "However, I *did* look for the unusual."

"And found nothing?"

"And found nothing. The room had a ghastly air of interrupted normality."

They were ploughing through a small drift. The snow yielded, mounted in a wall in front of the radiator and splashed across the windscreen. They felt a familiar and ominous quiver and in a moment had come to a standstill.

"Out comes wold shovel agin," said James cheerfully. "She's not a bad 'un this time, sir."

Mandrake backed out of the drift and again James set to work.

"There's one detail," said Mandrake, "that for some reason annoys me. No doubt there's nothing in it."

"What's that?"

"You saw it. Do you remember the drawing-pin in the sole of my shoe? I picked it up in the smoking-room. There's dried paint on it and it's the same as the ones that are stuck in the lid of William's paint-box."

"I'm afraid I don't see . . ."

"I said there was nothing in it. The only thing is, why should William have had a drawing-pin in the study? He did no painting at Highfold."

"Yes, he did," Chloris contradicted. "At least he did a drawing of me yesterday before lunch. It was while he was doing it that we had our row. And the paper was pinned down to a bit of board. And he dropped one of the pins."

"Oh," said Mandrake, flatly. "Well, you might add that to the notes. That's a flop then. What do we think of now?"

"Well, I can't think of anything," said Chloris hopelessly.

"What the devil," said Mandrake, "is that old mountebank doing?"

James Bewling, having cleared a passage in front of the car, had, with great difficulty, climbed the bank under the buried hedgerow and now stood waving his arms and pointing down the road. Mandrake sounded his horn and James instantly plunged down the bank and across the intervening snowdrift to the car. He climbed into the back seat, shouting excitedly as he came.

"Road's clear, down-along," shouted James. "There's a mort of chaps with shovels and one of they scrapers. On 'ee go, sir, us'll be there in ten minutes."

"Thank God!" said Mandrake and Chloris sincerely.

IV

Dinah Copeland trudged down the side path and pressed her face against the French window, instantly obscuring it with her breath. Alleyn put down his book and let her in.

"You *do* look wholesome," he said.

"Did you hear me ring the Angelus?" she demanded. "Was it all right, Daddy?"

"Very nice, my dear," said the Rector out of the corner of his mouth, "but I mustn't talk. Mrs. Alleyn's doing my bottom lip."

"I've finished," said Troy.

"For the morning?"

"Yes. Would you like to look?"

Dinah kicked off her snow-boots and hurried round the easel. Troy grinned at her husband, who upon that signal joined her. She thrust her thin arm in its painty sleeve through his and with Dinah they looked at the portrait.

"Pleased?" Alleyn asked his wife.

"Not so bad from my point of view, but what about Dinah?"

"It's Heaven," said Dinah emphatically.

"Not quite what the church-hen ordered, I'm afraid," Troy murmured.

"No, thank the Lord. I *was* wondering if by any chance you'd gone surrealist and would mix Daddy up with some nice symbols. I've got rather keen on surrealism since I've been working with Aubrey Mandrake. But now I see it, I'm quite glad you haven't put in any eggshells or phallic trimmings."

"Dinah!"

"Well, Daddy, everybody recognizes the frightful importance—all right, darling, I won't. I do wish my young man was here to see it," said Dinah. "Daddy, aren't you glad we scraped acquaintance with Mr. Alleyn over our murder?"

"I'm very glad, at all events," said Troy. "Do you know this is the only time since we were married that he's let me meet any of his criminal acquaintances?" She laughed, squinted at her work and asked: "Do you think it's all right, Roderick?"

"I like it," said Alleyn gravely.

The Rector, who wore the diffident simper of the subject, joined the group at Troy's easel. Alleyn, gripping his pipe between his teeth and humming gently to himself, began to roll up and put away his wife's tubes of paint. She lit a cigarette and watched him.

"For a long time," said Troy, "he endured my paint-box in silence, and then one day he asked me if dirt was an essential to self-expression. Since then it's got more and more like the regulation issue for investigating officers at C.I."

"Whereas before, it was a test case for advanced students at Hendon. I found," said Alleyn, "characteristic refuse from Fiji, Quebec, Norway, and the Dolomites. Hullo! What's that?"

"What's what?" asked Troy.

"There's a car struggling outside in the church lane."

"Church lane!" Dinah ejaculated. "It must be driven by a lunatic if it's come from anywhere round Cloudyfold. They've cleared the lane up to the first turning but above that it's thick snow. Your car must have come in from the main road, Mr. Alleyn. It'll very soon have to stop."

"It has stopped," said Alleyn. "And I fancy at your gate. Oh, dear me!"

"What's the matter with you?" asked his wife.

"By the pricking of my thumbs! Well, it can't be for me, anyway."

"Somebody's coming up the side path," cried Dinah, and a moment later she turned an astonished face upon the others. "It's Aubrey Mandrake."

"Mandrake?" said Alleyn sharply. "But he ought to be on the other side of Cloudyfold."

"It can't be Mandrake, my dear," said the Rector.

"But it *is*. And the car's driven away. Here he comes. He's seen me and he's coming to this window." Dinah stared at Alleyn. "I think there must be something wrong," she said. "Aubrey looks—different."

She opened the French window and in another moment Aubrey Mandrake walked in.

"Alleyn!" said Mandrake. "Thank God you're here. There's been a most appalling tragedy at Highfold, and we've come to get you."

"You detestable young man," said Alleyn.

V

"So you see," Mandrake said, "there really was nothing for it but to come to you."

"But it's *not*—" Alleyn protested piteously, "it's really *not* my cup of tea. It's the Chief Constable's cup of tea, and old Blandish's. Is Blandish still the Superintendent at Great Chipping, Rector?"

"Yes, he is. This is an appalling thing, Mandrake. I—I simply can't believe it. William Compline seemed such a nice fellow. We don't know them very well, they're rather beyond our country at Penfelton, but I liked what I saw of William."

"Mrs. Compline's in desperate case. If we don't get back quickly—" Mandrake began, and Alleyn cut in crisply: "Yes, of course." He turned to Mr. Copeland. "I've forgotten the name of your Chief Constable, sir."

"Lord Hesterdon. Miles and miles away to the north; and if, as Mandrake says, the telephone wires over Cloudyfold are down, I'm afraid you won't get him."

"I'll get Blandish if I have to wade to Great Chipping," Alleyn muttered. "May I use your telephone?"

He went into the hall.

"I'm sorry," said Mandrake. "He's livid with rage, isn't he?"

"Not really," said Troy. "It's only his pretty little ways. He'll do his stuff I expect. He'll have to be asked, you know, by the local police. C.I. people don't as a rule just nip in and take a case wherever they happen to be."

"Red tape," said Mandrake gloomily. "I guessed as much. Murderers can ramp about country houses, women can kill themselves with overdoses of veronal, well-intentioned guests can wallow in and out of snow-drifts in an effort to help on an arrest, and when, after suffering the most disgusting privations, they win home to the fountain-head, it is only to become wreathed, Laocoön-like, in the toils of red tape."

"I don't think," said Troy, "that it will be quite as bad as that." And Dinah, who was listening shamelessly at the door, said: "He's saying: 'Well, you'll have to ring up C.I., blast you.' "

"Dinah, darling," said her father, "you really mustn't."

"It's all right," said Dinah, shutting the door. "He's cursing freely and asking for Whitehall 1212. When do you think your girl-friend will get back, Aubrey?"

"She'll have to beat up the Little Chipping chemist. We only remembered it was Sunday when we heard your bell."

"That was me," said Dinah. "Mr. Tassy is our chemist and he lives over his shop, so that'll be all right. The road from here to Chipping has been cleared pretty well but I hear there are masses of frightful drifts beyond, on the way to Great Chipping. So I don't see how you'll get the police-surgeon or Mr. Blandish."

"If you'll excuse me," said Troy, "I believe I'll pack my husband's bag."

"Then you think he'll come?" cried Mandrake.

"Oh, yes," said Troy vaguely, "he'll come, all right."

She went out and as the door opened they heard Alleyn's voice saying: "I haven't got a damn' thing. I'll ring up the local chemist and get some stuff from him. Is Dr. Curtis *there?* At the Yard? Well, get him to speak to me. You'd better find out . . ." The door shut off the rest of his remarks.

"Daddy," said Dinah, "hadn't we better give Aubrey a drink?"

"Yes, yes, of course. My dear boy, forgive me, of course you must be exhausted. I'm so sorry. You must have a glass of sherry. Or—"

"You'd better have a whiskey, Aubrey. It's almost lunchtime, so why not eat while you're waiting? And if you can't wait for Miss Wynne, when she comes, we can at least send something out to the car. I'll bustle them up in the kitchen. Bring him along to the dining-room, Daddy."

She hurried out and met Alleyn in the hall. "I'm so sorry," Alleyn said, "nobody could want to go away less than I do, but here's Blandish gibbering at Great Chipping with a cracked water-tank in his car and a story of drifts six feet between us and him. He's going to get hold of a doctor, commandeer a car, and ginger up the road-clearing gang, but in the meantime he wants me to go ahead. I've rung up my atrocious superior and he's all for it, blast his eyes. May Troy stay on, as we originally planned, and finish her portrait?"

"Of course. We'd never forgive you if you put her off her stroke. I say, this *is* a rum go, isn't it?"

"Not 'alf," said Alleyn. "It's a damned ugly go by the sound of it."

"Awful. Your wife's upstairs."

"I'll find her."

He ran to his dressing-room and found his wife on her knees before a small suit-case.

"Pyjamas, dressing-gown, shaving-things," Troy muttered. "I suppose you'll be there tonight won't you? What'll you do for all those things in the case bag? Squirts and bottles and powders and stuff for making casts?"

"My darling oddity, I can't think. At least I've got a camera and I've rung up the chemist at Chipping. Miss Wynne was in the shop. He's going to give her some stuff for me—iodine and whatnot. Can you lend me a soft brush, darling? One of the sort you use for water colour. And scissors? And some bits of charcoal? For the rest, I'll have to trust Fox and Co. getting through by train. They're looking out a route, now. It'll be detecting in the raw, won't it? Case for the resourceful officer."

"I'm a rotten packer," said Troy, "but I think that's all you'll want."

"My dear," said her husband who was at the writing-table, helping himself to several sheets of notepaper and some envelopes, "almost you qualify for the role of clever little wife."

"You go to the devil," said Mrs. Alleyn amiably.

He squatted down beside her, looked through the contents of the suit-case, refrained from improving on the pack and from saying that he did not think it likely he would need his pyjamas. "Admirable," he said. "Now I'd better swathe myself in sweaters and top-coats. Give me a kiss and say you're sorry I'm going out on a beastly case."

"Did you ever see such a change in anyone as appears in the somewhat precious Mandrake?" asked Troy, hunting in his wardrobe.

"It takes murder to mould a man."

"Do you think the statement he's written is dependable?"

"As regards fact, yes, I should say so. As regards his interpretation of fact, I fancy it wanders a bit. For a symbolic expressionist, he seems to have remained very firmly wedded to a convention. But perhaps that's the secret of two-dimensional poetic drama. I wouldn't know. Is that a car?"

"Yes."

"Then I must be off." He kissed his wife, who was absently scrubbing at her painty nose with the collar of her smock. She looked at him, scowling a little.

"This is the worst sort of luck," said Alleyn. "It was being such a good holiday."

"I hate these cases," said Troy.

"Not more than I do, bless you."

"For a different reason."

"I'm so sorry," he said quickly. "I know."

"No, you don't, Rory. Not squeamishness, nowadays—exactly. I wish Brer Fox was with you."

She went downstairs with him and saw him go off with Mandrake, his hat pulled down over his right eye, the collar of his heavy raincoat turned up, his camera slung over his shoulder and his suit-case in his hand.

"He looks as if he was off on a winter sports holiday," said Dina. "I don't mean to be particularly callous, but there's no denying a murder *is* rather exciting."

"Dinah!" said her father automatically.

They heard the car start up the lane.

CHAPTER XII

Recapitulation

I

ALLEYN SAT IN THE BACK seat and read through Mandrake's notes. He was parted from Mr. Bewling by a large luncheon basket provided by Dinah Copeland. "We'll open it," said Chloris Wynne, "at our first breakdown. If The Others overheard me saying that, I daresay they won't let us have a breakdown, so that they can collar the lunch."

"What *can* you mean?" asked Mandrake.

"Don't you know about The Others?" said Chloris in a sprightly manner. "They're the ones that leave nails and broken glass on the road. They hide things when you're in a hurry. They've only got one arm and one leg each, you know. So they take single gloves and stockings, and they're frightfully keen on keys and unanswered letters."

"My God, are you being whimsical?" Mandrake demanded, and Alleyn thought he recognized that particular shade of caressing rudeness which is the courtship note among members of the advanced intelligentsia. He was not mistaken. Miss Wynne made a small preening movement.

"Don't pretend you're not interested in The Others," she said. "I bet they take the top of your fountain-pen often enough." She turned her beautifully arranged head to look at Alleyn. "Bleached," he thought automatically, "but I daresay she's quite a nice creature."

"Do they ever get into Scotland Yard, Mr. Alleyn?" she asked.

"Do they not? They are the authors of most anonymous letters, I fancy."

"There!" she cried. "Mr. Alleyn doesn't think I'm whimsical." He saw, with some misgivings, that Mandrake had removed his left hand from the driving-wheel, and reflected, not for the first time, that affairs of sentiment will flourish under the most unpropitious circumstances. "But she's rattled all the same," he thought. "This brightness is all my eye. I wonder how well she knew the young man who is dead." His reflections were interrupted by James Bewling, who cleared his throat portentously.

"Axcuse me, sir," said James. "I bin thinking."

"Indeed?" said Mandrake, apprehensively. "What's the matter, James?"

"I bin thinking," repeated James: "Being this-yurr is a lethal matter, and being this gentleman is going into the thick of it with his eyes only half-open like a kitten, and being he'll be burning in his official heart and soul to be axing you this and axing you that, I bin thinking it might be agreeable if I left the party along to Ogg's Corner."

"Whatever do you mean, James?" asked Chloris. "You can't just walk out into a snowdrift from motives of delicacy."

"It's not so bad as that, Miss. My wold aunty, Miss Fancy Bewling, bides in cottage along to Ogg's Corner. Her's ninety-one yurrs of age and so cantankerous an old masterpiece as ever you see. Reckon her'll be pleased as Punch to blow me up at her leisure until Mr. Blandish and his chaps comes along, when I'll get a lift and direct 'em best way to Highfold."

"Well, James," said Mandrake, "it's not a bad idea. We'll be all right. I know the way and we've ploughed a sort of path for ourselves. What do you think, Mr. Alleyn?"

"If there's any danger of Blandish missing his way," said Alleyn, "I'd be very glad to think you were there, Bewling."

"Good enough, sir. Then put me down if you please, souls, at next turning but one. Don't miss thicky little twiddling lane up to Pen Gidding, Mr. Mandrake, sir, and be bold to rush 'er up when she skiddles."

So they dropped him by his aunt's cottage, and it seemed to Alleyn that Miss Wynne watched him go with some regret. She said that Mandrake might despise James, but that she considered he had shown extraordinary tact and forbearance. "He must have been dying to know more about the disaster," she said, "but he never so much as asked a leading question."

"We talked pretty freely without him having to bother," Mandrake pointed out. "However, I agree it was nice of James. Is there anything you want to ask us, Alleyn? By dint of terrific concentration I can manage to keep the car on its tracks and my mind more or less on the conversation."

Alleyn took Mandrake's notes from his pocket and at the rustle of paper he saw Chloris turn her head sharply. Something about the set of Mandrake's shoulders suggested that he too was suddenly alert.

"If I may," said Alleyn, "I should like to go over these notes with you. It's fortunate for me that you decided to make this very clear and well-ordered summary. I'm sure it gives the skeleton of events as completely as possible, and that is invaluable. But I should like, with your help, to clothe the bones in a semblance of flesh."

This was spoken in what Troy called "the official manner," and it was the first Chloris and Mandrake had heard of this manner. Neither of them answered, and Alleyn knew that with one short speech he had established an atmosphere of uneasy expectation. He was right. Until this moment Chloris and Mandrake had wished above all things for the assurance that Alleyn would take charge. Now that, with a certain crispness and a marked change of manner, he had actually done so, each of them felt an icy touch of apprehension. They had set in motion a process which they were unable to stop. They were not yet nervous for themselves but instinctively they moved a little nearer to each other. They had called in the Yard.

"First of all," said Alleyn, "I should like to go over the notes, putting them into my own words to make quite sure I've got hold of the right ends of all the sticks. Will you stop me if I'm wrong? The death of this young man, William Compline, occurred at about ten minutes past ten yesterday evening. He was sitting in a room which communicates with a library, a small sitting-room, and a hall. Just before the discovery of his body, the library was occupied by his host, Mr. Jonathan Royal, by Lady Hersey Amblington, by Miss Chloris Wynne, by Mr. Aubrey Mandrake, and by Mr. Nicholas Compline. The small sitting-room had been occupied by Dr. Francis Hart; but, on his own statement and that of the footman Thomas, it appears that Dr. Hart left the sitting-room—you call it a 'boudoir,' I see—at the same time that Thomas came into the hall with a grog tray which he took into the library. That was some minutes after Nicholas Compline had left his brother and joined the party in the library, and quite definitely before you all heard the wireless turned on in the smoking-room. The wireless was turned on after the drinks came in. You agreed you would like to hear it, and Nicholas Compline opened the door and called out to his brother. A screen hid William but Nicholas heard someone cross the room and a moment later the wireless struck up 'Boomps-a-Daisy.'"

"That's it," said Chloris. "Nick left the door open."

"Yes. You endured the dance music and in a minute or so the news came on the air. At about this moment Mr. Royal went out to reassure himself that Dr. Hart was not in the 'boudoir.' He states that he did not enter the 'boudoir,' but saw there was no light under the door. He visited a cloak-room and, having met no one in the hall, returned before the news ended."

"Yes."

"All right. Well now, I understand that the wireless had been in use not long before. It's not likely, then, that the music was delayed by any warming-up process?"

"No," said Chloris. "I thought of that but it seems that the radio had been switched on all the time and wouldn't need to warm up. As soon as Bill turned the volume control it'd come up."

"As soon as the volume control was turned, at all events," said Alleyn, "and it must have been turned."

"By William," said Mandrake, "or his murderer. Exactly."

"And you see," Chloris added, "we *asked* for it and it was at once turned on. By *Somebody*."

"Yes. We now come to the curious episode of the dancing footman. The music follows Thomas' re-entry into the hall when he saw Dr. Hart on the stairs. Therefore, it seems, Dr. Hart did not turn up the volume control. Now it appears that Thomas, arrested by the strains of a composition known as 'Boomps-a-Daisy,' was moved to dance. As long as the music continued, Thomas, a solitary figure in the hall, capered, clapped his hands, slapped his knees and stuck out his stern in a rhythmic sequence. When the music stopped, so did Thomas. He left the hall as the news bulletin began. Then we have Mr. Royal's short excursion; and lastly, some minutes later, Lady Hersey Amblington, carrying a tumbler, walked from the library into the smoking-room, re-appeared in the doorway, returned into the smoking-room and switched off the radio. She then called out to her cousin, Mr. Royal, who joined her. Finally she came back to the library and summoned you, Mr. Mandrake. You went into the smoking-room and found William Compline there, dead. It was somewhere about this time that you trod on a drawing-pin which stuck in the sole of your shoe."

"Yes."

"The instrument used by the assailant," said Alleyn with a private grimace over the police-court phrase, "seems to have been a Maori *mere* which was one of a collection of weapons hanging on the smoking-room wall. Which wall?"

"What? Oh, on the right from the library door. There's a red leather screen inside the door and this unspeakable club was just beyond it."

"I see you've given me a very useful sketch-plan. Would you mark the position on the wall? I'll put a cross and you shall tell me if it's in the right place."

Chloris took the paper and showed it to Mandrake, who slowed down, glanced at it, nodded, and accelerated. James Bewling had got hold of a set of chains in Chipping, and the wheels bit well into their old tracks.

"Right," said Alleyn. "During this time, two members of the party were upstairs. They were Mrs. Compline and Madame Lisse, who you tell me is actually Mrs. Francis Hart." He paused. Neither Chloris nor Mandrake spoke.

"That's right, isn't it?"

"Yes," said Chloris, "that's it."

"As far as we know," said Mandrake unwillingly.

"As far as we know," Alleyn agreed. "At all events we know that neither of them could have come downstairs while Thomas was there. If it was anybody other than William Compline who turned up the wireless, this person must have entered the room after Nicholas Compline left it and remained there until after Thomas left the hall. If, on the other hand, it was William himself who turned up the wireless, his murderer must have entered the room after Thomas left the hall, and made his get-away before Lady Hersey went in with the drink."

"Avoiding Jonathan Royal," added Mandrake. "Don't forget he crossed the hall twice."

"Oh," said Alleyn vaguely, "I hadn't forgotten that. Now before we leave these, the crucial periods as I see them, I pause to remind myself that the communicating door between the smoking-room and the 'boudoir' was locked on the smoking-room side."

"Yes," said Mandrake. "I ought to have said, I think, that there is nowhere in the smoking-room where anybody could hide. The screen's no good because of the door into the library. I think I'm right in saying the murderer must have come in by the hall door."

"It looks like it," Alleyn agreed. "Avoiding the dancing footman and Mr. Royal."

"Somebody could hide in the hall," said Chloris suddenly. "We'd thought of that."

"There's still the dancing footman. He defines the periods when it would have been possible for the murderer to enter or leave the smoking-room."

"Yes," agreed Mandrake. "Thomas continued his antics until the music stopped, and that leaves a margin of a few minutes before Lady Hersey entered the room. The 'boudoir' is no good, because the door was still locked. I know that."

"Then," said Chloris slowly, "doesn't it look as if the crucial time is the time when the murderer *left* the room? Because, whether he worked the wireless or not, he could only have got away after Thomas had left the hall."

"Top marks for deduction, Miss Wynne," said Alleyn.

"It's a grim notion," said Mandrake suddenly, "to think of us all sitting there calling for the news. If it was Hart, imagine him having to pull himself together and turn up the wireless!"

"Don't," said Chloris.

Alleyn had, with some difficulty in the jolting car, made a series of marginal notes. He now glanced up and found Chloris leaning her arm along the front seat and looking at him.

"I'd like to get Lady Hersey's movements fixed in my head," he said. "She went into the smoking-room with the drink, disappeared round the screen, returned to the doorway, said something you couldn't hear, disappeared again, and called out to Mr. Royal, who then joined her. Finally she re-entered the library and asked you, Mandrake, to go to your host."

"That's it." Mandrake changed down and crawled the car over its own skid marks. Chloris drew in her breath audibly. "It's all right," he said. "No trouble this time." But Alleyn, who had been watching her, knew that it was not their progress that had scared her. She looked quickly at him and away again. "Lady Hersey," she said, "is an old friend of the Complines. She's terribly nice and she's been absolutely marvellous since it happened. She was helping Dr. Hart with Mrs. Compline. She couldn't be more sorry and upset about it all."

These somewhat conventional phrases were shot out at nobody in particular and were followed by an odd little pause.

"Ah," Alleyn murmured, "those are the sort of touches that help to clothe the bare bones of a case. We'll collect some more, I hope, as we go along. I'm working backwards through your notes, Mandrake, and arrive at the booby-trap. A heavy brass Buddha, of all disagreeable objects, is perched on the top of a door, so that when the door is opened it is bound to fall on the person who pushes the door. The room is Nicholas Compline's and it is upon his arm the Buddha falls. This trap was set, you say, during a visit Compline paid to Madame Lisse. You've worked out a time check on two clocks; the grandfather clock at the top of the stairs and the drawing-room clock which agrees with it. On this reckoning it appears that the trap was set some time between half-past seven, which struck as Nicholas Compline left his room, and a minute or so past twenty to eight, when you heard him cry out as the Buddha struck his arm. You suggest that you have found alibis during this period for everybody but Dr. Hart, who was in the bathroom. Lady Hersey gives Mrs. Compline her alibi, Mr. Royal gives you yours, Mandrake. Can you return the gesture?"

"I can say that I think he arrived in the drawing-room some little time before the crash."

"Ten minutes before?"

"I feel sure it must have been. I—we were talking. Yes, it must have been at least ten minutes."

"There's no way by which you could come a little nearer to it? For example, did he light a cigarette when he came into the room?"

"Let me think. No. No, I don't believe he did. But I did. I'd forgotten to bring my case down and I was helping myself to one of his when he came into the room. I remember that," said Mandrake and Alleyn saw the back of his neck go red, "because I felt—" He stopped and made rather a business of adjusting his wind-screen wiper which at that moment was not needed.

"Yes?"

"What? Oh, I merely felt, very stupidly, a little embarrassed." Mandrake's voice trailed off and then he said loudly: "I was not born into the purple, Mr. Alleyn. Until a few years ago, I lived in the odour of extreme economy, among people who waited to be invited before they smoked other people's cigarettes."

"I should call that a sign of courtesy rather than penury," said Alleyn, and received a brilliant smile from Miss Wynne. "Well, you lit your cigarette, then. That's a help. Was it still going when you heard Nicholas Compline yell?"

"Was it, now? Yes. Yes, I remember throwing it in the fire before I went upstairs but it was almost smoked out, I'm sure. Yes, I'm sure of that."

"Good. Well, now, Madame Lisse's alibi is vouched for by Nicholas Compline and looks pretty well cast-iron. William Compline was in the smoking-room listening to the news bulletin. He heard Mr. Royal speak to the butler in the hall, and was prepared to give the gist of the bulletin which does not come on until seven-thirty."

"Surely that's of academic interest, only," said Mandrake, "considering what has happened to William Compline."

"You are probably quite right, but you know what policemen are. Dr. Hart has no alibi. Wait a bit, I must count up. Who haven't I got? Oh, there's you, Miss Wynne."

"I haven't got one," said Chloris quickly. "I was in my room and I had a bath next door and I changed. But I can't prove it."

"Oh, well," said Alleyn, "it'd be an odd state of affairs if everybody could prove all the things they hadn't done every minute of the day. Is there to be no privacy, not even in the bathroom? That leaves Lady Hersey Amblington."

"But she was with Mrs. Compline," said Mandrake. "Nicholas saw her go past his door on her way to Mrs. Compline's room. It's there in the notes. We've been over that."

"Have we? Then I've got myself into a muddle, no doubt. Lady Hersey gives Mrs. Compline an alibi. Does Mrs. Compline do as much for Lady Hersey? I mean did Mrs. Compline agree that Lady Hersey was in her room from seven-thirty until the alarm?"

"Well, she—Well, I mean she wasn't there when we talked about alibis. Lady Hersey saw her afterwards and may have spoken about it then."

"But actually nobody else questioned Mrs. Compline about it?"

"No, but of course it's all right. I mean it's out of the question that Lady Hersey—"

"I expect it is," said Alleyn. "But you see just at the moment we're dealing with hard facts, aren't we? And the actual fact, which may be of no importance whatever, is that Lady Hersey vouches for Mrs. Compline but Mrs. Compline doesn't happen to have corroborated her account. Is that it?"

"She can't," said Chloris. "She can't, now. She may never . . ."

"We won't jump that fence," said Alleyn, "until we meet it."

II

So far the return journey had not presented many difficulties. The new set of chains worked well and Mandrake kept to his own tracks where the snow had packed down hard and was already freezing over again. They ran into desultory flurries of snow, but the rain had not crossed Cloudyfold. Beyond the hills, the sky was still terraced with stormclouds, prolonged at their bases into down-pouring masses, as if some Olympian painter had dragged at them with a dry brush.

At Alleyn's suggestion they broached Dinah's luncheon hamper and he continued his examination of Mandrake's notes in an atmosphere of ham and hard-boiled egg, plying Chloris with food and both of them with questions.

"The oddest thing about this beastly business," he said, "seems to be your plunge in the pond, Mandrake. You say here that Dr. Hart had the best chance of bringing it off unobserved, and that he saw Compline leave the house wearing Mr. Royal's cape which is the double of your cape which incidentally seems to be Hart's cape. Having absorbed those fancy touches, I learn that Nicholas Compline saw you through the window of the pavilion, where he was undressing in order to plunge into the ornamental waters in pursuance of a wager. He recognized you, and you exchanged waves. Then comes your plunge, attended by the Compline brothers, Hart, Miss Wynne, and Mr. Royal, in that order. Again Mrs. Compline, Madame Lisse and Lady Hersey are absent. The first two breakfasted in their rooms. Lady Hersey says she was in the smoking-room. I understand you have read these notes, Miss Wynne?"

"Yes."

"Have you formed any theory about the footprints which Mandrake says he saw in the snow? The small prints that led out to the top of the terrace from the house and returned to the house, suggesting that the person who made them stood on the terrace for a time at a spot from which she—apparently it must have been a woman—had a full view of the pond and the pavilion?"

"I?" said Chloris. "Why, I've thought a lot about it ever since Aubrey told me but I'm afraid I've no ideas at all. It might have been one of the maids, even, though I suppose that's not very likely."

"Did you notice these prints as you went down?"

"I'm not sure. I stood on the top of the terrace for a bit and noticed Aubrey's and some other big footprints—William's they must have been—and I thought I might walk down inside them, do you know? I've got a sort of feeling I did notice something out of the tail of my eye. I've got a sort of after-flavour of having fancied there must be someone else about but it's much too vague to be useful. On the way back I was too concerned about Aubrey to notice."

"Were you?" asked Mandrake with unmistakable fervour. Alleyn waited philosophically through an exchange of inaudible phrases, and remarked the air of complacency that characterizes persons who have arrived at a certain stage of mutual attraction.

"The smoking-room is on that side of the house, isn't it?" he said at last.

"Yes," agreed Chloris uncomfortably, "but so are the visitors' rooms upstairs."

"Do they overlook the lake and pavilion?"

"Madame Lisse's room doesn't," said Mandrake. "I asked Jonathan that, and he said some tall evergreens on the bank would be in the way. I imagine they'd interrupt Mrs. Compline's view too."

"And you definitely connect these three strange events? You feel certain that the same person is behind all of them?"

"But—yes," said Chloris blankly. "Of course we do. Don't you?"

"It looks like it, certainly," said Alleyn absently.

"Surely," said Mandrake, acidly, "it would be too fantastic to suppose there has been more than one person planning elaborate deaths for Nicholas Compline during the week-end?"

"For Nicholas Compline?" Alleyn repeated. "Oh, yes. It would, wouldn't it?"

"I assure you I had no enemies at Highfold. I'd never met a single one of the guests before."

"Quite so," said Alleyn mildly. "Going back still farther, we come to the first hint of trouble, the rather childish message on the Charter form which you say Dr. Hart handed to Nicholas Compline, together with a form that had been correctly filled in. 'You are warned. Keep off.' You say that there is no question of anyone else handing this paper to Compline."

"No possibility of it. Nicholas simply took the paper from Hart," said Mandrake, "and, on looking at it, found this second one underneath. Hart's explanation was that he must have torn two papers off at once. Nicholas didn't say, at the time, what was on the paper, but he was obviously very much upset and, later that evening, he told Jonathan he thought he ought to go. The following day, and good God it's only yesterday, he actually tried to go and nearly drowned himself in a drift."

"Yes. And that completes the skeleton." Alleyn folded the notes and put them in his pocket. "As they used to say in Baker Street: 'You are in possession of the facts.' I'd like a little news about the people. You say that, with the exception of your host, you had met none of them before. That's not counting Miss Wynne, of course."

"Yes, it is," said Chloris, and with an air of great demureness she added: "Aubrey and I are complete strangers."

"I don't suppose I shall know her if I meet her again." Alleyn sighed as Mandrake once more removed his left hand from the driving-wheel. "He will resent everything I say to her," thought Alleyn, "and she will adore his resentment. Blow!" However, he introduced the subject of motive, which Mandrake, in his notes, had dealt with illusively, unconsciously supposing the reader would be almost as familiar as himself with the relationships of the eight guests to each other and to their host. In a very short time Alleyn discovered that these two were quite ready to talk about Madame Lisse and Lady Hersey, about Mrs. Compline and Dr. Hart, and about William's fury when he discovered that Hart was the author of his mother's disfigurement. They were less ready to discuss in detail Hart's enmity to Nicholas, though they never tired of stressing it. Hart had threatened Nicholas. Nicholas had goaded Hart until he completely lost control of himself. That was the burden of their song. It was on account of Nicholas' attentions to Madame Lisse, they said. When Alleyn asked if Nicholas knew that Madame Lisse was Madame Hart, they said they hadn't asked him, and Chloris added, with a new edge to her voice, that it was highly probable. Alleyn said mildly that it appeared that Nicholas had acted like a fool. "He seems to have baited Hart to the top of his bent and at the same time been rather frightened of him."

"But that's Nicholas all over," said Chloris quickly. "It was exactly that. The small boy tweaking the dog's tail. That's Nicholas." Mandrake cut in rather hurriedly but Alleyn stopped him. "You know Compline well, Miss Wynne?" She took so long to answer that he was about to repeat the question, which he was certain she had heard, when without turning her head, she said: "Yes. Quite well. I was engaged to him. You'd better hear all about it, I suppose."

"I can't see . . ." Mandrake began, but this time it was Chloris who stopped him: "It hasn't anything to do with it, I know, but I think Mr. Alleyn would rather see for himself."

"An admirable conclusion," said Alleyn lightly, and he heard without further comment the story of the two engagements. When she had finished, he made her a little speech, saying he was sorry under such tragic circumstances to be obliged to pester her with questions. Nothing could have been more uncomfortable than their reception of this simple offer of sympathy. Their silence was eloquent of embarrassment. Chloris did not turn her head and when Alleyn caught sight of Mandrake's face in the driving glass it was scarlet and scowling.

"You needn't bother," said Chloris in a high voice. "I wasn't in love with William. Didn't you guess that? As I have already explained to Aubrey, I did it on the rebound from Nicholas." In spite of herself, her voice lost composure and she ended up shakily: "That doesn't say I'm not terribly sorry. I liked old Bill. I liked him tremendously."

"I liked him too," said Mandrake. "He was an oddity, wasn't he?" Chloris nodded, and Alleyn thought that in making this unemphatic comment on William Compline, Mandrake had shown sureness of touch and a certain delicacy of understanding. He went on quietly: "He would have interested you, I believe, Alleyn. He was one of those people who speak a thing almost at the same time as they think it, and as he had a curious simplicity about him, some of the things he said were odd and disconcerting. He was quite like his brother to look at. The shape of his head—" Mandrake stumbled a little and then went on rather hurriedly. "From behind, as I explained in those notes, it was difficult to tell them apart. But they couldn't have been more unalike in temperament, I should say."

"And he painted?"

"Yes. I haven't seen any of his works."

"They were queer," Chloris said. "You might like them, Aubrey. They might be quite your cup of tea, but most people thought his pictures too embarrassingly bad. I must say I always felt rather shy when I saw them. I never knew what to say."

"What are they like?" asked Alleyn.

"Well, a bit as if a child had done them, but not quite like that."

"*Very* thick oil paint," said Mandrake, under his breath.

"Why, have you seen one?" asked Chloris, in astonishment.

"No. He told me. He said it rather quaintly. If there was something childlike in his painting, it must have come from himself."

"Yes, that's true," said Chloris, and they began quite tranquilly to discuss William. Alleyn wondered how old they were. Miss Wynne was not more than twenty, he thought, and he remembered a critique of one of Mandrake's poetic dramas in which the author had been described as extremely young. Perhaps he was twenty-six. They were fortified with all the resilience that youth presents to an emotional shock. In the midst of murder and attempted suicide, they had managed, not only to behave with address and good sense, but also to fall in love with each other. Very odd, thought Alleyn, and listened attentively to what they had to say about William Compline. They were discussing him with some animation. Alleyn was pretty sure they had almost forgotten his presence. This was all to the good, and a firm picture of the murdered and elder Compline began to take form. With owlish gravity, Chloris and Mandrake discussed poor William's "psychology" and decided that unconscious jealousy of Nicholas, a mother-fixation, an inferiority complex, and a particularly elaborate Œdipus complex were at the bottom of his lightest action and the sole causes of his violent outburst against Hart. "Really," said Mandrake, "it's the Ugly Duckling and Cinderella themes. Extraordinarily sound, those folk tales." "And of course the painting was simply an effort to overcome the inferiority complex—er, on the pain-pleasure principle," added Chloris uncertainly. Mandrake remarked that Mrs. Compline's strong preference for Nicholas was extremely characteristic, but of what, Alleyn could not quite make out. However he did get a clear picture of two unhappy people dominated by the selfish, vain, and, according to the two experts in the front seat, excessively oversexed Nicholas. Shorn of intellectual garnishings it was still a sufficiently curious story. One phrase of Chloris' struck him as being particularly illuminating. "I would have liked to be friends with her," she said, "but she hated me from the beginning, poor thing. First because I was engaged to Nick, and secondly and even more violently, because, as she made herself suppose, I jilted him for William. I think she knew well enough that Nick hadn't been exactly the little gent, but she wouldn't let herself believe that he could do anything that wasn't perfect. For her he just *had* to be heroic, don't you know, and she had a fantastic hatred for anyone who made him look shabby."

"Did she know about *l'affaire Lisse,* do you suppose?" asked Mandrake.

"I don't know. I daresay he kept it dark. He could be pretty quiet about his philanderings when it suited him. But even if she did know I believe she would have taken it as a perfectly natural obsession on Madame Lisse's part. In her eyes, Nicholas was really rather like one of those Greek gods who lolled about on clouds and said 'I'll have *that* one!' "

Alleyn coughed, and Miss Wynne became aware of him. "I suppose," she said, "you think it revolting of us to talk about him like this."

"No," he said, "I would find a show of excessive distress much more disagreeable."

"Yes, I know. All the same it's pretty ghastly not being able to get back quicker. I suppose you can't rush her up a bit Aubrey, can you? It's terribly important that Dr. Hart should get these things. I mean, in a sort of way, everything depends on us."

"I'm banging along as fast as I dare. There's Pen Gidding ahead. We're making much better time. Look, there's the rain still over the Highfold country. We'll be running into it again soon. If I stick in Deep Bottom it's only about half a mile from the house."

"Return to horror," said Chloris, under her breath.

"Never mind, my dear," whispered Mandrake. "Never mind."

"There's one thing that strikes me as being very odd," said Alleyn, "and that is the house-party itself. What persuaded your host to collect such a gang of warring elements under his roof? Or didn't he know they were at war?"

"Yes," said Mandrake, "he knew."

"Then why—"

"He did it on purpose. He explained it to me on the night I arrived. He wanted to work out his æsthetic frustration in a flesh-and-blood medium."

"Good Lord!" Alleyn ejaculated. "How unbelievably rum!"

III

There was no wind over Cloudyfold that afternoon, but the rain poured down inexorably. By half-past two the rooms at Highfold had begun to assume a stealthy dimness. The house itself, as well as the human beings inside it, seemed to listen and to wait. Highfold was dominated by two rooms. Behind the locked doors of the smoking-room, William Compline now sat as rigidly as if he had been made of iron, his hands propped between his feet and his head fixed between his knees. In the principal visitor's room lay his mother in bed, breathing very slowly, scarcely responding, now, to Dr. Hart when he slapped the face he had marred twenty years ago, or when he advanced his own white face close to hers and called her name as if he cried for admittance at the door of her consciousness. Hersey Amblington, too, cried out to her old friend. Three times Nicholas had come. It had been difficult for Nicholas to obey Hart and call loudly upon his mother. At first his voice cracked grotesquely into a sobbing whisper. Hart kept repeating: "Loudly. Loudly. To rouse her, you understand. She must be roused." And Hersey: "If she hears it's you, Nick, she may try. You must, Nick, you must." Mrs. Pouting in her sitting-room, and Thomas in the hall, and Caper in the pantry, and Madame Lisse in the green "boudoir," and Jonathan Royal on the stairs had all heard Nicholas shout as though across a nightmare of silence: "*Mother! It's Nicholas!* Mother!" They had all waited, listening intently, until his voice cracked into silence and they became aware once more of the hard beat of rain on the house. Jonathan, from his place on the stairs, had heard Nicholas leave his mother's room and cross the landing. He had seen him stop at the stairhead, raise his clasped hands to his lips, and then, as if some invisible cord had been released, jerk forwards until his head rested on his arms across the balustrade. Jonathan started forward, but at the sound of harsh sobbing paused and finally stole downstairs, unseen by Nicholas. He crossed the hall, and after some hesitation, entered the green "boudoir."

Between Hersey Amblington and Dr. Hart there had arisen a curious feeling of comradeship. Hersey had proved herself to be an efficient nurse, obeying Hart's instructions without a question or fuss. There were certain unpleasant things that could be attempted and between them they had made the attempts. Hart had not pretended to any experience of veronal poisoning. "But the treatment must be on general common-sense lines," he said. "There, we cannot go wrong. Unfortunately there has not been the response. We have not eliminated the poison. If only they would return from the chemist!"

"What's the time now?"

"Nearly two o'clock. They should have returned."

He bent over the bed. Hersey watched him and in a minute or two she said: "Am I mistaken, Dr. Hart, or is there a change?"

"You are not mistaken. The pupils are now contracted, the pulse is 120. Do you notice the colour of the finger-nails, a dusky red?"

"And her breathing."

"It is gravely impeded. We shall take the temperature again. God be thanked that at least this old Pouting had a thermometer."

Hersey fetched the thermometer and returned to the window where she waited, looking through rain across the terrace and down to the bathing-pool. Cypress trees had been planted at intervals along the terrace, and one of these hid the far end of the pool and the entrance to the pavilion. "She could not have seen Mandrake go overboard," thought Hersey, "but she could have seen him leave the house and go down." And she looked at the wardrobe where yesterday she had found a wet coat.

"The temperature is 102.8°," said Hart. "It has risen two points. Well, we must try the emetic again, but I am afraid she is now quite unable to swallow."

Hersey rejoined him, and again they worked together to no avail. After a time she suggested that he should leave her in charge. "You've eaten nothing and you haven't sat down since they brought you here hours ago. I can tell you if there's any change." Hart glanced up with those prominent eyes of his and said: "And where should I go, Lady Hersey? To my room? Should I not be locked up again? Ever since I came to the patient, I believe there has been someone on guard in the passage or on the stairs. Is that not so? No, let me remain here until the car returns. If they have brought a medical man I shall go back to my cell."

"I don't believe you killed William Compline," Hersey said abruptly.

"No? You are a sensible woman. I did not kill him. . . . There is no doubt, I am afraid, that the condition is less satisfactory. She is more comatose. The reflexes are completely abolished. Why do you look at me in that fashion, Lady Hersey?"

"You seem to have no thought for your own position."

"You mean that I am not afraid," said Dr. Hart, who was again stooping over his patient. "You are right, Lady Hersey, I am an Austrian refugee and a Jew, who has become a naturalized Briton. I have developed what I believe you would call a good nose for justice. Austrian justice, Nazi justice, and English justice. I have learned when to be terrified and when not to be terrified. I am a kind of thermometer for terror. At this moment I am quite normal. I do not believe I shall be found guilty of a murder I did not commit."

"Do you believe," asked Hersey Amblington, after a long pause, "that the murderer will be arrested?"

"I do believe so." He straightened his back, but he still watched his patient.

"Dr. Hart," Hersey said harshly, "do you think you know who killed William Compline?"

"Oh, yes," said Hart, and for the first time he looked directly at her. "Yes. I believe I know. Do you wish me to say the name?"

"No," she said. "Let us not discuss it."

"I agree," said Dr. Hart.

IV

Down in the green sitting-room, Jonathan Royal listened to Madame Lisse. An onlooker with a taste for irony might have found something to divert him in the scene, particularly if he liked his irony laced with a touch of the macabre. A nice sense of the fitness of things had prompted Madame to dress herself in black, a dead crapy black that gloved her figure with adroitness. She looked and smelt most expensive. She had sent a message to her host by Mrs. Pouting, asking for an interview. Jonathan, fresh from seeing Nicholas Compline's breakdown on the upstairs landing, eyed his beautiful guest with a certain air of wariness.

"It is so kind of you to see me," said Madame Lisse. "Ever since this terrible affair I have felt that of all our party you would remain the sanest, the best able to control events, the one to whom I must instinctively turn."

Jonathan touched his glasses and said that it was very nice of her. She continued in this strain for some time. Her manner conveyed, as an Englishwoman's manner seldom conveys, a sort of woman-to-man awareness that was touched with camaraderie. With every look she gave him,—and her glances were circumspect,—she flattered Jonathan, and, although he still made uncomfortable little noises in his throat and fidgeted with his glasses, he began to look sleek; into his own manner there crept an air of calculation that would have astonished his cousin Hersey or Chloris Wynne. He and Madame Lisse were very polite to each other, but there was a hint of insolence in their civility. Madame began to explain her reasons for keeping her marriage to Hart a secret. It had been her idea, she said. She had not wished to give up her own business, which was a flourishing one, but on the other hand Dr. Hart, before they met, had, under his own name, published a book in which he exposed what he had called the "beauty-parlour racket." "The book has had considerable publicity and is widely associated with his name," she said. "It would have been impossible for me as his wife to continue my business. Both of us would have appeared ridiculous. So we were married very quietly, in London, and continued in our separate ménages."

"An ambiguous position," Jonathan said with a little smile.

"Until recently it has worked quite well."

"Until Nicholas Compline was transferred to Great Chipping, perhaps?"

"Until then," she agreed, and for a time both of them were silent while Jonathan looked at her steadily through those blank glasses of his. "Ah, well," said Madame Lisse, "there it is. I was quite powerless. Francis became insanely jealous. I should never have allowed this visit, but he guessed that Nicholas had been asked and he accepted. I had hoped that Nicholas would be sensible and that Francis would become reassured. But as it was, both of them behaved like lunatics. And now the brother and the disfigured mother too, perhaps—it is too horrible. I shall blame myself to the end of my life. I shall never recover from the horror," said Madame Lisse, delicately clasping her hands, "never."

"Why did you wish to speak to me?"

"To explain my own position. When I heard last night of this tragedy, I was shattered. All night I stayed awake thinking—thinking. Not of myself, you understand, but of that poor gauche William, killed, as it seems, on my account. That is what people will say. They will say that Francis mistook him for Nicholas and killed him because of me. It will not be true, Mr. Royal."

At this remarkable assemblage of contradictory data, Jonathan gaped a little, but Madame Lisse leant towards him and gazed into his spectacles, and he was silent.

"It will not be true," she repeated.

"But—who do you suggest—"

"Do not misunderstand me. There can be no doubt who struck the blow. But the motive—the motive! You heard that unfortunate young man cry out that all the world should learn it was Francis who ruined his mother's beauty. Why did she try to kill herself? Because she knew that it was on her account that Francis Hart had killed her son."

Jonathan primmed his lips. Madame Lisse leant towards him. "You are a man of the world," said this amazing lady, "you understand women. I felt it the first time we met. There was a *frisson*—how shall I describe it? We were *en rapport*. One is never mistaken in these things. There is an instinct." She continued in this vein for some time. Presently she was holding one of Jonathan's hands in both her own, and imperceptibly this state of affairs changed into Jonathan holding both hers in one of his. Her voice went on and on. He was to understand that she was the victim of men's passions. She could not help it. She could not stop Nicholas falling in love with her. Her husband had treated her exceedingly ill. But the murder had nothing to do with her or with Nicholas. There were terrible days ahead, she would never recover. But—and here she raised Jonathan's hand to her cheek—he, Jonathan, would protect her. He would keep their secret. "What secret?" cried Jonathan in alarm. The secret of Nicholas' infatuation. Her name need never be brought into the picture. "You ask the impossible!" Jonathan exclaimed. "My dear lady, even if I—" She wept a little and said it was evident he did not return the *deep, deep* regard she had for him. She swayed very close indeed and murmured something in his ear. Jonathan changed colour and spluttered: "If I could . . . I should be enchanted, but it is beyond my power." He wetted his lips. "It's no good," he said. "Mandrake knows. They all know. It's impossible."

While he still stared at her they both heard the sound of a car coming slowly up the last curve of the drive.

CHAPTER XIII

Examination

I

ALLEYN WENT ALONE to the smoking-room. On their arrival Mandrake had gone at once to find Jonathan and had returned to say he would be down in a minute or two. "And in the meantime," Mandrake said, "I am deputed to show you anything you want to see. I suppose—I mean, I've got the keys . . ." Alleyn thanked him, took the keys, and let himself into the smoking-room. He drew back the curtains from the windows and a very cold light discovered the body of William Compline. The greenstone blade lay on the floor about two feet from William's left shoe. The striking edge was stained. There was a short thong around the narrow grip. Alleyn had seen Maori *meres* in New Zealand museums and had reflected on the deadly efficiency of this beautifully shaped and balanced weapon. "The nearest thing," he murmured as he bent over it, "to the deadly Gurkha *kukri* that is possible in stone, and that only in the extremely hard and tough New Zealand greenstone. Unless this expert is a lunatic there'll be no prints, of course." He looked very closely at the wireless. It was an all-wave instrument made by a famous firm. There were five bakelite control knobs under the dial. From left to right the knobs were marked Brilliance, Bass, Tuner, Wave-band and Volume. The screws that attached them were sunk in small holes. The tuner control, placed above the others, was formed by a large quick-turning knob from the centre of which a smaller knob, for more delicate tuning, projected. The main switch was on the side facing the "boudoir" door. Alleyn noted the position of the tuning indicator and reflected that if a time check was needed he could get one from the B.B.C. He turned from the wireless to a writing-desk that stood against the same wall, between two windows. Above this desk was hung an array of weapons, a Malay kris, a boomerang, a Chinese dagger, and a Javenese knife; the fruits, thought Alleyn, of some Royal tour through the East to Oceania. An empty space on the extreme left of the group suggested the position of the *mere* and an unfaded patch on the wall gave a clear trace of its shape. It had been in full view of William as he sat fiddling with the radio control. This conjured up a curious picture. Was William so absorbed in the radio that he did not notice his assailant take the weapon from its place on the wall? That was scarcely credible. Had his assailant removed the weapon some time previously? Or did William notice the removal and see no cause for alarm? In that case the assailant could surely not have been Hart since William's antagonism to Hart was so acute that it was impossible to imagine him regarding such a move with anything but the deepest suspicion. Had Hart, then, previously removed the *mere*? But when? Before Mandrake spoke to him in the "boudoir"? Not afterwards, because William was there with Nicholas, who locked the communicating door in his face. Again he looked from the volume control to the space on the wall and wondered suddenly if Hart's ignorance of radio could possibly be assumed. But suppose Hart removed the *mere*? He had not been present at dinner. Had he taken it while the others were dining? Alleyn turned from the wall to the desk, a small affair with two drawers, one of which was not quite closed. He opened it with his finger-nail. Inside were a number of small pads. "Charter forms, by gum," Alleyn muttered.

He had brought with him the parcel ordered by telephone from the chemist. He opened it and transferred the contents to his own attaché-case. Among them were two pairs of tweezers. With these he took the Charter pads, one by one, from the drawer and laid them out on the desk. There were nine, and most of them were complete with their own small pencils. At the back of the drawer he found a number of India-rubbers.

"A little dreary labour," he thought, "should no doubt be expended. Later, perhaps." And taking great pains not to touch the pads, he transferred them, together with the pencils and India-rubbers, to an empty stationery box he found in another drawer. This he placed in his attaché-case. He then moved on from the desk toward the library door. A four-fold red leather screen stood in front of the library door. It almost touched the outside wall and extended, at an angle, some five or six feet out into the room. Alleyn went round it and faced the door itself, which was in the corner of the room. The door-knob was on his right. He unlocked it, glanced into the library, and shut it again. As he stooped to the lock he noticed a small hole in the white paint on the jamb. At first sight it resembled the usual marks left by wood-rot. The one tool of his trade that Alleyn had about him was his pocket lens. He took it out, squatted down and squinted through it at the hole. Alleyn fetched a disgruntled sigh and moved to the fireplace. Above the mantelpiece, the wall was decorated with an old-fashioned fishing-rod, complete with reel. Beneath it hung a faded photograph in an Oxford frame. It presented a Victorian gentleman wearing an ineffable air of hauteur and a costume which suggested that he had begun to dress up as Mr. Sherlock Holmes but, suddenly losing interest, had gone out fishing instead. With sorry success, it seemed, as from his right hand depended a large languid trout, while with his left hand he supported a rod. Across this gentleman's shins, in faded spidery letters, was written the legend: "Hubert St. John Worthington Royal, 1900. 4½ lbs. Penfelton Reach." This brief but confusing information was supplemented by a label which hung from the old rod. "With this rod," said the label dimly, "and this fly, an Alexandra, I caught a four-and-a-half-pounder above Trott's Bridge in Penfelton Reach. It now enters an honourable retirement. H. St. J. W. Royal, 1900."

"Well done, H. St. J. W. R.," said Alleyn. "Would you be Jonathan's papa, now, or his grandpapa? Not that it matters. I want to have a look at your reel."

It appeared that somebody else had been interested in the reel. For whereas the rod and the reel itself had escaped the attention of Jonathan's housemaids, the mass of rolled line was comparatively free from dust; and although, on the one side, this roll of line was discoloured and faded, the centre and the other side were clean and new-looking. Alleyn saw that the loose end of line that hung down had a clean cross-section. He caught this end in his tweezers, pulled out a good stretch of line, cut it off with Troy's nail-scissors, which he had pocketed before leaving, and put it away in another envelope. Mandrake was an observant fellow, he thought, but evidently he had missed the trout line.

Alleyn now examined the fireplace and, looking at the dead ash in the grate, sighed for his case bag and his usual band of assistants. It had been a wood fire and, in burning out, had missed the two side logs which had fallen apart, showing their charred inner surfaces. Between these were a heap of ash and small pieces of charcoal. Alleyn squatted down and peered through his pocket lens at this heap without disturbing it. Lying across the surface, broken at intervals but suggesting, rather than forming, a thread-like pattern, trailed a fine worm of ash. It was the ghost of some alien substance that had been thrown on the fire not long before it died out. Alleyn decided to leave the ash for the moment and continued his prowl round the room. The door into the library was a massive affair, felted, and lined, on the library side, with shelves and dummy books, bearing titles devised by some sportive Royal.

"I fancy the radio'd have to blast its head off before you'd hear much of it in the library," thought Alleyn. "Damn, I'd like to try. Better not, though, till I've printed the knobs and trimmings."

He hunted over the floor, using his torch and pressing his fingers into the pile of the carpet. He found nothing that seemed to him to be of interest. He completed his examination of the room and returned at last to the body of William Compline.

Alleyn's camera was a very expensive instrument. He had brought it with him to make records of his wife's work during its successive stages. He now used it to photograph William Compline's body, the area of floor surrounding his feet, his skull, the *mere,* the wireless cabinet, the ash in the fireplace, and the library door-jamb. "In case," he muttered, "Thompson and Co. don't get through tonight." Detective-Sergeant Thompson was his photographic expert.

Having taken his pictures he stood for a time, looking down at William. "I don't imagine *you* knew anything about it." And he thought, "Life's going to be pretty cheap when summer comes, but you've caught a *Blitzkrieg* of your own and so for you it's different. You've conjured up the Yard, you poor chap. You've cranked up the majesty of the law and by the time *your* killer reaches the dock, Lord knows how many of your friends will be there to give evidence. There ought to be a moral lurking somewhere round this but I'm damned if I know what it is." He replaced the sheet, looked round the room once more, locked the two inner doors, gathered up his possessions and went into the hall. As he was locking the door he heard a sort of male twittering, and turning round saw on the stairs a small rotund gentleman dressed in plus fours and wearing thick-lensed glasses.

"I'm so awfully sorry to keep you waiting," said this person. "Mandrake looked after you?"

"Very well indeed, thank you."

"Yes. He told me you were here," said Jonathan. "I begged him to—to give you the keys of that terrible room. I—I find myself very much upset. I'm quite ashamed of myself."

"A very natural reaction, sir," said Alleyn politely. "May we have a word or two somewhere?"

"Eh? Yes. Yes, of course. Er—in the drawing-room, shall we? This way."

"I fancy Mandrake and Miss Wynne are in the drawing-room. Perhaps the library?"

Jonathan nervously agreed to the library and Alleyn had a notion that he would have preferred somewhere farther away from the smoking-room.

He saw Jonathan look quickly at the communicating door and then turn away abruptly to the fire.

"Before anything else," Alleyn said, "I must ask how Mrs. Compline is. Mandrake will have told you that the local police are trying to find a doctor. In the meantime I hope—"

"She's very ill indeed," said Jonathan. "That's why you find me so greatly upset. She—they think she's going to die."

II

Jonathan was not easy to deal with. He was both restless and lugubrious and it was with difficulty that Alleyn contrived to nail him down to hard facts. For five minutes he listened to a recital in which such matters as Jonathan's affection for the Complines, his bewilderment, the sacred laws of hospitality and the infamy of Dr. Hart were strangely mingled. At last, however, Alleyn managed to pin him down to giving direct answers to questions based on Mandrake's notes. Jonathan gave a fairly coherent account of his own talks with Nicholas, and laid great stress on the point of Hart's practically admitting that he had written threatening letters. "And in *my* house Alleyn, in *my* house he had the effrontery to make use of a round game—" Alleyn cut short this lament with a direct question.

"Who is with Mrs. Compline at the moment?"

"Hart!" Jonathan exclaimed. "There it is, you see! Hart! I know it's a most improper, a monstrous arrangement, but what could we do?"

"Nothing else, sir, I'm sure. Is he alone?"

"No. No, my cousin, Lady Hersey Amblington, who is an experienced V.A.D., is there. I spoke to her on my way down. I did not go in. She came to the door. They—ah—they're doing something—I understand you brought—but Hart appears to think she is almost beyond help."

"In that case," said Alleyn, "as soon as it's possible, I should like to see Dr. Hart. At once, if he can leave his patient."

"I don't think he can do so just yet. There's one other thing, Mr. Alleyn." Jonathan's hand went to the inside pocket of his coat. He drew out a long envelope.

"This," he said, "contains the letter she left behind for Nicholas. He has read it, but nobody else has done so. I persuaded him to place it in this envelope in the presence of my cousin, Hersey Amblington, and myself. We have signed a statement to that effect on the outside. I now," said Jonathan with a small bow to Alleyn, "hand it to you."

"That's very correct, sir," said Alleyn.

"Oh well, I'm a J.P. you know, and if, as we fear, poor Sandra does not recover . . ."

"Yes, of course. I think I should see Mr. Compline before I open the letter. It's more important at the moment that I should talk to Dr. Hart. Perhaps we had better go upstairs. Dr. Hart may be able to come out for a moment. Will you take me up, please?"

"But—is it absolutely necessary . . ."

"I'm afraid Mrs. Compline's condition makes it imperative, sir. Shall we go?"

Jonathan pulled at his lower lip, eyed Alleyn over the top of his glasses, and finally made a little dart at him. "In your hands," he chattered, "unreservedly. Come on."

He led the way upstairs. They turned off to the left and came up to the visitors' wing. Alleyn paused at the stairhead. A little to his right and facing the stairs, he saw an empty niche in the wall and, remembering the plan Mandrake had sketched in the margin of his notes, he recognized this as the erst-while perch of the brass Buddha. The men's rooms, then, would be down the passage. Madame Lisse's, he remembered, was opposite the stairhead, and Mrs. Compline's next door to the left. Indeed Jonathan now pointed to the door of this room and, with a wealth of finicking gestures, indicated that Alleyn should wait where he stood. "Just a moment, Alleyn," he mouthed. "Better just—if you don't mind—one doesn't know . . ."

He tiptoed to the door and, staring apprehensively at Alleyn, tapped very gently, paused, shook his head and tapped again. In a moment or two the door opened. Alleyn saw a tallish woman, with a well-groomed head and a careful make-up on a face that wore an expression of extreme distress. Jonathan whispered and the lady looked quickly over his shoulder at Alleyn. "Not now, Jo," she said. "Surely, not now." Jonathan whispered again and she said with a show of irritation: "There's no need to do that. *She* can't hear, poor dear."

Alleyn moved towards them. "I'm so sorry," he said, "but I'm afraid I must see Dr. Hart as soon as possible."

Jonathan said hurriedly and rather ludicrously: "You don't know Mr. Alleyn, Hersey. My cousin, Lady Hersey Amblington, Alleyn."

"If he's still—" Alleyn began, and Hersey said quickly: "He's done everything possible. I'm afraid he doesn't think it's going to be any use. He's been rather marvellous, Mr. Alleyn."

Before Alleyn could reply to this unexpected tribute or to the petulant little cluck with which Jonathan received it, the door was suddenly pulled wide open from within and there stood a heavy pale man, wearing no jacket, his shirt sleeves rolled up, his face glistening.

"What *is* all this?" demanded Dr. Hart. "What now! Lady Hersey, you have no business to stand chattering in doorways when perhaps I may need you."

"I'm sorry," said Hersey meekly, and disappeared into the room. Hart glared at Alleyn. "Well?" he said.

"I'm an officer of Scotland Yard, Dr. Hart. May I speak to you?"

"Why, in God's name, haven't you brought a medical man with you? Well, well, come in here. Come in."

So Alleyn went into the room and Hart very neatly shut the door in Jonathan's face.

III

The bed had been moved out from the wall and the light from a large window fell across it and directly upon the face of the woman who lay there. Her eyes were not quite closed, nor was her mouth which, Alleyn saw, was crooked, dragged down on one side as though by an invisible cord. So strong was the light that coming from the dark passage he saw the scene as a pattern of hard whites and swimming blacks, and some moments passed before his eyes found, in the shadows round the bed, a litter of nursing paraphernalia which Hersey at once began to clear away. Alleyn became aware of a slow, deep, and stertorous rhythm, the sound of the patient's breathing.

"Is she deeply unconscious?" he asked.

"Profound coma," said Hart. "I have, I think, done everything possible in the way of treatment. Mr. Mandrake gave me your notes, which I understand came from a surgeon at Scotland Yard. They confirmed my own opinion as regards treatment. I am deeply disappointed that you have not brought a medical man with you, not because I believe he could do anything, but because I wish to protect myself."

"Was the stuff from the local chemist no use?"

"It enabled me to complete the treatment, but the condition has not improved. Have you pencil and paper?" demanded Dr. Hart surprisingly.

"I have." Alleyn's hand went to his pocket.

"I wish you to record the treatment. I am in a dangerous position. I wish to protect myself. Lady Hersey Amblington will be witness to my statement. I have administered injections of normal saline and of Croton oil. Every attempt to obtain elimination—You are not taking notes," said Dr. Hart accusingly.

"Dr. Hart," said Alleyn, "I shall take exhaustive notes in a little while and you will be given every opportunity to make statements. At the moment I am concerned with your patient. Is there the smallest hope of her recovery?"

"In my opinion, none. That is why—"

"I think I understand your position. Has she, at any time since you have attended her, regained consciousness?"

Dr. Hart turned down his shirt sleeves and looked about for his aggressively countrified coat. Hersey at once brought it and helped him into it, and Alleyn found a moment in which to appreciate Dr. Hart's unconscious acceptance of her attention.

"At first," he said, "she could be made to wince by slapping the face. Twice she opened her eyes. The last time was when her son tried to rouse her. Otherwise there has been nothing."

Hersey made a sharp movement and Alleyn said: "Yes, Lady Hersey? You were going to say something, weren't you?"

"Only that she did speak once. Dr. Hart was at the far end of the room and I don't think he heard her."

"What is this?" said Hart sharply. "You should have told me immediately. When did the patient speak?"

"It was when Nicholas was here. You remember he shouted. You told him to. And he shook her. There was no response, she had closed her eyes again, and you—you sort of threw up your hands and walked away. Do you remember?"

"Of course I remember!"

"Nicholas leant forward and put his hand against her cheek—the disfigured cheek. He did it quite gently, but it seemed to rouse her. She opened her eyes and said one word. It was the faintest whisper. You couldn't have heard."

"Well, well, well, what was this one word?" Hart demanded. "Why did you not call me, at once? What was it?"

"It was your name." There was a short silence and Hersey added: "She didn't speak again."

Alleyn said: "Did you get the impression that she spoke with any intention?"

"I—don't think so. Perhaps she realized Dr. Hart was attending her," said Hersey, and Alleyn thought: "You don't believe that." He moved nearer to the bed and Dr. Hart joined him there. "How long?" Alleyn murmured.

"Not very long, I think."

"Should I fetch Nicholas?" said Hersey.

"Does he wish to return?" asked Hart coolly.

"I don't think so. Not unless—I promised I would tell him when—"

"It will not be just yet, I think."

"Perhaps I'd better tell him that. He's in his room. I shall be there if you want me."

Alleyn opened the door for her. When he moved back into the room, Dr. Hart was stooping over his patient. Without turning his head, but with a certain deepening of his voice, he said: "I would have given much—I would have given something that I have struggled greatly to retain—if by doing so I could have saved this case. Do you know why that is?"

"I think perhaps I might guess."

"Come here, Inspector. Look at that face. For many years I used to dream of those disfigurements, for a long time I was actually afraid to go to sleep for fear I should be visited by a certain nightmare, a nightmare of the re-enactment of my blunder and of the terrible scene that followed her discovery of it. You have heard, of course, that she recognized me and that the elder son, who has been killed, reacted most violently to her story?"

"I've been given some account of it," said Alleyn without emphasis.

"It is true that I was the Franz Hartz of Vienna who blundered. If I could have saved her life I would have felt it to be an atonement. I always knew," said Dr. Hart, straightening his back and facing Alleyn, "I always knew that some day I should meet this woman again. There is no use in concealing these things from you, Inspector. These others, these fools, will come screaming at you, eager to accuse me. I have refused to discuss my dilemma with any one of them. I am ready to discuss it with you."

Alleyn reflected with faint amusement that this, from a leading suspect, was just as well. He complimented Dr. Hart on his decision, and together they moved away from the bed to a more distant window, where Jonathan's bouquet of everlasting flowers, papery little mummies, still rustled in their carefully chosen vase. And now Alleyn did produce a pocket notebook.

"Before we begin," he said. "Is there any possibility that Mrs. Compline will regain consciousness?"

"I should say there is not the remotest possibility. There may be a change. I expect, and your police-surgeon's advice confirms my suspicion, that the respiration may change. I should prefer to remain in this room. We shall conduct the interview here, if you please."

And, while the light from a rain-blurred window imperceptibly thickened and grew cold upon the face of Dr. Hart's patient, he answered Alleyn's questions. Alleyn had had official dealings with aliens for many years. Since the onset of Nazidom he had learned to recognize a common and tragic characteristic in many of them, and that was a deep-seated terror of plain-clothes police officers. Dr. Hart's attitude surprised him very much. As he carried forward his questions he found that in the face of what appeared to be an extremely nasty position, Hart showed little nervousness. He answered readily but with a suggestion of impatience. Alleyn was more than usually careful to give him the official warnings. Hart listened to them with an air of respect, nodding his head gravely but showing no inclination to consider his answers more carefully. If he was indeed innocent, he was the ideal witness, but in this case his belief in his own safety was alarming. If he was guilty, he was a very cool customer indeed. Alleyn decided to try him a little further.

"It comes to this, then," he said. "You can offer no explanation of how this extra Charter form, containing the warning, reached Mr. Compline. Nor have you any theory as to who pushed Mr. Mandrake into the pond, though you agree that you saw Mr. Compline leave for the pond wearing precisely the same kind of cape. Is that right?"

"It is true that I do not know who pushed Mr. Mandrake into the pond," said Hart slowly. "As for the Charter form, I suggested at the time that I might have torn two forms off together and that the bottom form had been written by somebody else."

"Someone who made letters reminiscent of your own writing?"

"I have not seen the form. I do not know what was written on it."

"Five words. 'You are warned. Keep off.' "

A dull red crept into those heavy cheeks. For the first time he seemed disconcerted. For the first time Alleyn saw the nervous tic flutter under his lip.

"Dr. Hart," Alleyn said, "of all the people in that room, who had most cause to send such a message to Nicholas Compline?"

"Two people had cause. His brother and myself. His brother had cause. Had he not practised his goat's tricks upon the girl, the brother's fiancée?"

"And only on her?" Hart was silent. "Is it true," Alleyn asked, "that you had written to Nicholas Compline, objecting to his friendship with your wife and threatening to take certain steps if this friendship continued?"

"Did *he* tell you that?" Hart demanded.

"I haven't seen him yet, but if you wrote such letters he's not likely to keep it a secret."

"I do not deny that I wrote them. I deny that I wrote this ridiculous message. And I object most strongly to the introduction into this affair of matters that concern only myself."

"If they prove to be irrelevant they will not be made public. Dr. Hart, you tell me you have nothing to fear and nothing to conceal from me. At the same time you don't deny that you threatened Nicholas Compline. I must tell you that I've had a very full account of this week-end from a member of your party. I've warned you that your statements, if relevant, may be used in subsequent proceedings. I'm going to ask you certain questions and I shall do my best to check your answers. We shall get on a good deal faster if you don't challenge my questions, but either refuse or consent to give plain answers to them."

There was a pause and then Hart said hurriedly: "Very well, very well. I do not seek to obstruct you. It is only that there is one matter that is most painful to me. Unendurably painful."

"I'm sorry. Do you agree that you were at enmity with Compline?"

"I objected to his behaviour in regard to—my wife."

"Did he know she was your wife?"

"I desired to tell him so."

"But you didn't tell him?"

"No. My wife did not wish me to do so."

"Have you quarrelled with him since you came to Highfold?"

"Yes. Openly. I have not attempted to conceal my mistrust and dislike of him. Would a man who was planning a murder behave in such a manner? Would he not rather simulate friendship?"

Alleyn looked at the pale face with its twitching lip. "If he was in full command of his emotions, no doubt he would attempt to do so." Hart found no answer to this and he went on: "Did you meet anyone on your way from the house to the pond?"

"No."

"I have had a very brief look at that part of the garden. You went by a path that comes out at the back of the pavilion?"

"Yes."

"What did you see as you came round the pavilion?"

"I heard shouts and I saw William Compline, Nicholas Compline, Miss Wynne and Mr. Royal gesticulating on the edge of the pond."

"Yesterday evening when you came upstairs to dress, did you see anybody after you went to your room?"

"Nobody."

"Have you ever touched the brass Buddha that injured Nicholas Compline?"

"Never. But—wait a moment . . . Yes. Yes, my God, I have touched it!"

"When?"

"It was the first night. We went up to our rooms. I remember I drew back because I did not wish to accompany Nicholas Compline, who walked a little ahead with his brother. Mr. Royal drew my attention to this Buddha. He asked me if I knew anything of Oriental art. As an excuse to delay, I feigned an interest. I reached out my hands and touched it. Compline made some remark on the obesity of the Buddha. It was an insult to me. Whenever he could insult me he did so. So I have touched it."

"Coming back to last night. Will you describe your movements from the time you entered the green 'boudoir' until the time you went upstairs for the last time?"

Hart did this and his description tallied with Mandrake's note. "I felt I could not dine with them. They suspected me. It was an intolerable situation. I spoke to Mr. Royal and he suggested that I remain in that room. When, as I have told you, I finally left it, it was for the first time. I went straight to my room. The footman saw me."

"Had you been into the smoking-room at any time yesterday?"

"I do not think so. That insufferable machine was there. In the morning he had driven me crazy with it. First one horrible noise, then another, and all of them distorted. I cannot endure radio. I have a radio-phobia. I did not go into the room at all yesterday."

"But you have been there at some time?"

"Oh, yes. The first night we played this Charter game in that room."

"Will you describe the room to me?"

"Describe it? But you have seen it. Why should I?"

"I should like you to do so if you will."

Hart stared at Alleyn as if he were insane and began a laborious catalogue. "First, then, if you must have it, there is this detestable radio close to the 'boudoir' door. When I think of the room I think of the radio by which it is made hideous. There are English leather chairs. There is a red leather screen. There are pictures, English sportings, I think. And photographs, very old and faded. There is such a photograph above the mantelpiece of an old fellow with a fish. He wears an absurd costume. There is also hanging on the wall a fishing-rod. Surely this is a great waste of time, Inspector."

"Are you a fisherman?"

"*Gott im Himmel,* of what importance is it whether I fish or do not fish! I do not fish. I know nothing of fishing." Hart stared irritably at Alleyn and then added: "If I lose my temper you will forgive me. I have heard of the efficiency of Scotland Yard. No doubt there is some reason which I do not follow for these questions of interior decoration and fishing. I can tell you little more of the room. I did not particularly observe this room."

"The colour of the walls?"

"A light colour. A neutral colour. Almost white."

"And the carpet?"

"I cannot tell you—dark. Green, I think. Dark green. There are, of course, three doors. The one into the 'boudoir' was locked by Nicholas Compline after I requested that he should not use that machine of hell."

"What else did you see on the walls?"

"What else? Ah, the weapons, of course. Mr. Royal drew our attention to the weapons, I remember, Friday night. It was before dinner. Some of the men were in the room. He described the travels of his father in the Antipodes where he collected some of them. He showed me . . ."

"Yes, Dr. Hart?"

Hart paused with his mouth open and then turned away. "I have just remembered," he muttered. "He took down the stone club from the wall, saying it was—I forget—a Polynesian or New Zealand native weapon. He gave it to me to examine. I was interested. I—examined the weapon."

"Both the *mere* and the Buddha?" said Alleyn, without particular stress. "I see."

IV

It was twenty to four when Alleyn finished with Dr. Hart. Hart made another examination of his patient. He said her condition was "less satisfactory." Her temperature had risen and her respiration was more markedly abnormal. Alleyn would have been glad to escape from the rhythm of deep and then shallow breaths, broken by terrible intervals of silence. Hersey Amblington returned, Hart said he thought that Nicholas should be warned of the change in his mother, and she went to fetch him. Obviously Hart expected Alleyn to go. He had told him there was no possibility of Mrs. Compline regaining consciousness before she died, but Alleyn did not feel justified in acting upon this assurance. He remained, standing in shadow at the far end of the room, and Hart paid no more attention to him. The rain drove in sighing gusts against the closed windows and found its way in through the open ones, so that Alleyn felt its touch upon his face. A vast desolation filled the room and still there came from the bed that sequence of deep breath, shallow breath, interval; and then again, deep breath, shallow breath.

The door opened and Hersey Amblington came in with Nicholas.

Alleyn saw a tall young man in uniform who carried his left arm in a sling. He noticed the lint-coloured hair, the blankly good-looking face with its blond moustache and faintly etched lines of dissipation, and he wondered if normally it held any trace of colour. He watched Nicholas walk slowly towards the bed, his gaze fixed, his right hand plucking at his tie. Hersey moved forward a chair and, without a word, Nicholas sat beside his mother. Hersey stooped over the bed and presently Alleyn saw that she had drawn Mrs. Compline's hand from under the sheets and laid it close beside Nicholas. It was so flaccid it seemed already dead. Nicholas laid his own hand over it and at the touch broke down completely, burying his face beside their joined hands and weeping bitterly. For several minutes Alleyn stood in the shadow, hearing the wind and rain, the sound of distorted breathing, and the heavy sobs of Nicholas Compline. Then there was a lessening of sound. Hart moved to the head of the bed, looked at Hersey, and nodded. She had laid her hand on Nicholas' shoulder but, before he raised his head, Alleyn had slipped out of the room.

It was darkish now in the passage and he almost collided with Jonathan Royal, who must have been standing close to the door. Jonathan had his finger to his lips. As they faced each other there, they heard Nicholas, beyond that closed door, scream out: "Don't touch her, you ——! Keep your hands off her. If it hadn't been for you she'd never have done it."

"My God!" said Jonathan in a whisper. "What now? What's he doing to her?"

"Nothing that can hurt her," said Alleyn.

CHAPTER XIV

Interrogation

I

AT FIVE O'CLOCK the telephone in the library rang out. Alleyn, who was there, answered it. It was a police call from London for himself, and he took it with the greatest satisfaction. The Yard reported that Detective-Inspector Fox, together with a surgeon, a finger-print expert and a photographer, had left London at three o'clock and would reach Penfelton by way of a branch line, at seven-thirty. The Chipping constabulary had arranged for a car to bring them on to Highfold.

"I'm damn' glad to hear it," said Alleyn warmly. "I'm here with a couple of bodies and seven lunatics. D'you know what's happened to the Chipping people?"

"They got stuck somewhere, sir, and had to walk back. We'd have reported before, but the line's only just fixed."

"The whole thing's damn' silly," said Alleyn. "We might be marooned in Antarctica. Anyway, thank Heaven for Fox and Co. Good-bye."

He hung up the receiver, drove his hands through his hair, and returned to Mandrake's notes. As a postscript, Mandrake had added a sort of tabulated summary (opposite).

Alleyn shook his head over the last name. "Industrious Mr. Mandrake! But he's not to be trusted there," he thought. "We have a young woman who has been jilted by Nicholas, who attracted her. As soon as she engages herself to William, who does not attract her, Nicholas begins to make amorous antics at her all over again. A wicked young woman might wish to get rid of William. A desperate young woman might wish to get rid of Nicholas. And is it *quite* impossible that Miss Wynne darted down to the pond before making her official arrival with Jonathan? Perhaps it is. I'll have to go down to that pond." He lit a cigarette and stared dolefully at the row of "Yeses" against Hart. "All jolly fine, but how the devil did he rig a booby-trap that neither Nicholas nor William noticed? No, it's

	If the Murderer mistook William for Nicholas				If the Murderer recognized William	
	Motive	Opp. 1st attempt	Opp. 2nd attempt	Opp. 3rd attempt	Motive	Reason for other attempts
Dr. Hart	Yes	Yes	Yes	Booby-trap?	Yes	Made against Nicholas
Nicholas Compline	——	——	——	——	None	None
Jonathan Royal	None	Possibly	Improbable	Yes?	None	None
Lady Hersey	None	Yes	Yes?	Yes	None	None
Mrs. C.	None	Yes	No	Yes	?	None
Aubrey Mandrake	None	Yes!	No	No	None	None
Madame Lisse	None	Yes	No	Yes	?	None
Chloris Wynne	None	No	Yes	No	None	None

not a bad effort on Master Mandrake's part. But I fancy he's made one error. Now, I *wonder*." And taking up his pen he put a heavy cross against one of Mandrake's entries. He wandered disconsolately about the library, and finally, with a grimace, let himself into the smoking-room. He went straight to the radio, passing behind the shrouded figure in the chair. This time he did not draw back the curtains from the windows but turned up the lights and used his torch. The wireless cabinet stood on a low stool. Alleyn's torch-light crawled over the front surface and finally came to rest on the bakelite volume control which he examined through his lens. He found several extremely faint lines inside of the screw-hole. There were also faint scratches across the surface outside the hole, making tracks in a film of dust.

The stillness of the room was interrupted by a small murmur of satisfaction. Alleyn got out his pair of tweezers, introduced them delicately into the hole in the volume control. Screwing his face into an excruciating grimace he manipulated his tweezers and finally drew them out. He squatted on the carpet quite close to the motionless folds of white linen. These followed so closely the frozen posture of the figure they concealed that an onlooker might have been visited by the horrid notion that William imitated Alleyn and, under his shroud, conducted a secret scrutiny of the carpet. Alleyn had laid an envelope on the carpet and on its surface he dropped the minute fragment he had taken in his tweezers. It was scarcely larger than an eyelash. He peered at it through his glass.

"Scarlet. Feather, I *think*. And a tiny scrap of green," said Alleyn. And whistling soundlessly he sealed his find up in the envelope.

Next he peered into the crevice between the large and small tuning controls. "Not so much as a speck of dust," he muttered, "although there's plenty in the screw-hole. There's the actual shaft which rotates, of course. It's reminiscent of a pulley." He found one or two scratches on the surface of the tuning control. It was just possible through the lens to see that each of these marks had a sharp beginning and a gentler tail, suggesting that some very fine pointed object had struck the surface smartly and fallen away. Alleyn re-examined the carpet. Directly below the wall where the *mere* had hung, he found one or two marks that he had missed on his first examination. They occurred beneath the small desk that stood under the weapons. Here the pile of the carpet was protected and thick. Across its surface, running roughly parallel with the wall, were a series of marks which, when he examined them through his glass, looked like the traces of some sharp object that had torn across the surface of the pile. In one place he found a little tuft of carpet that had become detached. He photographed this area, fenced it in with chairs, and returned to the library.

Here he found a young footman with a tea-tray.

"Is that for me?" Alleyn asked.

"Yes, sir. I was to ask if there was anything further you required, sir."

"Nothing, at the moment, thank you. Are you Thomas?"

"Yes, sir," said Thomas with a nervous simper.

"I'd like a word with you." Alleyn poured out a cup of tea. "Still keen on 'Boomps-a-Daisy'?"

Thomas did not answer and Alleyn glanced up at him.

"Never want to hear it again s' long as I live, sir," said Thomas ardently.

"You needn't regret your burst of good spirits, you know. It may be very valuable."

"Beg pardon, sir," said Thomas, "but I don't want to be mixed up in nothing unpleasant, sir. I've put my name down, sir, and I'm waiting to be called up. I don't want to go into the army, sir, with an unpleasantness hanging over me, like."

Alleyn was only too familiar with this attitude of mind and was careful to reassure Thomas.

"There ought to be no unpleasantness about furthering the cause of justice, and that's what I hope you may be able to do. I only want you to repeat an assurance you have already given Mr. Royal and Mr. Mandrake. I'm going to put it this way, and I hope you'll agree that it couldn't be put more candidly. Would you be prepared to swear that between the time you passed through the hall to the library and the time when you left off dancing, Dr. Hart could not have entered the smoking-room?"

"Yes, sir, I would."

"You've thought it over carefully, I expect, since Mr. Royal spoke to you last night."

"I have indeed, sir. I have been over and over it in my brain till I can't seem to think of anything else. But it's the same every time, sir. Dr. Hart was crossing the hall when I took the tray in, and I wasn't above a few seconds setting it down, and when I come out, sir, he was half-way up the stairs."

"Was there a good light on the stairs?"

"Enough to see him, sir."

"You couldn't have mistaken somebody else for Dr. Hart?"

"No sir, not a chance, if you'll excuse me. I saw him quite distinct, sir, walking up with his hands behind his back. He turned the corner and I noticed his face looking sort of—well it's difficult to describe."

"Try," said Alleyn.

"Well, sir, as if he was very worried. Well, kind of frantic, sir. Haunted almost," added Thomas with an air of surprising himself. "I noticed it particular, sir, because it was just the same as he looked when he was walking in the garden yesterday morning."

Alleyn's cup was half-way to his lips. He set it down carefully.

"Did you see Dr. Hart in the garden yesterday morning? Whereabouts?"

"Behind that bathing-shed—I mean that pavilion, sir. We'd heard about the bet Mr. William Compline had on with his brother, sir, and I'm afraid I just nipped out to see the fun, sir. One of the maids kind of kidded me on, if you'll excuse the expression, sir."

"I'll excuse it," said Alleyn. "Go on, Thomas. Tell me exactly what you did see."

"Well, sir, I knew Mr. Caper wouldn't be all that pleased if he knew, so I went out by the east wing door and walked round to the front of the house by a path in the lower gardens. It comes out a little way down the drive, sir."

"Yes."

"I dodged across the drive, sir, and up through the trees towards the terrace. I was just above the pavilion, sir, and I looked down and there was the doctor gentleman, with his hands behind his back, walking towards the rear of the pavilion. I'd seen him go out by the front door before I left, sir. Mr. Royal saw him off."

"Did you continue to watch him?"

"No, sir, not for long. You see, while I was looking at him, I heard a splash and a great to-do and I ran on to where I could see the pond and there was Mr. Nicholas throwing in one of them floating birds and yelling for help and Mr. Mandrake half drowning in the pond and Mr. William running down the steps, with the young lady and Mr. Royal just crossing the terrace. But the Doctor must have come along as quick as he could, sir, because he got there, just as they hauled Mr. Mandrake out."

"Did you see anyone else on the terrace? A lady?"

"No, sir." Thomas waited for a moment and then said: "Will there be anything further, sir?"

"I fancy not, Thomas. I'll get that down in writing and ask you to sign it. It'll do very nicely indeed, to go on with."

"Thank you, sir," said Thomas primly, and withdrew.

II

"Dr. Hart," Alleyn muttered after a long cogitation: "Opportunity for first attempt!" He altered the entry in Mandrake's tables and rang the bell. It was answered by Caper, a condescension that Alleyn imagined must have been prompted by curiosity. He divided butlers into two classes, the human and the inhuman. Caper, he thought, looked human.

"You rang, sir?" said Caper.

"To send a message to Mr. Nicholas Compline. I don't want to worry him too much, but I should like to see him if he's free."

"I'll make enquiries, sir," said Caper. Inhuman butlers, Alleyn reflected, always "ascertained."

"Thank you. Before you go, I'd like your opinion on the footman."

"On Thomas, sir?"

"Yes. I expect he's told you all about his interviews with Mr. Royal."

"He has mentioned them, sir."

"What's your opinion of him?"

Caper drew down his upper lip, placed Alleyn's cup and saucer on the tray, and appeared to deliberate. "He's not cut out for service, sir," he said finally. "In a manner of speaking he's too high-spirited."

"Ah," Alleyn murmured, "you've heard about 'Boomps-a-Daisy.' "

"I have, sir. I was horrified. But it's not that alone, not by any means. He's always up to something. There's no harm in the lad, sir. He's a nice open truthful lad, but not suitable. He'll do better in the army."

"Truthful?" Alleyn repeated.

"I should say exceptionally so, sir. Very observant and bright in his ways, too."

"That's a useful recommendation."

"Will that be all, sir?"

"Not quite." Alleyn waited for a moment and then looked directly at Caper. "You know why I'm here, of course."

"Yes, sir."

"There is no doubt whatever that Mr. William Compline has been murdered. This being so, it appears that his murderer is now at large in this house. I am sure that the members of Mr. Royal's staff will want to give us all the help they can in a difficult and possibly even a dangerous situation."

"I'm sure we'll all do our duty by the master, sir," said Caper, and if this were not a direct answer, Alleyn chose to regard it as one. He began, very delicately, to probe. He believed that the servants in a large household had a seventy-per-cent working knowledge of everything that happened on the other side of the green baize door. This uncanny awareness, he thought, was comparable to the secret communications of prisoners, and he sometimes wondered if it was engendered in the bad old days of domestic servitude. To tap this source of information is one of the arts of police investigation, and Alleyn, who did not care overmuch for the job, sighed for Inspector Fox, who had a great way with female domestics. Fox settled down comfortably and talked their own language, a difficult task and one which it was useless for Alleyn to attempt. Caper had placed him in Jonathan's class and would distrust and despise any effort Alleyn made to get out of it. So he went warily to work, at first with poor results. Caper remembered speaking to Mr. Royal in the hall, before dinner on the previous evening. Mr. Royal ordered the wine for dinner and asked the time, as there was some question of letting the port settle after it was decanted. It was twenty-five minutes to eight. It would be about five minutes later that Caper heard, somewhere upstairs, a heavy thud, followed by a shout from Mr. Nicholas. Mr. Royal had gone to the big drawing-room when he left Caper. Alleyn tried for an account of the quarrel between Hart and Nicholas Compline on Friday night after dinner. Caper said he had heard nothing of it. Alleyn groped about, watching his man, and at last he found an opening. Caper, true to his class, disliked foreigners. Something in the turn of his voice, when Hart's name was introduced, gave Alleyn his cue.

"I suppose," Alleyn said, "Dr. Hart and Madame Lisse have often visited Highfold?"

"No, sir. Only once previously. We had a ball in aid of the Polish refugees, and they both attended. That was in December, sir."

"Has Mr. Royal visited them?"

"I believe so, sir. I believe Mr. Royal dined with Mrs. Lisse, if that is the lady's name, not long after the ball. I understand the Doctor was present on that occasion. Shortly afterwards he presented Mr. Royal with That Garment, sir."

"The Tyrolese cape?"

"Exactly so, sir," said Caper after closing his eyes for a second.

"It wouldn't be right, then, to say that the entire party was well known to the staff?"

"No, sir. Her ladyship and Mrs. Compline and the two young gentlemen are old friends of Mr. Royal's, and Mr. Mandrake has often visited."

"He's an old friend of Mr. Royal's too, then?"

"I understand there is some business connection, sir," said Caper, and a kind of quintessence of snobbery overlaid the qualification.

"Did it strike you that it was a curiously assorted party?" Alleyn ventured. "Mr. Royal tells me you've been with him since you were a boy. Frankly, Caper, have you ever known another week-end party quite like this one?"

"Frankly, sir," said Caper, coming abruptly into the open, "I haven't." He paused for a moment and perhaps he read a friendly interest in Alleyn's face. "I don't mention the hall out of the hall as a rule, sir," he said, "but, as you say, this is different. And I will say that Mrs. Pouting and myself never fancied them. Never."

"Never fancied who, Caper?"

"The foreigners, sir. And what's been seen since they came, hasn't served to change our opinion."

With a certain distaste, Alleyn recognized his opening and took it. "Well, Caper, what *has* been seen? Hadn't you better tell me?"

Caper told him. There had been stories of Dr. Hart and Madame Lisse, stories that had percolated from Great Chipping. Caper digressed a little to throw out dark references to the Fifth Column and was led back gently to the burden of his song. There had been other stories, it seemed, of visits in the dead of night from Dr. Hart to Madame Lisse, and Mrs. Pouting had given it as her opinion that if they were not married they ought to be. From this it was an easy step to Nicholas. It was "common knowledge," said Caper, that Mr. Nicholas was paying serious court to Madame Lisse. "If it had been the elder brother she'd have taken him, sir, and it's the opinion of some that if poor Mr. William had come along first it would have been another story." It was obvious that Nicholas passed the test of the servants' hall. Caper said they were always very pleased to hear he was coming. The impression Alleyn had got from Mandrake and Chloris Wynne was of a vain, shallow fellow with a great deal of physical attraction for women. The impression he had got from his own brief glimpse of Nicholas was of a young man bewildered and dazed by a profound emotional shock. Jonathan, when he spoke coherently, had sketched a picture of a somewhat out-of-date rip. Caper managed to suggest a spirited grandee. Mr. William, he said, was the quiet one. Strange in his ways. But Mr. Nicholas was the same to everybody, always open-handed and pleasant. He was very well liked in the district. Alleyn led him back to Madame Lisse and soon discovered that Mrs. Pouting and Caper believed she was out to catch Nicholas. That, in Caper's opinion, was the beginning of the trouble.

"If I may speak frankly, sir, we'd heard a good deal about it before Mrs. Lisse came. There was a lot of talk."

"What did it all add up to?"

"Why, sir, that the lady was taken up with this Dr. Hart until she saw something a good deal better come along. Mrs. Pouting says—"

"Look here," said Alleyn, "suppose you ask Mrs. Pouting to come in for a moment."

Mrs. Pouting was fetched and proved to be a large capable lady with a good deal of jaw and not very much lip. With her entrance it became clear that the servants had determined that Madame Lisse and Dr. Hart, between them, were responsible for the whole tragedy. Alleyn recognized very characteristic forms on loyalty, prejudice and obstinacy. Jonathan and his intimate friends were not to be blown upon, they had been deceived and victimized by the foreigners. The remotest suggestion of Jonathan's complicity was enough to set Mrs. Pouting off. She was very grand. Her manner as well as her skirts seemed to rustle, but Alleyn saw that she was big with a theory and meant to be delivered of it.

"Things have been going on," said Mrs. Pouting, "which, if Mr. Royal had heard of them, would have stopped certain persons from remaining at Highfold. Under this very roof, they've been going on."

"What sort of things?"

"I cannot bring myself . . ." Mrs. Pouting began, but Alleyn interrupted her. Would it not be better, he suggested, for her to tell him what she knew, here in private, than to have it dragged out piecemeal at an inquest? He would not use information that was irrelevant. Mrs. Pouting then said that there had been in-goings and out-comings from "Mrs. Lisse's" room. The house-maids had made discoveries. Dr. Hart had been overheard accusing her of all sorts of things.

"What sorts of things?" Alleyn repeated, patiently.

"She's a bad woman, sir. We've heard no good of her. She's treated her ladyship disgracefully over her shop. She made trouble between Mr. Nicholas and his young lady. She's out for money, sir, and she doesn't care how she gets it. I've my own ideas about what's at the bottom of it all."

"You'd better tell me what these ideas are, Mrs. Pouting."

Caper made an uncomfortable noise in his throat. Mrs. Pouting glanced at him and said: "Mr. Caper doesn't altogether agree with me, I believe.

Mr. Caper is inclined to blame *him* more than *her*, whereas I'm quite positive it's *her* more than *him*."

"What is?"

"If I may interrupt, sir," said Caper, "I think it would be best for us to say outright what's in our minds, sir."

"So do I," said Alleyn heartily.

"Thank you, sir. Yesterday evening after the accident with the brass figure, Dr. Hart came downstairs and sat in the small green room, the one that opens into the smoking-room, sir. It happened that Mrs. Pouting had gone into the smoking-room to see if everything was to rights there, the flower vases full of water and the fire made up and so on. The communicating door was not quite closed and—"

"I hope it will be clearly understood," Mrs. Pouting struck in, "that I had *not* realized anybody was in the 'boudoir.' I was examining the radio for dust—the maids are *not* as thorough as I could wish—when quite suddenly, a few inches away as it seemed, I heard Dr. Hart's voice. He said: 'Let them say what they like, they can prove nothing.' And Mrs. Lisse's voice said: 'Are you sure?' I was very awkwardly placed," continued Mrs. Pouting genteelly. "I scarcely knew what to do. They had evidently come close to the door. If I made my presence known they would think, perhaps, that I had heard more and—well, really, it was very difficult. While I hesitated, they began to speak again, but more quietly. I heard Mrs. Lisse say: 'In that event I shall know what to do.' He said: 'Would you have the courage?' and she said: 'Where much is at stake, I would dare much.' And then," said Mrs. Pouting, no longer able to conceal her relish for dramatic values, "*then*, sir, he said almost admiringly, sir: '*You devil, I believe you would.*' And she said: 'It's not "I *would*," Francis, it's "I *will*."' Then they moved away from the door and I went out. But I repeat now what I said shortly afterwards to Mr. Caper: she sounded murderous."

III

"Well," said Alleyn after a pause, "that's a very curious story, Mrs. Pouting." He looked from one to the other of the two servants, who still kept up their air of contained deference. "What's your interpretation of it?" he asked.

Mrs. Pouting did not reply, but she slightly cast up her eyes and her silence was ineffably expressive. Alleyn turned to Caper.

"Mrs. Pouting and I differ a little, sir," said Caper, exactly as if they had enjoyed an amiable discussion on the rival merits of thick and thin soup. "Mrs. Pouting, I understand, considers that Dr. Hart and Mrs. Lisse are adventurers who were working together to entrap Mr. Nicholas Compline, but that Dr. Hart had become jealous and that they had fallen out. Mrs. Pouting considers that Mrs. Lisse took advantage of Dr. Hart's two attempts on Mr. Nicholas to kill Mr. William and make it look as if Dr. Hart had done it, mistaking him for his brother. With a mercenary motive, sir."

"Extremely Machiavellian!" said Alleyn. "What do you think?"

"Well, sir, I don't know what to think but somehow I can't fancy the lady actually struck the blow, sir."

"That," said Mrs. Pouting vigorously, "is because you're a man, Mr. Caper. I hope I know vice when I see it," she added.

"I'm sure you do, Mrs. Pouting," said Alleyn absently. "Why not?"

Mrs. Pouting clasped her hands together and, by that simple gesture, turned herself into an anxious human creature. "Whether it's both of them together or her alone," she said, "they're dangerous, sir. I know they're dangerous. If they'd heard me telling you what I have told you . . . ! But it's not for myself, sir, but for Mr. Royal that I'm worried. He's made no secret of what he thinks. He says openly that Dr. Hart—though why 'Doctor,' when he's no more than a meddler with Heaven's handiwork, I'm sure I don't know—that Dr. Hart struck down Mr. William and that he'll see him hanged for it, and there they both are, free to deal another blow."

"Not quite," said Alleyn. "Dr. Hart, at his own suggestion, is once more locked in his room. I said I'd see Mr. Compline next, Caper, but I've changed my mind. Will you find out if Madame Hart is disengaged?"

"*Madame Hart!*" they both said together.

"Ah, I forgot. You haven't heard that they are man and wife."

"His wife!" whispered Mrs. Pouting. "That proves I'm right. She wanted to be rid of him. She wanted to catch the heir to Penfelton. That's why poor Mr. William was killed. And if the man is hanged for it, mark my words, Mr. Caper, she'll marry Mr. Nicholas."

And with this pronouncement, delivered with sibylline emphasis, Mrs. Pouting withdrew, sweeping Caper away in her train.

Alleyn noted down the conversation, pulled a grimace at the result and fell to thinking of former cases when the fantastic solution had turned out to be the correct one. "It's the left-and-right theory," he thought. "A wishes to be rid of B and C. A murders B in such a fashion that C is arrested and hanged. Mrs. Pouting casts Madame for the role of A. A murderess on the grand scale. What do murderesses on the grand scale look like?"

The next moment he was on his feet. Madame Lisse had made her entrance.

Nobody had told Alleyn that she was a remarkably beautiful woman and for a brief moment he experienced the strange feeling of awed astonishment that extreme physical beauty may bring to the beholder. His first conscious thought was that she was lovely enough to stir up a limitless amount of trouble.

"You sent for me," said Madame Lisse.

"I asked if I might see you," said Alleyn. "Won't you sit down?"

She sat down. The movement was like a lesson in deportment, deliberately executed and ending in stillness, her back held erect, her wrists crossed on her lap. "I wonder," thought Alleyn, "if William ever wanted to paint her." With every appearance of tranquillity, she waited for him to begin. He took out his note-book and flattened it on his knee.

"First," he said, "I think I should have your name in full."

"Elise Lisse."

"I mean," said Alleyn, "your legal name, Madame. That should be Elise Hart, I understand." And he thought: "Golly! That's shaken her!" For a moment she looked furious. He saw the charming curve of her mouth harden and then compose itself. After a pause she said, very sedately: "My legal name. Yes, of course. I do not care to use it and it did not occur to me to give it. I am separated from my husband."

"Ah, yes," said Alleyn. "Legally separated?"

"No," she said placidly. "Not legally."

"I hope you will forgive me if I ask you questions that may seem irrelevant and impertinent. You are under no obligation to answer them: I must make that quite clear and perhaps I should add that any questions which you refuse to answer will be noted."

This uncompromising slice of the official manner seemed to have very little effect on Madame Lisse. She said: "Of course," and leant a little towards him. He got a whiff of her scent and recognized it as an expensive one.

"You are separated from your husband, but one supposes, since you go to the same house-parties, that it is an amicable arrangement."

There was a considerable pause before she answered: "Not precisely. I didn't care for accepting the same invitation but did so before I knew he had been invited."

"Were his feelings in the matter much the same as yours?"

"I can't tell you," said Madame Lisse. "I think not."

"You mean that you have not discussed the matter with him?"

"I don't enter into discussions with him if I can avoid doing so. I have tried as far as possible to avoid encounters."

Alleyn watched her for a moment and then said: "Did you drive here, Madame Lisse?"

"Yes."

"In your own car?"

"No. My—my husband drove me. Mr. Royal unfortunately made the suggestion, which I couldn't very well refuse."

"Could you not? I should have thought you might have found a way out."

She surprised him by leaning still farther forward and putting her hand on the arm of his chair. It was a swift intimate gesture that brought her close to him.

"I see I must explain," said Madame Lisse.

"Please do," said Alleyn.

"I am a very unhappy woman, Mr.—I do not know your name."

Alleyn told her his name and she managed to convey, with great delicacy, a suggestion of deference. "Mr. Alleyn. I didn't know—I am so sorry. Of course I have read of your wonderful cases. I'm sure you will understand. It will be easy to explain to you, a relief, a great relief to me." Her finger-tips brushed his sleeve. "There are more ways than one," Alleyn thought, "of saying, 'Dilly, dilly, dilly, come and be killed.'" But he did not answer Madame Lisse and in a moment she was launched. "I have been so terribly unhappy. You see, although I had decided I could no longer live with my husband, it wasn't possible for either of us to leave Great Chipping. Of course it is a very large town, isn't it? I hoped we would be able to avoid encounters but he has made it very difficult for me. You will understand what I mean. He is still devoted to me."

She paused, gazing at him. The scene was beginning to develop in the best tradition of the French novel. If the situation had been less serious and she had been less beautiful, he might have found it more amusing, but he had a difficult job to do, and there are few men who are able to feel amusement at overwhelming beauty.

"He has haunted me," she was saying. "I refused to see him but he lay in wait for me. He is insane. I believe him to be insane. He rang me up and implored that I should allow him to drive me to Highfold. I consented, hoping to bring him to reason. But all the way here, he begged me to return to him. I said that it was impossible and immediately he began to rave against Mr. Nicholas Compline. Nicholas Compline and I have seen a good deal of each other and he, my husband, became madly jealous of our friendship. I am a lonely woman, Mr. Alleyn, and Mr. Compline has been a kind and chivalrous friend to me. You do believe me, don't you?" said Madame Lisse.

Alleyn said: "Is it true that some time ago you gave a dinner party to which you invited your husband and Mr. Royal, who, by the way, did not know Dr. Hart was your husband?"

He saw her eyes turn to flint but she scarcely hesitated: "It was my one attempt," she said, "to try and establish friendly relations. I hoped that they would take pleasure in each other's company."

"By gum," thought Alleyn, "you've got your nerve about you!"

"Madame," he said, "I am going to ask you a very direct question. Who, do you think, committed this murder?"

She clasped her hands over the arm of his chair. "I had hoped," she whispered, "that I might be spared that question."

"It is my duty to ask it," said Alleyn solemnly.

"I must refuse to answer. How can I answer? I loved him once."

By this remarkable statement Alleyn learned that if, as Mrs. Pouting considered, Dr. and Madame Hart were joint adventurers, the lady displayed a most characteristic readiness to betray her partner when the necessity arose.

"You will understand," he said, "that I must question each member of the party about his or her movements on three occasions. The first is the occasion when Mr. Mandrake was thrown into the bathing-pool. Where were you at that time, Madame Lisse?"

"In bed, in my room."

"Was anybody else in your room?"

"I believe a maid came in with my breakfast. I remember it was a very little while after she left the room that I heard voices on the terrace beneath my window and not long after that, I was told of the accident."

"Who told you, please?"

She waited for a moment, and then, very delicately, shrugged her shoulders.

"It was Mr. Compline," she said. "You will think it strange that I permitted the visit, but I have adopted the English custom in such matters. He was agitated and felt that he must warn me."

"Warn you?"

"Of this exhibition on the part of my husband."

"Suppose," said Alleyn, "that I told you I had convincing evidence that your husband was not responsible for this affair. What would you say?"

For the first time she looked frightened and for a moment she had no answer to give him. Her hands were clenched and her arms rigid. "I am afraid that I should not believe you," she said. "It is horrible to have to say these things. I find it unbearable. But one must protect oneself, and other innocent persons."

Alleyn was beginning to get a sort of enjoyment out of Madame Lisse.

"I am to understand," he said, "that it was a very unusual event for Mr. Compline to pay you such an informal visit?"

"The circumstances were extraordinary."

"Were they extraordinary when he again visited you at half-past seven that same evening?"

"Of course. I had asked him to come. I was most anxious to see him alone. By that time I was convinced that my husband meant to do him an injury. My husband had told me as much." Perhaps Alleyn looked a little incredulous, for she said quickly: "It is quite true. He said that he had come to the end of his endurance and could not trust himself. I was terrified. I warned Mr. Compline and begged him to be careful. When he left me, I looked after him and I saw that horrible figure fall from the top of his door. His hand was almost on the door. I screamed out and at the same moment it struck his arm. It might have killed him."

"No doubt," said Alleyn, who had already taken possession of the Buddha. "Then you and Mr. Compline were together from the time he left his room and walked down the passage to yours, until he returned and received his injury?"

"Yes. He has told me he came straight to my room."

"You were together," Alleyn repeated slowly, "the whole time?"

Again he thought he had frightened her. Again there was an odd little pause before she said: "Yes, certainly. I never left my room until he went."

"And did he?"

"He?" she said readily. "Oh no, *he* didn't, of course. I had to send him away in the end."

There was something here, Alleyn felt sure, that she had concealed from him, but he decided to leave it for the moment and went on to the time of the murder. Again Madame Lisse had been in her room. "I was in agony. I suffer from the *migraine* and this was a terrible attack, brought on, no doubt, by nervous suspense. I went to bed before dinner and remained there until I was told of the tragedy."

"Who told you of the tragedy, Madame?"

"Nicholas Compline. He broke it to me after he had told his mother."

"And what was your reaction?"

"I was horrified, of course." She leant back again in her chair and it seemed to him that she marshalled a series of sentences she had previously rehearsed. "At first I thought it was a mistake, that he had meant to kill Nicholas, but then it dawned upon me that it was William's threats to expose him that had driven him to do it. I realized that it had nothing to do with me, nothing at all. No other explanation is possible."

"You believe that it was impossible that William could be mistaken for Nicholas?"

"Of course. They were not so alike. Even the backs of their heads. There was a small thin patch in William's hair, just below the crown of his head."

"Yes," said Alleyn, watching her trembling lips. "There was."

"Whereas Nicholas has thick hair, like honey. And the nape of William's neck—it was—" She caught her breath and her voice seemed to die on her lips.

"You must have observed him very closely," said Alleyn.

CHAPTER XV

Document

I

ALLEYN'S INTERVIEW WITH NICHOLAS was an uncomfortable affair. They had not been together for two minutes before he realized that he had to deal with a man who had pretty well reached the end of his tether. Nicholas was bewildered and dazed. He answered Alleyn's questions abruptly and almost at random. Even when the question of the murderer's identity was directly broached, Nicholas merely flared up weakly like a damp squib and went out. Alleyn became insistent and Nicholas made an effort to concentrate, saying that Hart must have done it and escaped after Thomas left the hall. When Alleyn asked if he thought it was a case of mistaken identity, he said he did and spoke incoherently of the two earlier attempts. "It was me all along," he said, "that he was after. I thought, at first, Bill's fiddling about with the radio had sent him off his head; but Mandrake pointed out that Hart must have come in by the door from the hall and that, leaning over like that, the back of Bill's head and tunic would look like mine. And he must have heard me tell Bill to go to bed."

"When was that?"

Nicholas passed his hand across his eyes, pressing down with his finger-tips. "Oh, God," he said, "when was it? I can't sort of think. It was when Hart turned bloody-minded over the radio. He and Mandrake were in the room they call the 'boudoir.' He opened the door and raised hell about the wireless. I slammed the door in his face and Mandrake yelled out that I was to turn off the radio. I got suddenly fed up with the whole show. I said to my brother something like: 'Oh, all right, the wireless is no go. Get to bed, Bill.' Mandrake and Hart must have heard. I turned the radio down to a whisper. We didn't say anything and I suppose he thought Bill did go away. I heard him switch off the light. He must have done it as a blind or something, to make us think he had gone."

"Was that long afterwards?"

"I don't know. I heard Mandrake go out. It was after that."

"Did you and your brother not speak at all?"

"Yes. When, as I thought, I heard Hart go, I said it was all right now if Bill wanted to use the wireless. He was furious with Hart, you know. We both were, but I saw I'd been making a fool of myself. I was suddenly sick of the whole thing. I tried to calm Bill down. He'd turned pretty grim and wouldn't talk. I hung about a bit and then I came away."

"Can you tell me exactly what he was doing when you left?"

Nicholas went very white. "He was sitting by the fire. He didn't look up. He just grunted something, and I went into the library."

"Did you shut the door?" Alleyn had to repeat this question. Nicholas was staring blankly at him.

"I don't remember," he said at last. "I suppose so. Yes, I did. They all began asking me about my brother. Whether he was still livid with Hart, that kind of thing. I sort of tried to shut them up because of Bill hearing us, but I think I'd shut the door. I'm sorry, I'm not sure about that. Is it important?"

"I'd like an exact picture, you know. You are certain, then, that the door was shut?"

"I think so. Yes, I'm pretty sure it was."

"Do you remember exactly at what moment Mr. Royal left the library?"

"How the devil should I remember?" said Nicholas with a sort of peevish violence. "He can tell you that himself. What *is* all this?" He stared at Alleyn and then said quickly: "Look here, if you're thinking Jonathan . . . I mean it'd be too preposterous. Jonathan! Good God, he's our greatest friend. God, what *are* you driving at?"

"Nothing in the world," said Alleyn gently. "I only want facts. I'm sorry to have to hammer away at details like this."

"Well, all I can tell you is that at some time during the news bulletin Jonathan went into the hall for a minute or two."

"The red leather screen in the smoking-room was stretched in front of the door, as it is now?"

"I suppose so."

"Yes. To get back to the wireless. You tell me that you turned it down after the outburst from Dr. Hart. Did you look closely at it?"

"Why the hell should I look closely at it?" demanded Nicholas, in a fury. "I turned it down. You don't peer at a wireless when you turn it down."

"You turned it *down*," Alleyn murmured. "Not off. Down."

"You've grasped it. Down," said Nicholas, and burst into hysterical laughter. "I turned it down, and five minutes later somebody turned it up, and a little while after that Hart murdered my brother. You're getting on marvellously, Inspector."

Alleyn waited for a moment. Nicholas had scrambled out of his chair and had turned away, half weeping, half laughing. "I'm sorry," he stammered, "I can't help it. He's in there, murdered, and my mother—my mother. I can't help it."

"I'm sorry, too," said Alleyn. "All this insistence on detail must seem unbearably futile, but I promise you it has its purpose. You see, this is unhappily a police matter; a matter, if you can stomach the phrase, of serving justice, and in that cause very many things must be sacrificed, including the nerves of the witnesses."

"I'm all to pieces," Nicholas mumbled. "I'm no good. It must be shock or something." His voice died away in a trail of inaudibilities: ". . . can't concentrate . . . enough to send you mad . . ." He pulled out his handkerchief and retired to the window, where he blew his nose very violently, caught his breath in a harsh sob, and stared out at the teeming rain, beating his uninjured hand on the sill. Alleyn waited for a little while and presently Nicholas turned and faced him. "All right," said Nicholas. "Go on."

"I've nearly done. If you would rather, I can wait. . . ."

"No, no. For God's sake, get it over."

Alleyn went back to the incidents of the pond and the Buddha and at first learnt nothing new from Nicholas. He had seen Mandrake through the pavilion window and they had waved to each other. He had then turned away and gone on with the dismal business of undressing. He had heard the sound of a splash but had not immediately looked out, thinking that Mandrake might have thrown something into the pond. When he did go out to the rescue he had seen nobody else, but the assailant would have had time to dodge behind the pavilion. He had not noticed any footprints. When Hart came upon the scene, Nicholas had already thrown the seriocomic life-belt into the pond. As for his escape from the brass Buddha, it had fallen out exactly as Madame Lisse had described it. He had felt the door resist him and then give way suddenly. Almost simultaneously with this, he had started back and immediately afterwards something had fallen on his forearm. "It's damned sore," said Nicholas querulously, and didn't need much persuasion to exhibit his injury, which was sufficiently ugly. Alleyn said it should have a surgical dressing and Nicholas, with considerable emphasis, said he'd see Hart in hell before he let him near it.

"Madame Lisse watched you as you walked down the passage?"

It appeared that he had glanced back and seen her in the doorway. He said that but for this distraction he might have noticed the Buddha, but he didn't think he would have done so. Alleyn asked him the now familiar questions: Had he gone straight to her room on leaving his own and had they been together the whole time?

"Yes, the whole time," said Nicholas, and looked extremely uncomfortable. "We were talking. She wanted to see me, to warn me about him. I hope to Heaven you'll keep her name out of this as much as possible, Alleyn."

Alleyn blandly disregarded this.

"You heard nothing suspicious? No noise in the passage outside?"

"We did, as a matter of fact. I thought it was somebody at the door. It was a very slight sound. We sort of—sensed it. You don't want to get a wrong idea, you know," said Nicholas. "I suppose you've heard how he's made life hideous for her. She told me all about it." For the first time Alleyn saw a wan shadow of Nicholas' old effrontery. He stroked the back of his head and there was a hint of complacency in the gesture. "I wasn't going to be dictated to by the fellow," he said.

"What did you do?" Alleyn enquired. Nicholas began to stammer again and Alleyn had some little trouble in discovering that he had taken cover behind a screen while the lady looked into the passage.

"So, in point of fact, you were not together the whole time?"

"To all intents and purposes, we were. She was away only for about a minute. Of course what we had heard was Hart going past the door with that blasted image in his hands. I suppose when Elise looked out he was in my room. She'll tell you it was only for a minute."

Alleyn did not tell him that in giving her account of their meeting, Madame Lisse had made no mention of this incident.

II

Before he let Nicholas go, Alleyn asked him, as he had asked Hart, to give a description of the smoking-room. Nicholas appeared to find this request suspicious and distressing and at first made a poor fist of his recital. "I don't know what's in the ghastly place. It's just an ordinary room. You've *seen* it. Why do you want to ask me for an inventory?" Alleyn persisted, however, and Nicholas gave him a list of objects, rattling it off in a series of jerks: "The wireless. Those filthy knives. There are seven of them and the thing that did it"—he wetted his lips—"hung in the middle. I remember looking at it while we were talking. There were some flowering plants in pots, I think. And there's a glass-topped case with *objets d'art* in it. Medals and miniatures and things. And sporting prints and photographs. There's a glass-fronted cupboard with china and old sporting trophies inside, and a small bookcase with *Handley Cross* and *Stonehenge* and those sort of books in it. Leather chairs and an occasional table with cigars and cigarettes. I can't think of anything else. My God, when I think of that room I see only one thing and I'll see it to the end of my days!"

"You've given me a very useful piece of information," Alleyn said. "You told me that when you left your brother, the Maori *mere* was still in its place on the wall."

Nicholas stared dully at him. "I hadn't thought of it before," he said. "I suppose it was."

"Are you quite certain?"

Nicholas passed his hand over his eyes again. "Certain?" he repeated. "I thought I was, but now you ask me again I'm not so sure. It might have been when Bill and I were in the smoking-room in the morning. What were we talking about? Yes. Yes, we were talking about Mandrake in the pond. Yes, it *was* in the morning. Oh, hell, I'm sorry. I can't say it was there in the evening. I don't think I looked at the wall, then. I can't remember."

"There's only one other thing," Alleyn said. "I must tell you that Mr. Royal has given me the letter that was found in your mother's room."

"But," said Nicholas, "that's horrible! It was for me. There's nothing in it—Can't you—Must you pry into everything? There's nothing in it that can help you."

"If that's how it is," said Alleyn, "it will go no further than the inquest. But I'm sure you will see that I must read it."

Nicholas' lips had bleached to a mauve line. "You won't understand it," he said. "You'll misread it. I shouldn't have given it to them. I should have burnt it."

"You'd have made a really bad mistake if you'd done that." Alleyn took the letter from his pocket and laid it on the desk.

"For God's sake," Nicholas said, "remember that when she wrote it she was thinking of me and how much I'd miss her. She's accusing herself of deserting me. For God's sake remember that."

"I'll remember," Alleyn said. He put the letter aside with his other papers and said that he need keep Nicholas no longer. Now that he was free, Nicholas seemed less anxious to go. He hung about the library looking miserably at Alleyn out of the corners of his eyes. Alleyn wrote up his notes and wondered what was coming. He became aware that Nicholas was watching him. For some little time he went on sedately with his notes but at last looked up to find, as he had expected, those rather prominent grey eyes staring at him.

"What is it, Mr. Compline?" said Alleyn quietly.

"Oh, nothing. It's just—there doesn't seem anywhere to go. It gets on your nerves, wandering about the house. This damned mongrel rain and everything. I—I was going to ask you where he was."

"Dr. Hart?"

"Yes."

"He's locked up at the moment, at his own request."

"So long as he *is* locked up. Mandrake and Hersey seem to have gone silly over him. Because he attended my mother! God, she was at his mercy! Hart! The man who ruined her beauty and had just murdered her son. Pretty, wasn't it! How do I know what he was doing to her?"

"From what Lady Hersey tells me, his treatment was exactly what the doctor I spoke to prescribed. I'm sure you need not distress yourself by thinking that any other treatment would have made the smallest difference."

"Why didn't Mandrake get here sooner? They wanted the stuff from the chemist urgently, didn't they? What the hell was he doing? Nearly four hours to go sixty miles! My mother was dying and the best they could do was to send a bloody little highbrow cripple with a false name."

"A false name!" Alleyn ejaculated.

"Yes. Didn't Jonathan tell you? He told me. He's as common as dirt, is Mr. Aubrey Mandrake, and his name's Footling. Jonathan put me up to pulling his leg about it, and he's had his knife into me ever since."

The door opened and Aubrey Mandrake looked in.

"Sorry," he said, "I didn't know you were still engaged."

"We've finished, I think," said Alleyn. "Thank you so much, Mr. Compline. Come in, Mr. Mandrake."

III

"I only came in," said Mandrake, "to say Lady Hersey is free now, if you want to see her. She asked me to tell you."

"I shall be glad to see her in a minute or so. I just want to get my notes into some sort of order. I suppose you can't do shorthand, can you?"

"Good Heavens, no," said Mandrake languidly. "What an offensive suggestion."

"I wish I could. Never mind. I've been going through your notes. They're of the greatest help. You haven't signed them and I'll get you to do so, if you don't mind."

"I don't mind, of course," said Mandrake uneasily, "but you must remember they're based on hearsay as well as on my own observations."

"I think you've made that quite clear. Here they are."

He gave Mandrake his pen and pressed the notes out flat for him. It was a decorative affair, the signature, with the tail of the "y" in "Aubrey" greatly prolonged and slashed forward to make the up-stroke of the "M" in "Mandrake." Alleyn blotted it carefully and looked at it.

"This is your legal signature?" he said, as he folded the notes.

When Mandrake answered, his voice sounded astonishingly vicious. "You've been talking to the bereaved Nicholas, of course," he said. "It seems that even in his sorrow he found a moment for one of his little pleasantries."

"He's in a condition that might very well develop into a nervous crisis. He's lashing out blindly and rather stupidly. It's understandable."

"I suppose he told you of the incident at dinner? About my name?"

"No. What was the incident at dinner?"

Mandrake told him. "It's too squalidly insignificant and stupid, of course," he ended rapidly. "It was idiotic of me to let it get under my skin, but I happen to object rather strongly to that particular type of wholesome public-school humour. Possibly because I did not go to a public school." Before Alleyn could answer he went on defiantly: "And now, of course, you are able to place me. I'm the kind of inverted snob that can't quite manage to take the carefree line about my background. And I talk far too much about myself."

"I should have thought," said Alleyn, "you'd have worked all that off with your writing. But then I'm not a psychologist. As for your name, you've had the fun of changing it, and all I want to know is whether you did it by deed poll or whether I've got to ask for the other signature."

"I haven't, but I'm going to. 'The next witness was Stanley Footling, better known as Aubrey Mandrake.' It'll look jolly in the papers, won't it?"

"By the time this case comes off, the papers won't have much room for fancy touches, I believe," said Alleyn. "If you don't mind my mentioning it, I think you're going to find that your particular bogey will be forgotten in a welter of what we are probably going to call 'extreme realism.' Now write your name down like a good chap, and never mind if it is a funny one. I've a hell of a lot to do."

Mandrake said with a grin: "How right you are, Inspector," and re-signed his notes. "All the same," he added, "I could have murdered Nicholas." He caught his breath. "How often one uses that phrase! Don't suspect me, I implore you. I could have, but I didn't. I didn't even murder poor William. I liked poor William. Shall I fetch Lady Hersey?"

"Please do," said Alleyn.

IV

Motive apart, Lady Hersey was, on paper, the likeliest suspect. She had opportunity to execute both attempts, if they had been attempts, as well as the actual murder. During the long journey in the car, Alleyn had found his thoughts turning to this unknown woman, as to a figure which, conjecturally, might be the key piece in a complicated pattern. In all police investigations, there is such a figure; and sometimes, but not always, it is that of the criminal himself. Though none of the interviews had disclosed the smallest hint of a motive in Lady Hersey's case, he was still inclined to think she occupied a key position. She was the link common to the Complines, Jonathan Royal, and the two Harts. "The one person who could have done it," Alleyn muttered, "and the one person who didn't want to." This was an inaccurate statement but it relieved his feelings. The case was developing along lines with which Alleyn was all too familiar. He had now very little doubt as to the identity of William Compline's murderer and also very little substantial proof to support his theory or to warrant an arrest. The *reductio ad absurdum* method is not usually smiled upon by the higher powers at New Scotland Yard, and it can be a joyous romping-ground for defending counsel. Alleyn knew that a bungling murderer can give more trouble than a clever one. "And the murderer of William Compline is a bungler if ever there was one," he thought. He was turning over Mrs. Compline's letter to her son when he heard Lady Hersey's voice on the stairs. He hesitated, returned the letter to his pocket and fished out the length of line he had cut from the reel in the smoking-room. When Hersey Amblington came in, he was twisting this line through his long fingers and when he rose to greet her, it dangled conspicuously from his hands.

"I'm sorry if I've kept you waiting, Mr. Alleyn," she said. "There were things to do upstairs and nobody else to do them."

He pushed forward a chair and she sat down slowly and wearily, letting her head fall back against the chair. A sequence of fine lines appeared about her mouth and eyes, and her hands looked exhausted. "If you're going to ask me to provide myself with three nice little alibis," said Hersey, "you may as well know straight away that I can't do it. I seem to remember reading somewhere that that makes me innocent and I'm sure I hope it's true."

"It's in the best tradition of detective fiction, I understand," said Alleyn with a smile.

"That's not very comforting. Am I allowed to smoke?"

Alleyn offered her his case and lit her cigarette for her, dropping his length of fishing line over her wrist as he did so. He apologized and gathered it into his hand.

"Is that a clue or something?" asked Hersey. "It looks like fishing line."

"Are you a fisherman, Lady Hersey?"

"I used to be. Jonathan's father taught me when I was a child. He's the old party in the photograph in that ghastly room next door."

"Hubert St. John Worthington Royal, who caught a four-and-a-half-pounder in Penfelton Reach?"

"If I wasn't so tired," said Hersey, "I'd fall into a rapture over your powers of observation. That's the man. And the rod on the wall is his rod. Now I come to think of it, your bit of string looks very much like his line."

Alleyn opened his hand. Without moving her head or her hands she looked languidly at it.

"Yes," she said, "that's it. It's been looped back from the point of the rod to the reel, for years." She looked up into Alleyn's face. "There's something in this, isn't there? What is it?"

"There's a lot in it," Alleyn said, slowly. "Lady Hersey, will you try to remember, without straining at your memory, when you last saw the line in its customary position?"

"Friday night," said Hersey instantly. "There was an old cast on it, shrivelled up with age, and a fly. I remember staring at it while I was trying to fit in a letter in that foul parlour game of Jo's. It was the cast that caught the famous four-and-a-half-pounder. Or so we've always been told."

"You went into the smoking-room last night some little time before the tragedy, but when the two brothers were there?"

"Yes. I went in to see if they had calmed down. That was before the row over the radio."

"You didn't, by any chance, look at the old rod, then?"

"No. No, but I did at lunch-time. Just before lunch. I was warming my toes at the fire, and I stared absently at it as one does at things one has seen a thousand times before."

"And there was the line looped from the tip of the reel?"

Hersey knitted her brows, and for the first time her full attention seemed to be aroused. "Now you ask me," she said, "it wasn't. I remember thinking vaguely that someone must have wound it up or something."

"You are positive?"

"Yes. Yes, absolutely positive."

"Suppose I began to heckle you about it."

"I should dig my toes in."

"Good!" said Alleyn heartily, and wrote it down.

When he looked up, Hersey's eyes were closed, but she opened them and said: "Before I forget or go to sleep there's one thing I must say. I don't believe the face-lifter did it."

"Why?" asked Alleyn, without emphasis.

"Because I've spent a good many hours working for him up there in Sandra Compline's room. I like him and I don't think he's a murderer, and anyway I don't see how you can get over the dancing footman's story." Alleyn dropped the coil of fishing line on the desk. "That little man's no killer," Hersey added. "He worked like a navvy over Sandra, and if she'd lived she'd have done her best, poor darling, to have him convicted of homicidal lunacy. He knew that."

"Why are you so sure she would have taken that line?"

"Don't forget," said Hersey, "I was the last person to see her alive. I gave her a half-dose of that stuff. She wouldn't take more and she said she had no aspirin. I suppose she wanted—wanted to make sure later on. Nick had broken Bill's death to her. She seemed absolutely stunned, almost incredulous if that's not too strange a word to use. Not sorrowful so much as horrified. She wouldn't say anything much about it, although I did try gently to talk to her. It seemed to me it would be better if she broke down. She was stony with bewilderment. But just as I was going she said: 'Dr. Hart is mad, Hersey. I thought I could never forgive him but I think my face has haunted him as badly as it has haunted me.' And then she said: 'Don't forget, Hersey, he's out of his mind.' I haven't told anyone else of this. I can't tell you how strange her manner was, and how astonished I was to hear her say all that so deliberately when a moment before she had seemed so confused."

Alleyn asked Hersey to repeat this statement and wrote it down. When he had finished she said: "There's one other thing. Have you examined her room?"

"Only superficially. I had a look round, after Compline went out."

"Did you look at her clothes?" asked Hersey.

"Yes."

"The blue Harris tweed overcoat?"

"The one that is still very damp? Yes."

"It was soaking wet yesterday afternoon, and she told me she hadn't stirred out of the house all day."

V

Alleyn opened Mrs. Compline's letter to her son in the presence of Jonathan Royal, Nicholas Compline, and Aubrey Mandrake. He did not read it aloud, but he showed it to Mandrake and asked him to make a copy. While they waited, in an uncomfortable silence, Mandrake performed this office and at Alleyn's request re-sealed the original in a fresh envelope, across the flap of which Jonathan was asked to sign his name. Alleyn then tied a string round the envelope and sealed the knot down with wax from his chemist's parcel. He said that he would be obliged if Jonathan and Nicholas would leave him alone with Mandrake. Jonathan seemed perfectly ready to comply with this request, but Nicholas treated them to a sudden and violent outbreak of hysteria. He demanded that the letter should be returned, stormed at Alleyn, threatened Hart, and at last, sobbing breathlessly, flung himself into a chair and refused to move. As the best means of cutting this performance short, Alleyn gathered up his possessions and, followed by a very much shaken Mandrake, moved to the green "boudoir." Here he asked Mandrake to read over the copy of the letter.

My darling [Mandrake read],

You must not let this make you very sad. If I stayed with you, even for the little time there would be left to me, the memory of these terrible days would lie between us. I think that during these last hours I have been insane. I cannot write a confession. I have tried but the words were so terrible I could not write them. What I am going to do will make everything clear enough, and the innocent shall not suffer through me. Already Hersey suspects that I went out of the house this morning. I think she knows where I went. I cannot face it. You should have been my eldest son, my darling. If I could have taken any other way—but there was no other way. All my life, everything I have done has been for you, even this last terrible thing is for you, and however wicked it may seem, you must always remember that. And now, darling, I must write down what I mean to do. I have kept the sleeping powders they took from that man's room, and I have an unopened bottle of aspirins. I shan't feel anything at all. My last thoughts and my last prayers are for you.

MOTHER

I sign this with my full name because you will have to show it.

SANDRA MARY COMPLINE

CHAPTER XVI

Arrest

I

ALLEYN HAD ASKED Mandrake to say nothing of the contents of the letter. "Under ordinary circumstances," he said, "I would have had another officer with me when I opened it. I want you to fix the contents firmly in your mind, and I want you to be prepared, if necessary, to swear that it is the original letter which I have sealed in this envelope, the letter which I opened in your presence and from which you made this copy. All this may be quite unnecessary but as the most detached member of the party I thought it well to get your assistance. I'll keep the copy, if you please."

Mandrake gave him the copy. His hand shook so much that the paper rattled and he muttered an apology.

"It's horrible," Mandrake said. "Horrible. Mother love! My God!" He stared at Alleyn. "This sort of thing"—he stammered—"it can't happen. I never dreamed of this. It's so much worse—it's ever so much worse."

Alleyn watched him for a moment. "Worse than what?" he asked.

"It's real," said Mandrake. "I suppose you'll think it incredible but until now it hasn't been quite real to me. Not even," he jerked his head towards the smoking-room door, "not even—that. One works these things out in terms of an æsthetic, but for them to *happen* . . . ! God, this'll about kill Nicholas."

"Yes."

"To have it before him for the rest of his life! I don't know why it should affect me like this. After all, it's better that it should end this way. I suppose it's better. She's ended it. No horrible parade of justice. She's spared him that. But I can't help suddenly *seeing* it. It's as if a mist had cleared, leaving the solid reality of a disfigured woman writing that letter, mixing the poison, getting into bed and then, with God knows what nightmare of last memories, drinking it down." Mandrake limped about the room and Alleyn watched him. "At least," said Mandrake, "we are spared an arrest. But Nicholas saw the letter. He *knew*."

"He still insists that Dr. Hart killed his brother."

"Let me see the copy of that letter again."

Alleyn gave him the copy and he muttered over the phrases. "What else can it mean? 'You should have been my eldest son!' 'Hersey suspects.' 'I cannot face it.' 'Everything I have done has been for you.' What else but that she did it? But I can't understand. Why the other two attempts? It doesn't make sense." He looked up. "Alleyn, for God's sake tell me. Does it make sense?"

"I'm afraid it makes sense, all right," said Alleyn.

II

From five o'clock until seven, Alleyn worked alone. First of all he inspected the Charter blocks, handling them with tweezers and wishing very heartily for Bailey, his finger-print expert. The blocks were made of thinnish paper and the impression of heavily pencilled letters appeared on the surfaces of the unused forms. The smoking-room waste-paper baskets had been emptied, but a hunt through a rubbish bin in an outhouse brought to light several of the used forms. The rest, it appeared, had been thrown on the fire by the players after their scores had been marked. Mandrake had told him that after the little scene over the extra form, Jonathan had suddenly suggested that they play some other game, and the Charter pads had been discarded. By dint of a wearisome round of questions, Alleyn managed to identify most of the used forms. Dr. Hart readily selected his, admitting placidly that he had used "threats" as a seven-square word. Alleyn found the ghost of this word on one of the blocks, which he was then able to classify definitely as Hart's. The Doctor had used a sharp pencil and had pressed hard upon it, so that the marks persisted through two or three of the under-papers. But neither on his used form nor on the rest of the pages did Alleyn find the faintest trace of the words: "You are warned. Keep off." This was negative evidence. Hart might have been at pains to tear off that particular form and fill it in against the card back of the block, which would take no impression. At this stage Alleyn went to Jonathan and asked if he had a specimen of Hart's writing. Jonathan at once produced Hart's note accepting the invitation to Highfold. Alleyn shut himself up again and made his first really interesting discovery: The writing in the note was a script that still bore many foreign characteristics. But in his first Charter form, Dr. Hart had used block capitals throughout, though his experimental scribblings in the margin were in his characteristic script. Turning to the warning message, which was written wholly in script, Alleyn discovered indications that the letters had been slowly and carefully formed, and he thought that it began to look very much like the work of someone who was familiar with Hart's writing and had deliberately introduced those characteristic letters.

Of the other players, an exhaustive process of enquiry and comparison showed that Mrs. Compline, Hersey and Jonathan had written too lightly to leave impressions, while William's and Mandrake's papers had been burnt after being marked. Alleyn could find no trace of the message on any of the blocks. At last he began to turn back the pages of each one, using his tweezers and going on doggedly, long after the faintest trace had faded, to the last leaf of each block. At the third block, about half-way through, he made his discovery. Here, suddenly, he came upon the indented trace of those five words; and a closer inspection showed him that the page before the one so marked had been torn away. Owing to its position, the perforations had not been followed and when he fitted the crumpled message to the torn edge, the serrations tallied. This, then, was the block upon which the message had been written—and it was not Dr. Hart's block. He turned back to the first pages and gave a little sigh. They held no impressions. Alleyn got a picture of the writer hurriedly using the mass of pages as a cover, scribbling his message on the central leaf and wrenching it free of the pad. Either this writer had written his legitimate Charters with a light hand, or else he had torn away the additional pages that held an impression. The pad had belonged neither to William nor to Mandrake, for theirs bore marks that Mandrake himself had identified. Two of the remaining pads were marked by certain faint traces, visible through the lens, and these, he thought, must have been used by Madame Lisse and Chloris Wynne, whose finger-nails were long and pointed.

"Not so bad," he murmured and, whistling softly, put the Charter pads away again.

He went up to Mrs. Compline's room, taking the not very willing Mandrake with him.

"I like to have a witness," he said vaguely. "As a general rule we work in pairs over the ticklish bits. It'll be all right when Fox comes, but in the meantime you, as an unsuspected person, will do very nicely."

Mandrake kept his back turned to the shrouded figure on the bed and watched Alleyn go through the clothes in the wardrobe. Alleyn got him to feel the shoulders and skirts of a Harris tweed overcoat.

the threshold, his face like parchment against the dim scarlet of the screen. Bailey came past him and sat on a low stool just inside the door.

"Did you come straight in?" Alleyn asked Nicholas.

"I don't know. I expect I did."

"Does anyone else remember?"

"I do," said Mandrake. "I remember, Compline, that you came in and shut the door. I suppose you paused for a moment with your hand on the knob."

"Is it agreed that Mr. Compline shut the door?" Alleyn asked.

"Yes, yes, yes," Jonathan cried out shrilly. "It was shut."

"Then will you please go on?" said Alleyn quietly.

"Will somebody be very kind," said Nicholas in a high voice, "and tell me precisely what I did next? It would be a pity if I stepped off on the wrong foot, wouldn't it?"

"We may as well keep our tempers, Nick," said Hersey.

"You made a face as if to say Bill was still pretty tricky. I did 'Thumbs up?' and you did 'Thumbs down,' and then you sat in that chair by the door and we talked about Bill. After a bit, Jo offered you a drink."

"Agreed?"

"Agreed," said Mandrake. Jonathan uttered an impatient sound and added very querulously: "Yes. Oh, yes." Nicholas said: "Oh, by all means, agreed," and laughed.

"There's the chair," said Alleyn.

Nicholas dropped into the armchair on the opposite side of the door from Bailey's stool.

"Jonathan asked me to ring for drinks," said Mandrake, "but, before I could do so, we heard a clink of glasses in the hall and—"

He stopped short. Fox had opened the door into the hall and in the complete silence that followed they all heard the faint jingling of glasses.

Thomas came in with the grog tray.

He set it on the table and went out, shutting the door behind him.

"He is now tidying the hall," said Alleyn.

"I'm not enjoying this," said Hersey Amblington loudly. "I'm hating it."

"It will not be much longer," said Alleyn. Mandrake heard his own voice saying: "But it *is* horrible. We're creating it all over again. It's as if we were making something take form—in there."

"Oh, *don't,*" Hersey whispered.

"There is no one in the smoking-room," said Alleyn, and he spoke with unexpected emphasis. "The other doors are locked. There is no one in there. Please go on. Did you have your drinks?"

Nobody answered. At last Mandrake forced himself to speak. "Jonathan poured them out and then he said: 'What about William?' "

"One moment. You should be at the table, then, Mr. Royal."

Jonathan went to the table. Mandrake's voice went on: "He said: 'What about William?' meaning would he like a drink, and Compline stuck his head in at the door and sang out: 'Coming in for a drink, Bill?' "

Nicholas reached out and opened the door. He made an attempt to speak, boggled over it, and finally said: "I asked him to come in. I think he sort of grunted. Then I asked him to turn on the news. Mandrake had suggested that we might listen to it."

"What exactly did you say?"

"I can't remember the precise words."

"I can," said Mandrake. "Or pretty nearly. You said: 'D'you mind switching on the wireless? It's time for the news and we'd like to hear it.' Then there was a slight pause."

Nicholas said: "I waited, and heard someone walk across the floor; and I called out: 'Thanks!' "

Another heavy silence fell upon the room. Fox stood motionless by the door into the hall, Bailey by the door into the smoking-room, Alleyn close to Jonathan by the table.

"And then?" Alleyn asked.

"And then we heard the wireless," said Mandrake.

Bailey's hand moved.

And in the empty smoking-room a voice roared:—

> "*. . . out the barrel,*
> *Roll out the barrel again.*"

Jonathan Royal screamed out an oath and backed away from the table, his hand to his mouth.

He was almost knocked over. Nicholas had stumbled towards the door, where he was checked by Bailey. He struck at Bailey, turned, and made for the door into the hall, where Alleyn barred the way. Nicholas mouthed at him.

"Steady," said Alleyn. Nicholas stretched out his uninjured arm, pointing back to the empty room: "I didn't touch it," he gabbled, "I didn't touch it. Hart did it. It's the second booby-trap. Don't look at me like that. You can't prove anything against me." He fell back a pace. Alleyn made a move and Nicholas sprang at him. Bailey and Fox closed in on Nicholas Compline.

CHAPTER XVII

Departure

I

THE RAIN FELL STEADILY over Highfold all through that night. When in the dead light of dawn Alleyn shaved and washed in the downstairs cloakroom, the house still drummed faintly to the inexorable onslaught of the rain. At five o'clock the Great Chipping police had telephoned to say they were coming through by the Pen-Gidding road and that an ambulance was already on its way. At half-past five, Nicholas Compline lifted a blotched face from his arm and, breaking a silence of six hours, told Fox he wished to make a statement. At six o'clock, Dr. Francis Hart had an interview with Alleyn. He arrived fully dressed and said that with the permission of the authorities he would attempt to drive home by the long route. "My wife has asked me to take her with me," he said. "I have agreed to do so, if you allow." Alleyn consented readily. Dr. Hart then made him a formal speech, causing him acute embarrassment by many references to the courtesy and integrity of the British police.

"Never for a moment," Dr. Hart said, "was I in doubt of the issue. As soon as I heard of William Compline's death I knew that it must be his brother."

"You seem to have been the only member of the party who refused to be bamboozled by fancy touches," said Alleyn. "Why were you so certain?"

"I understand my wife," said Dr. Hart simply. He clasped his hands over his waistcoat, frowned judicially, and continued: "My wife is extremely mercenary and an almost perfect egoist. She was in love with Nicholas Compline. That I perceived and with that knowledge I tortured myself. She loved him as much as she could love anyone other than herself and obviously he was quite determined to have her. Whether she was his mistress or not I am unable to decide, but in any case my own suspicious attitude and the scenes I created so continually must have been very irksome. I have no doubt he wished to see her break with me and if possible obtain a divorce. That, of course, she would refuse to do. A young man with little money would never persuade her to embark on a damaging scandal. But a young man with a large estate and fine prospects—how different! No doubt she told him so. I do not believe she was aware of his guilt, still less that she was a partner in his crime. She would never risk such a proceeding. No. She thought I killed William Compline, and that when I was hanged she would wait for a discreet period and then marry his brother. She will now strain every nerve to disassociate herself from Nicholas."

"I'm afraid," said Alleyn grimly, "that she will *not* succeed."

"Of course not. But if you interview her she will try to persuade you that his motive was purely mercenary and that she was the victim of his importunities. She will also offer to return to me."

Alleyn glanced up quickly. "No," said Dr. Hart. "I have recovered from that sickness. She would have betrayed me. In our last interview before the crime she told me that if anything happened to Compline she would accuse me. I said she would not have the courage and she replied that where much was at stake she would dare much. I felt as a man might feel if some possession he had treasured was suddenly proved to be worthless. I have lost all desire for my wife."

"You have been very frank," said Alleyn, after a pause. "When this is all over what do you mean to do?"

"I am a surgeon. I think in a little while there will be a need for many surgeons in England. Perhaps, who knows, I may do more admirable work than the patching-up of faded women's faces." Dr. Hart pulled at his lips with his finger. "All the same," he said, "I wish I had been able to save her life."

"It would have been no great service to her, you know."

"I suppose not." He held out his hand. "Good-bye, Chief-Inspector," he said, and bowed stiffly from the waist. Alleyn watched him go, an almost arrogantly foreign figure in his English tweeds. A little while later he heard a car drive round the house. Bailey came in to say that Madame Lisse wished to see him before she left. Alleyn grimaced. "I'm engaged," he said. "Tell her Mr. Fox will see her. I think she'll say it doesn't matter."

II

At half-past six, Mandrake and Chloris came into the library with their top-coats over their arms, and asked if they too might leave Highfold.

"Yes," Alleyn said. "You'll be asked to attend the inquest, you know, so I'll have to keep in touch with you."

"I know," Mandrake agreed, "we'd thought of that. When will it be?"

"Wednesday, I should think."

"Jonathan's asked us to stay but we thought we'd like to go up to London for a slight change of scene. We might look in at the rectory. The road'll be all right now. Can we take a message for you?"

Alleyn gave his message. Mandrake and Chloris still hung off and on.

"We also thought," said Mandrake at last, "that we'd like a few of the worst knots unravelled by a master hand. Or doesn't one ask?"

"What knots?" said Alleyn with a smile.

"Well," said Chloris, "why Aubrey was shoved in the pond, for one. Did Nicholas shove him?"

"He did."

"But he recognized Aubrey."

"Because he recognized him."

"Oh."

"But," said Mandrake, "we'd worked that out quite differently. After the evidence of the footprints and her letter, we decided that Mrs. Compline had followed out to stop Nicholas taking the plunge and had thought I was William gloating and, on a wave of long pent-up resentment, had shoved me overboard."

"And then," said Chloris, "we thought that when she heard Bill was dead, she'd gone out of her mind and imagined that in some way she had killed him. That's how we read the letter."

"It's a very ingenious reading," said Alleyn with the ghost of a smile, "but it doesn't quite fit. How could she have gone down the steps without your seeing her? And even suppose she did manage to do that, she would have had a very clear view of you, as you stood facing the pond. Moreover she watched William go downstairs. And, finally, she had a full account of the whole affair afterwards and heard you being brought upstairs and all the rest of it. Even if she had pushed you overboard she must have very soon heard of her mistake, so how on earth could she think she'd killed William?"

"But the letter?" said Chloris.

"The letter is more tragic and less demented than you thought. The evidence of the footprints tells us that Mrs. Compline stood on the terrace and looked down. A few moments later a housemaid saw her return looking terribly upset. I believe that Mrs. Compline saw her son Nicholas make his assault upon you, Mandrake. At the time she may have thought it a dangerous piece of horseplay, but what was she to think when she heard him declare that Hart had done it, believing the victim to be Nicholas himself? And what was she to think when the booby-trap was set and again Nicholas accused Hart? Don't you think that through the hysteria she displayed, ran some inkling of the truth? Last of all, when Nicholas went to her last night and told her William had been killed *in mistake for himself*, what was she to think then? With her secret knowledge how could she escape the terrible conclusion? Her adored son had murdered his brother. She made her last effort to save him and the legend she had made round his character. She wrote a letter that told him she knew and at the same time accused herself to us. She could not quite bring herself to say, in so many words, that she had killed her son; but Nicholas understood—and so did we."

"I never thought," said Mandrake after a long silence, "that Nicholas did it."

"I must say I'd have thought you'd have guessed. Compline gave you the cape, Mandrake, didn't he? He looked out of the pavilion window and recognized you as you came down. He might have been looking at himself when you stood there in the other cloak. I think at that moment he saw his chance to bring off his tom-fool idea."

"What tom-fool idea?"

"To stage a series of apparent attempts on his own life based on an idea of mistaken identity. He planted that idea in all your heads. He insisted on it. He shoved you in and rescued you and then went about shouting that Hart had tried to drown him. Evidently he'd some such plan in his head on the first night. Hart had written threatening letters and Compline followed up by writing himself a threatening message with a rather crude imitation of Hart's handwriting. Once we'd proved Hart didn't write the message on the Charter form it was obvious only Nicholas could have done so. Perhaps he chucked you that cape deliberately. Before the bathing incident he knew where you all were and no doubt he watched Hart set off alone down the drive. If the plan failed there wasn't much harm done. Next, he staged his own flight over country that he knew damned well was impassable. If nobody had gone with him he'd have come back half-drowned in snow and told the tale. Next he rigged up his own booby-trap, choosing a moment when you were all changing in your rooms. He hadn't bargained on Madame Lisse looking after him as he went down the passage. He was going to kick the door open and let the brass Buddha fall on the floor. But, knowing that she was watching, he had to go a bit further than was comfortable, and he mucked up the business. He chose the Buddha because he'd seen Hart handle it the night before. He chose the Maori *mere* for the same reason, but he smudged Hart's prints when he used it. He himself wore gloves, of course."

"But the wireless?" asked Chloris.

"Do you remember that Hart had complained bitterly of the wireless? That appears in Mandrake's most useful and exhaustive notes. Compline knew Hart loathed radio. After the fiasco at the pond he shut himself up in the smoking-room, didn't he, until he was turned out by William, who wanted to make his drawing? And discordant noises were heard? He was always at the radio? Yes; well, he was making himself very familiar with that wireless set. Do you remember the fishing-rod above the mantelpiece in the smoking-room?"

"Yes," they said.

"Complete with fly and cast and green line?"

"Yes."

"Well, when we came on the scene there was no fly and the line had been freshly cut. On the screw-hole on the volume control I found a number of almost invisible scratches, all radiating outwards. I also found some minute fragments of red and green feathers. The card on the rod tells us that the late Mr. St. J. Worthington Royal used that red-and-green fly when he caught his four-and-a-half-pounder. There were other marks on the double tuning control which, at its centre, was free of dust. In the jamb of the door into the library there was a hole which accommodated the drawing-pin Mandrake picked up in the sole of his shoe. You saw that William dropped one of his drawing-pins in the smoking-room. I fancy Nicholas found and used it. In Mrs. Compline's hat I found two flies, one red-and-green, rather the worse for wear. The maid who looked after her swears there was only one, a yellow-and-black salmon fly, when she arrived. Who went straight to his mother's room after the murder? Right," said Alleyn, answering their startled glances. "Well, yesterday evening we experimented. We found that if we used a length of fishing-line with a fly attached but without a cast, we could hook the fly in the screw-hole of the volume control, pass the green line under the wave band and over the tuning-control axis, which served as a sort of smooth-running pulley, and fix the other end of the line to the library door-jamb with a drawing-pin. When you tweaked the line the hook pulled the volume control from Zero to fairly loud, the line playing over the tuning control, which we had set in such a way that the slight pull turned it to the station. As the hook in the screw-hole reached the bottom of the circuit, it fell out and the wireless was given tongue."

There was a long silence, broken at last by Mandrake. "But anybody could have fixed it," said Mandrake.

"Only after William was dead. He would have seen it when he was tuning, wouldn't he? But this is the place, I see, to introduce Thomas, the dancing footman. Thomas set a limit to the time when the murderer departed. Incidentally he also proved, by a little excursion, that Hart couldn't have shoved you in the pond. Thomas was Nicholas Compline's undoing. If it hadn't been for Thomas we would have had a job proving that Hart didn't do exactly what Nicholas said he did: creep in by the door from the hall into the smoking-room and kill William. The mistaken identity stunt had to be supported by an approach from the rear. That was why Nicholas locked the door into the 'boudoir.' But as things stood it was perfectly clear from the start that only Nicholas could have benefited by the wireless alibi. Mr. Royal, whose trip into the hall looked rather fishy, left the library after the wireless started, and Dr. Hart would have gained nothing whatsoever by the trick since he was alone for the entire time. Lady Hersey, who had no motive, is the stock figure of thriller-fiction—the all-too-obvious suspect. Moreover the trout-line device would have been of no use to her, either, since she went in after the noise started."

"What *exactly* did he do, though?" asked Chloris.

"He killed his brother, rigged the wireless trick, came out and shut the door. Later, he opened the door, held a one-sided conversation with William, asked for the news, tweaked the string which he had pinned to the door-jamb and waited, with God knows what sensations, for someone to go into the smoking-room."

"What happened to the line?"

"You will remember, Mandrake, that while you and Mr. Royal were together by the body, Nicholas came in. He had shut the door after him and was hidden from you by the screen. He had only to stoop and pull the line towards him. The drawing-pin had jerked away and he had no time to hunt for it. The line was in heavy shadow and the same colour as the carpet. It throws back well towards the screen when the trick is worked.

He gathered it up and put it on the fire when he got the chance. You left him by the fire for a moment, perhaps?"

"He asked us to leave him to himself."

"I'll be bound he did. But a trout-line doesn't burn without leaving a trace and we found its trace in the ashes."

"I see," said Mandrake.

"I can't help thinking about his mother," said Chloris. "I mean, it was Nicholas she adored."

"And for that reason she killed herself. At the inquest you will hear the letter she wrote. Mandrake has already seen it. She hoped to save Nicholas by that letter. While seeming to make a confession, it tells him that she knew what he had done. No wonder he was upset when he read it. It was her last gesture of love—a very terrible gesture."

"I think," said Chloris shakily, "that he truly was fond of her."

"Perhaps," said Alleyn.

The library door opened and Hersey's face, very pale and exhausted, looked in. "Is it an official party?" she asked. Alleyn asked her to come in. "I have already been over a good deal of this with Lady Hersey and with Mr. Royal," he explained, and to Hersey: "I have not got as far as your visit with Nicholas Compline to his mother."

"Oh, yes. You asked me last night to tell you exactly what he did and I couldn't remember very clearly. That's why I've come in. I've remembered what happened after he'd tried to tell her about William. I'm afraid it's quite insignificant. He seemed frightfully upset, of course, and I suppose in a ghastly sort of way he was. He didn't make her understand and turned away. I had to tell her. I knelt by her bed and put my arms around her. We were old friends, you know. I told her as best I could. I remember, now, hearing him walk away behind me and I remember that in the back of my head I was irritated with him because he seemed to be fidgeting about by the wardrobe. He must have been in a pretty awful state of mind. He was swinging the wardrobe door, I thought. I supposed he didn't know what he was doing."

"I think he knew," said Alleyn. "The tweed hat was on the top shelf of the wardrobe. He was getting rid of a green-and-red Alexander trout-fly."

III

"Wasn't that rather a mad thing to do?" asked Hersey wearily, when Alleyn had explained about the trout-fly.

"Not quite as mad as it sounds. The hook was not an easy thing to get rid of. He couldn't burn it or risk putting it in a waste-paper basket. He would have been wiser to keep the hook until he could safely dispose of it, or merely leave it on the mantelpiece, but no doubt he was possessed by the intense desire of all homicides to rid himself of the *corpus delicti*. In the shock of William's death his mother would have been most unlikely to notice a second and very insignificant trout-fly in her hat-band."

"And that's all," said Mandrake after a long silence.

"That, I think, is all. You would like to go now, wouldn't you?"

"Shall we go?" Mandrake asked Chloris. She nodded listlessly but didn't move. "I think I should go if I were you," said Alleyn, looking very directly at Mandrake.

"Come along, darling," Mandrake said, gently. They bade good-bye to Hersey and Alleyn and went out.

" 'Darling'?" murmured Hersey. "But it means nothing, nowadays, does it? Why do you want to get rid of them, Mr. Alleyn?"

"We're expecting the police car and the ambulance. It won't be very pleasant. You would like to get away too, I expect, wouldn't you?"

"No, thank you," said Hersey. "I think I'll stay with my cousin Jo. He's pretty well cut up about this, you know. After all, he gave the party. It's not a pleasant thought." She looked at the door into the smoking-room, the door with its rows of dummy books. "Mr. Alleyn," she said, "he's a despicable monster, but I was fond of his mother. Would she perhaps have liked me to see him now?"

"I don't think I should if I were you. We can tell him you've offered to see him and we can let you know later on if he'd like it."

"I must ask you—has he confessed?"

"He has made a written statement. It's not a confession."

"But . . . ?"

"I can't tell you more than that, I'm afraid," said Alleyn, and before his imagination rose the memory of sheets of paper covered with phrases that had no form, ending abruptly or straggling off into incoherence, phrases that contradicted each other and that made wild accusations against Hart, against the mother who had accused herself. He heard Fox saying: "I've given him the warning over and over again, but he will do it. He's hanging himself with every word of it." He felt Hersey's gaze upon him, and looking up saw that she was white to the lips. "Mr. Alleyn," she said, "what will happen to Nicholas?" And when he did not answer Hersey covered her face with her hands.

Through the sound of pouring rain Alleyn heard a car coming up the drive and out on the sweep before the house.

Fox came in. "It's our people, Mr. Alleyn."

"All right," said Alleyn, and he turned to Hersey. "I must go." Hersey walked to the door. He opened it and he and Fox followed her into the hall.

Jonathan was standing there. Hersey went straight to him and he took her by the hands. "Well, dear," said Jonathan, "it—it's time, I think."

Fox had gone to the front door and opened it. The sound of rain filled the hall. A large man in plain clothes came in, followed by two policemen. Alleyn met him and the large man shook hands. Jonathan came forward.

"Well, Blandish," he said.

"Very sorry about this, sir," said Superintendent Blandish. Jonathan made a small waving of his hands and turned back to Hersey.

"All ready for us, Mr. Alleyn?"

"I think so," Alleyn said, and they went into the green sitting-room, shutting the door behind them.

"Hersey, my dearest," said Jonathan, "don't stay out here, now."

"Would you rather I went away, Jo?"

"I—it's for your sake."

"Then I'll stay."

So Hersey saw Nicholas come out between Bailey and Fox, the senior officers keeping close behind him. He walked stiffly with short steps, looking out of the corners of his eyes. His unshaven cheeks were creased with a sort of grin and his mouth was not quite shut. His blond hair hung across his forehead in dishevelled streaks. Without turning his head, he looked at his host. Jonathan moved towards him and at once the two men halted.

"I want to tell you," Jonathan said, "that if you wish me to see your solicitors or do anything else that I am able to do, you have only to send instructions."

"There now," said Fox, comfortingly, "that'll be very nice, won't it?"

Nicholas said, in an unrecognizable voice: "Stop them hanging me," and suddenly sagged at the knees.

"Come along, now," said Fox. "You don't want to be talking like that."

As they went out, Jonathan and Hersey saw the ambulance van outside by the police car, and men with stretchers waiting to come in.

IV

"He'd made up his mind to do it somehow, Jo," said Hersey that afternoon. "You mustn't blame yourself too much."

"I do blame myself dreadfully," said Jonathan. He had taken off his glasses and his myopic eyes, blurred with tears, looked childlike and helpless. "It's just as you said, Hersey. I had to learn my lesson. You see—I thought I'd have a dramatic party."

"Oh, *Jo,*" cried Hersey, with a sob that was almost a laugh. *"Don't."*

"I did. That was my plan. I thought Aubrey might make a poetic drama out of it. I'm a mischievous, selfish fellow, trying to amuse myself and never thinking—just as you said, my dear."

"I talk too much. I was cross. You couldn't know what was behind it all."

"No. I think perhaps I do these things because I'm a bit lonely."

Hersey reached out her hand and he took it uncertainly between both of his. For a long time they sat in silence, looking at the fire.

V

"What you've got to do," said Mandrake, "is to think about other things. Get a new interest. Me, for instance."

"But it isn't over. If it was over, it wouldn't be so awful. I've been so mixed up with the Complines," said Chloris. "I wanted to be free of them, and now—all this has happened. It sounds silly, but I feel sort of lonely."

Mandrake removed his left hand from the driving-wheel.